YAQUI DELGADO WANTS TO KICK YOUR ASS

THE GRAPHIC NOVEL

YAQUI DELGADO WANTS TO KICK YOUR ASS

THE GRAPHIC NOVEL

MEG MEDINA

adapted and illustrated by
MEL VALENTINE VARGAS

CANDLEWICK PRESS

A NOTE FROM MEG MEDINA

When I wrote *Yaqui Delgado Wants to Kick Your Ass* a decade ago, I had a movie playing in my head. It looked a lot like the neighborhood in Queens where I grew up, including the junior high school where I got my first sour taste of bullying at the hands of a girl who was a lot like Yaqui. The ladies at the factory where my mom worked morphed into the ladies at Salón Corazón. Boys I knew in childhood became Joey and Rob. The protector I longed for emerged from my imagination as Lila. As I saw it, my job was to turn that personal movie into words that could give readers the room to make their own images and impressions as they followed Piddy Sanchez's journey.

I'm happy to say that I think it worked. The book was well received, especially by the many readers who wrote to say that they saw themselves and their classmates in its pages. At a time when there were countless news reports about bullying and its extreme consequences, it seemed that seeing that awful reality of school life named and survived offered some comfort. And today, it continues to be a go-to title for young Latinas wrestling with their daily experience of intersecting identities. Adults may have balked at the title, but it felt clear to me—then as now—that this very personal story about inclusive Latina identity, bullying, and girls explored something important about growing up, something that kids were hungry to discuss.

When my editor and I considered how best to celebrate the book's anniversary, I was really intrigued by the idea of a graphic novel. I am not a visual artist, unfortunately, but I am a die-hard fan of sharing stories in all forms, whether through dance, music, words, or visual arts. But how would another artist see Piddy and her friends? What parts of the story would they choose to make resonant?

Enter Mel Valentine Vargas.

They have brought their own aesthetic and perspective here, their own mental movie of the people and events who make up this novel. In reading their retelling, I think you'll find a depth that feels at once respectful of my original work as well as fresh and new. A new generation of fans who like to experience their stories in pictures and words can find comfort in these pages thanks to Mel.

My deepest hope is that this graphic novel will inspire us all to continue the long and essential conversations about the emotional violence we may find along the road, about how we can strengthen ourselves to survive it, and most of all, about the kindness and compassion we owe one another as we grow up.

Thank you, Mel.

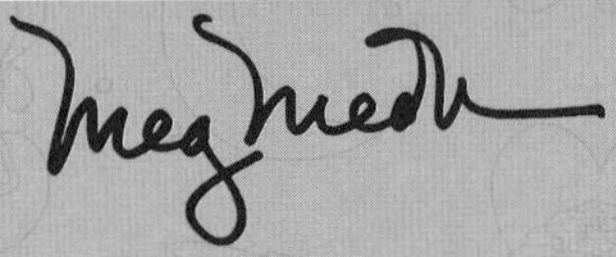

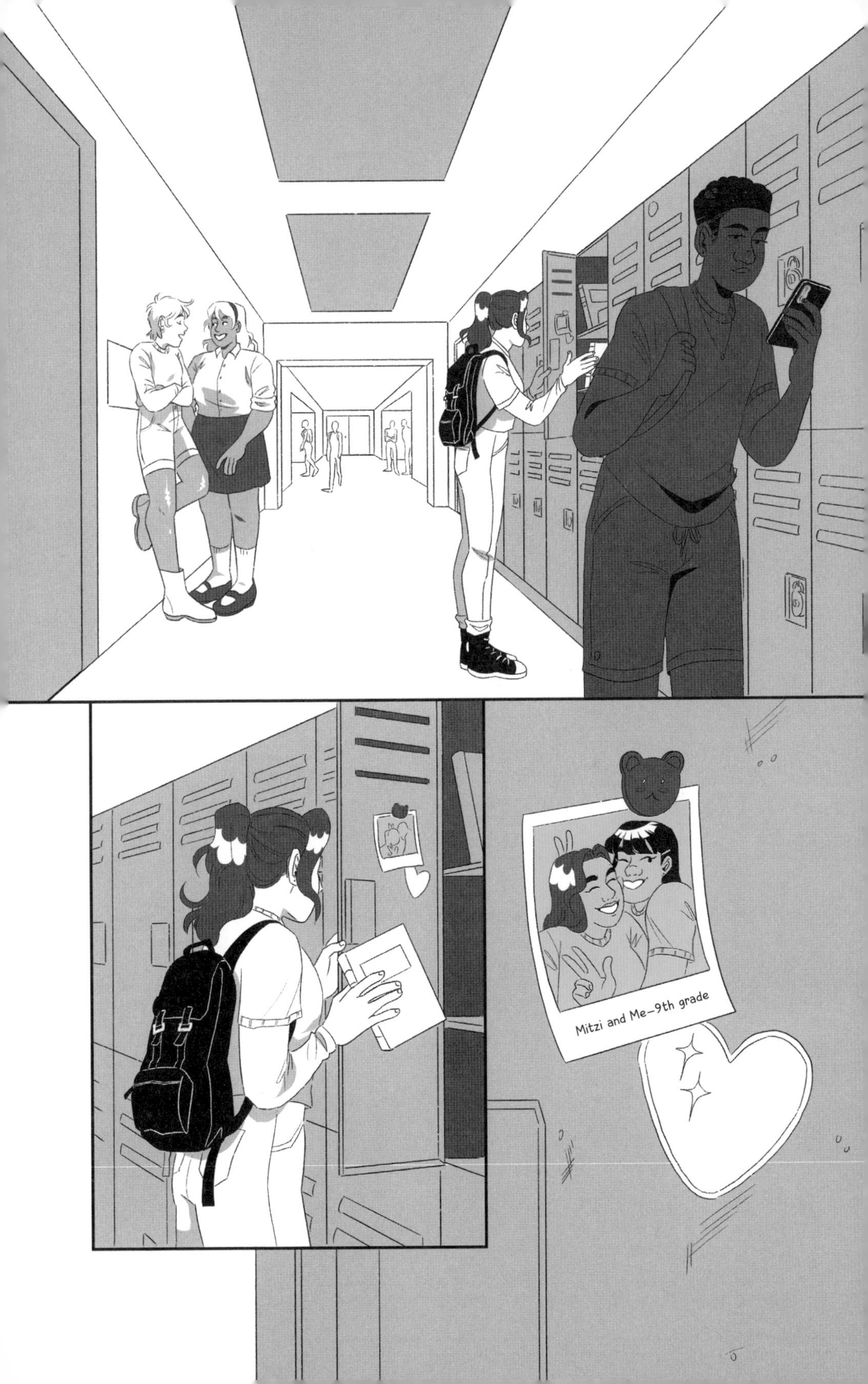
Mitzi and Me—9th grade

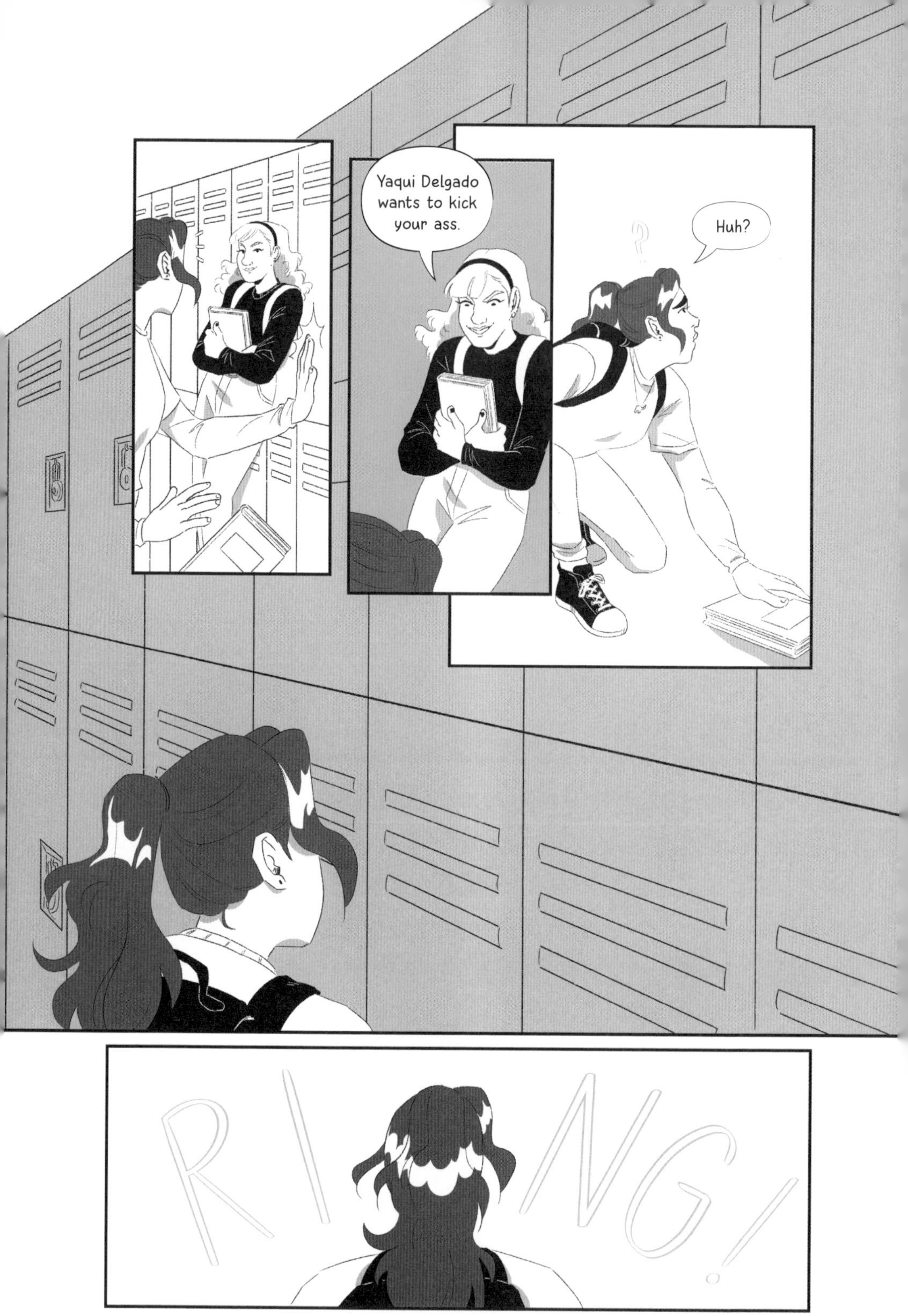
Yaqui Delgado wants to kick your ass.
?
Huh?
RING!

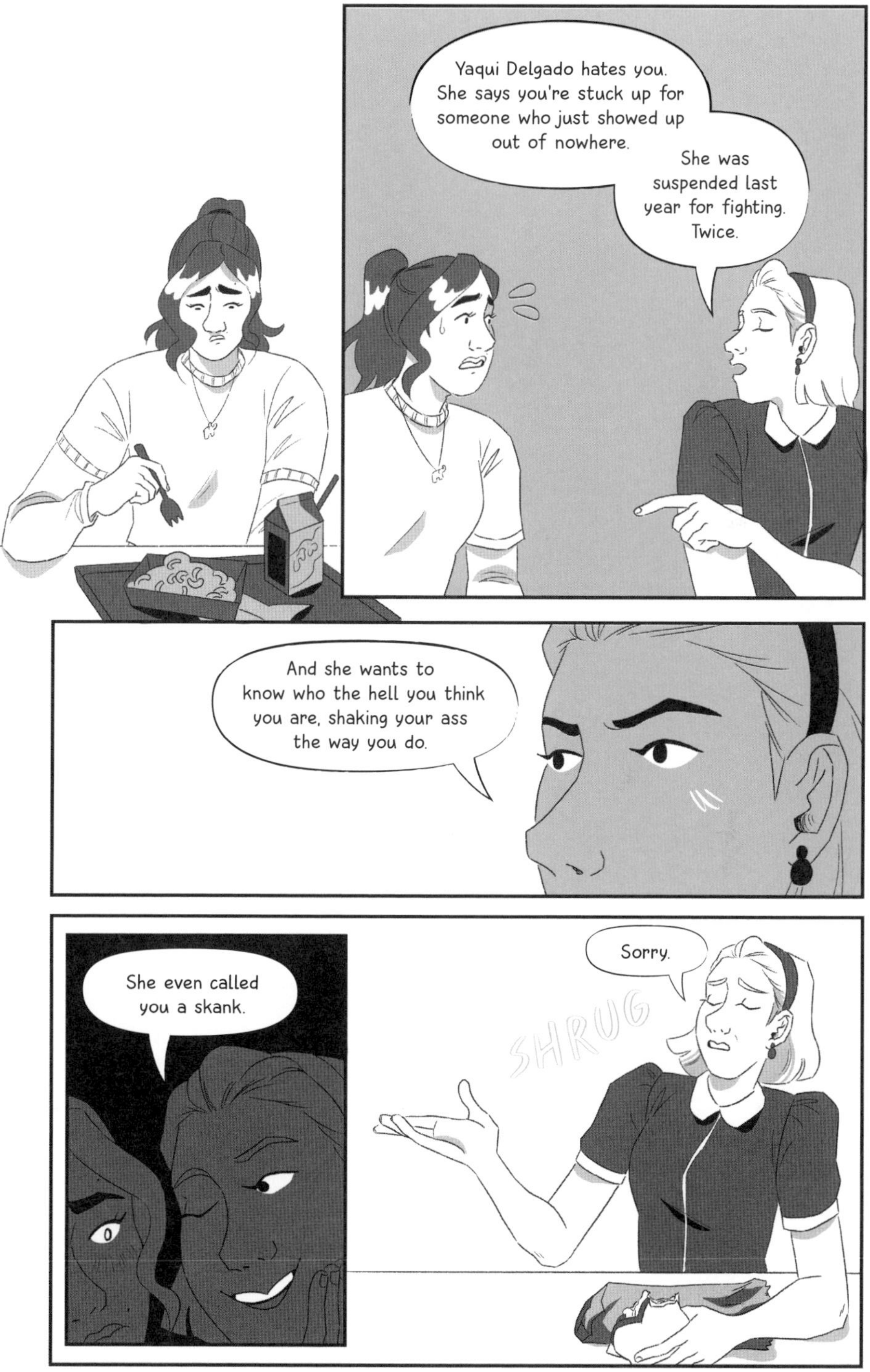
Yaqui Delgado hates you. She says you're stuck up for someone who just showed up out of nowhere.
She was suspended last year for fighting. Twice.
And she wants to know who the hell you think you are, shaking your ass the way you do.
She even called you a skank.
Sorry.
SHRUG

I shake my ass?

Definitely, yes.

Last year in ninth grade at my old school, I was a late bloomer. Planchadita. Wait till Mitzi hears about this.

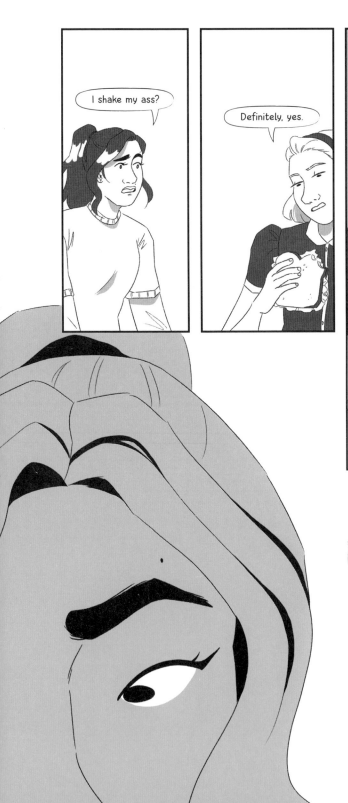

Ma noticed first.

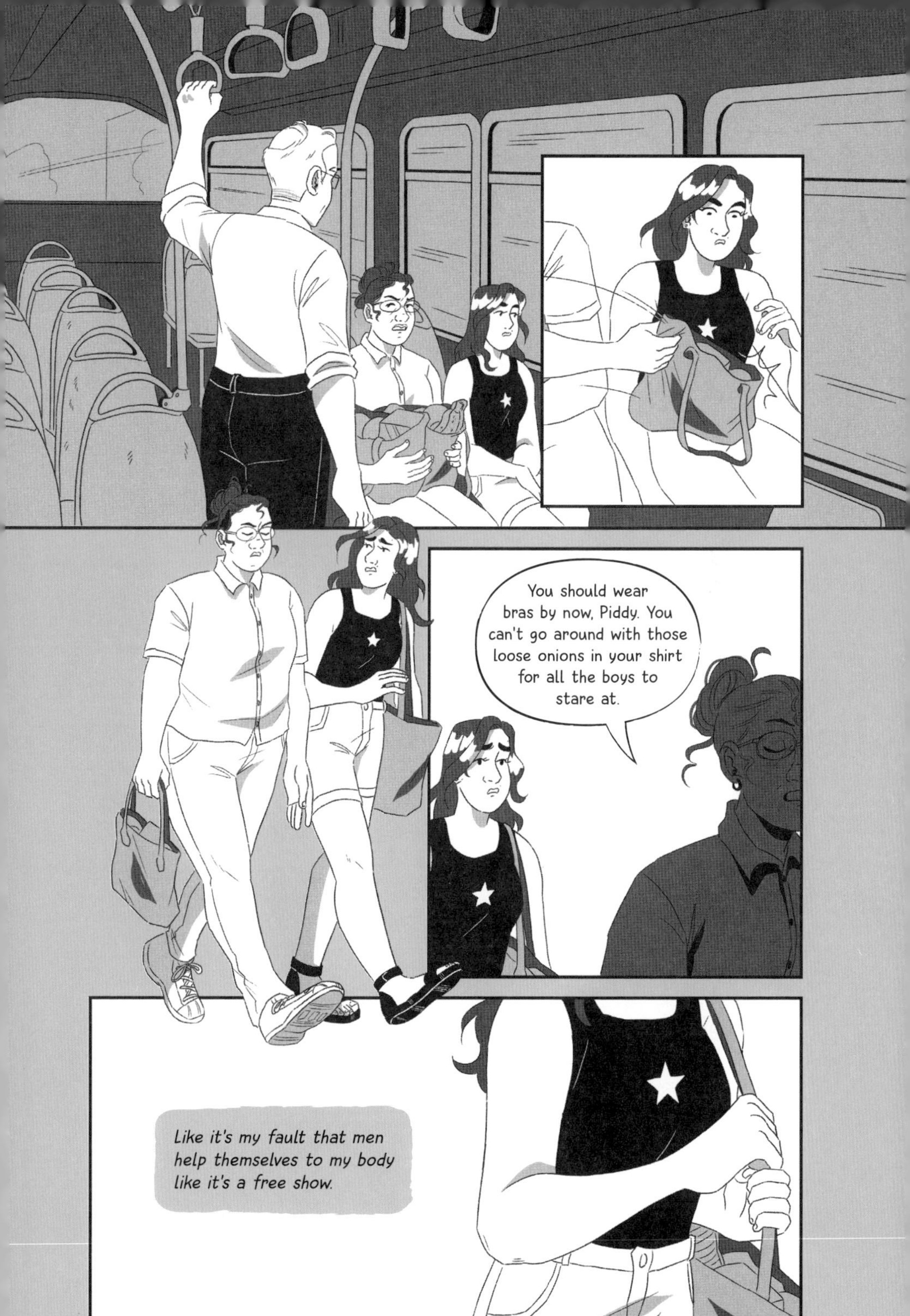
You should wear bras by now, Piddy. You can't go around with those loose onions in your shirt for all the boys to stare at.
Like it's my fault that men help themselves to my body like it's a free show.

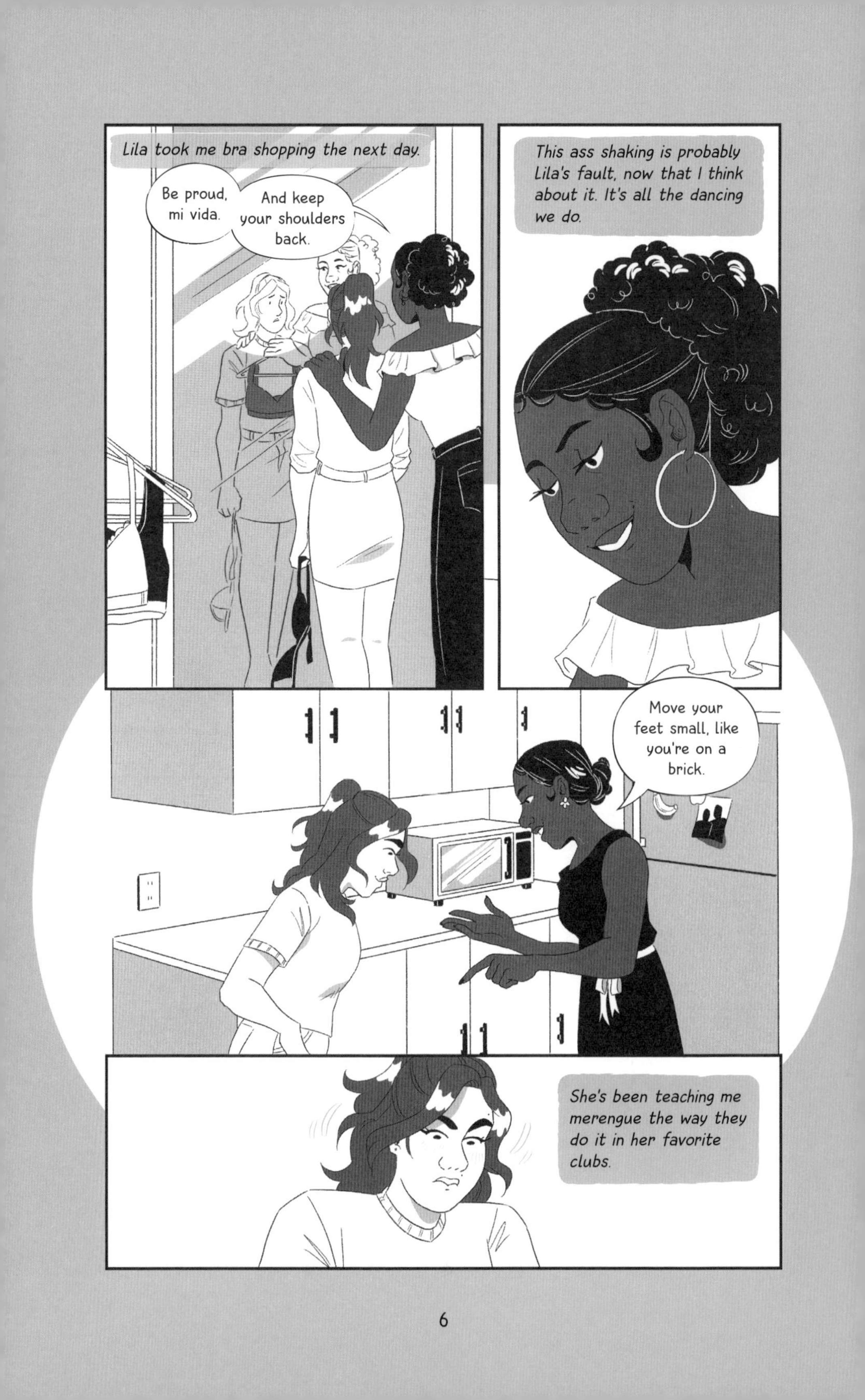
Lila took me bra shopping the next day.
Be proud, mi vida.
And keep your shoulders back.
This ass shaking is probably Lila's fault, now that I think about it. It's all the dancing we do.
Move your feet small, like you're on a brick.
She's been teaching me merengue the way they do it in her favorite clubs.

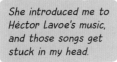 She introduced me to Héctor Lavoe's music, and those songs get stuck in my head.

But the hips? Shake them big, mami.

Maybe now my hips are always on swivel mode?

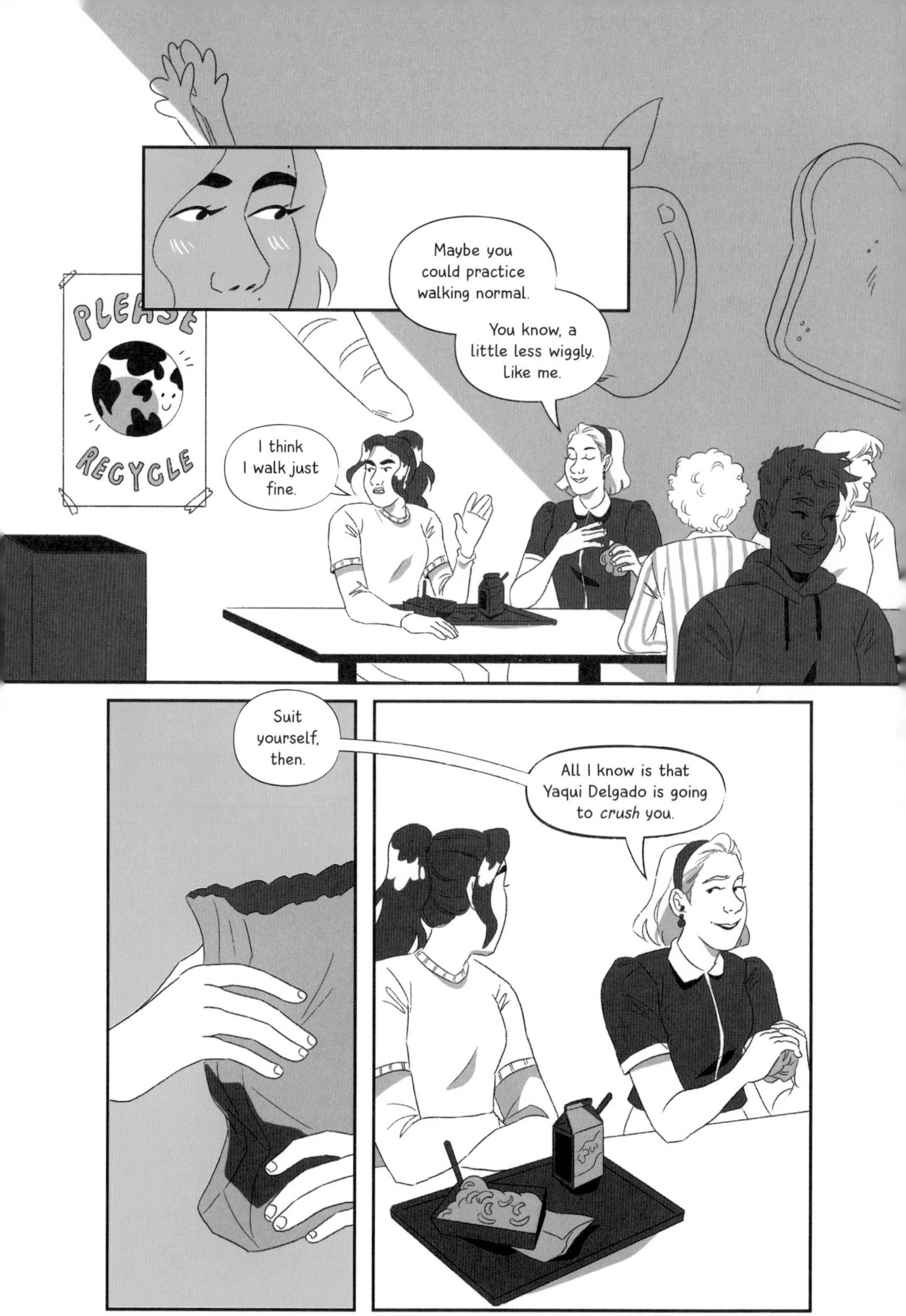
PLEASE RECYCLE
Maybe you could practice walking normal.
You know, a little less wiggly. Like me.
I think I walk just fine.
Suit yourself, then.
All I know is that Yaqui Delgado is going to *crush* you.

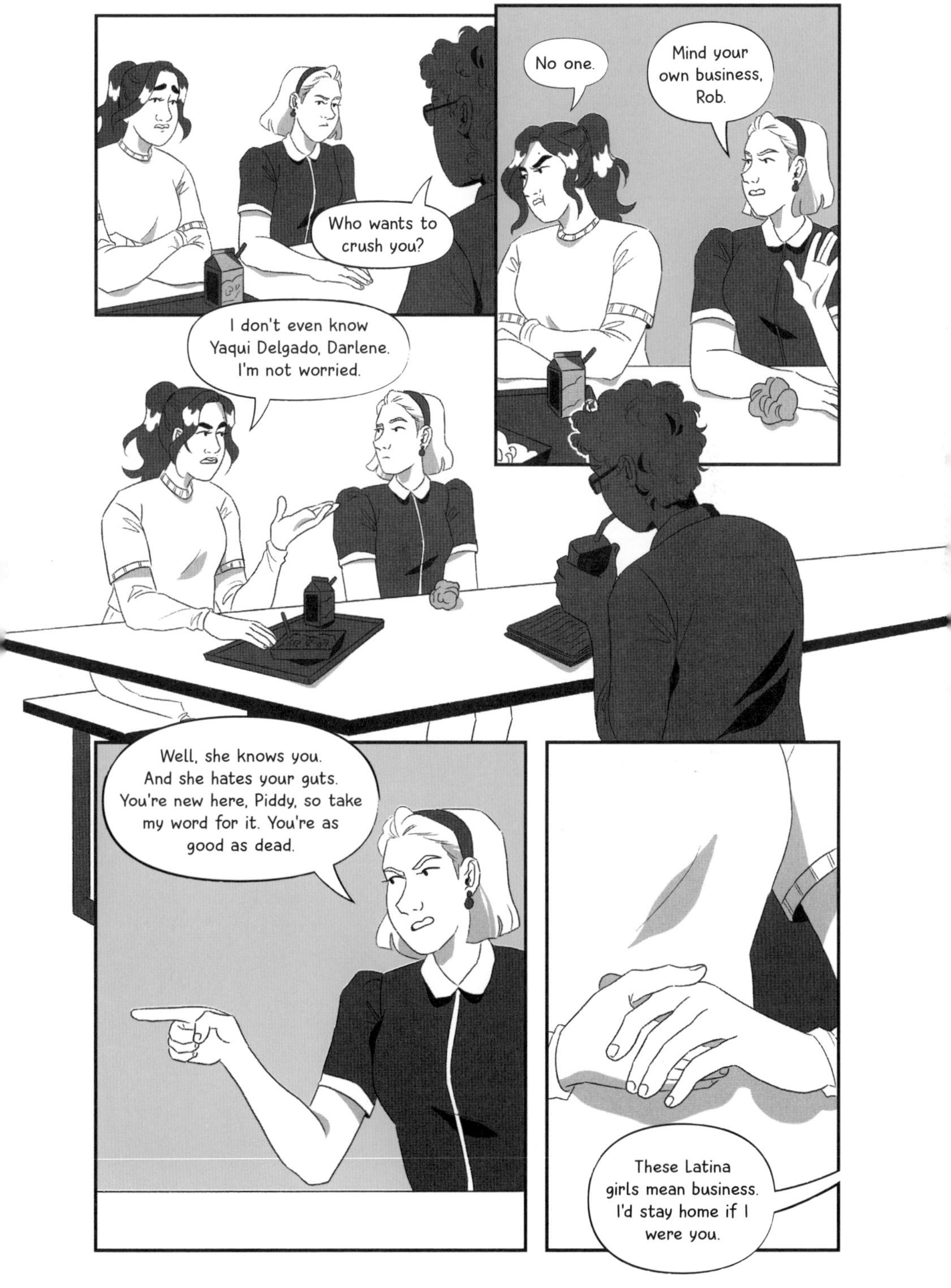
Who wants to crush you?
No one.
Mind your own business, Rob.
I don't even know Yaqui Delgado, Darlene. I'm not worried.
Well, she knows you. And she hates your guts. You're new here, Piddy, so take my word for it. You're as good as dead.
These Latina girls mean business. I'd stay home if I were you.

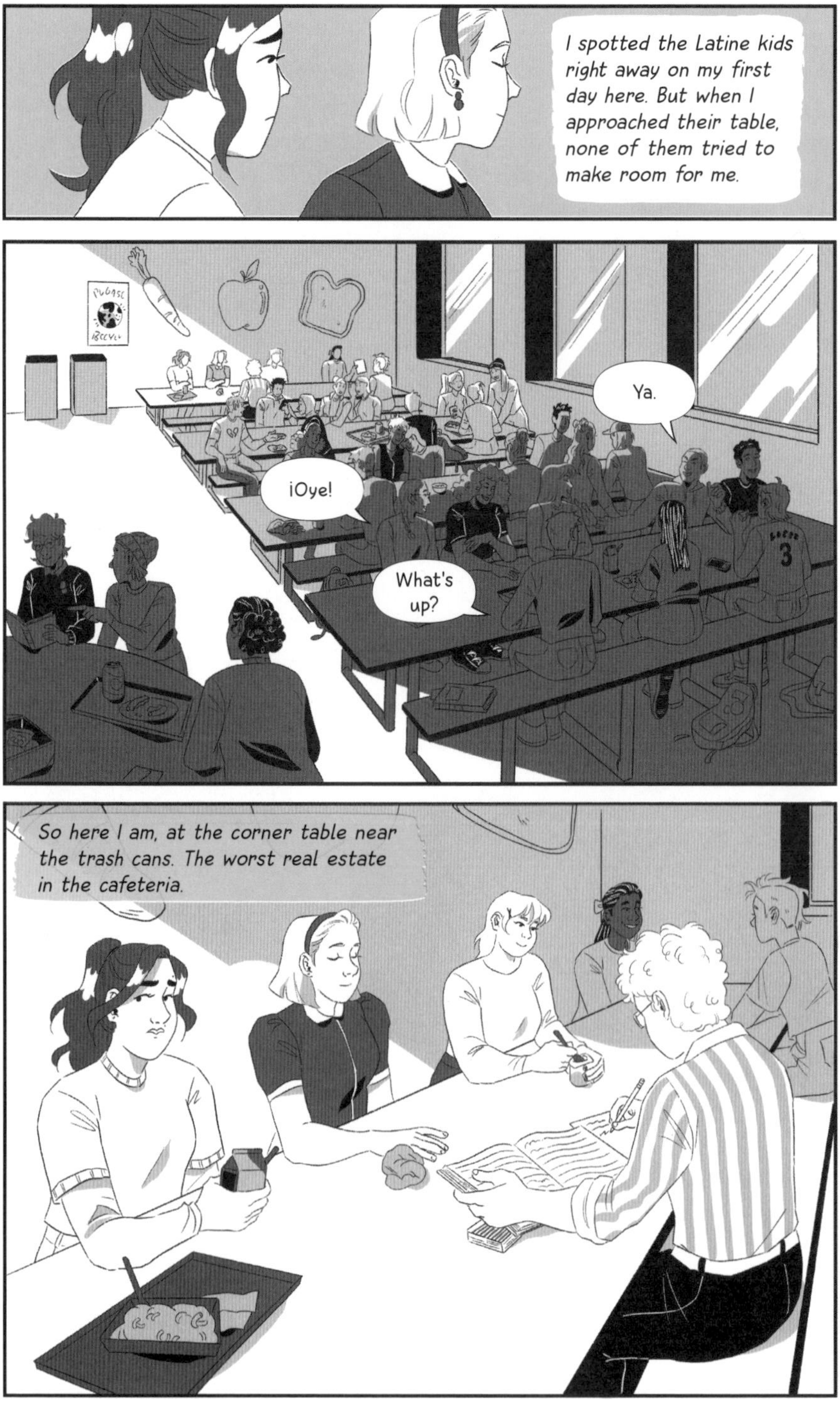
I spotted the Latine kids right away on my first day here. But when I approached their table, none of them tried to make room for me.
Ya.
¡Oye!
What's up?
So here I am, at the corner table near the trash cans. The worst real estate in the cafeteria.

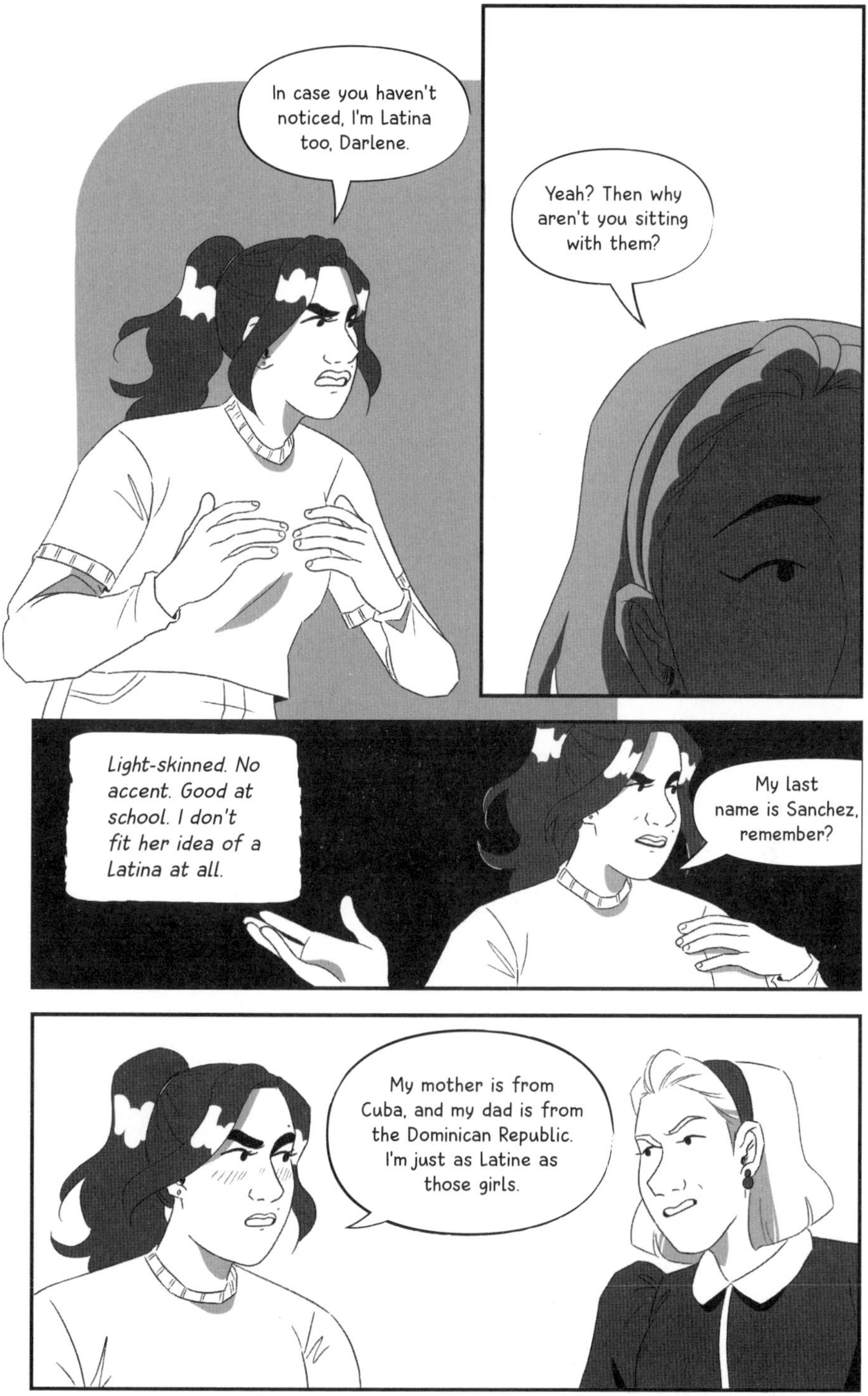
In case you haven't noticed, I'm Latina too, Darlene.
Yeah? Then why aren't you sitting with them?
Light-skinned. No accent. Good at school. I don't fit her idea of a Latina at all.
My last name is Sanchez, remember?
My mother is from Cuba, and my dad is from the Dominican Republic. I'm just as Latine as those girls.

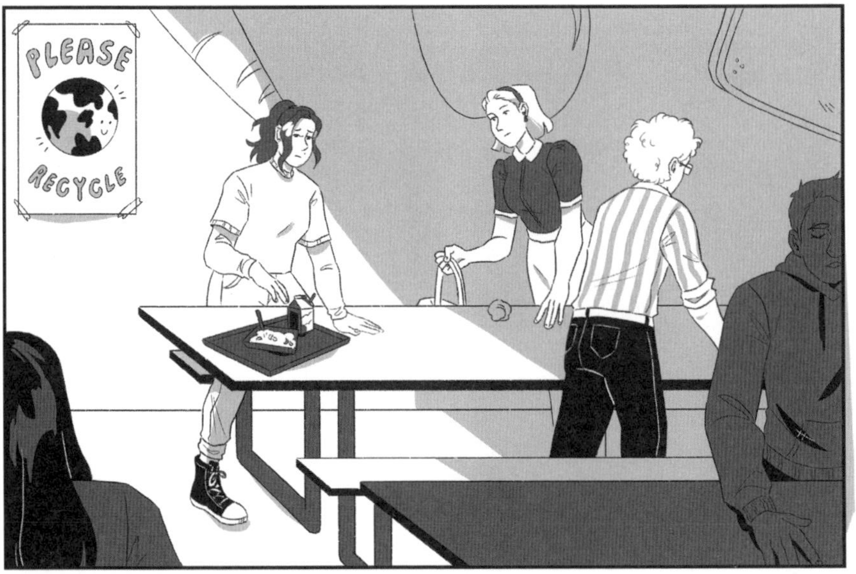
PLEASE
RECYCLE

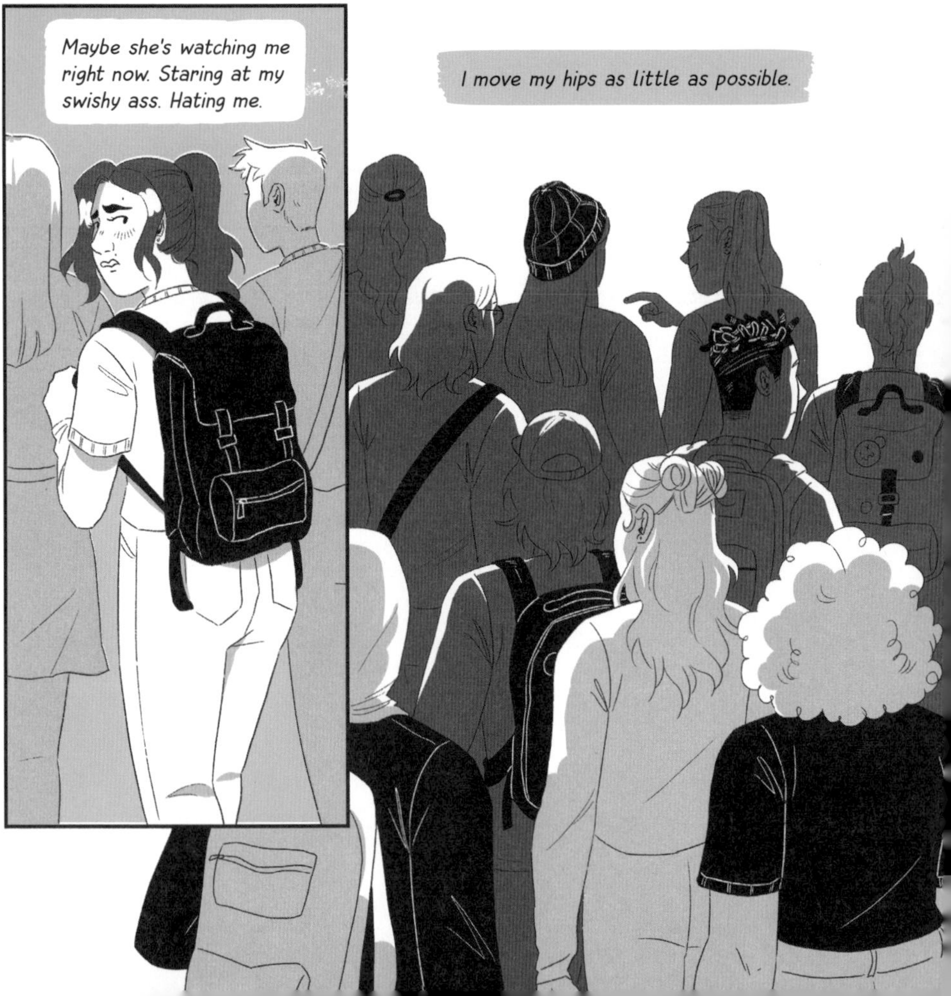
Maybe she's watching me right now. Staring at my swishy ass. Hating me.
I move my hips as little as possible.

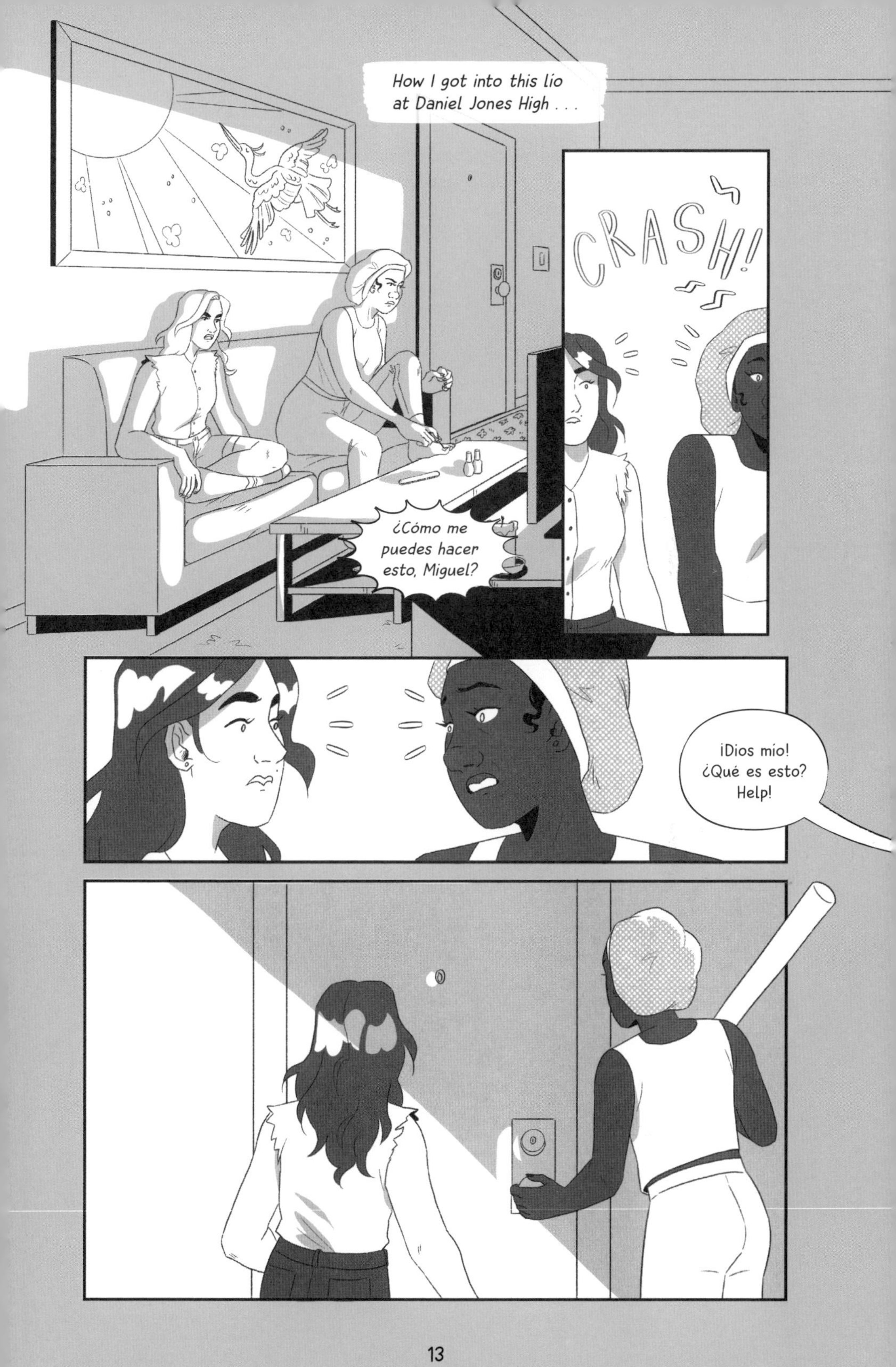
How I got into this lío at Daniel Jones High . . .
¿Cómo me puedes hacer esto, Miguel?
CRASH!
¡Dios mío! ¿Qué es esto? Help!

... is that the lobby staircase in our old apartment finally gave way.

¡Hasta aquí!

¡Sin vergüenza!

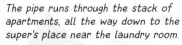

The pipe runs through the stack of apartments, all the way down to the super's place near the laundry room.

Calm yourself, Clara. You want a heart attack?

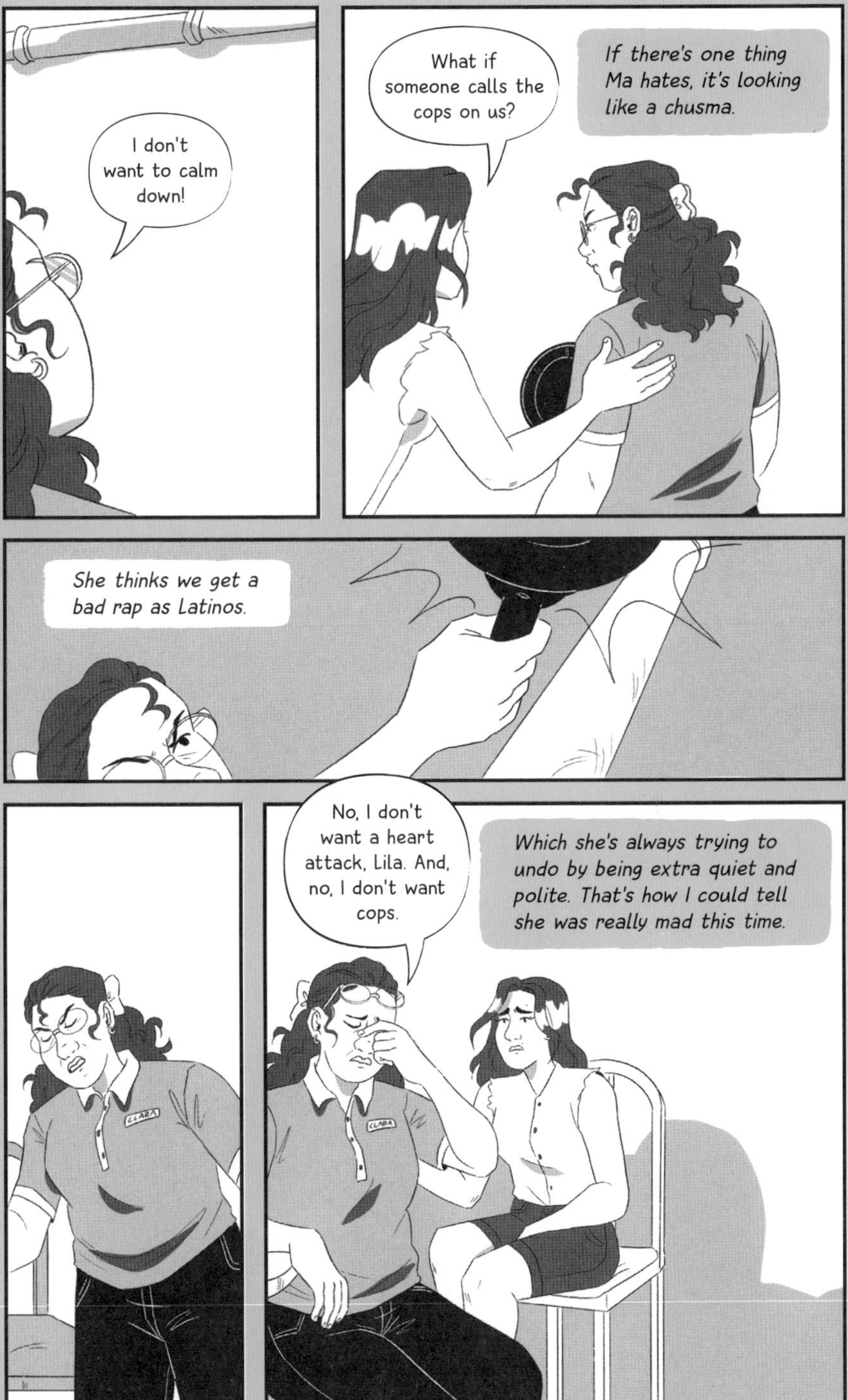
I don't want to calm down!
What if someone calls the cops on us?
If there's one thing Ma hates, it's looking like a chusma.
She thinks we get a bad rap as Latinos.
No, I don't want a heart attack, Lila. And, no, I don't want cops.
Which she's always trying to undo by being extra quiet and polite. That's how I could tell she was really mad this time.
CLARA
CLARA

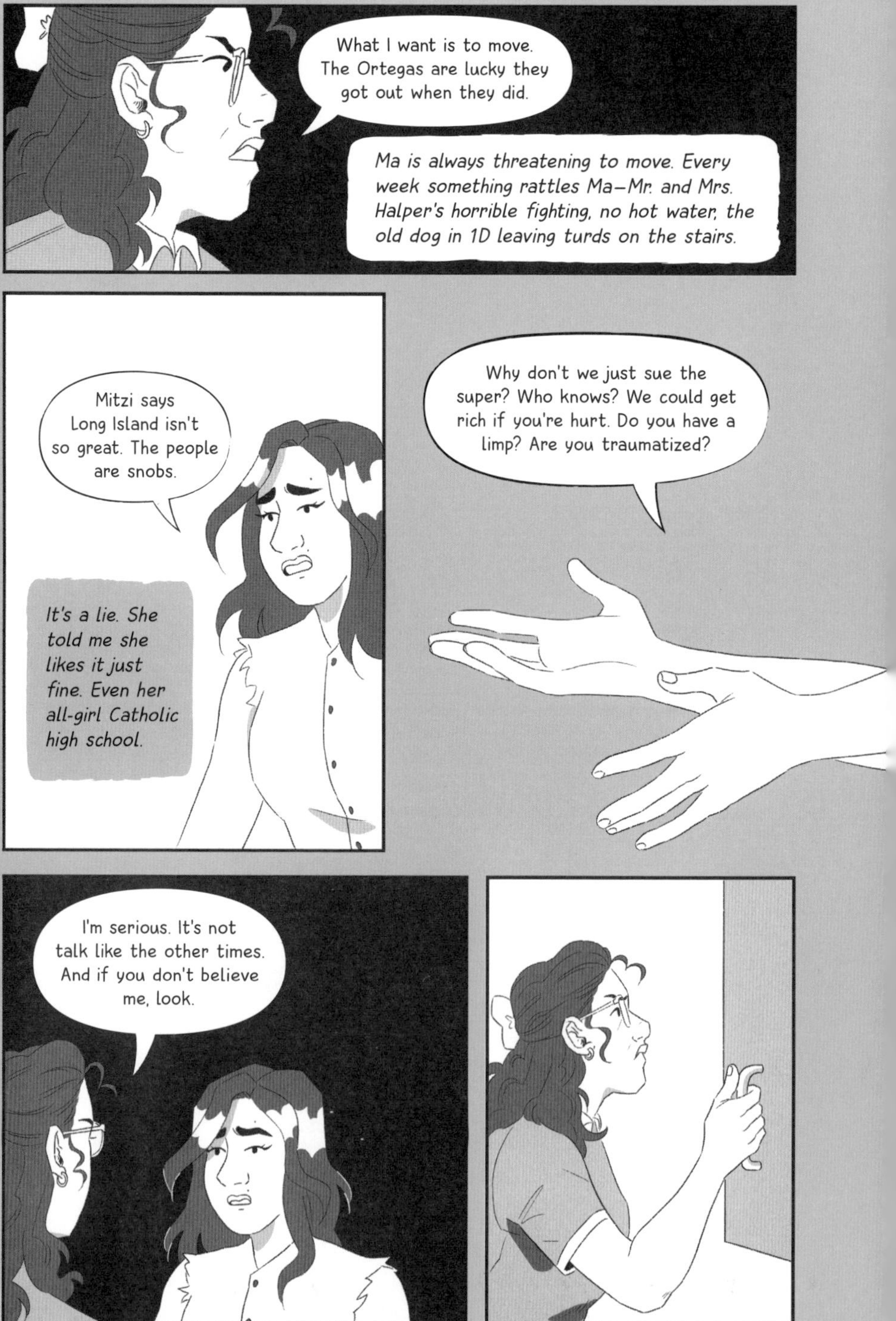
What I want is to move. The Ortegas are lucky they got out when they did.
Ma is always threatening to move. Every week something rattles Ma—Mr. and Mrs. Halper's horrible fighting, no hot water, the old dog in 1D leaving turds on the stairs.
Mitzi says Long Island isn't so great. The people are snobs.
It's a lie. She told me she likes it just fine. Even her all-girl Catholic high school.
Why don't we just sue the super? Who knows? We could get rich if you're hurt. Do you have a limp? Are you traumatized?
I'm serious. It's not talk like the other times. And if you don't believe me, look.

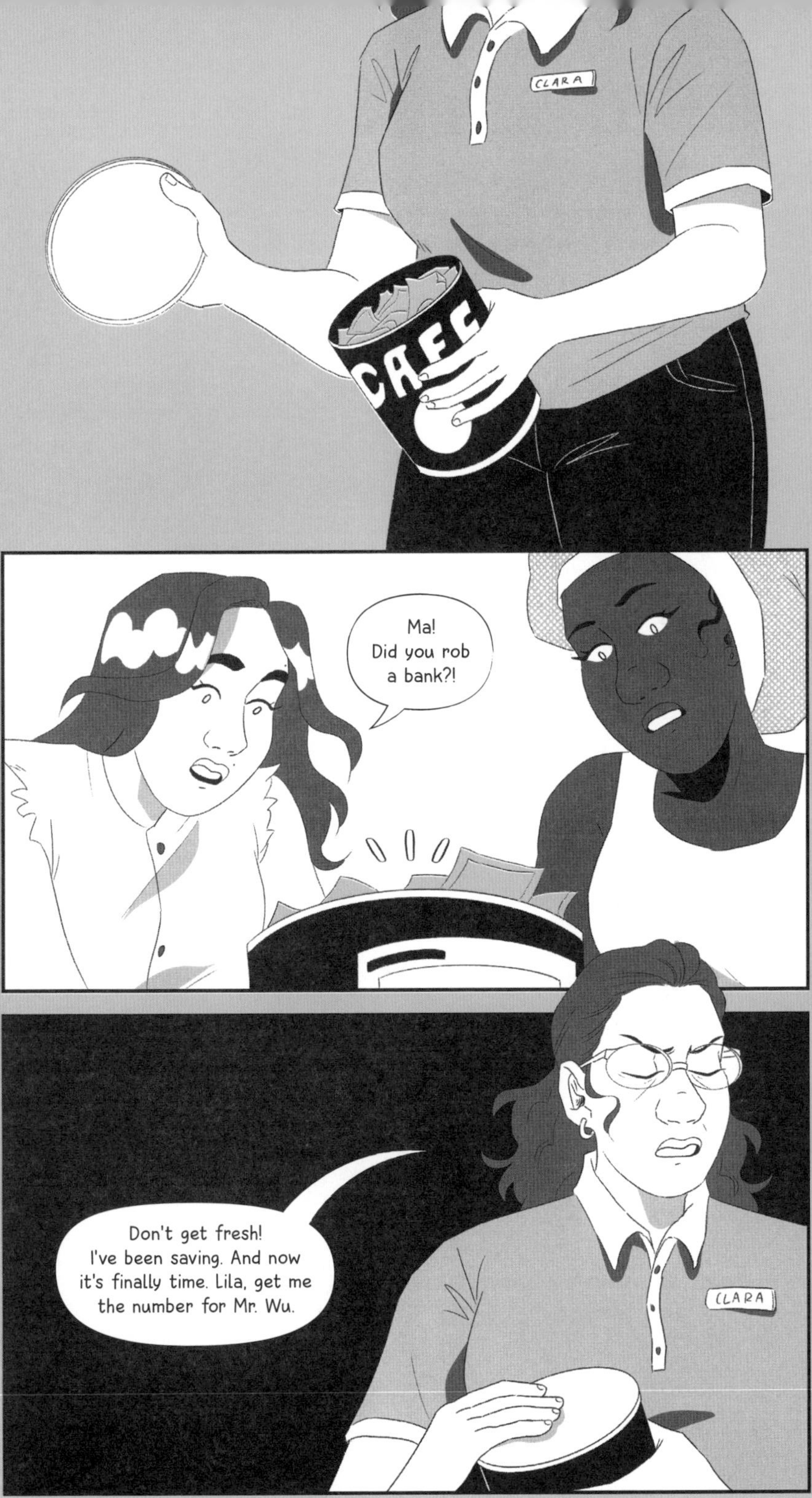
CLARA
CAFE
Ma! Did you rob a bank?!
CLARA
Don't get fresh! I've been saving. And now it's finally time. Lila, get me the number for Mr. Wu.

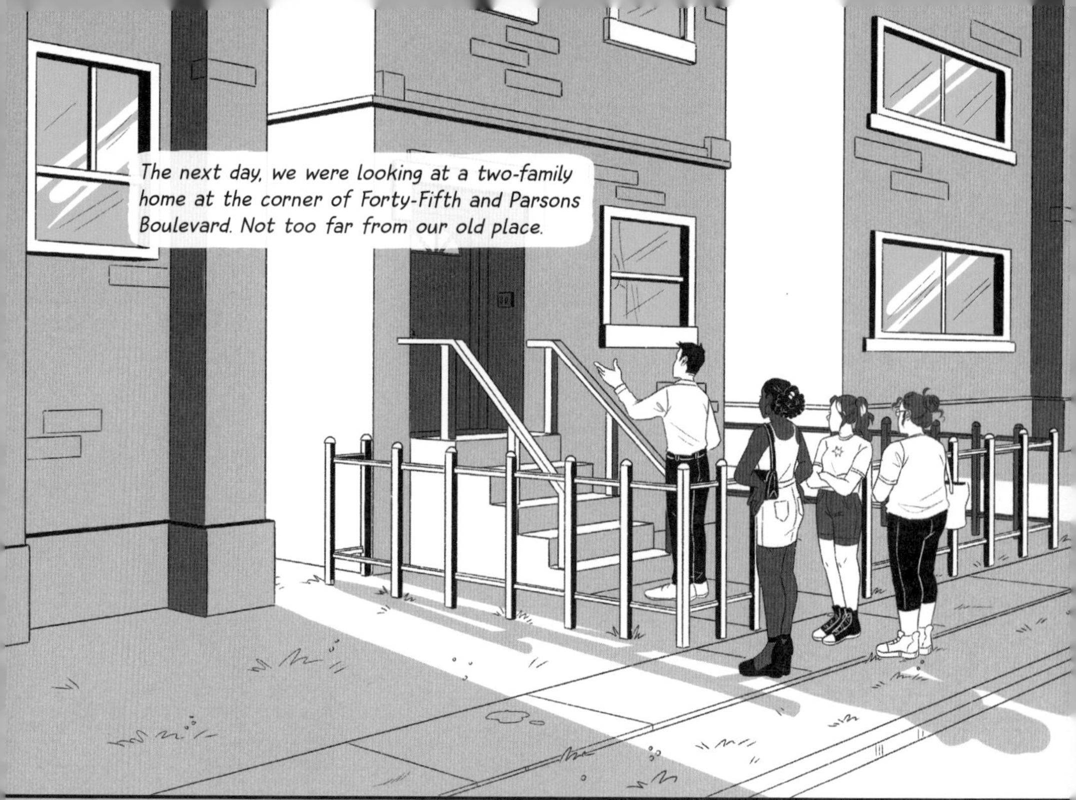
The next day, we were looking at a two-family home at the corner of Forty-Fifth and Parsons Boulevard. Not too far from our old place.

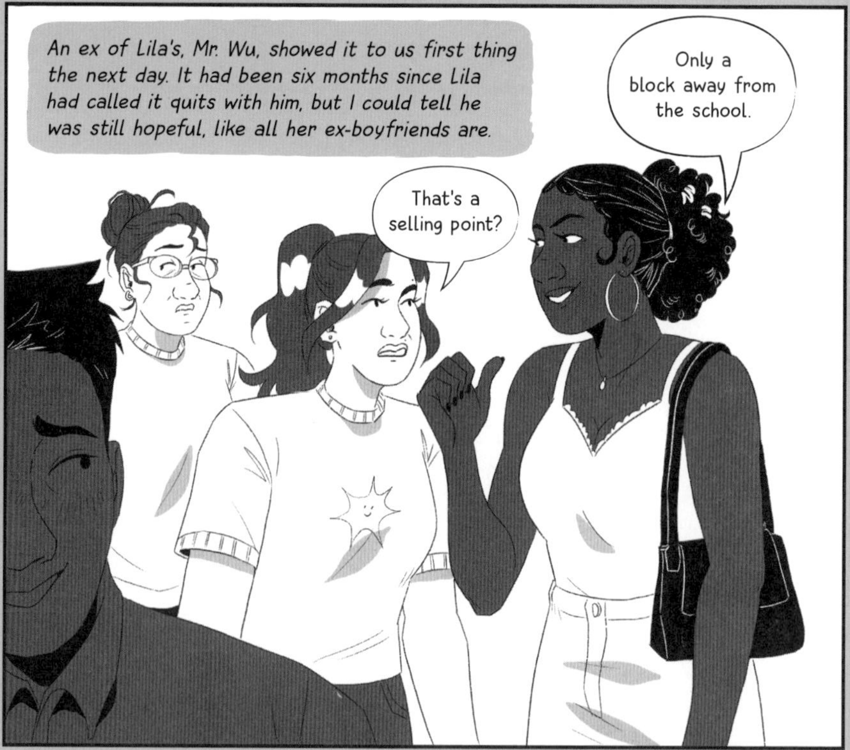
An ex of Lila's, Mr. Wu, showed it to us first thing the next day. It had been six months since Lila had called it quits with him, but I could tell he was still hopeful, like all her ex-boyfriends are.
Only a block away from the school.
That's a selling point?

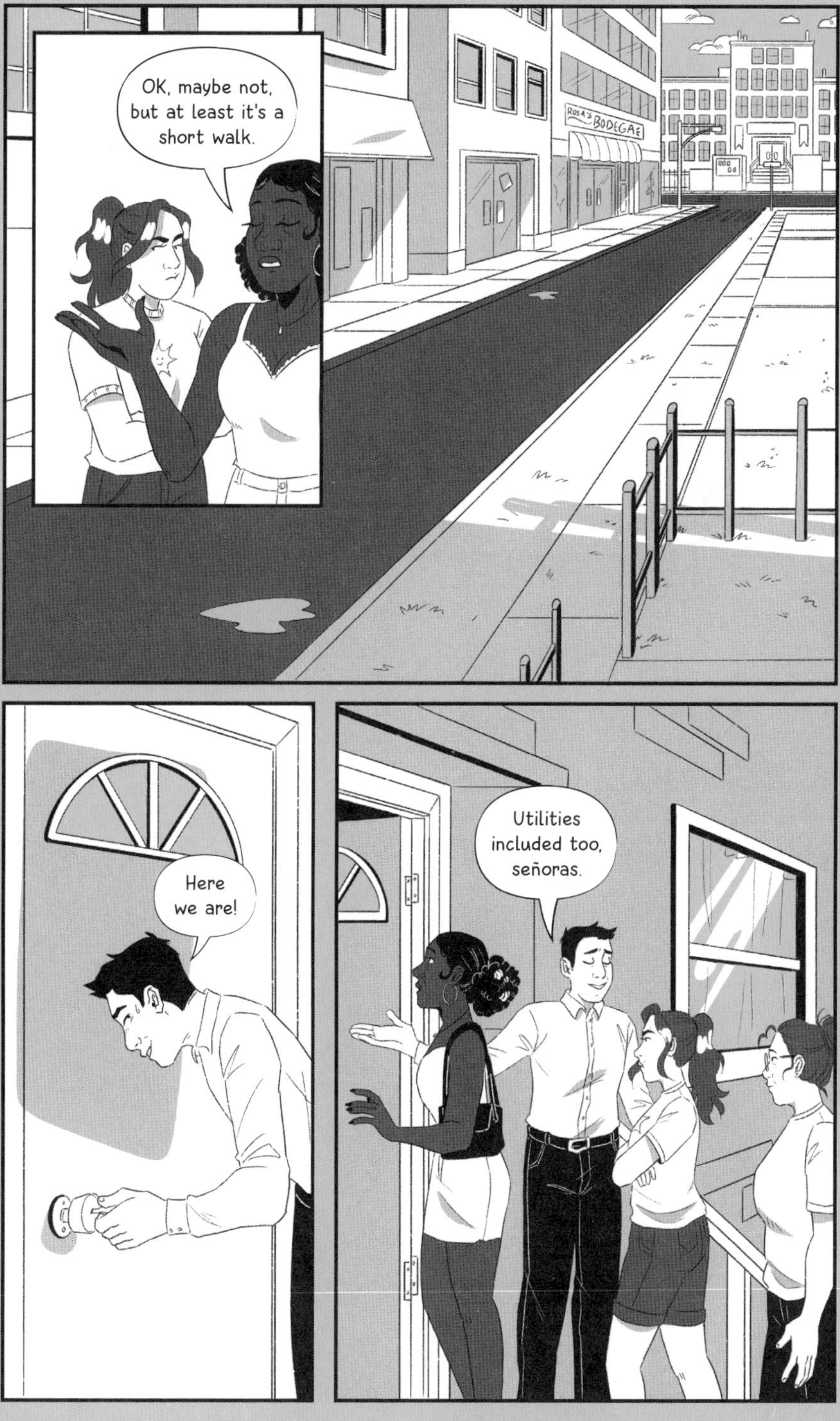
OK, maybe not, but at least it's a short walk.
ROSA'S BODEGA
Here we are!
Utilities included too, señoras.

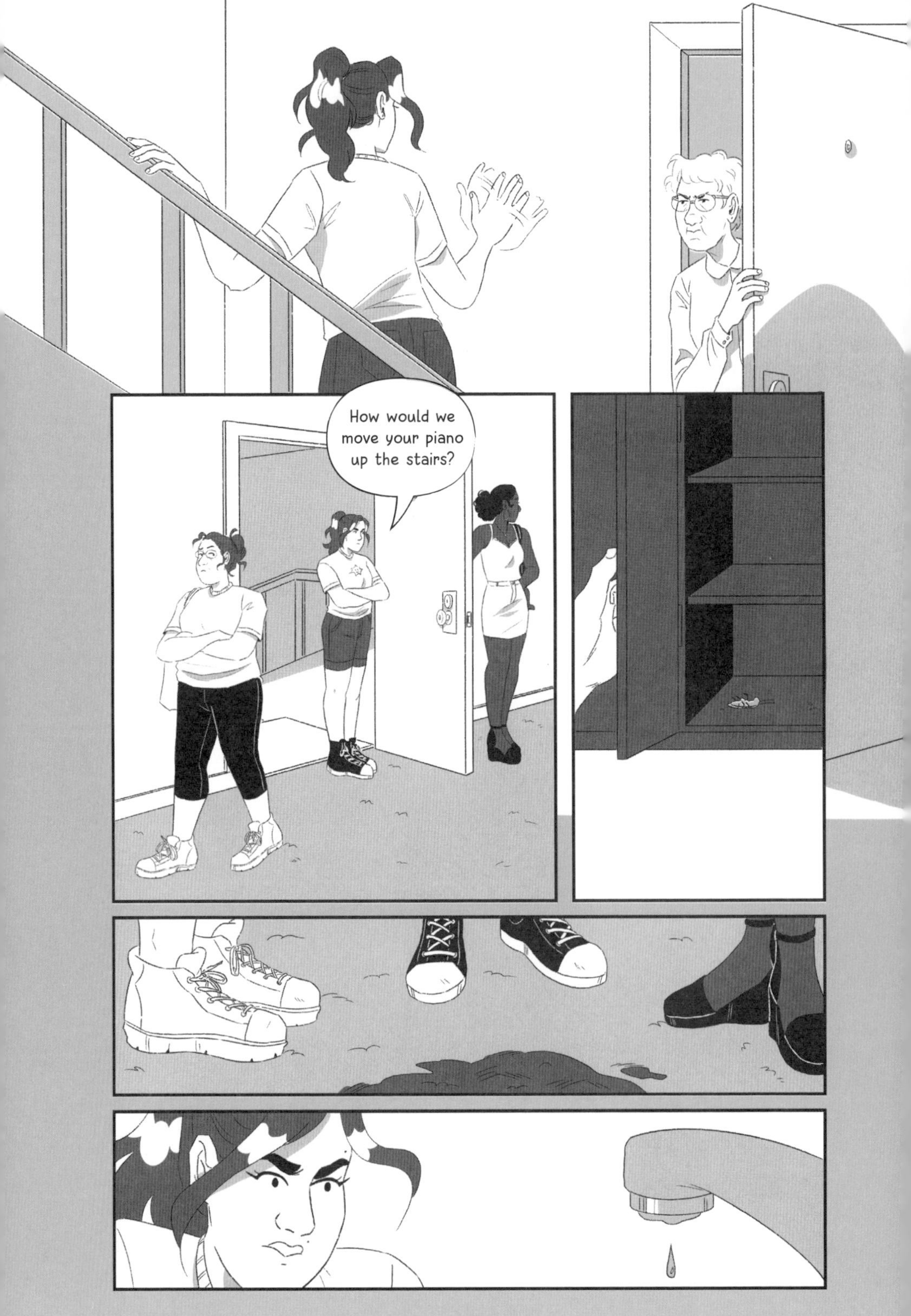
How would we move your piano up the stairs?

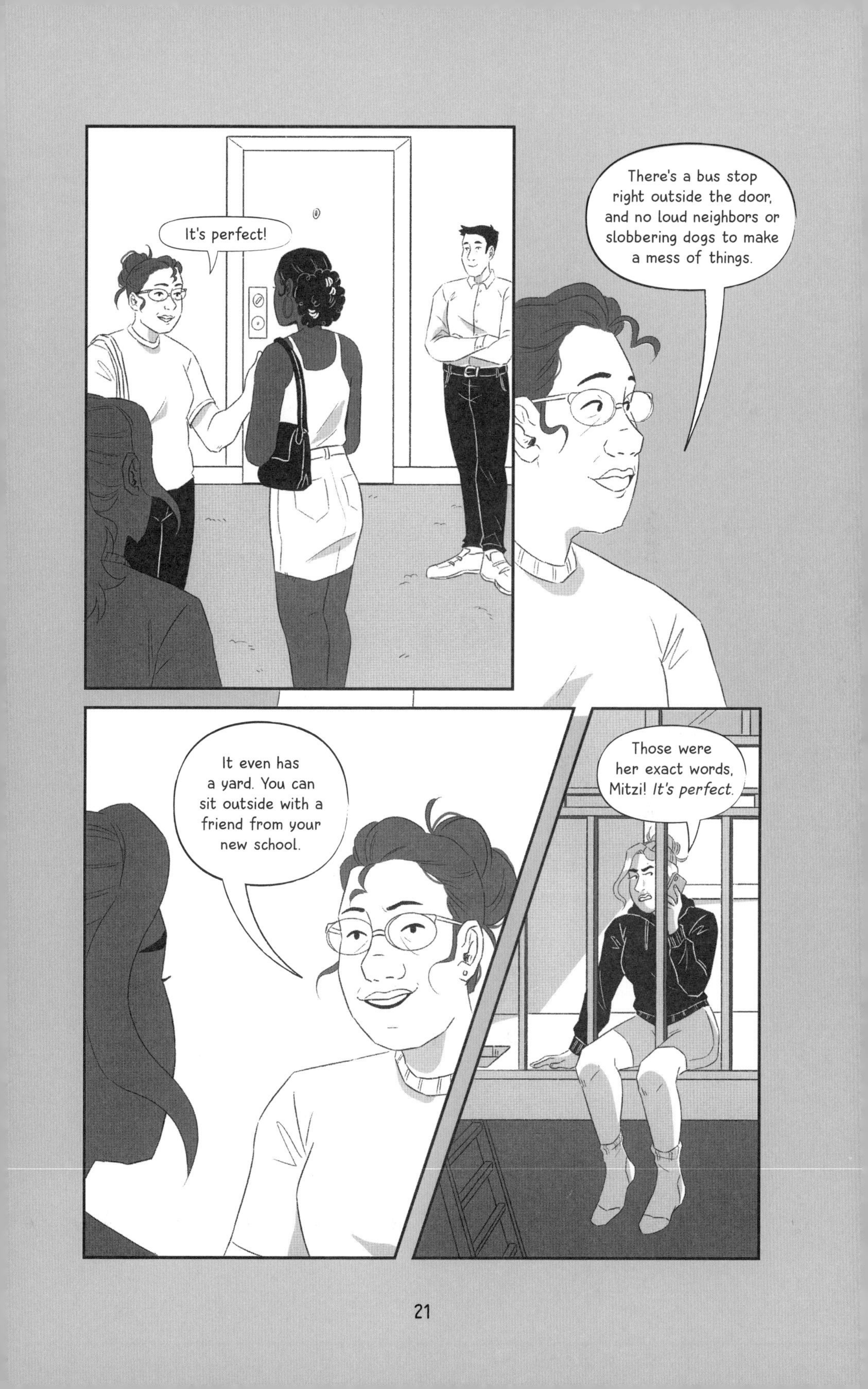
It's perfect!
There's a bus stop right outside the door, and no loud neighbors or slobbering dogs to make a mess of things.
It even has a yard. You can sit outside with a friend from your new school.
Those were her exact words, Mitzi! *It's perfect.*

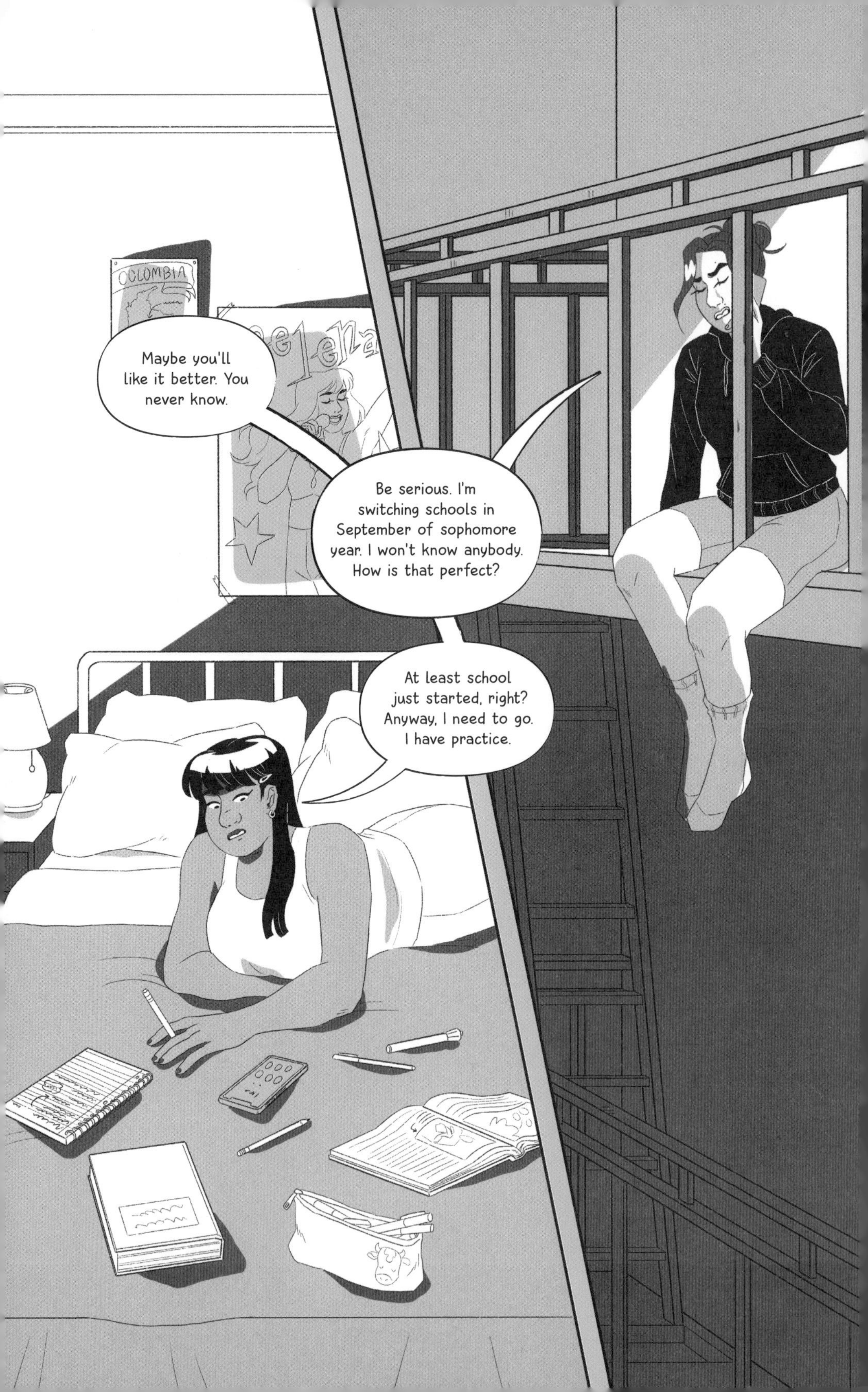
COLOMBIA
Maybe you'll like it better. You never know.
Be serious. I'm switching schools in September of sophomore year. I won't know anybody. How is that perfect?
At least school just started, right? Anyway, I need to go. I have practice.

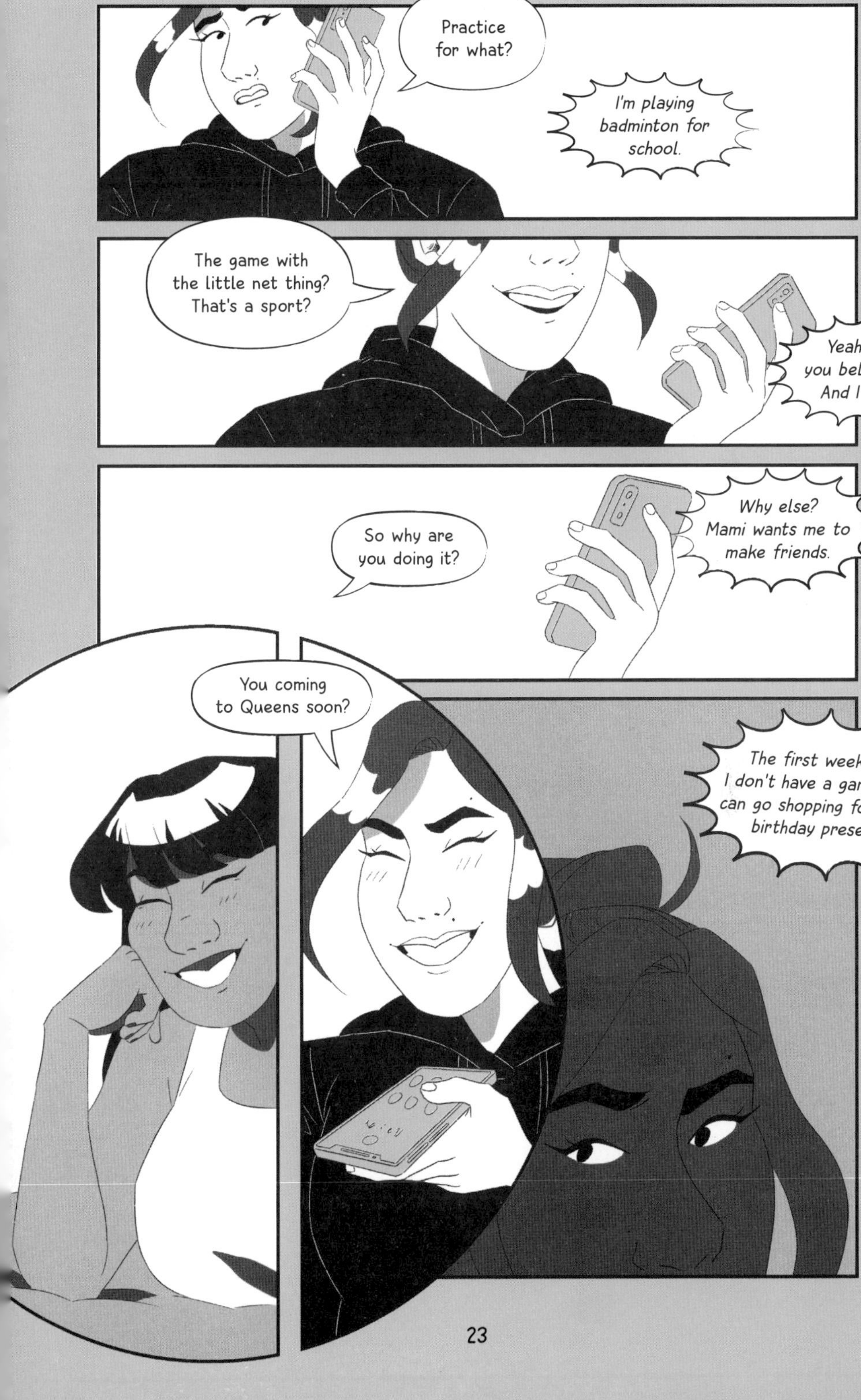
Practice for what?
I'm playing badminton for school.
The game with the little net thing? That's a sport?
Yeah, can you believe it? And I suck.
So why are you doing it?
Why else? Mami wants me to make friends.
You coming to Queens soon?
The first weekend I don't have a game. We can go shopping for your birthday present.

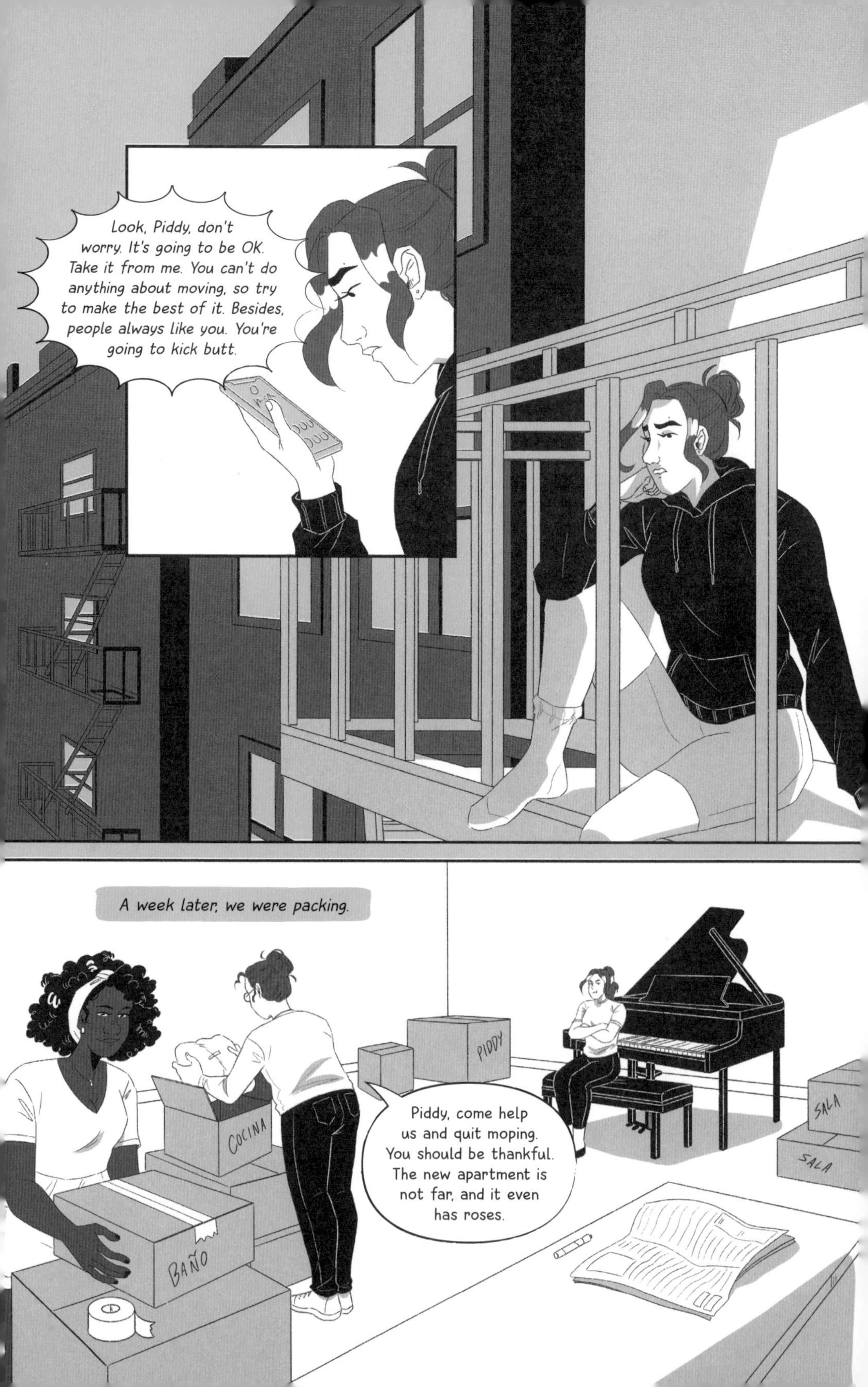
Look, Piddy, don't worry. It's going to be OK. Take it from me. You can't do anything about moving, so try to make the best of it. Besides, people always like you. You're going to kick butt.
A week later, we were packing.
PIDDY
COCINA
SALA
SALA
BAÑO
Piddy, come help us and quit moping. You should be thankful. The new apartment is not far, and it even has roses.

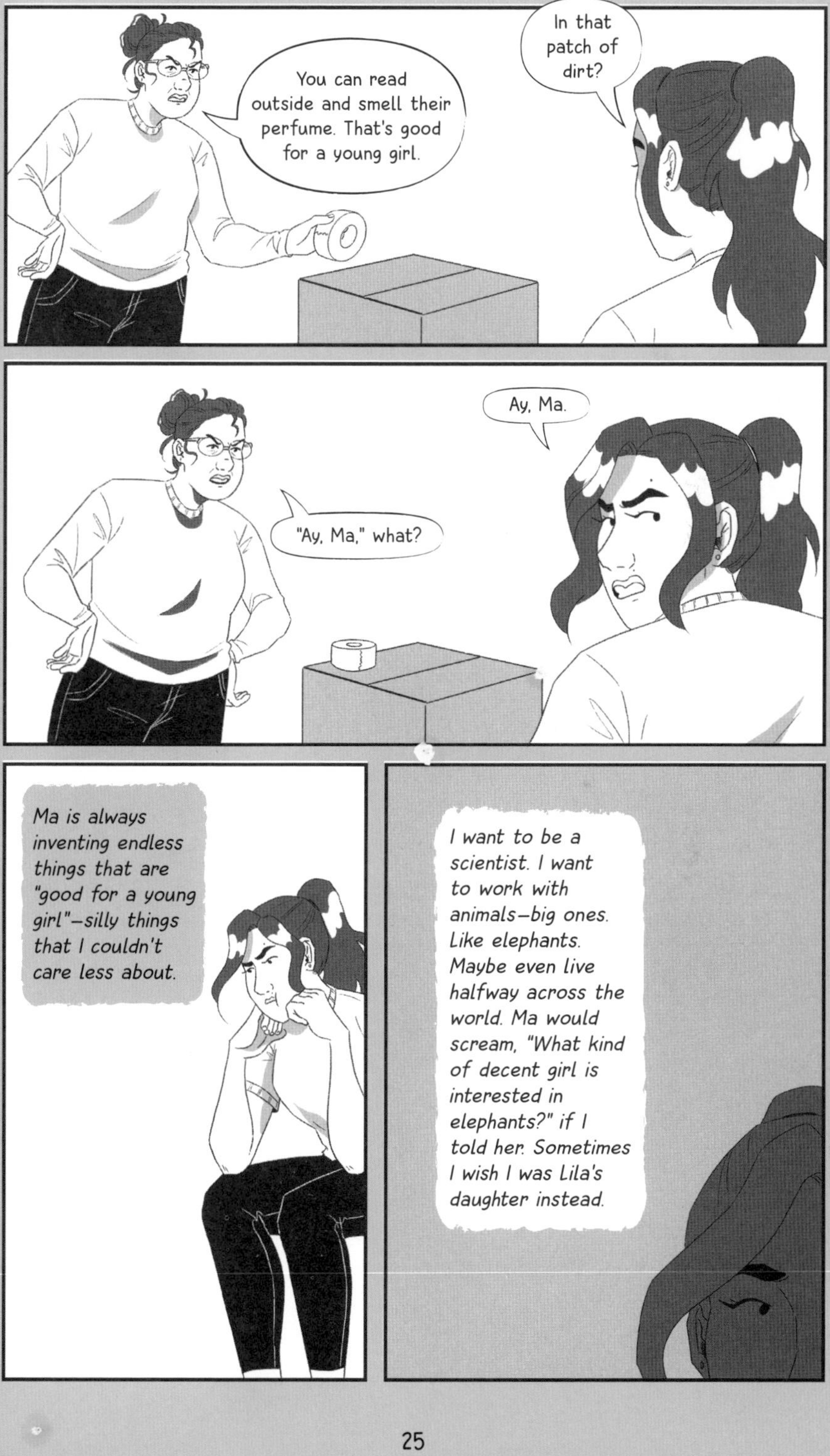

You can read outside and smell their perfume. That's good for a young girl.
In that patch of dirt?
Ay, Ma.
"Ay, Ma," what?
Ma is always inventing endless things that are "good for a young girl"—silly things that I couldn't care less about.
I want to be a scientist. I want to work with animals—big ones. Like elephants. Maybe even live halfway across the world. Ma would scream, "What kind of decent girl is interested in elephants?" if I told her. Sometimes I wish I was Lila's daughter instead.

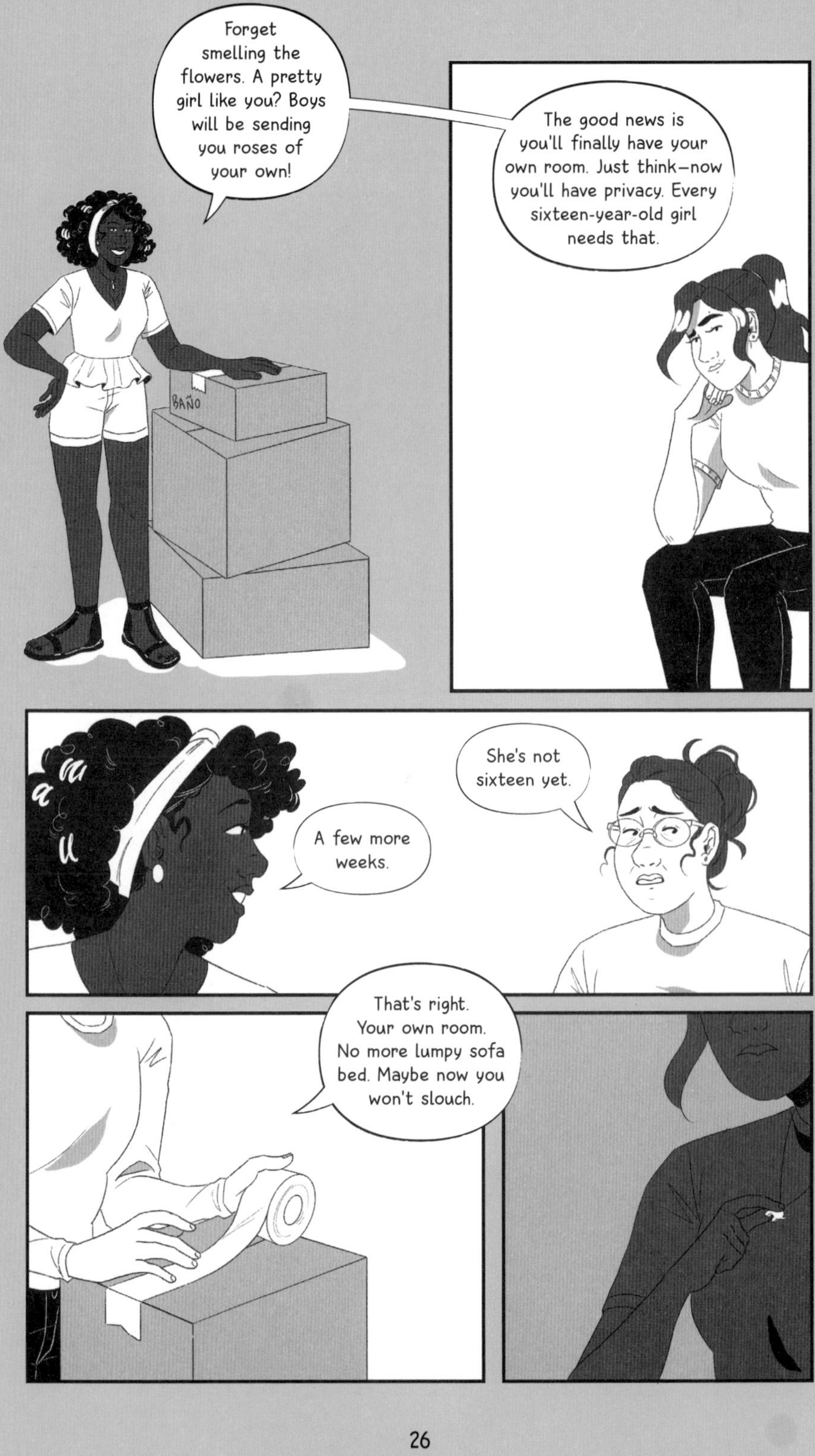
Forget smelling the flowers. A pretty girl like you? Boys will be sending you roses of your own!
The good news is you'll finally have your own room. Just think—now you'll have privacy. Every sixteen-year-old girl needs that.
BAÑO
She's not sixteen yet.
A few more weeks.
That's right. Your own room. No more lumpy sofa bed. Maybe now you won't slouch.

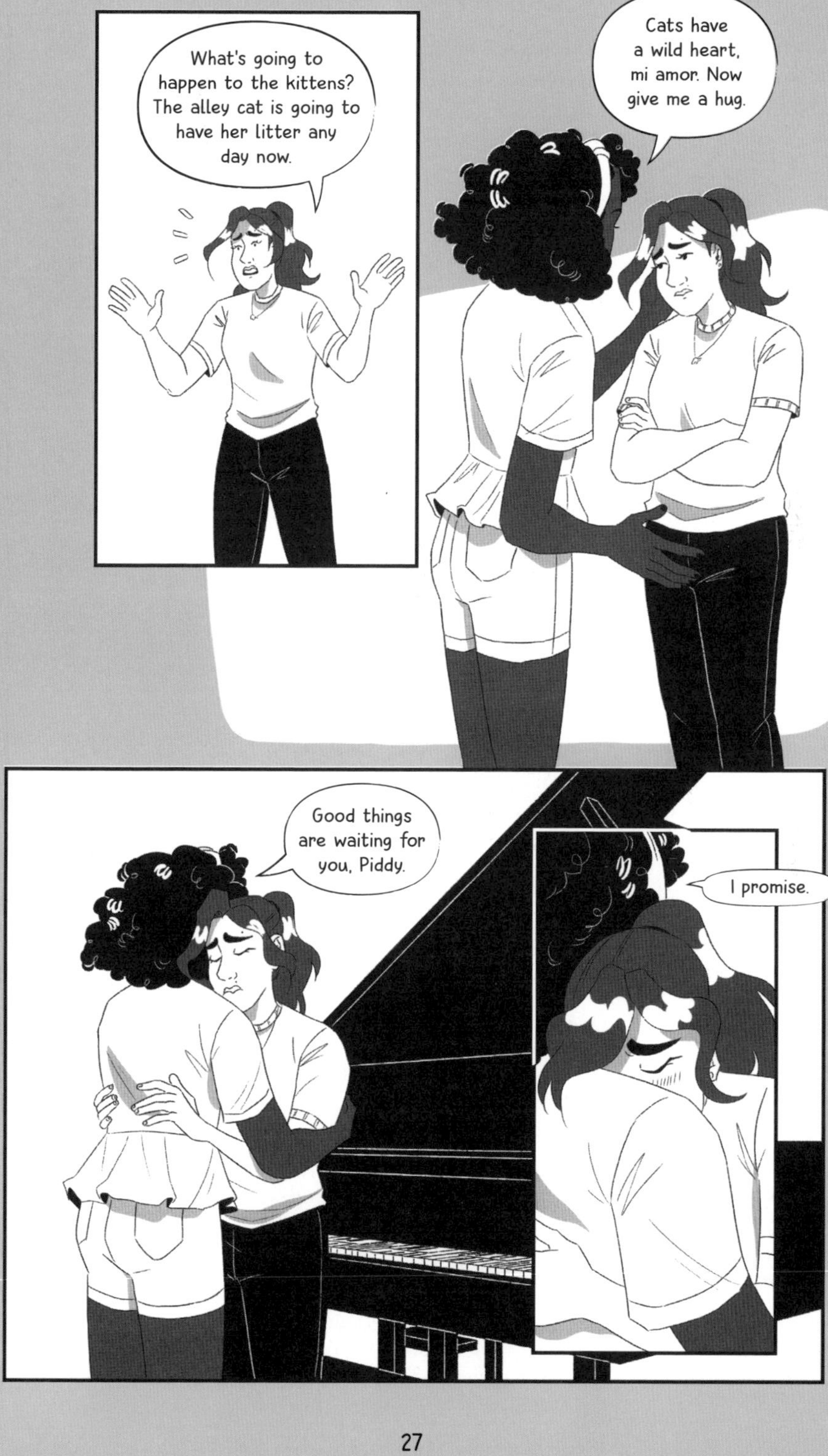
What's going to happen to the kittens? The alley cat is going to have her litter any day now.
Cats have a wild heart, mi amor. Now give me a hug.
Good things are waiting for you, Piddy.
I promise.

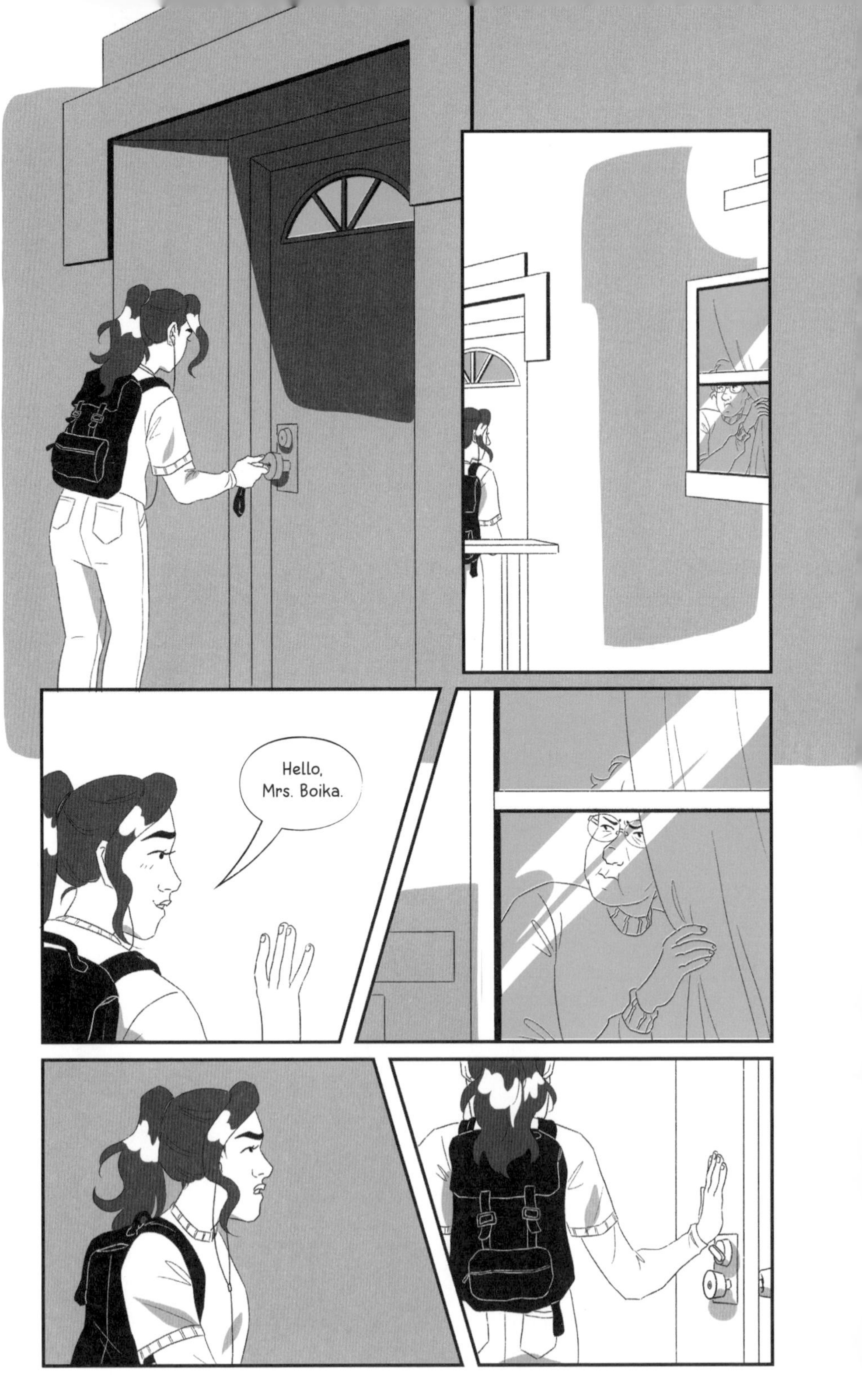
Hello, Mrs. Boika.

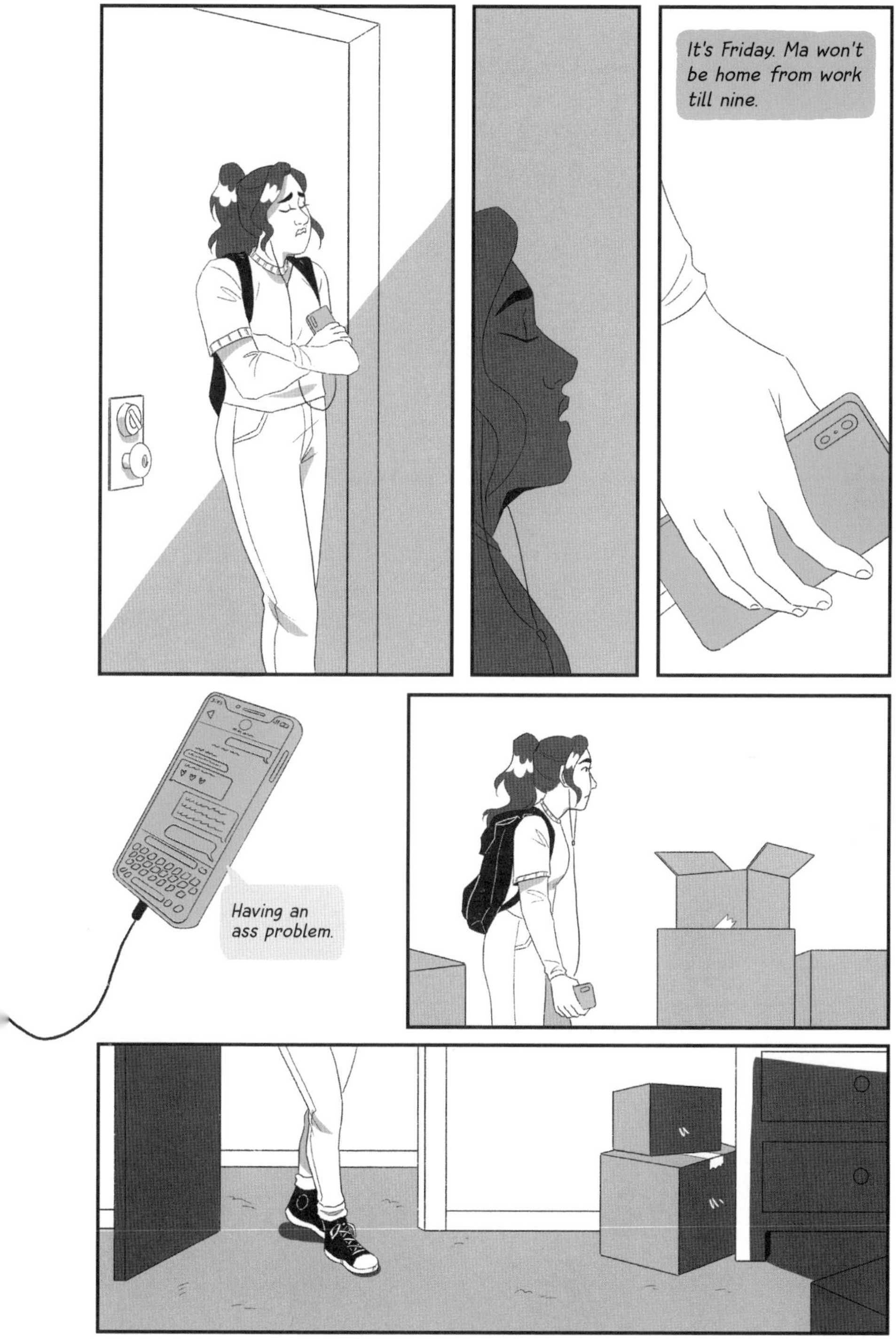
It's Friday. Ma won't be home from work till nine.
Having an ass problem.

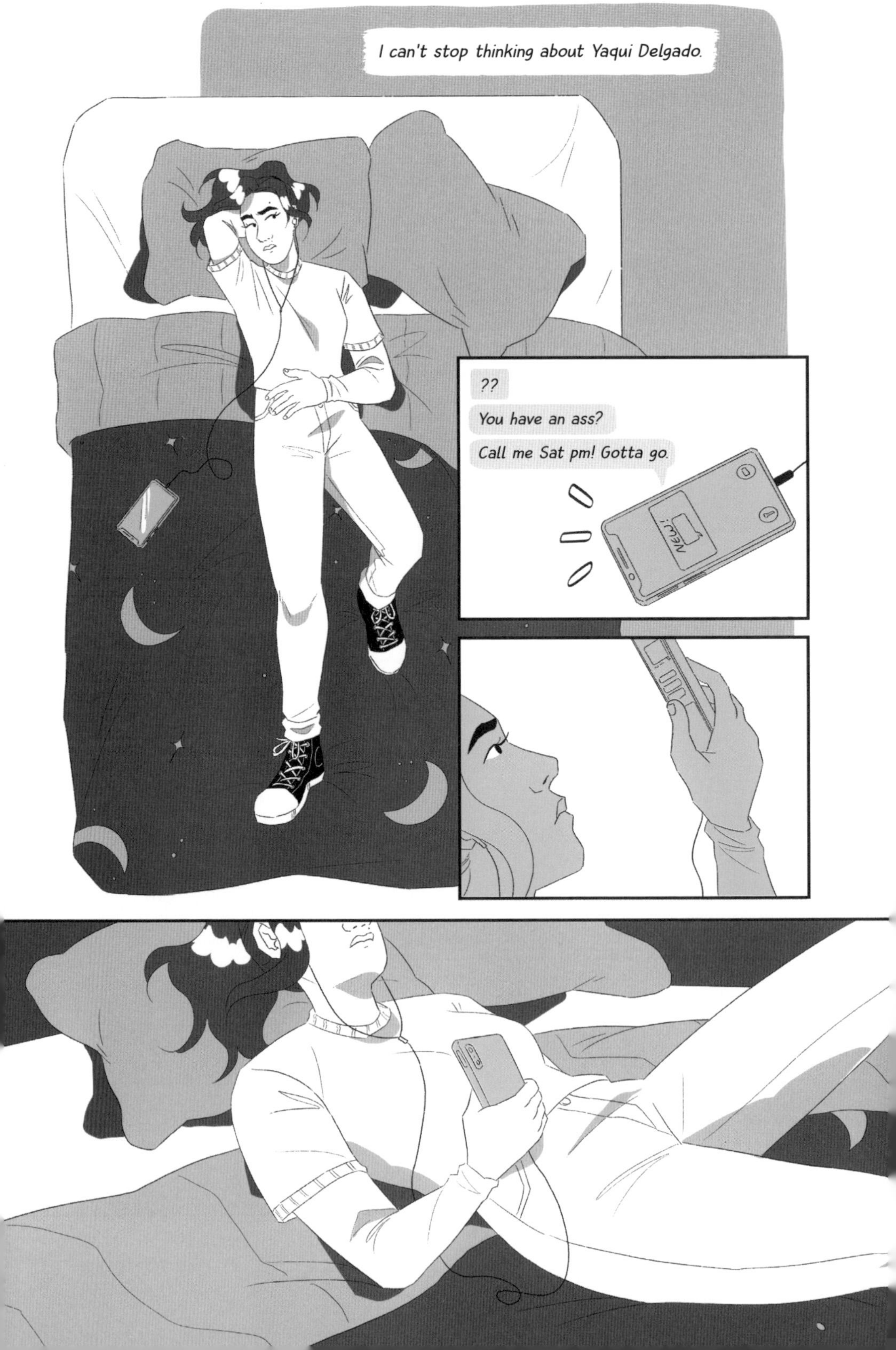
I can't stop thinking about Yaqui Delgado.
??
You have an ass?
Call me Sat pm! Gotta go.
NEW!

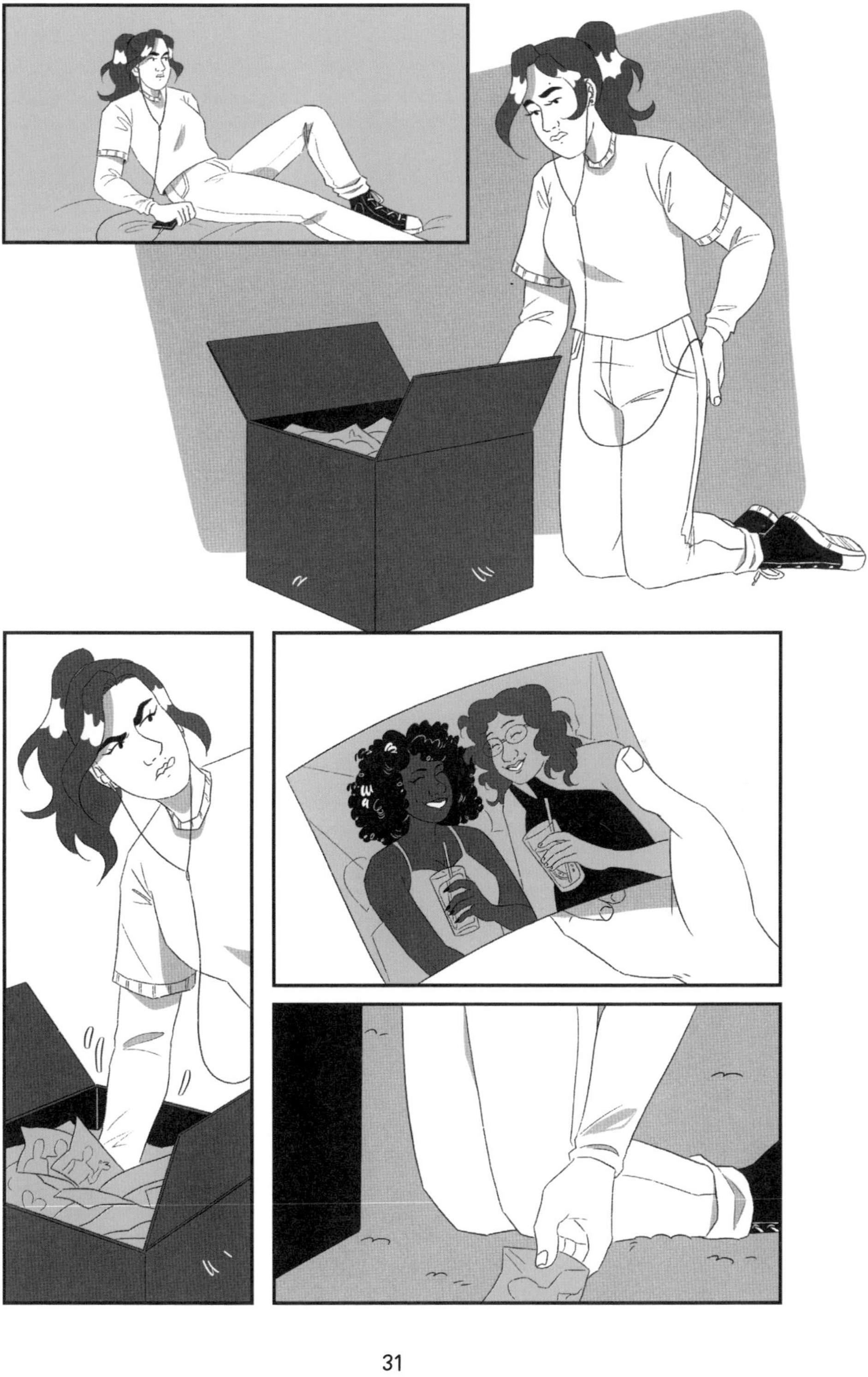

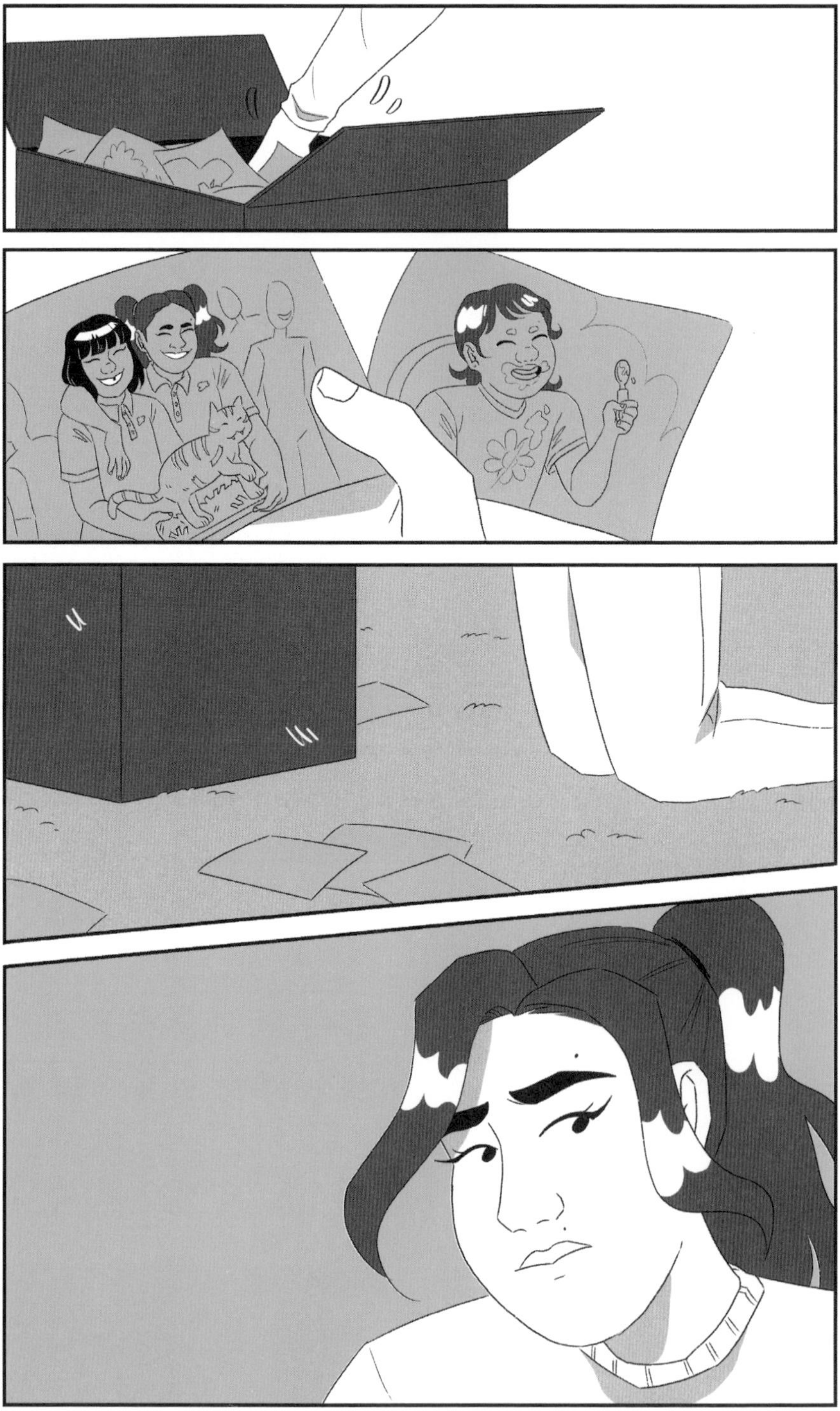

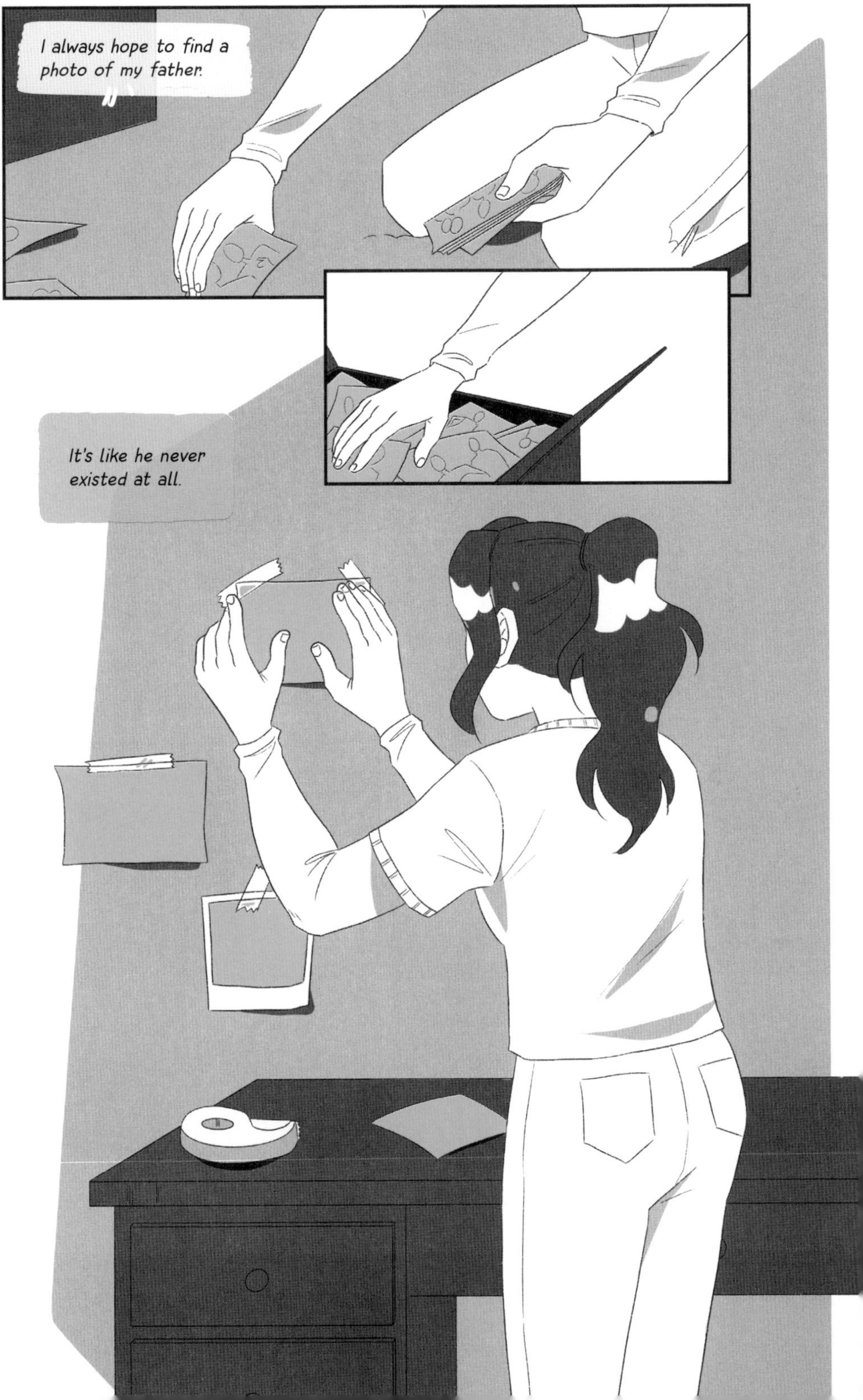
I always hope to find a photo of my father.
It's like he never existed at all.

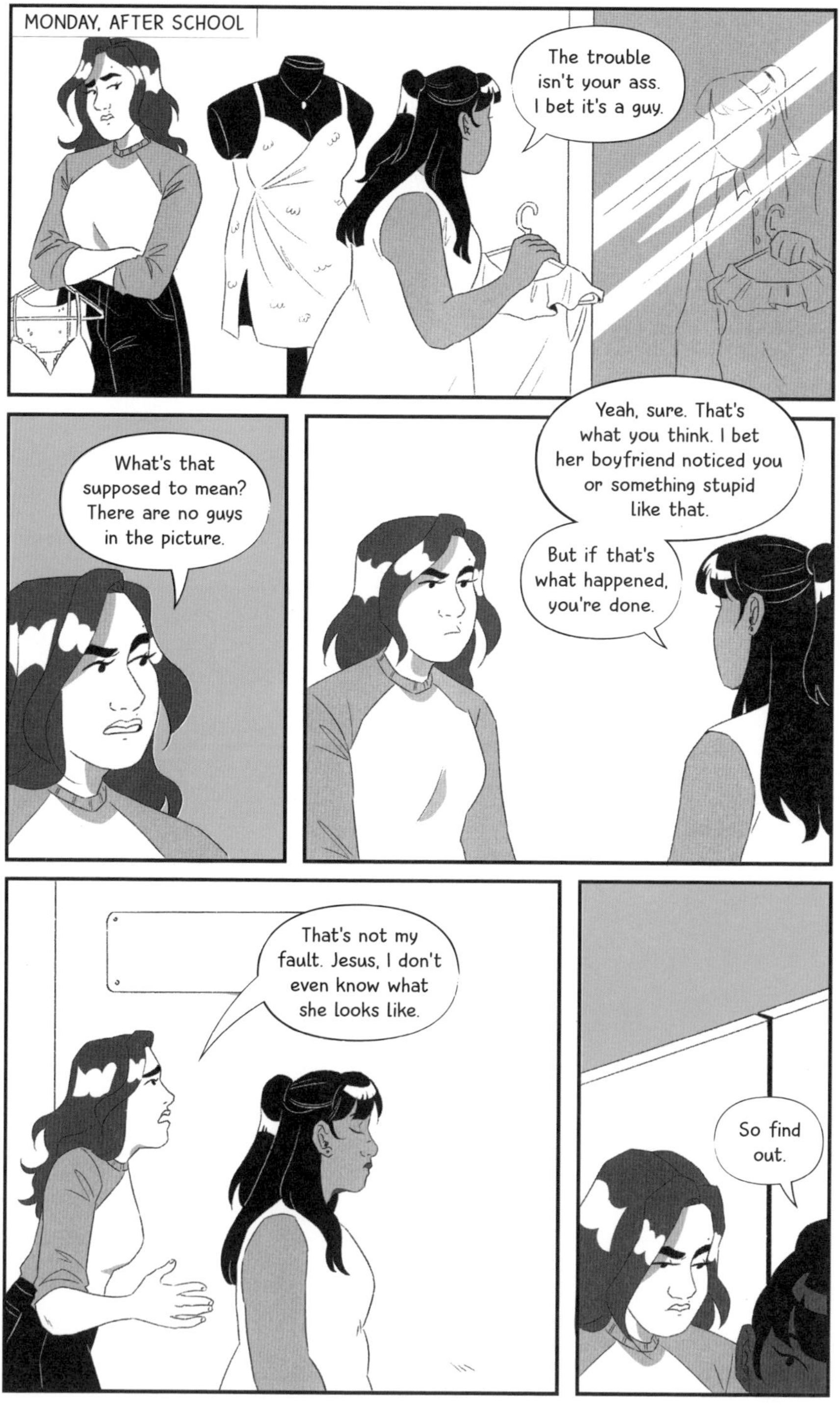
MONDAY, AFTER SCHOOL
The trouble isn't your ass. I bet it's a guy.
What's that supposed to mean? There are no guys in the picture.
Yeah, sure. That's what you think. I bet her boyfriend noticed you or something stupid like that.
But if that's what happened, you're done.
That's not my fault. Jesus, I don't even know what she looks like.
So find out.

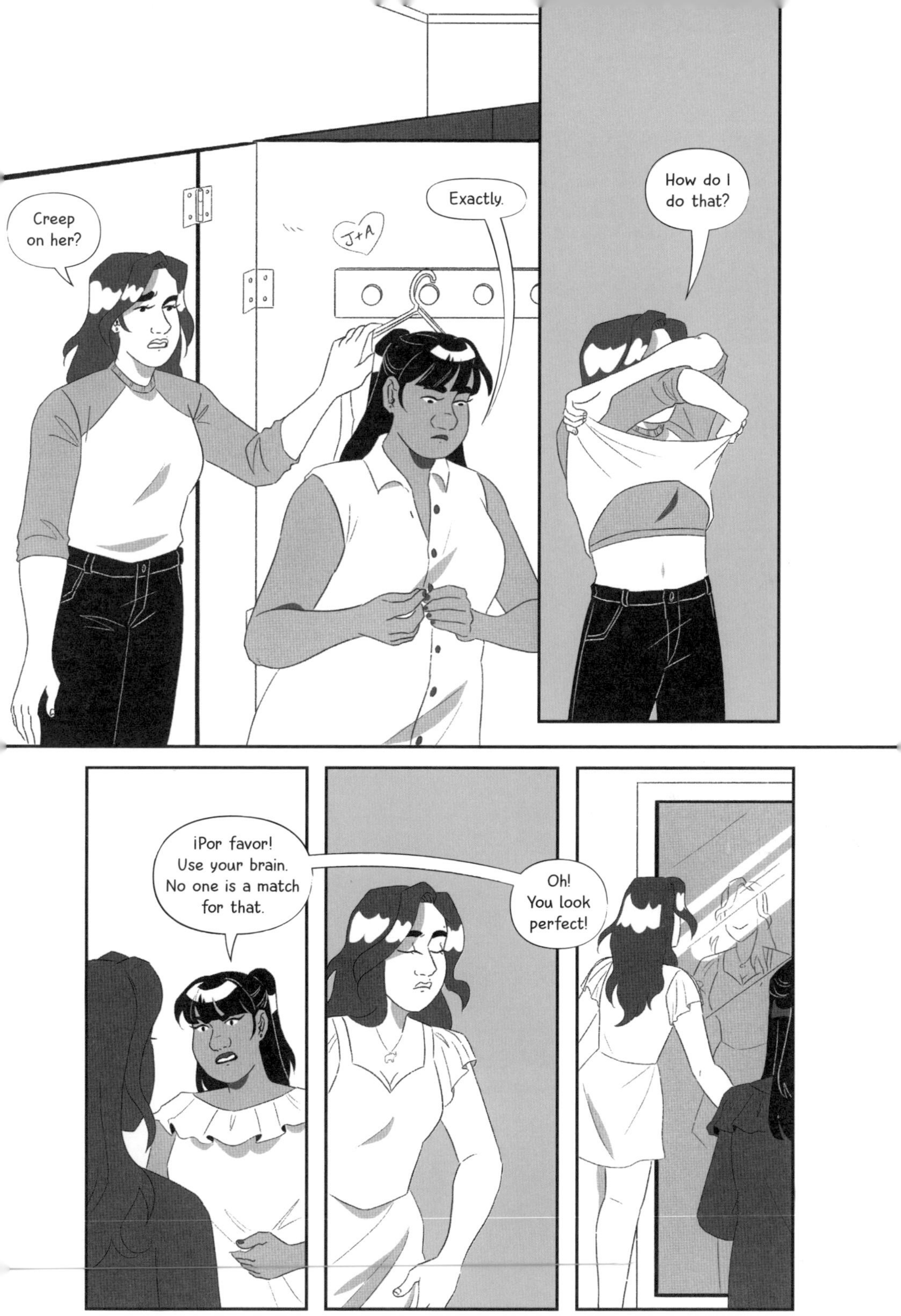
Creep on her?
Exactly.
J+A
How do I do that?
¡Por favor! Use your brain. No one is a match for that.
Oh! You look perfect!

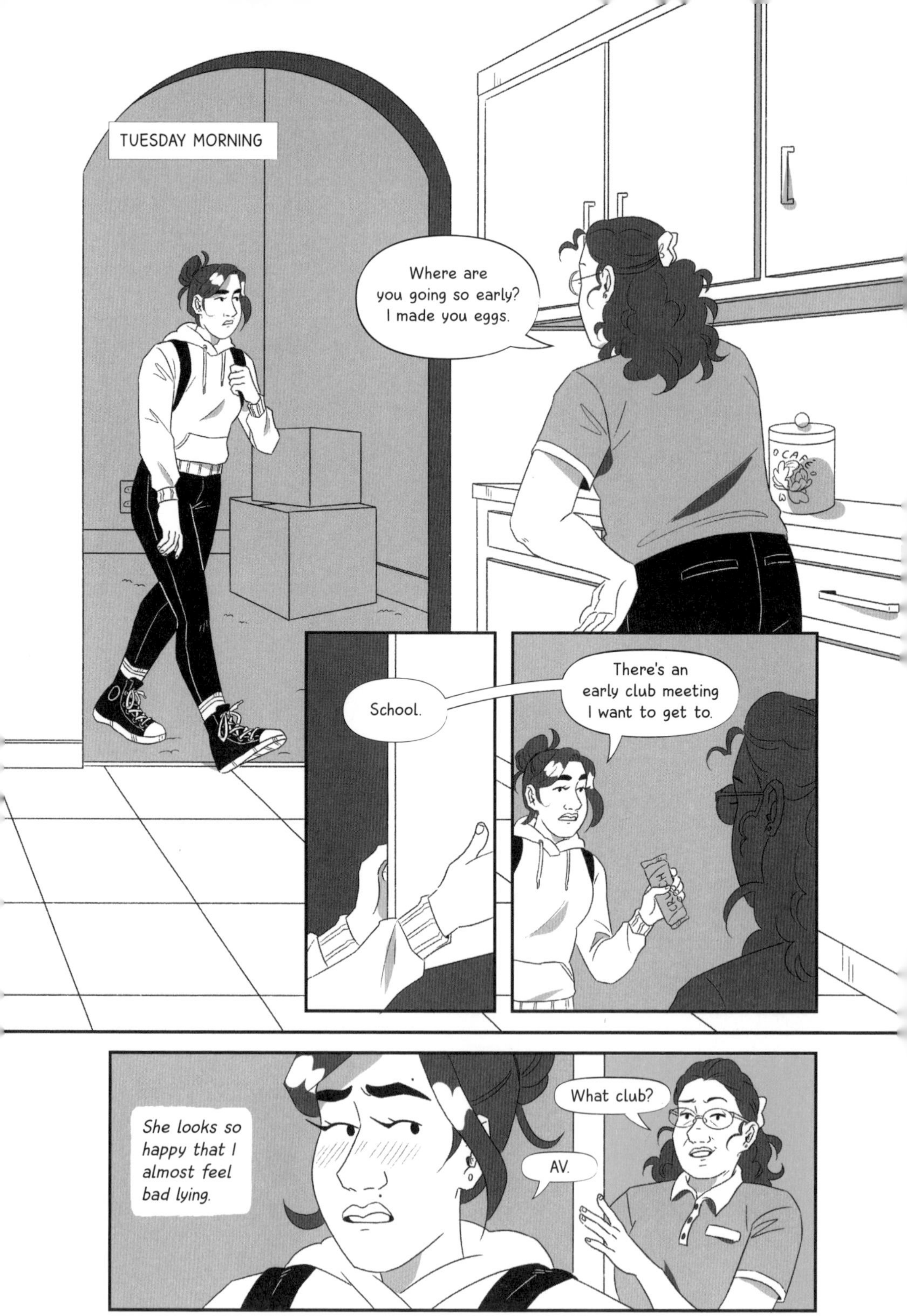
TUESDAY MORNING
Where are you going so early? I made you eggs.
School.
There's an early club meeting I want to get to.
CRUNCH
She looks so happy that I almost feel bad lying.
What club?
AV.

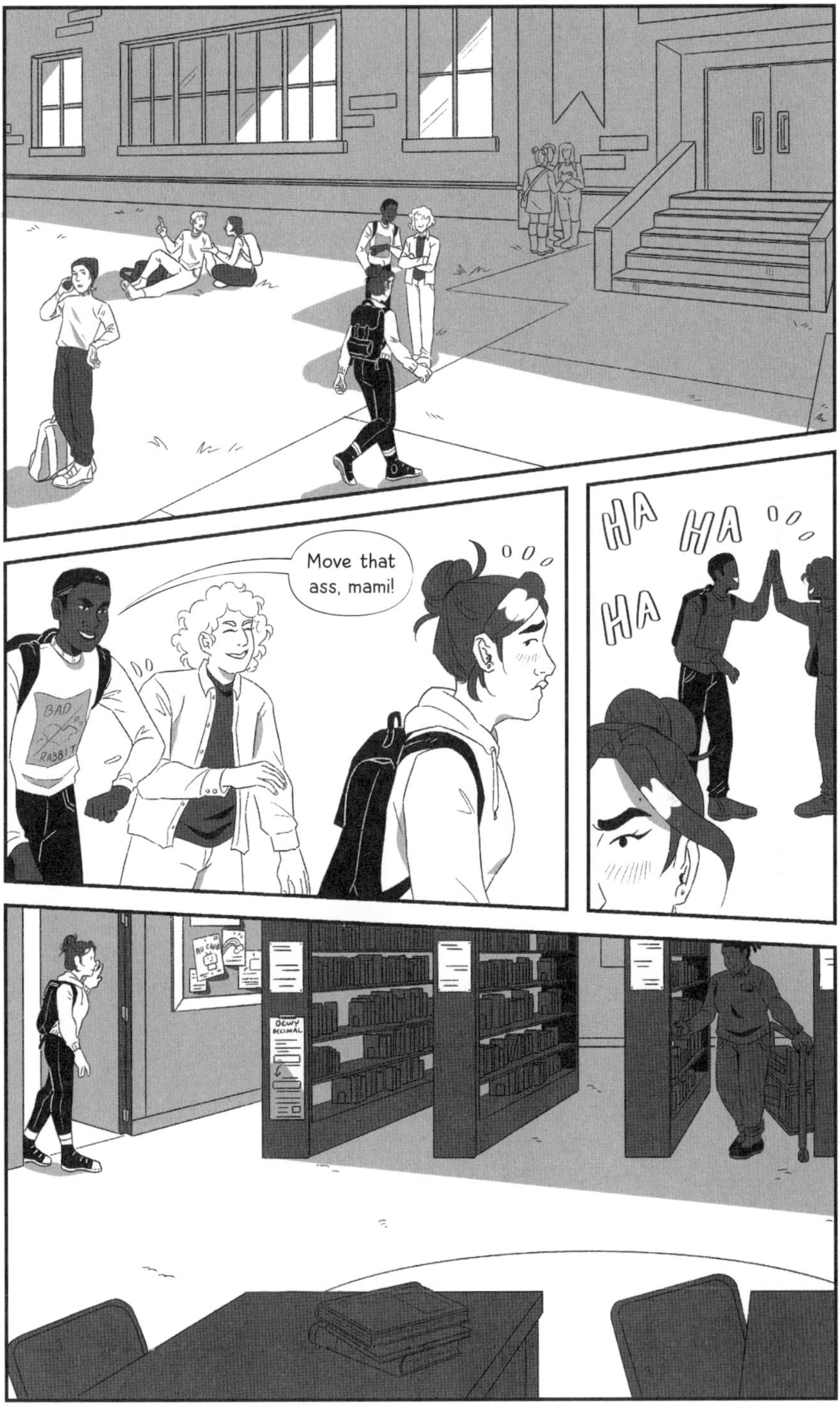
Move that ass, mami!
HA HA
HA
BAD RABBIT
DEWY DECIMAL

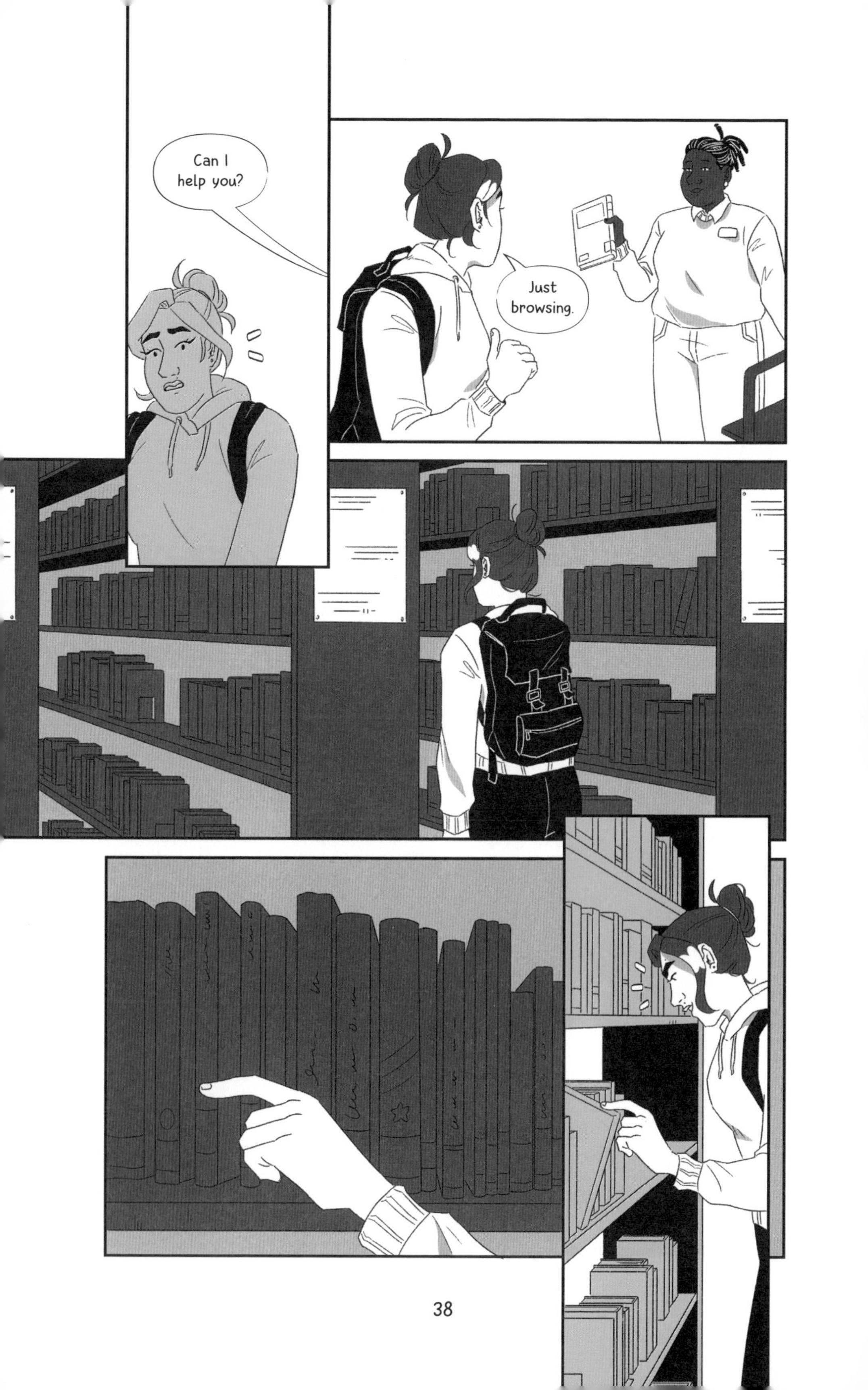
Can I help you?
Just browsing.

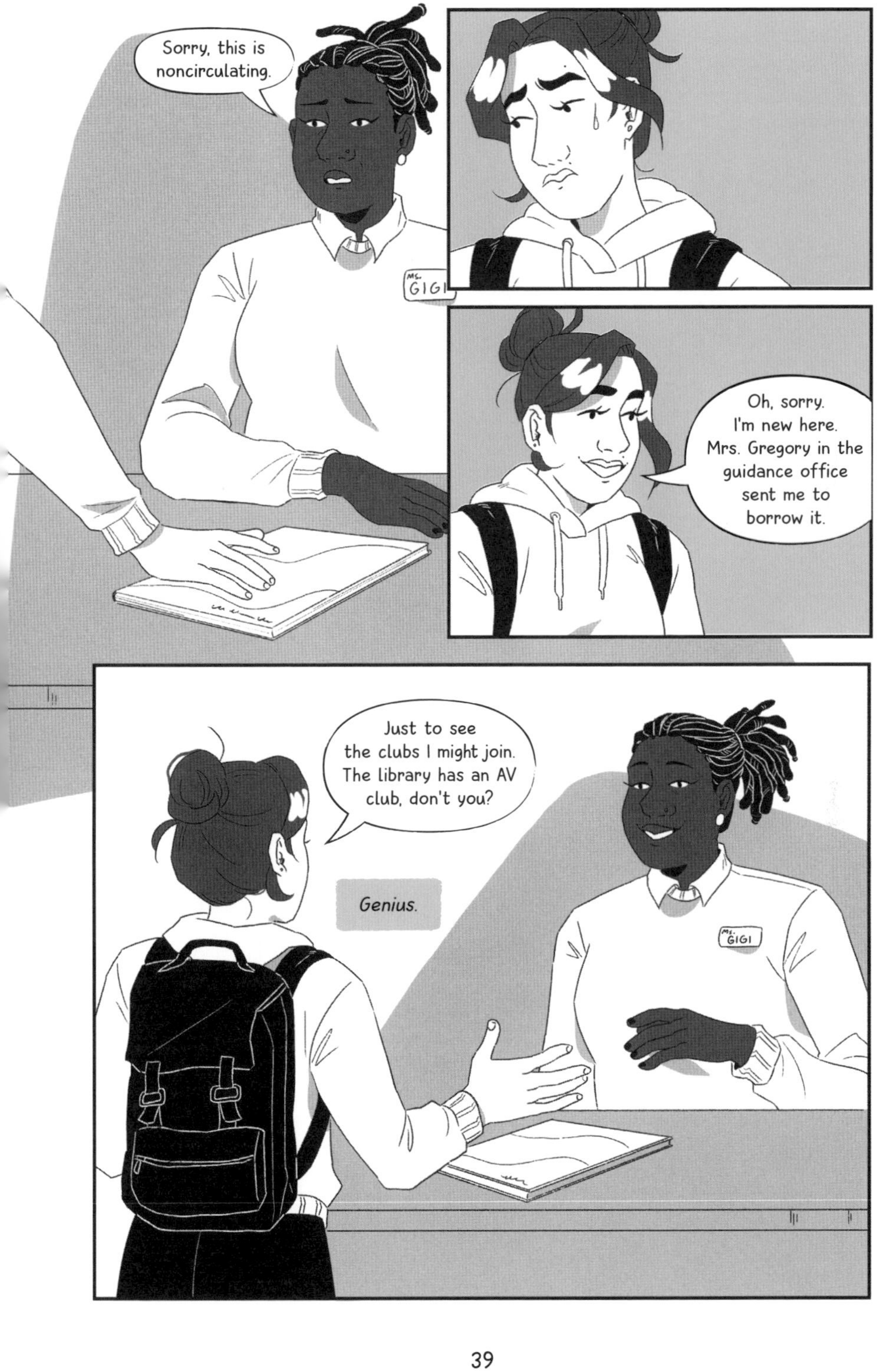
Sorry, this is noncirculating.
MS. GIGI
Oh, sorry. I'm new here. Mrs. Gregory in the guidance office sent me to borrow it.
Just to see the clubs I might join. The library has an AV club, don't you?
Genius.
MS. GIGI

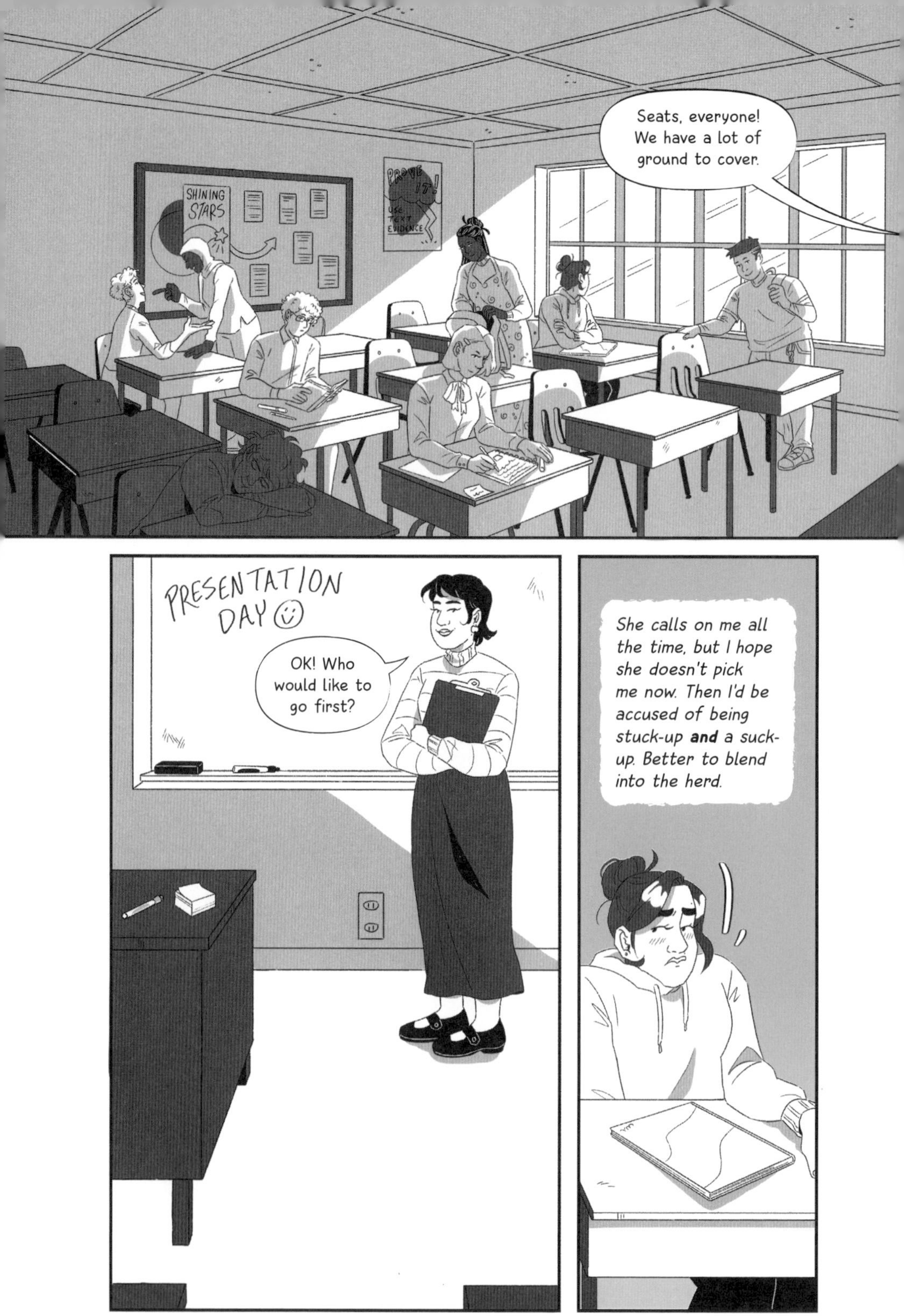
SHINING STARS
PROVE IT!
USE TEXT EVIDENCE
Seats, everyone! We have a lot of ground to cover.
PRESENTATION DAY
OK! Who would like to go first?
She calls on me all the time, but I hope she doesn't pick me now. Then I'd be accused of being stuck-up **and** a suck-up. Better to blend into the herd.

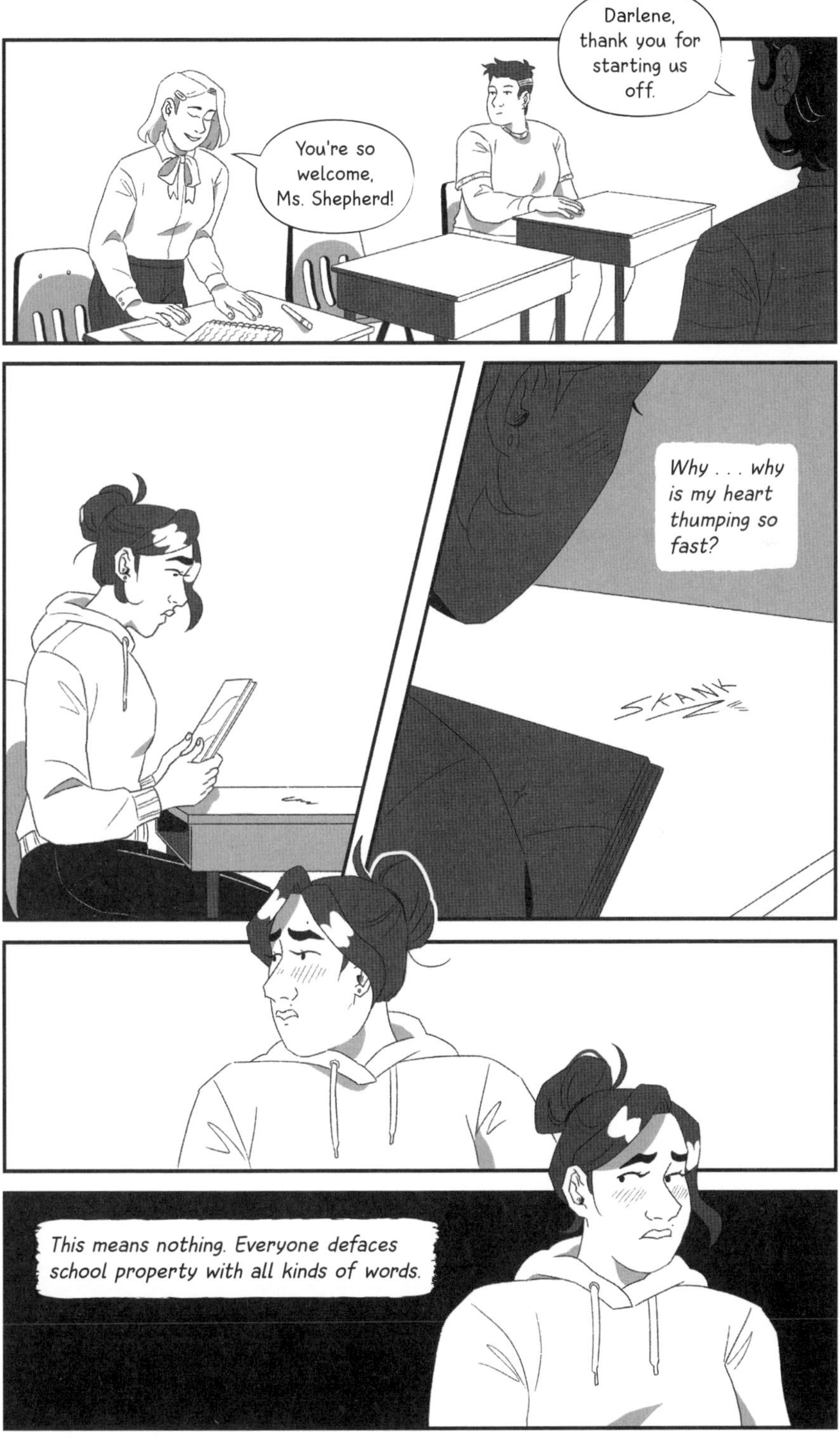
Darlene, thank you for starting us off.
You're so welcome, Ms. Shepherd!
Why . . . why is my heart thumping so fast?
SKANK
This means nothing. Everyone defaces school property with all kinds of words.

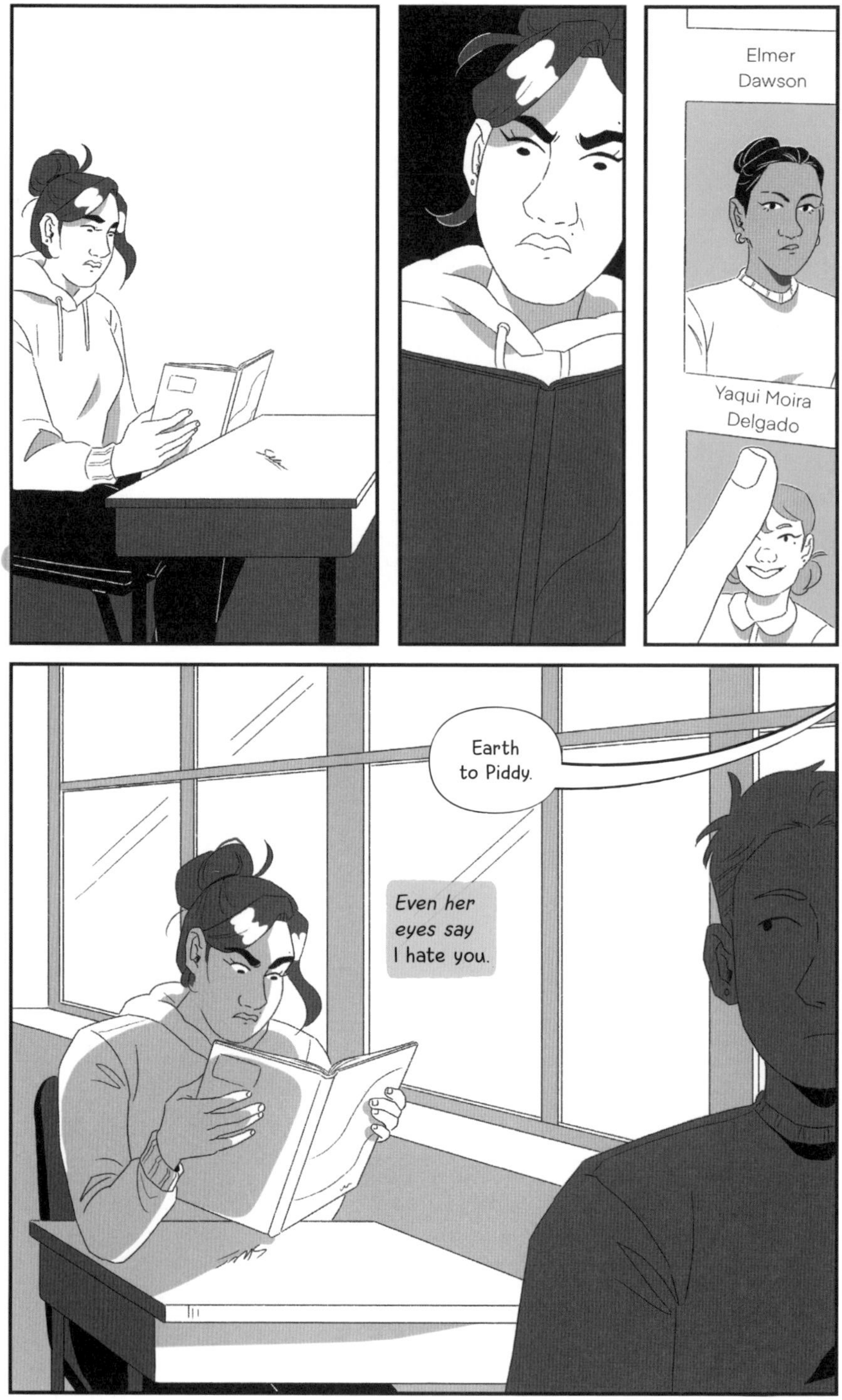
Elmer
Dawson
Yaqui Moira
Delgado
Earth to Piddy.
Even her eyes say I hate you.

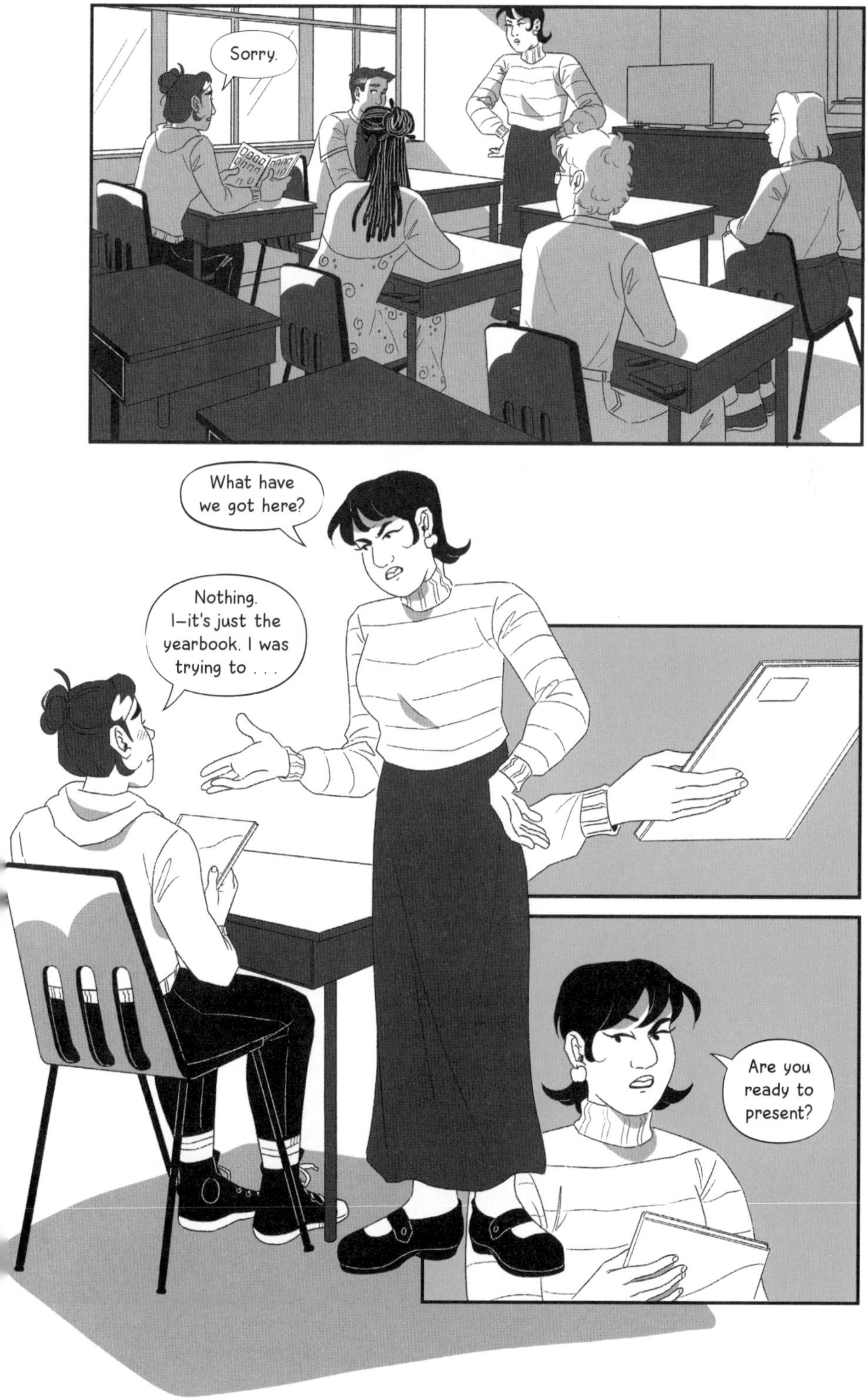
Sorry.
What have we got here?
Nothing. I—it's just the yearbook. I was trying to . . .
Are you ready to present?

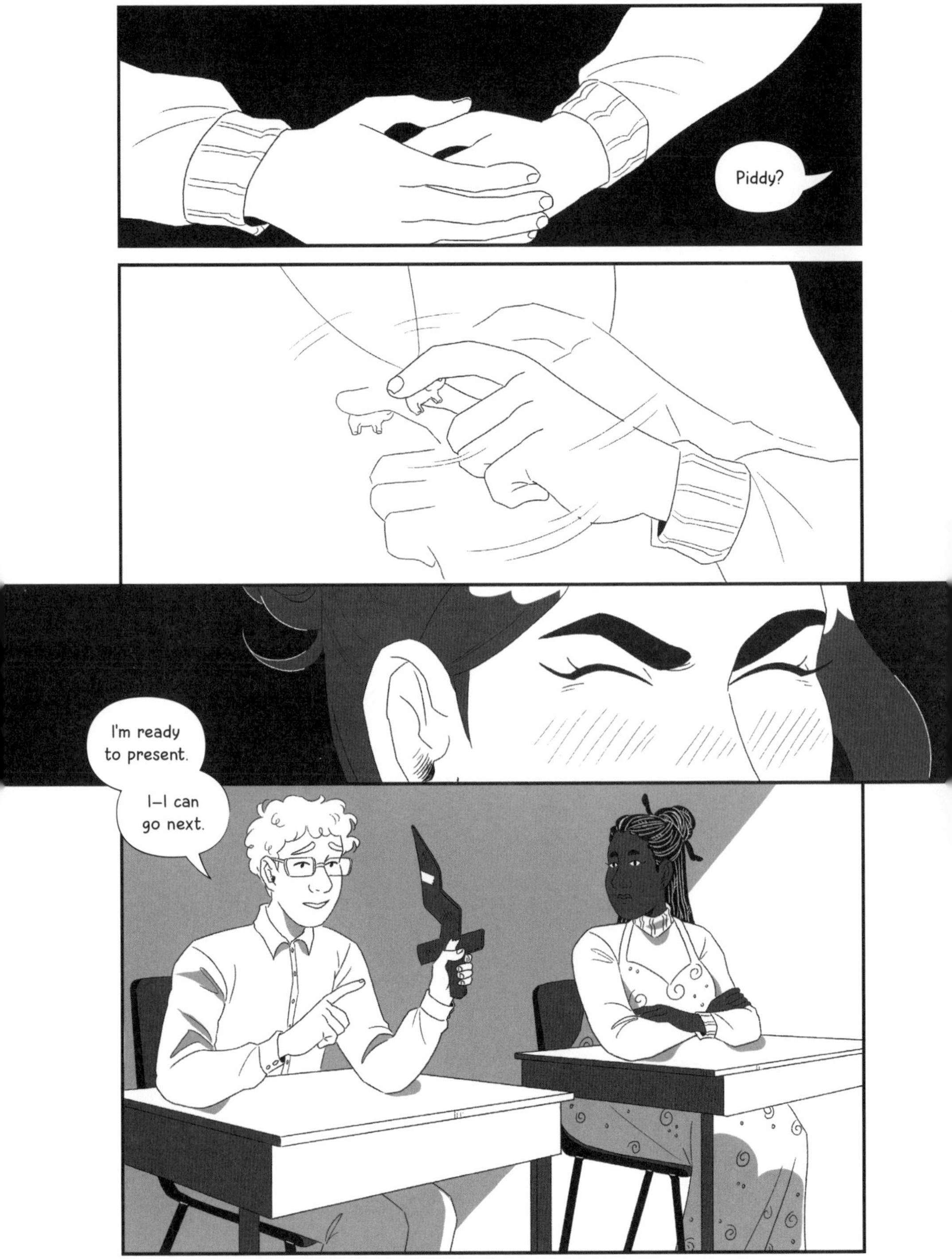

Piddy?
I'm ready to present.
I–I can go next.

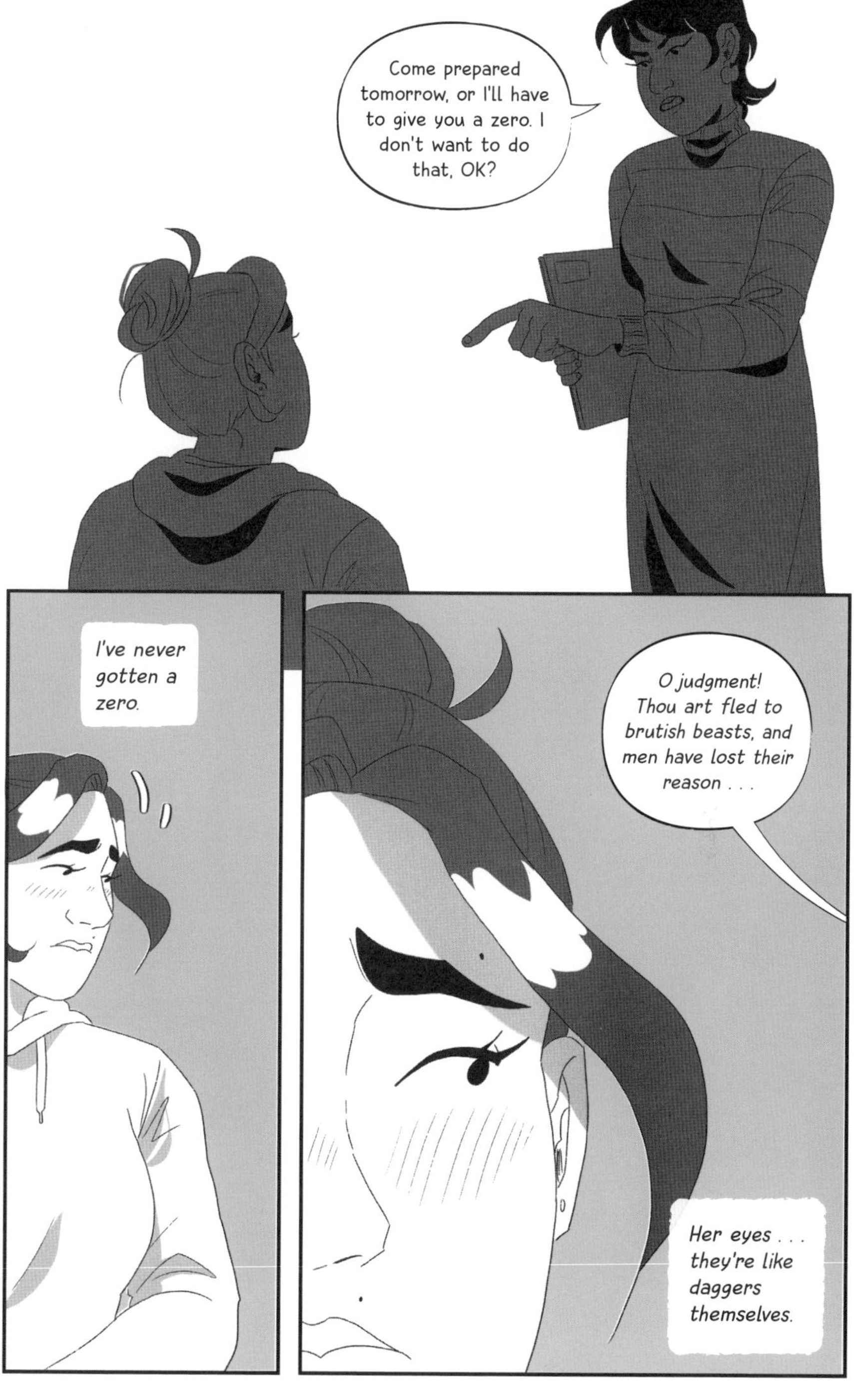

Come prepared tomorrow, or I'll have to give you a zero. I don't want to do that, OK?
I've never gotten a zero.
O judgment! Thou art fled to brutish beasts, and men have lost their reason . . .
Her eyes . . . they're like daggers themselves.

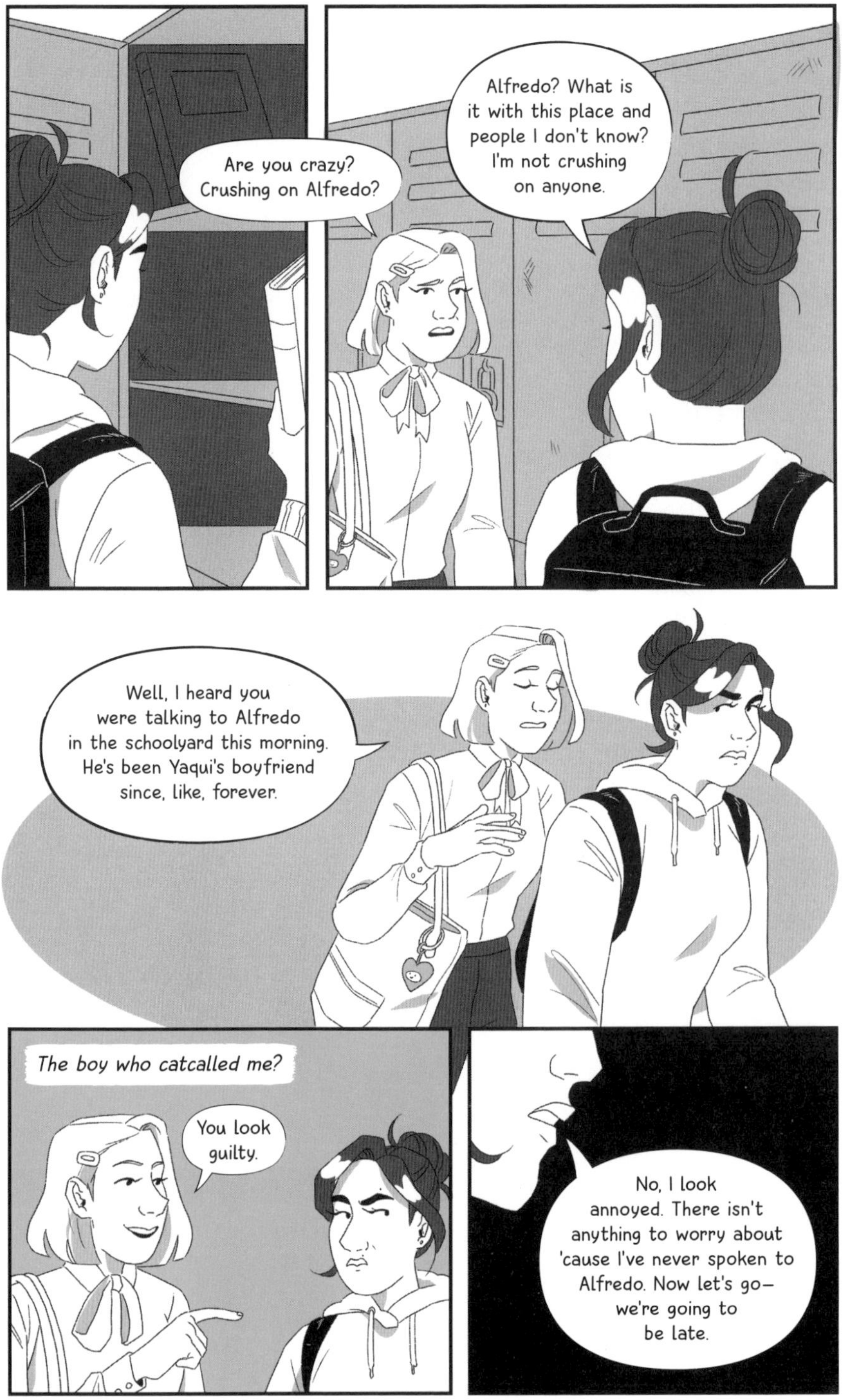
Are you crazy? Crushing on Alfredo?
Alfredo? What is it with this place and people I don't know? I'm not crushing on anyone.
Well, I heard you were talking to Alfredo in the schoolyard this morning. He's been Yaqui's boyfriend since, like, forever.
The boy who catcalled me?
You look guilty.
No, I look annoyed. There isn't anything to worry about 'cause I've never spoken to Alfredo. Now let's go— we're going to be late.

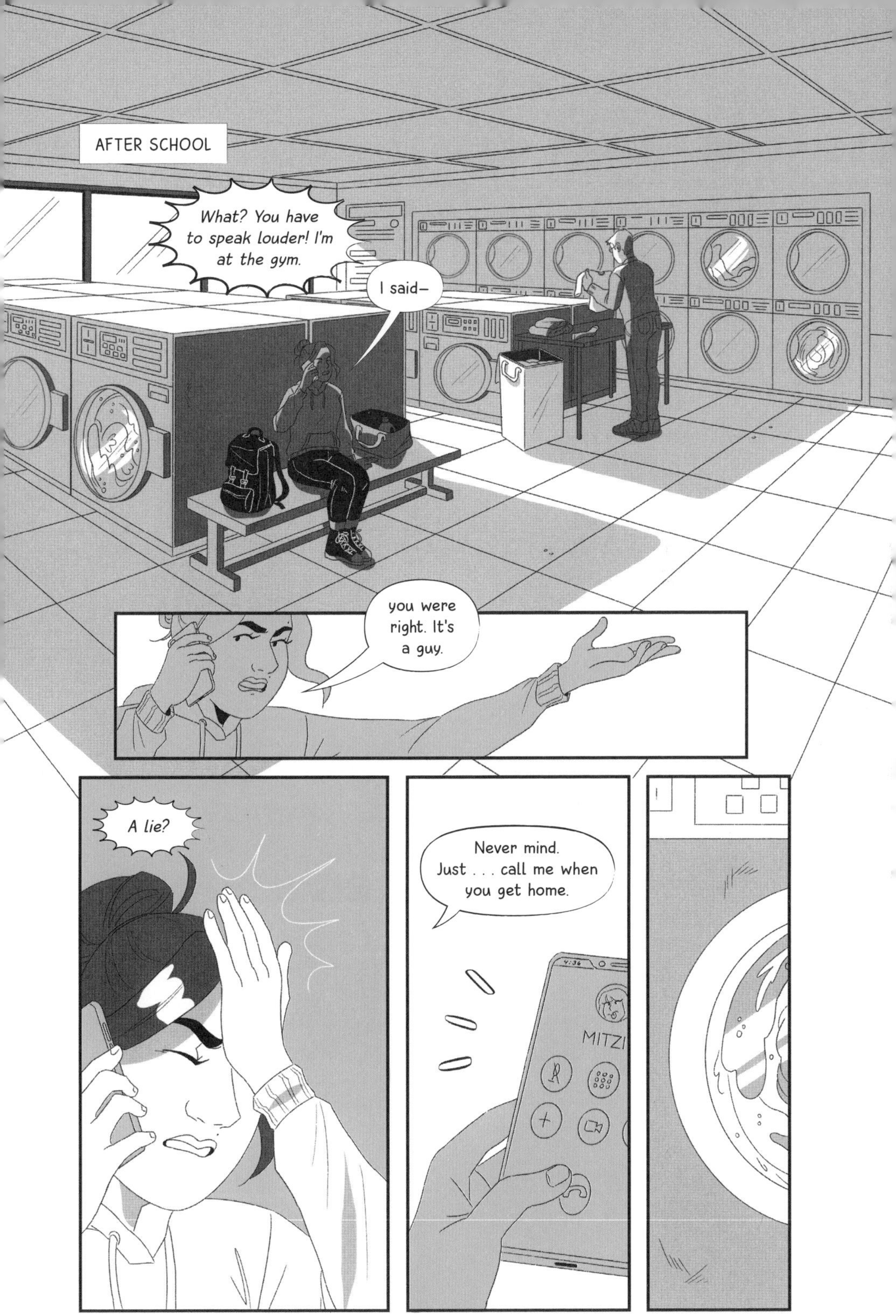
AFTER SCHOOL
What? You have to speak louder! I'm at the gym.
I said—
you were right. It's a guy.
A lie?
Never mind. Just . . . call me when you get home.
MITZI

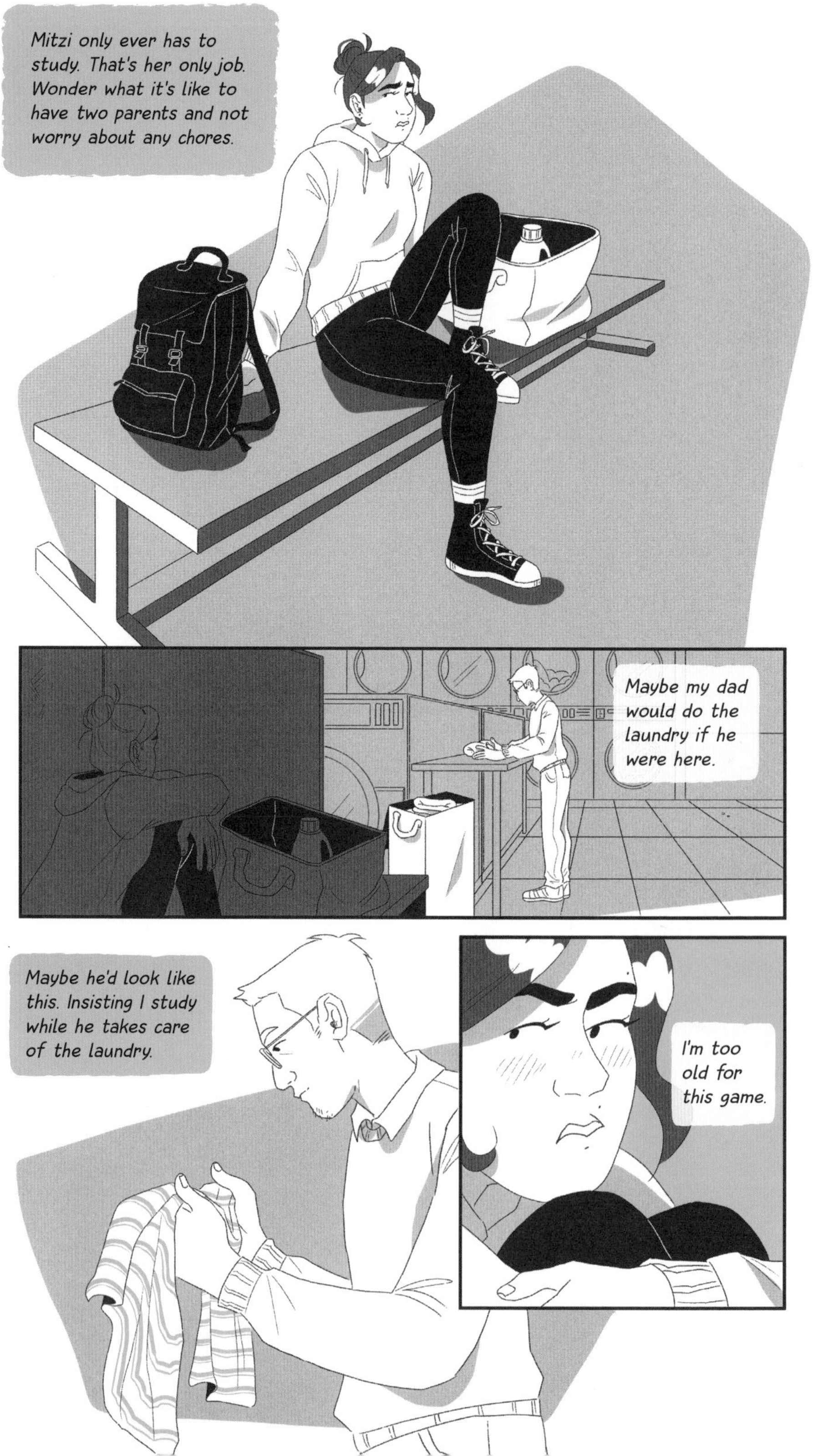
Mitzi only ever has to study. That's her only job. Wonder what it's like to have two parents and not worry about any chores.
Maybe my dad would do the laundry if he were here.
Maybe he'd look like this. Insisting I study while he takes care of the laundry.
I'm too old for this game.

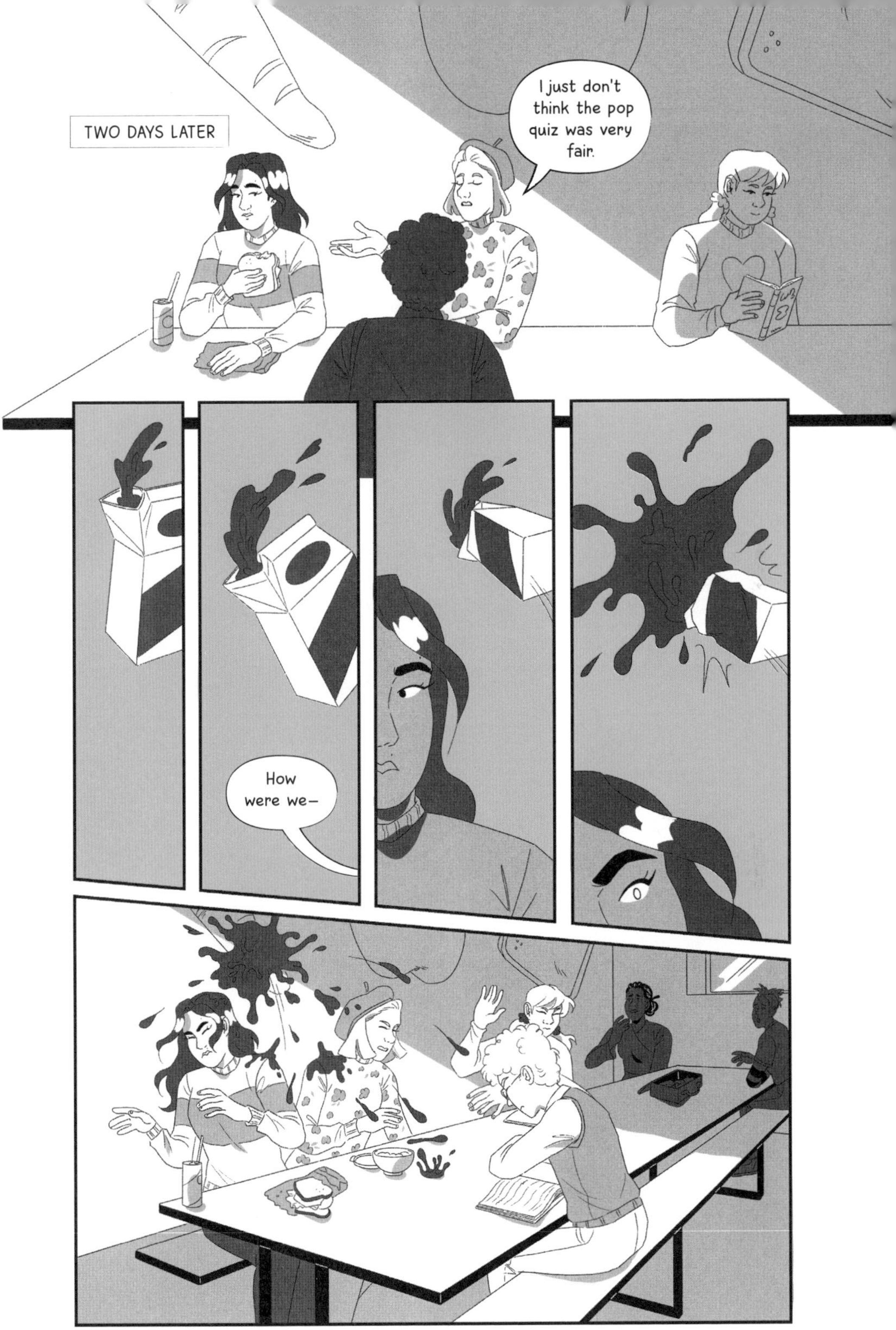
TWO DAYS LATER
I just don't think the pop quiz was very fair.
How were we–

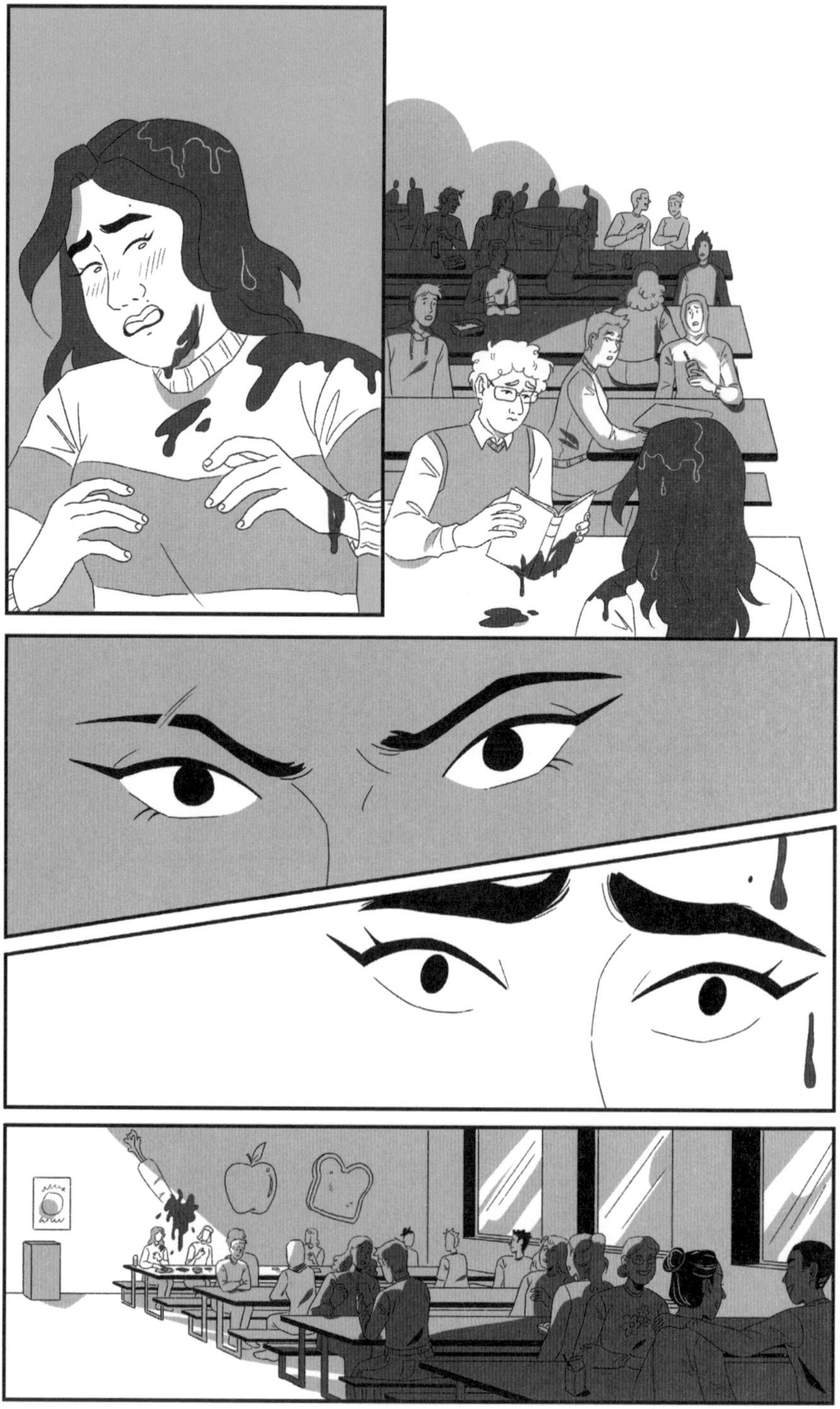

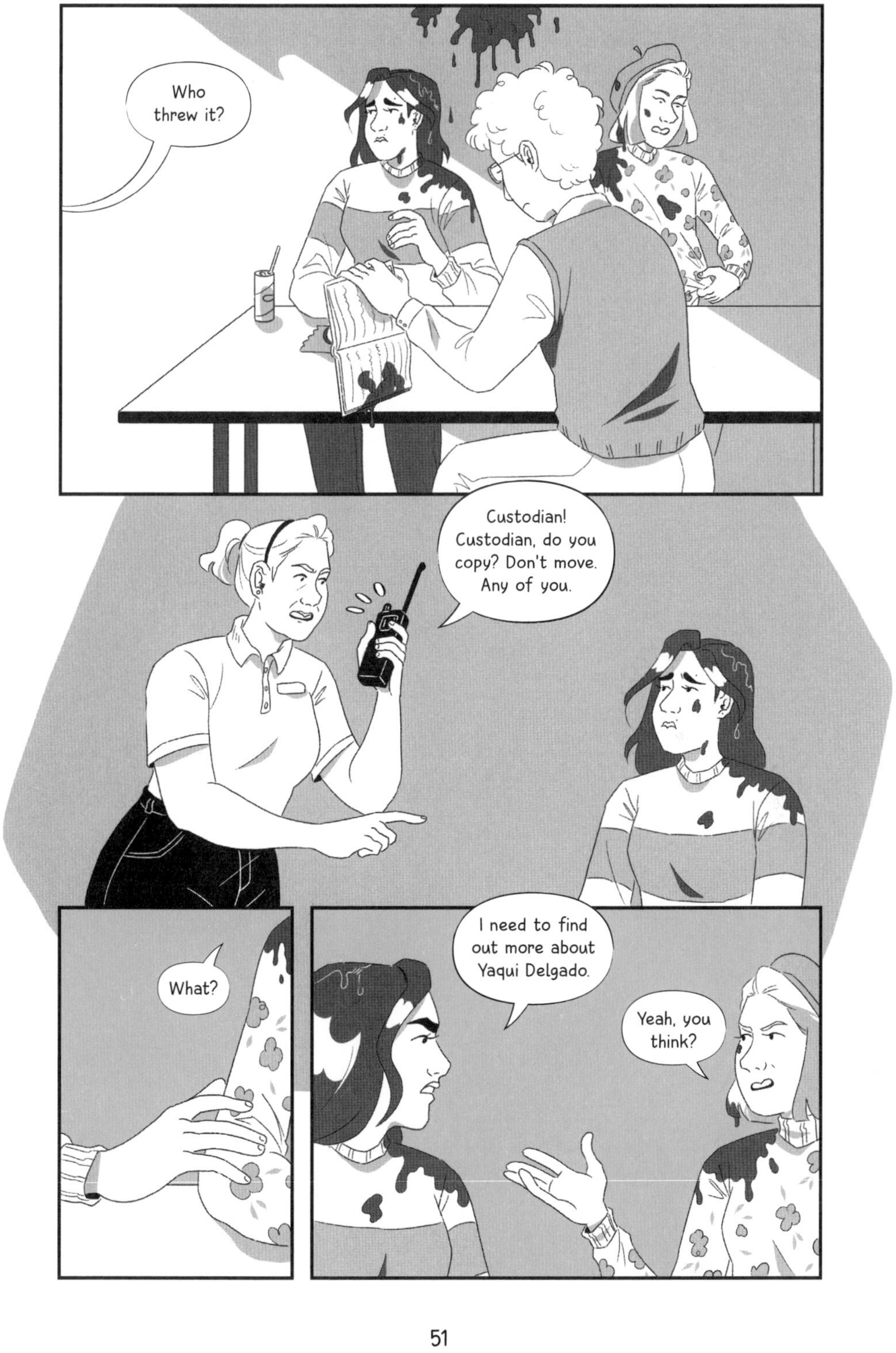
Who threw it?
Custodian! Custodian, do you copy? Don't move. Any of you.
What?
I need to find out more about Yaqui Delgado.
Yeah, you think?

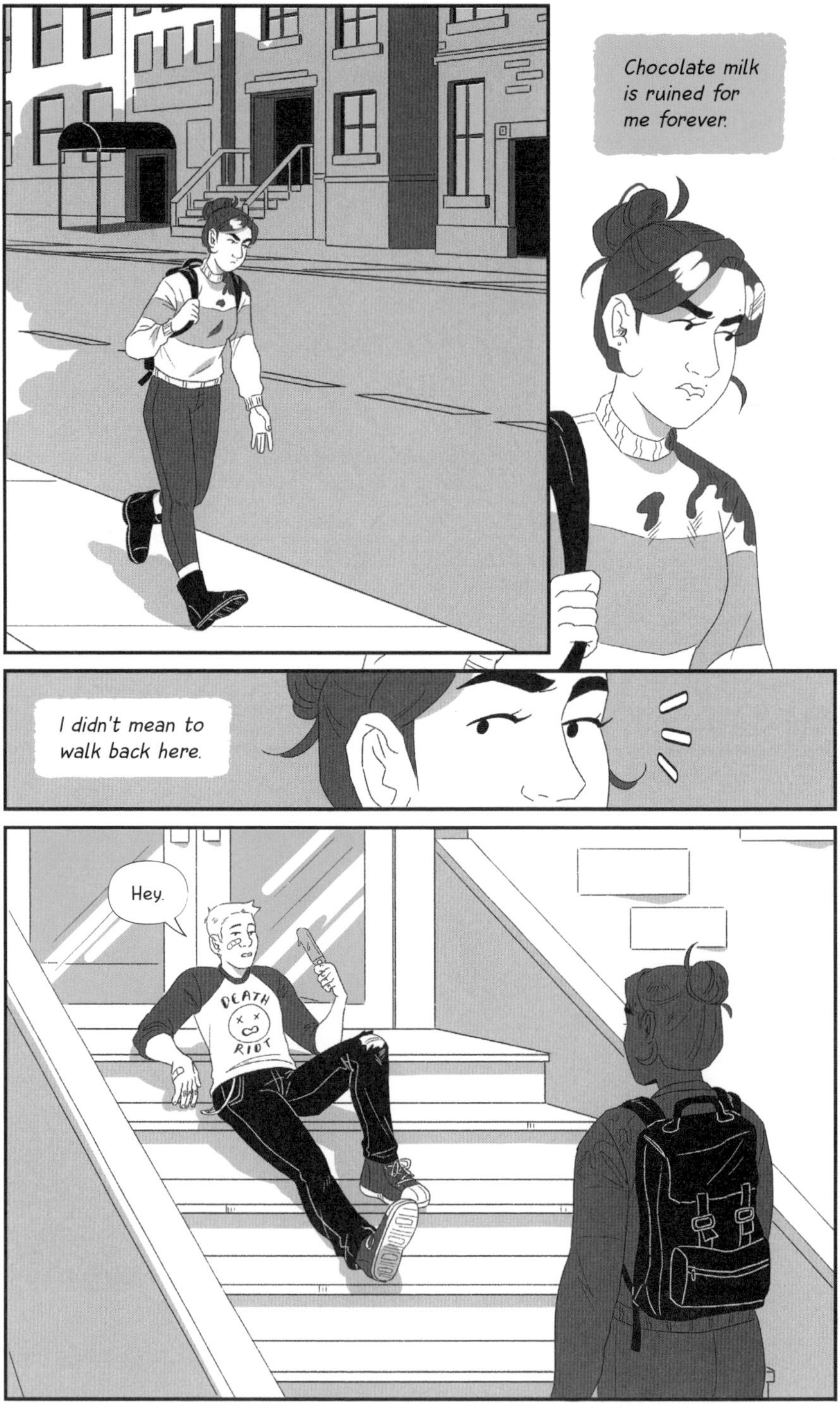
Chocolate milk is ruined for me forever.
I didn't mean to walk back here.
Hey.
DEATH RIOT

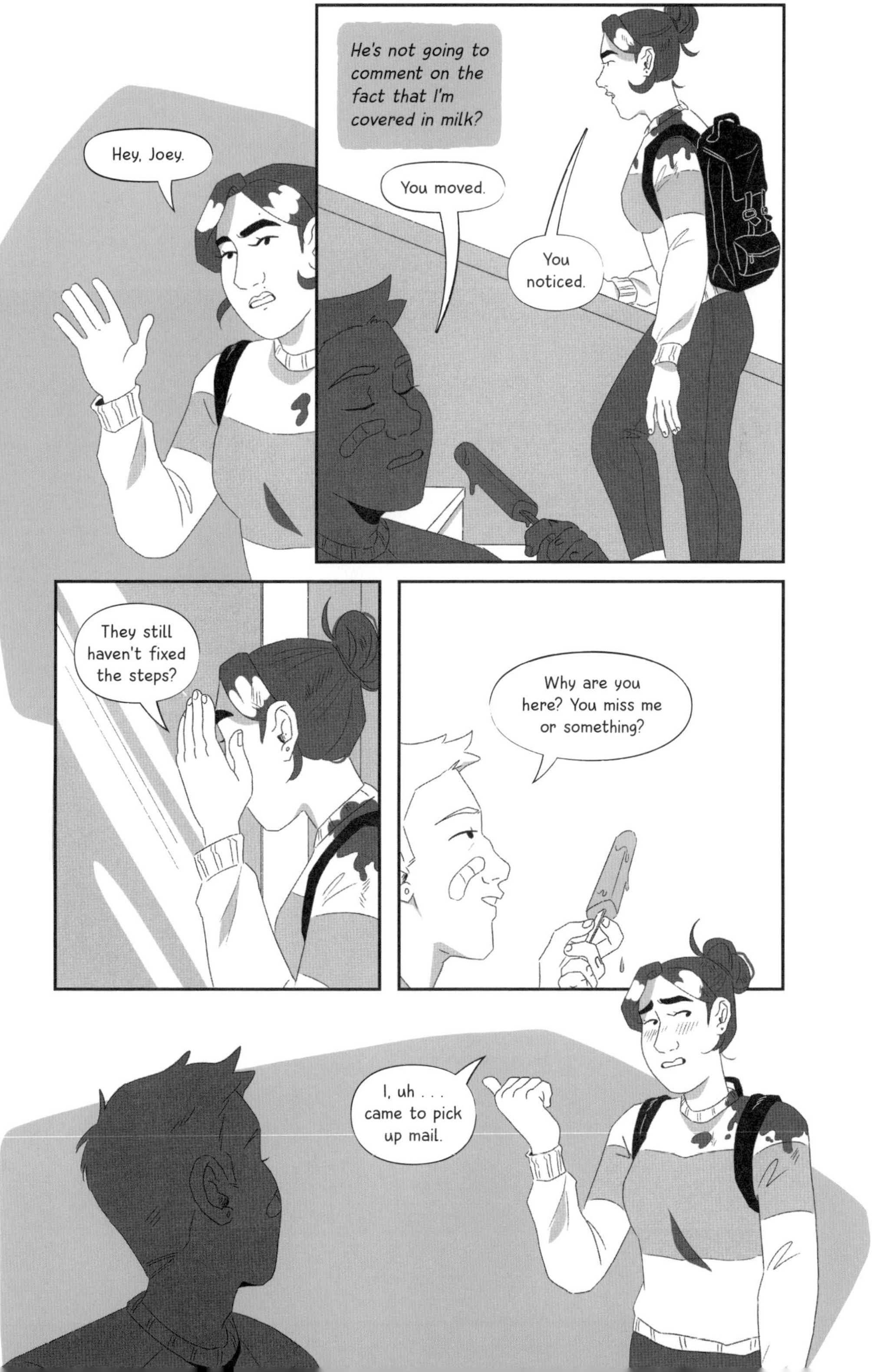
Hey, Joey.
He's not going to comment on the fact that I'm covered in milk?
You moved.
You noticed.
They still haven't fixed the steps?
Why are you here? You miss me or something?
I, uh . . . came to pick up mail.

Ha! No way anyone writes to you, Toad.

Funny. Who writes to you? Your probation officer?

Ribbit.

Lila, it's me. Buzz me in.

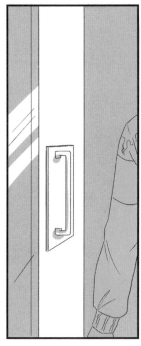

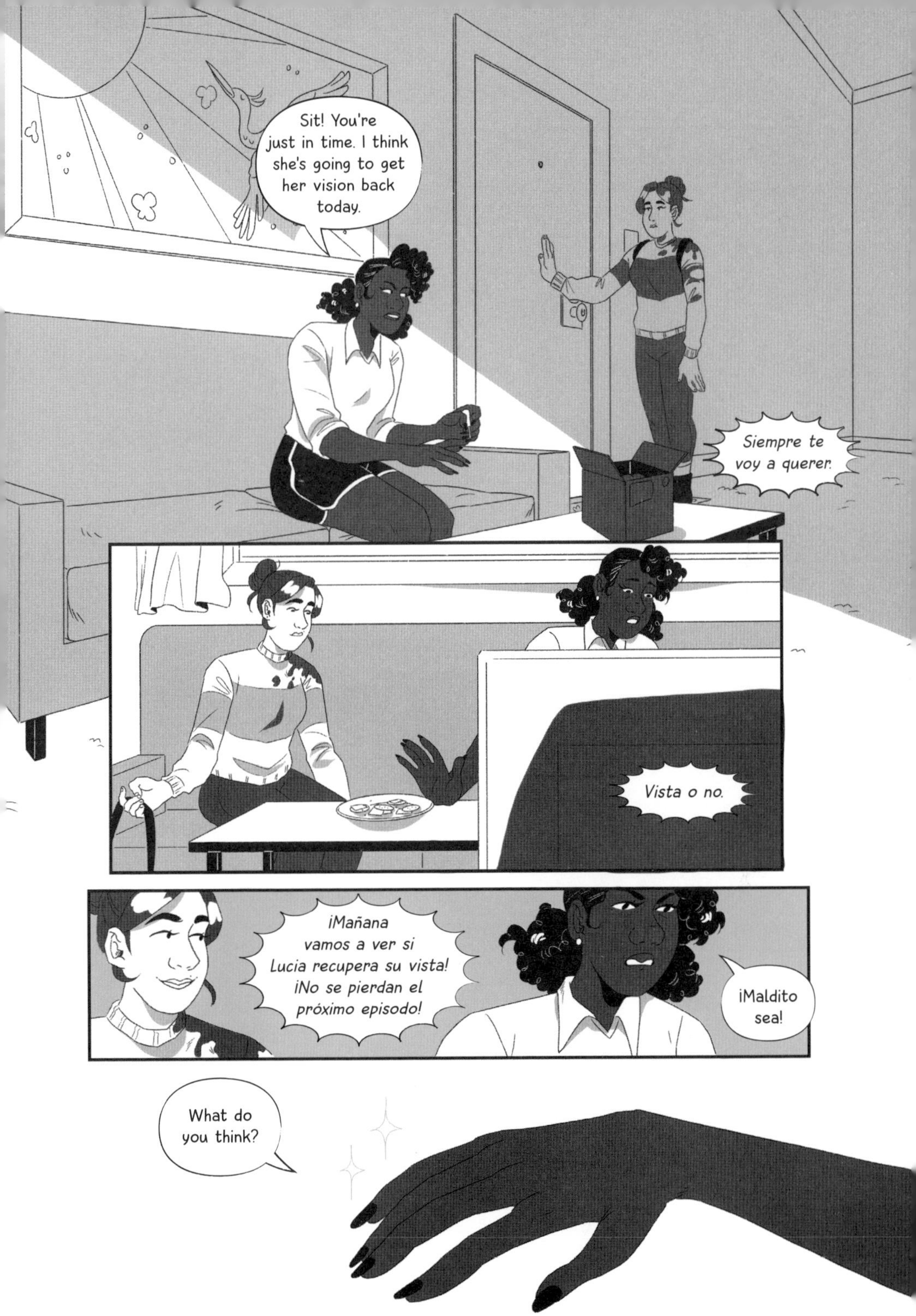

Sit! You're just in time. I think she's going to get her vision back today.
Siempre te voy a querer.
Vista o no.
¡Mañana vamos a ver si Lucia recupera su vista! ¡No se pierdan el próximo episodo!
¡Maldito sea!
What do you think?

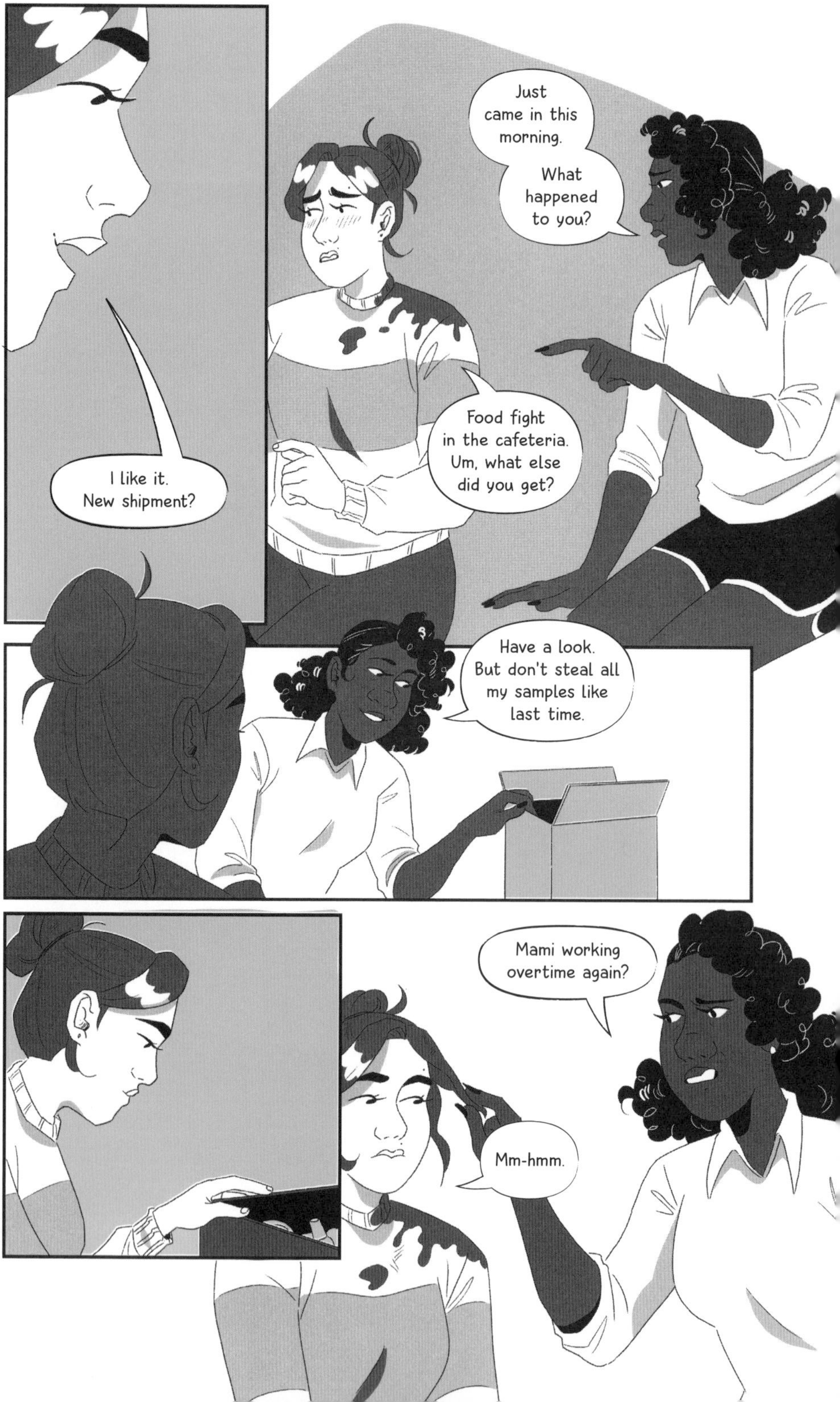
I like it. New shipment?
Just came in this morning.
What happened to you?
Food fight in the cafeteria. Um, what else did you get?
Have a look. But don't steal all my samples like last time.
Mami working overtime again?
Mm-hmm.

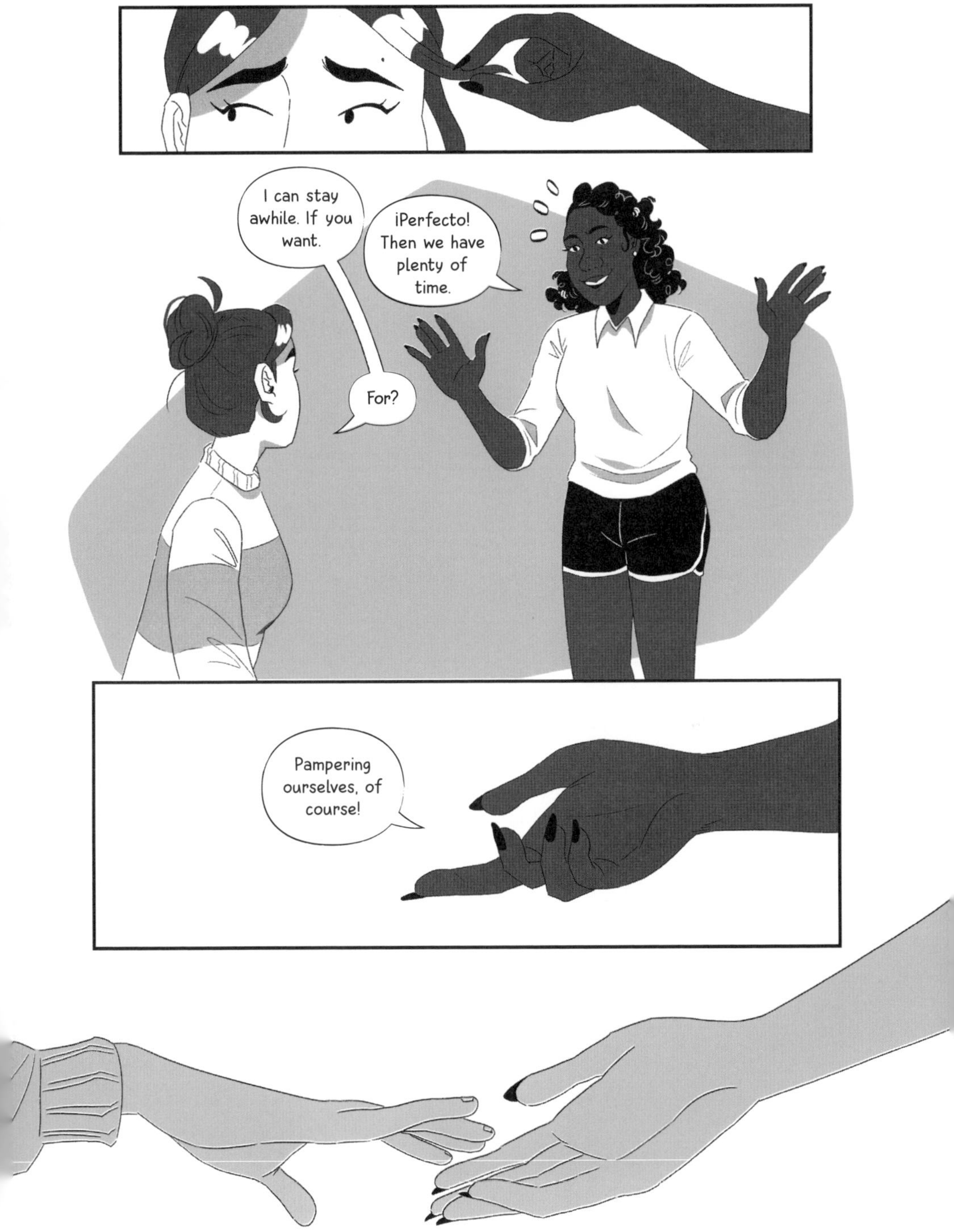
I can stay awhile. If you want.
¡Perfecto! Then we have plenty of time.
For?
Pampering ourselves, of course!

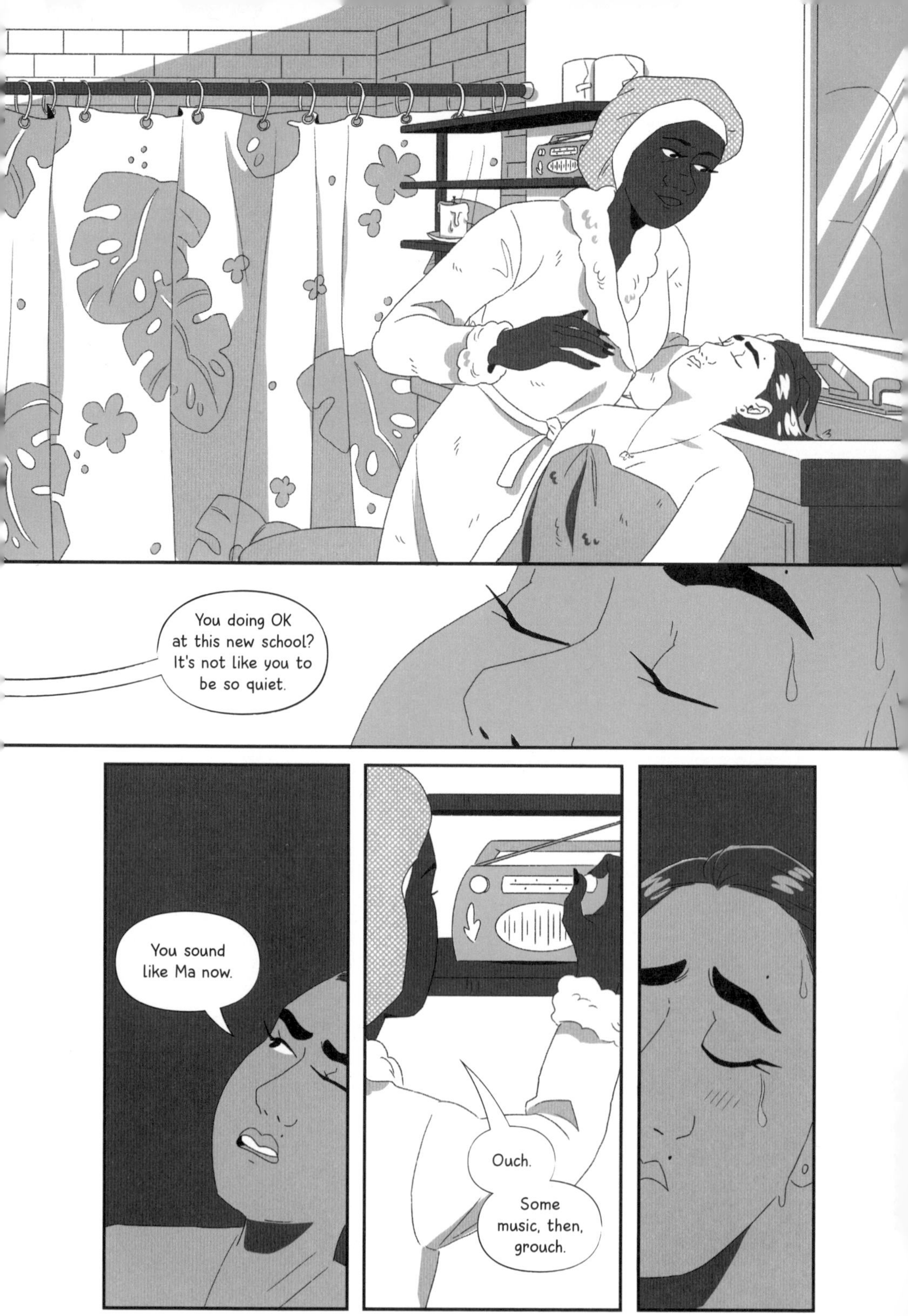

You doing OK at this new school? It's not like you to be so quiet.
You sound like Ma now.
Ouch.
Some music, then, grouch.

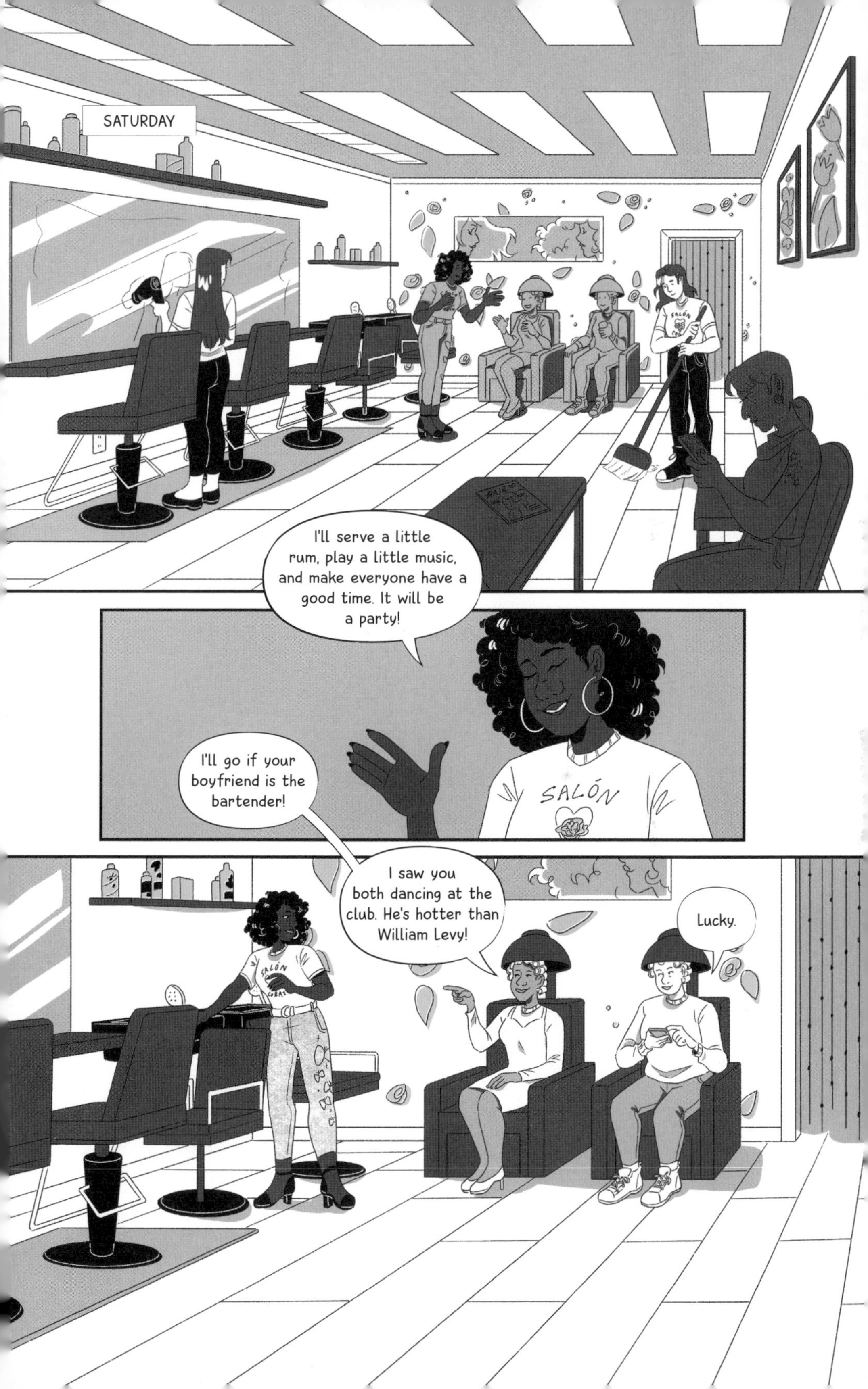
SATURDAY
I'll serve a little rum, play a little music, and make everyone have a good time. It will be a party!
I'll go if your boyfriend is the bartender!
SALÓN
I saw you both dancing at the club. He's hotter than William Levy!
Lucky.

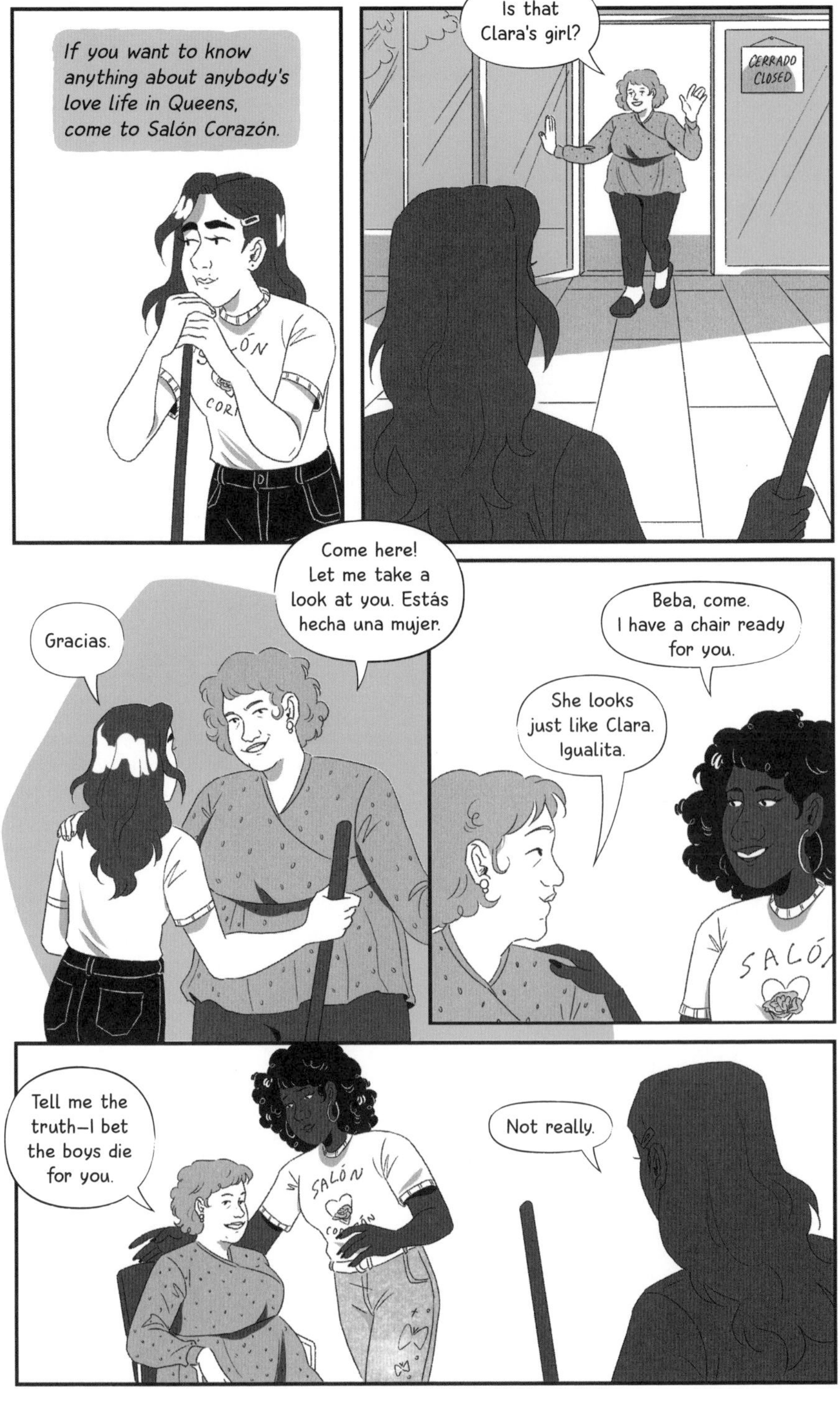
If you want to know anything about anybody's love life in Queens, come to Salón Corazón.
Is that Clara's girl?
CERRADO
CLOSED
Come here! Let me take a look at you. Estás hecha una mujer.
Gracias.
Beba, come. I have a chair ready for you.
She looks just like Clara. Igualita.
Tell me the truth—I bet the boys die for you.
Not really.

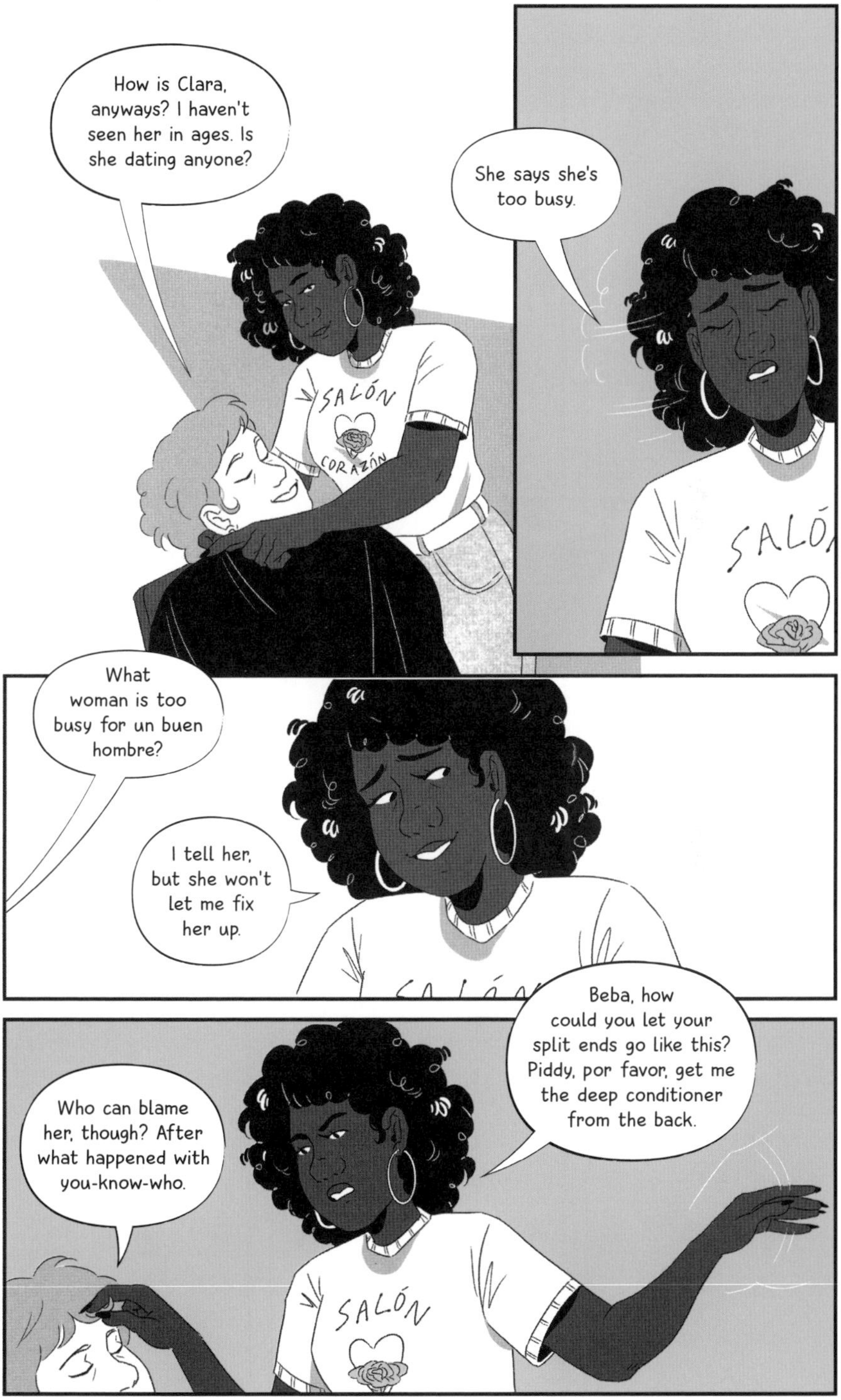
How is Clara, anyways? I haven't seen her in ages. Is she dating anyone?
She says she's too busy.
SALÓN CORAZÓN
What woman is too busy for un buen hombre?
I tell her, but she won't let me fix her up.
Who can blame her, though? After what happened with you-know-who.
Beba, how could you let your split ends go like this? Piddy, por favor, get me the deep conditioner from the back.

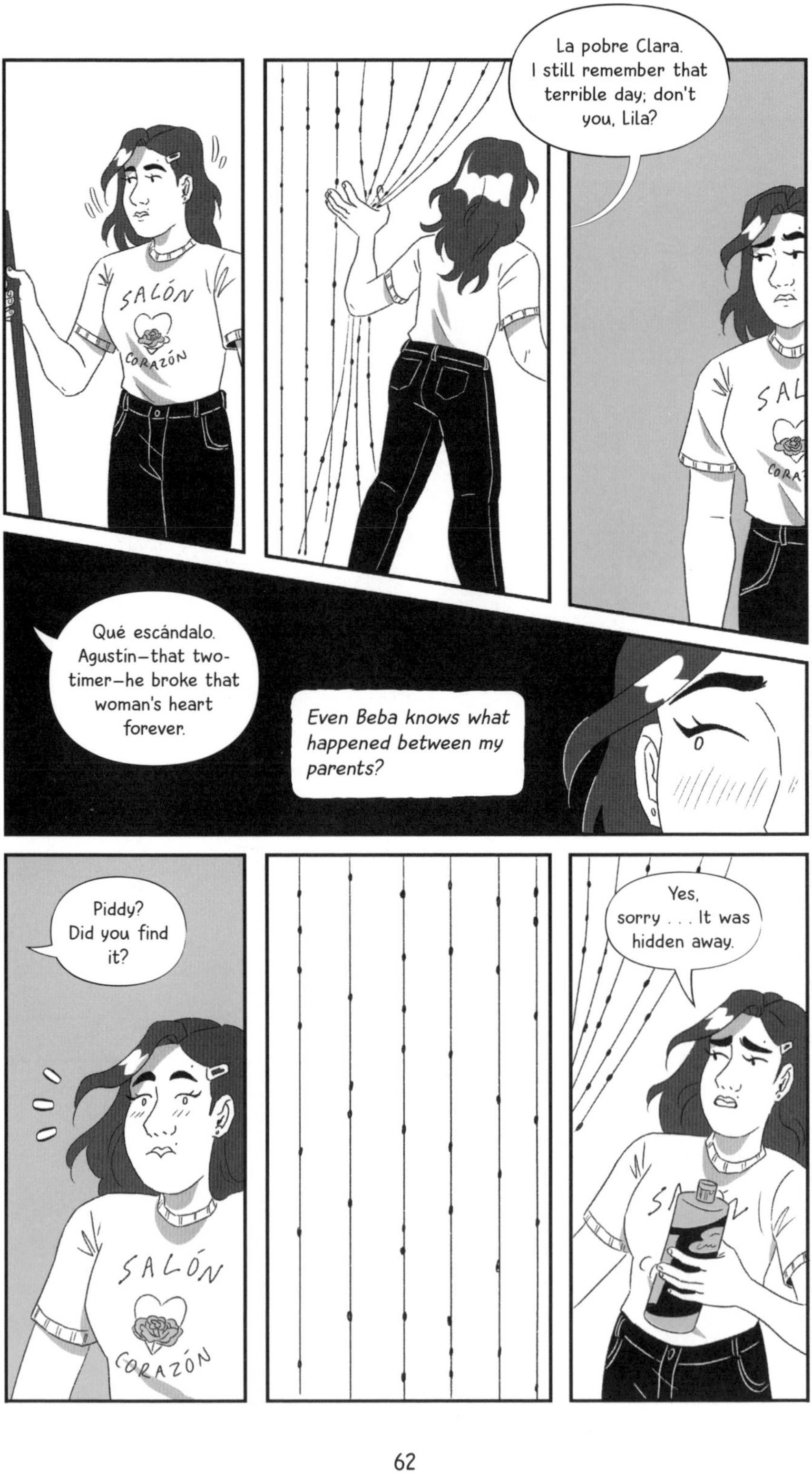
SALÓN CORAZÓN
La pobre Clara. I still remember that terrible day; don't you, Lila?
Qué escándalo. Agustín—that two-timer—he broke that woman's heart forever.
Even Beba knows what happened between my parents?
Piddy? Did you find it?
Yes, sorry . . . It was hidden away.

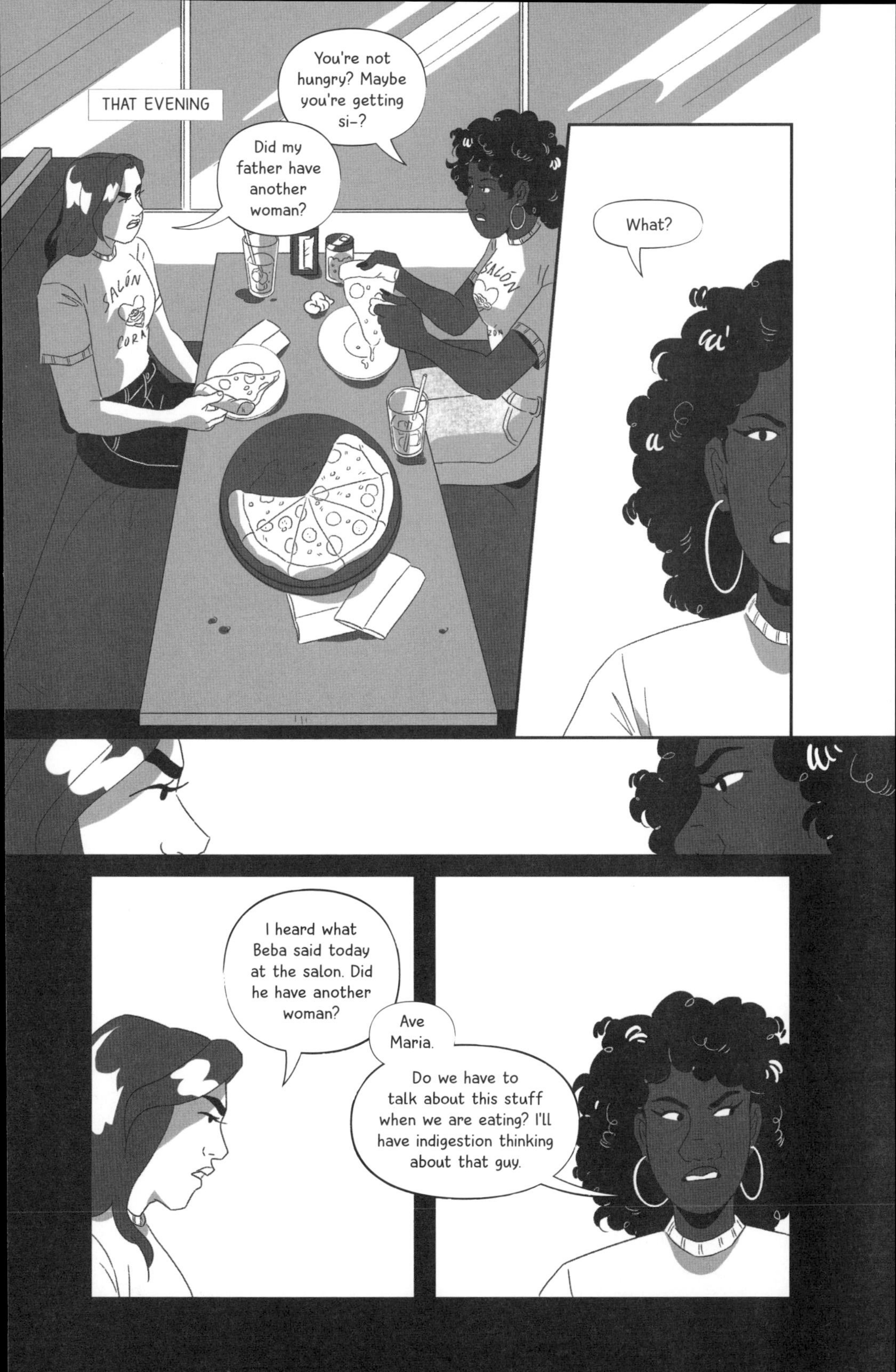
THAT EVENING
You're not hungry? Maybe you're getting si-?
Did my father have another woman?
What?
I heard what Beba said today at the salon. Did he have another woman?
Ave Maria.
Do we have to talk about this stuff when we are eating? I'll have indigestion thinking about that guy.

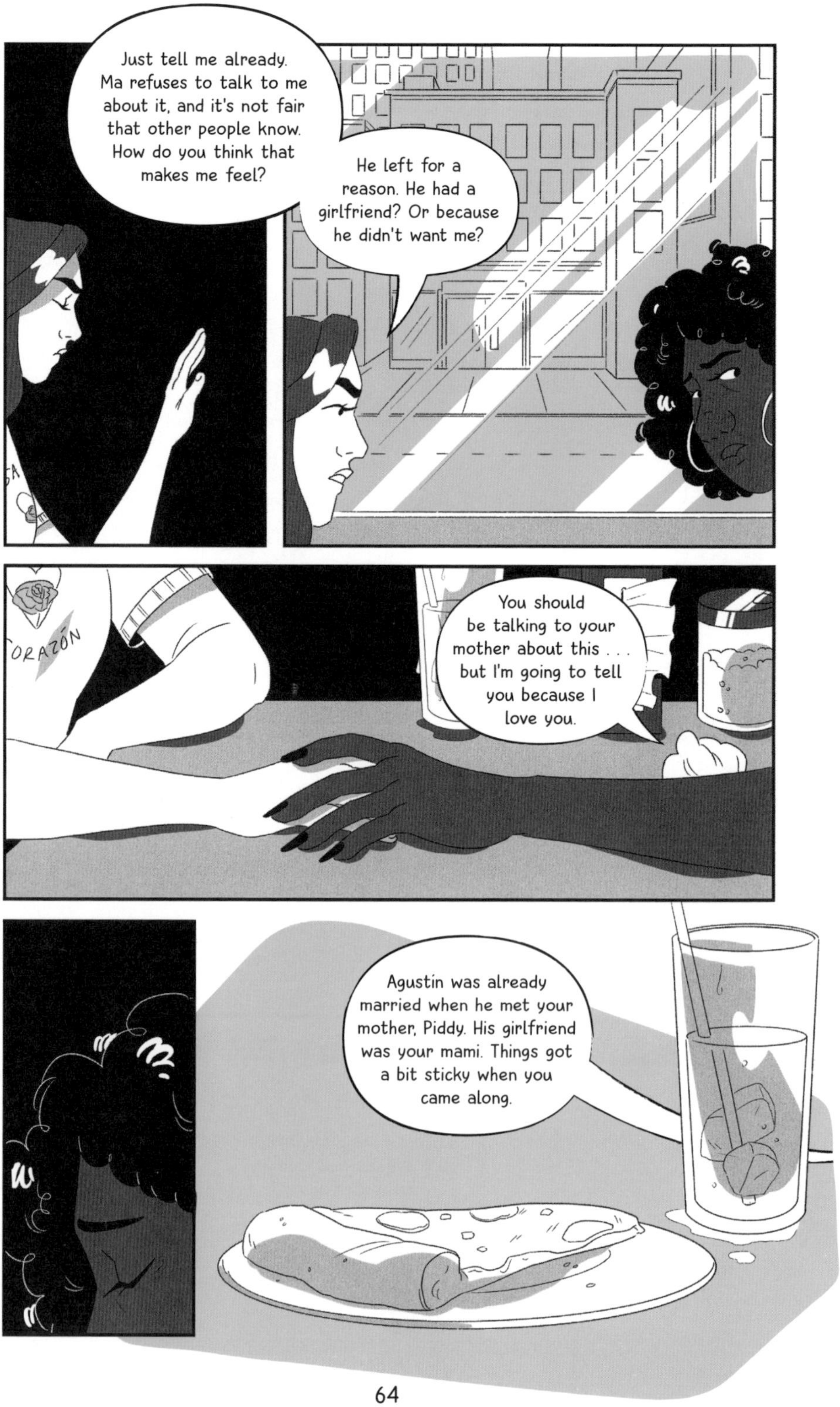
Just tell me already. Ma refuses to talk to me about it, and it's not fair that other people know. How do you think that makes me feel?
He left for a reason. He had a girlfriend? Or because he didn't want me?
CORAZÓN
You should be talking to your mother about this . . . but I'm going to tell you because I love you.
Agustín was already married when he met your mother, Piddy. His girlfriend was your mami. Things got a bit sticky when you came along.

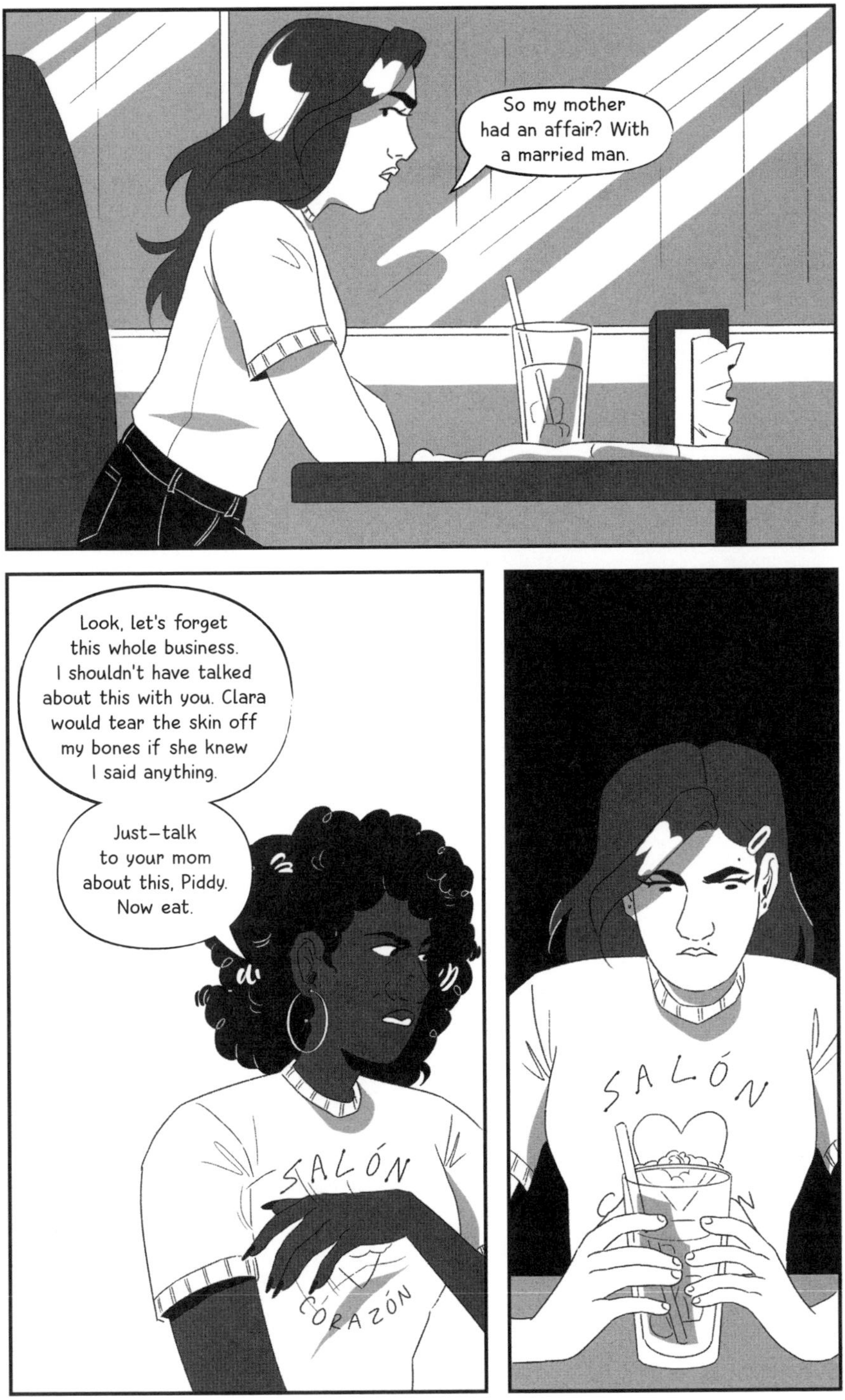
So my mother had an affair? With a married man.
Look, let's forget this whole business. I shouldn't have talked about this with you. Clara would tear the skin off my bones if she knew I said anything.
Just—talk to your mom about this, Piddy. Now eat.
SALÓN CORAZÓN
SALÓN

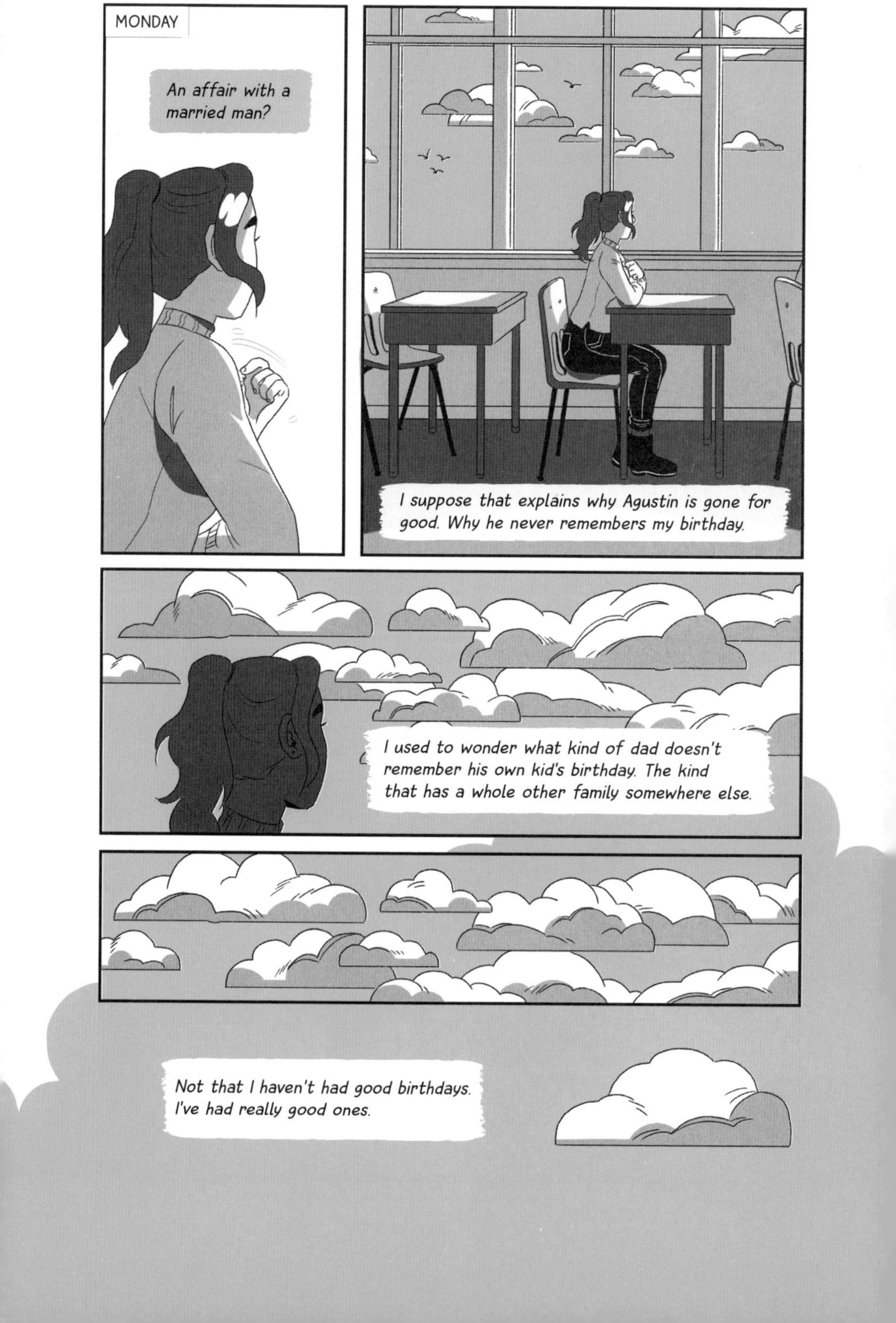
MONDAY
An affair with a married man?
I suppose that explains why Agustín is gone for good. Why he never remembers my birthday.
I used to wonder what kind of dad doesn't remember his own kid's birthday. The kind that has a whole other family somewhere else.
Not that I haven't had good birthdays. I've had really good ones.

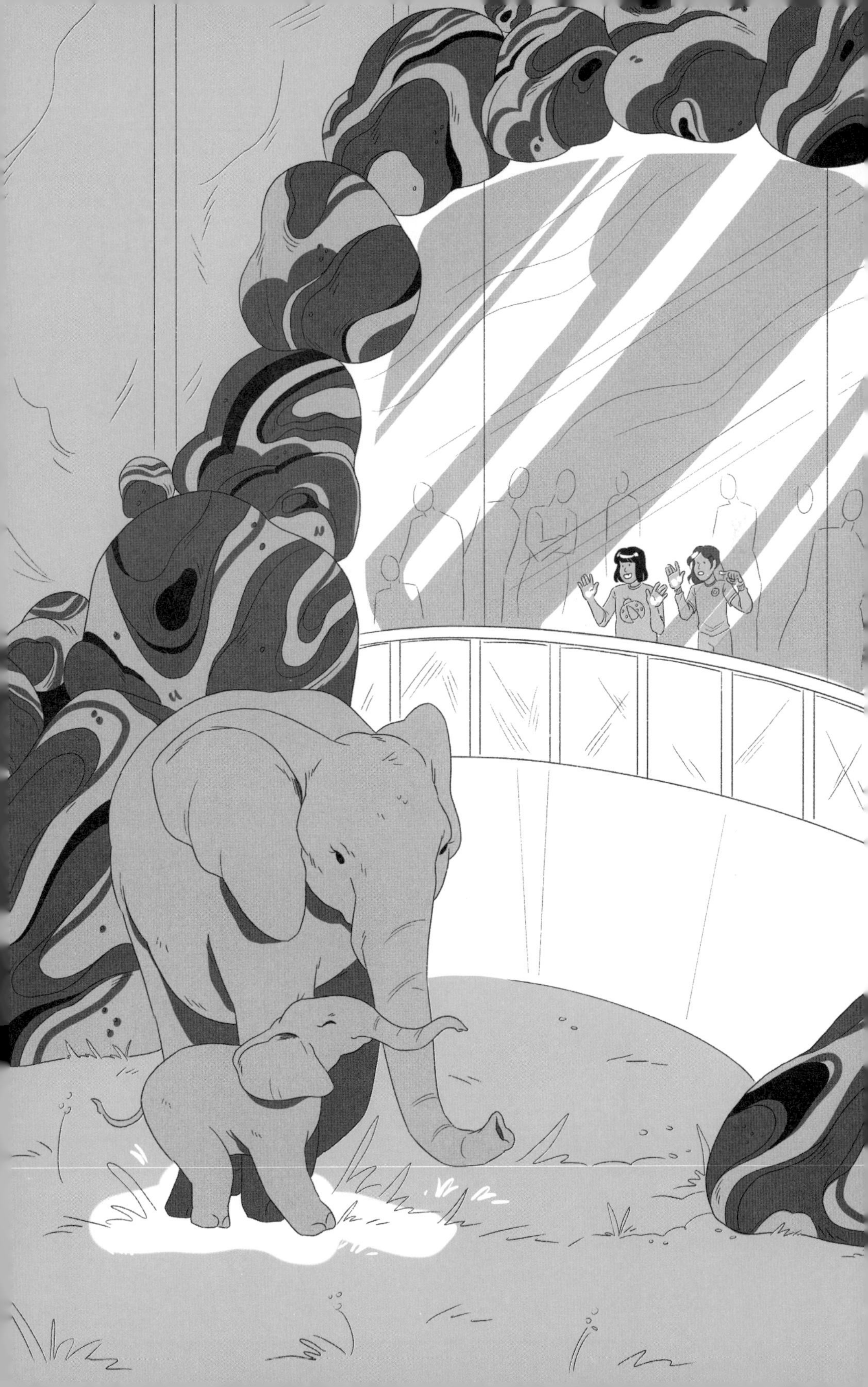

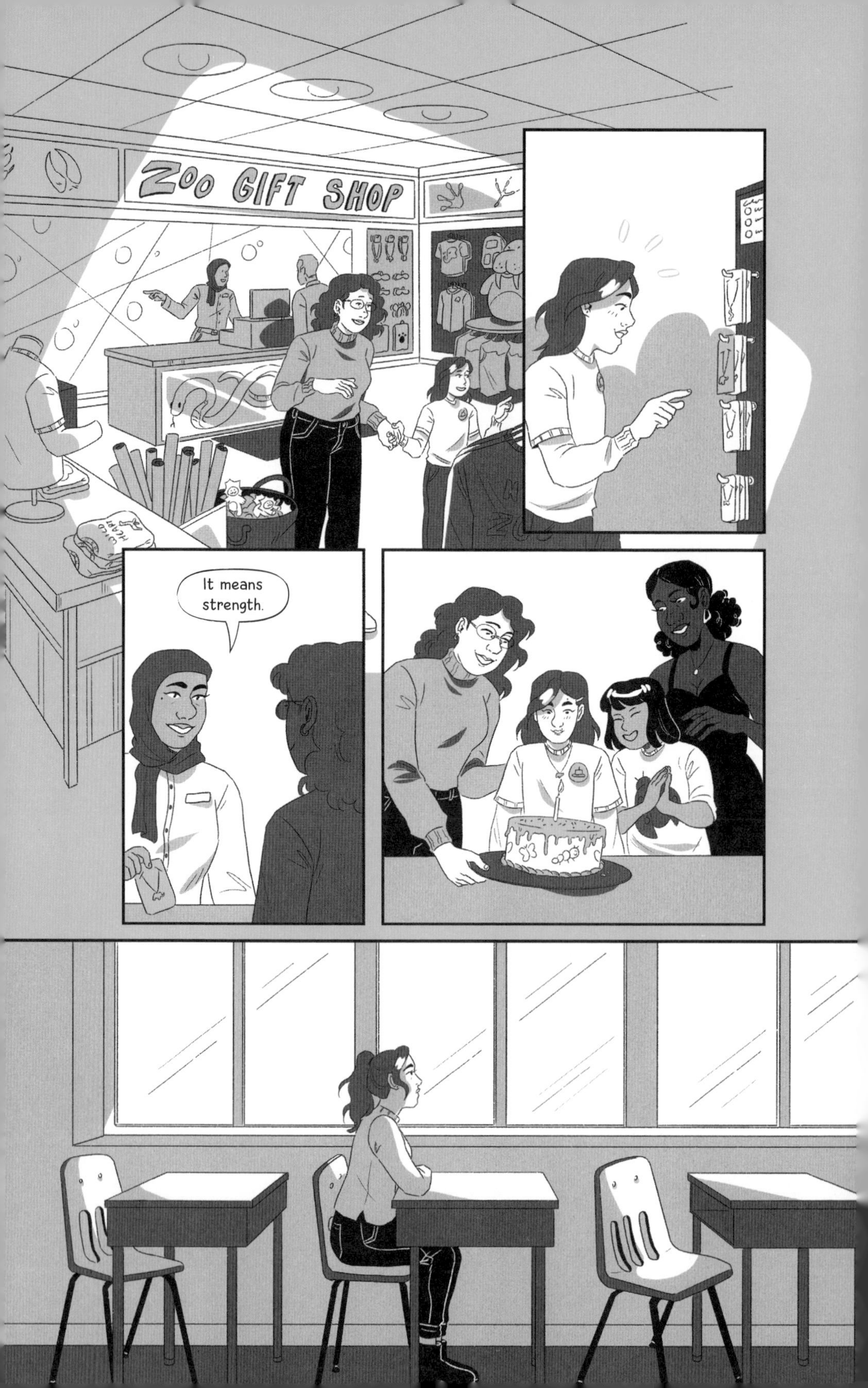
ZOO GIFT SHOP
It means strength.

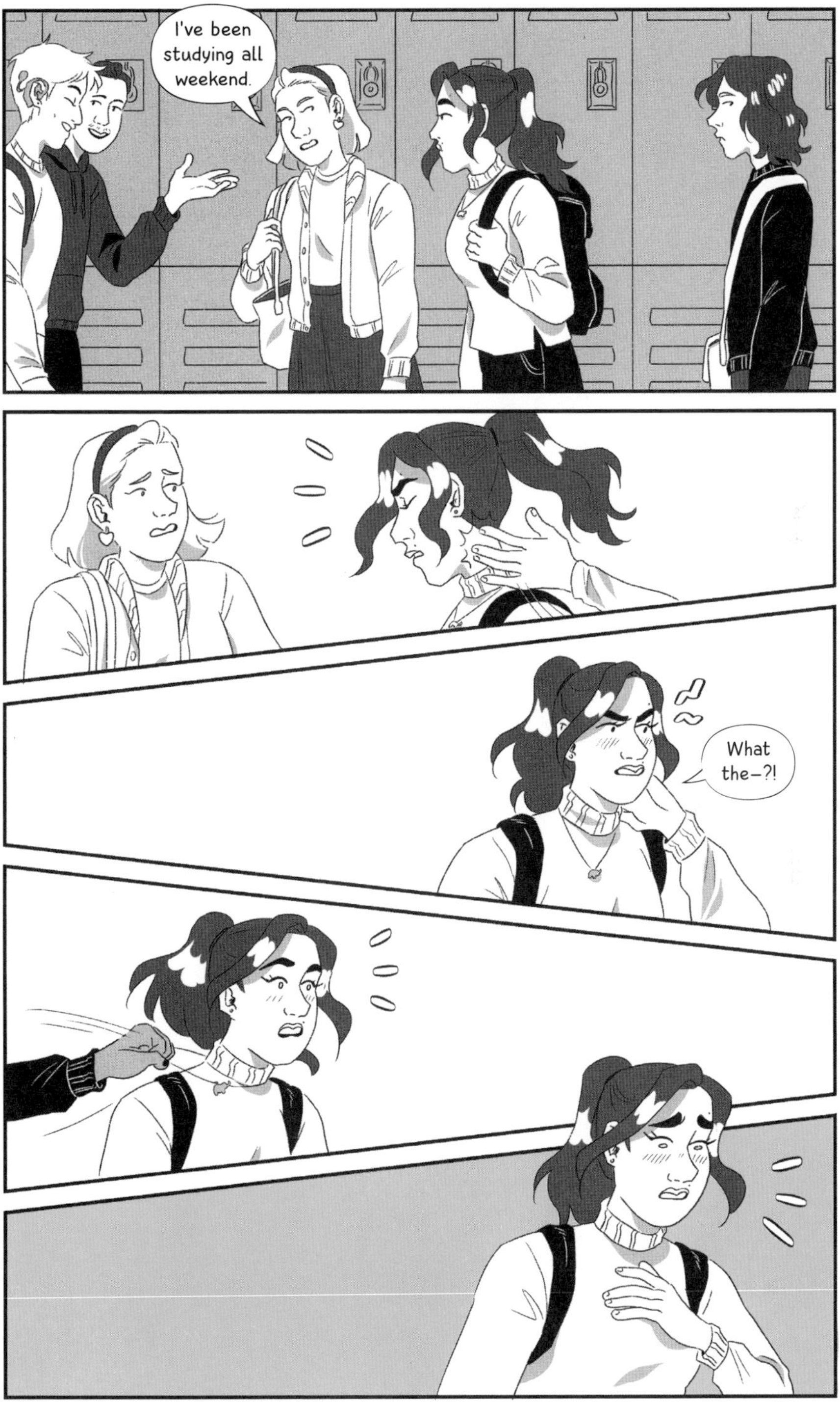
I've been studying all weekend.
What the–?!

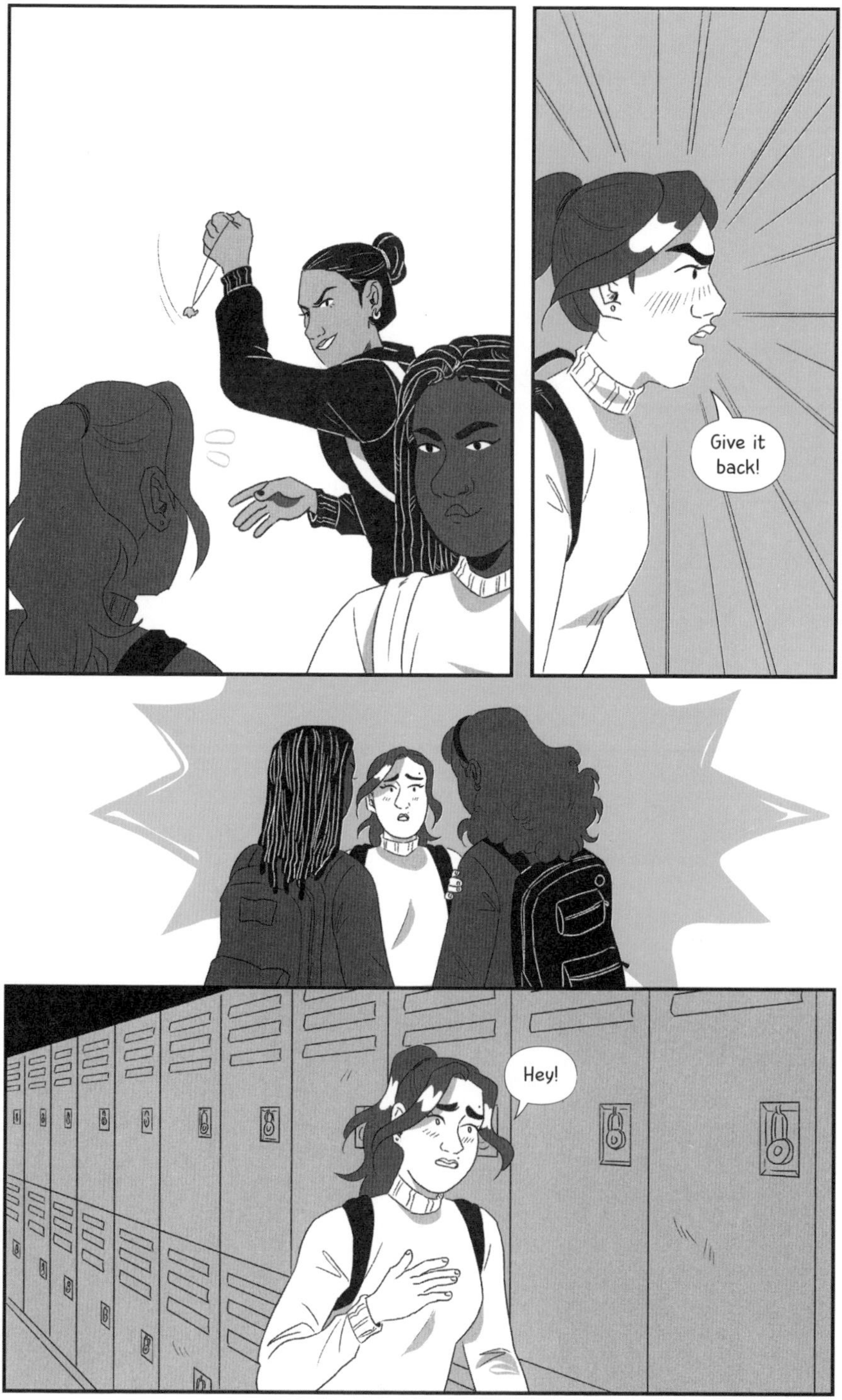
Give it back!
Hey!

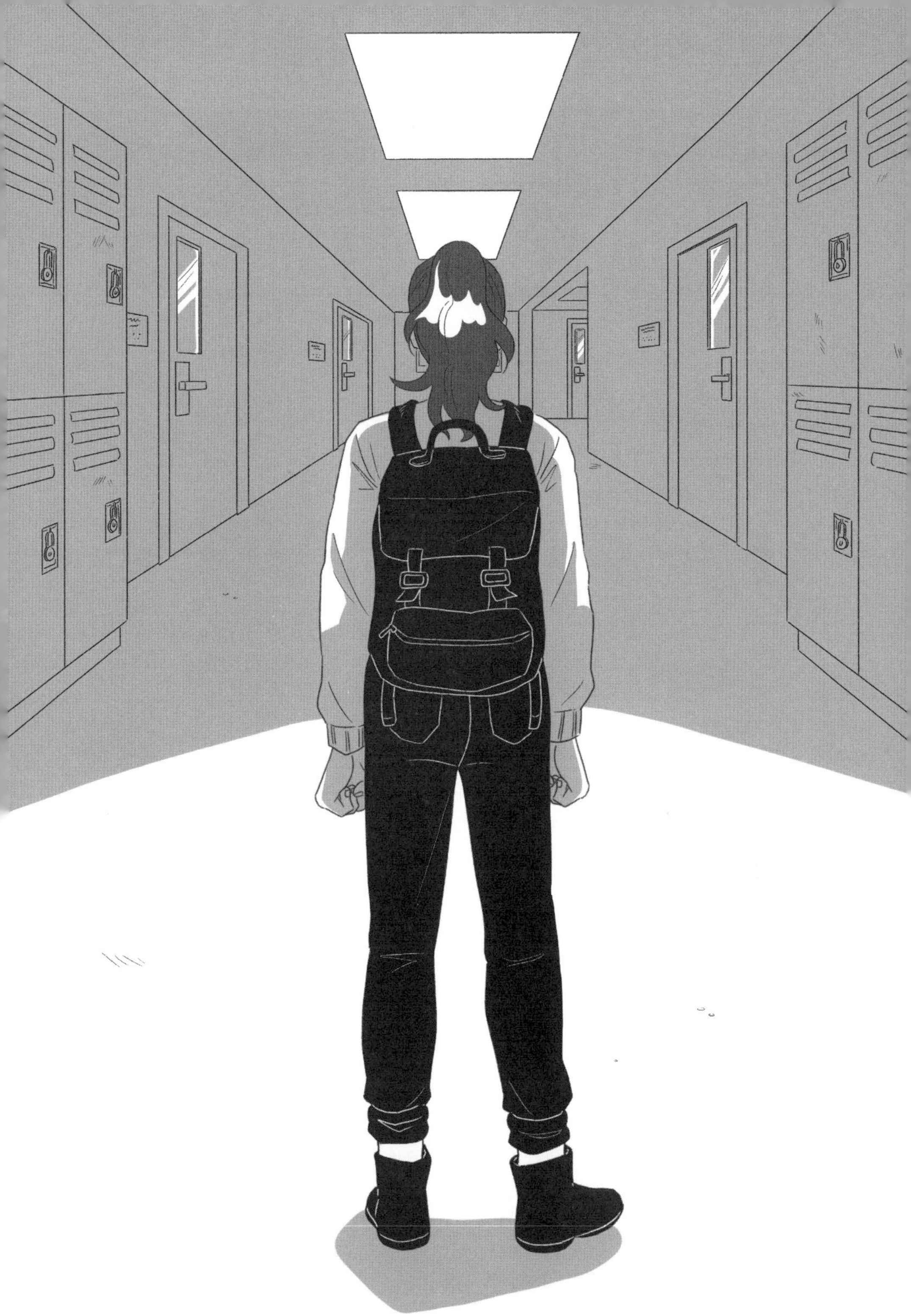

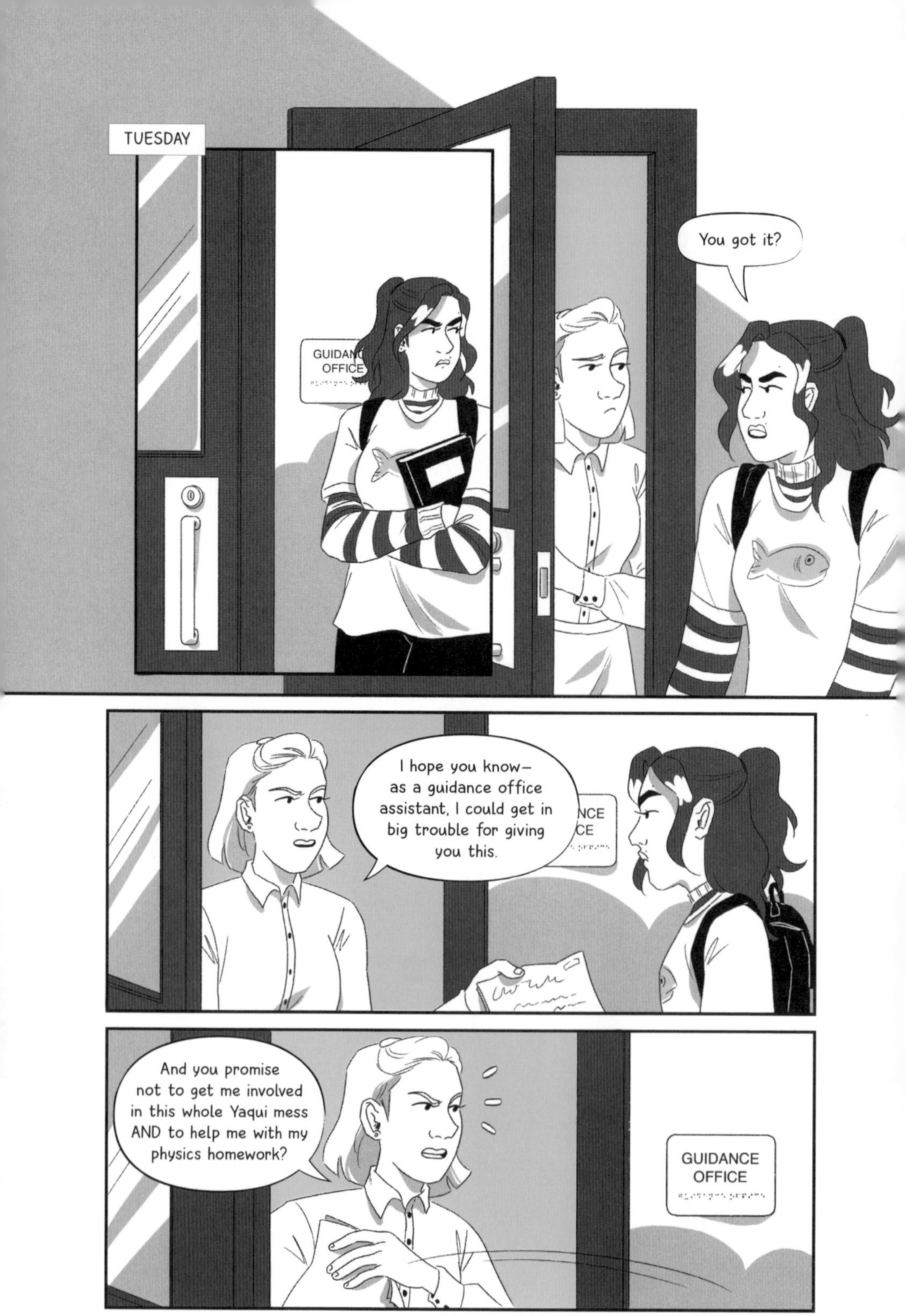
TUESDAY
GUIDANCE OFFICE
You got it?
I hope you know— as a guidance office assistant, I could get in big trouble for giving you this.
And you promise not to get me involved in this whole Yaqui mess AND to help me with my physics homework?
GUIDANCE OFFICE

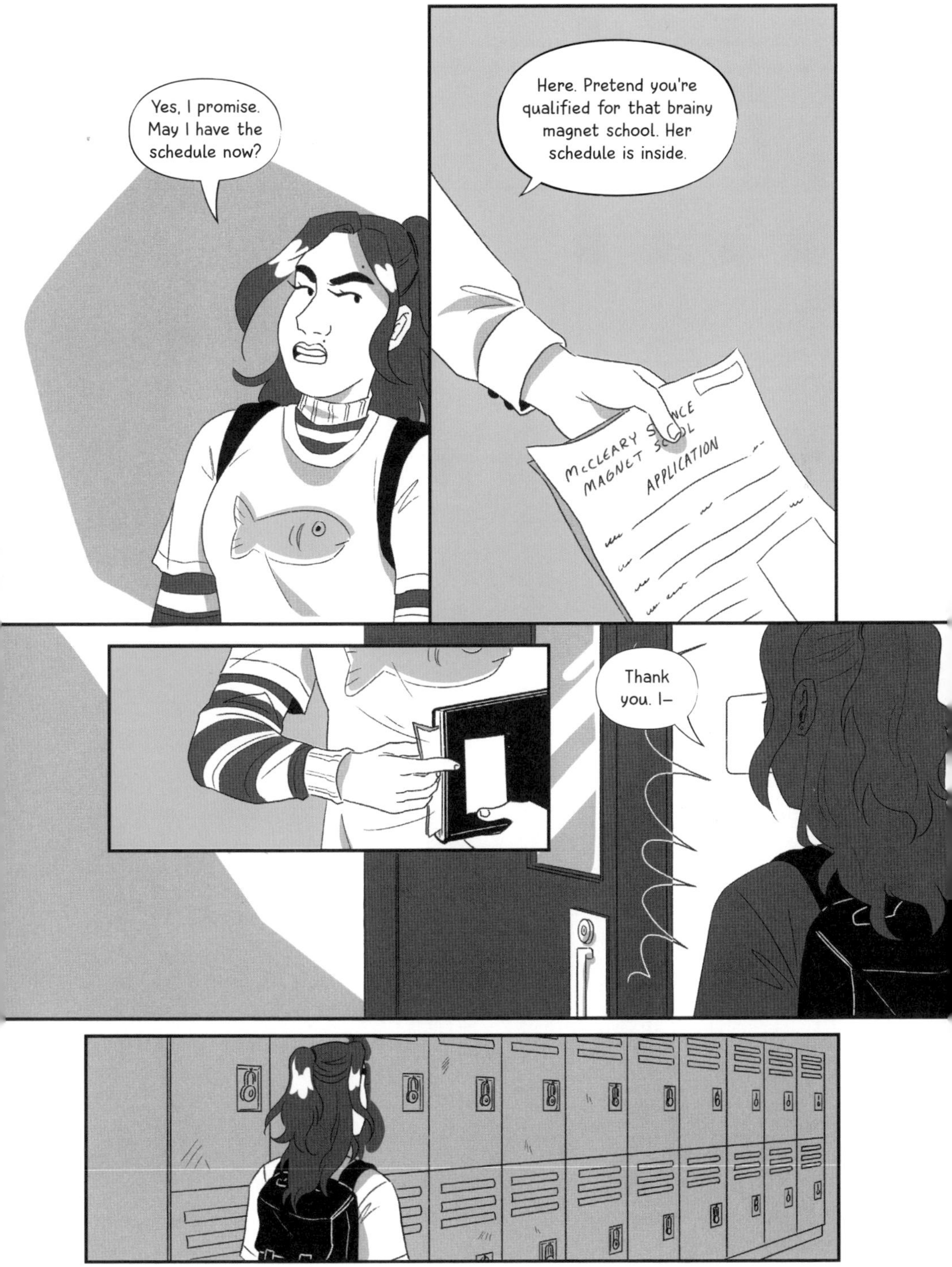
Yes, I promise. May I have the schedule now?
Here. Pretend you're qualified for that brainy magnet school. Her schedule is inside.
McCLEARY SCIENCE MAGNET SCHOOL APPLICATION
Thank you. I—

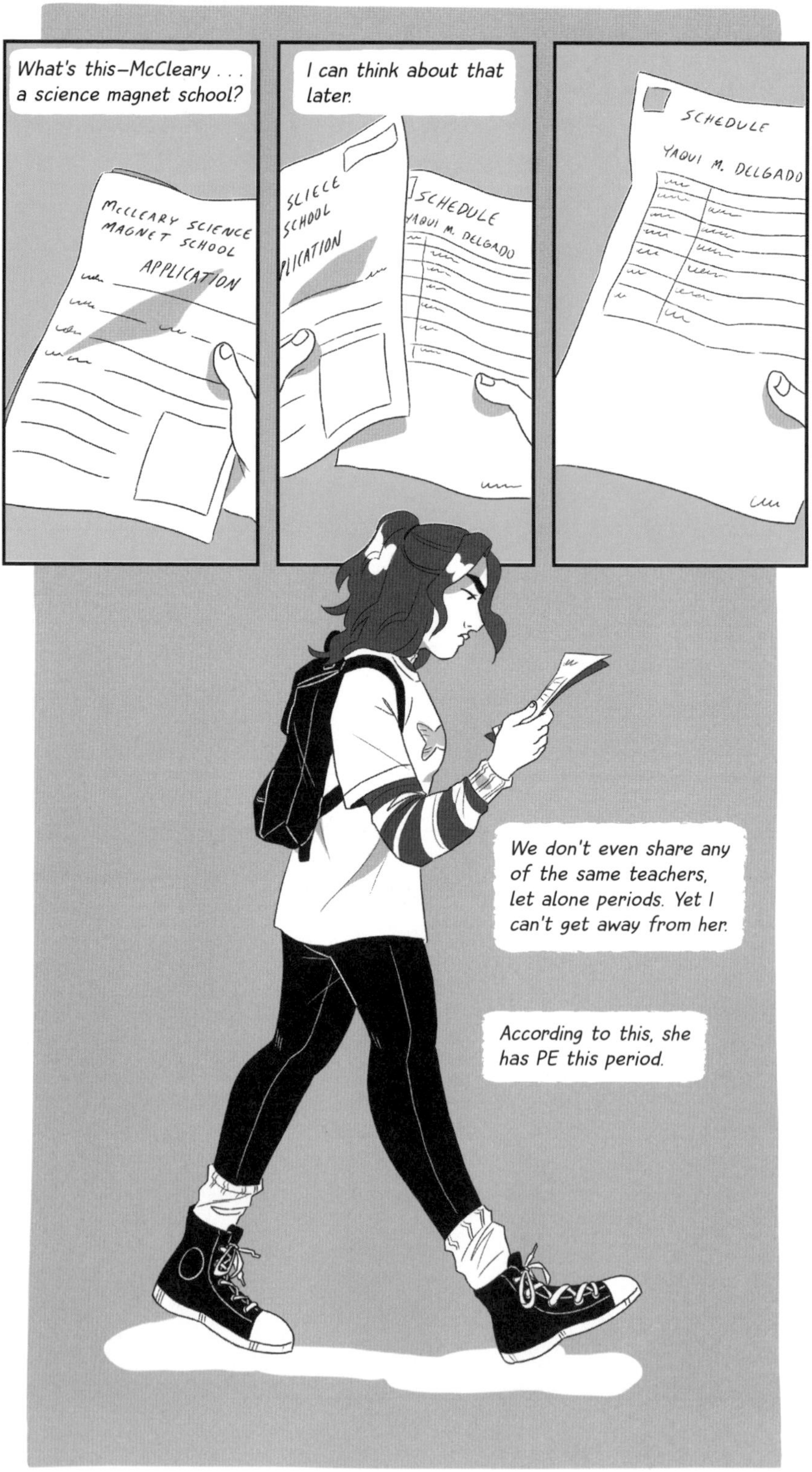

What's this—McCleary . . . a science magnet school?
McCLEARY SCIENCE MAGNET SCHOOL
APPLICATION
I can think about that later.
SCHEDULE
YAQUI M. DELGADO
We don't even share any of the same teachers, let alone periods. Yet I can't get away from her.
According to this, she has PE this period.

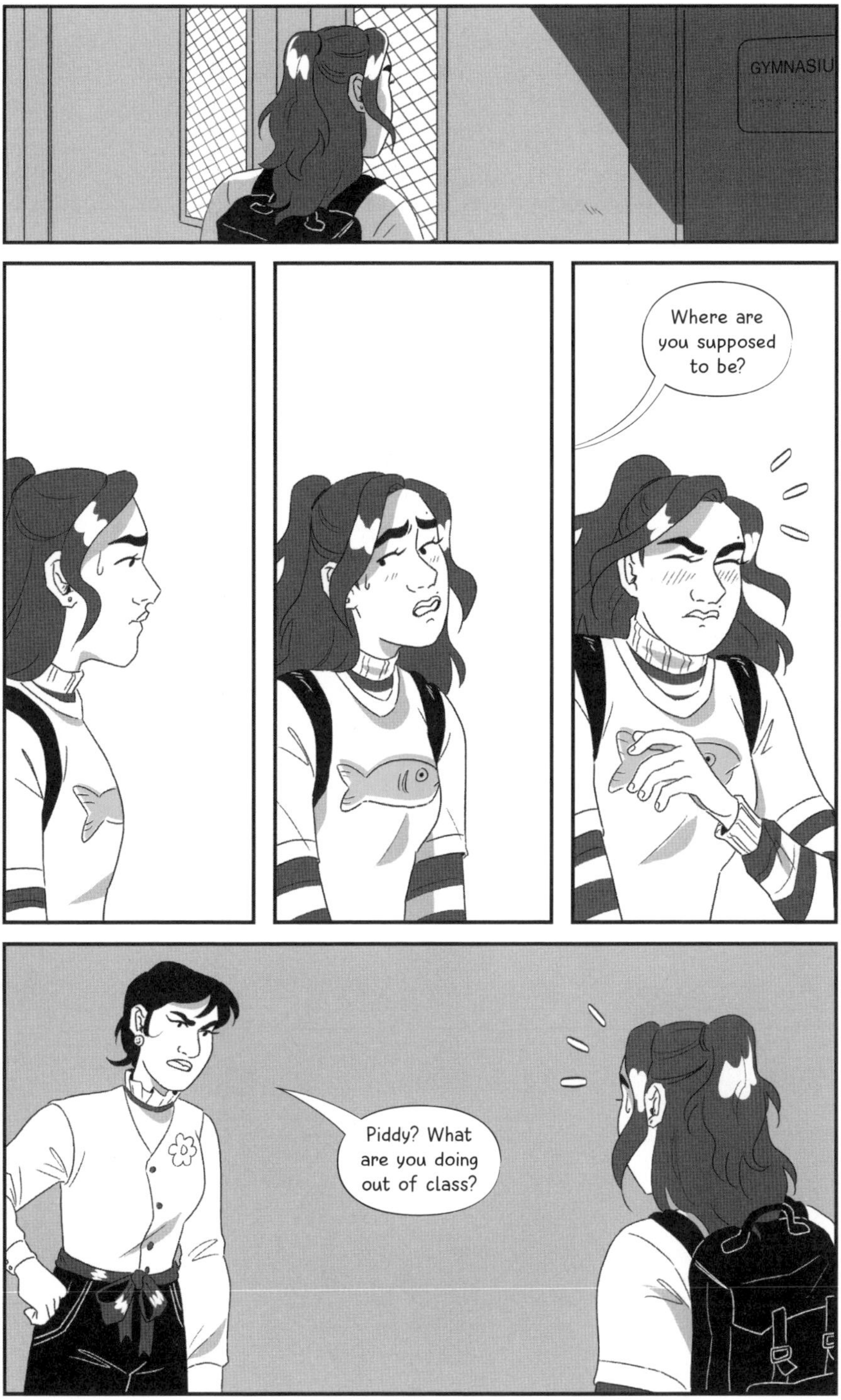
GYMNASIU
Where are you supposed to be?
Piddy? What are you doing out of class?

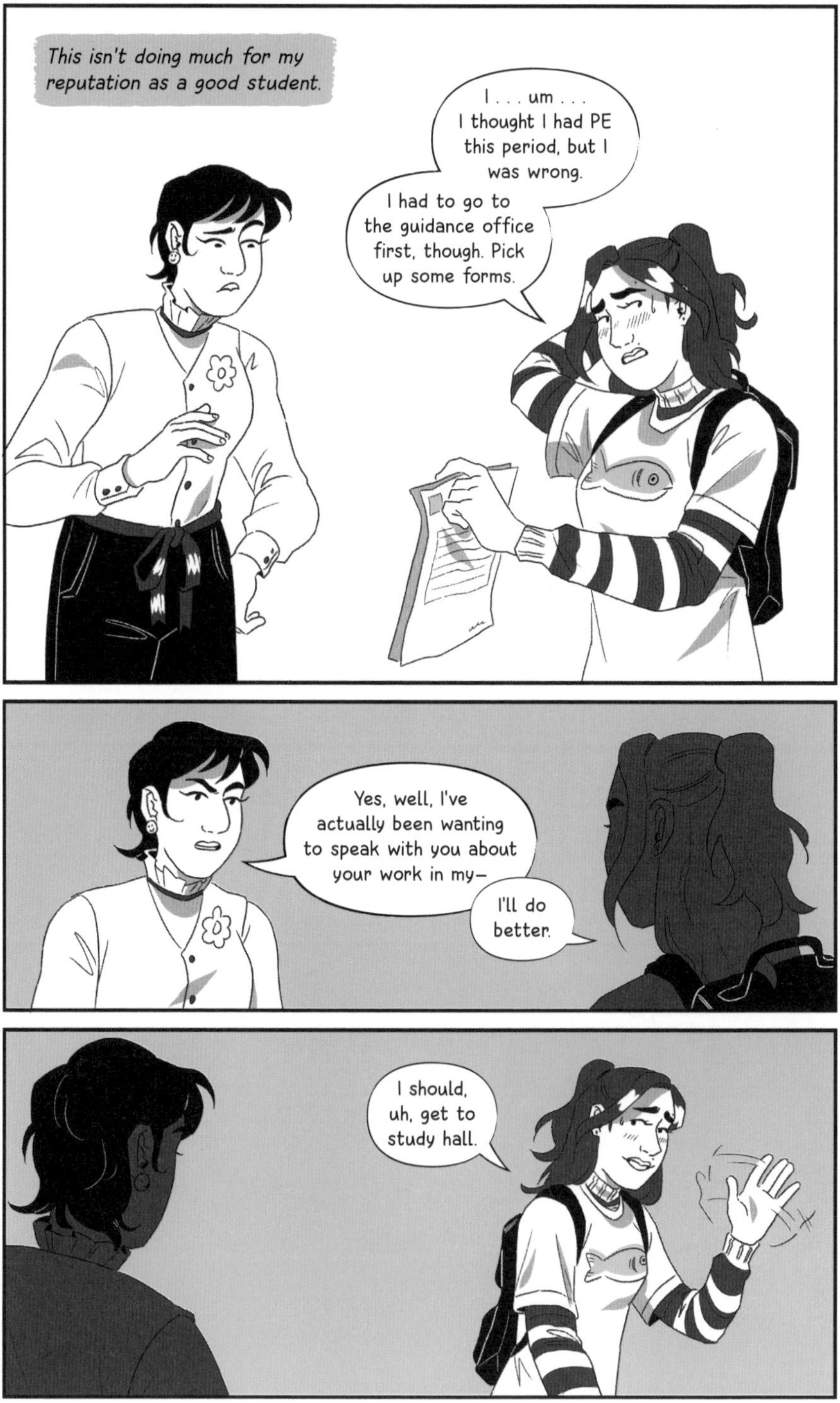
This isn't doing much for my reputation as a good student.
I . . . um . . . I thought I had PE this period, but I was wrong.
I had to go to the guidance office first, though. Pick up some forms.
Yes, well, I've actually been wanting to speak with you about your work in my—
I'll do better.
I should, uh, get to study hall.

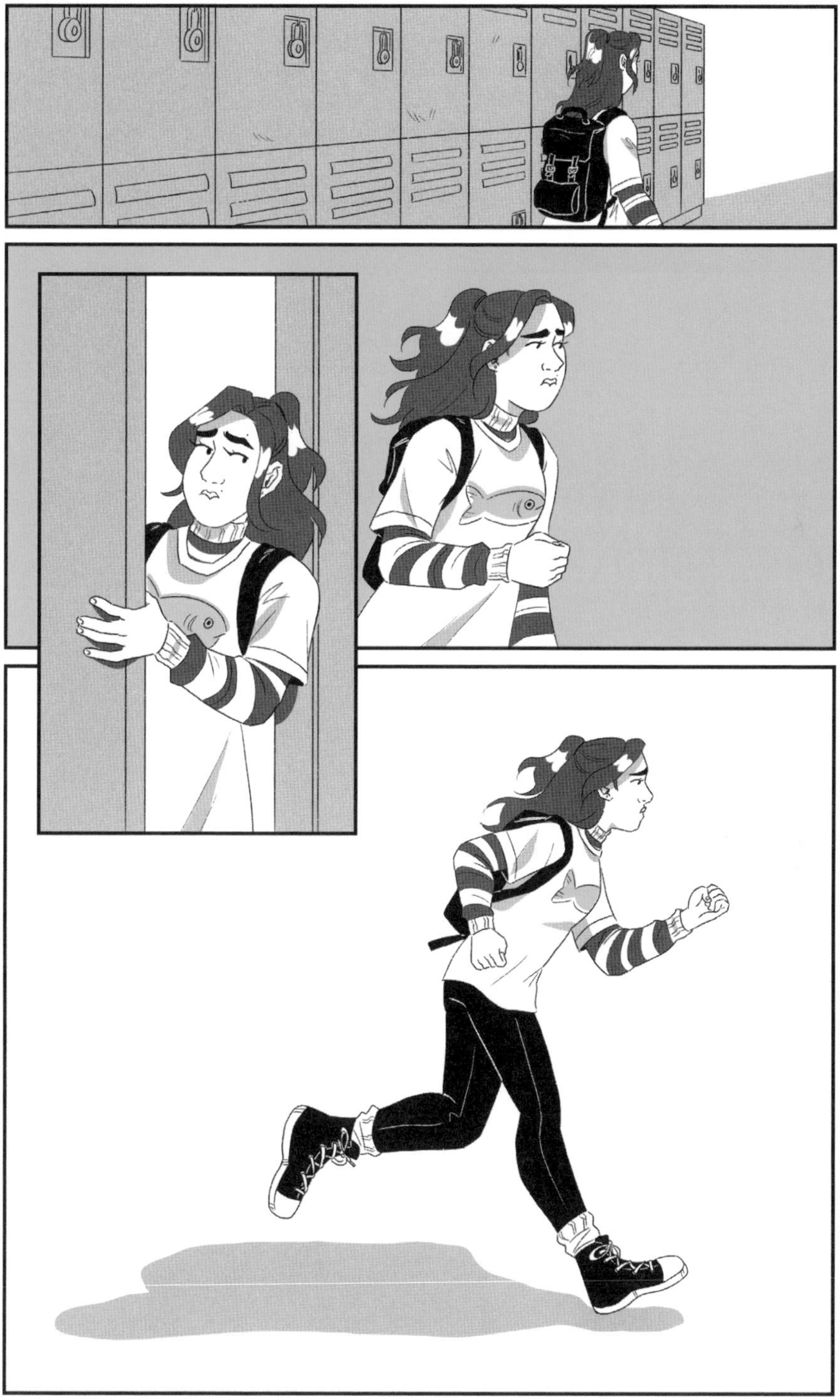

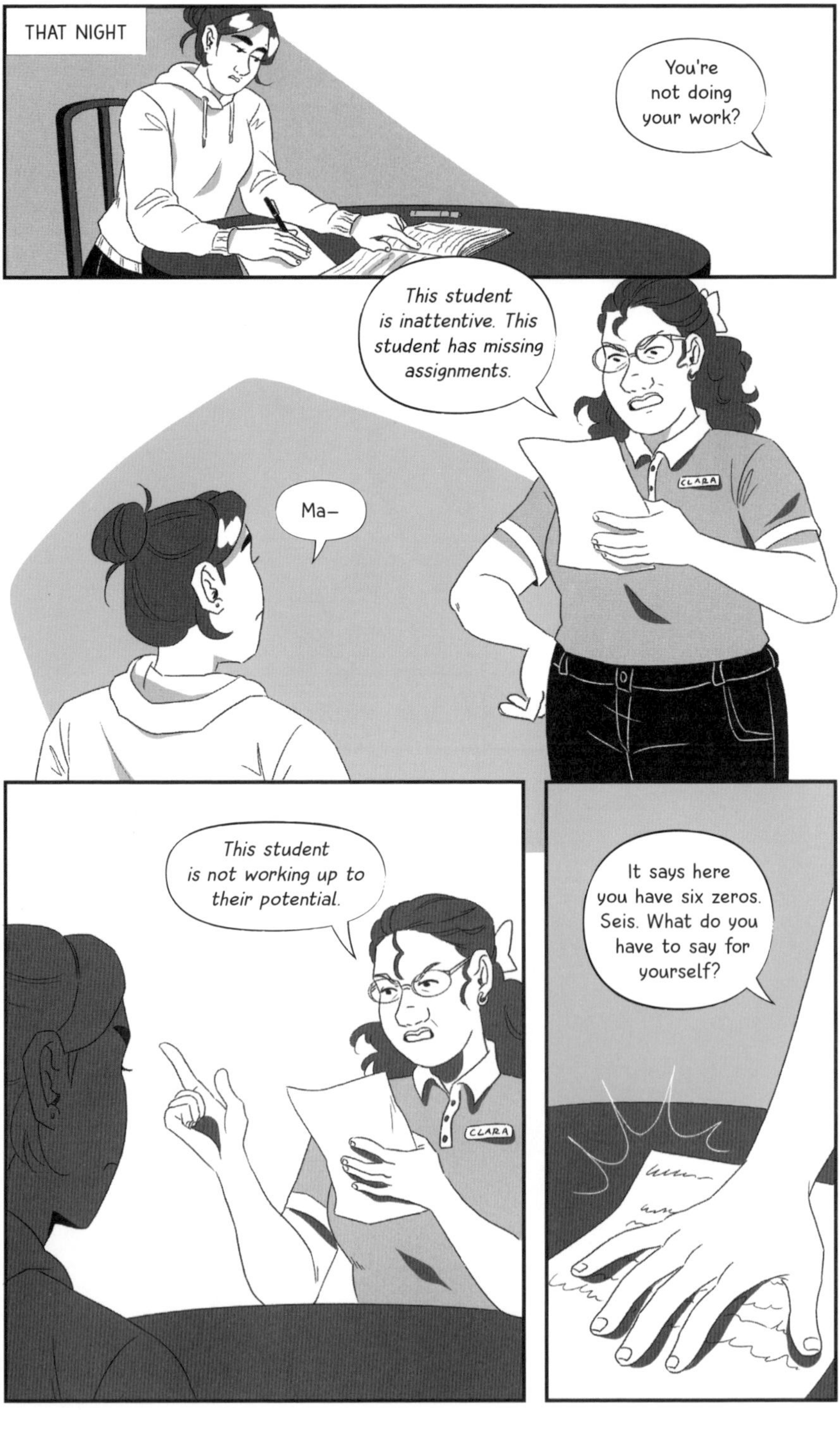
THAT NIGHT
You're not doing your work?
This student is inattentive. This student has missing assignments.
Ma–
CLARA
This student is not working up to their potential.
CLARA
It says here you have six zeros. Seis. What do you have to say for yourself?

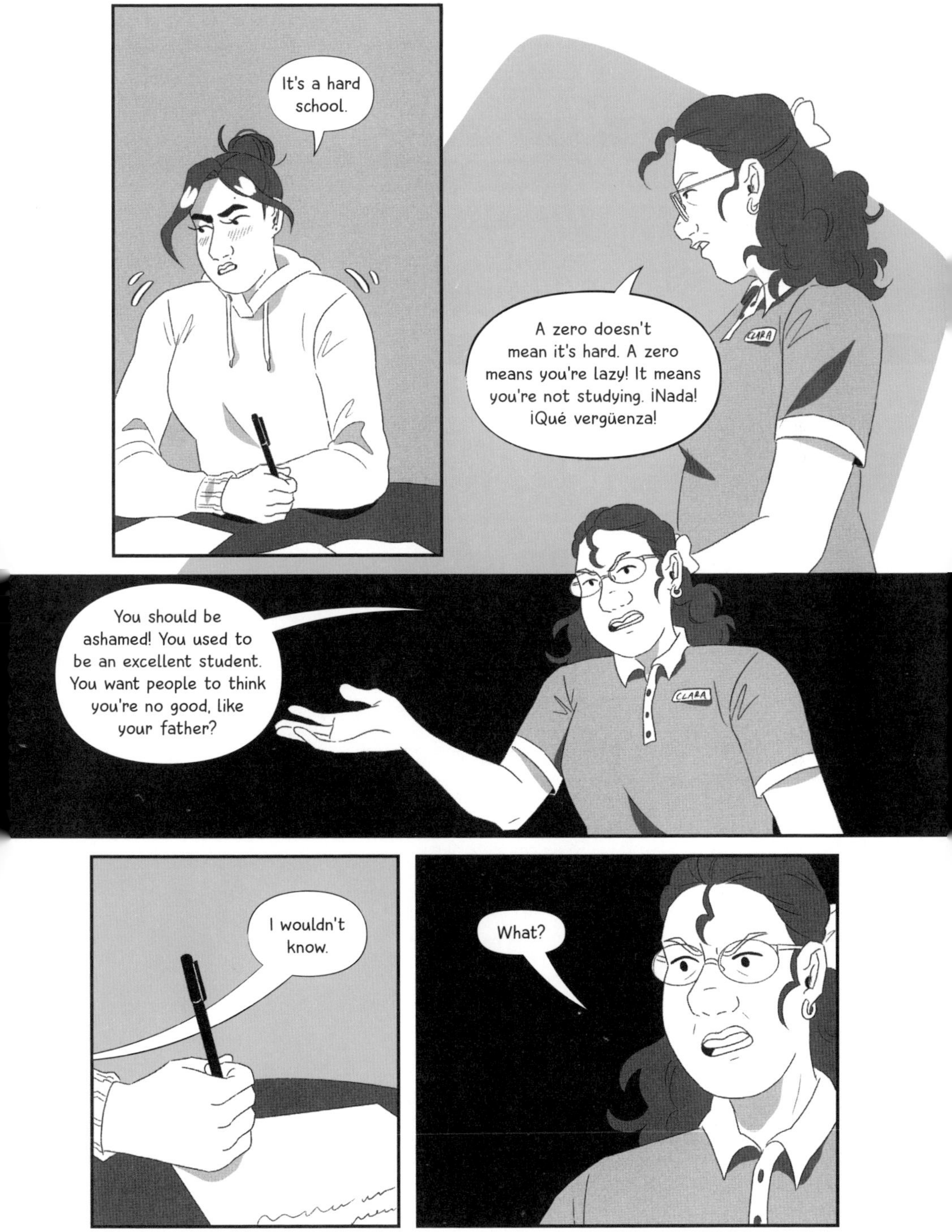

It's a hard school.
A zero doesn't mean it's hard. A zero means you're lazy! It means you're not studying. ¡Nada! ¡Qué vergüenza!
You should be ashamed! You used to be an excellent student. You want people to think you're no good, like your father?
I wouldn't know.
What?

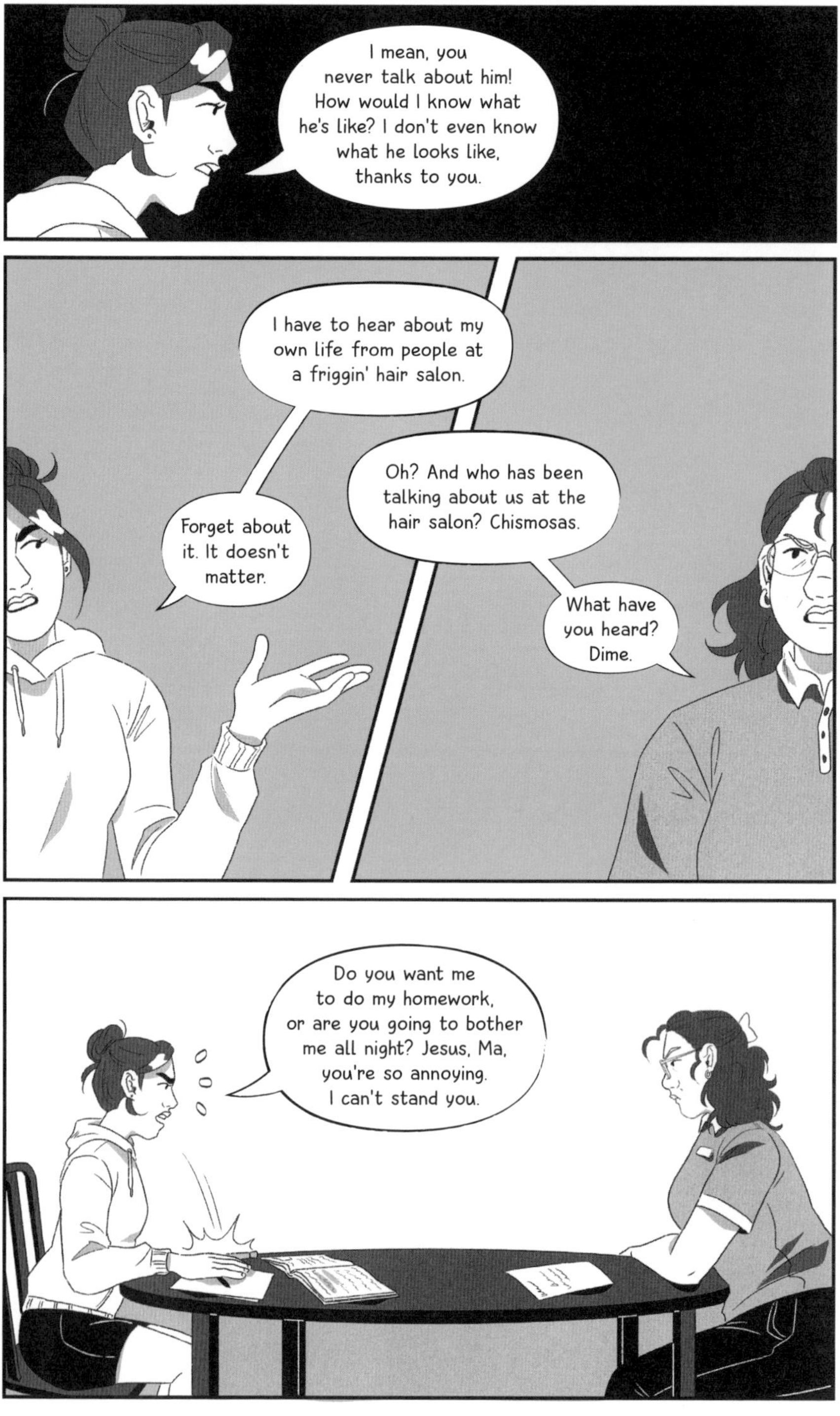
I mean, you never talk about him! How would I know what he's like? I don't even know what he looks like, thanks to you.
I have to hear about my own life from people at a friggin' hair salon.
Forget about it. It doesn't matter.
Oh? And who has been talking about us at the hair salon? Chismosas.
What have you heard? Dime.
Do you want me to do my homework, or are you going to bother me all night? Jesus, Ma, you're so annoying. I can't stand you.

You know what, Piedad Maria Sanchez? This isn't about Agustin—it has to do with you.

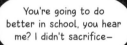

You're going to do better in school, you hear me? I didn't sacrifice—

Where are you going?

Away from you!

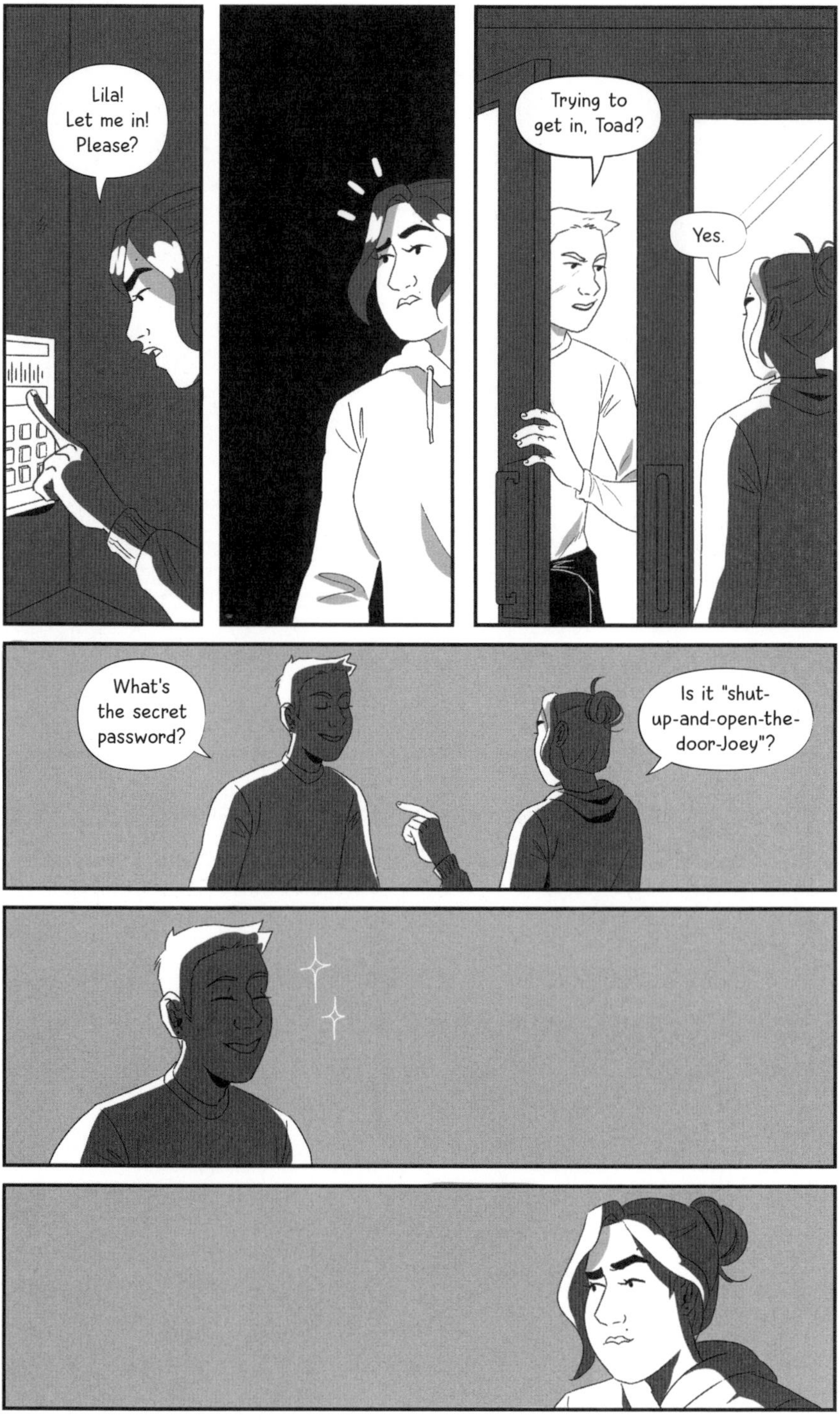
Lila!
Let me in!
Please?
Trying to get in, Toad?
Yes.
What's the secret password?
Is it "shut-up-and-open-the-door-Joey"?

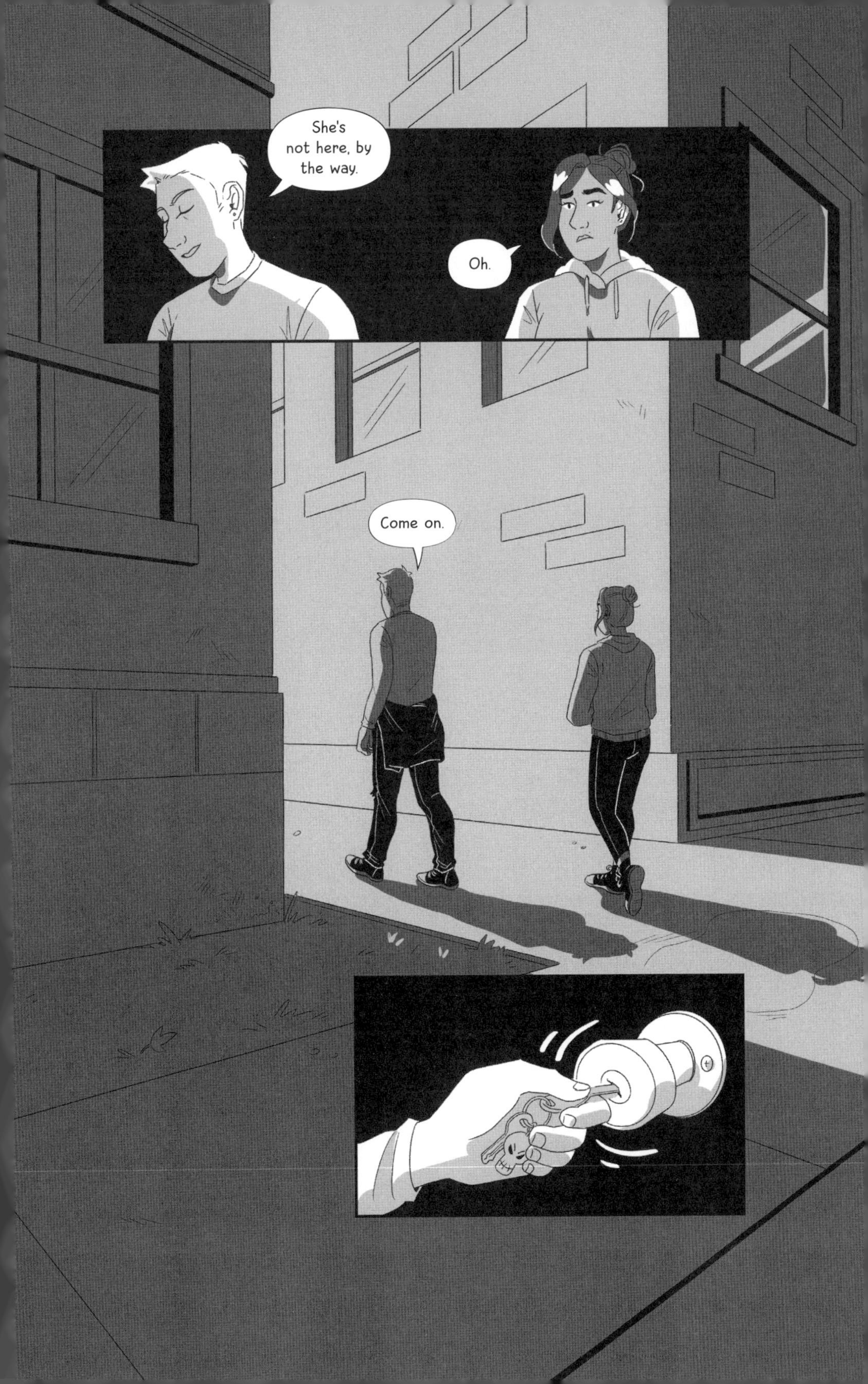
She's not here, by the way.
Oh.
Come on.

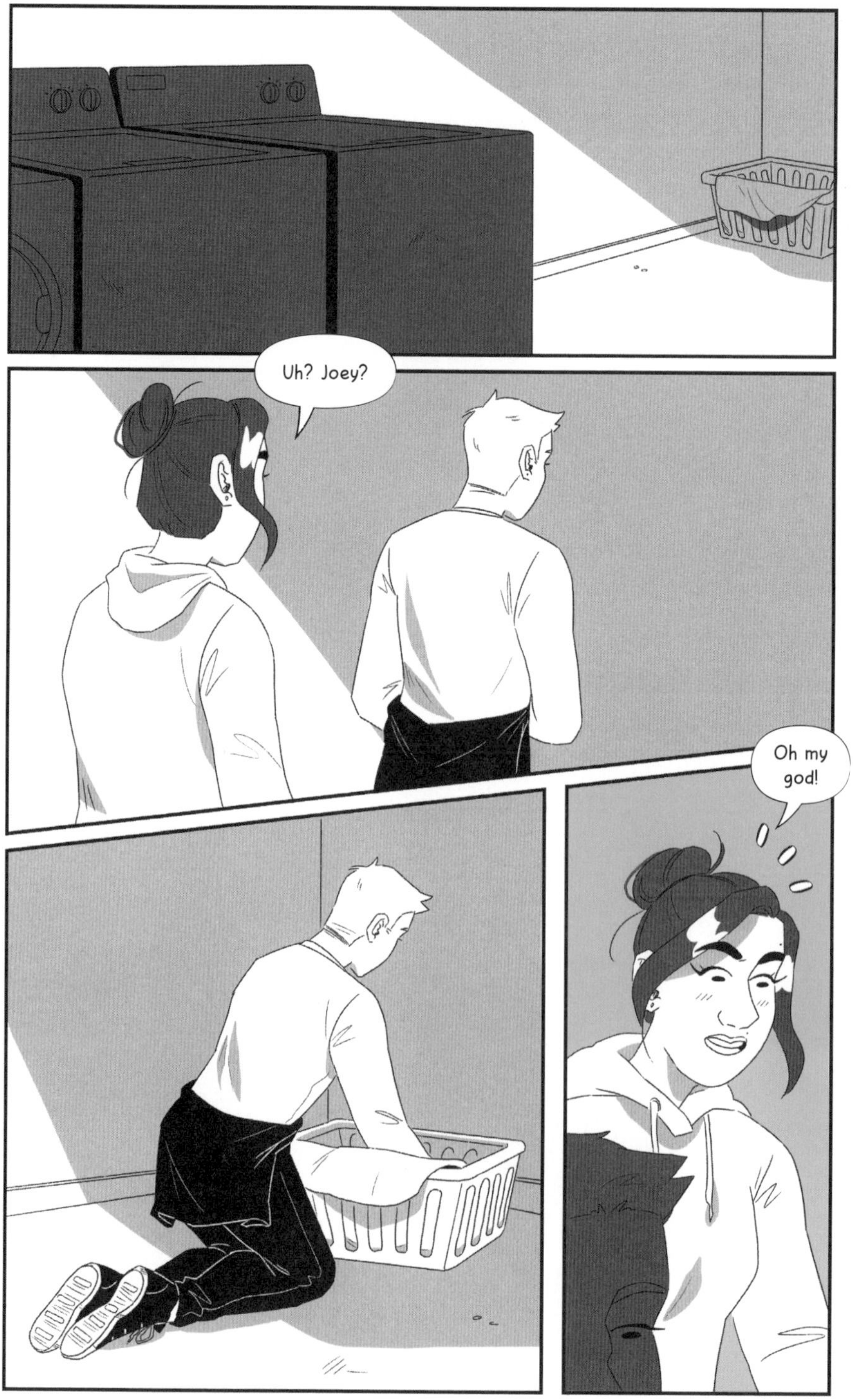
Uh? Joey?
Oh my god!

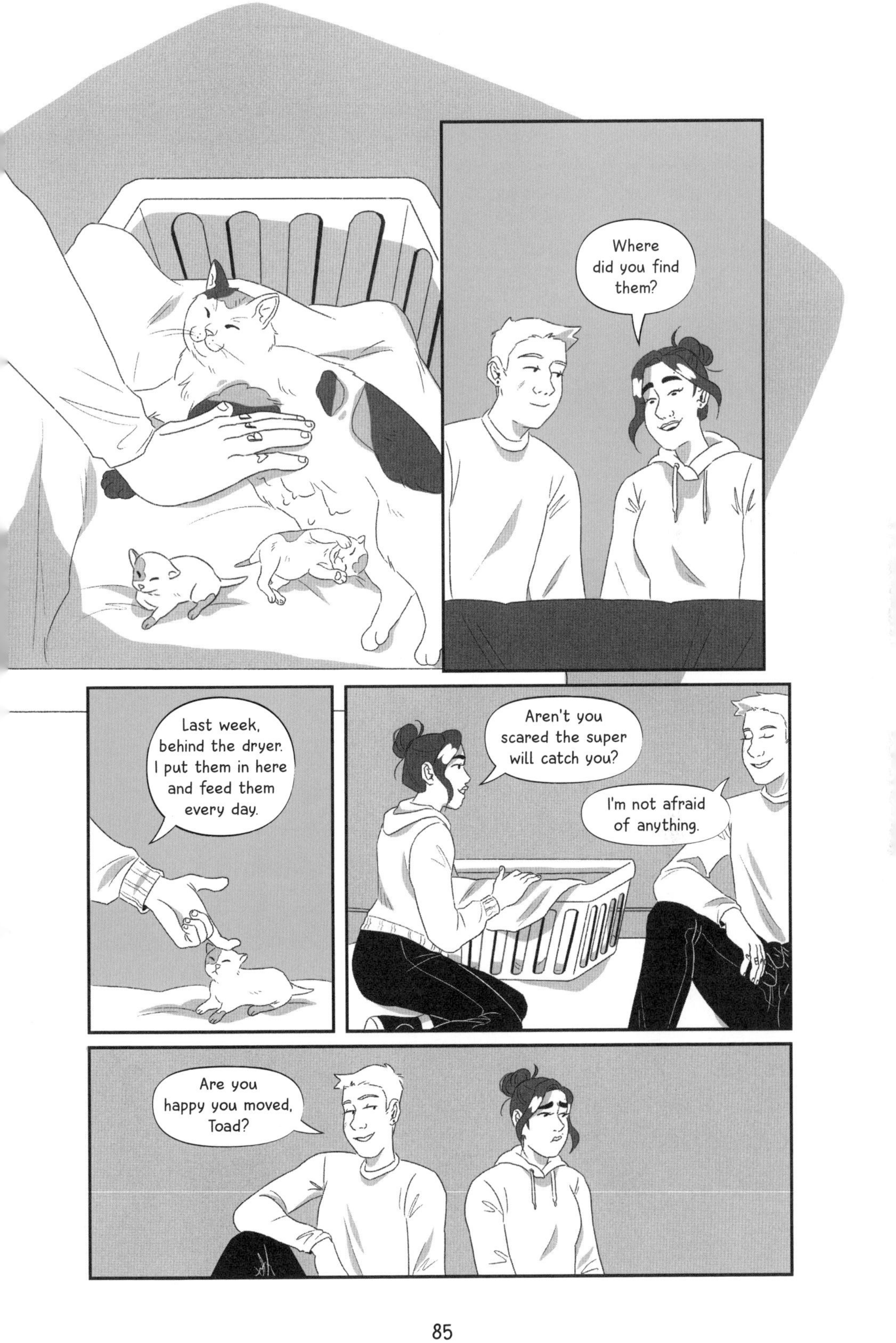
Where did you find them?
Last week, behind the dryer. I put them in here and feed them every day.
Aren't you scared the super will catch you?
I'm not afraid of anything.
Are you happy you moved, Toad?

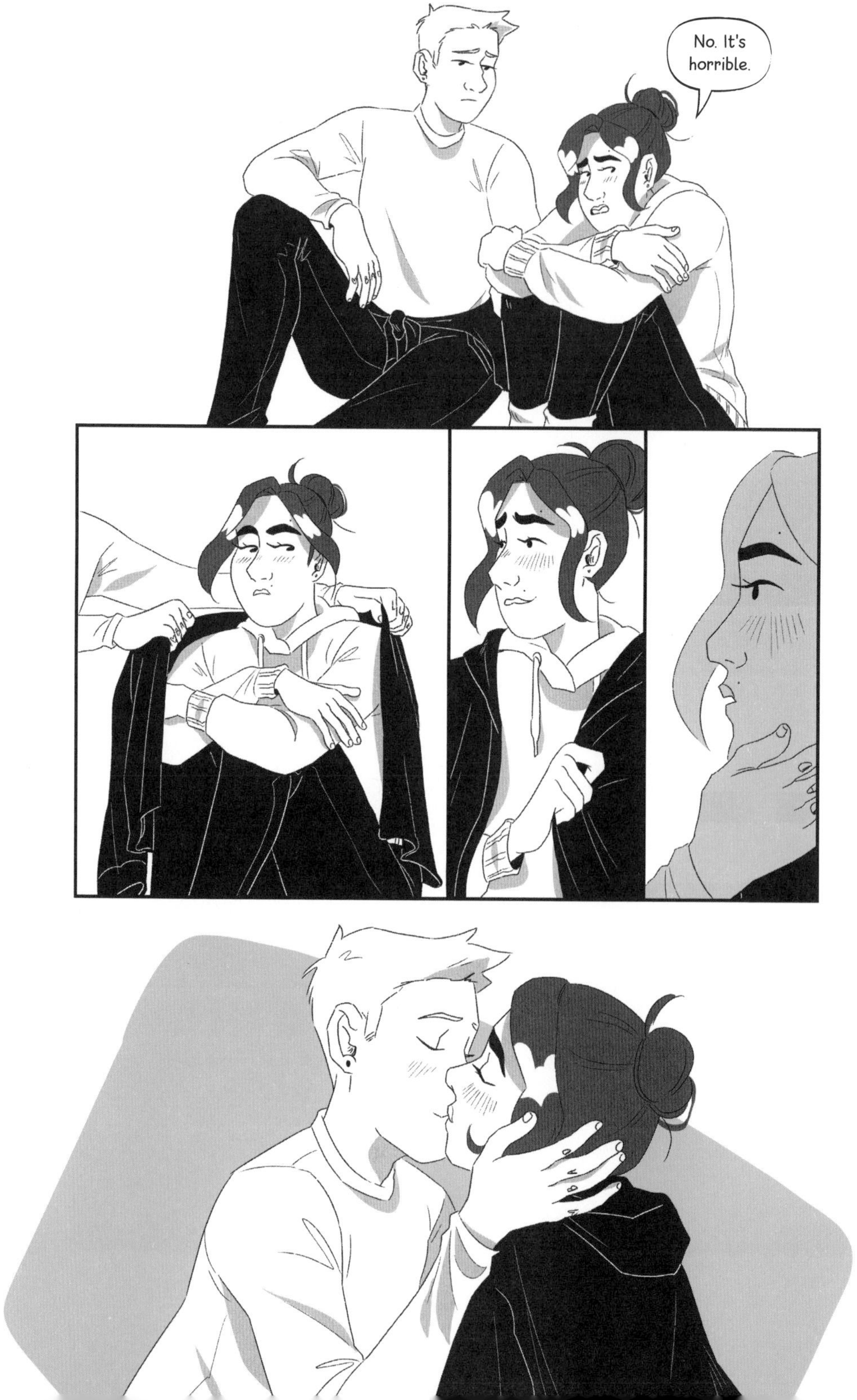
No. It's horrible.

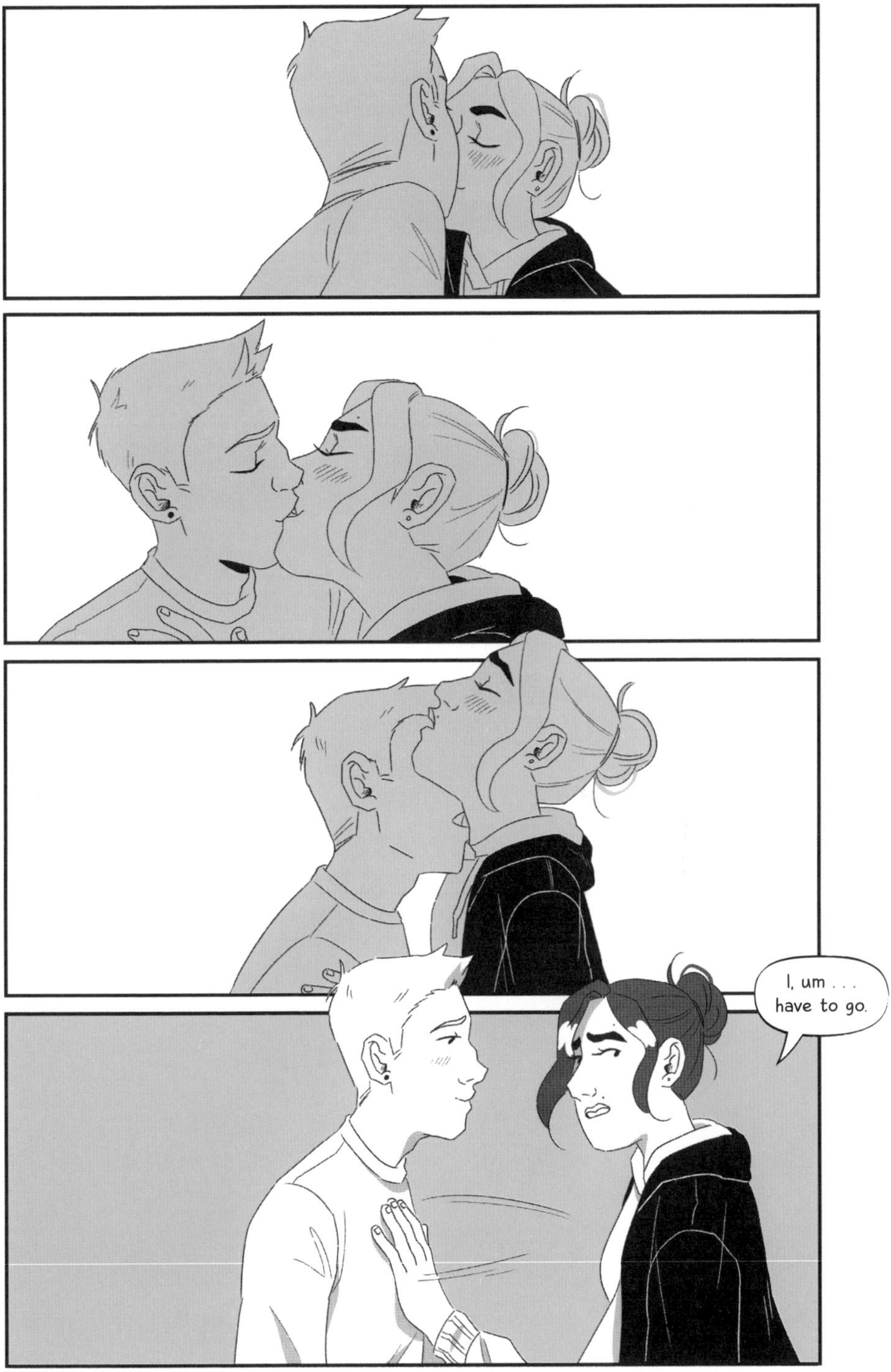
I, um . . . have to go.

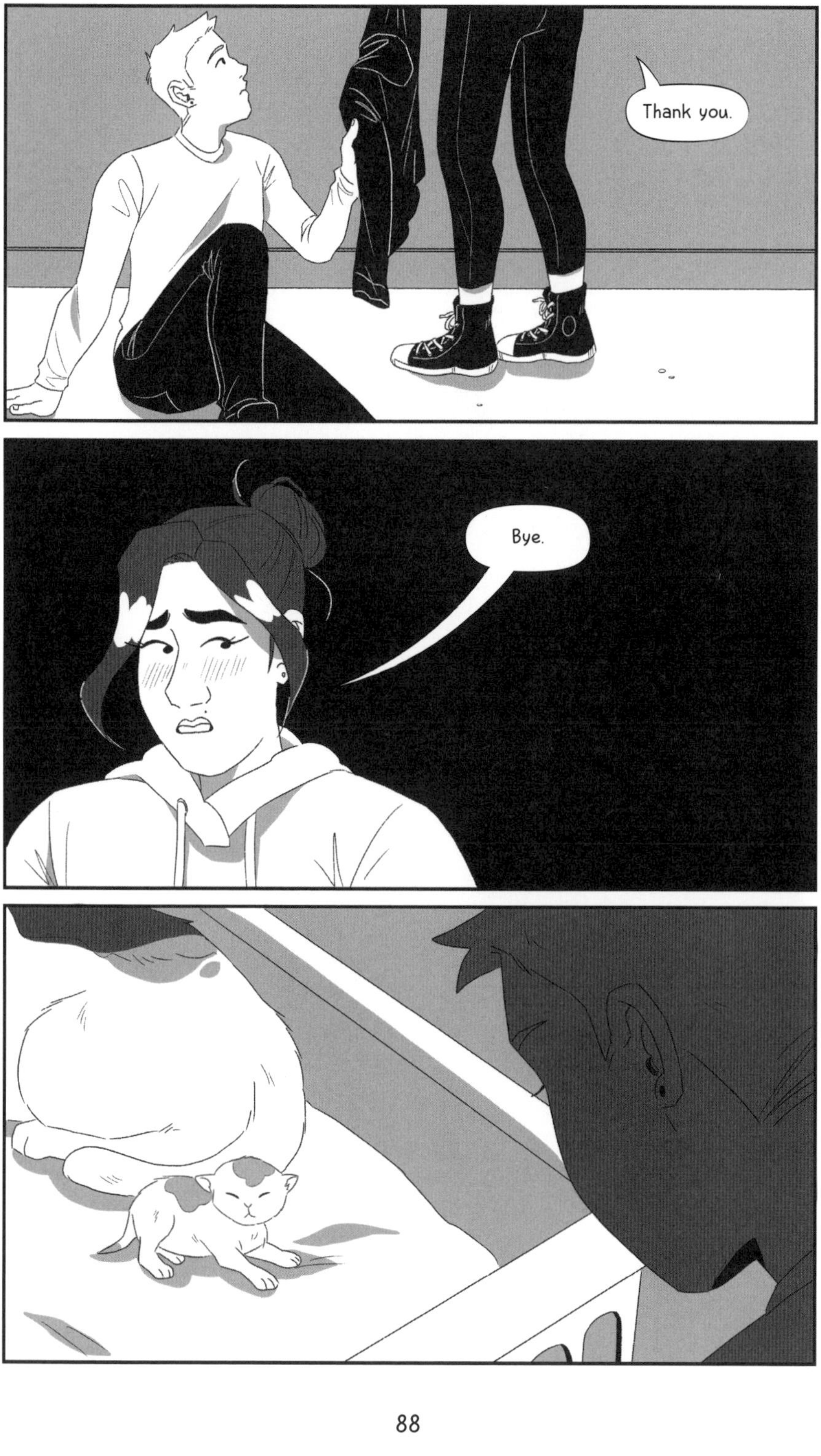
Thank you.
Bye.

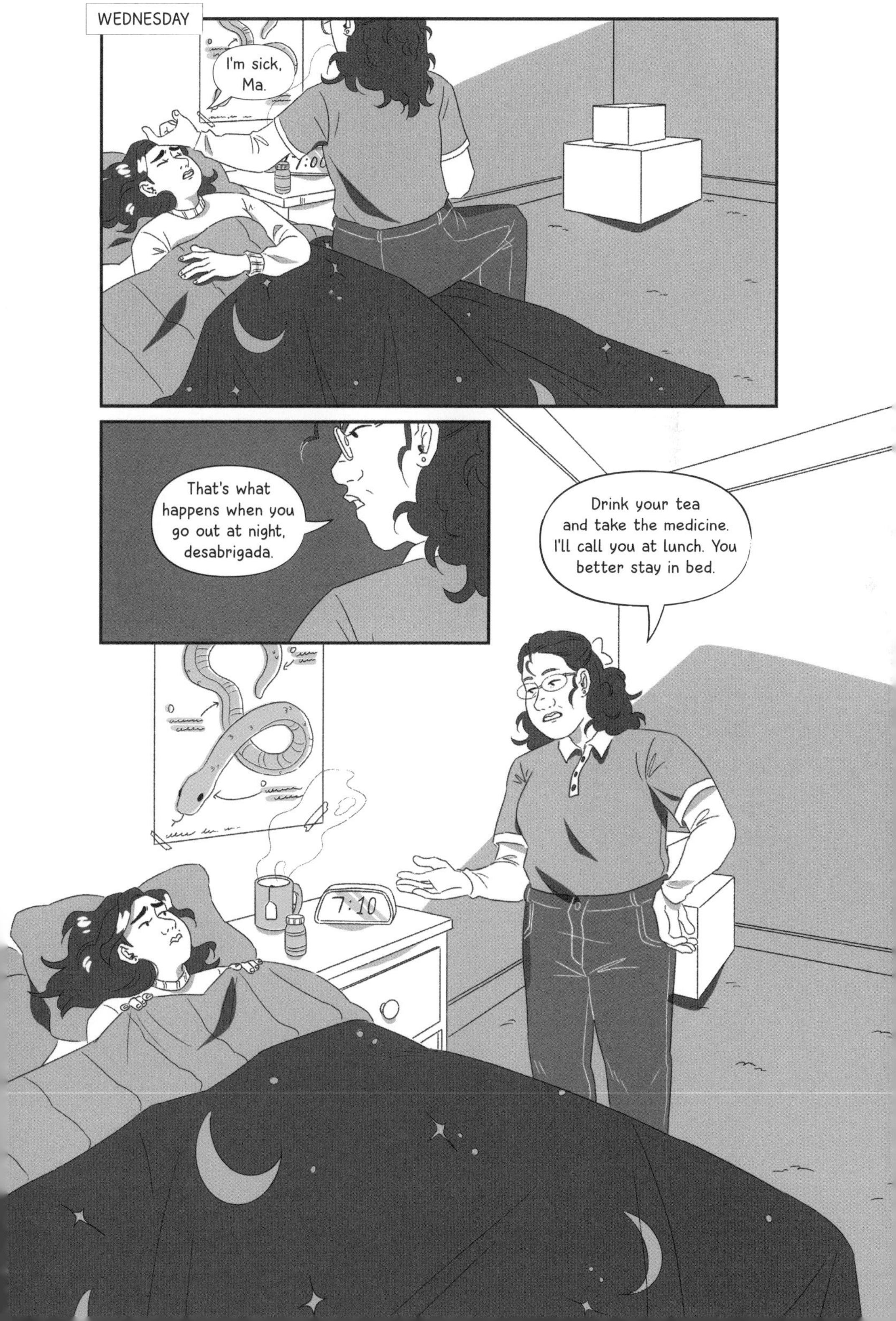
WEDNESDAY
I'm sick, Ma.
That's what happens when you go out at night, desabrigada.
Drink your tea and take the medicine. I'll call you at lunch. You better stay in bed.
7:10

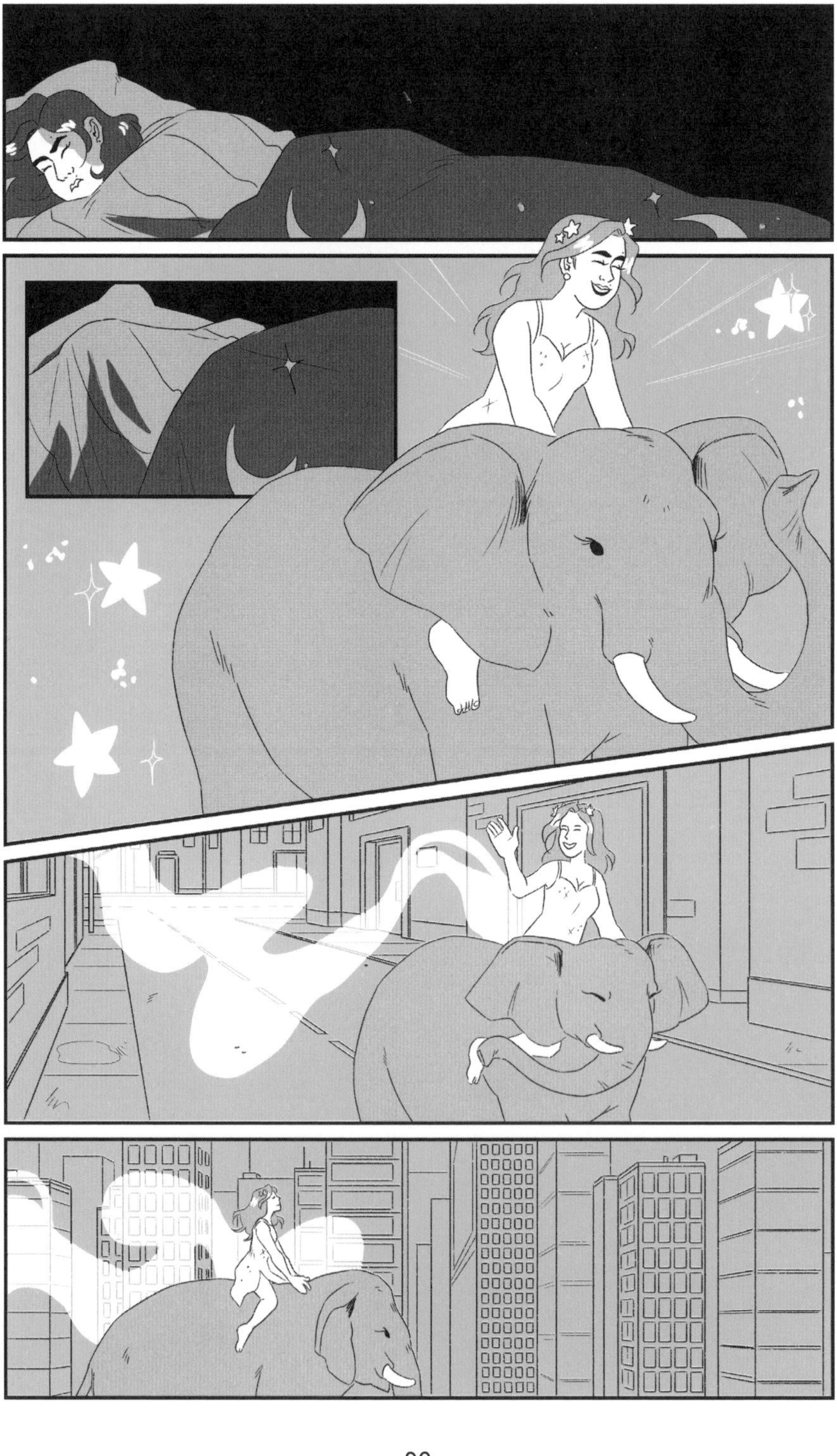

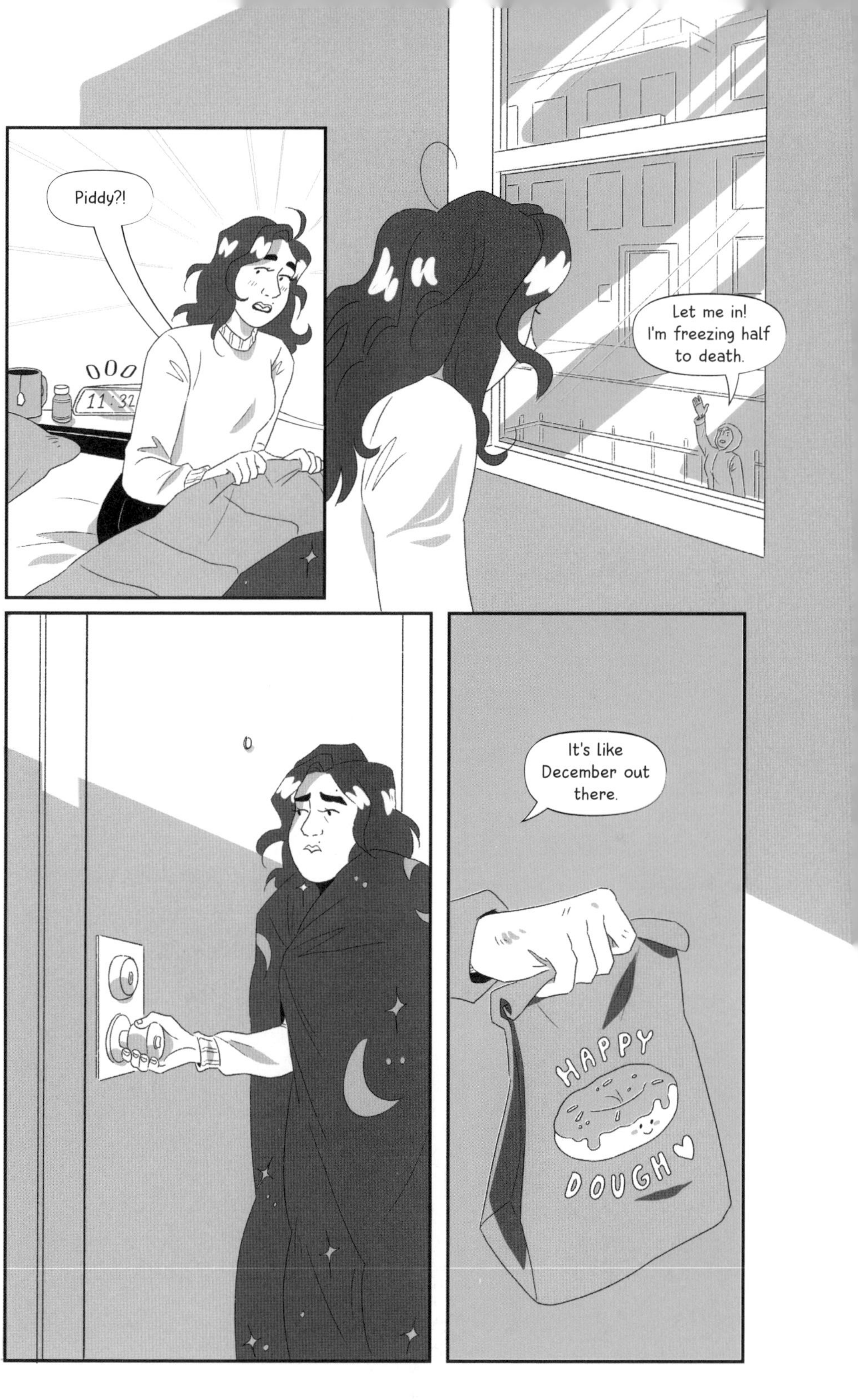
Piddy?!
11:32
Let me in! I'm freezing half to death.
It's like December out there.
HAPPY DOUGH

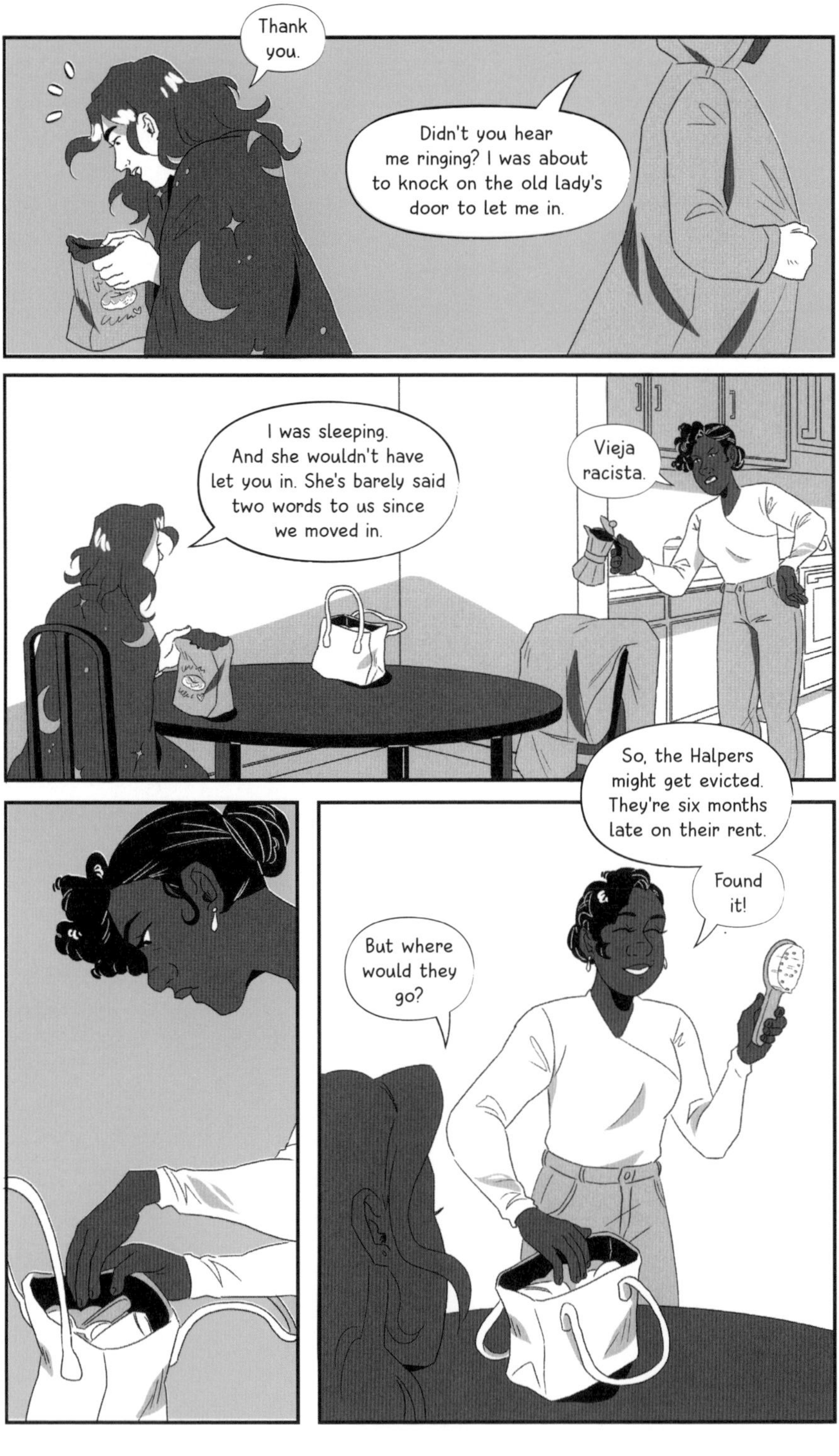
Thank you.
Didn't you hear me ringing? I was about to knock on the old lady's door to let me in.
I was sleeping. And she wouldn't have let you in. She's barely said two words to us since we moved in.
Vieja racista.
So, the Halpers might get evicted. They're six months late on their rent.
Found it!
But where would they go?

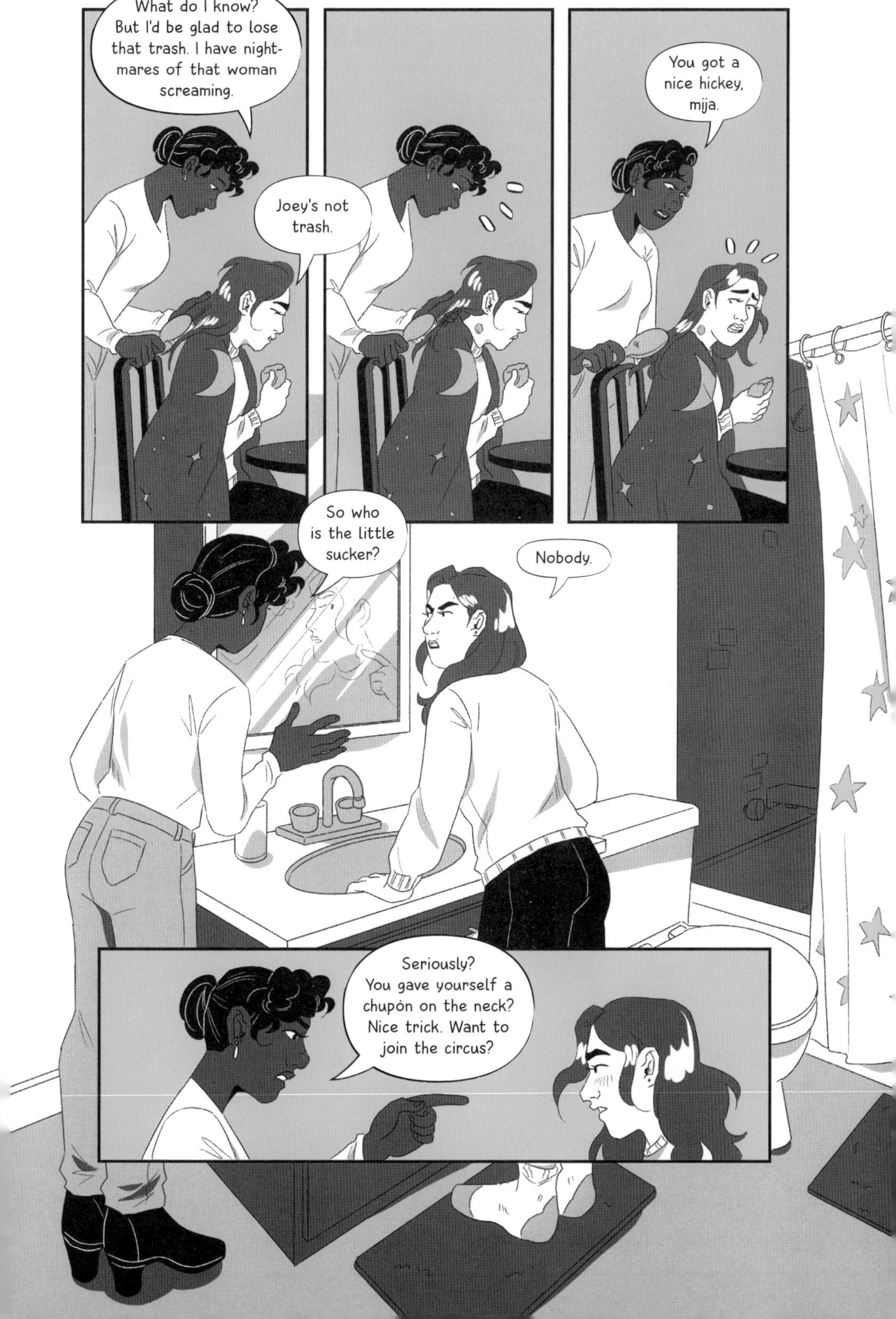
What do I know? But I'd be glad to lose that trash. I have night-mares of that woman screaming.
Joey's not trash.
You got a nice hickey, mija.
So who is the little sucker?
Nobody.
Seriously? You gave yourself a chupón on the neck? Nice trick. Want to join the circus?

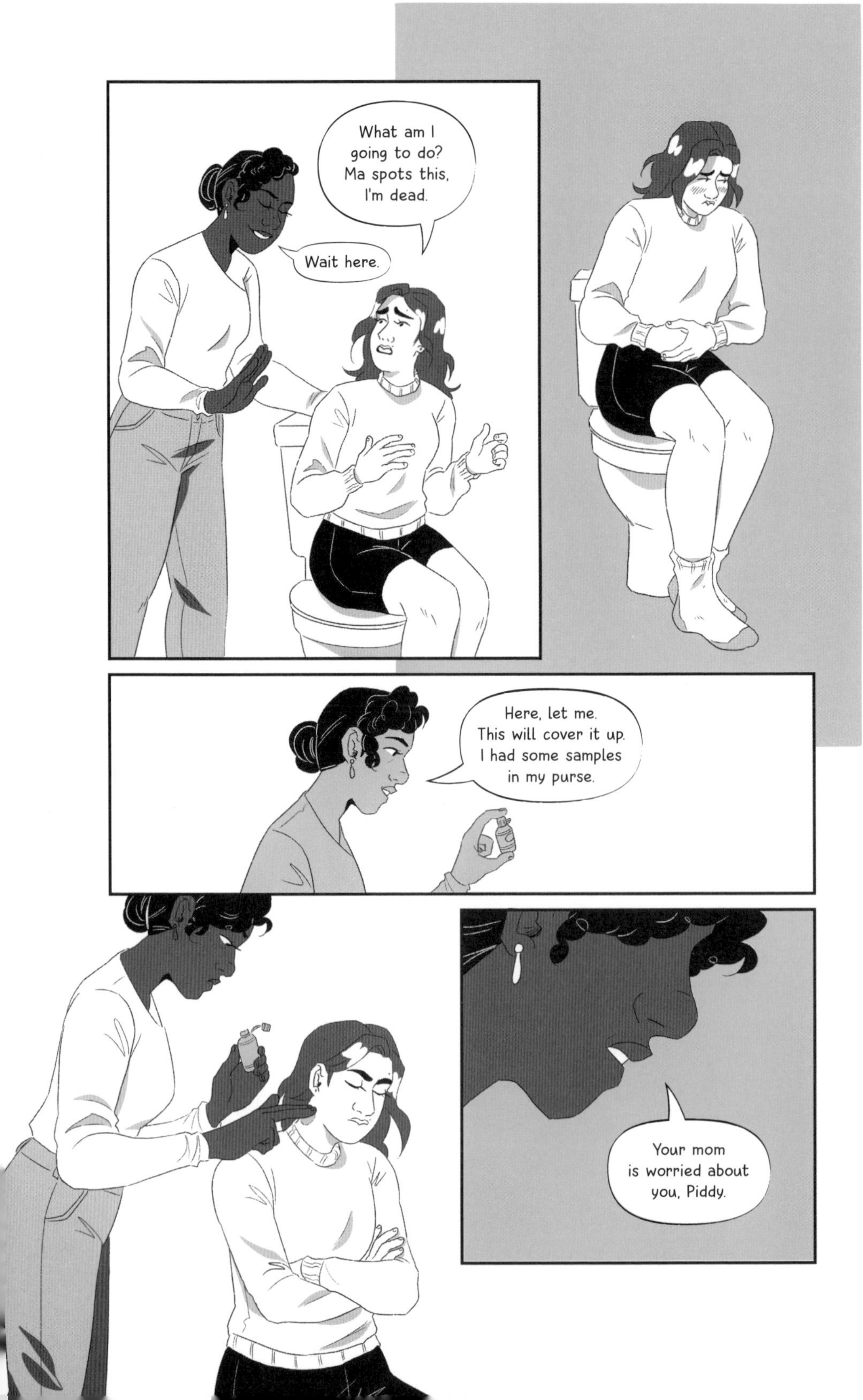

What am I going to do? Ma spots this, I'm dead.
Wait here.
Here, let me. This will cover it up. I had some samples in my purse.
Your mom is worried about you, Piddy.

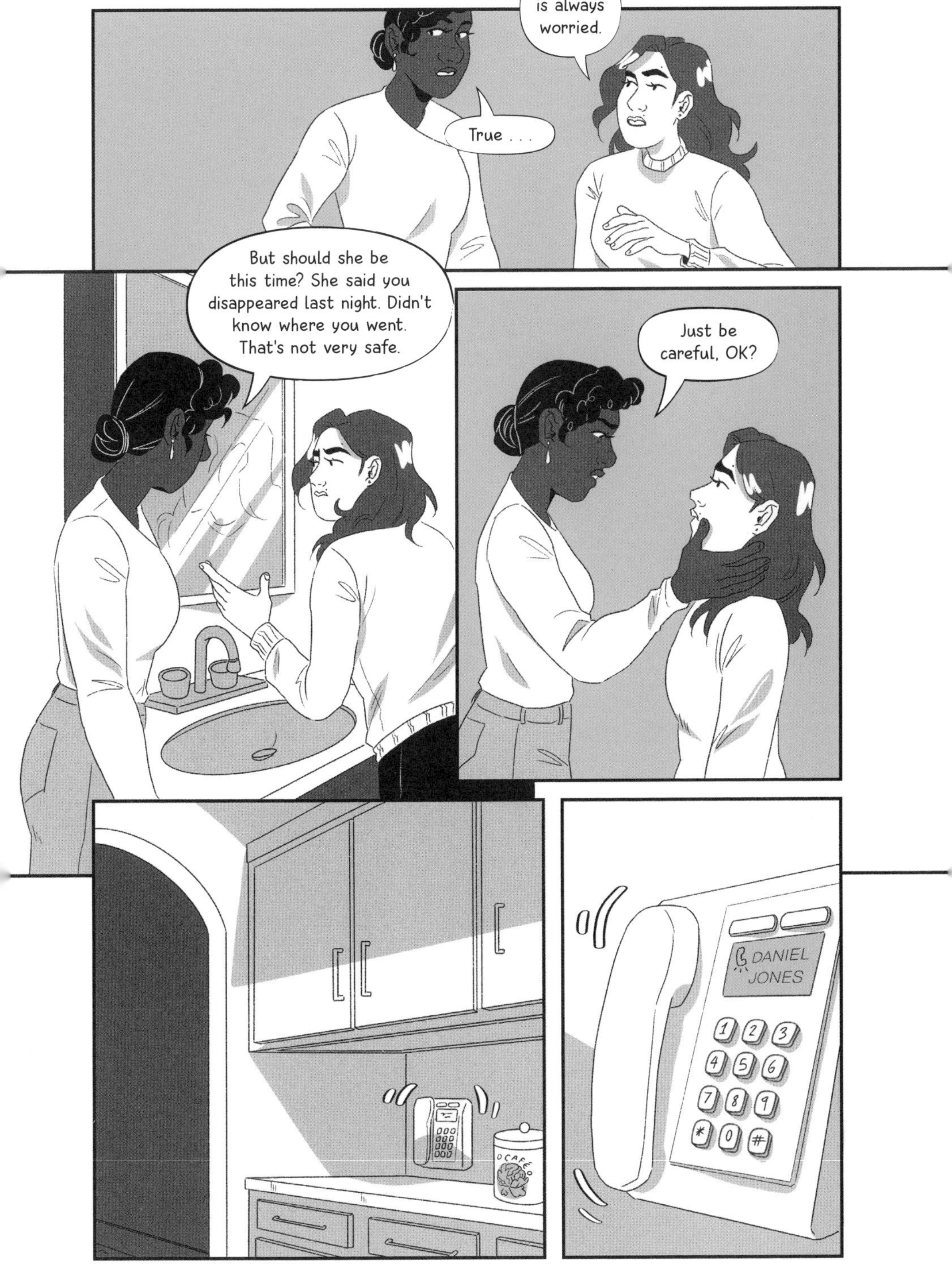
Ma is always worried.
True . . .
But should she be this time? She said you disappeared last night. Didn't know where you went. That's not very safe.
Just be careful, OK?
CAFÉ
DANIEL JONES
1 2 3 4 5 6 7 8 9 * 0 #

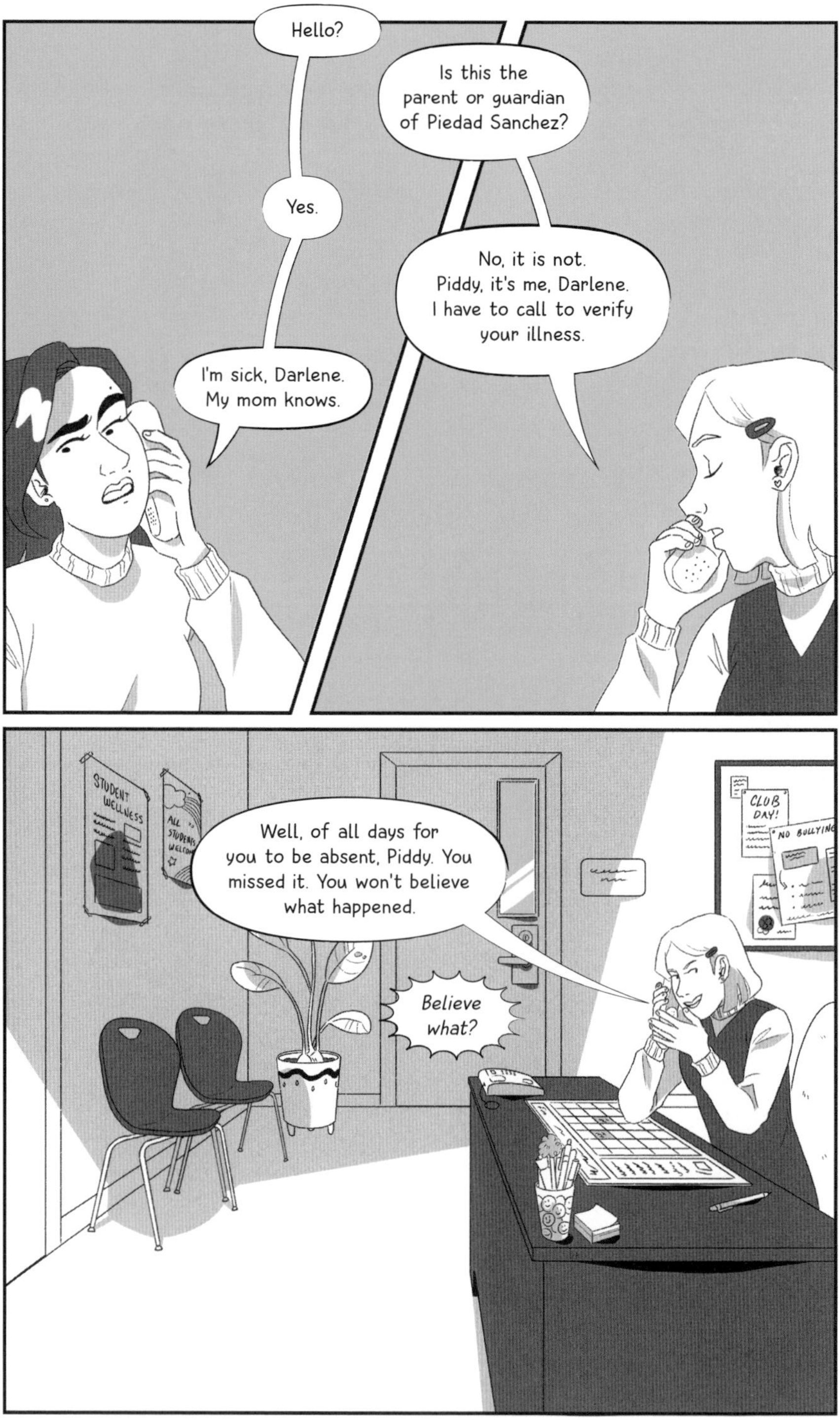
Hello?
Is this the parent or guardian of Piedad Sanchez?
Yes.
No, it is not. Piddy, it's me, Darlene. I have to call to verify your illness.
I'm sick, Darlene. My mom knows.
STUDENT WELLNESS
CLUB DAY!
Well, of all days for you to be absent, Piddy. You missed it. You won't believe what happened.
Believe what?

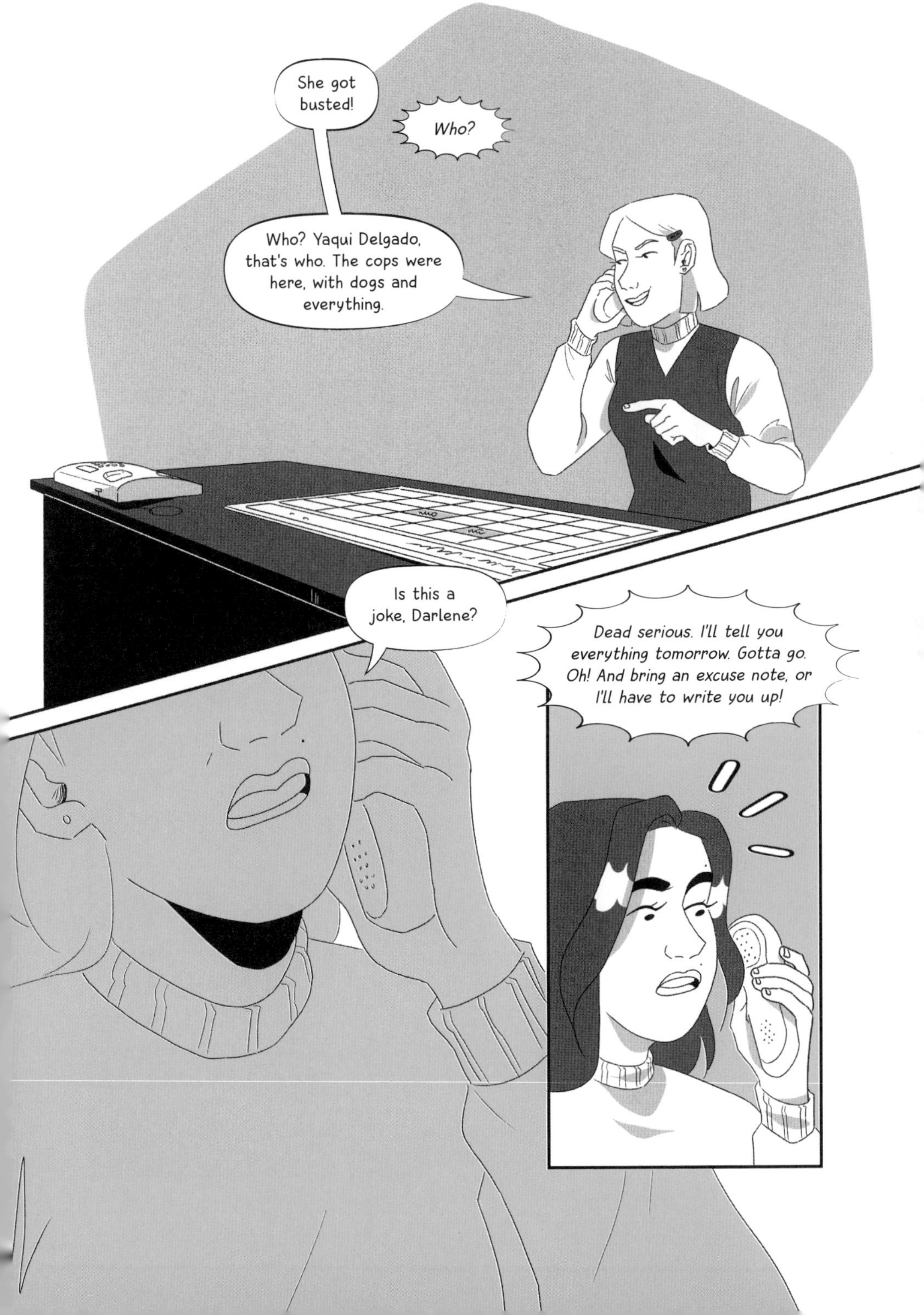
She got busted!
Who?
Who? Yaqui Delgado, that's who. The cops were here, with dogs and everything.
Is this a joke, Darlene?
Dead serious. I'll tell you everything tomorrow. Gotta go. Oh! And bring an excuse note, or I'll have to write you up!

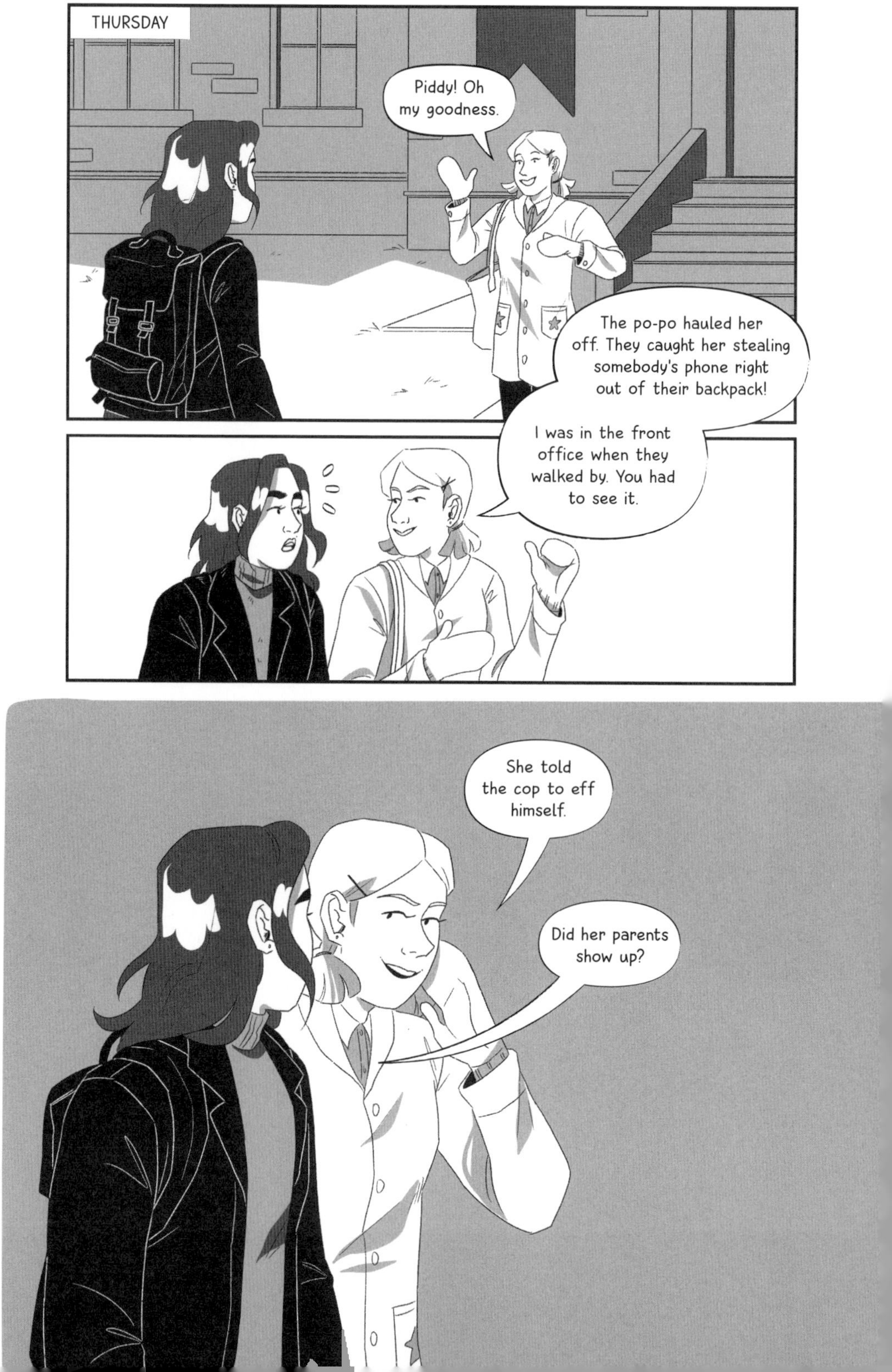
THURSDAY
Piddy! Oh my goodness.
The po-po hauled her off. They caught her stealing somebody's phone right out of their backpack!
I was in the front office when they walked by. You had to see it.
She told the cop to eff himself.
Did her parents show up?

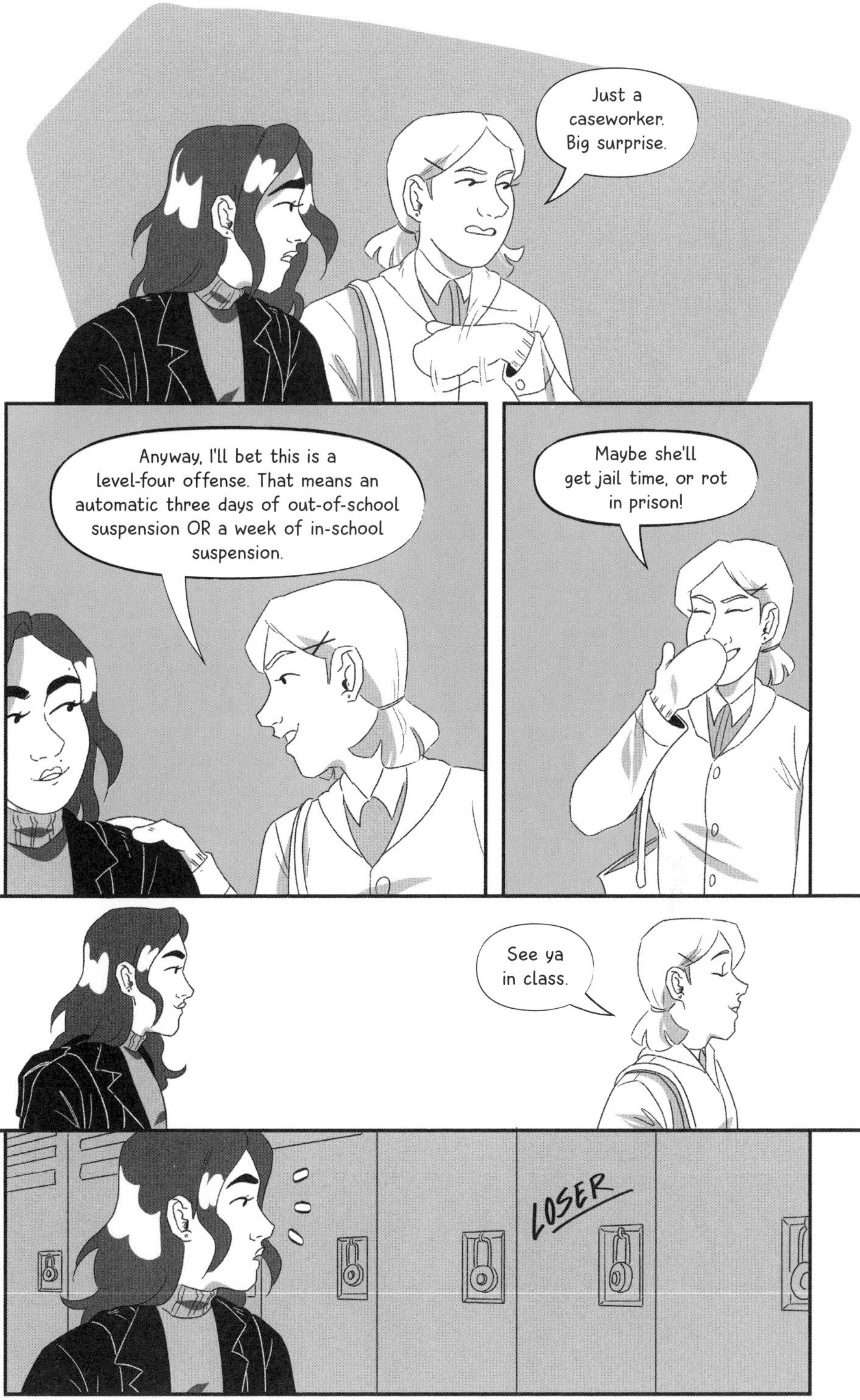
Just a caseworker. Big surprise.
Anyway, I'll bet this is a level-four offense. That means an automatic three days of out-of-school suspension OR a week of in-school suspension.
Maybe she'll get jail time, or rot in prison!
See ya in class.
LOSER

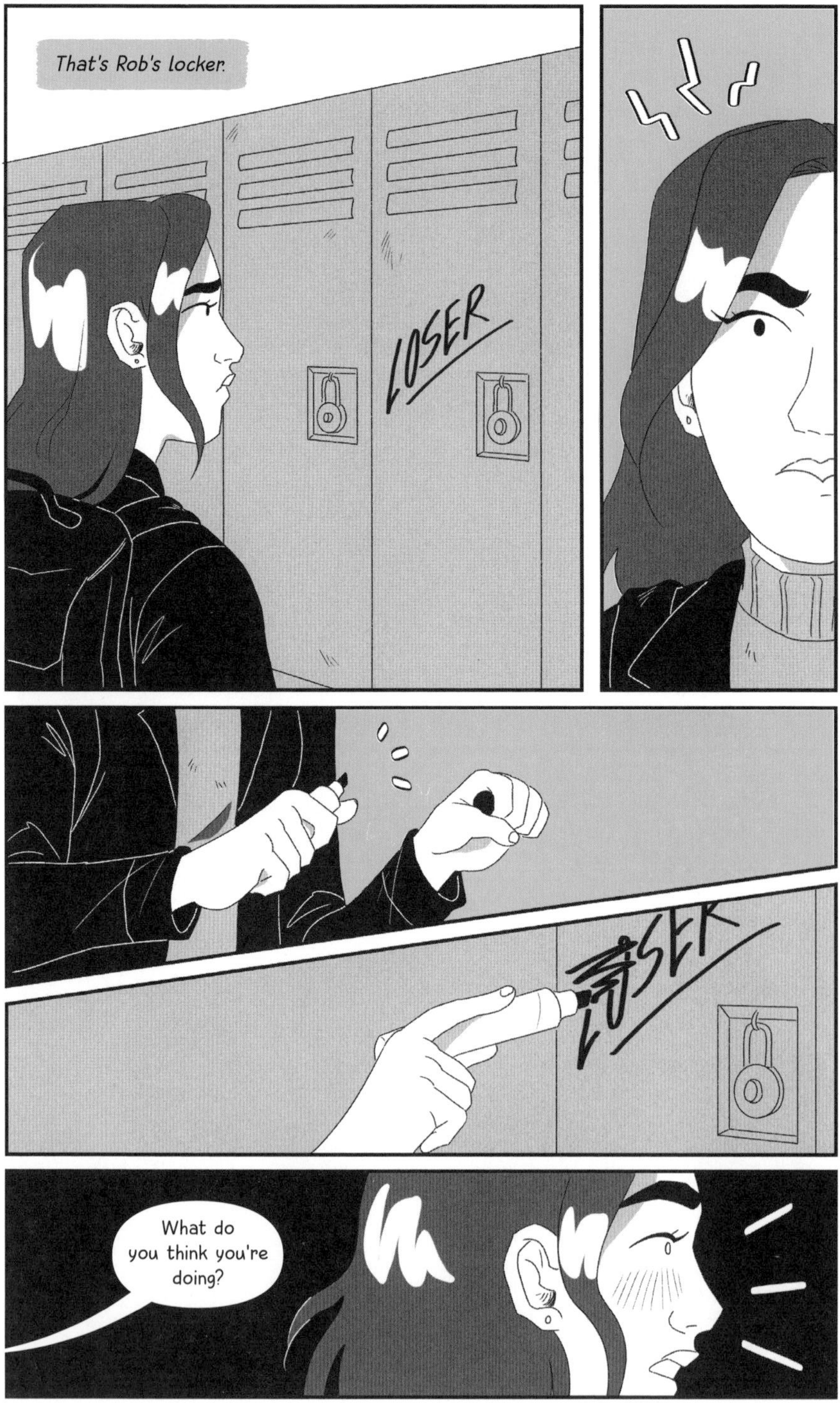
That's Rob's locker.
LOSER
What do you think you're doing?

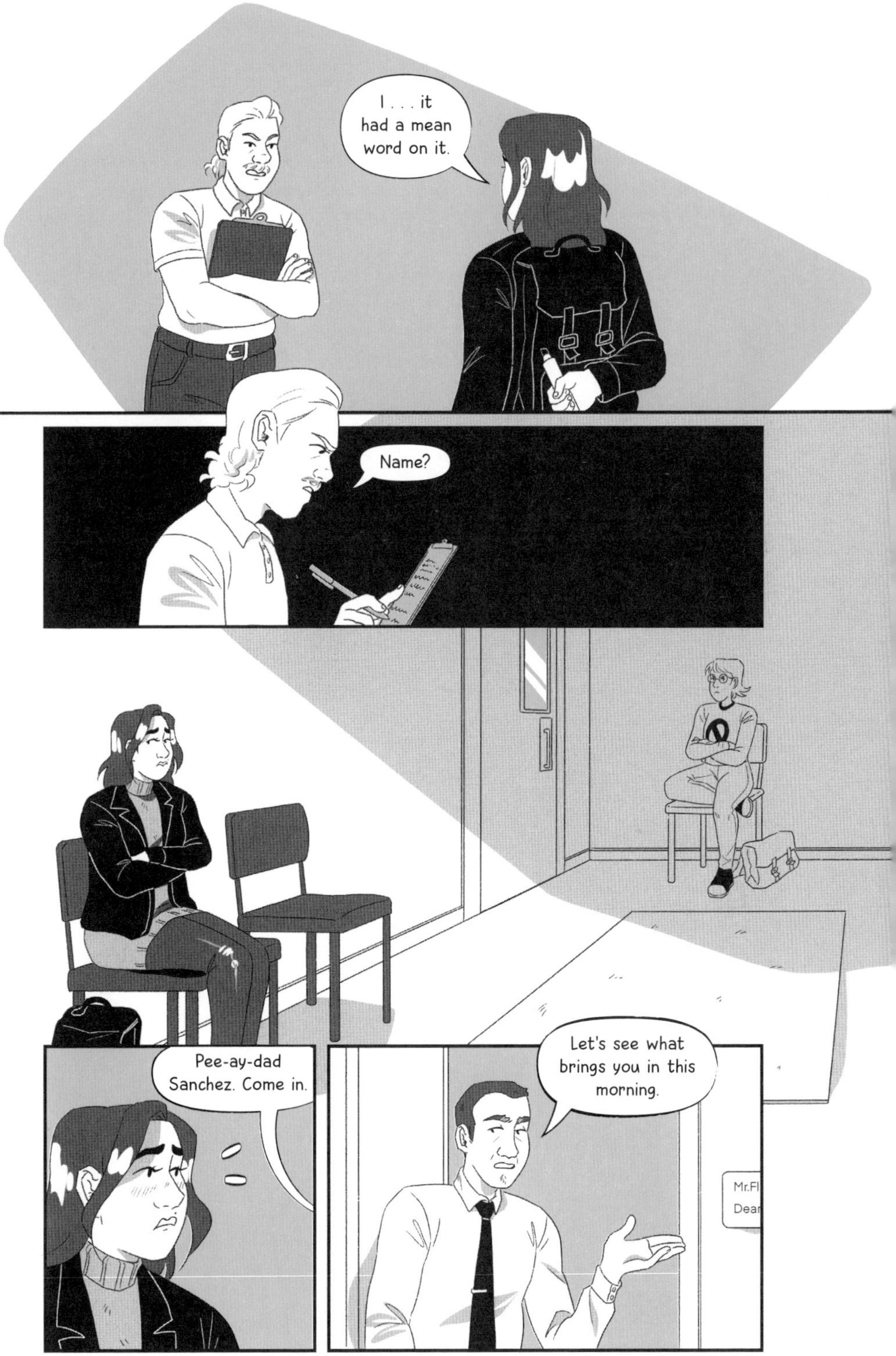
I . . . it had a mean word on it.
Name?
Pee-ay-dad Sanchez. Come in.
Let's see what brings you in this morning.

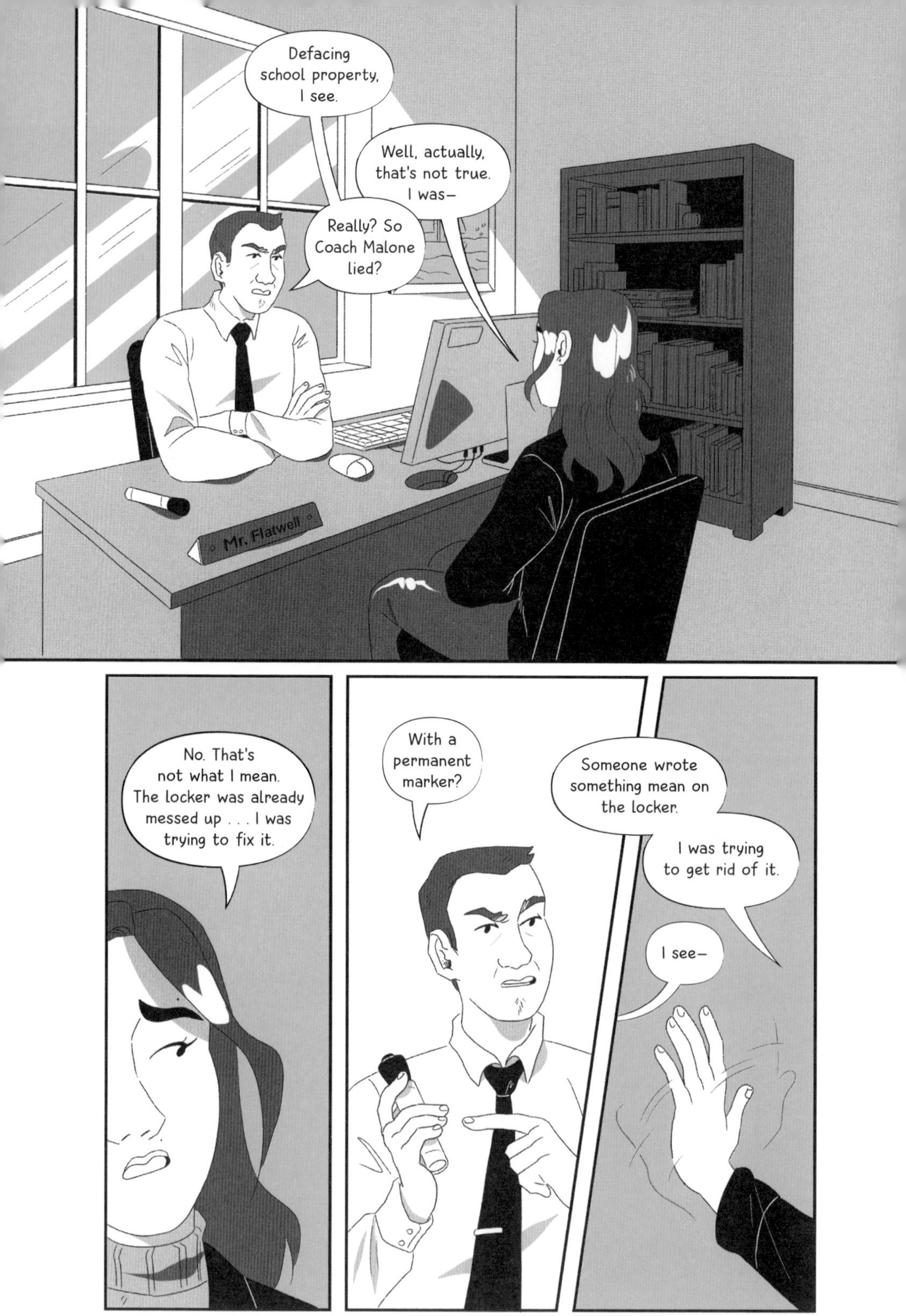
Defacing school property, I see.
Well, actually, that's not true. I was—
Really? So Coach Malone lied?
Mr. Flatwell
No. That's not what I mean. The locker was already messed up . . . I was trying to fix it.
With a permanent marker?
Someone wrote something mean on the locker.
I was trying to get rid of it.
I see—

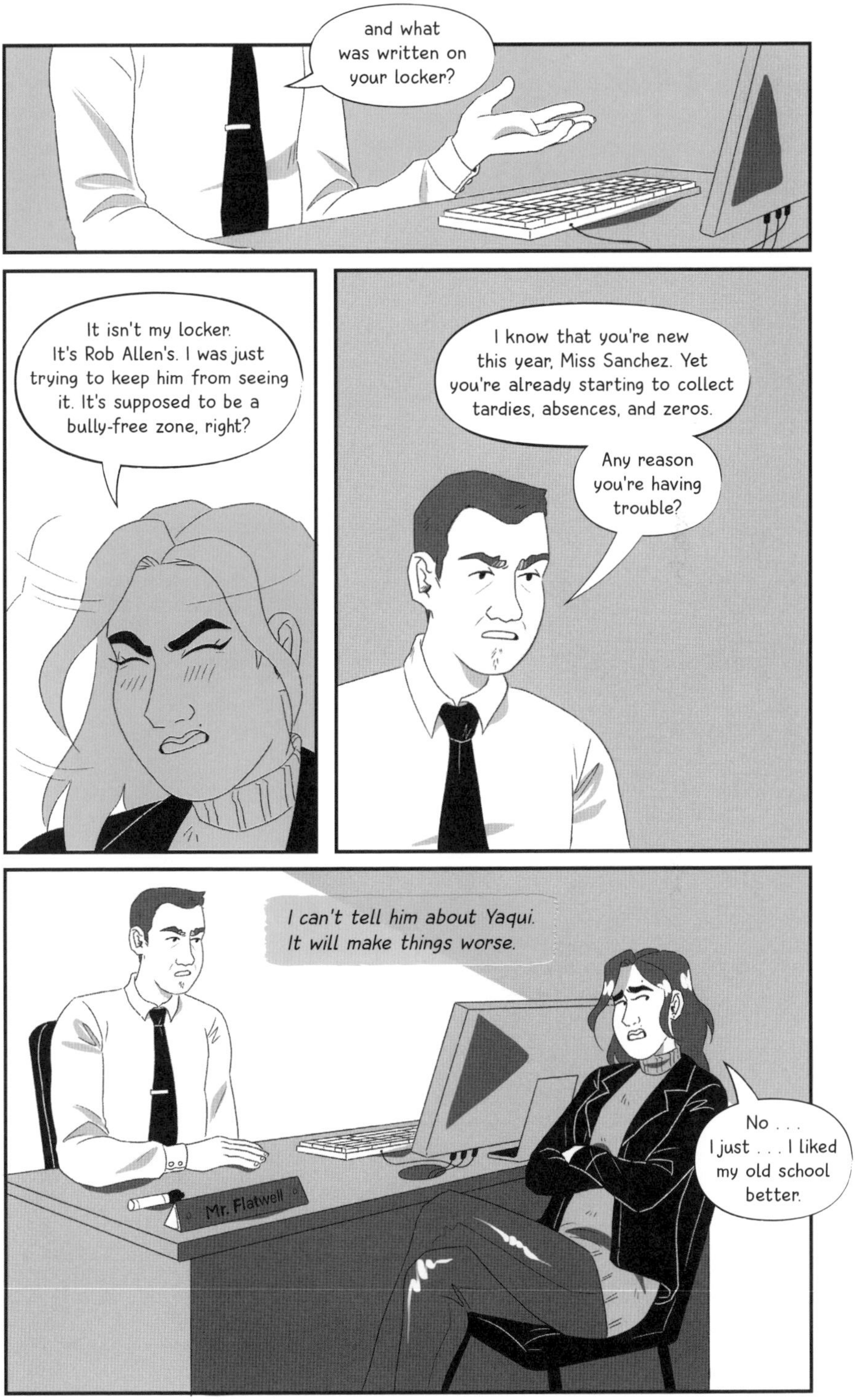
and what was written on your locker?
It isn't my locker. It's Rob Allen's. I was just trying to keep him from seeing it. It's supposed to be a bully-free zone, right?
I know that you're new this year, Miss Sanchez. Yet you're already starting to collect tardies, absences, and zeros.
Any reason you're having trouble?
I can't tell him about Yaqui. It will make things worse.
Mr. Flatwell
No . . . I just . . . I liked my old school better.

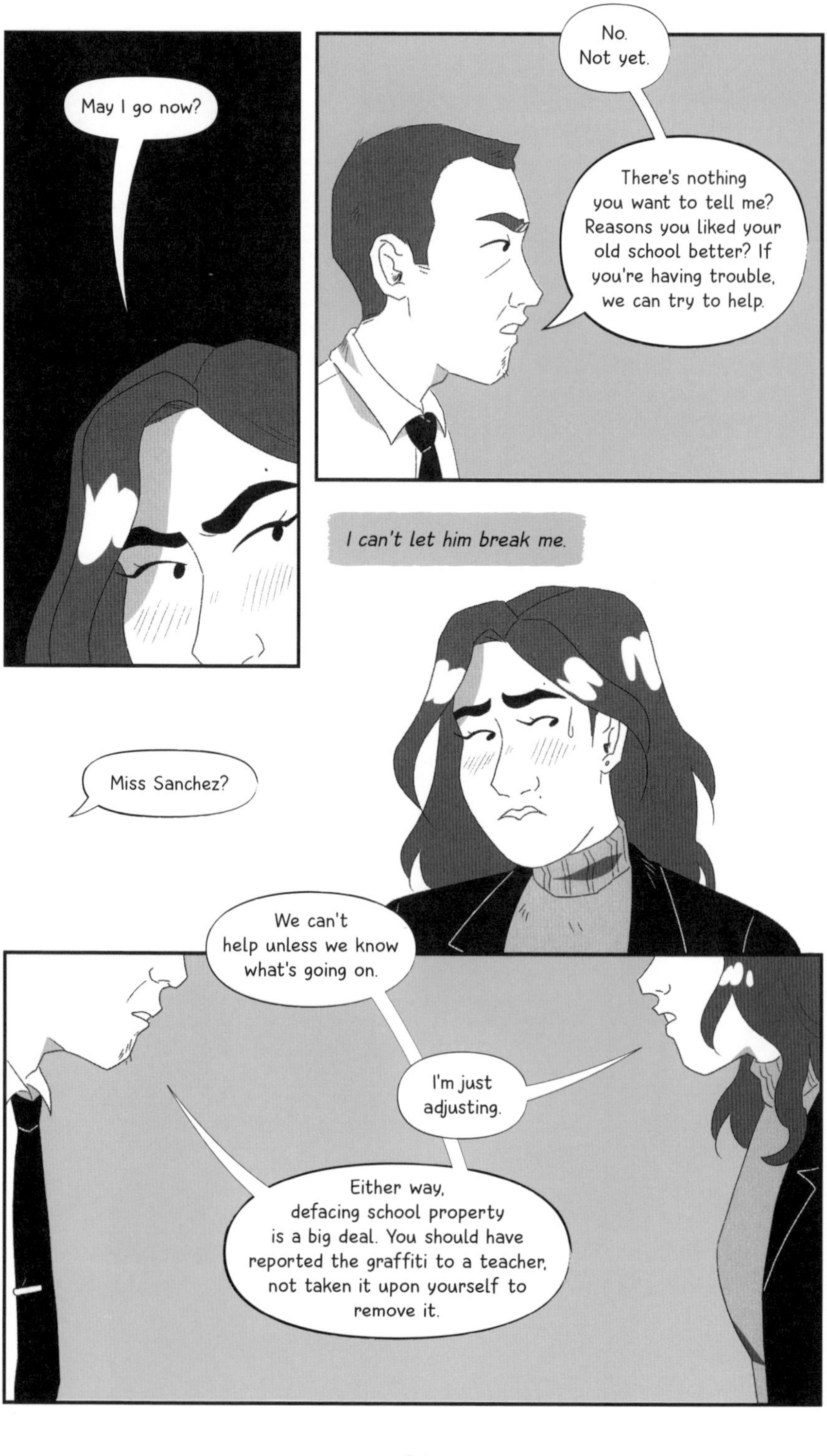
May I go now?
No.
Not yet.
There's nothing you want to tell me? Reasons you liked your old school better? If you're having trouble, we can try to help.
I can't let him break me.
Miss Sanchez?
We can't help unless we know what's going on.
I'm just adjusting.
Either way, defacing school property is a big deal. You should have reported the graffiti to a teacher, not taken it upon yourself to remove it.

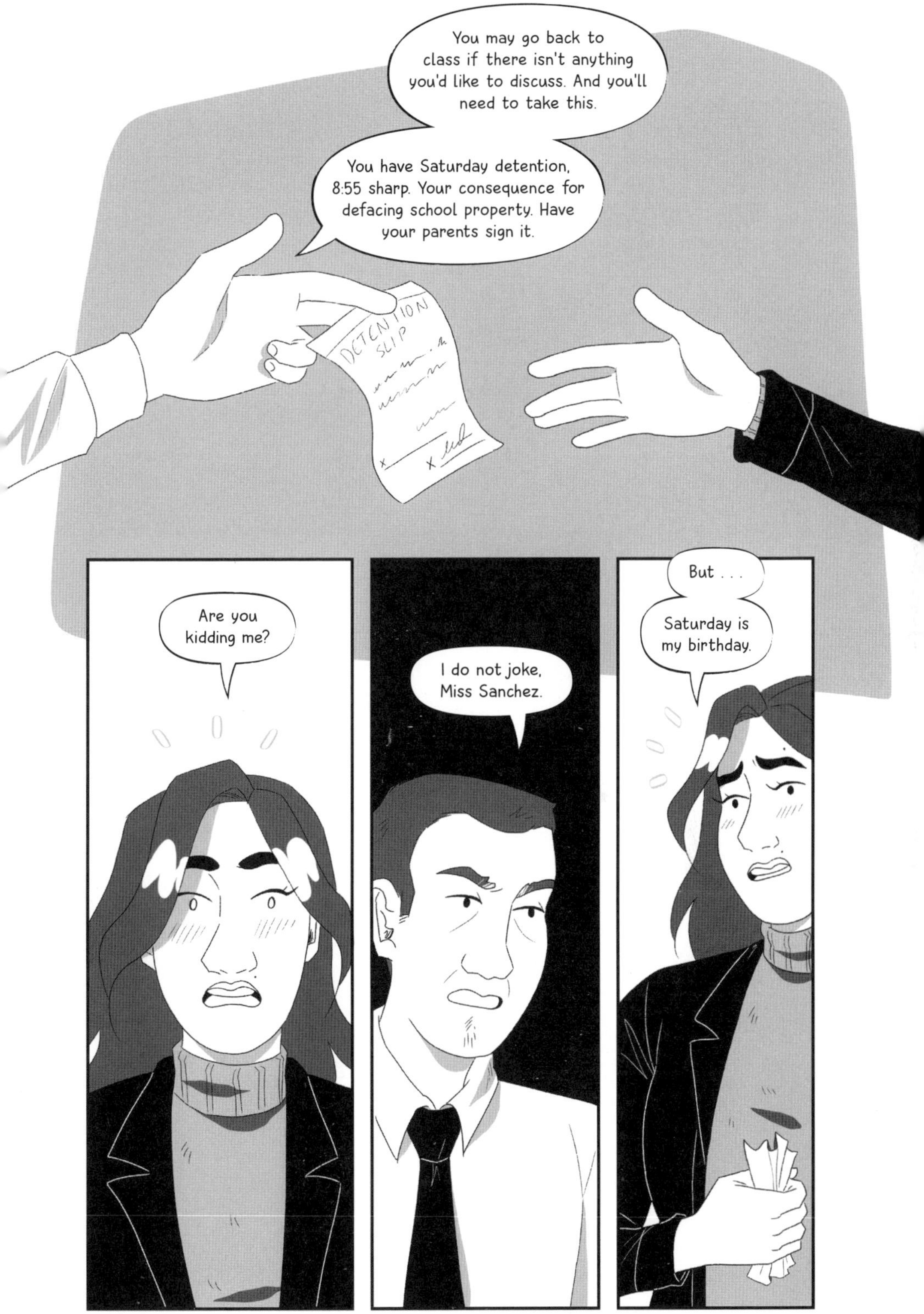
You may go back to class if there isn't anything you'd like to discuss. And you'll need to take this.
You have Saturday detention, 8:55 sharp. Your consequence for defacing school property. Have your parents sign it.
DETENTION SLIP
Are you kidding me?
I do not joke, Miss Sanchez.
But . . .
Saturday is my birthday.

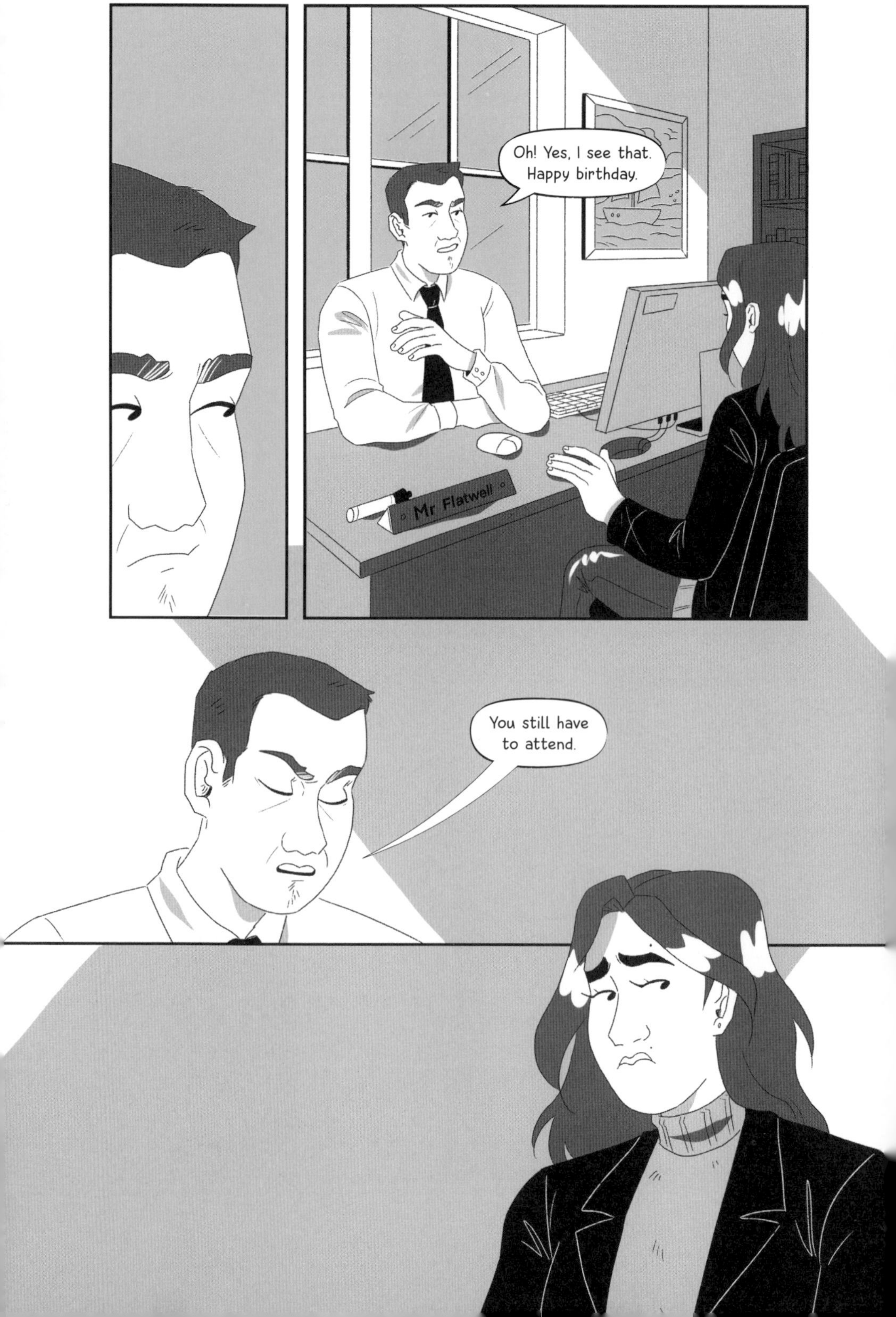
Oh! Yes, I see that. Happy birthday.
Mr Flatwell
You still have to attend.

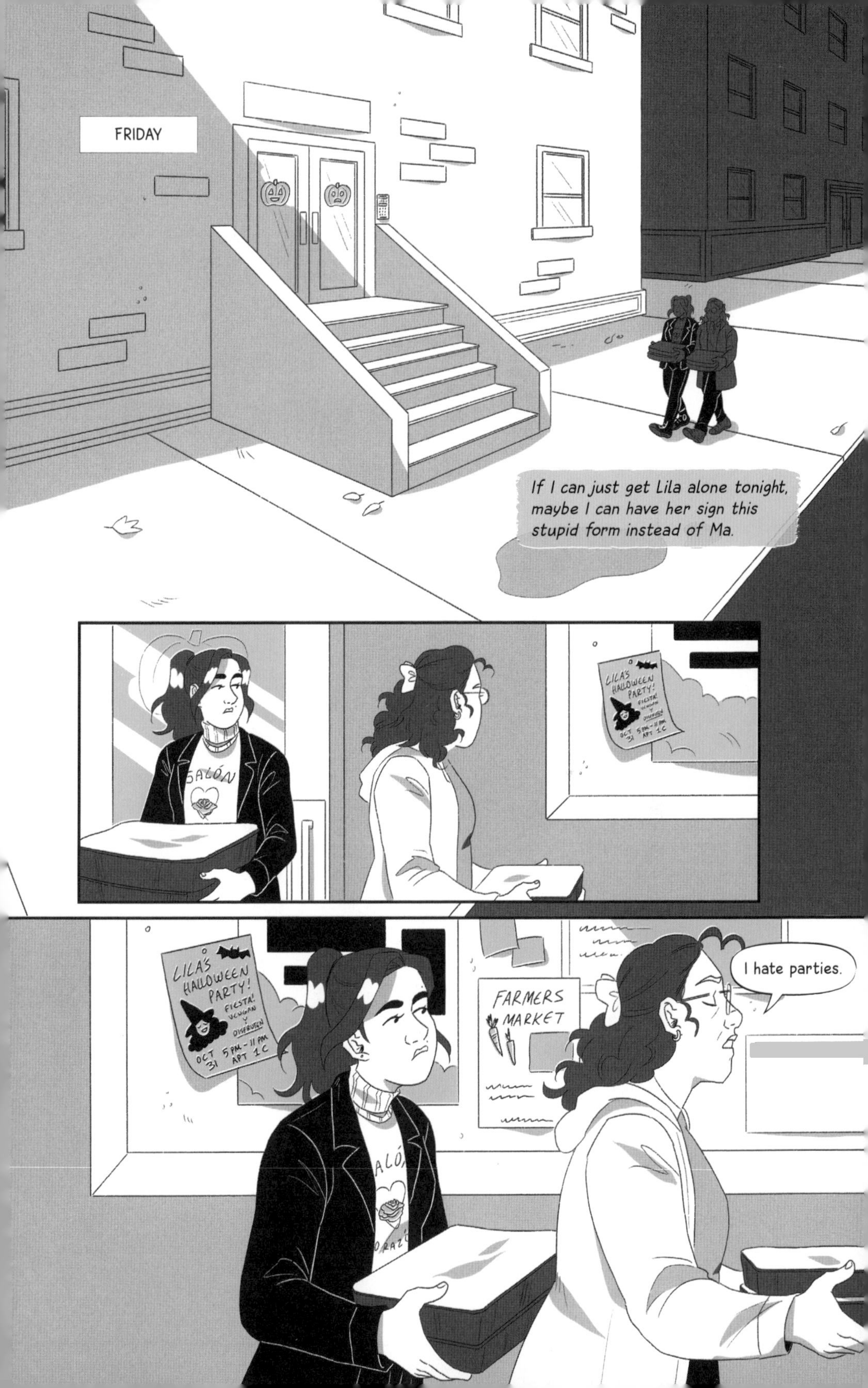
FRIDAY
If I can just get Lila alone tonight, maybe I can have her sign this stupid form instead of Ma.
LILA'S HALLOWEEN PARTY! FIESTA! VENGAN Y DISFRUTEN OCT 31 5PM–11PM APT 1C
FARMERS MARKET
I hate parties.

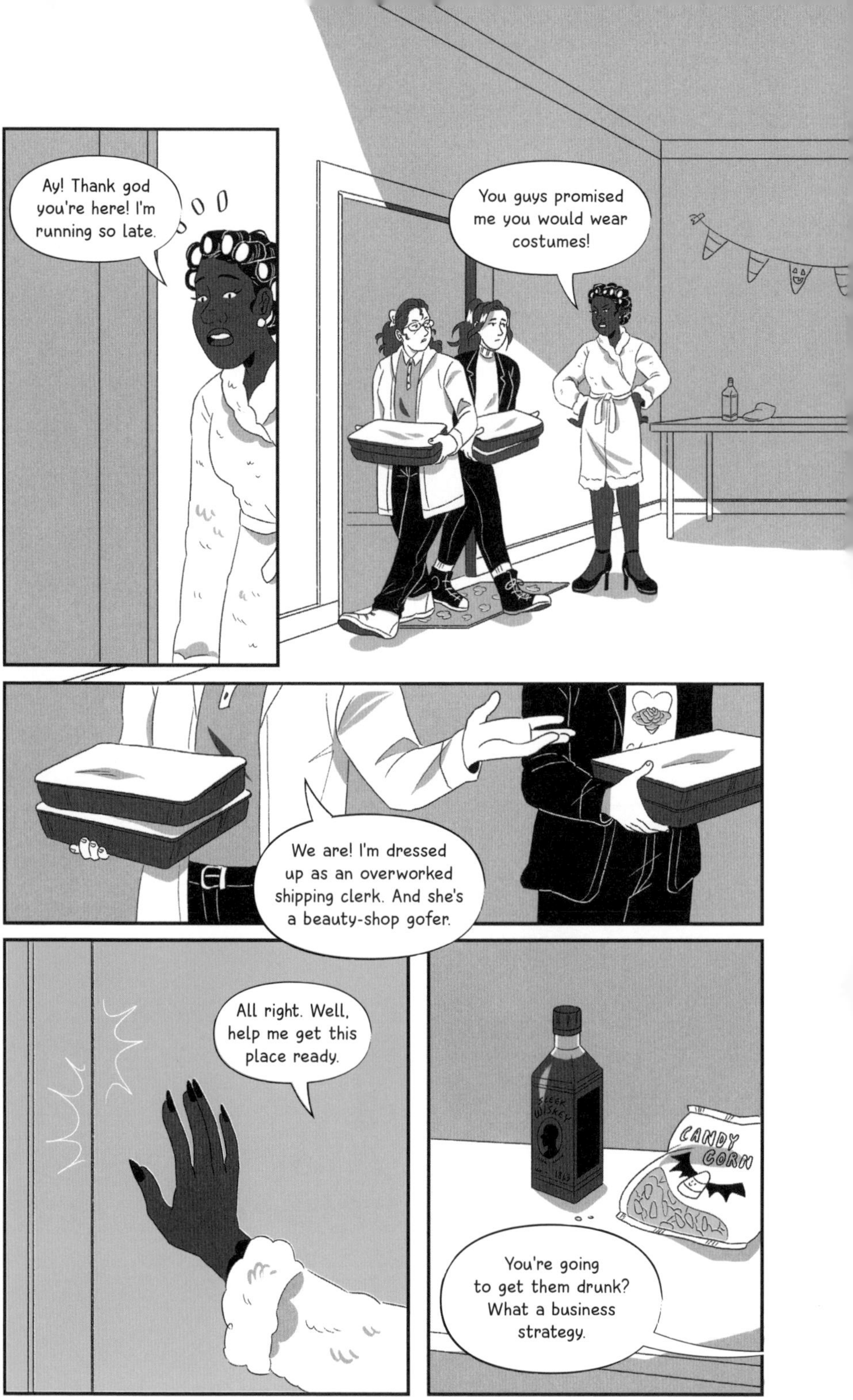
Ay! Thank god you're here! I'm running so late.
You guys promised me you would wear costumes!
We are! I'm dressed up as an overworked shipping clerk. And she's a beauty-shop gofer.
All right. Well, help me get this place ready.
CANDY CORN
You're going to get them drunk? What a business strategy.

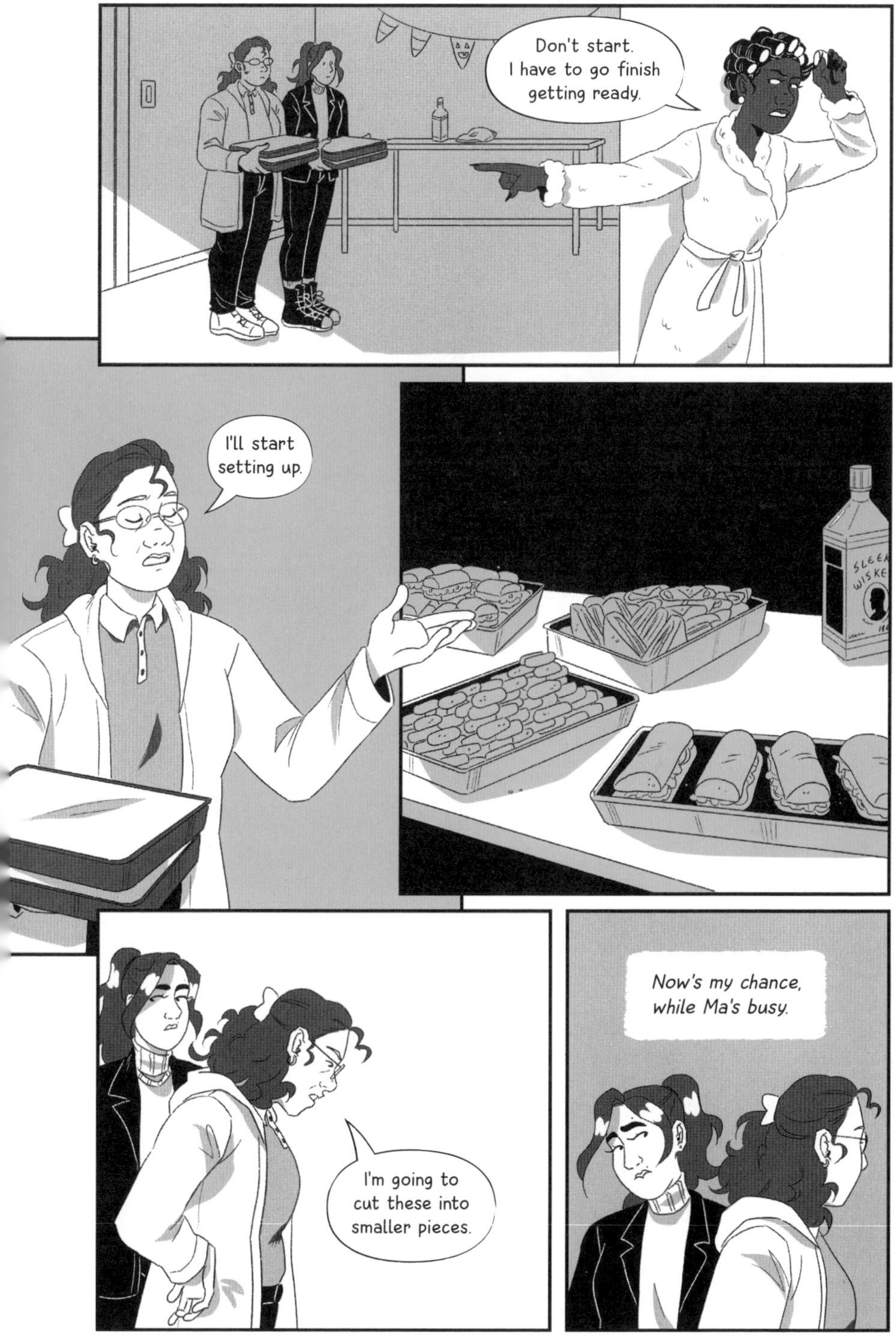
Don't start.
I have to go finish getting ready.
I'll start setting up.
SLEEK WISKE
I'm going to cut these into smaller pieces.
Now's my chance, while Ma's busy.

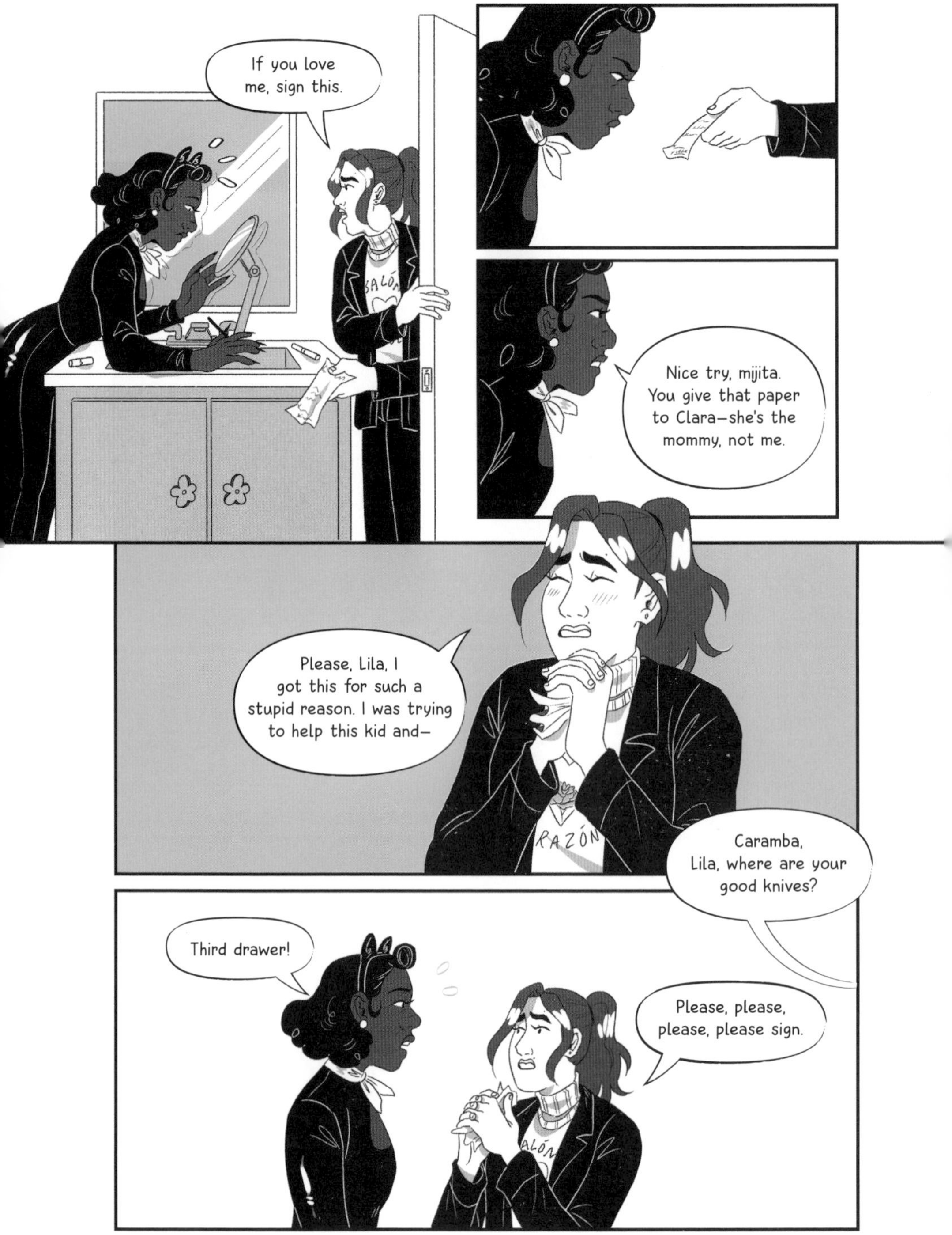
If you love me, sign this.
Nice try, mijita. You give that paper to Clara—she's the mommy, not me.
Please, Lila, I got this for such a stupid reason. I was trying to help this kid and—
Caramba, Lila, where are your good knives?
Third drawer!
Please, please, please, please sign.

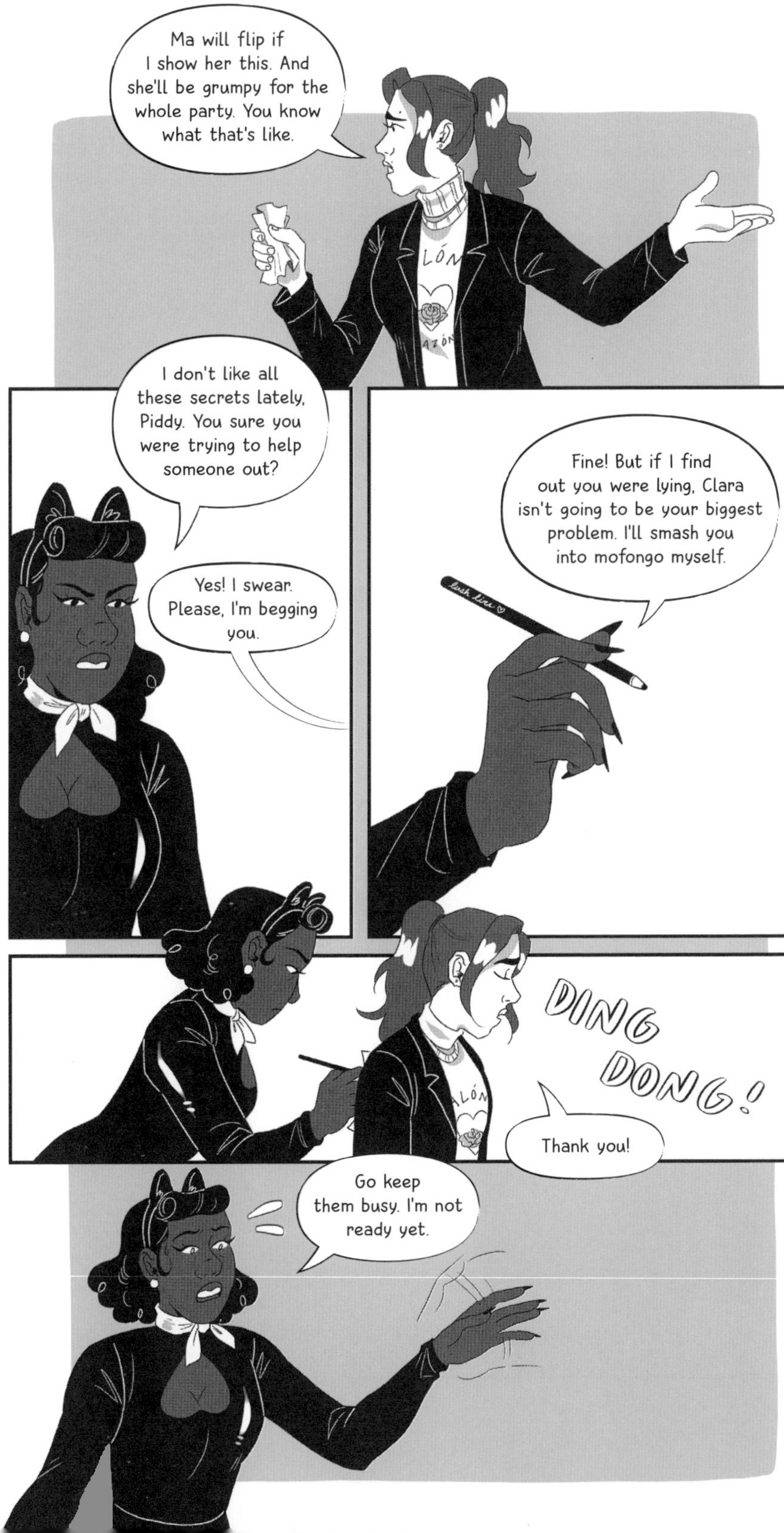
Ma will flip if I show her this. And she'll be grumpy for the whole party. You know what that's like.
I don't like all these secrets lately, Piddy. You sure you were trying to help someone out?
Yes! I swear. Please, I'm begging you.
Fine! But if I find out you were lying, Clara isn't going to be your biggest problem. I'll smash you into mofongo myself.
DING DONG!
Thank you!
Go keep them busy. I'm not ready yet.

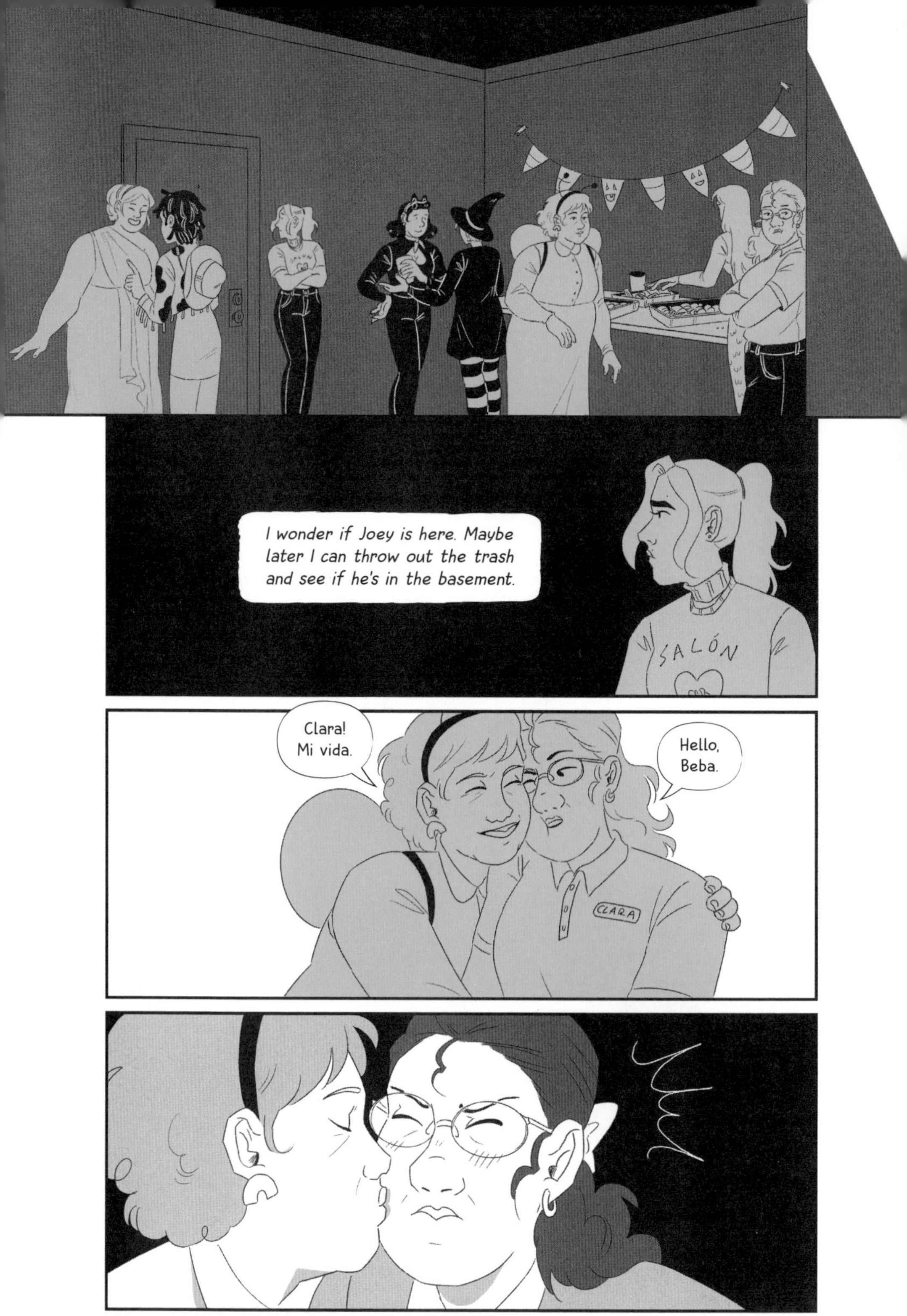

SALÓN
I wonder if Joey is here. Maybe later I can throw out the trash and see if he's in the basement.
SALÓN
Clara! Mi vida.
Hello, Beba.
CLARA

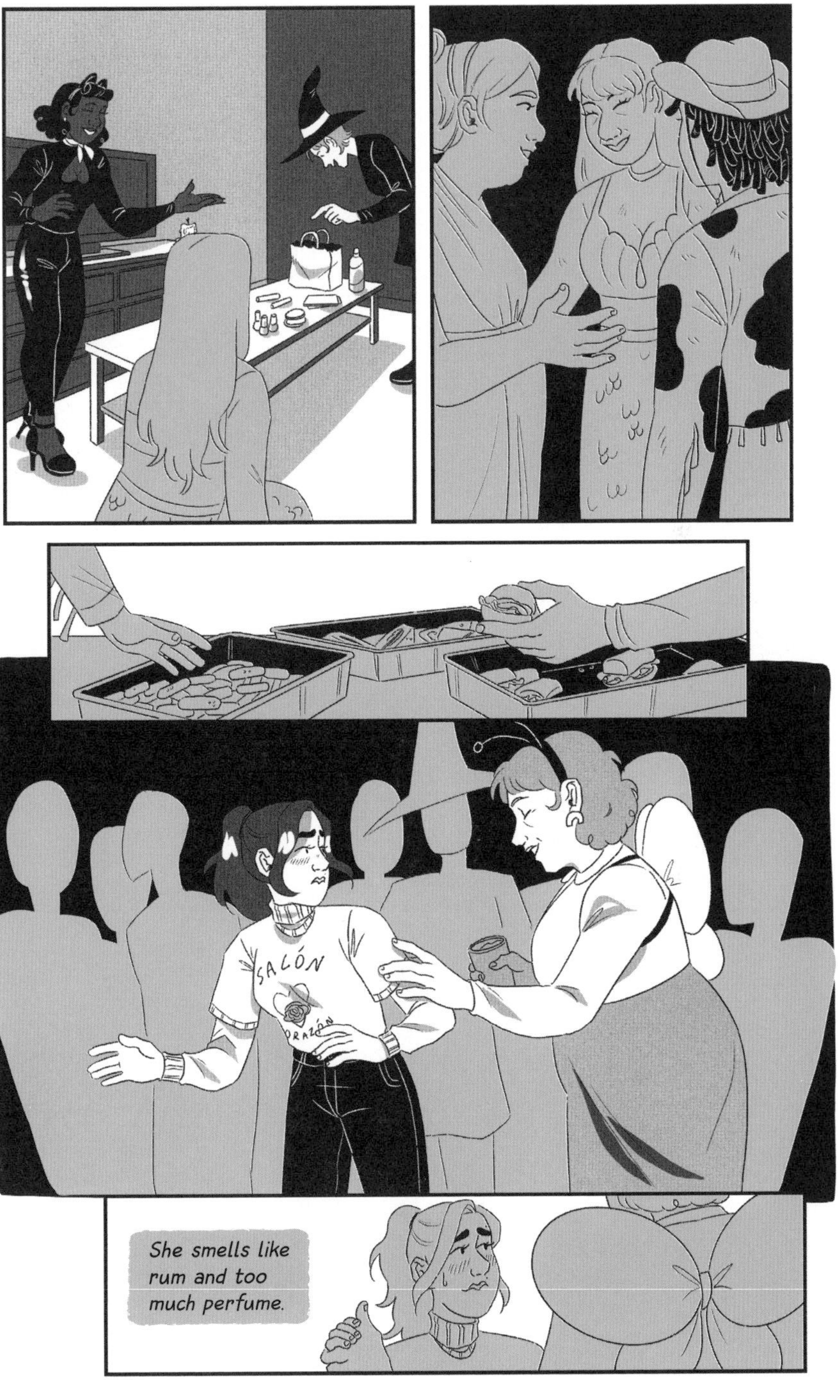
SALÓN
She smells like rum and too much perfume.

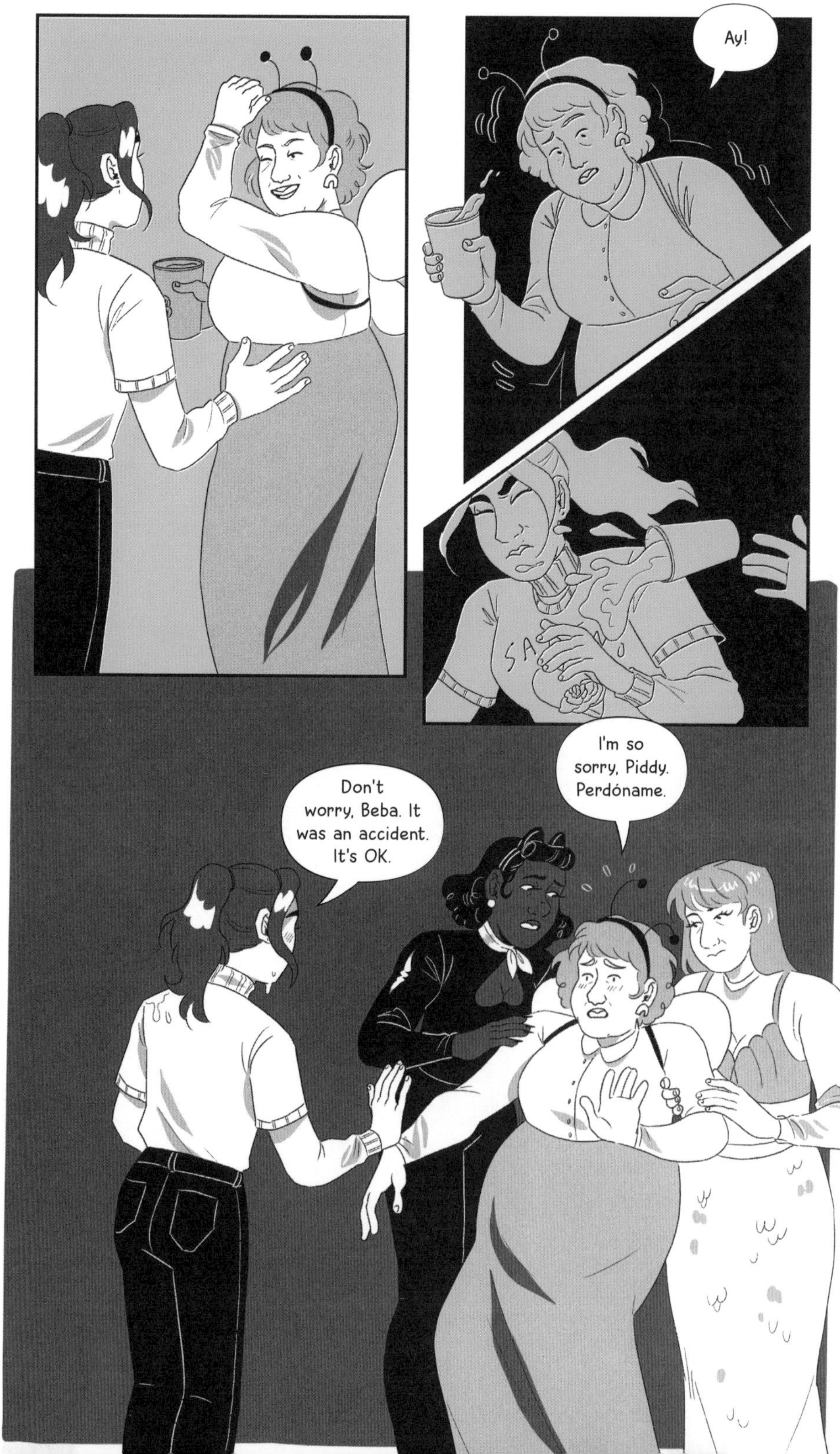
Ay!
Don't worry, Beba. It was an accident. It's OK.
I'm so sorry, Piddy. Perdóname.

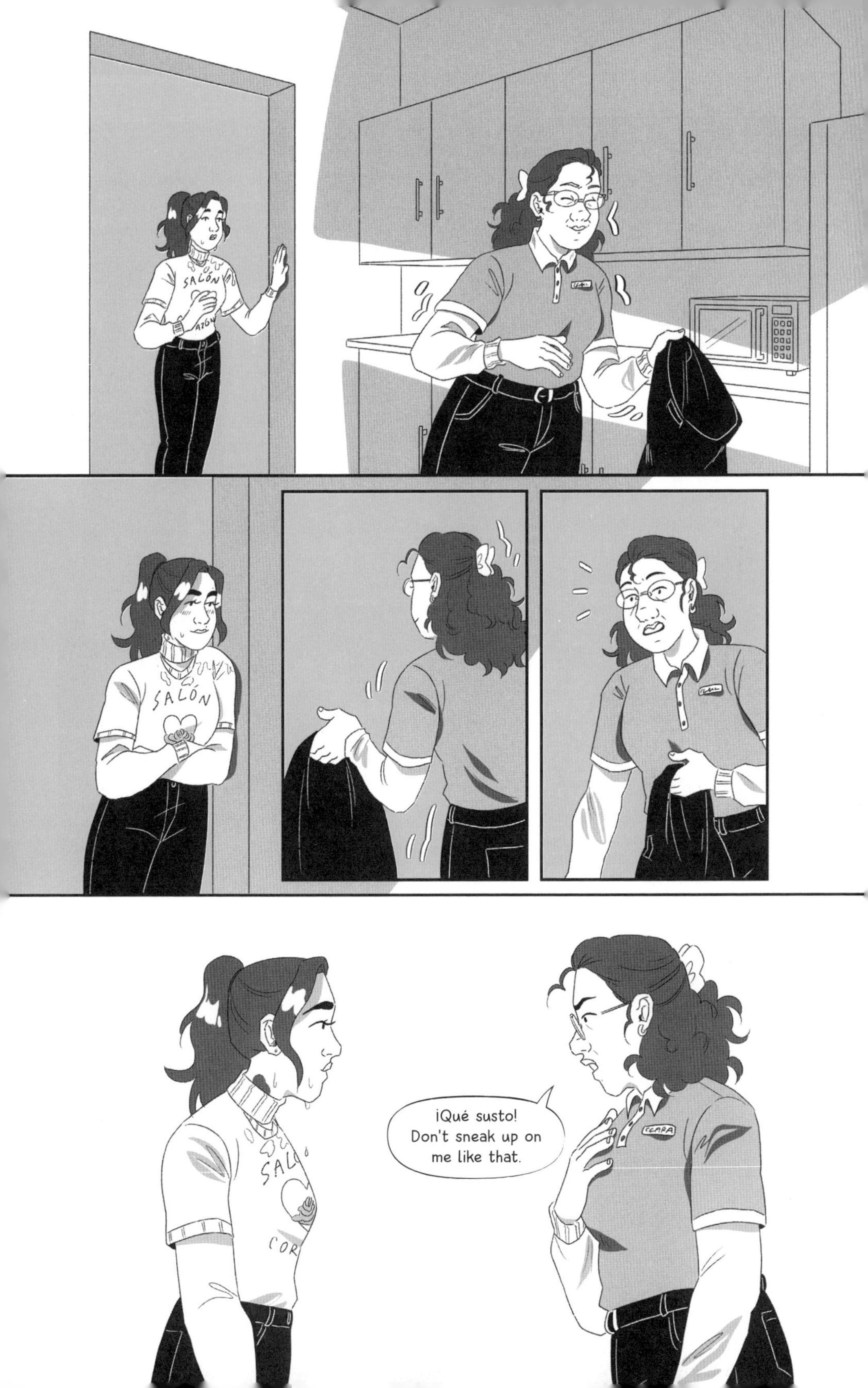
SALÓN
¡Qué susto!
Don't sneak up on
me like that.
CLARA

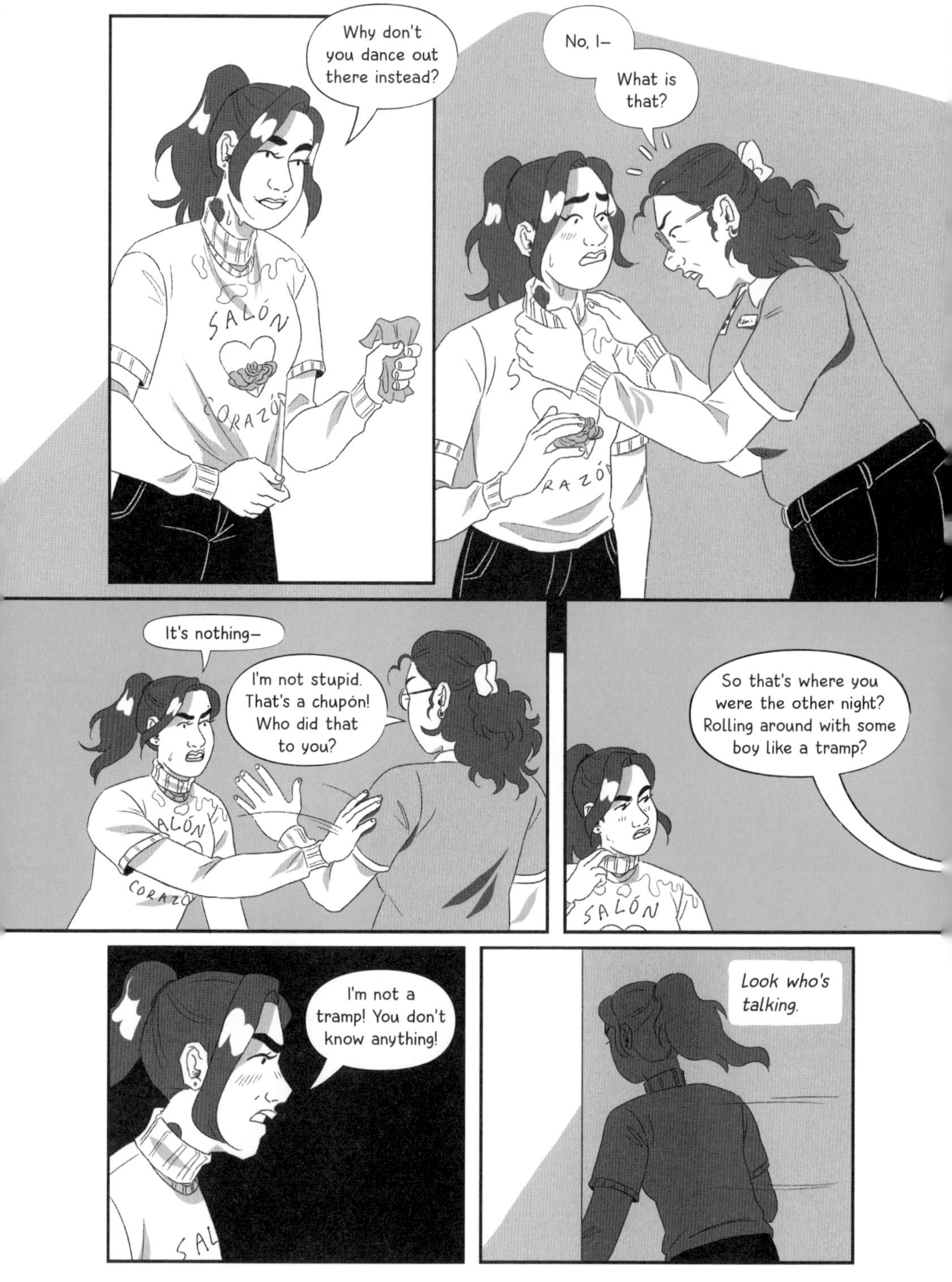

Why don't you dance out there instead?
No, I—
What is that?
It's nothing—
I'm not stupid. That's a chupón! Who did that to you?
So that's where you were the other night? Rolling around with some boy like a tramp?
I'm not a tramp! You don't know anything!
Look who's talking.

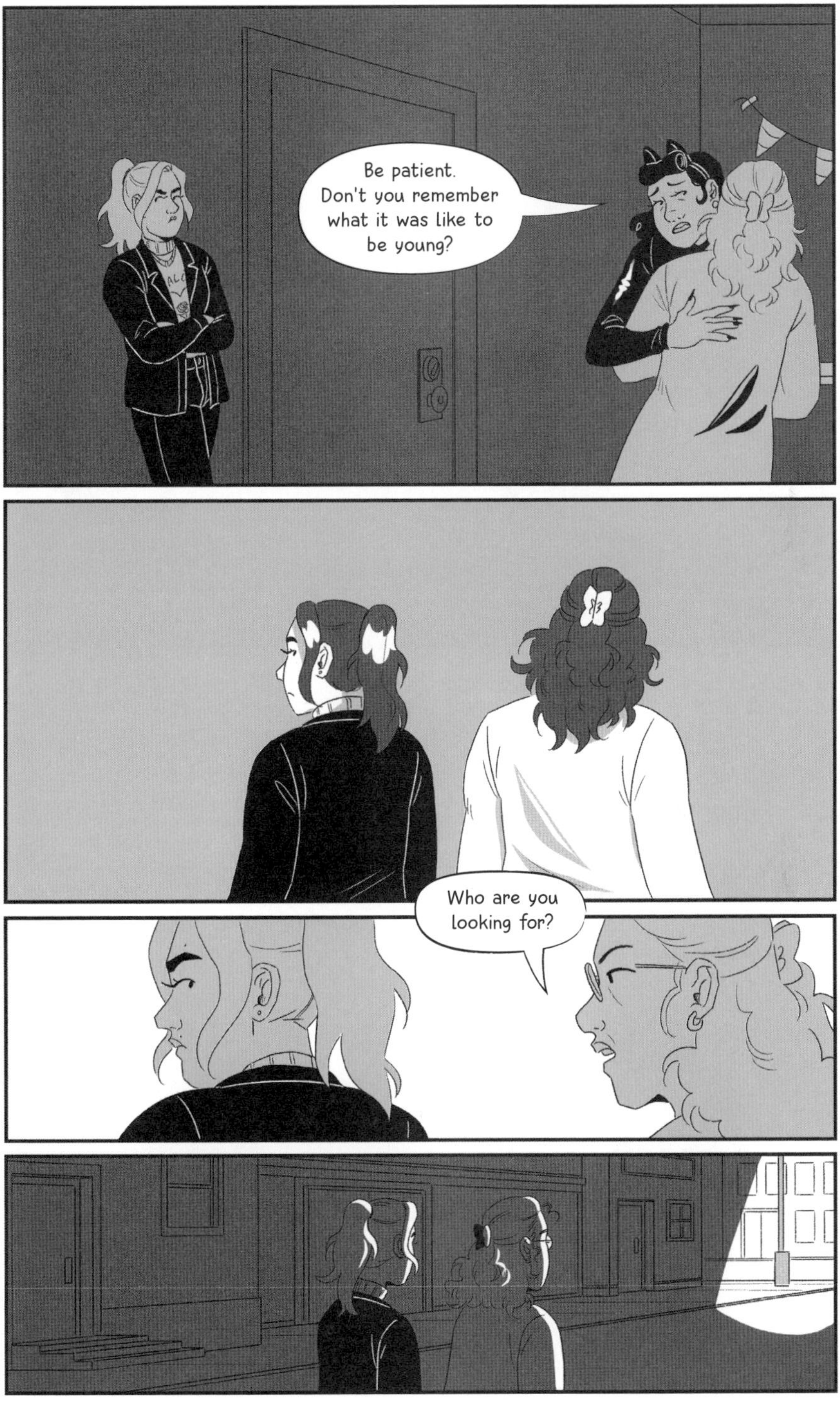
Be patient. Don't you remember what it was like to be young?
Who are you looking for?

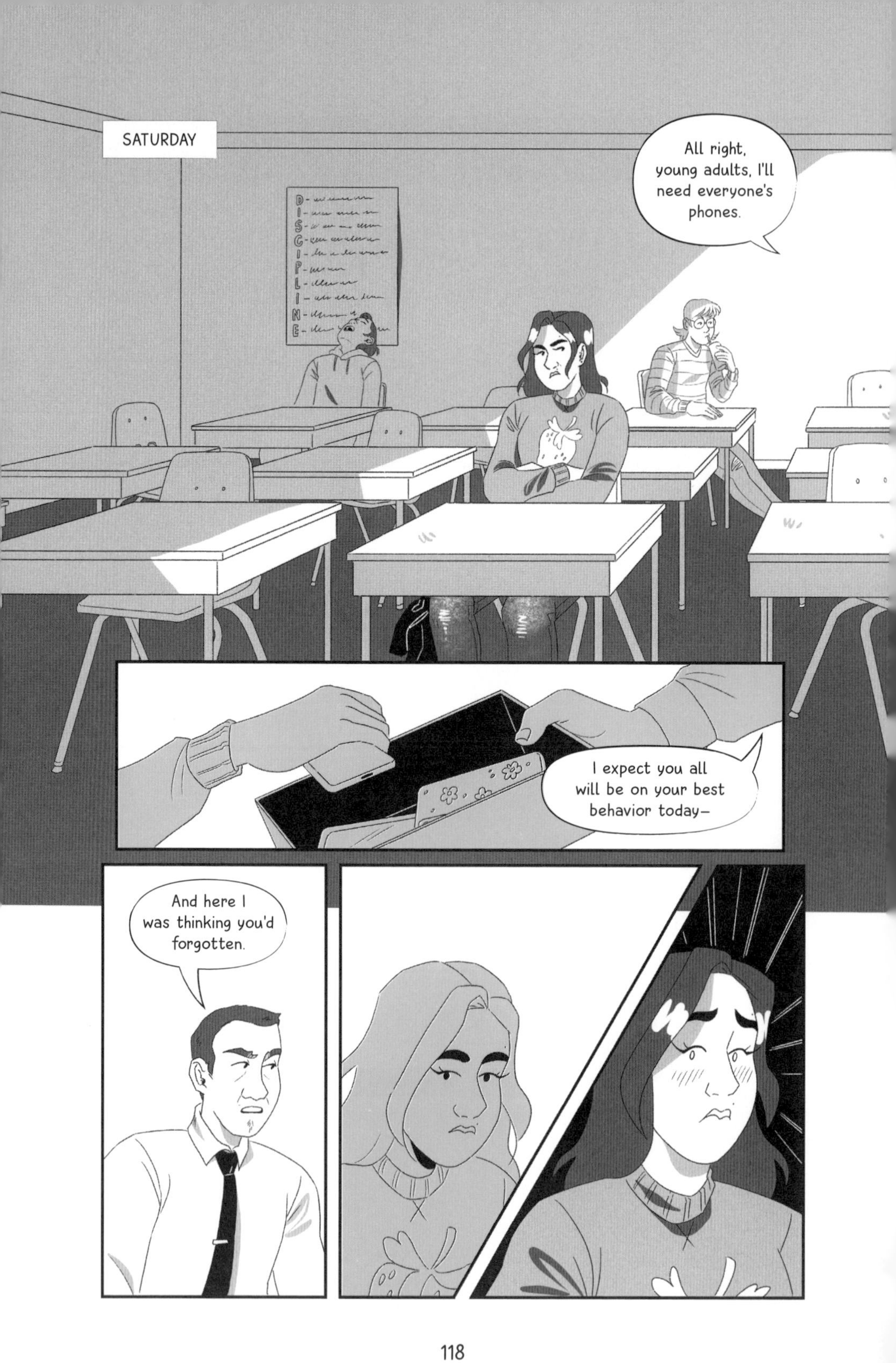
SATURDAY
All right, young adults, I'll need everyone's phones.
DISCIPLINE
I expect you all will be on your best behavior today—
And here I was thinking you'd forgotten.

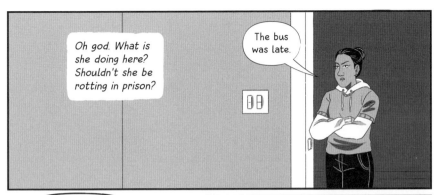

Oh god. What is she doing here? Shouldn't she be rotting in prison?

The bus was late.

The earlier one wasn't. You were ordered to arrive at 8:55 sharp, Miss Delgado.

You'll have to serve two more Saturdays now. See me Monday.

That's bull, I—

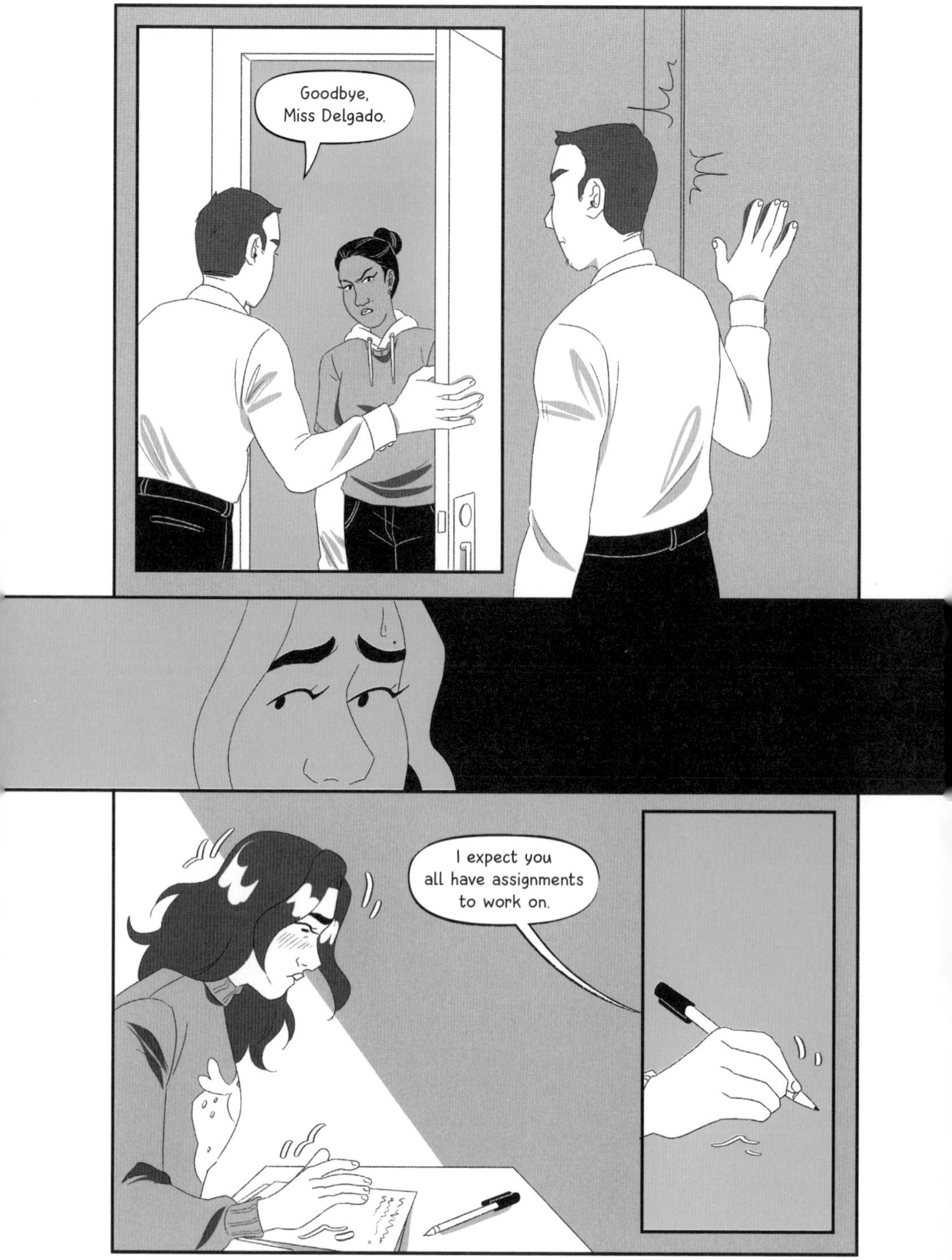
Goodbye,
Miss Delgado.
I expect you
all have assignments
to work on.

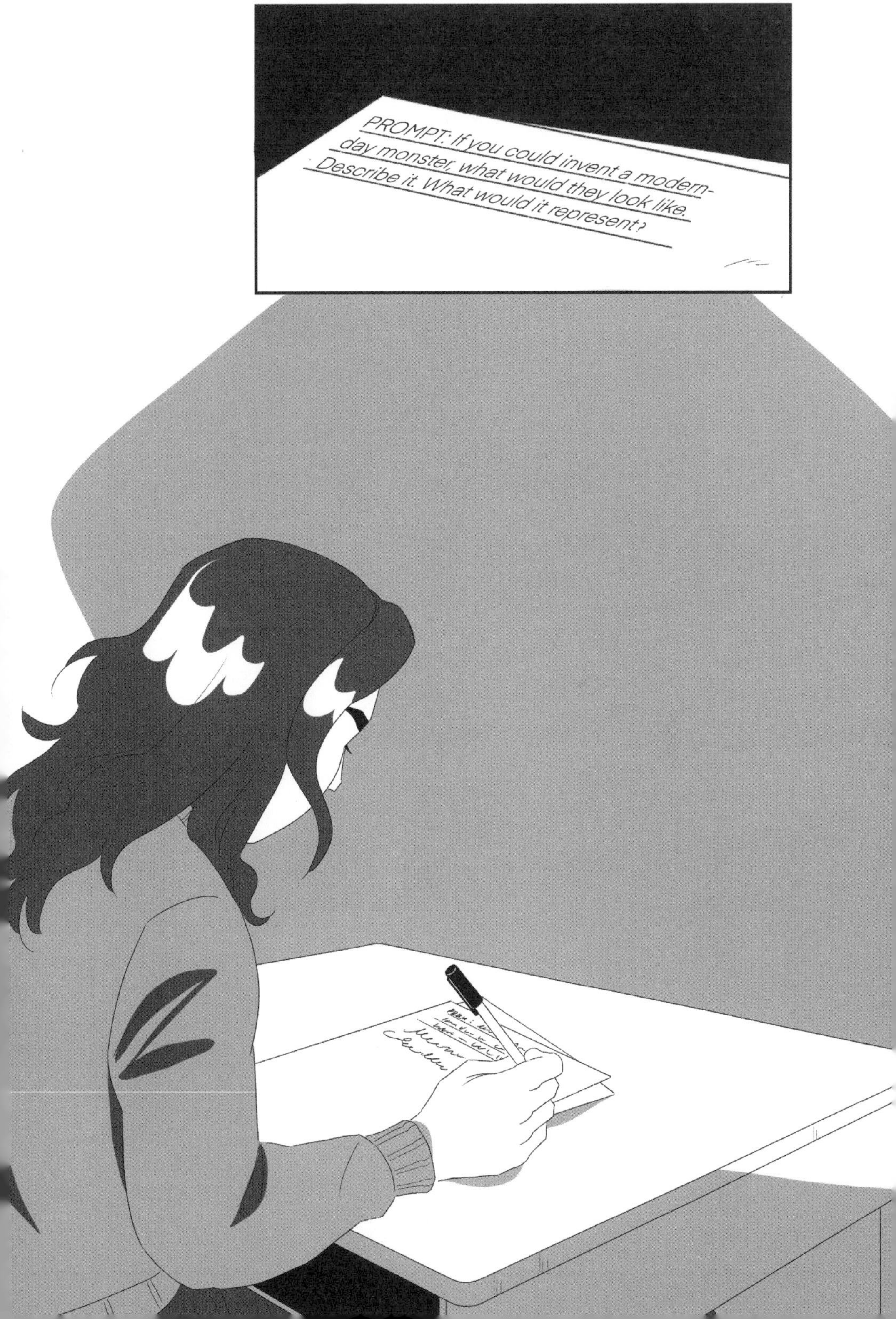
PROMPT: If you could invent a modern-day monster, what would they look like. Describe it. What would it represent?

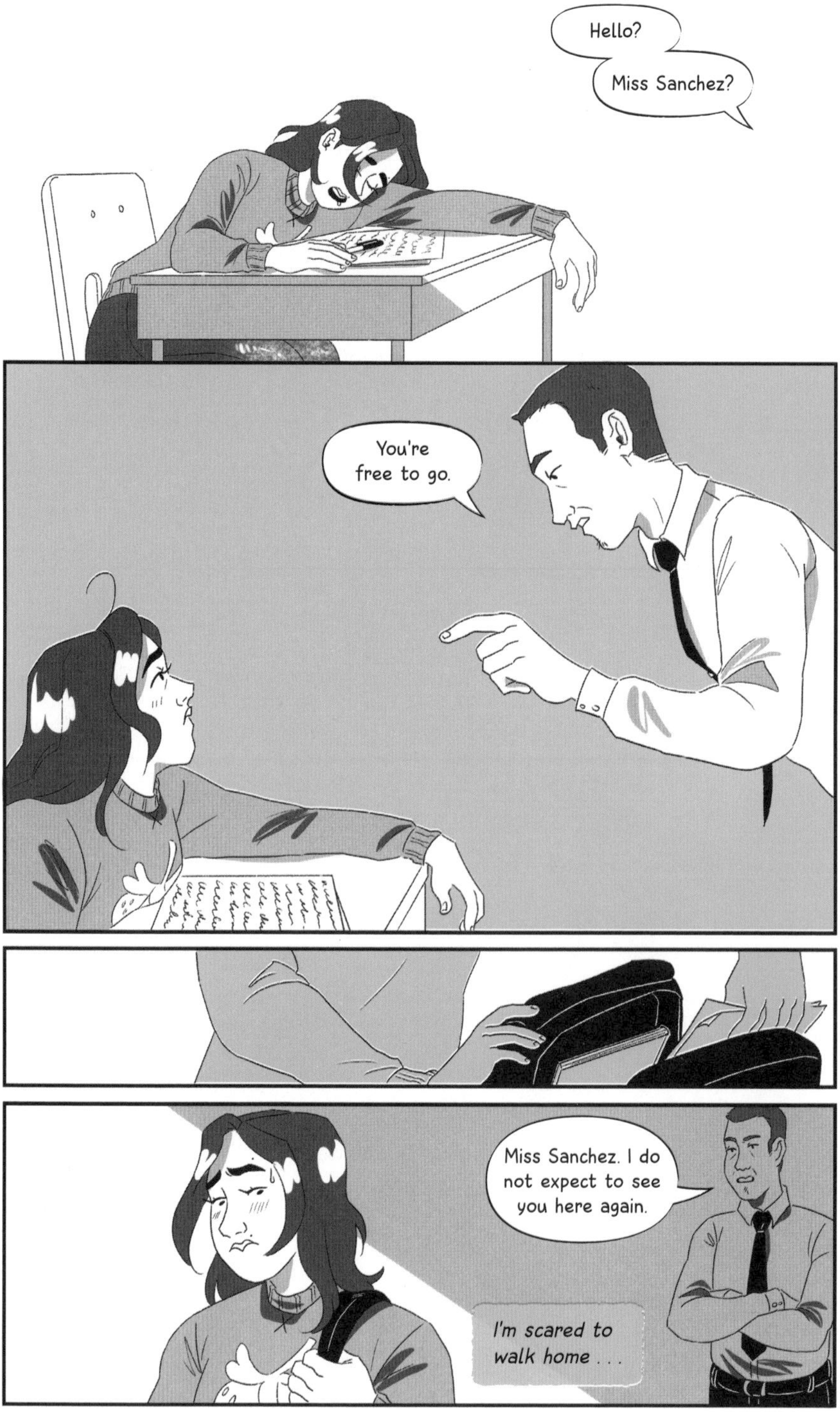
Hello?
Miss Sanchez?
You're free to go.
Miss Sanchez. I do not expect to see you here again.
I'm scared to walk home . . .

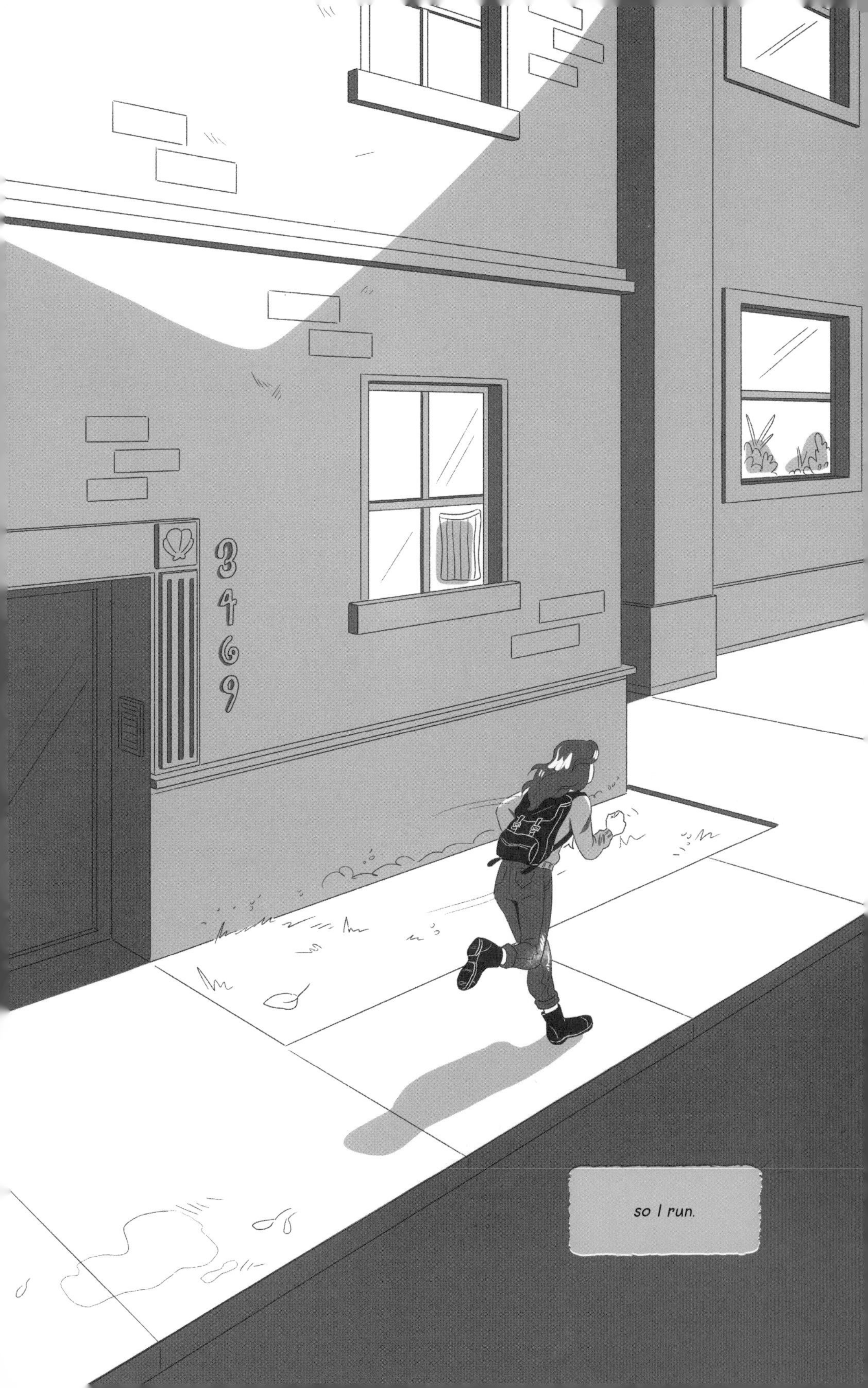
3469
so I run.

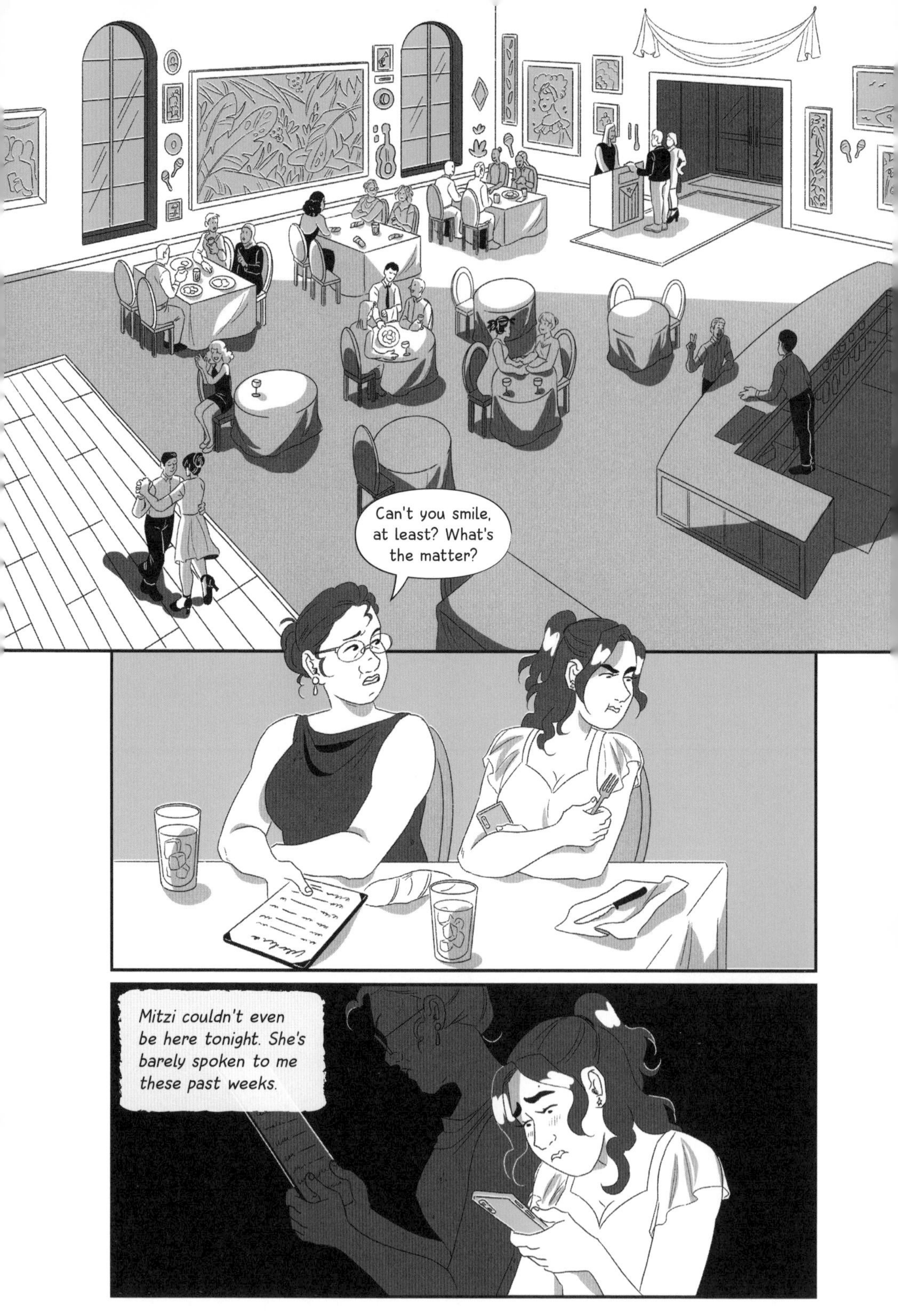
Can't you smile, at least? What's the matter?
Mitzi couldn't even be here tonight. She's barely spoken to me these past weeks.

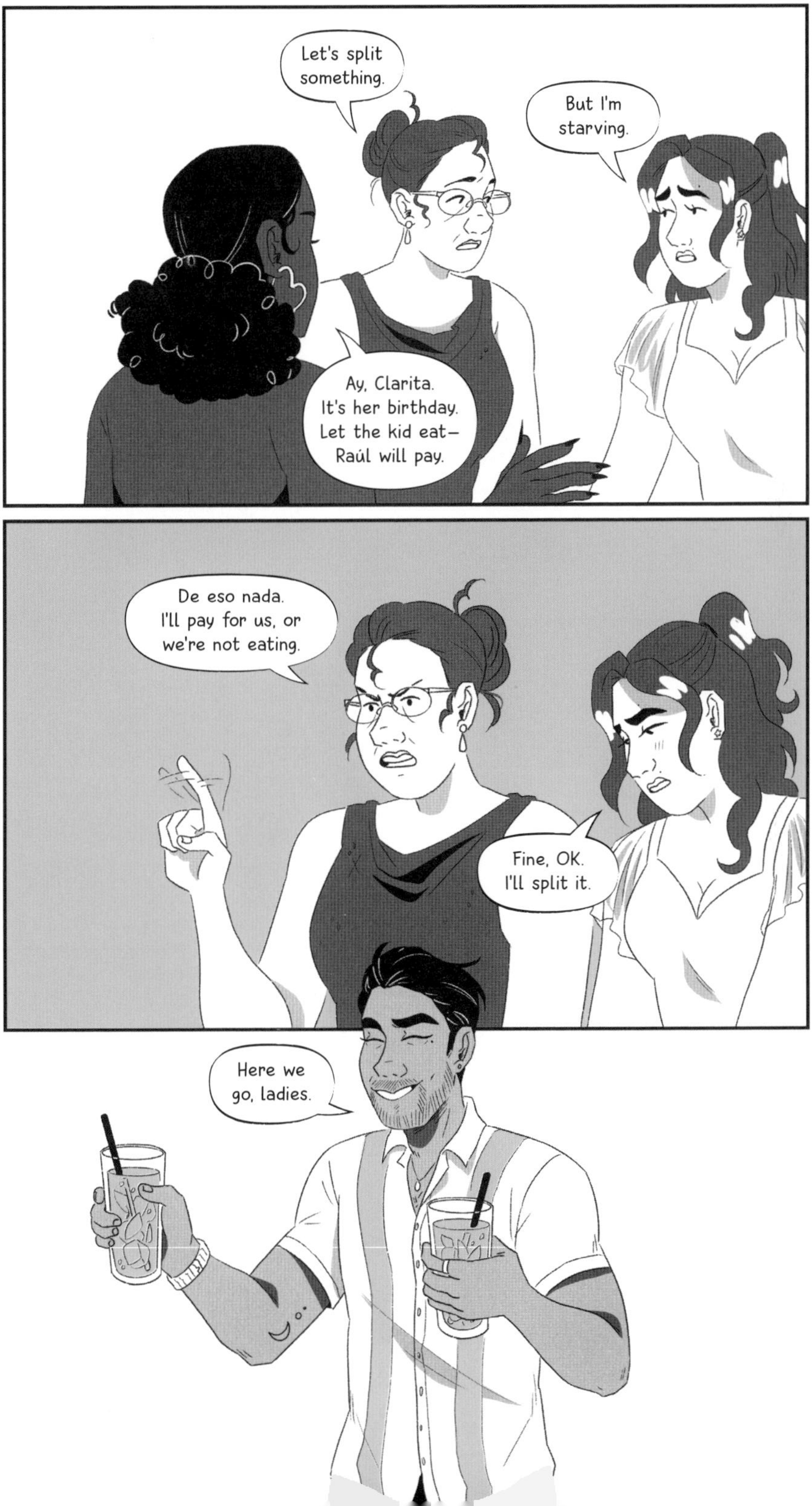
Let's split something.
But I'm starving.
Ay, Clarita. It's her birthday. Let the kid eat— Raúl will pay.
De eso nada. I'll pay for us, or we're not eating.
Fine, OK. I'll split it.
Here we go, ladies.

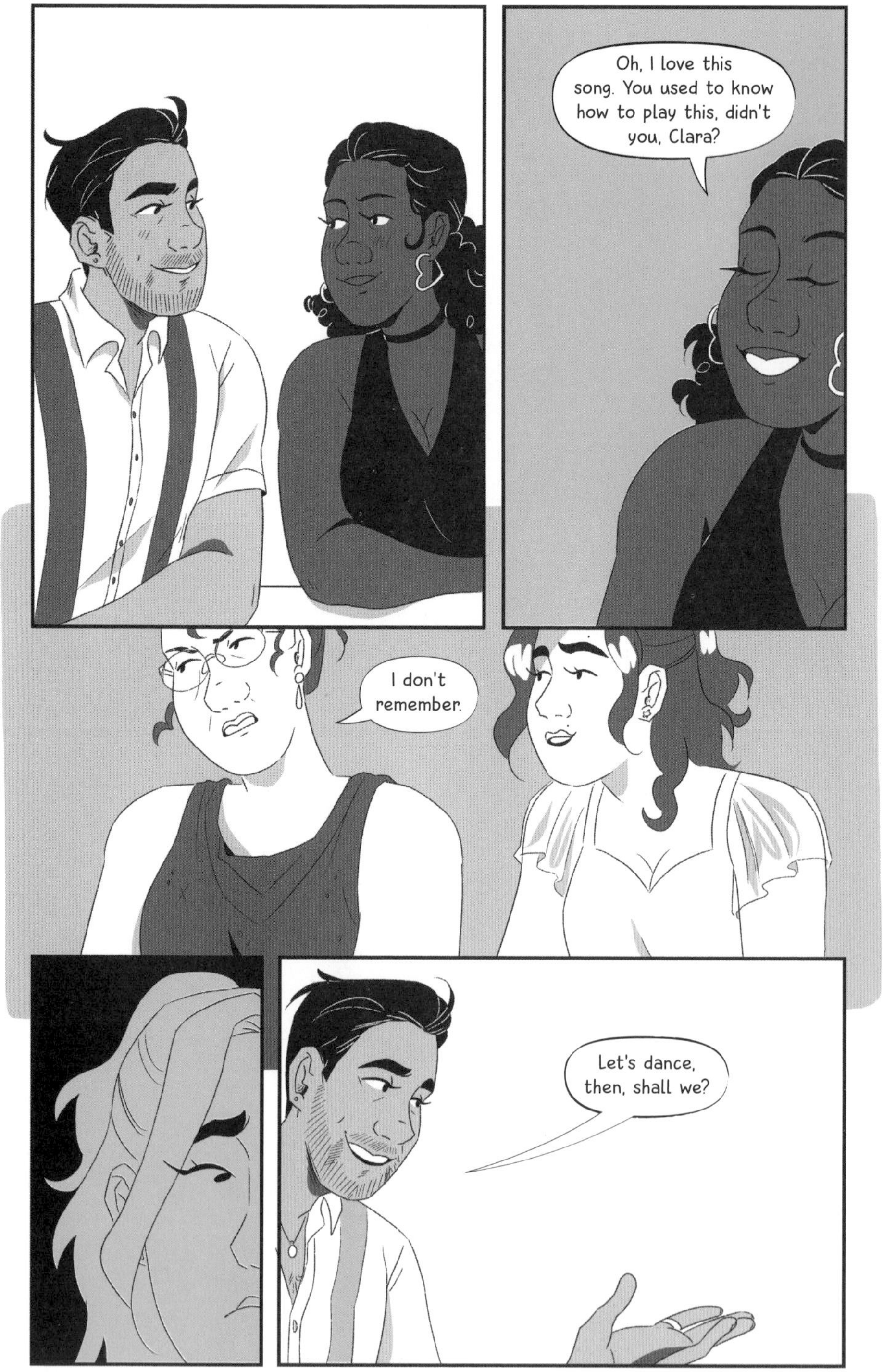
Oh, I love this song. You used to know how to play this, didn't you, Clara?
I don't remember.
Let's dance, then, shall we?

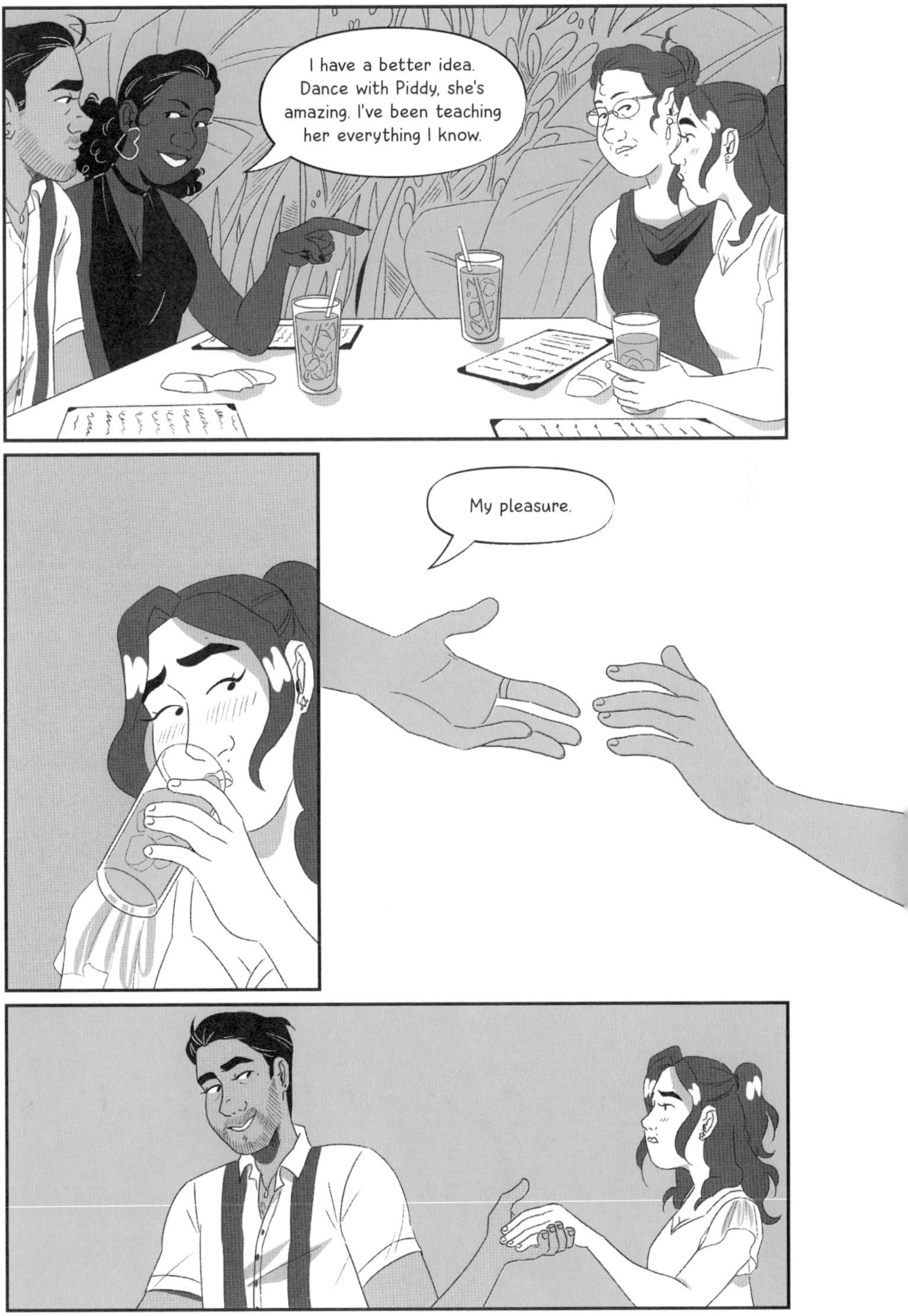
I have a better idea. Dance with Piddy, she's amazing. I've been teaching her everything I know.
My pleasure.

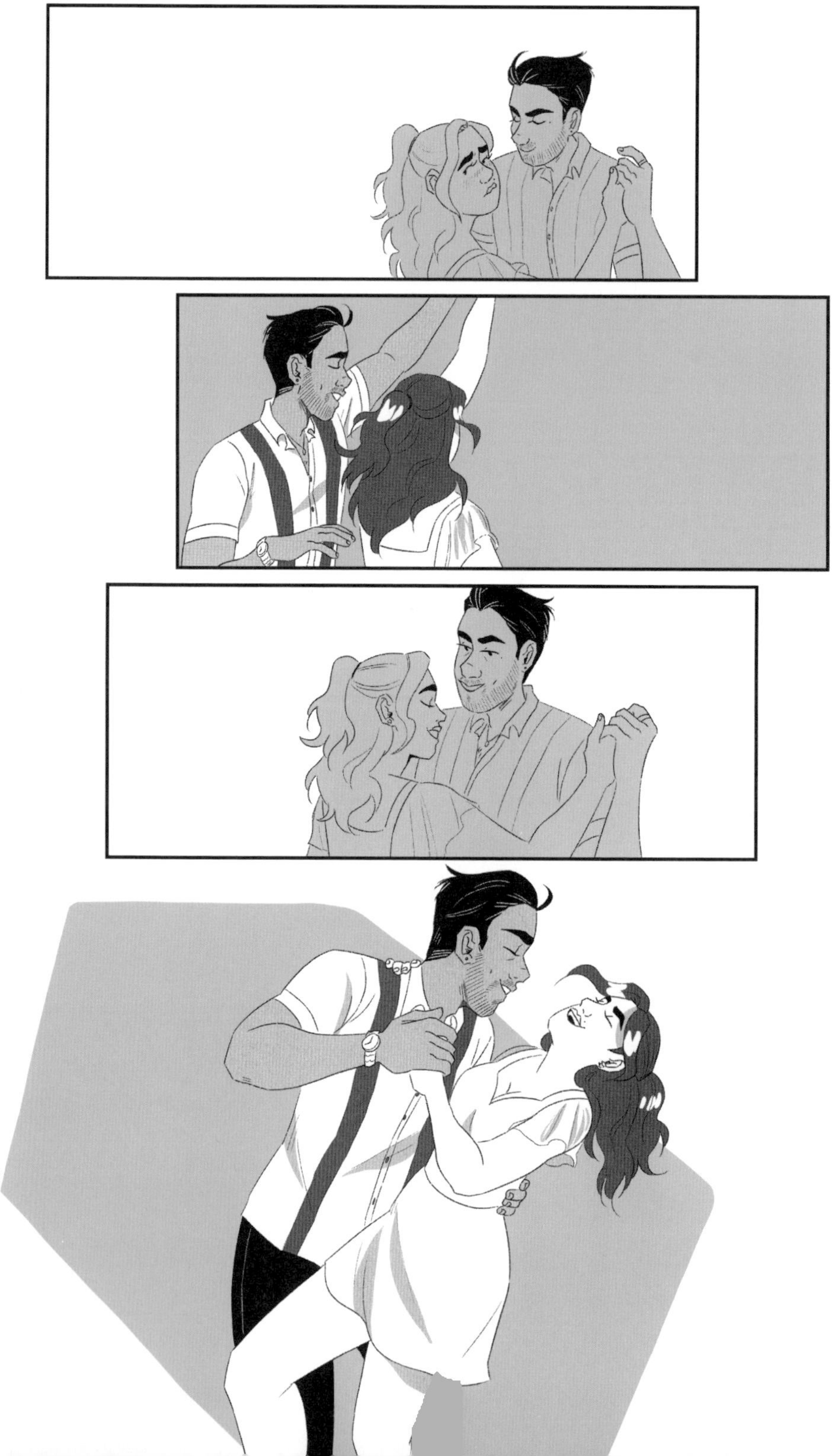

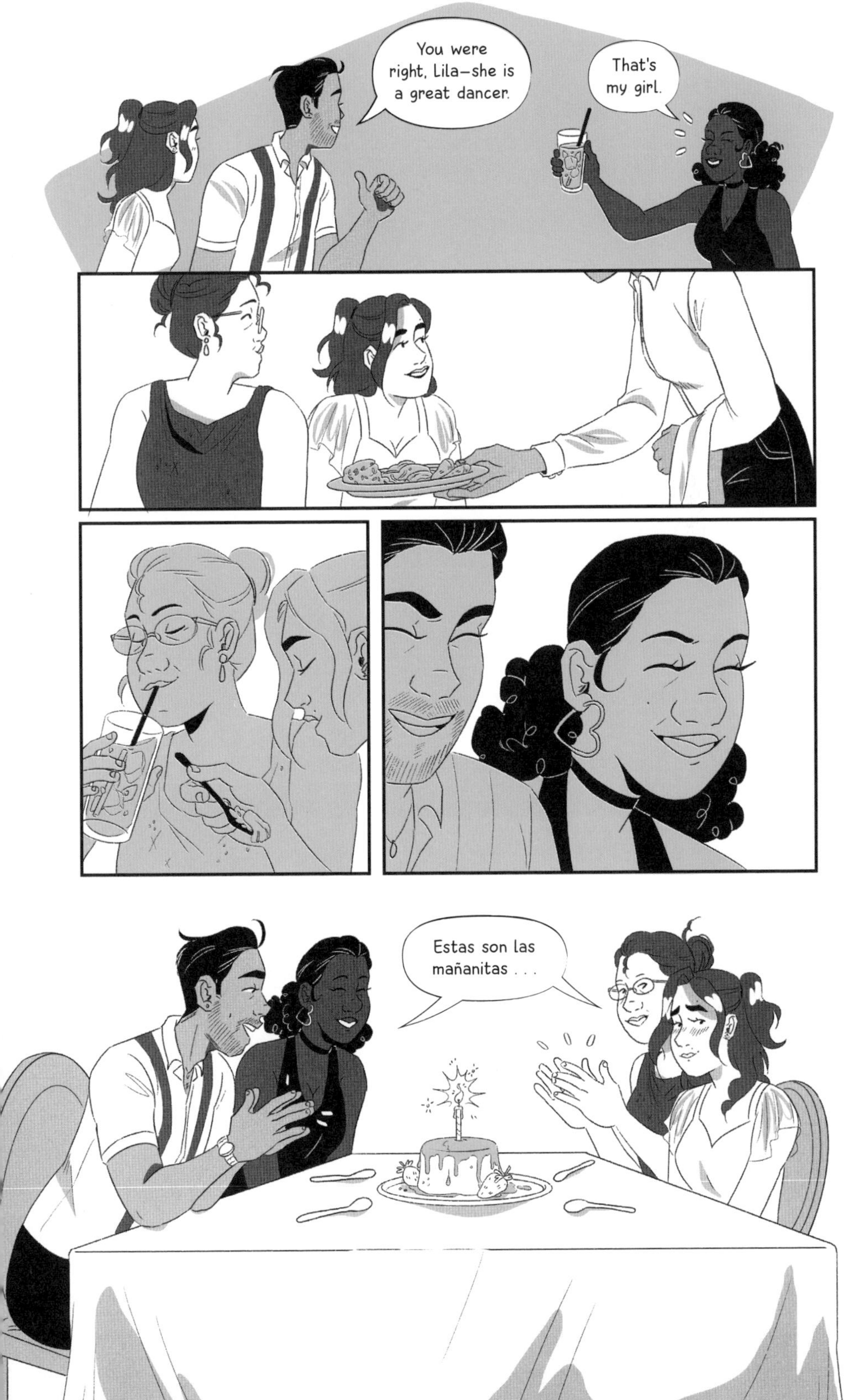
You were right, Lila—she is a great dancer.
That's my girl.
Estas son las mañanitas . . .

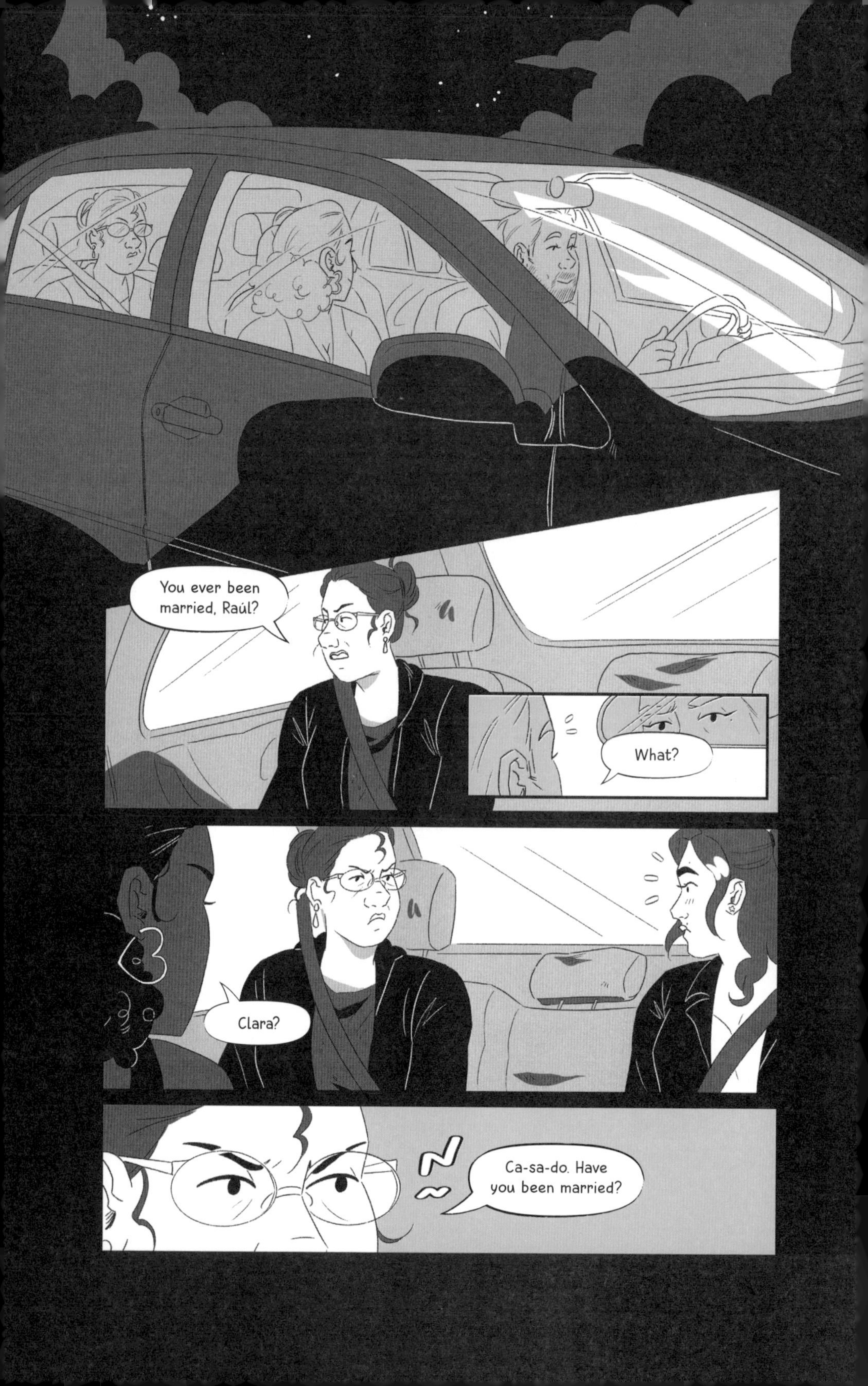
You ever been married, Raúl?
What?
Clara?
Ca-sa-do. Have you been married?

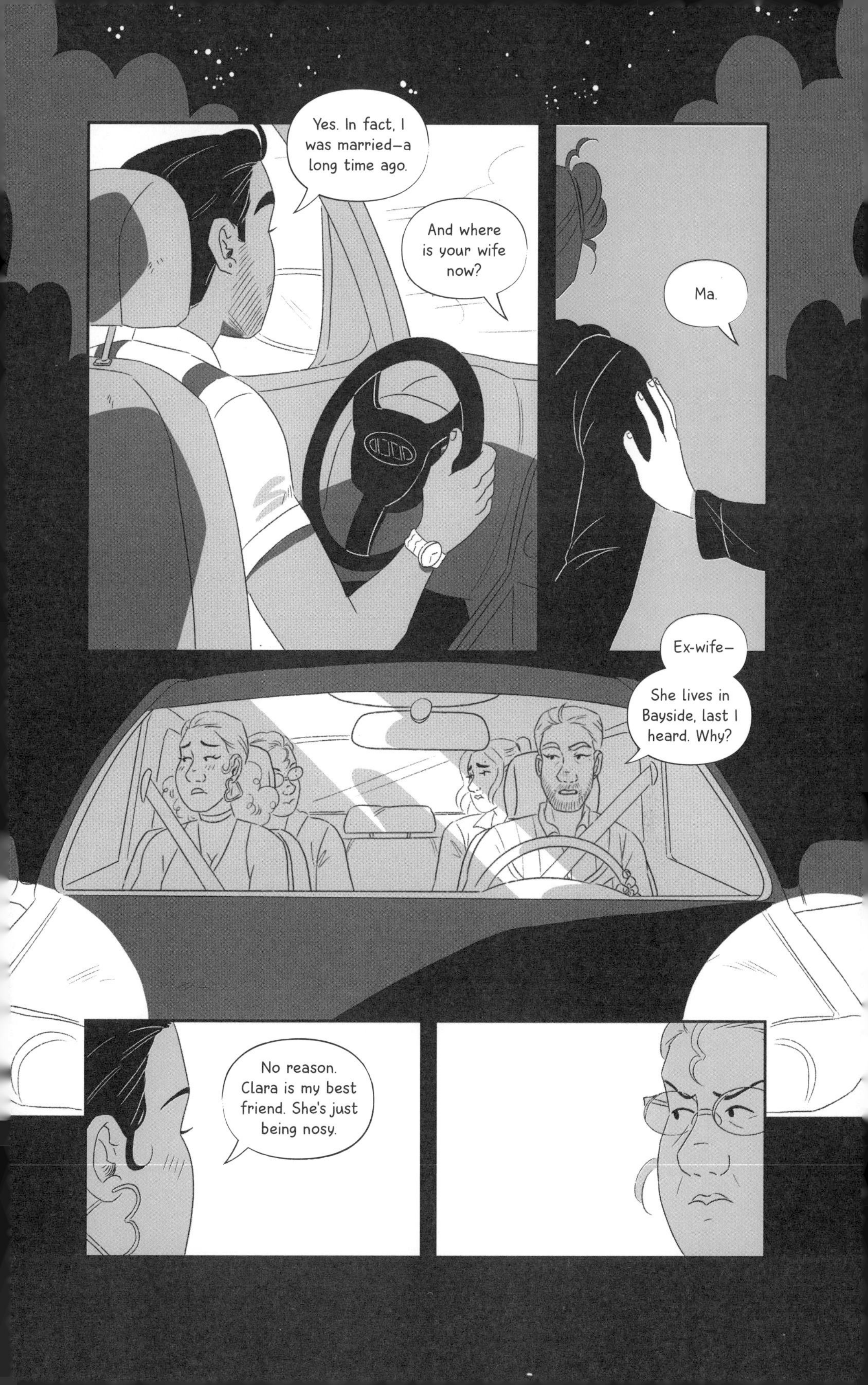
Yes. In fact, I was married—a long time ago.
And where is your wife now?
Ma.
Ex-wife—
She lives in Bayside, last I heard. Why?
No reason. Clara is my best friend. She's just being nosy.

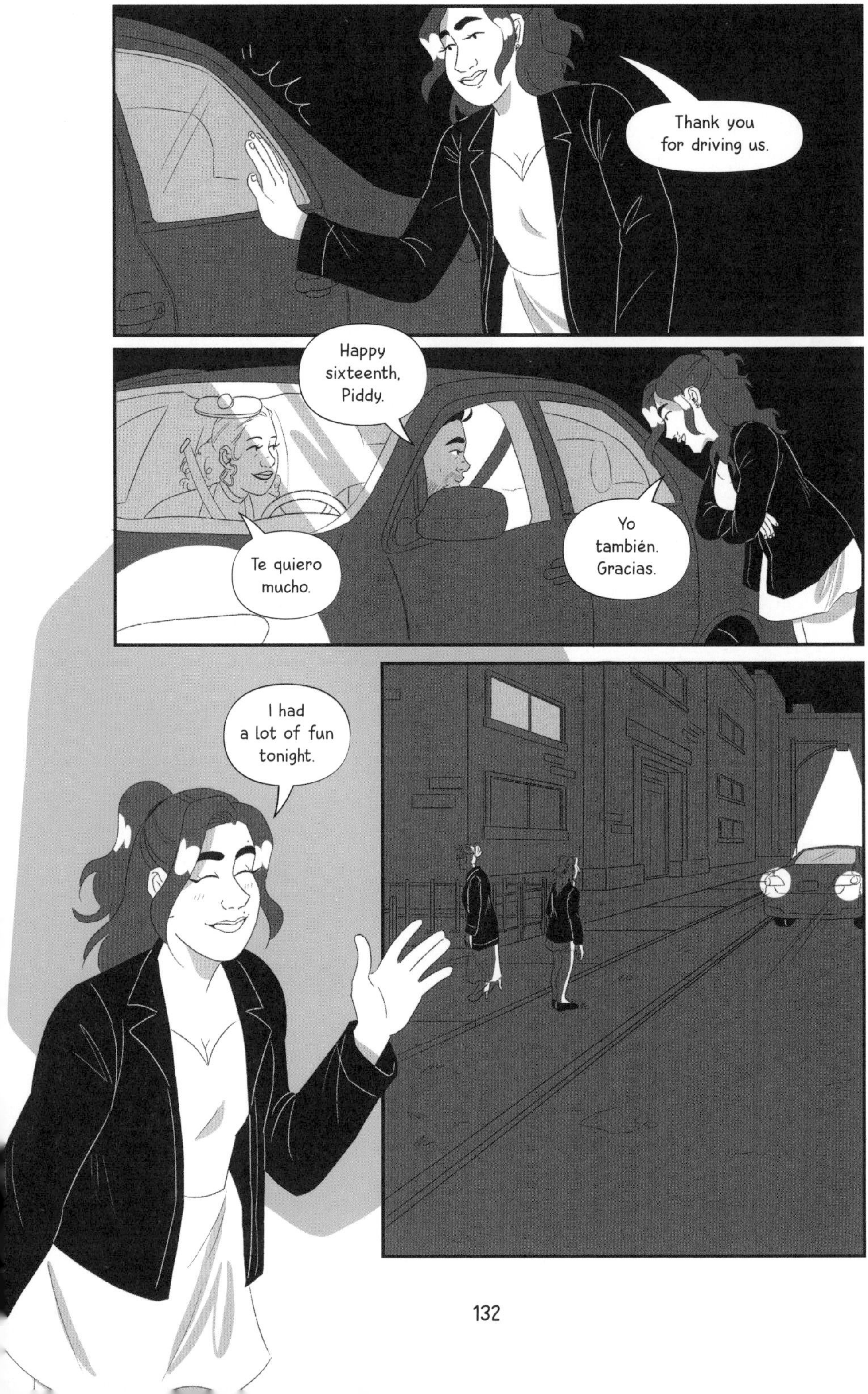
Thank you for driving us.
Happy sixteenth, Piddy.
Te quiero mucho.
Yo también. Gracias.
I had a lot of fun tonight.

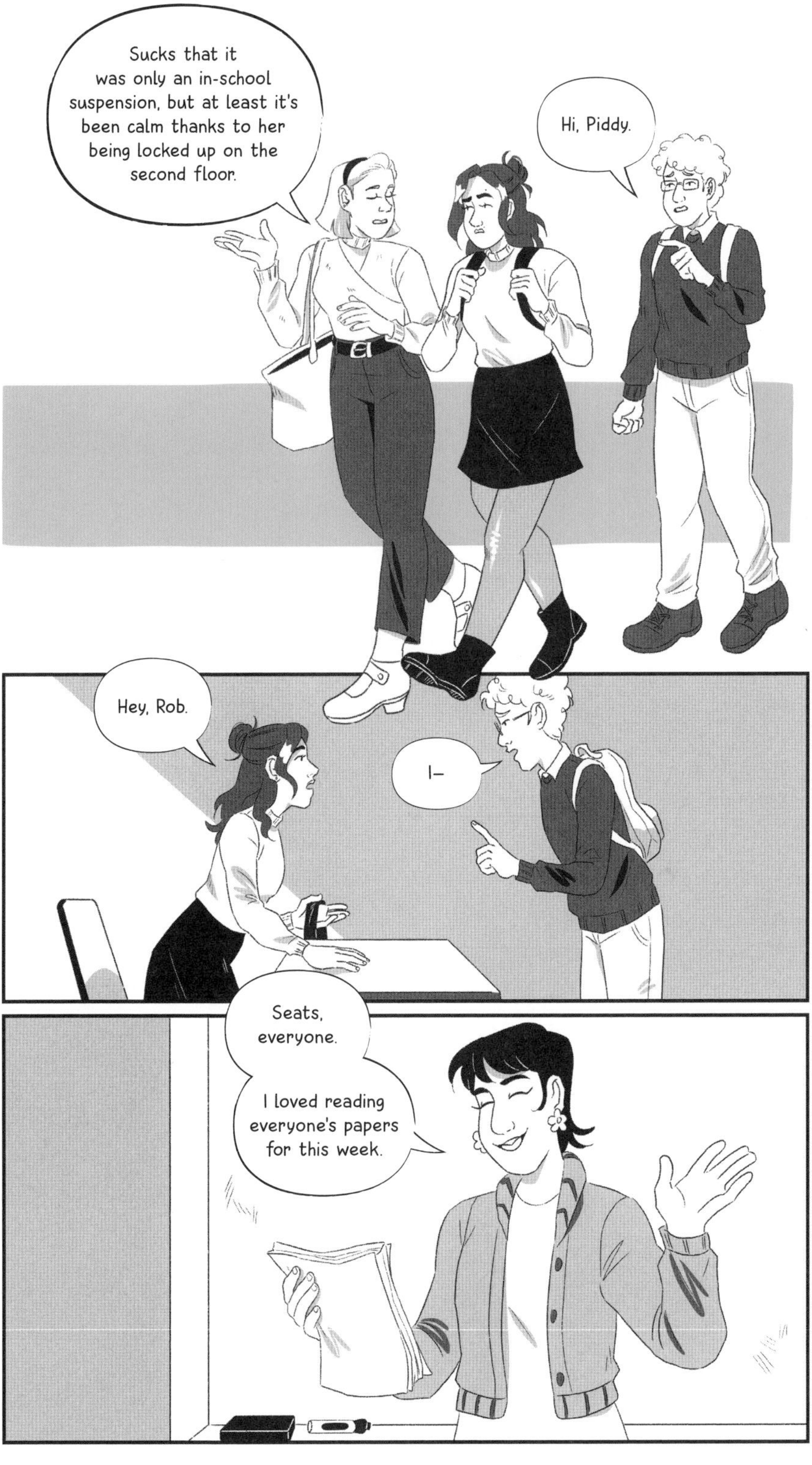
Sucks that it was only an in-school suspension, but at least it's been calm thanks to her being locked up on the second floor.
Hi, Piddy.
Hey, Rob.
I—
Seats, everyone.
I loved reading everyone's papers for this week.

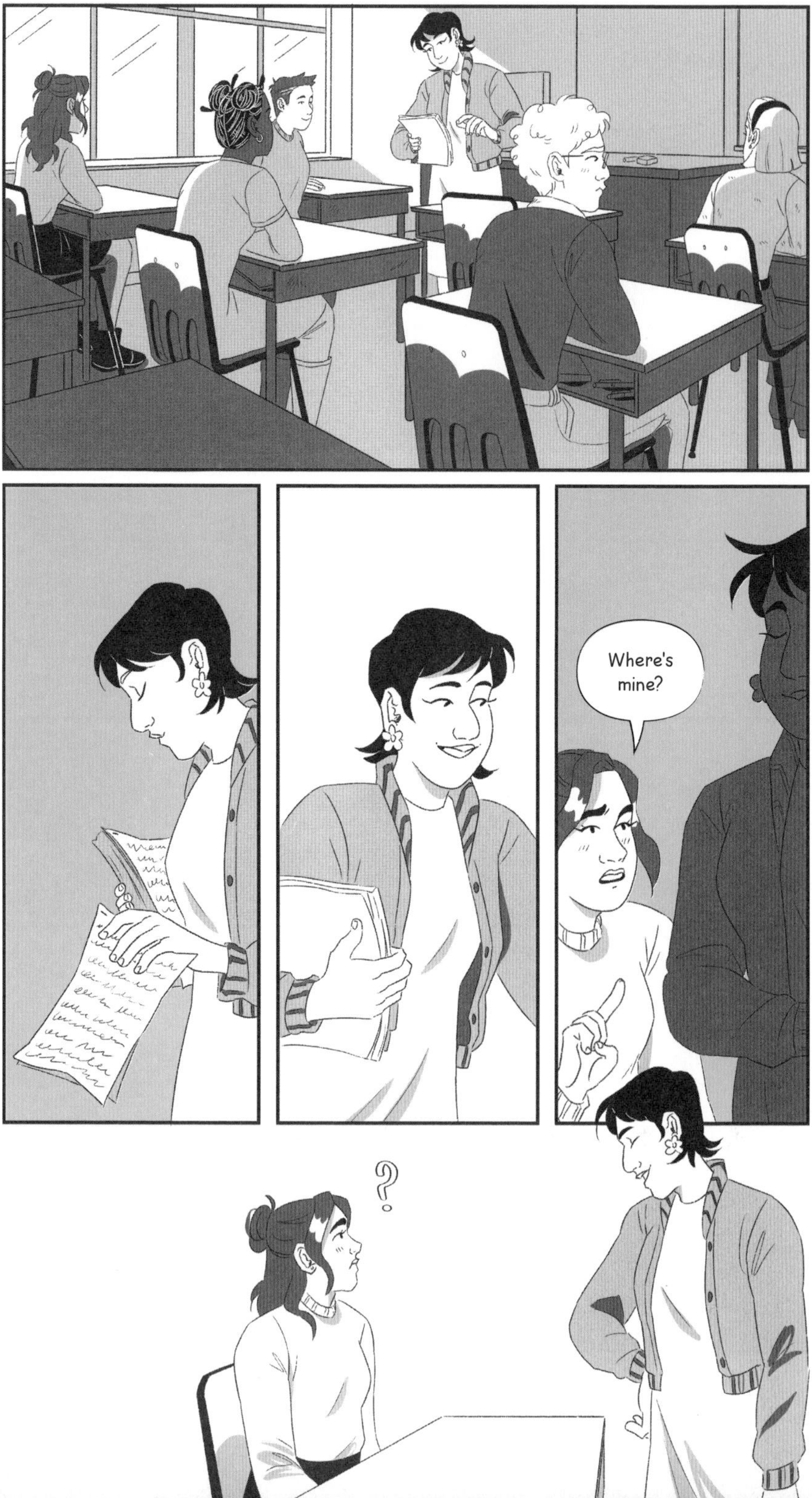
Where's mine?

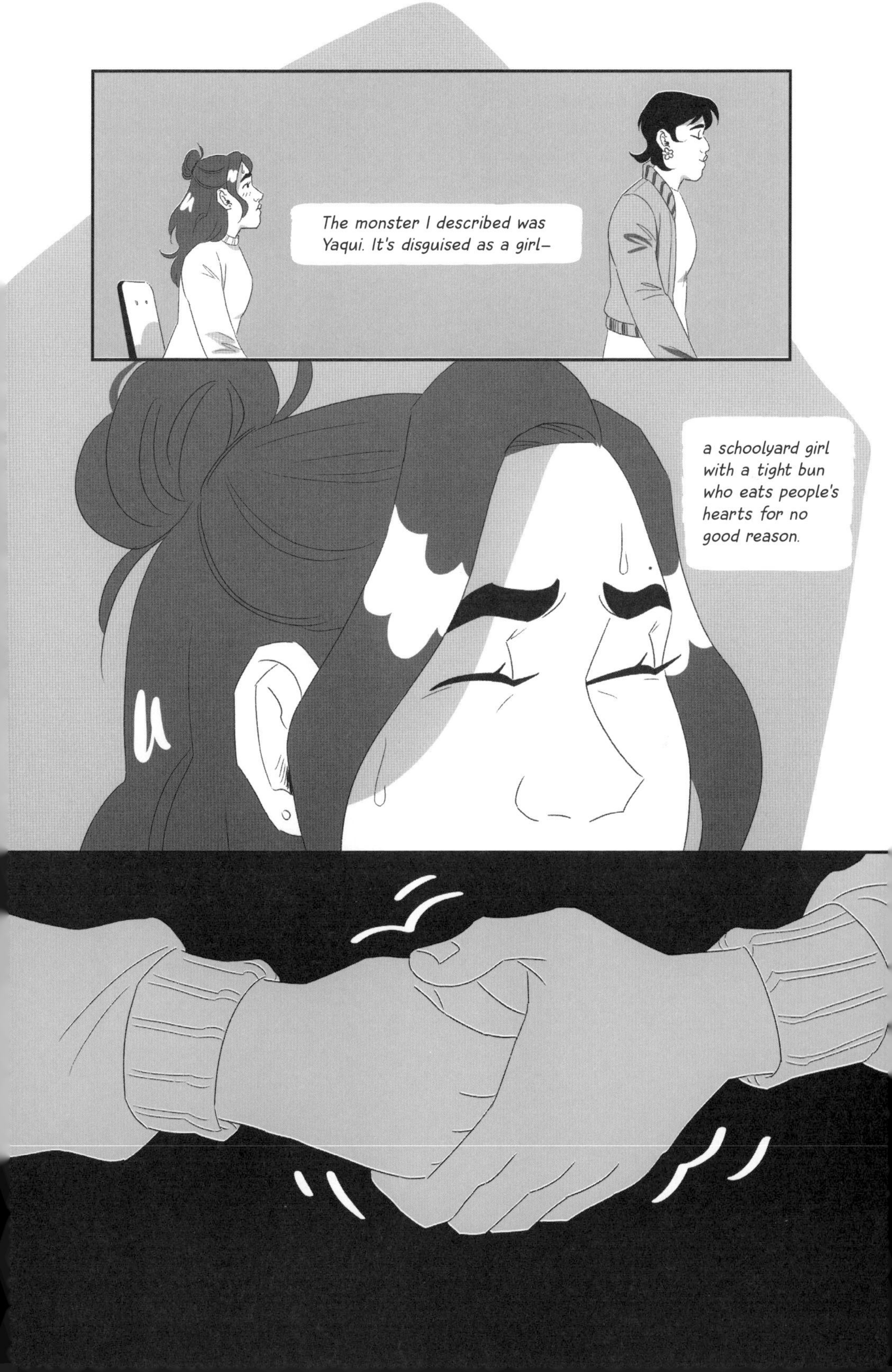
The monster I described was Yaqui. It's disguised as a girl—
a schoolyard girl with a tight bun who eats people's hearts for no good reason.

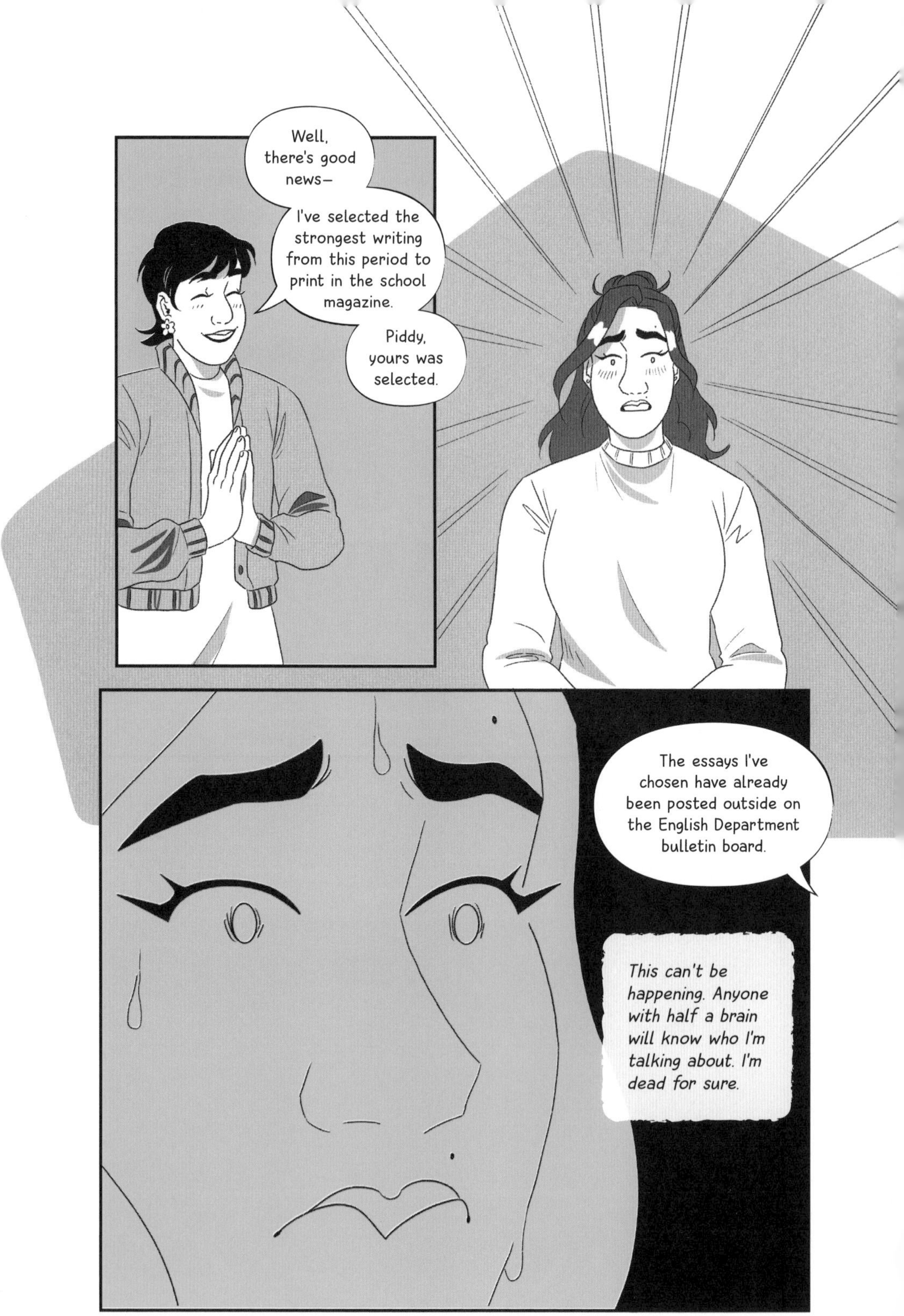
Well, there's good news—
I've selected the strongest writing from this period to print in the school magazine.
Piddy, yours was selected.
The essays I've chosen have already been posted outside on the English Department bulletin board.
This can't be happening. Anyone with half a brain will know who I'm talking about. I'm dead for sure.

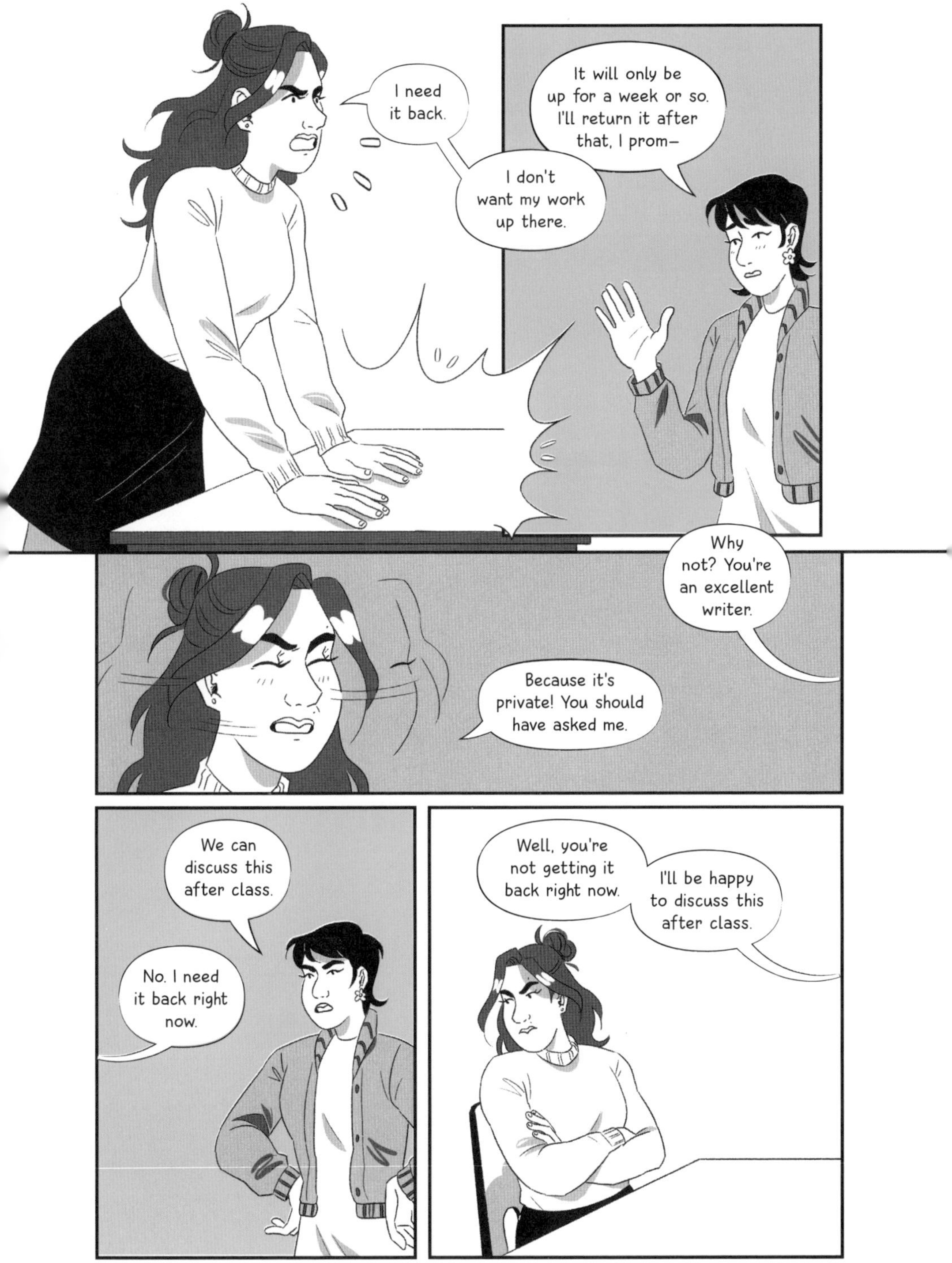

I need it back.
I don't want my work up there.
It will only be up for a week or so. I'll return it after that, I prom—
Why not? You're an excellent writer.
Because it's private! You should have asked me.
We can discuss this after class.
No. I need it back right now.
Well, you're not getting it back right now.
I'll be happy to discuss this after class.

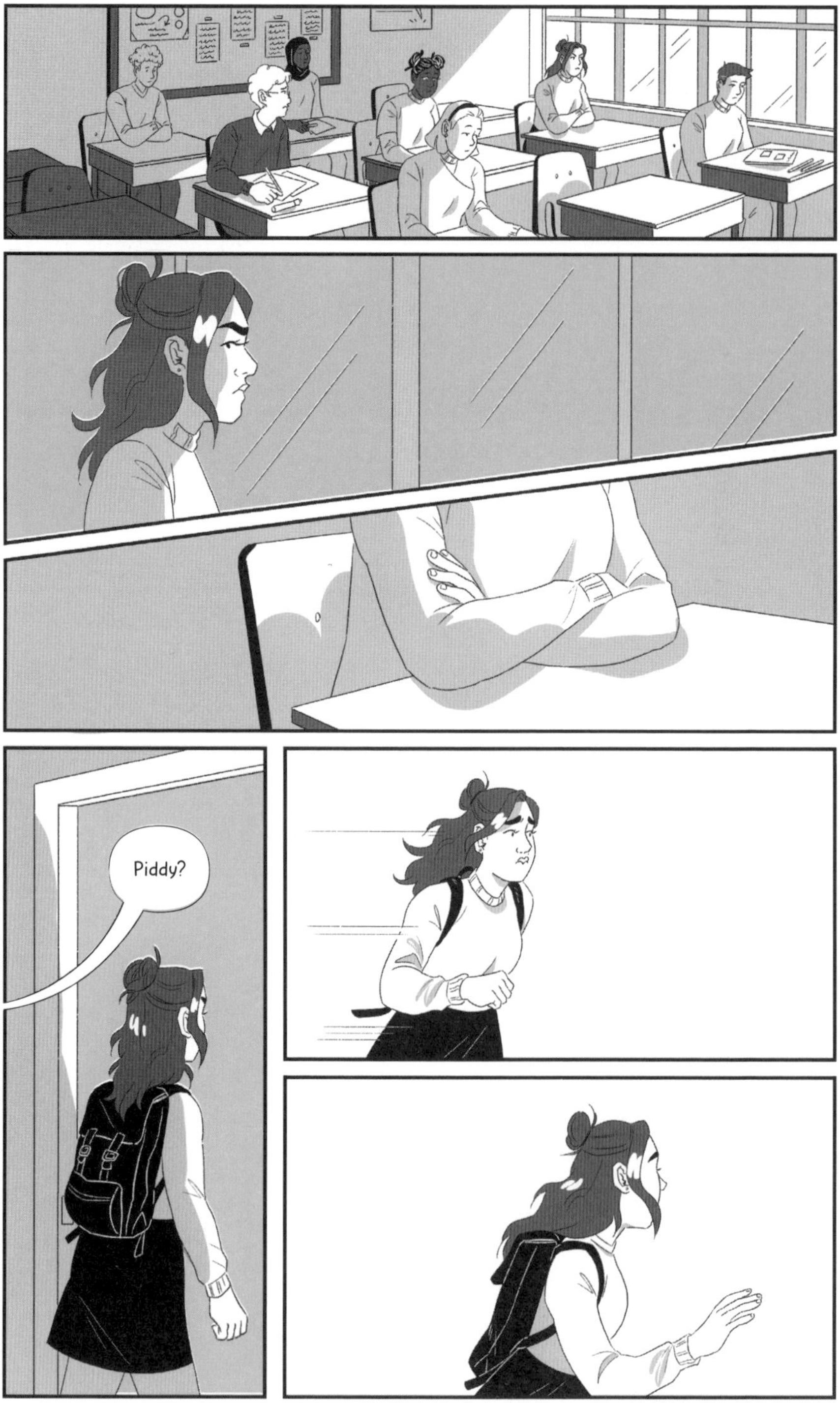
Piddy?

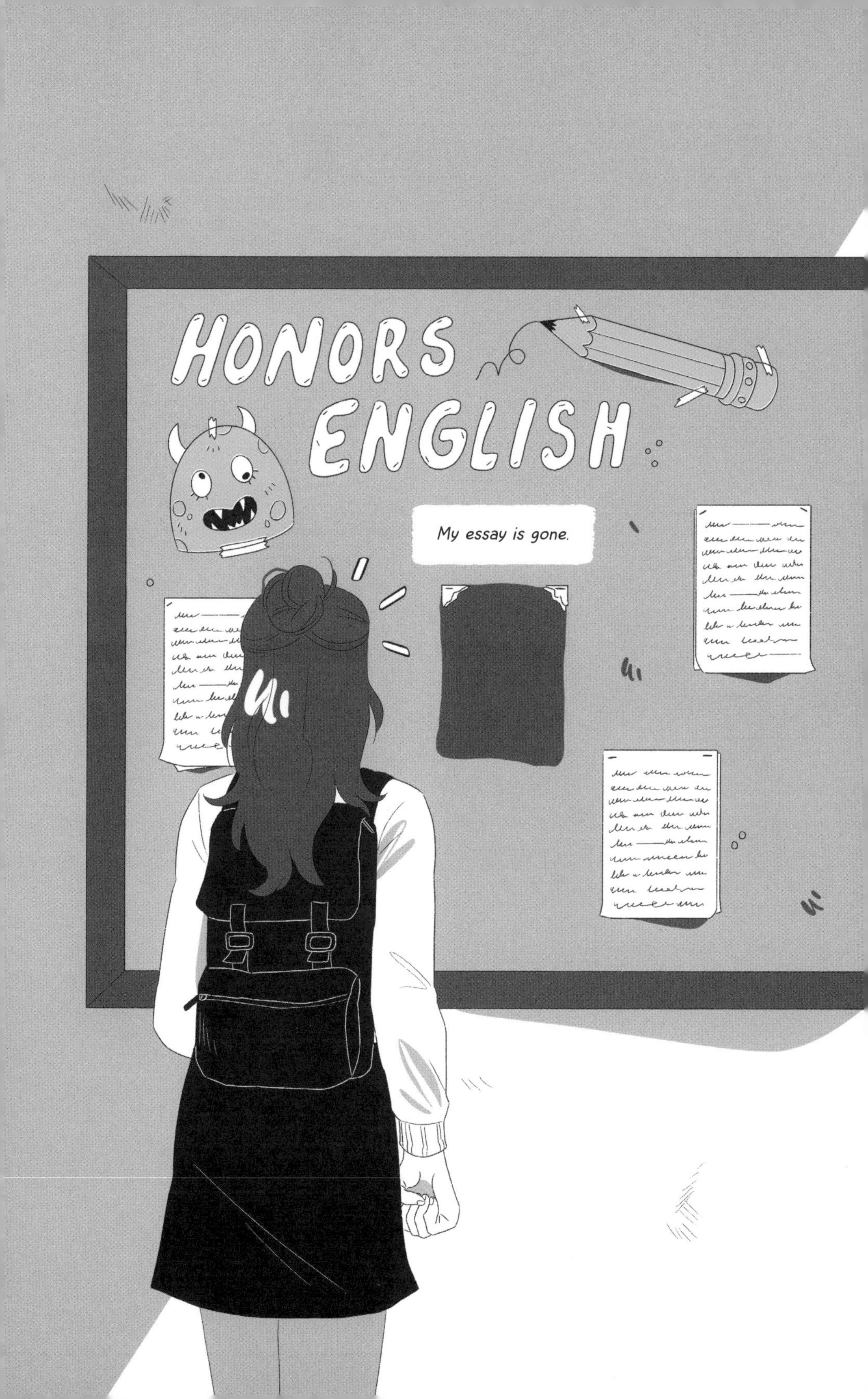
HONORS ENGLISH
My essay is gone.

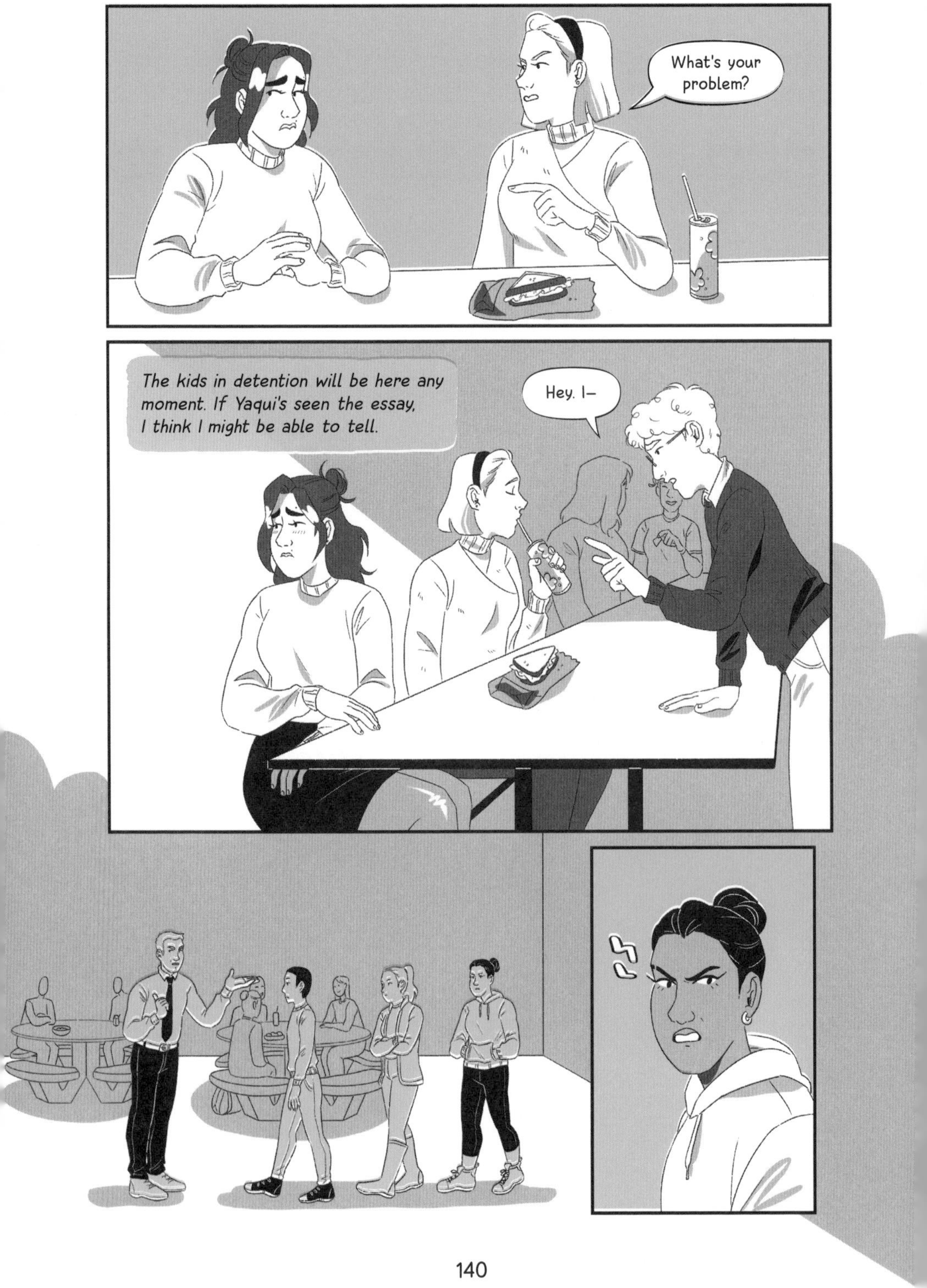
What's your problem?
The kids in detention will be here any moment. If Yaqui's seen the essay, I think I might be able to tell.
Hey. I–

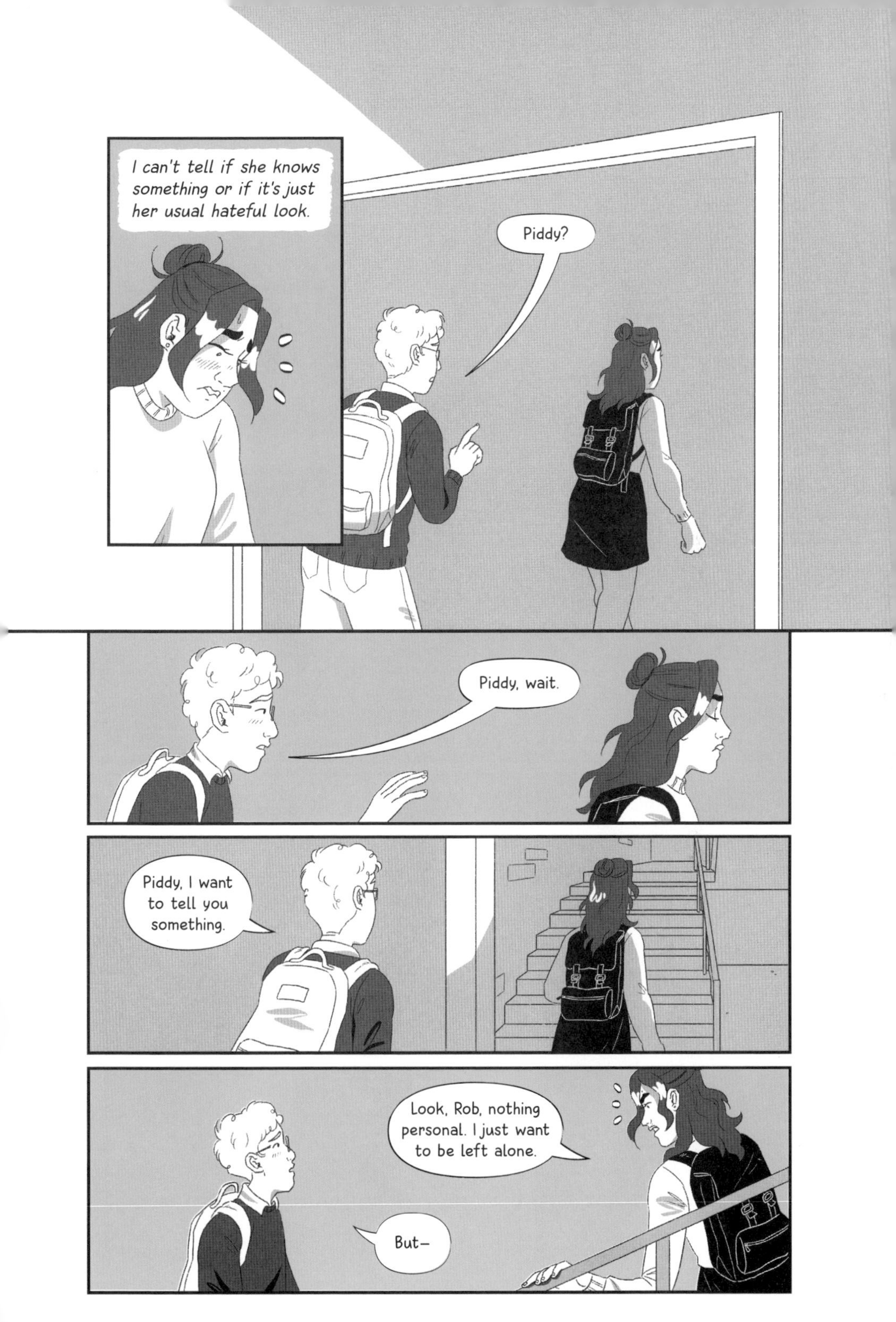
I can't tell if she knows something or if it's just her usual hateful look.
Piddy?
Piddy, wait.
Piddy, I want to tell you something.
Look, Rob, nothing personal. I just want to be left alone.
But—

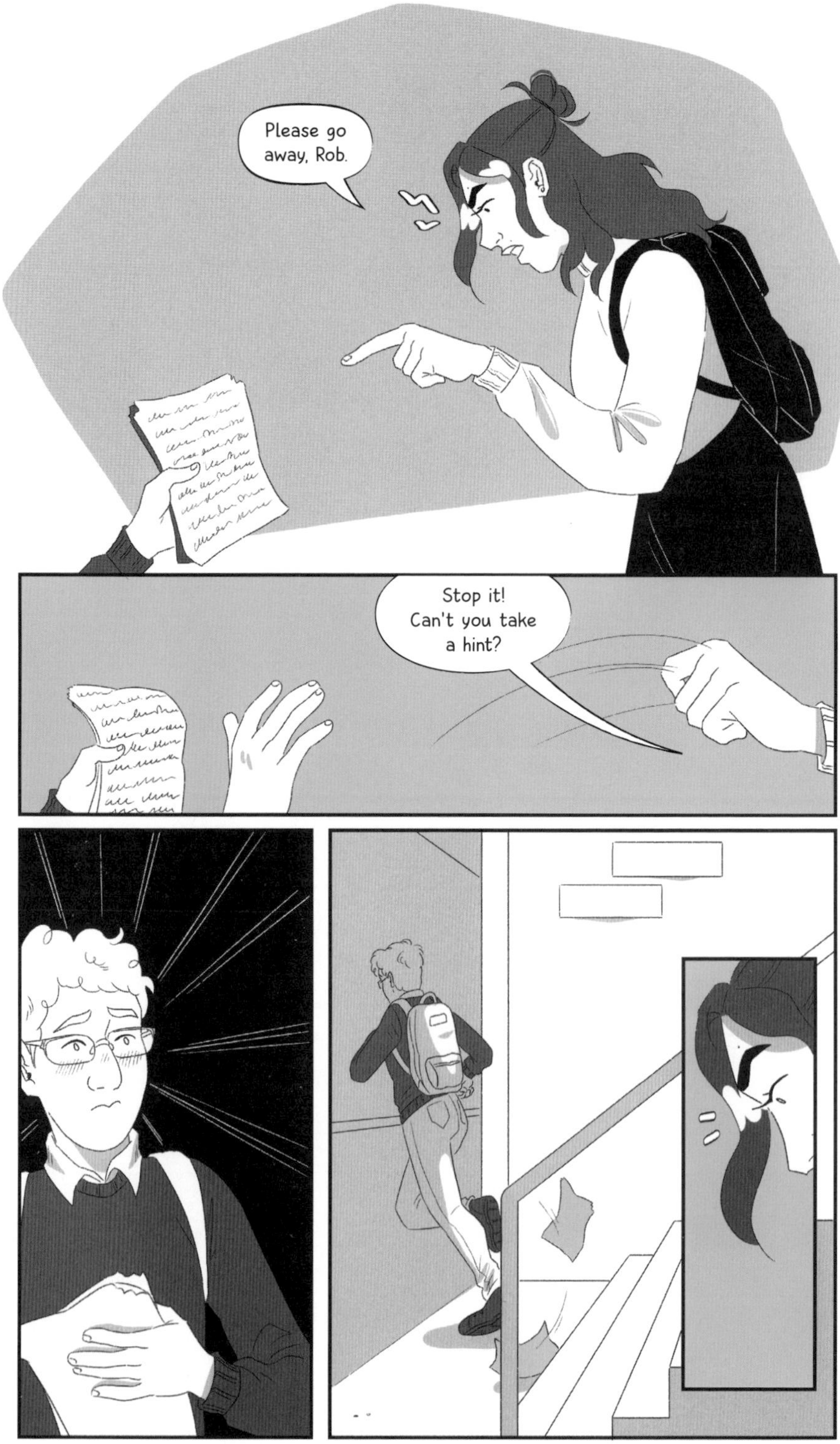
Please go away, Rob.
Stop it! Can't you take a hint?

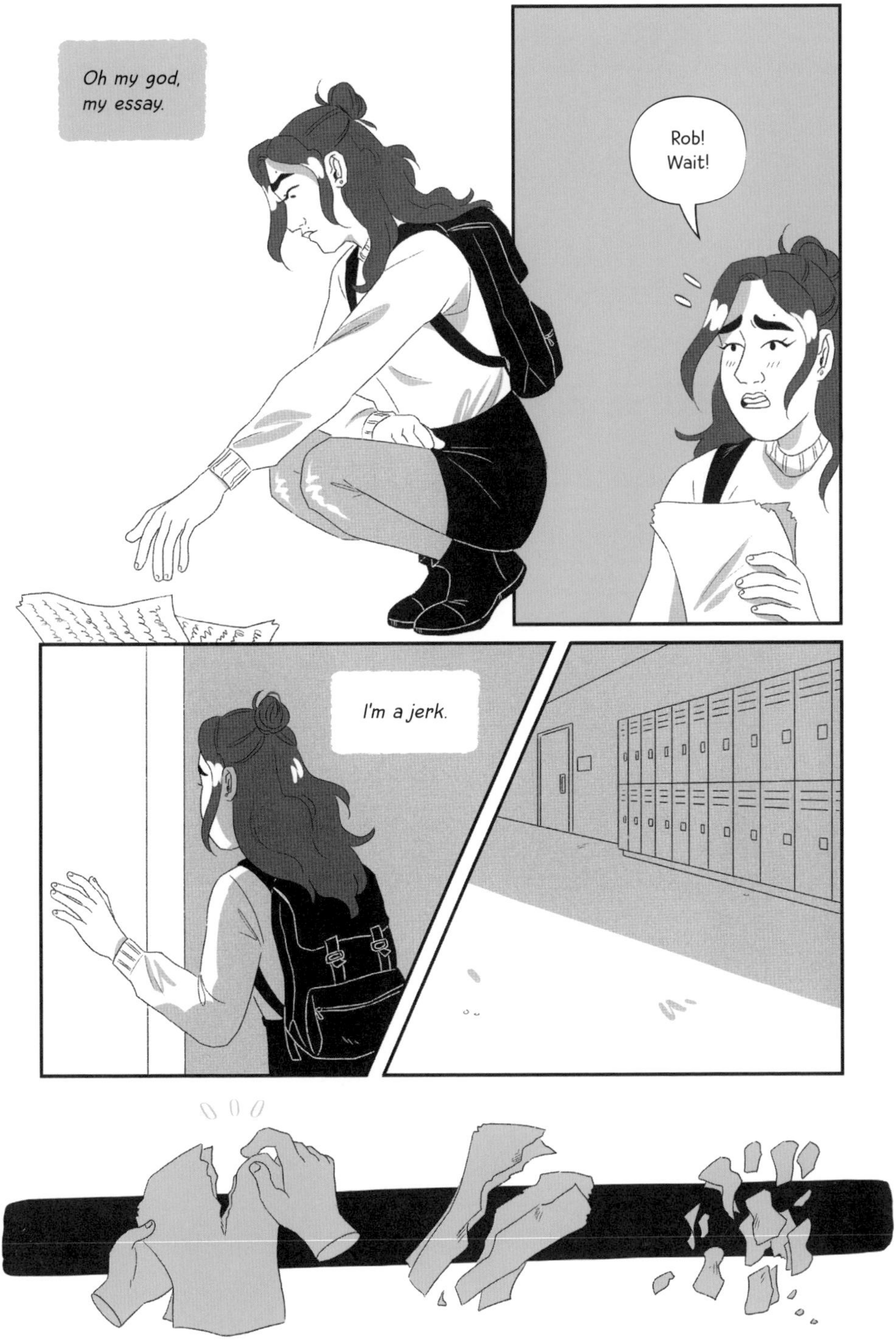
Oh my god, my essay.
Rob! Wait!
I'm a jerk.

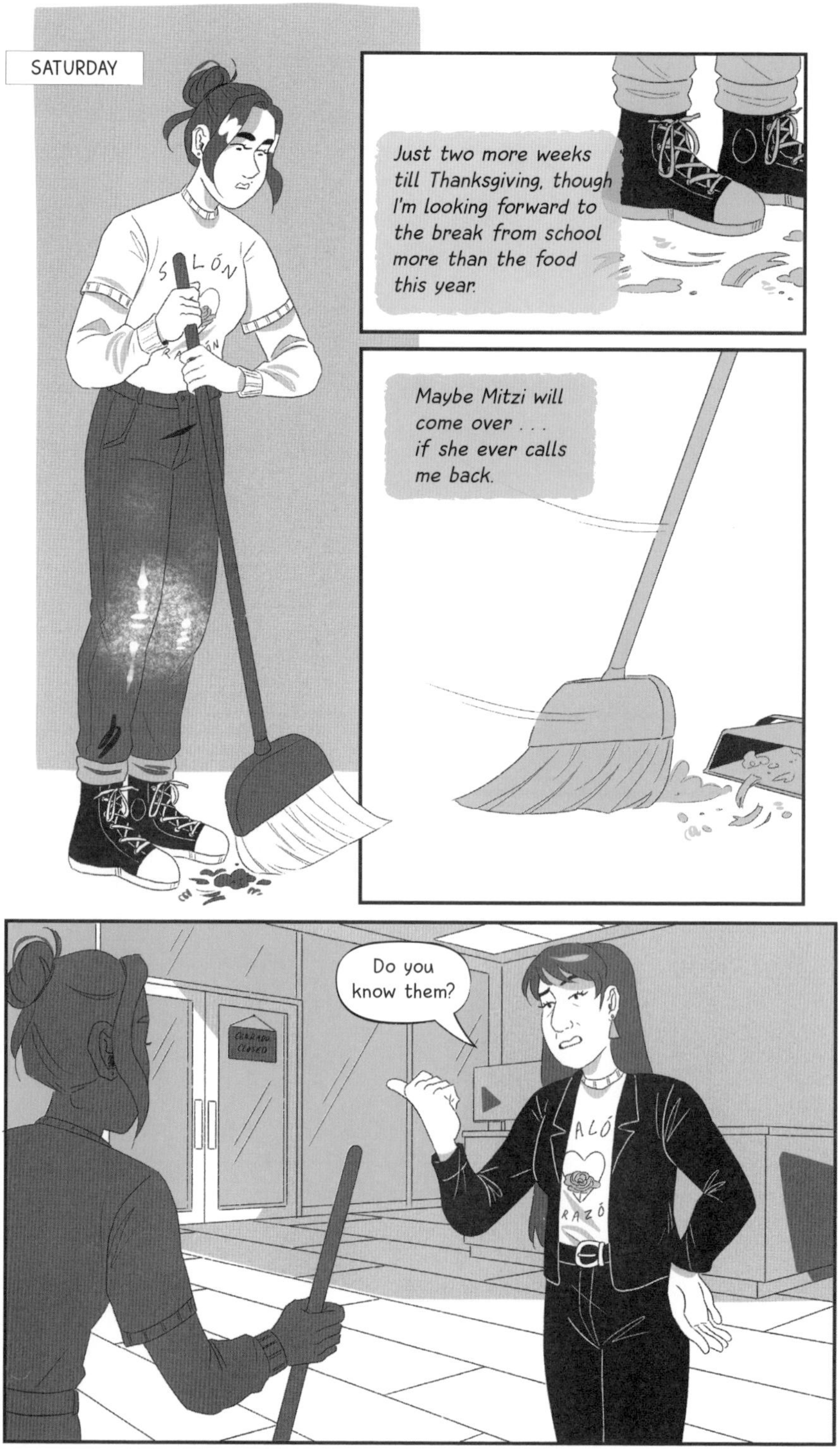

SATURDAY
Just two more weeks till Thanksgiving, though I'm looking forward to the break from school more than the food this year.
Maybe Mitzi will come over . . . if she ever calls me back.
Do you know them?
CLOSED

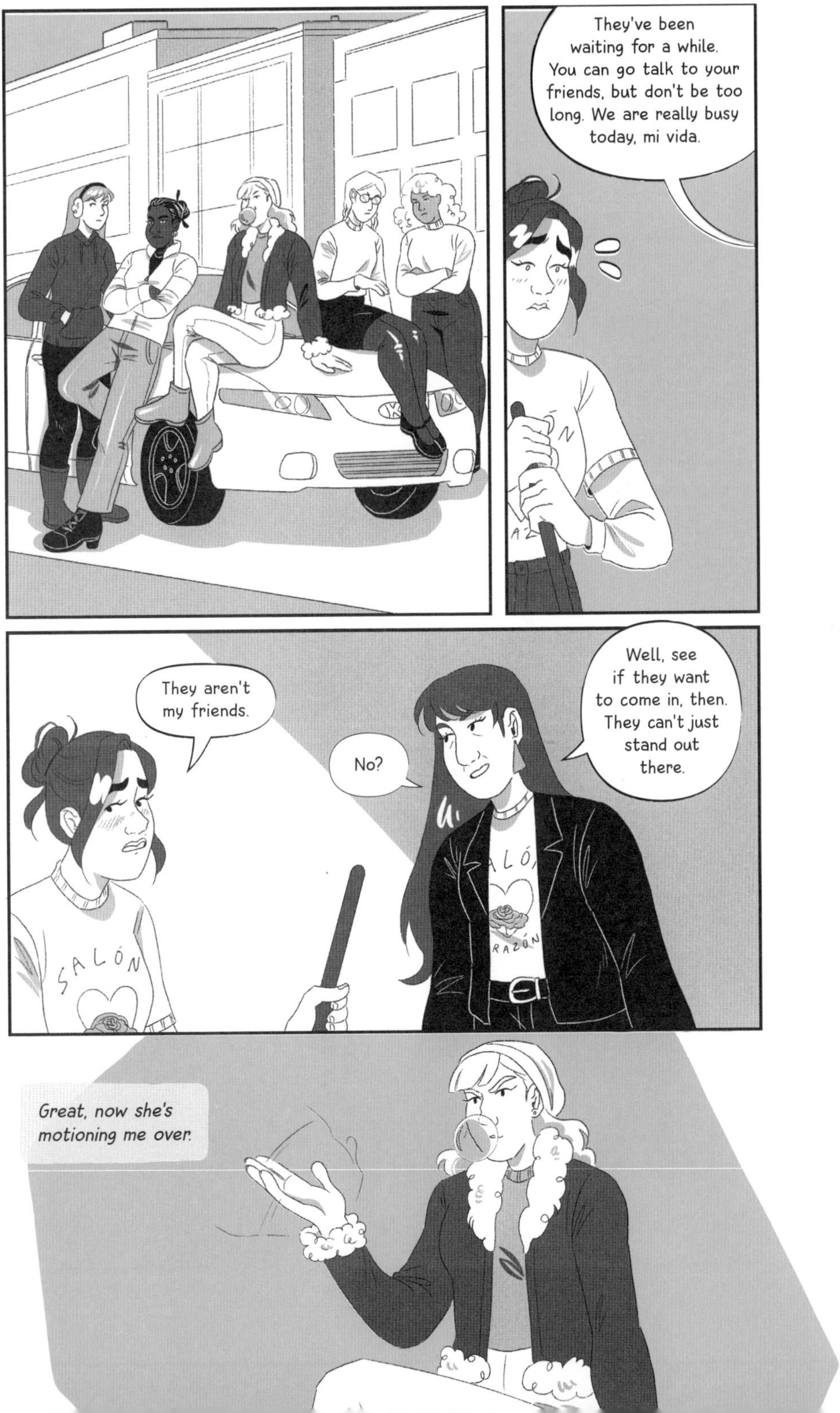
They've been waiting for a while. You can go talk to your friends, but don't be too long. We are really busy today, mi vida.
They aren't my friends.
No?
Well, see if they want to come in, then. They can't just stand out there.
Great, now she's motioning me over.

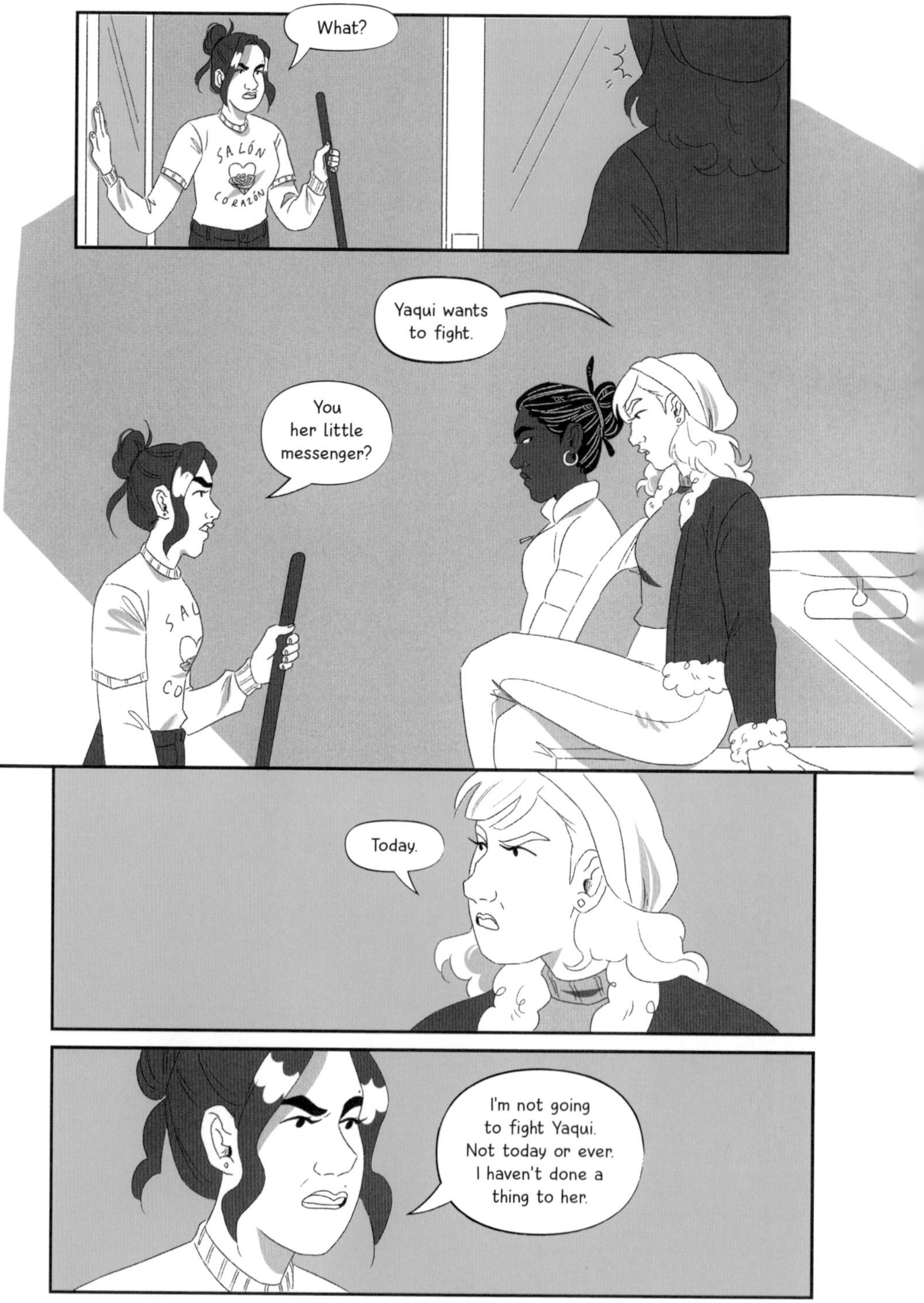
What?
Yaqui wants to fight.
You her little messenger?
Today.
I'm not going to fight Yaqui. Not today or ever. I haven't done a thing to her.

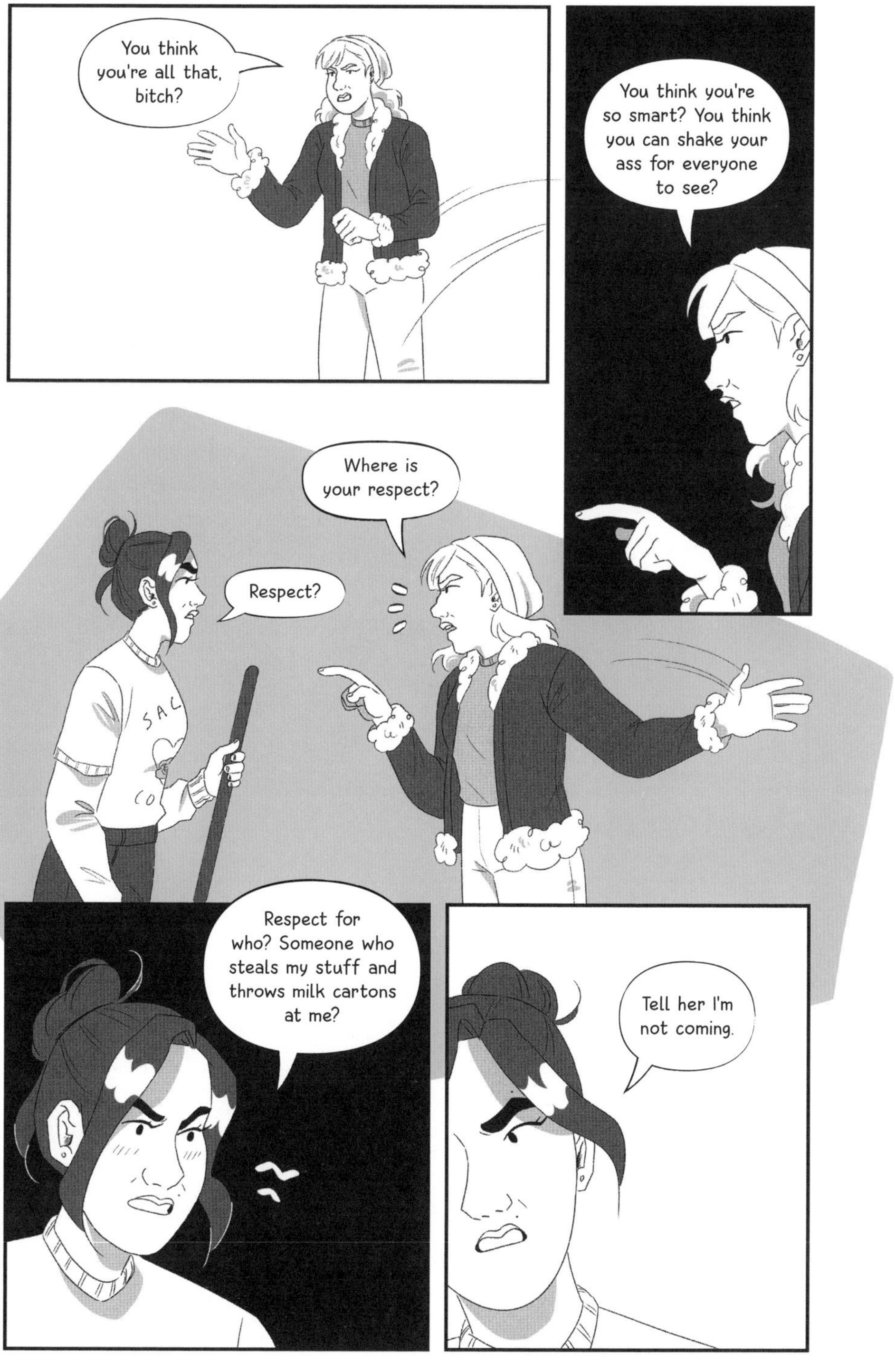
You think you're all that, bitch?
You think you're so smart? You think you can shake your ass for everyone to see?
Where is your respect?
Respect?
Respect for who? Someone who steals my stuff and throws milk cartons at me?
Tell her I'm not coming.

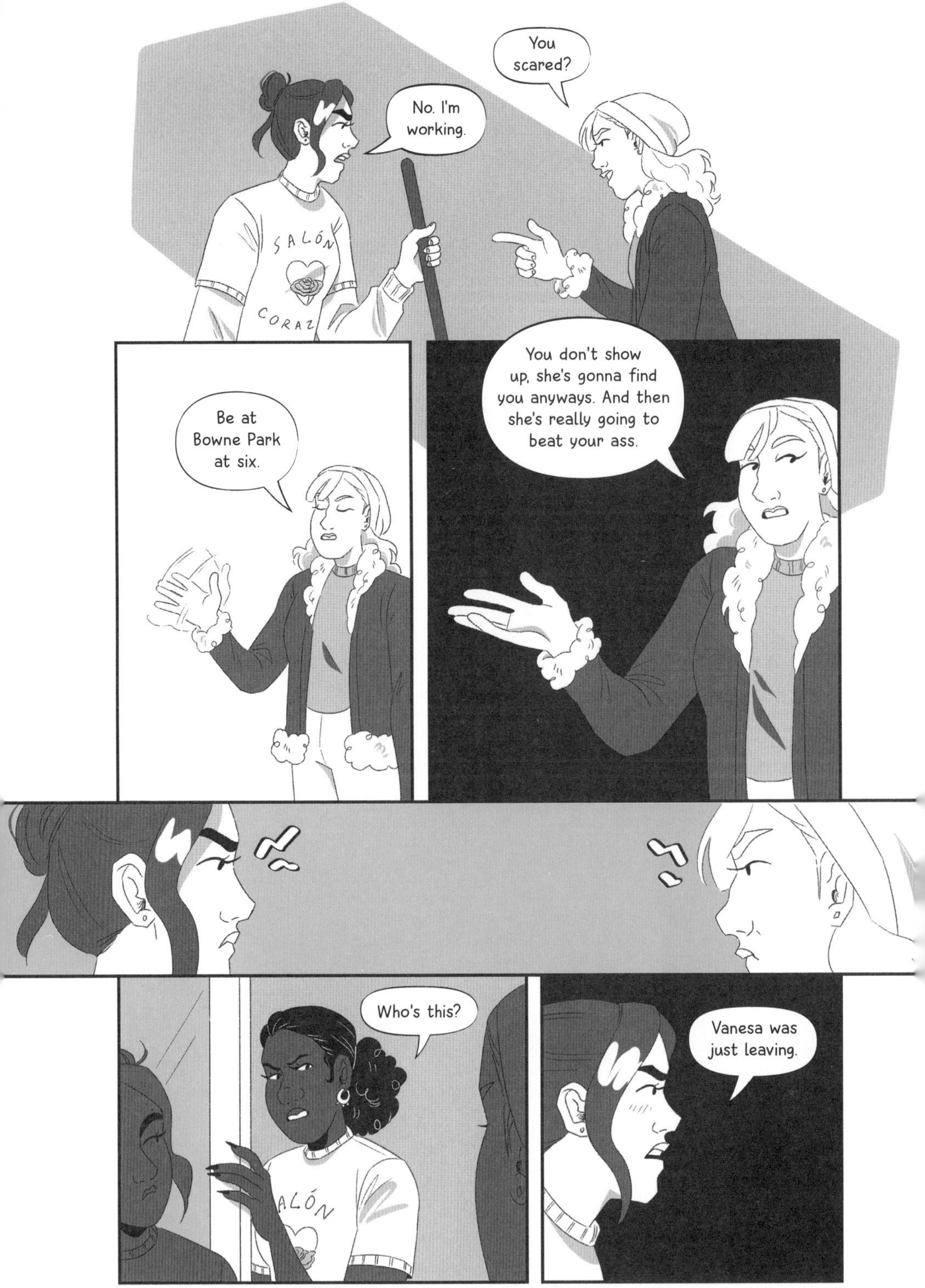
You scared?
No. I'm working.
SALÓN CORAZ
Be at Bowne Park at six.
You don't show up, she's gonna find you anyways. And then she's really going to beat your ass.
Who's this?
ALÓN
Vanesa was just leaving.

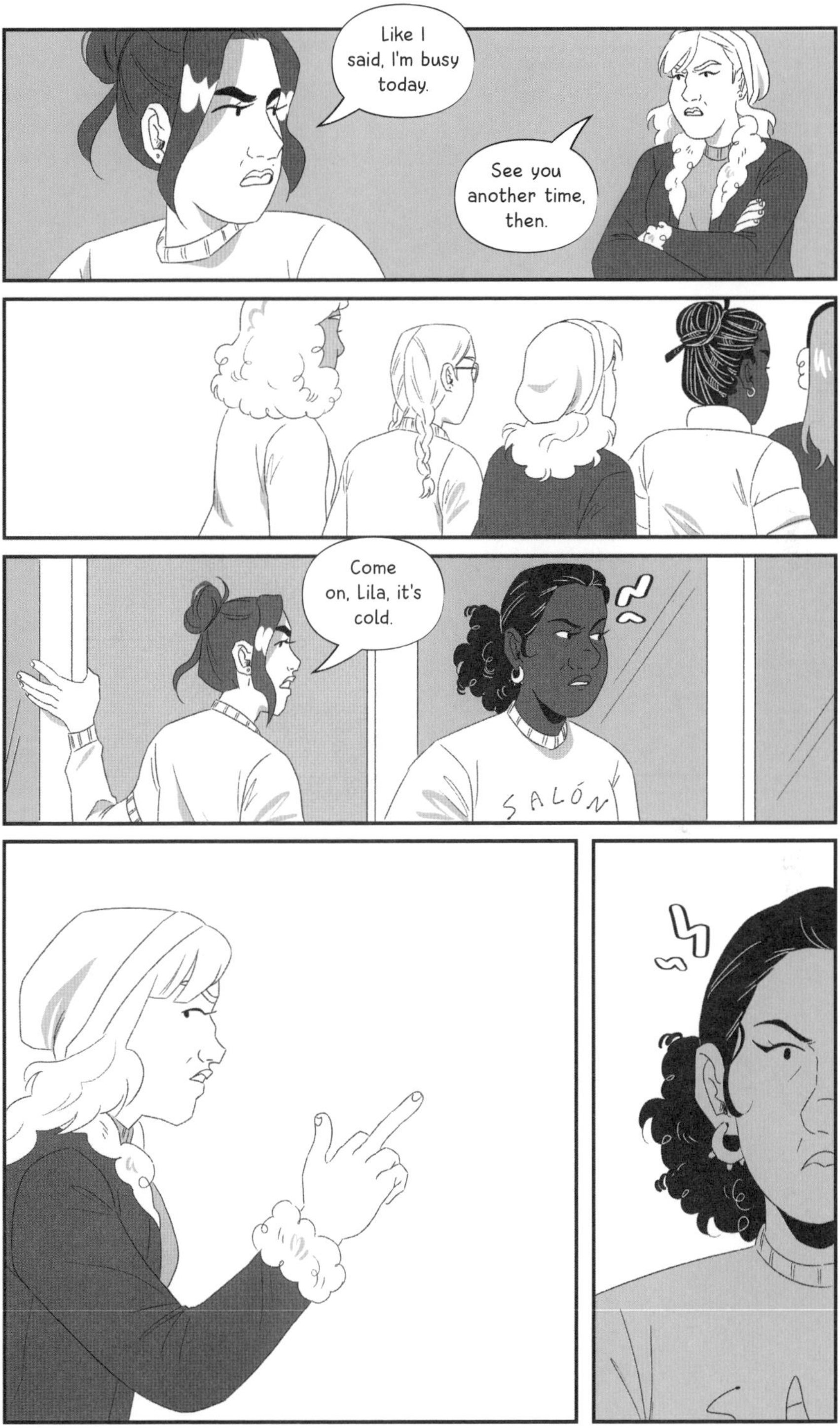
Like I said, I'm busy today.
See you another time, then.
Come on, Lila, it's cold.
SALÓN

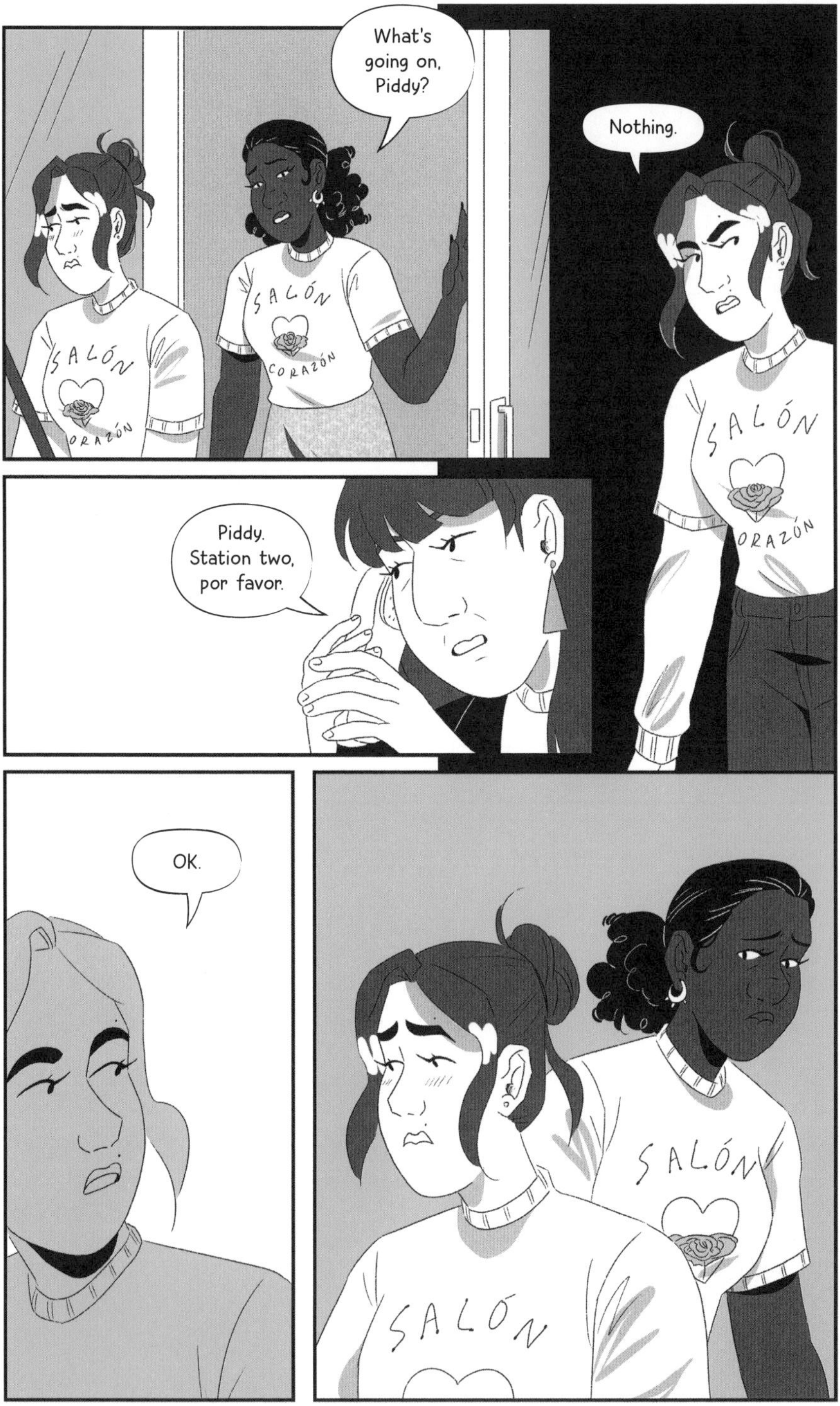

What's going on, Piddy?
Nothing.
Piddy. Station two, por favor.
OK.

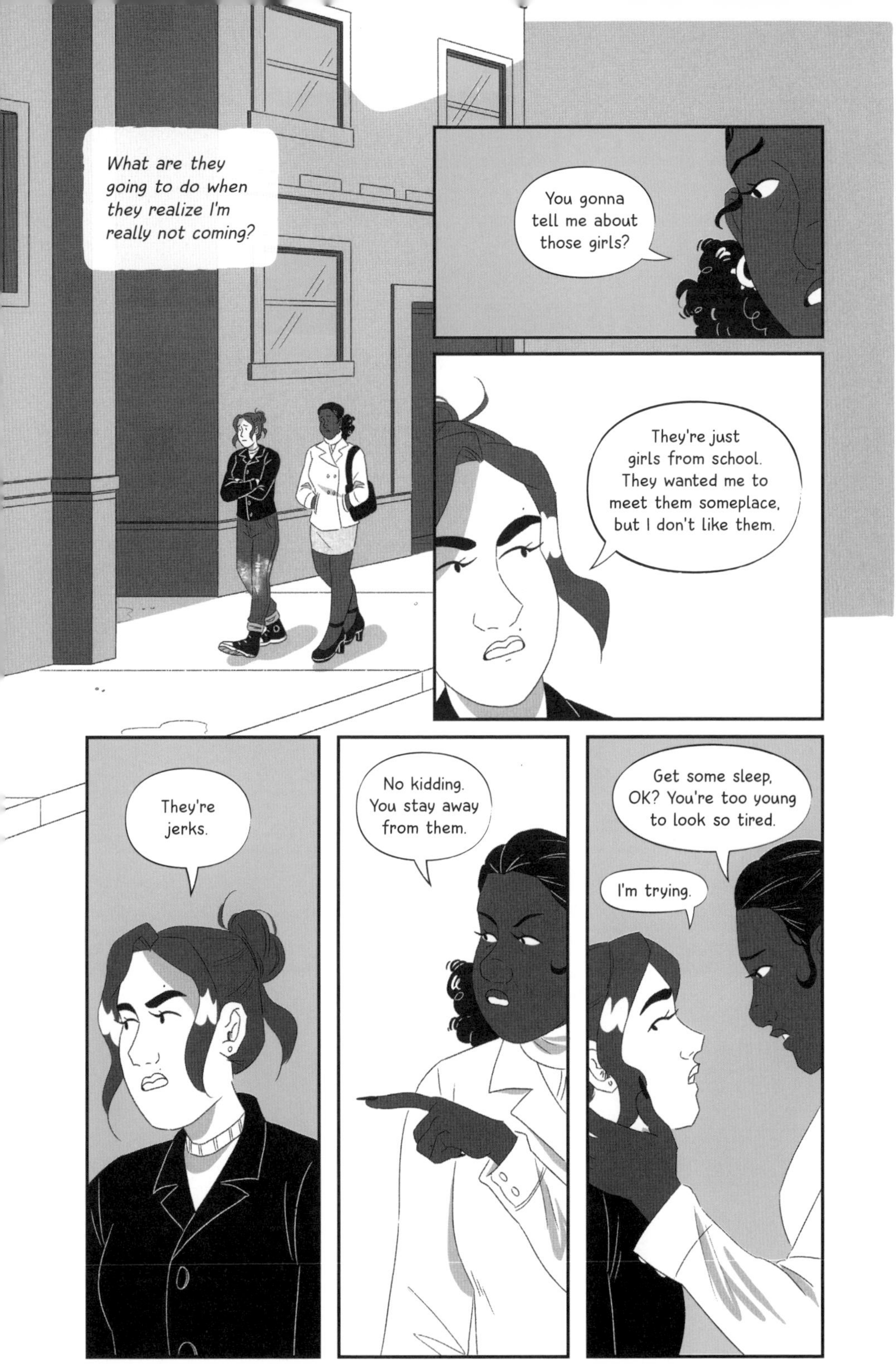
What are they going to do when they realize I'm really not coming?
You gonna tell me about those girls?
They're just girls from school. They wanted me to meet them someplace, but I don't like them.
They're jerks.
No kidding. You stay away from them.
Get some sleep, OK? You're too young to look so tired.
I'm trying.

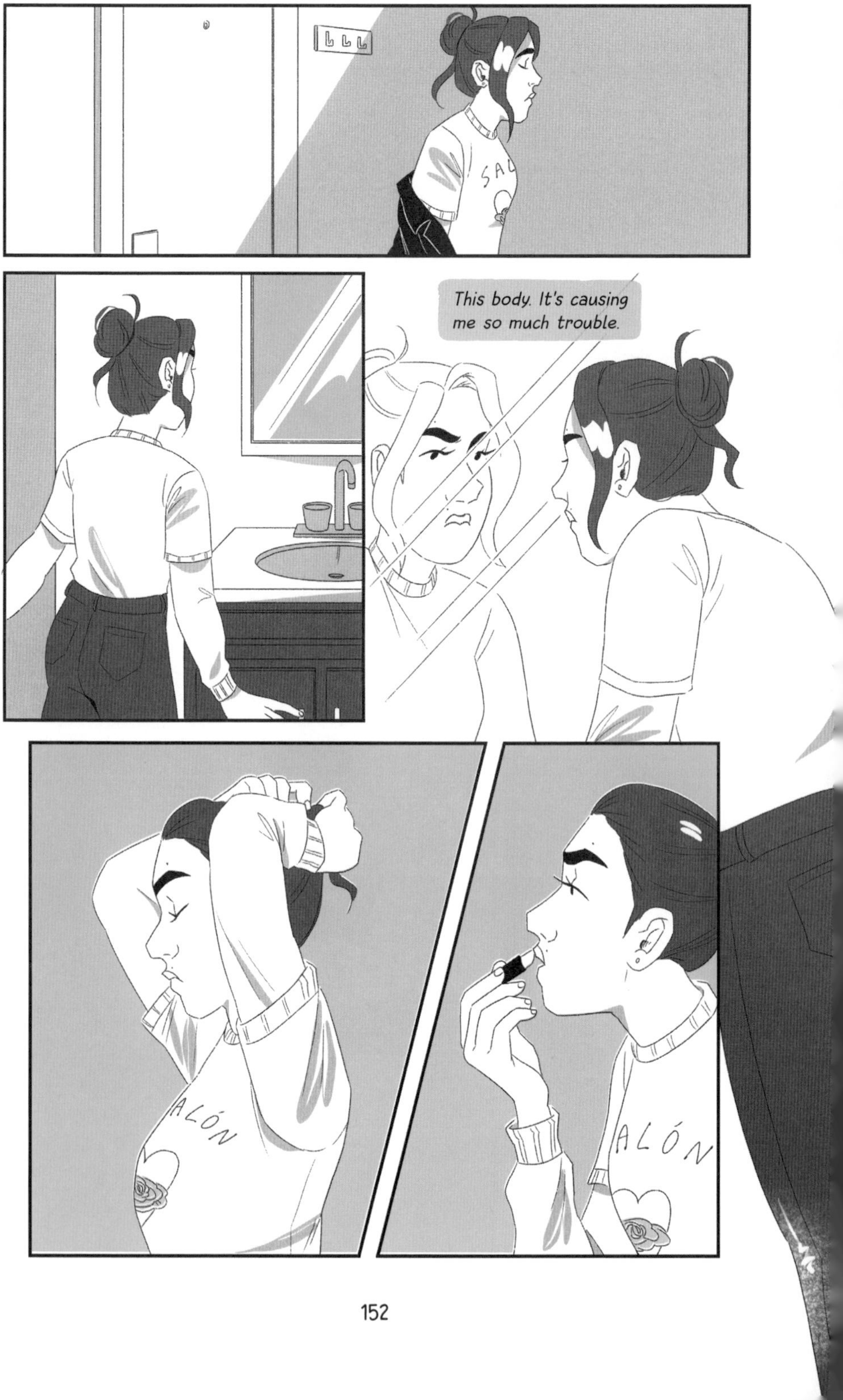
This body. It's causing me so much trouble.
SAL
ALÓN
ALÓN

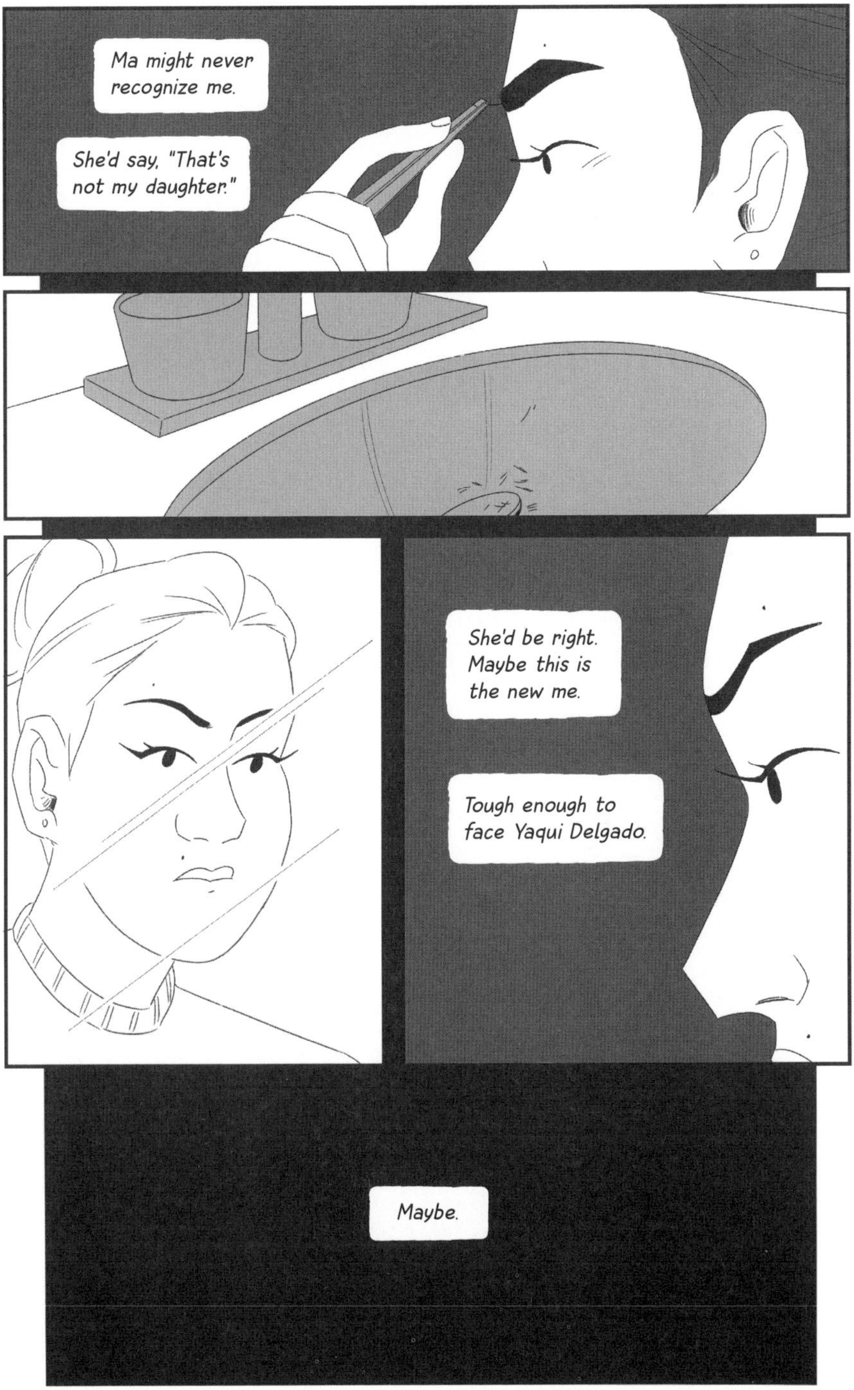
Ma might never recognize me.
She'd say, "That's not my daughter."
She'd be right. Maybe this is the new me.
Tough enough to face Yaqui Delgado.
Maybe.

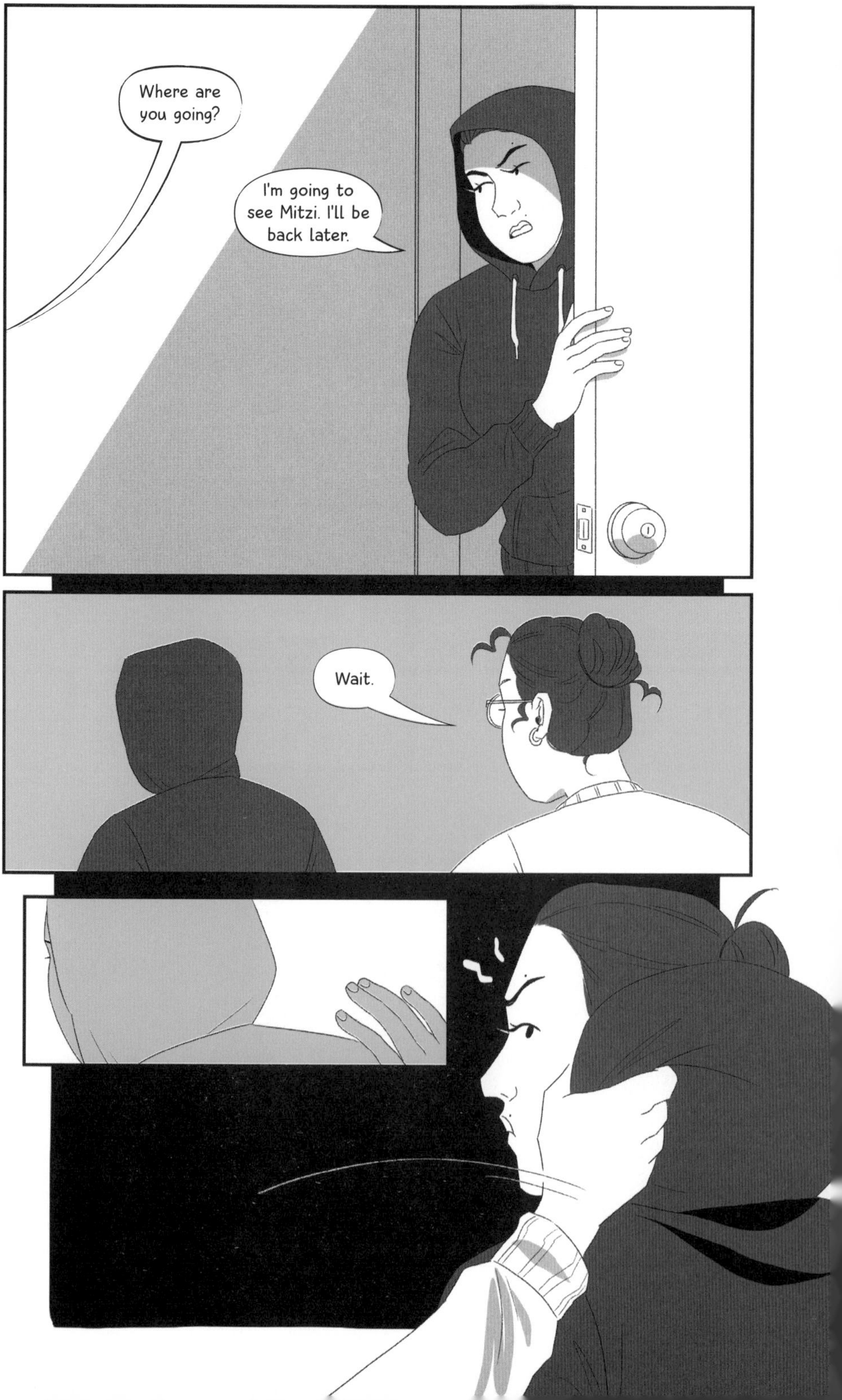
Where are you going?
I'm going to see Mitzi. I'll be back later.
Wait.

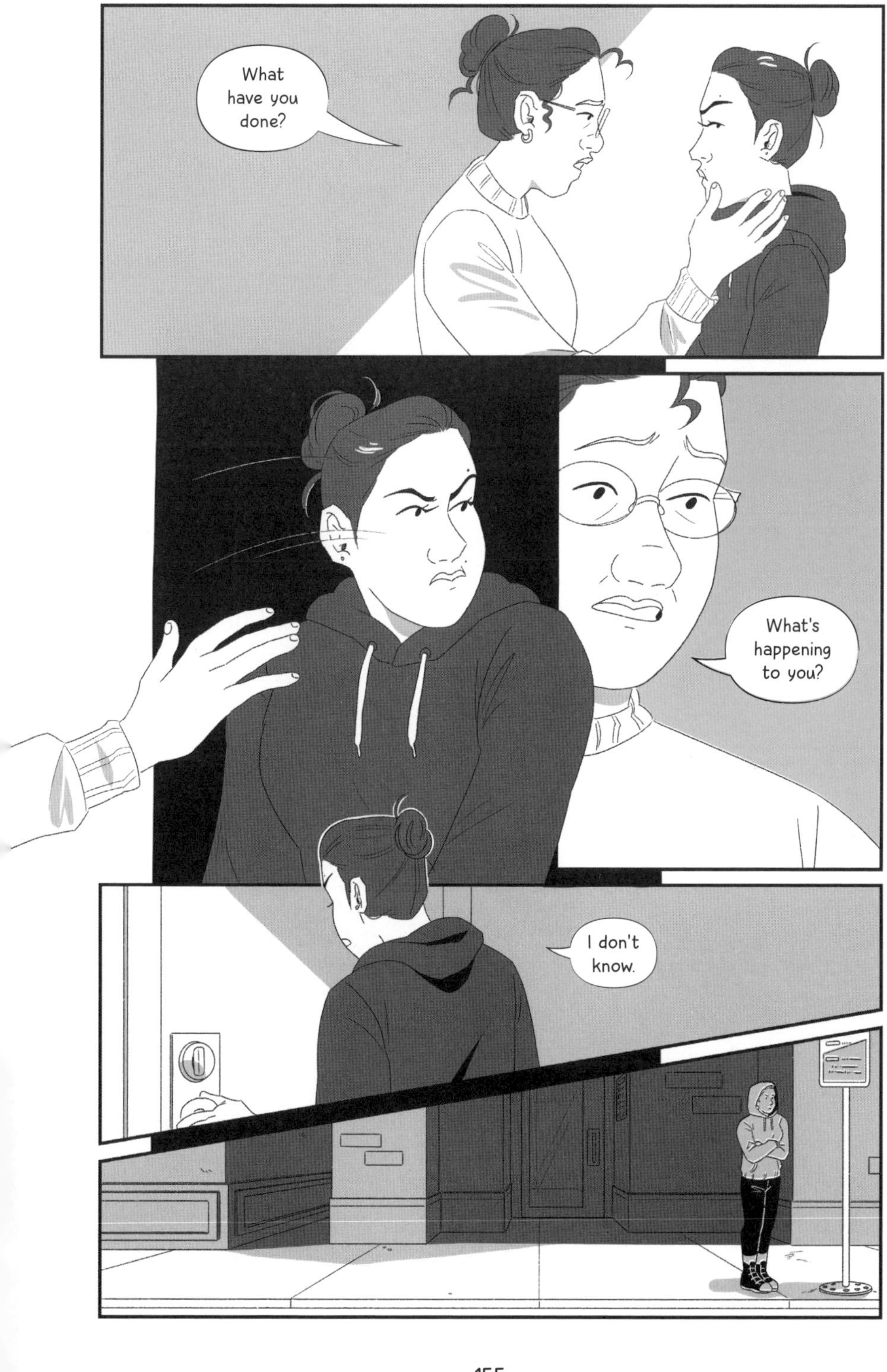

What have you done?
What's happening to you?
I don't know.

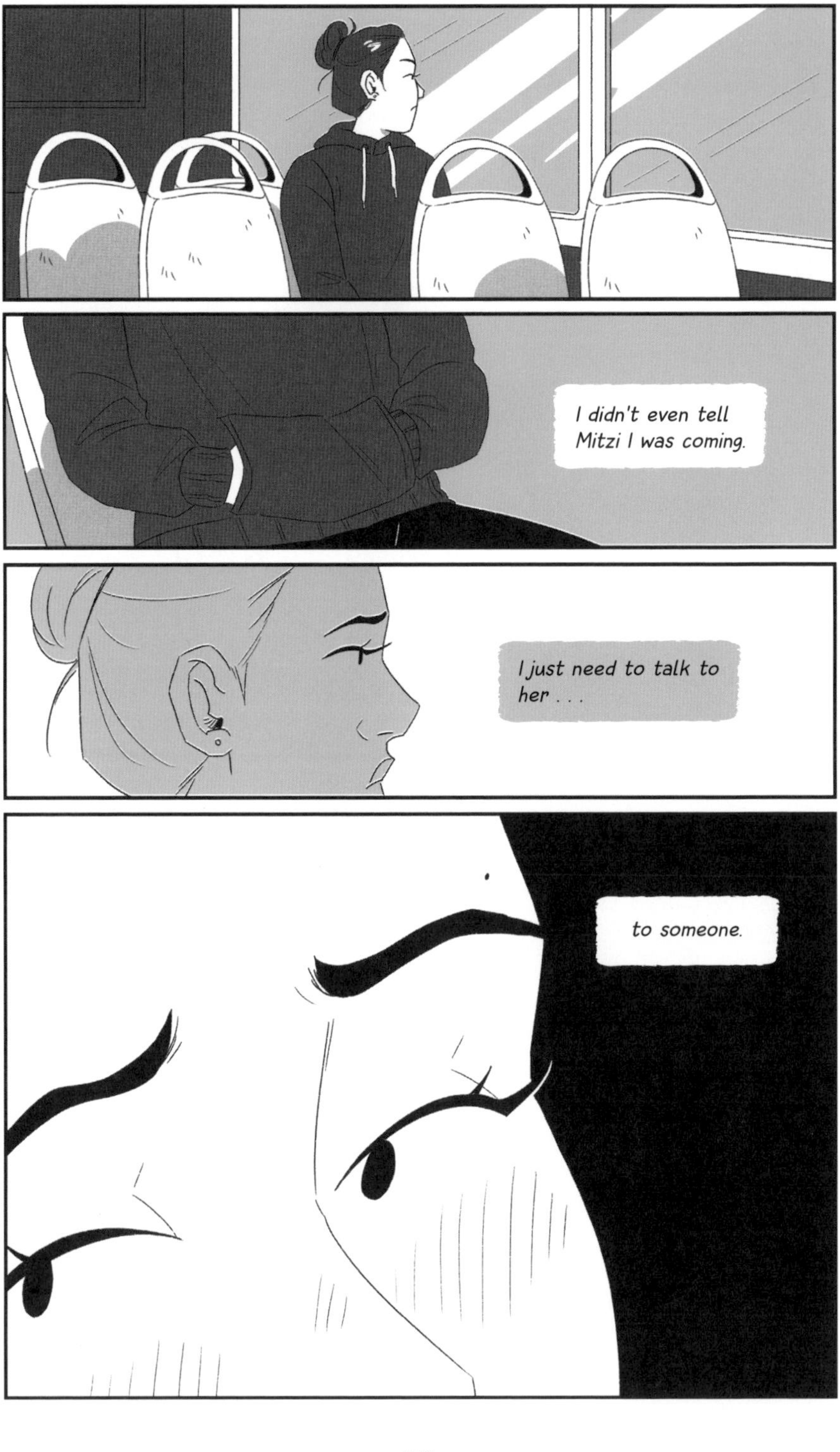

I didn't even tell Mitzi I was coming.
I just need to talk to her . . .
to someone.

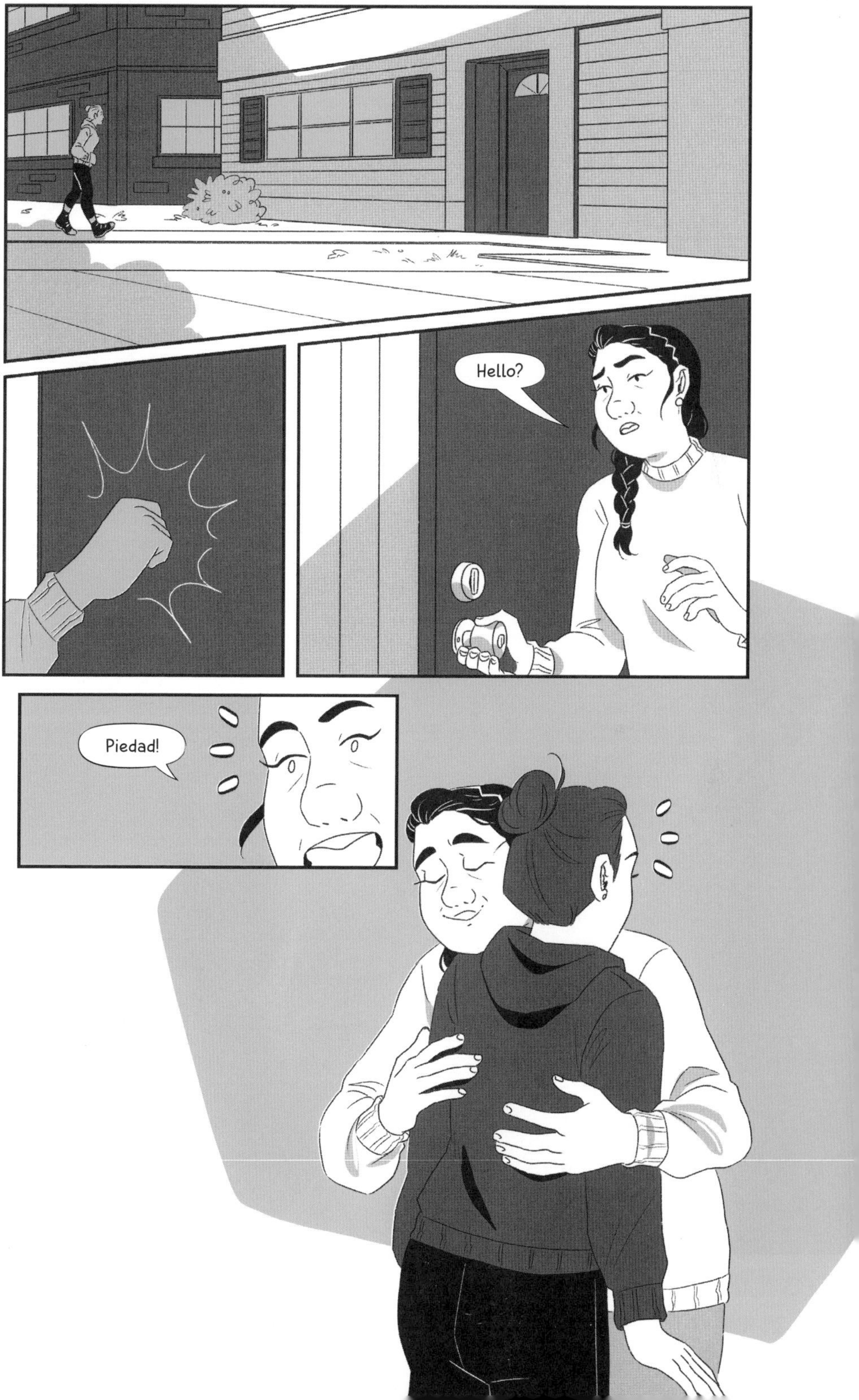
Hello?
Piedad!

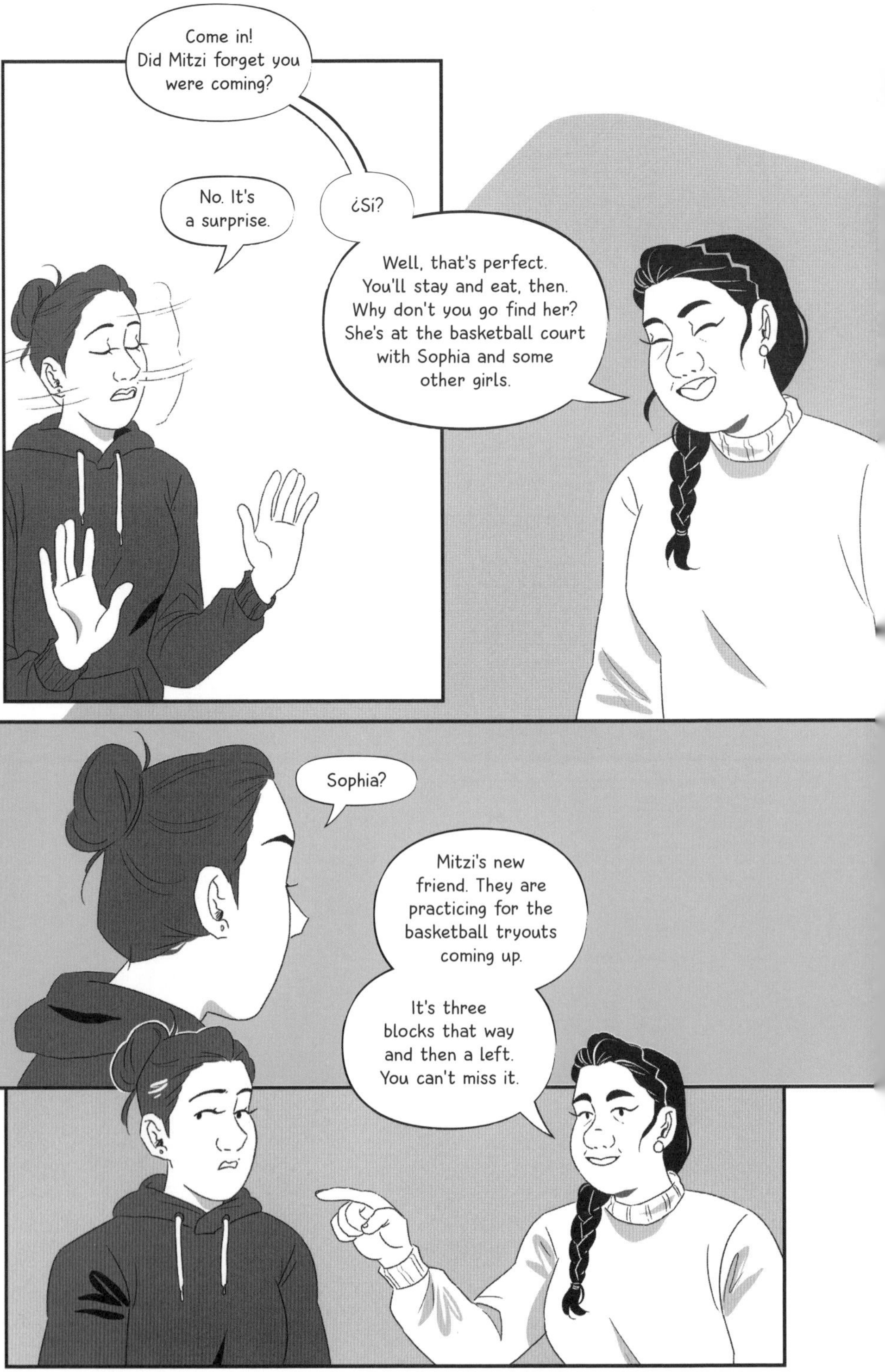
Come in! Did Mitzi forget you were coming?
No. It's a surprise.
¿Sí?
Well, that's perfect. You'll stay and eat, then. Why don't you go find her? She's at the basketball court with Sophia and some other girls.
Sophia?
Mitzi's new friend. They are practicing for the basketball tryouts coming up.
It's three blocks that way and then a left. You can't miss it.

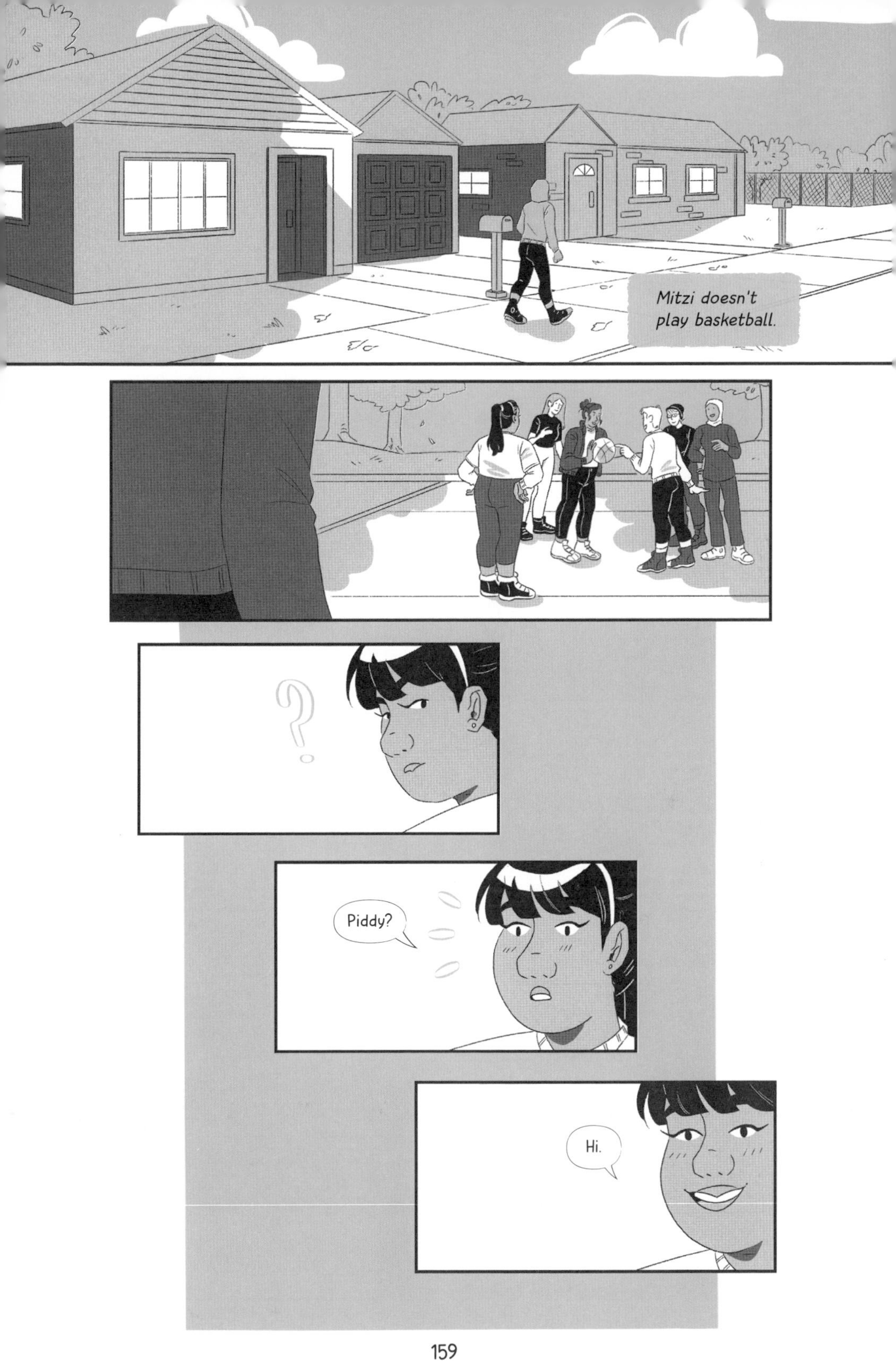
Mitzi doesn't play basketball.
Piddy?
Hi.

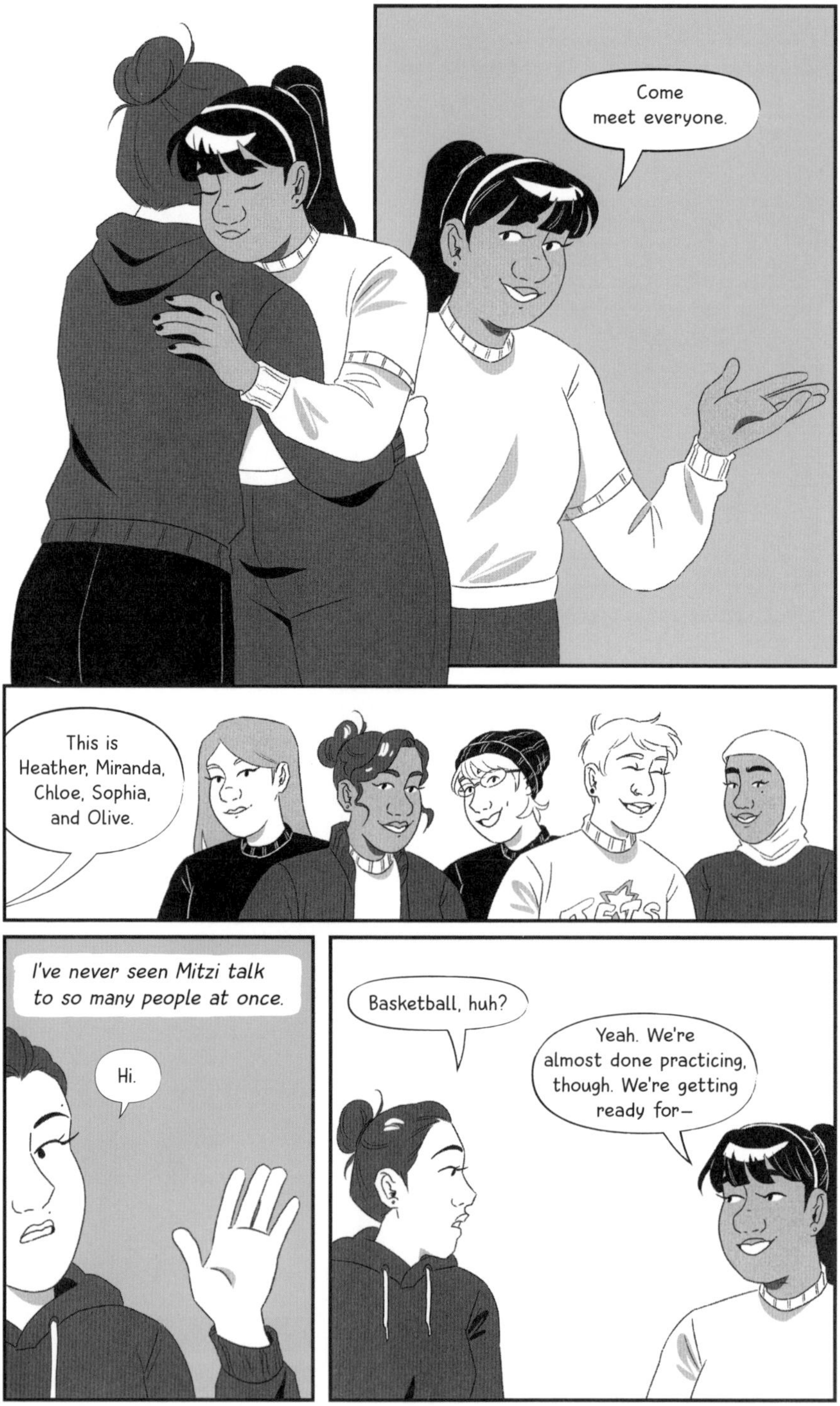
Come meet everyone.
This is Heather, Miranda, Chloe, Sophia, and Olive.
I've never seen Mitzi talk to so many people at once.
Hi.
Basketball, huh?
Yeah. We're almost done practicing, though. We're getting ready for—

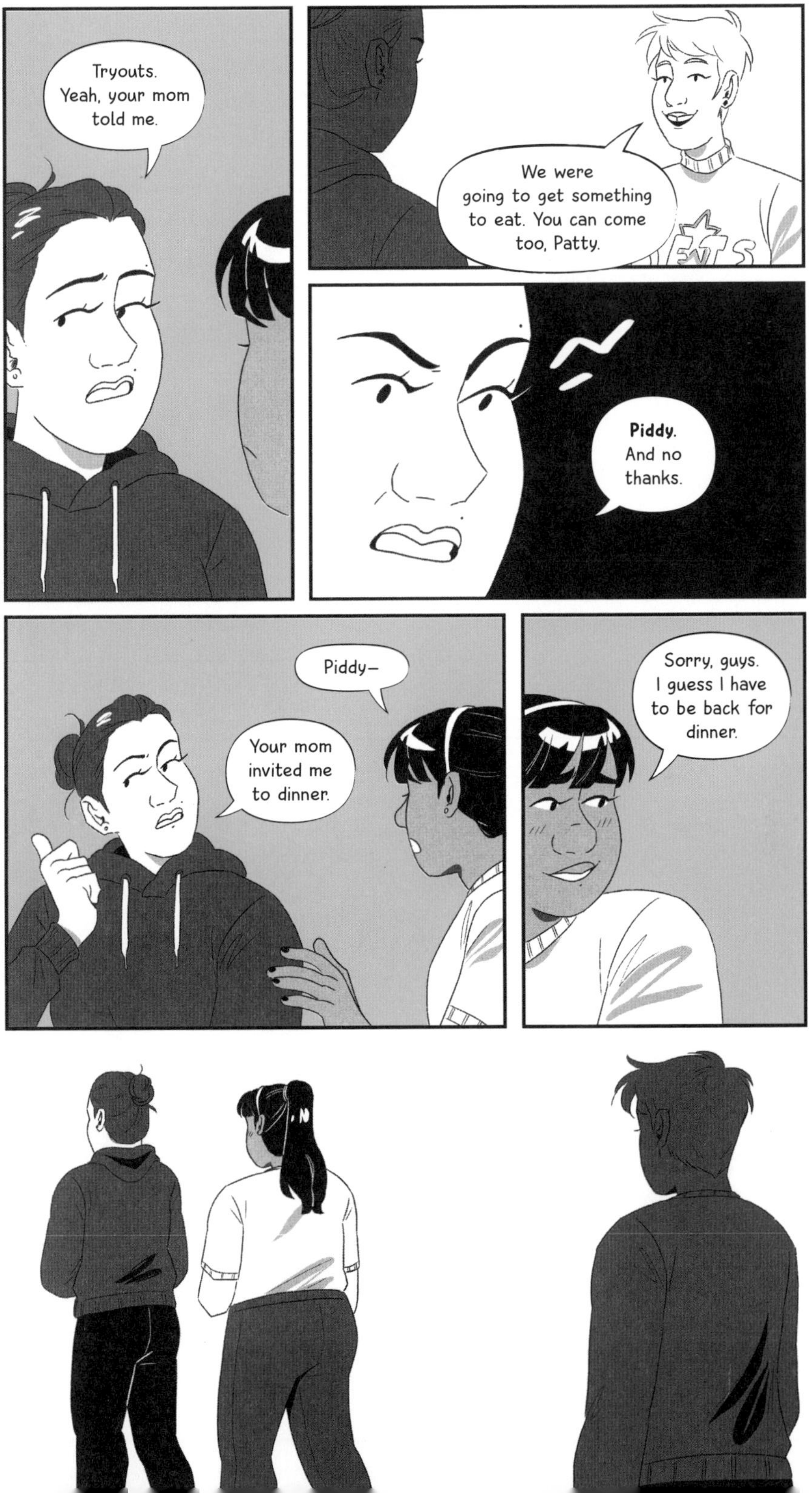
Tryouts. Yeah, your mom told me.
We were going to get something to eat. You can come too, Patty.
Piddy. And no thanks.
Piddy—
Your mom invited me to dinner.
Sorry, guys. I guess I have to be back for dinner.

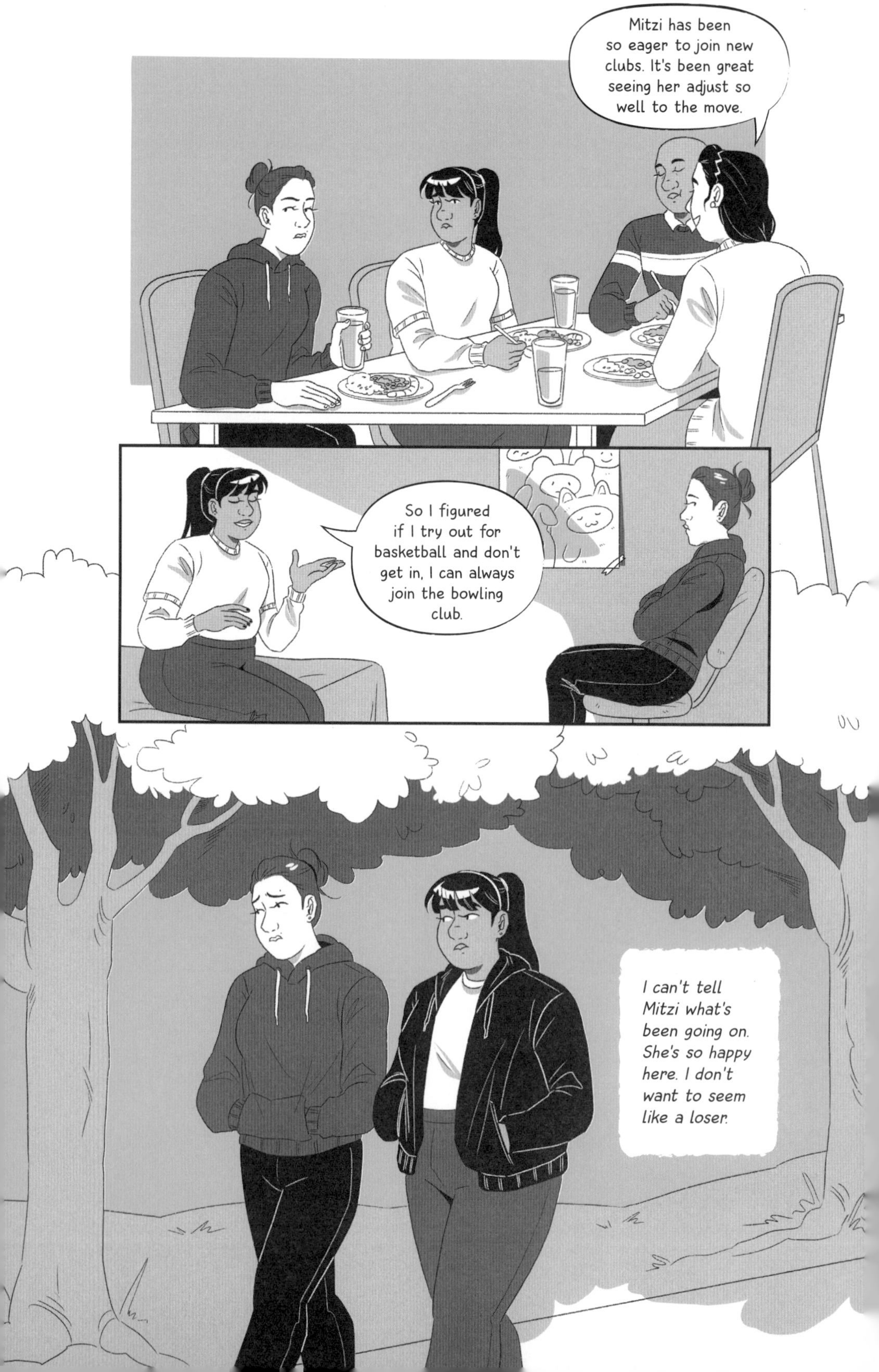
Mitzi has been so eager to join new clubs. It's been great seeing her adjust so well to the move.
So I figured if I try out for basketball and don't get in, I can always join the bowling club.
I can't tell Mitzi what's been going on. She's so happy here. I don't want to seem like a loser.

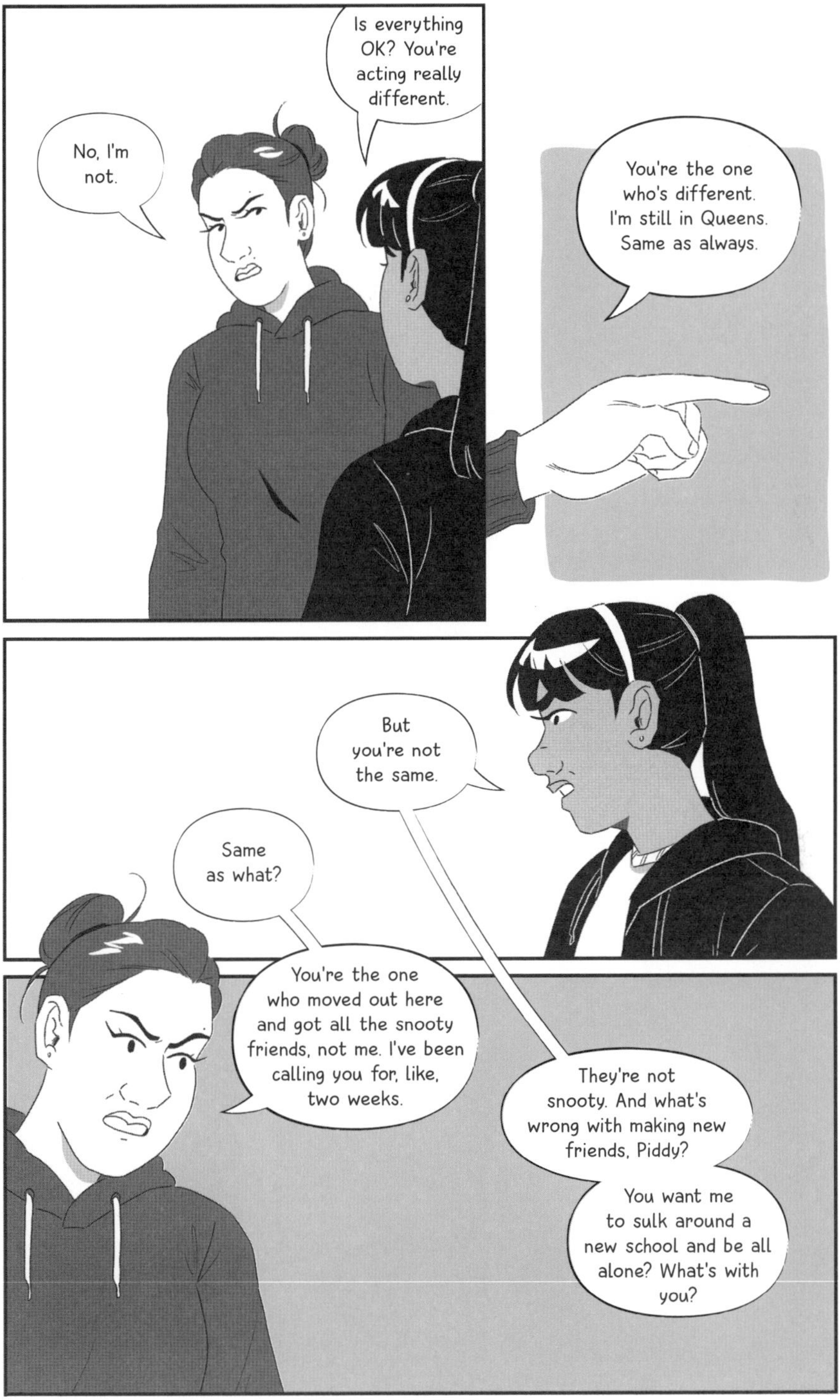
Is everything OK? You're acting really different.
No, I'm not.
You're the one who's different. I'm still in Queens. Same as always.
But you're not the same.
Same as what?
You're the one who moved out here and got all the snooty friends, not me. I've been calling you for, like, two weeks.
They're not snooty. And what's wrong with making new friends, Piddy?
You want me to sulk around a new school and be all alone? What's with you?

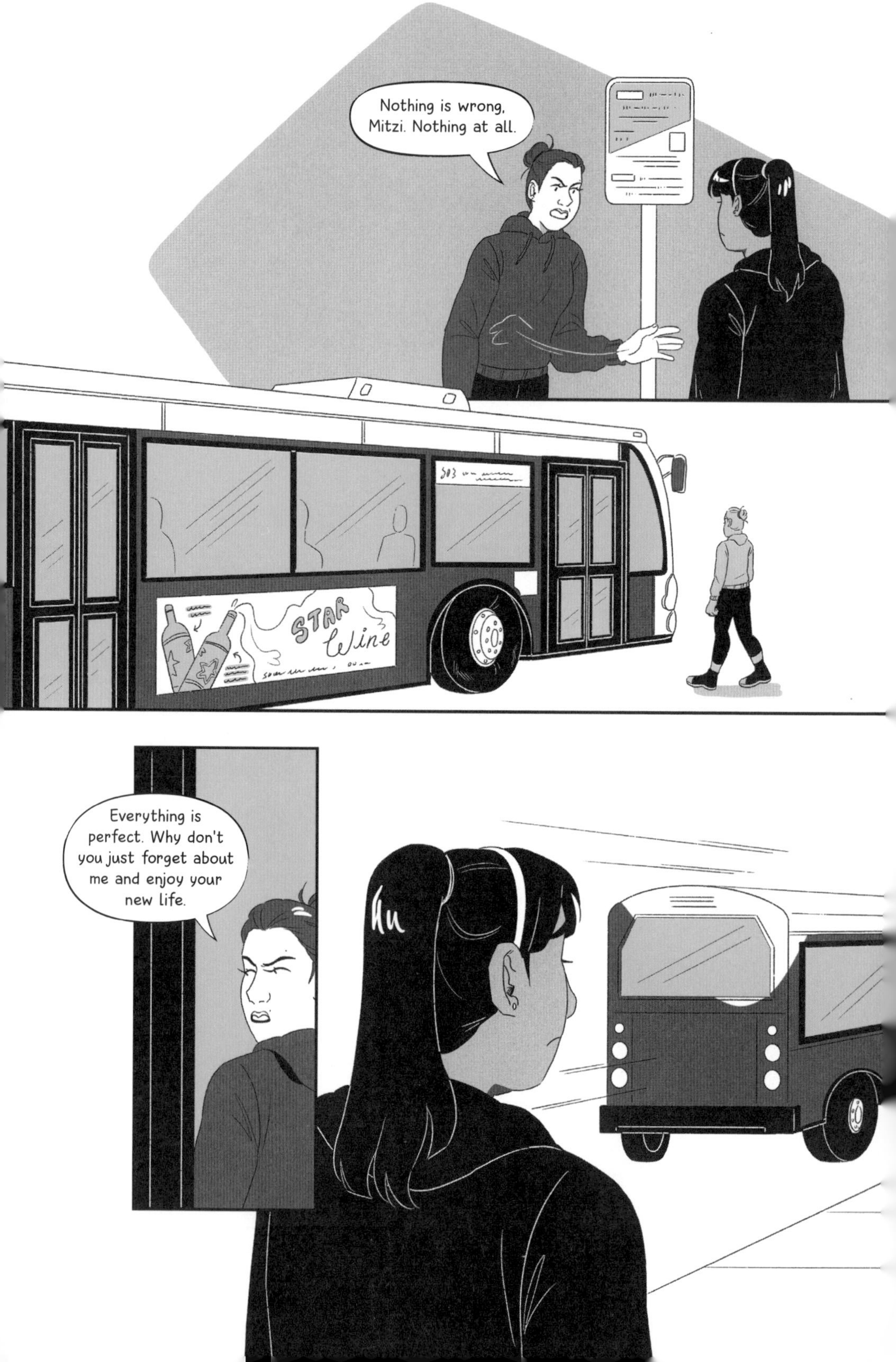
Nothing is wrong, Mitzi. Nothing at all.
STAR Wine
Everything is perfect. Why don't you just forget about me and enjoy your new life.

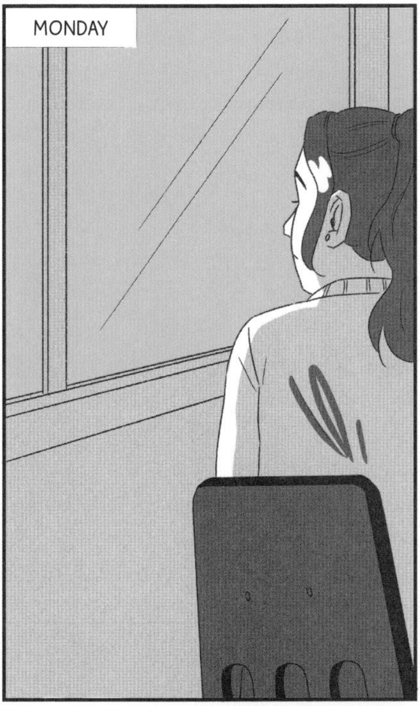
MONDAY

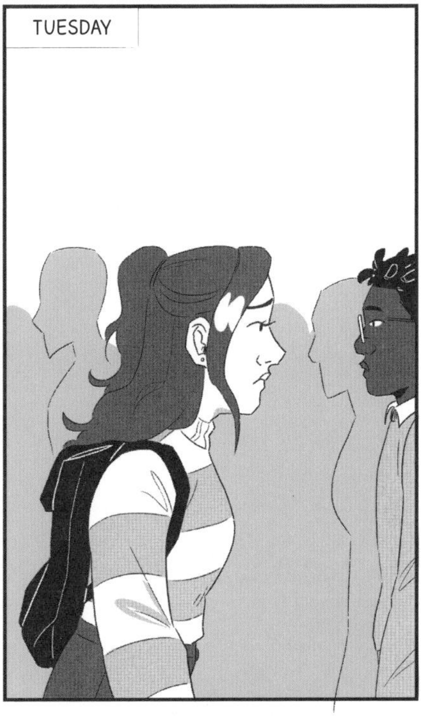
TUESDAY

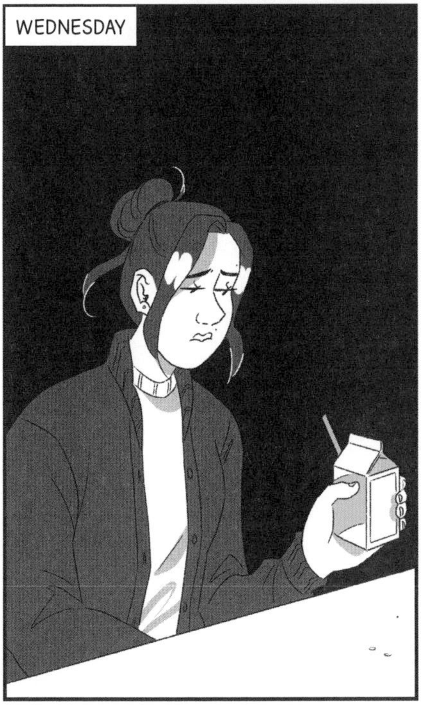
WEDNESDAY

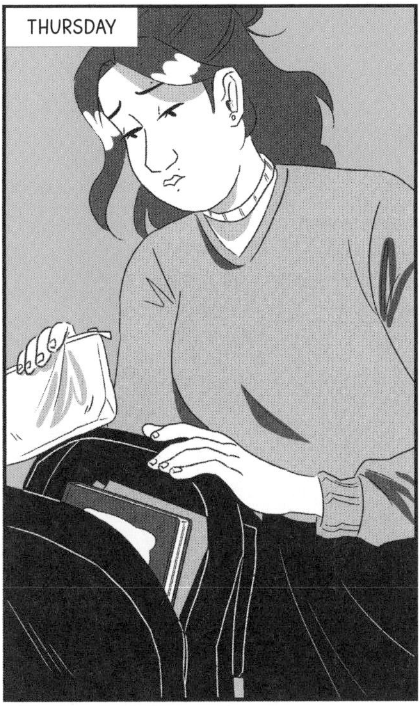
THURSDAY

FRIDAY

No one has messed with me all week.

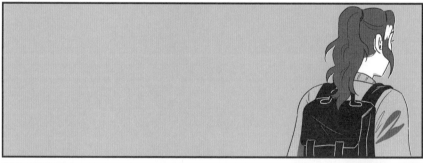

I knew it was too good to be true.

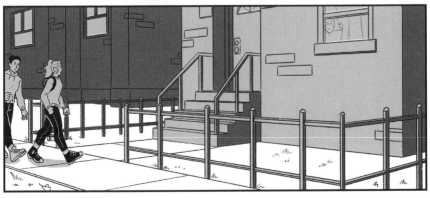

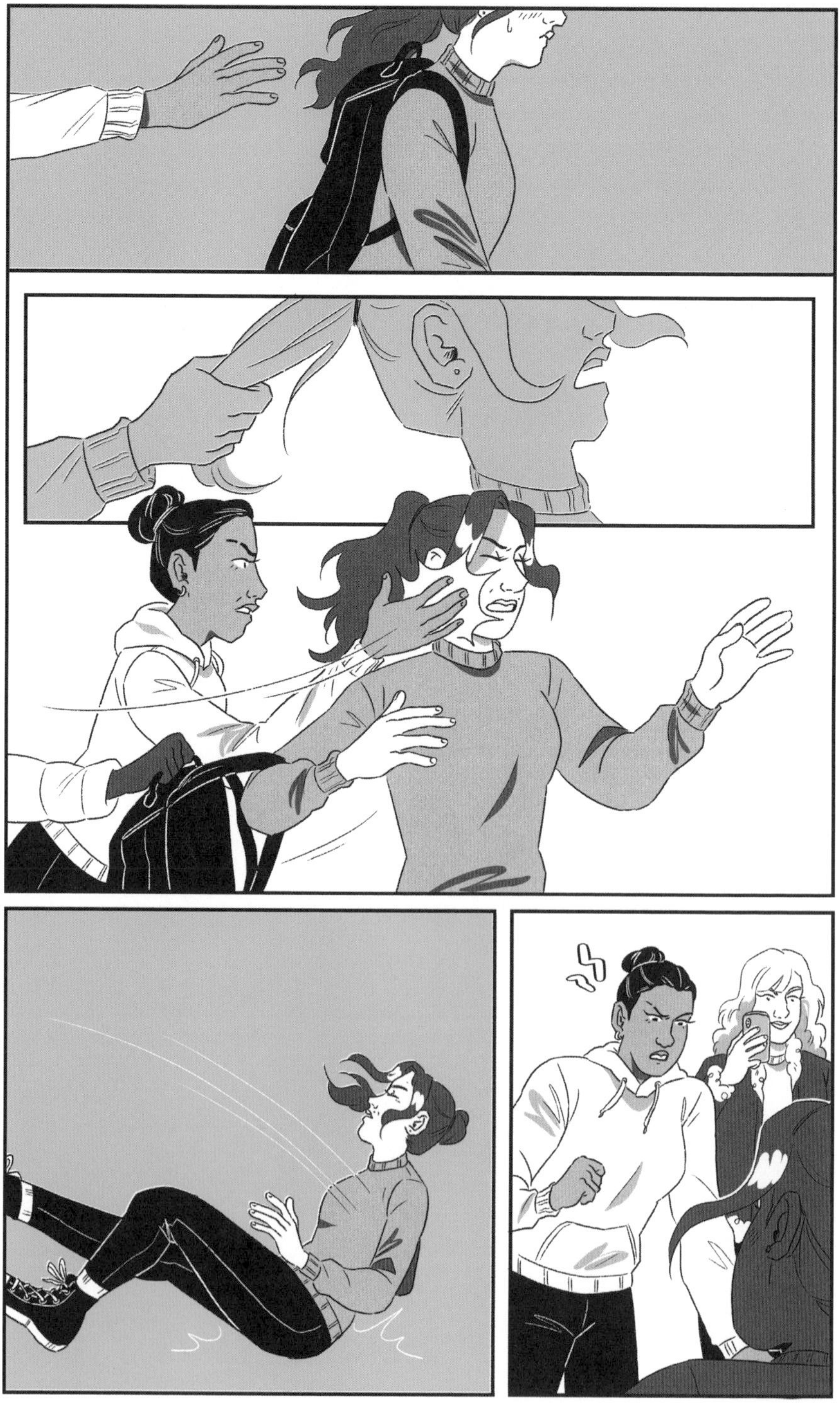

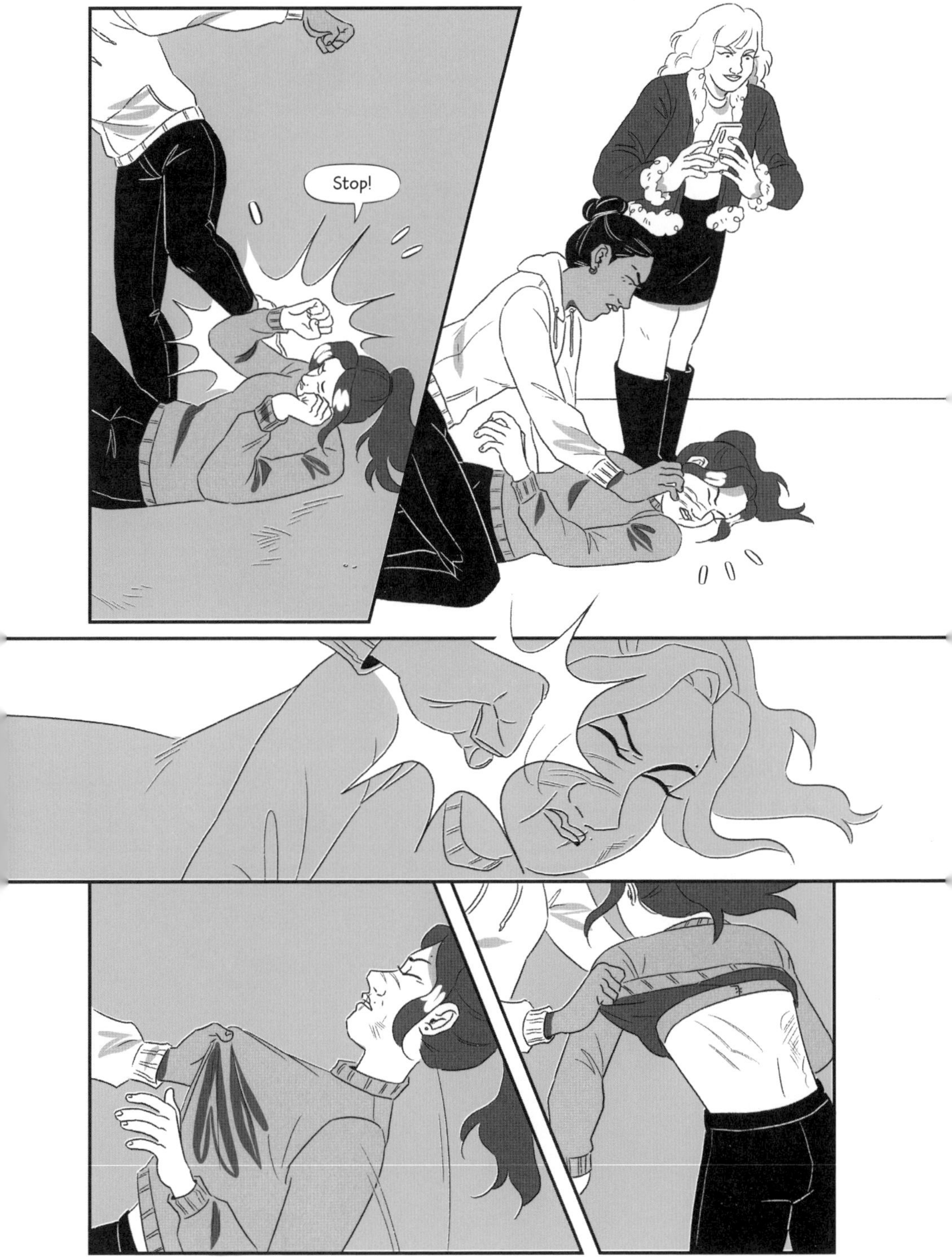
Stop!

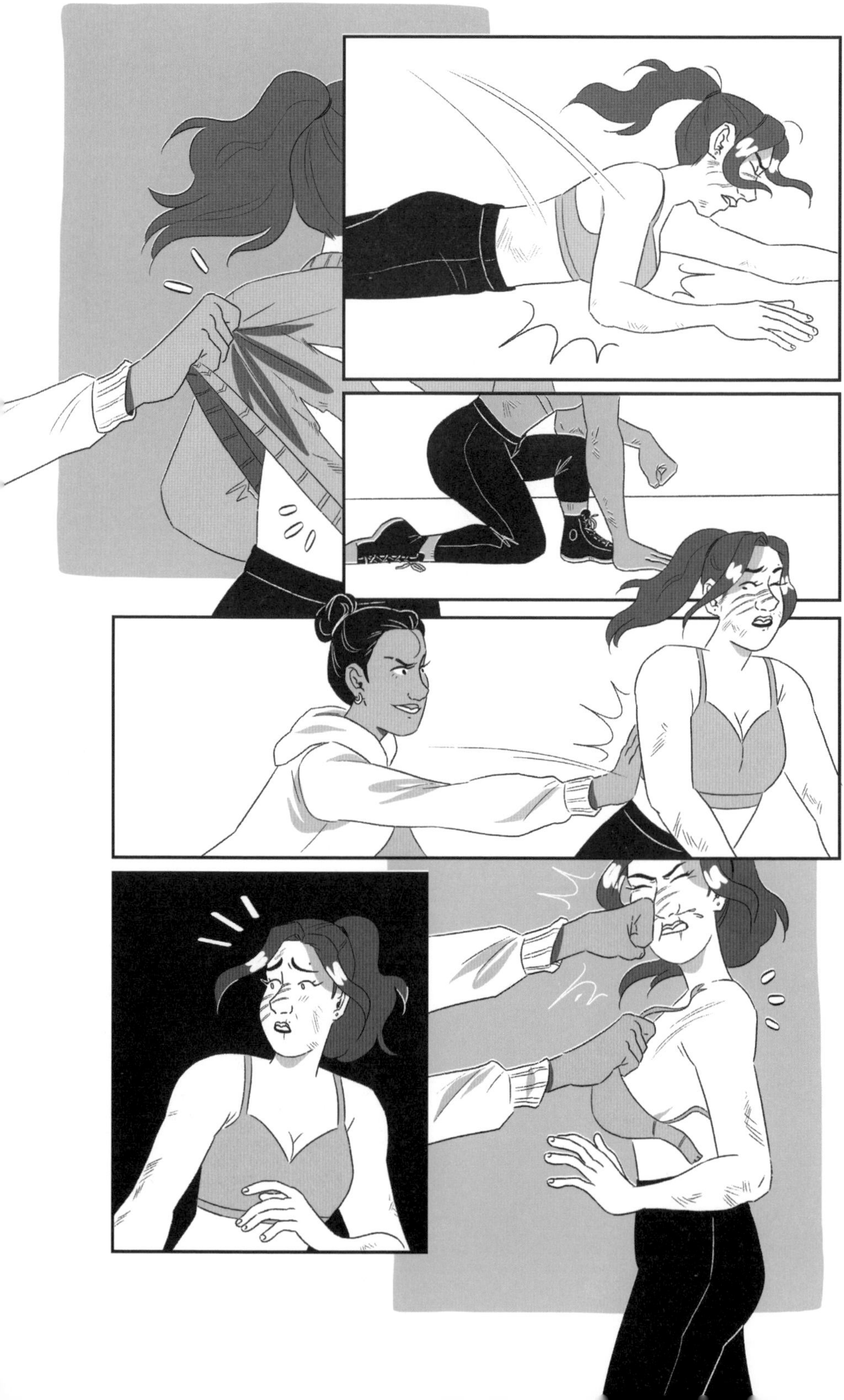

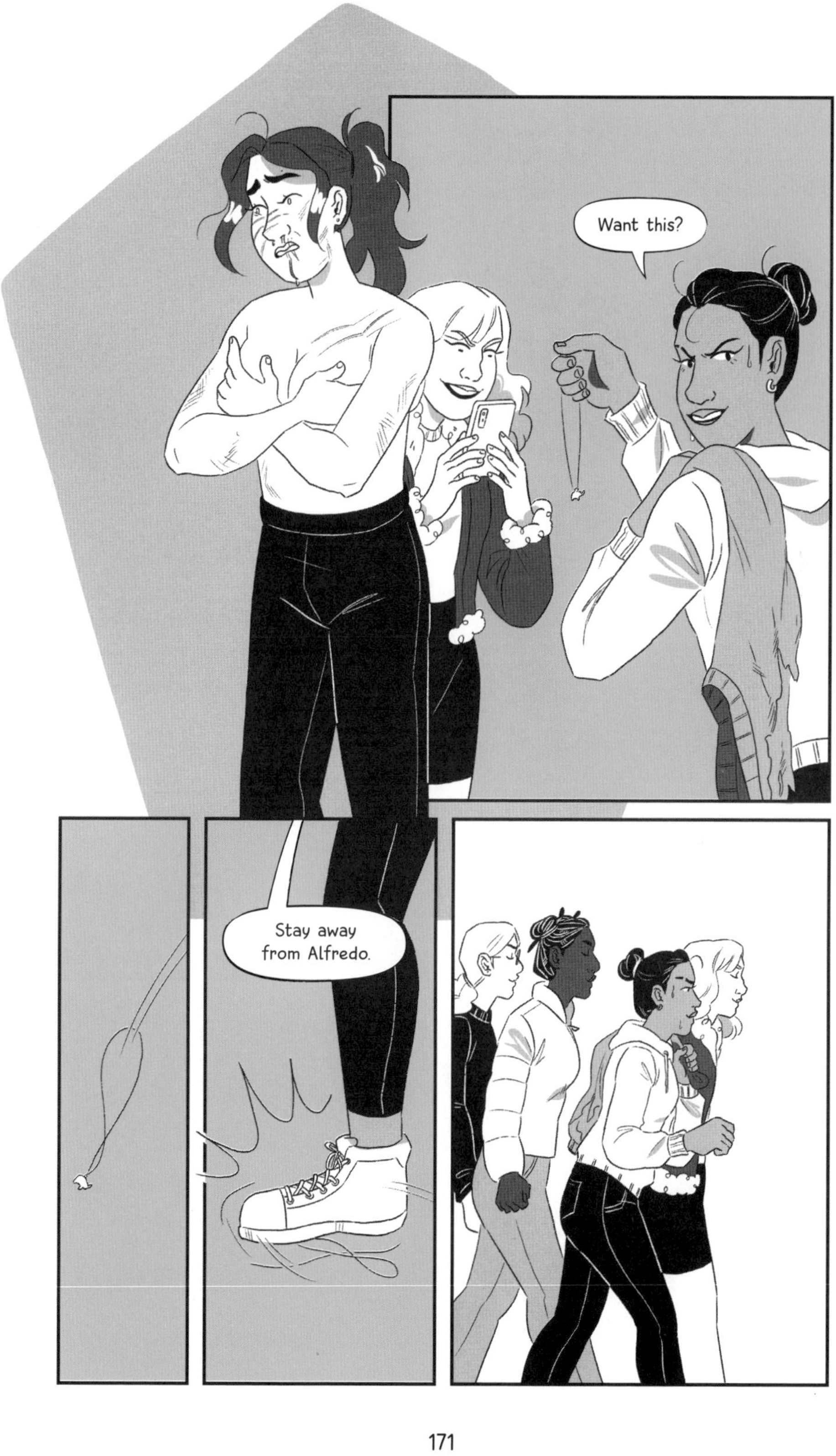
Want this?
Stay away from Alfredo.

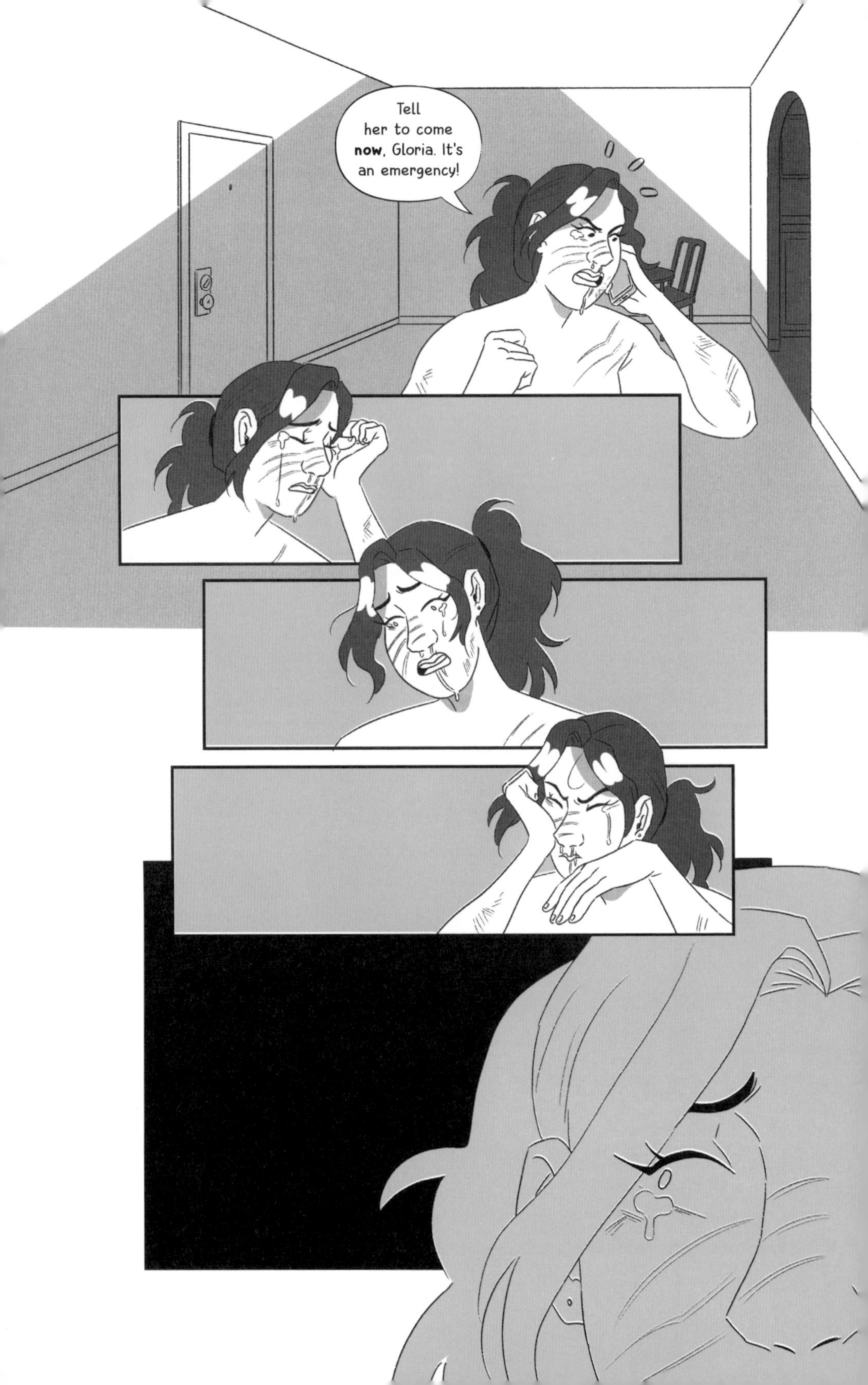
Tell her to come **now**, Gloria. It's an emergency!

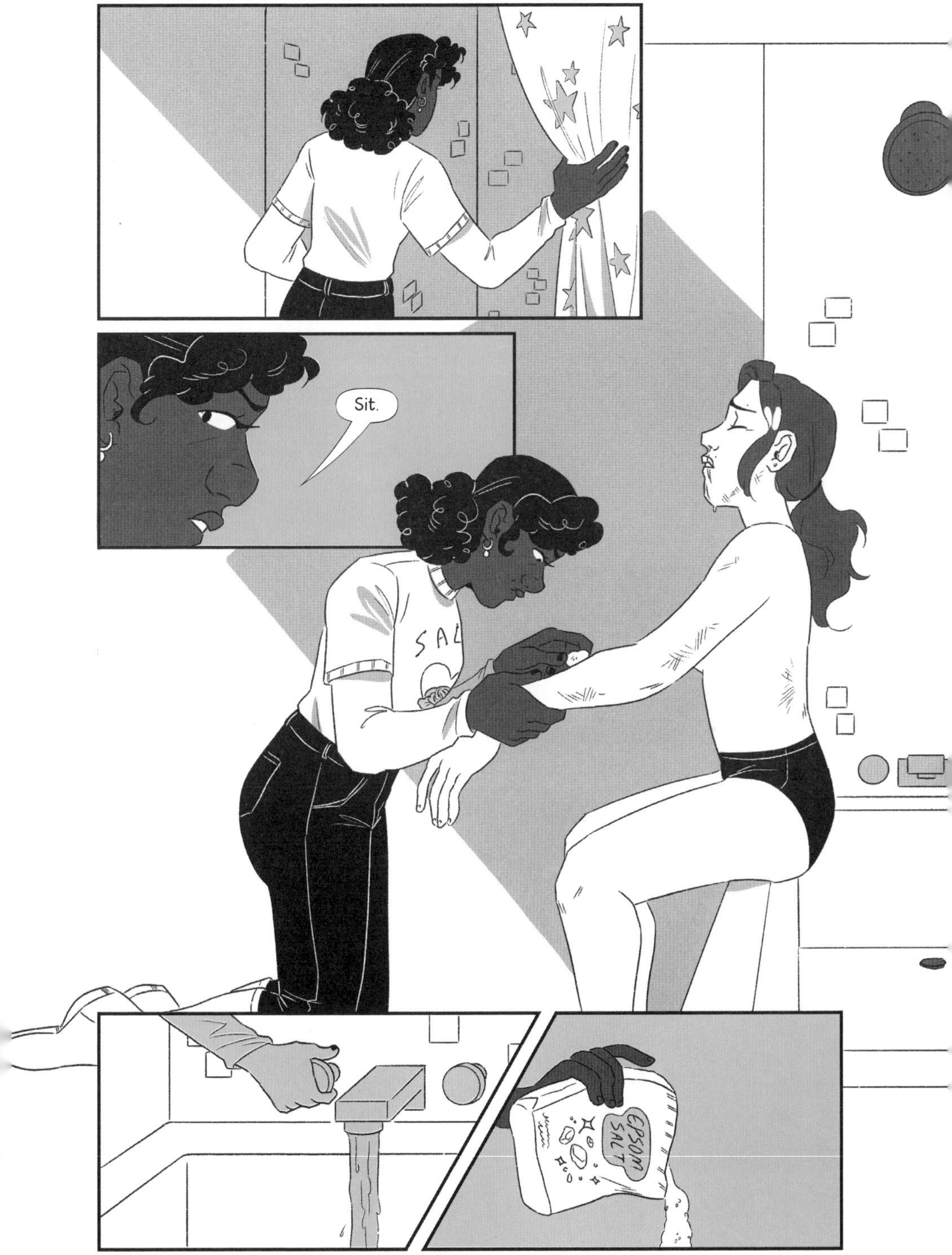
Sit.
SAL
EPSOM SALT

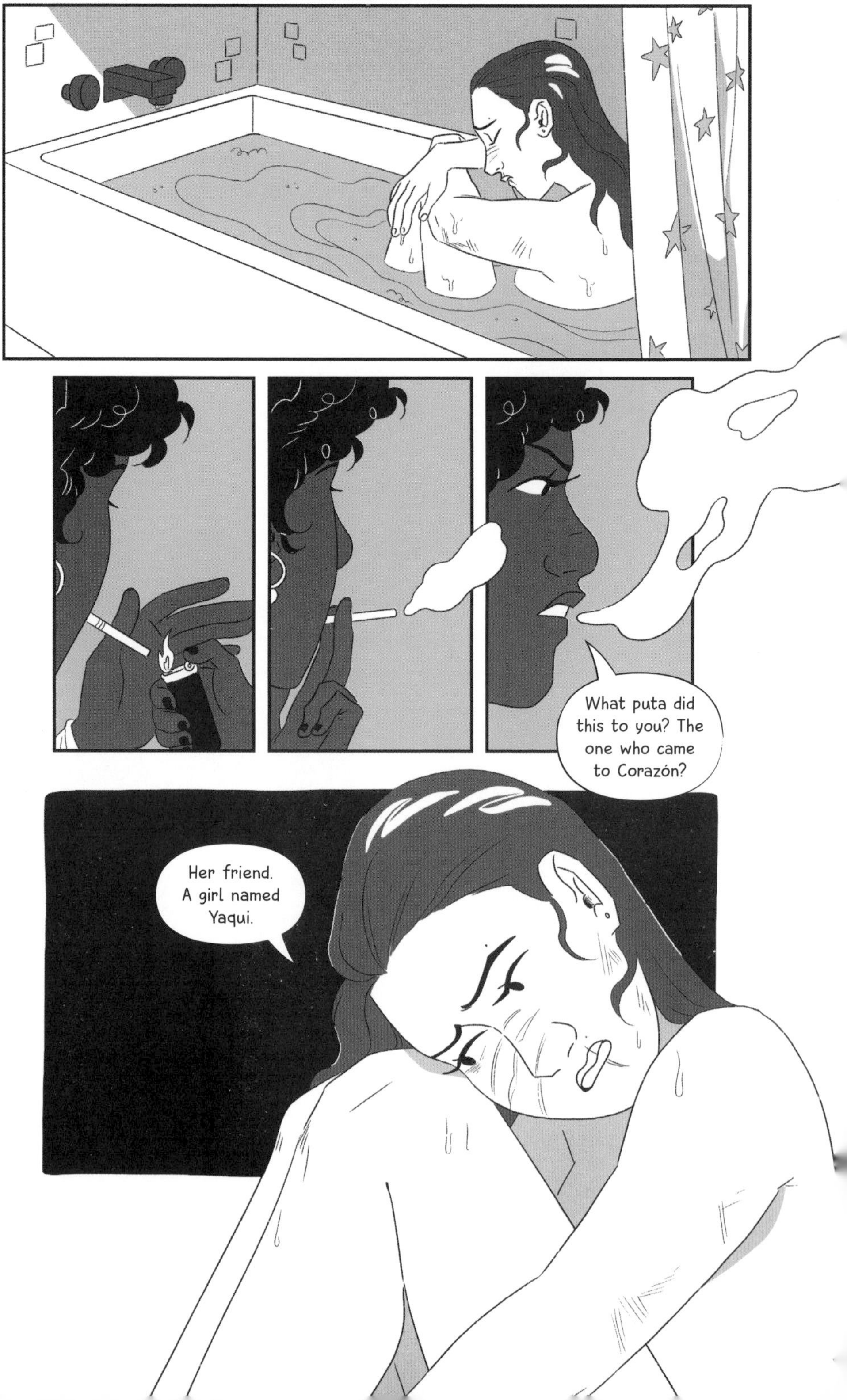
What puta did this to you? The one who came to Corazón?
Her friend. A girl named Yaqui.

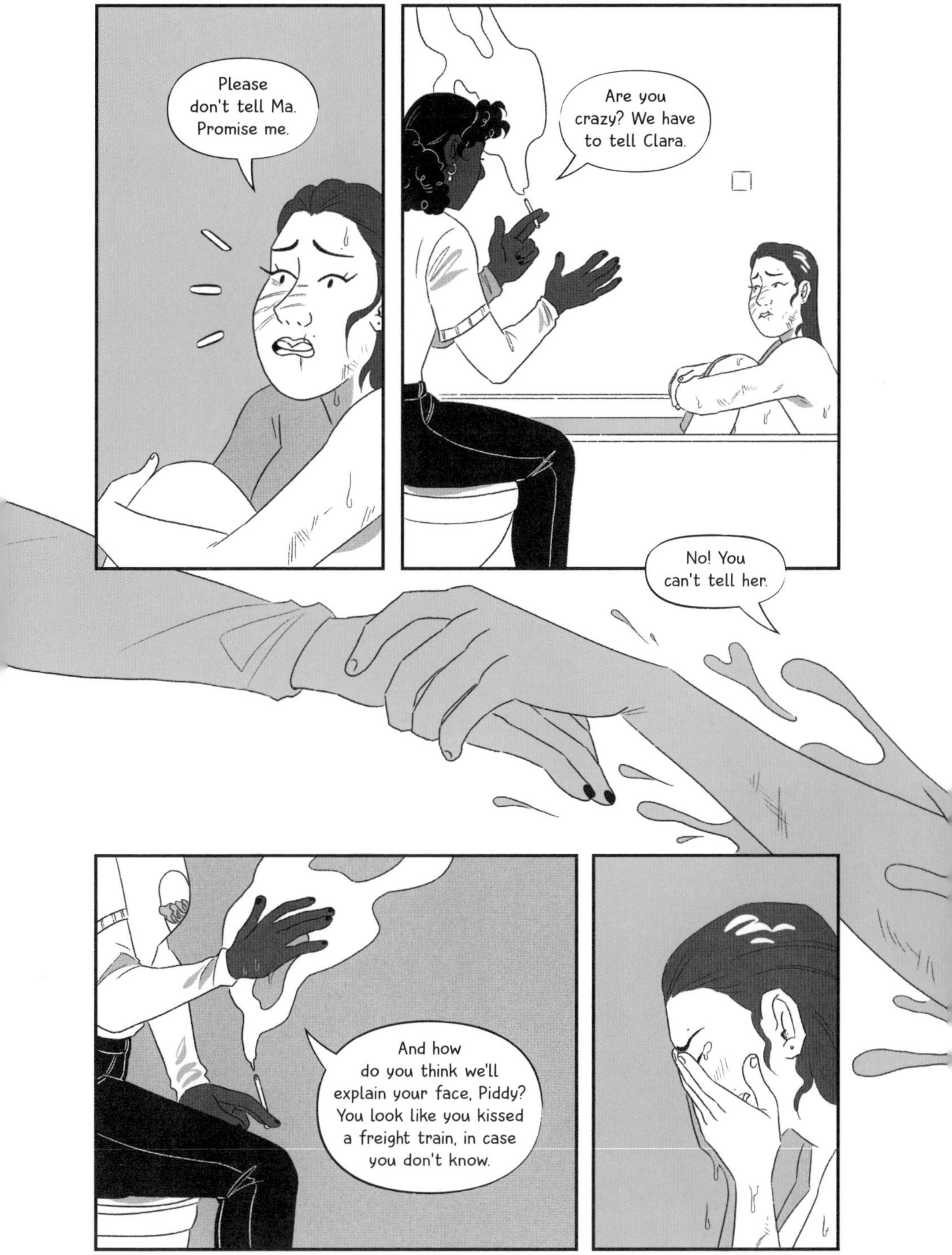
Please don't tell Ma. Promise me.
Are you crazy? We have to tell Clara.
No! You can't tell her.
And how do you think we'll explain your face, Piddy? You look like you kissed a freight train, in case you don't know.

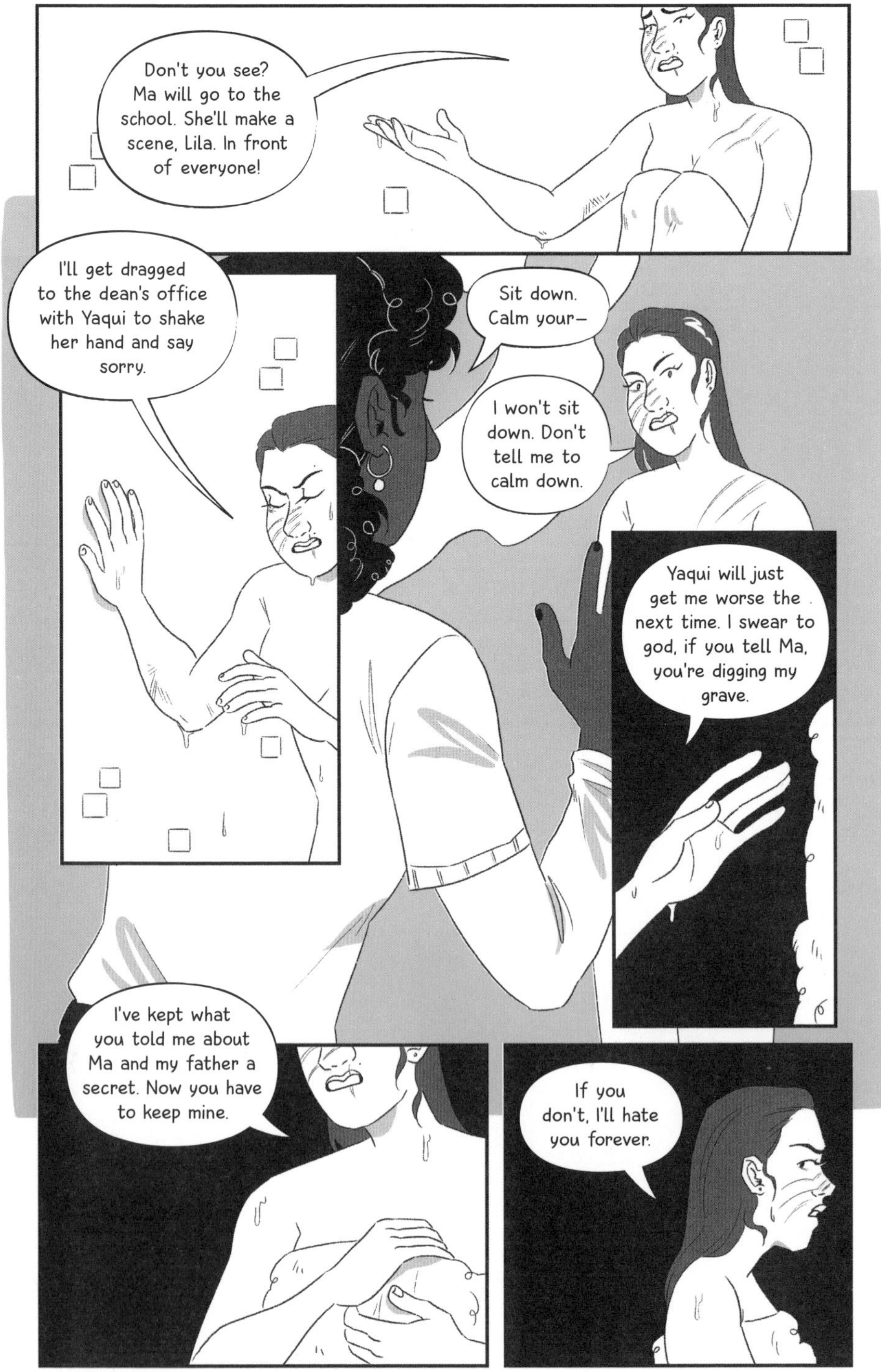
Don't you see? Ma will go to the school. She'll make a scene, Lila. In front of everyone!
I'll get dragged to the dean's office with Yaqui to shake her hand and say sorry.
Sit down. Calm your—
I won't sit down. Don't tell me to calm down.
Yaqui will just get me worse the next time. I swear to god, if you tell Ma, you're digging my grave.
I've kept what you told me about Ma and my father a secret. Now you have to keep mine.
If you don't, I'll hate you forever.

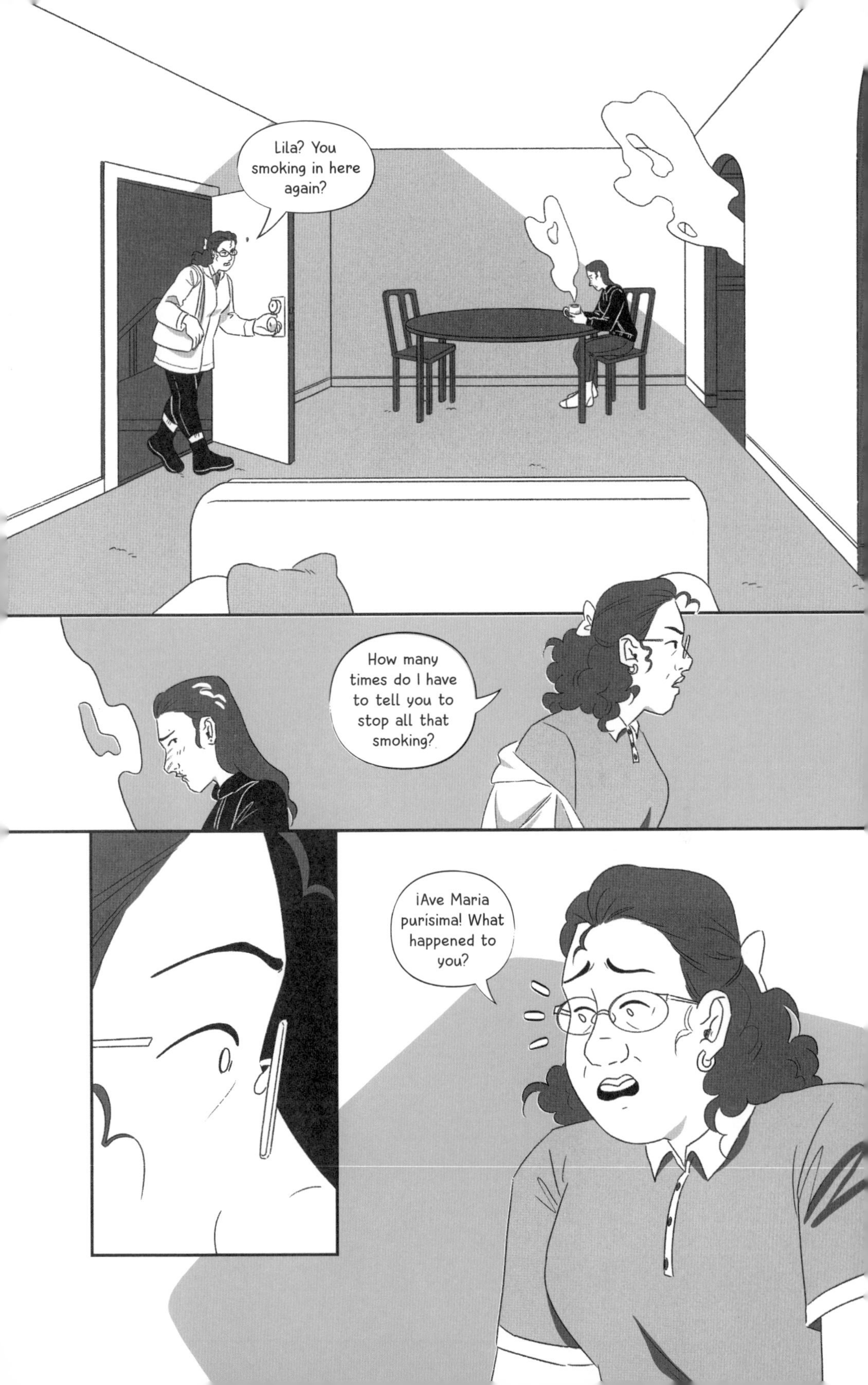
Lila? You smoking in here again?
How many times do I have to tell you to stop all that smoking?
¡Ave Maria purisima! What happened to you?

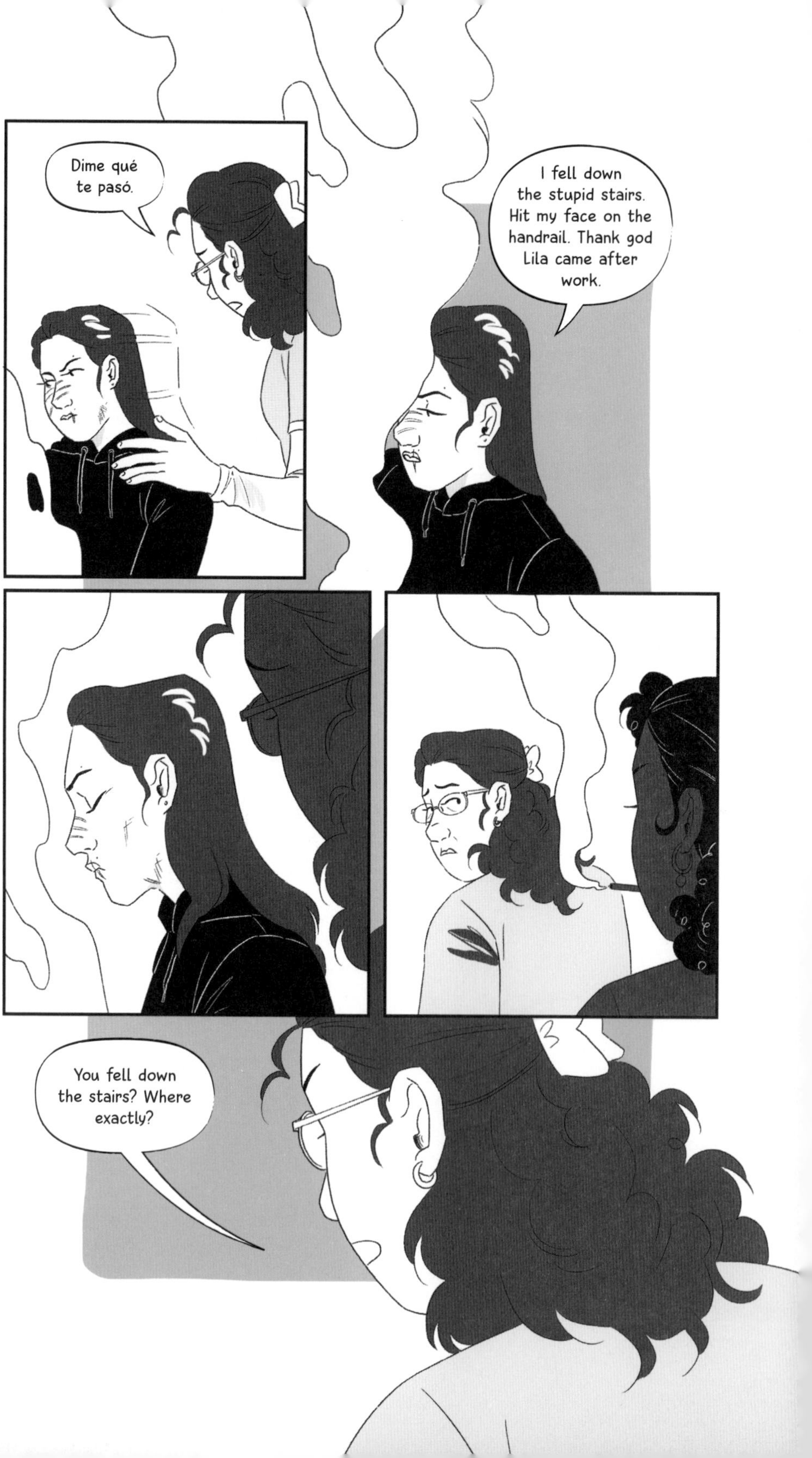
Dime qué te pasó.
I fell down the stupid stairs. Hit my face on the handrail. Thank god Lila came after work.
You fell down the stairs? Where exactly?

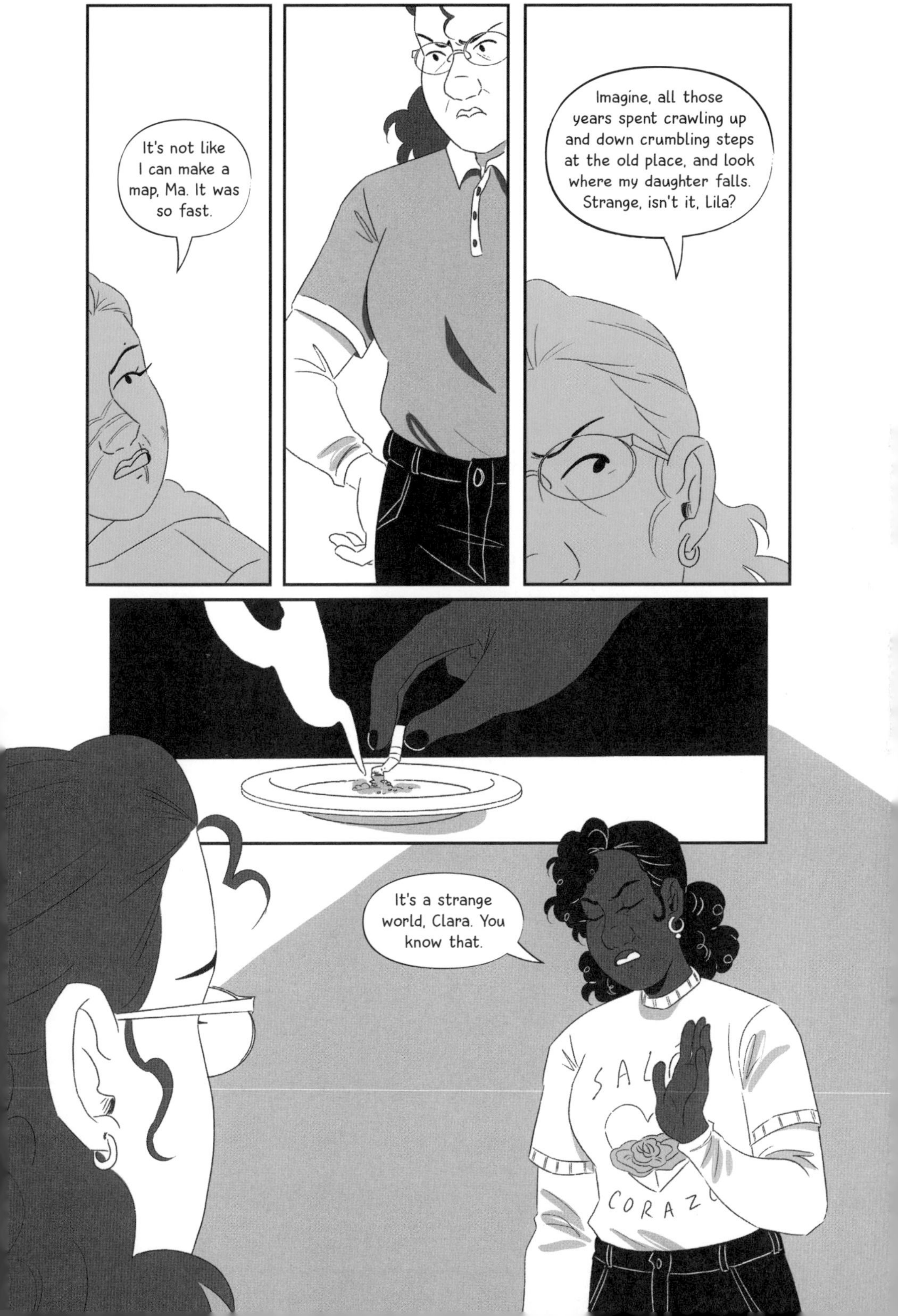
It's not like I can make a map, Ma. It was so fast.
Imagine, all those years spent crawling up and down crumbling steps at the old place, and look where my daughter falls. Strange, isn't it, Lila?
It's a strange world, Clara. You know that.
SAL
CORAZ

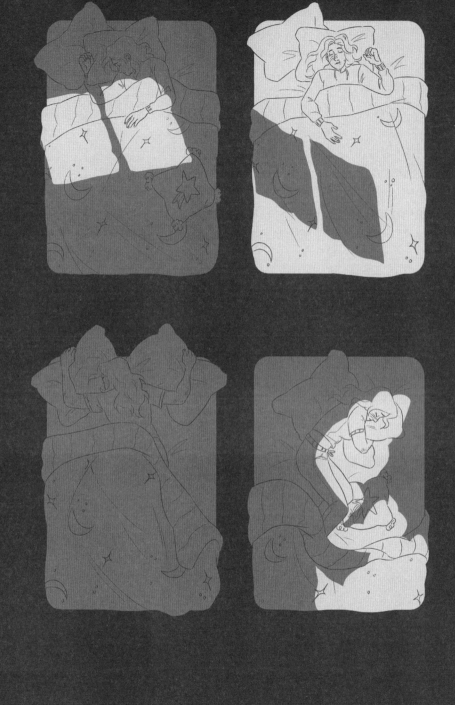

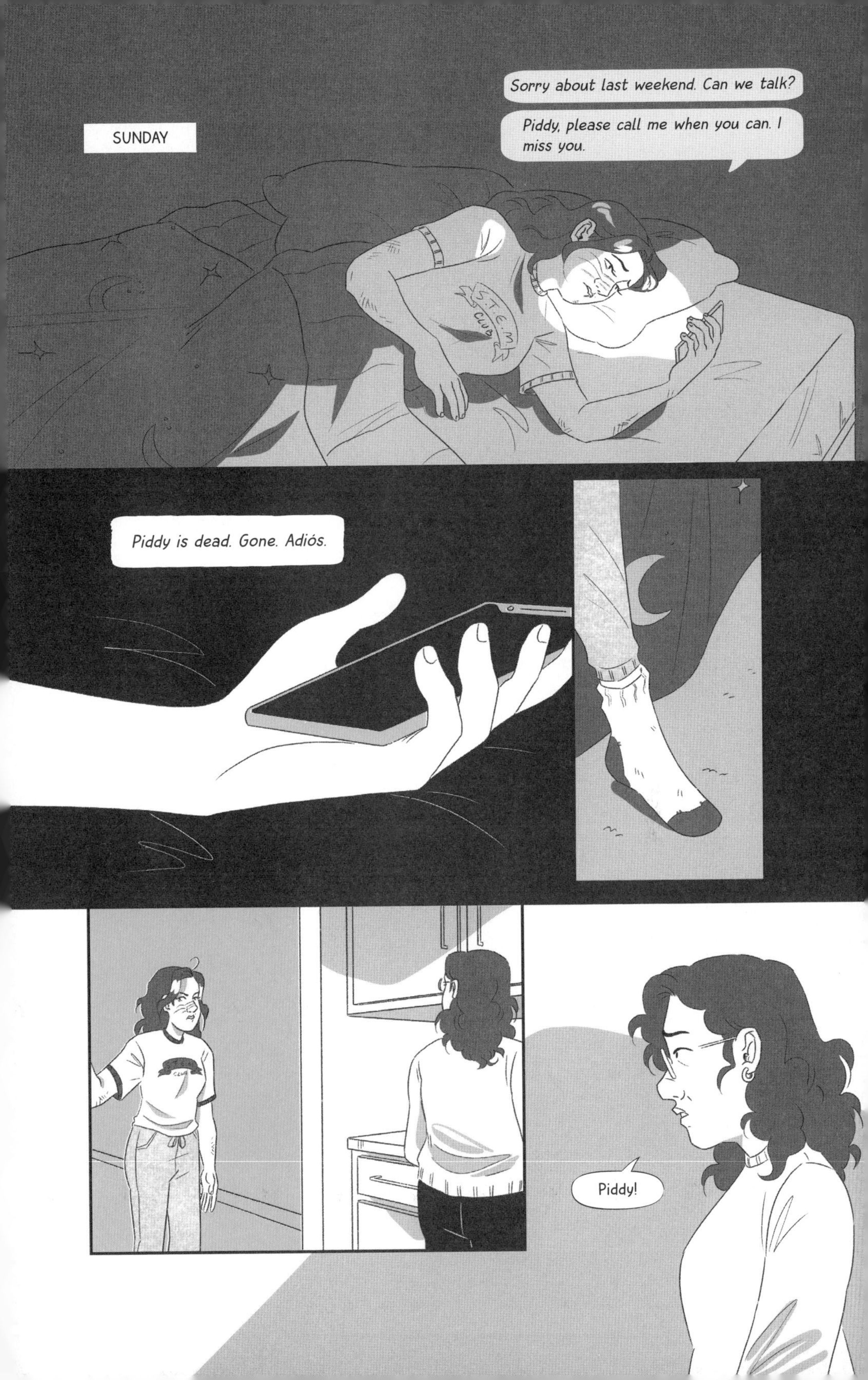
SUNDAY
Sorry about last weekend. Can we talk?
Piddy, please call me when you can. I miss you.
Piddy is dead. Gone. Adiós.
Piddy!

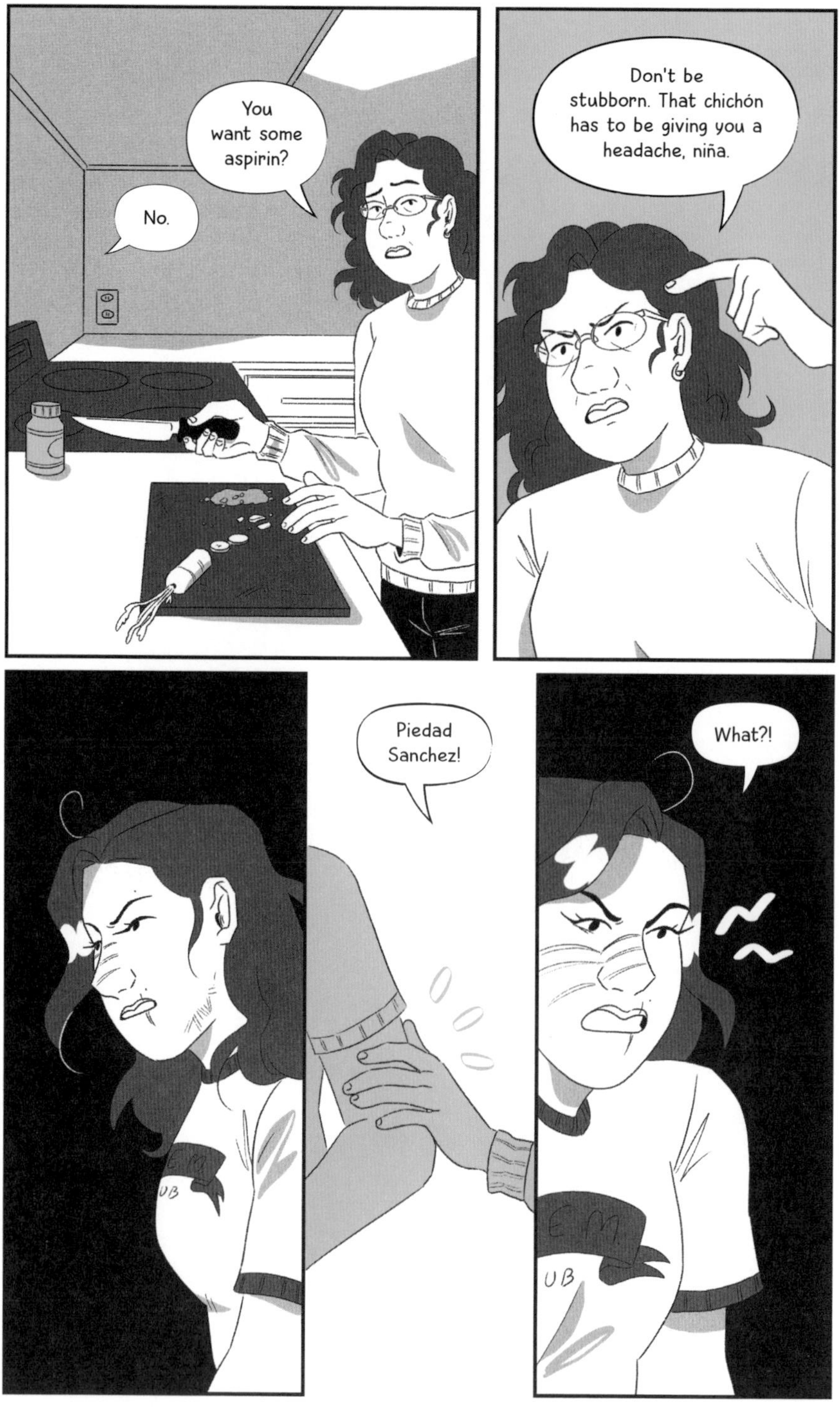
You want some aspirin?
No.
Don't be stubborn. That chichón has to be giving you a headache, niña.
Piedad Sanchez!
What?!

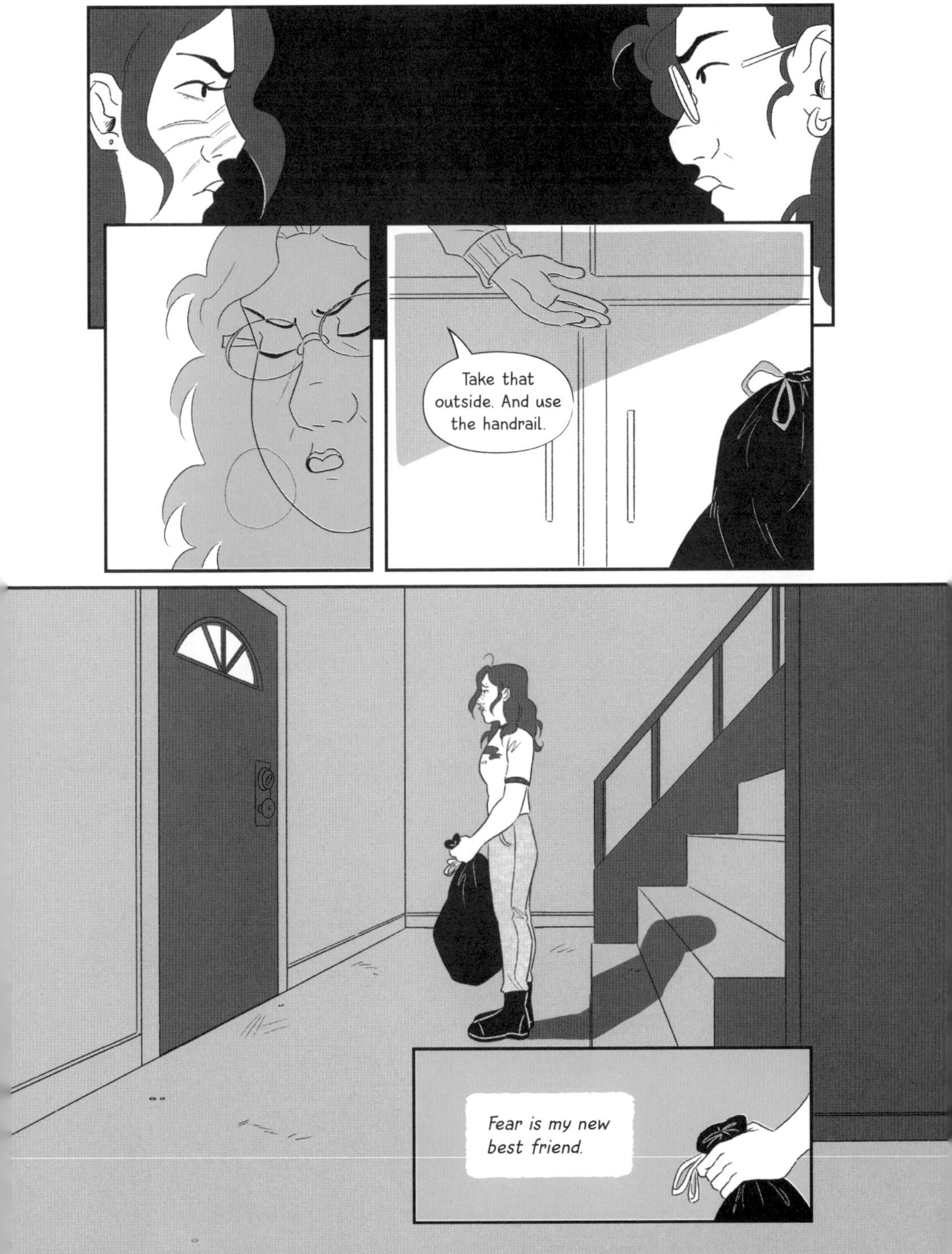
Take that outside. And use the handrail.
Fear is my new best friend.

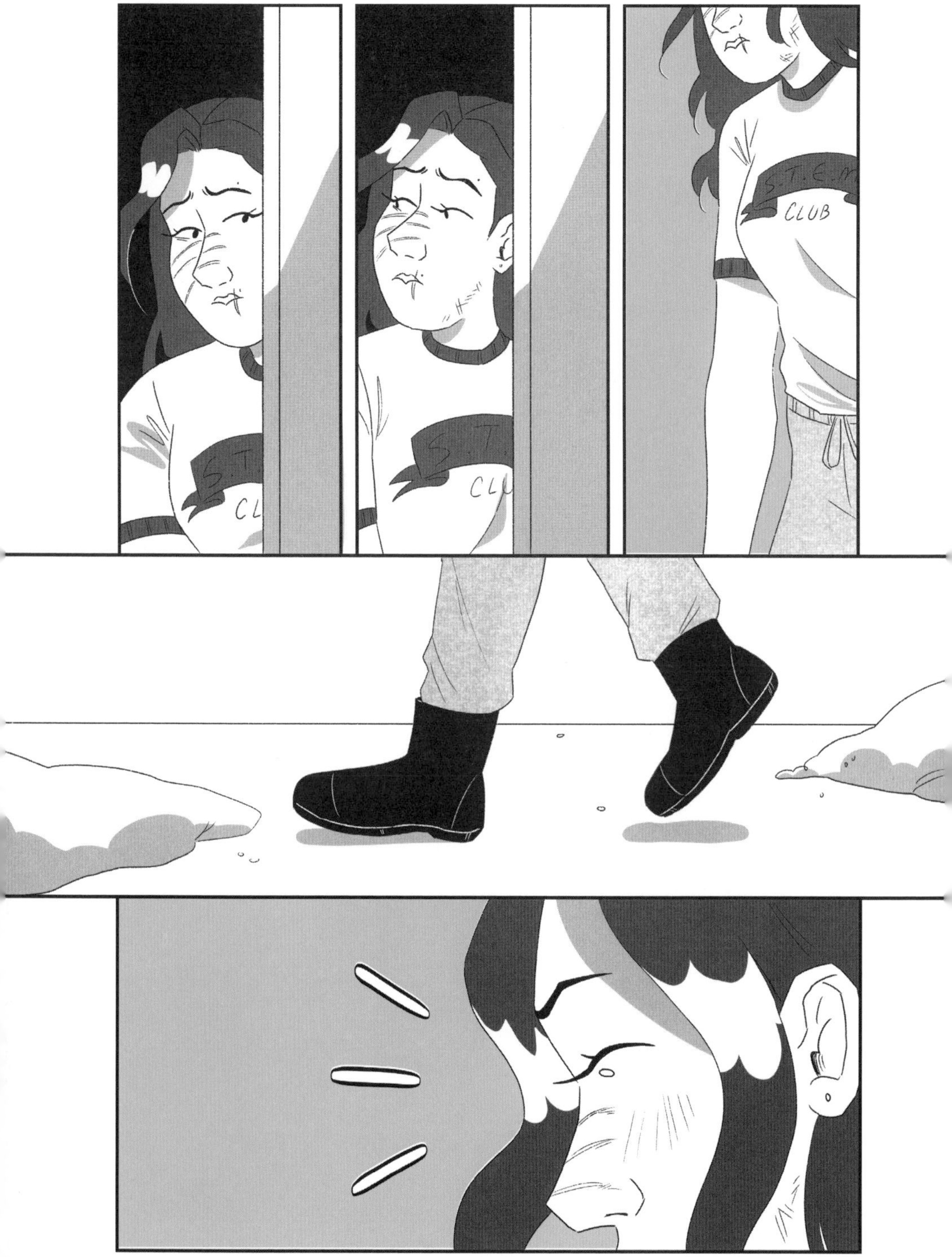
CLUB

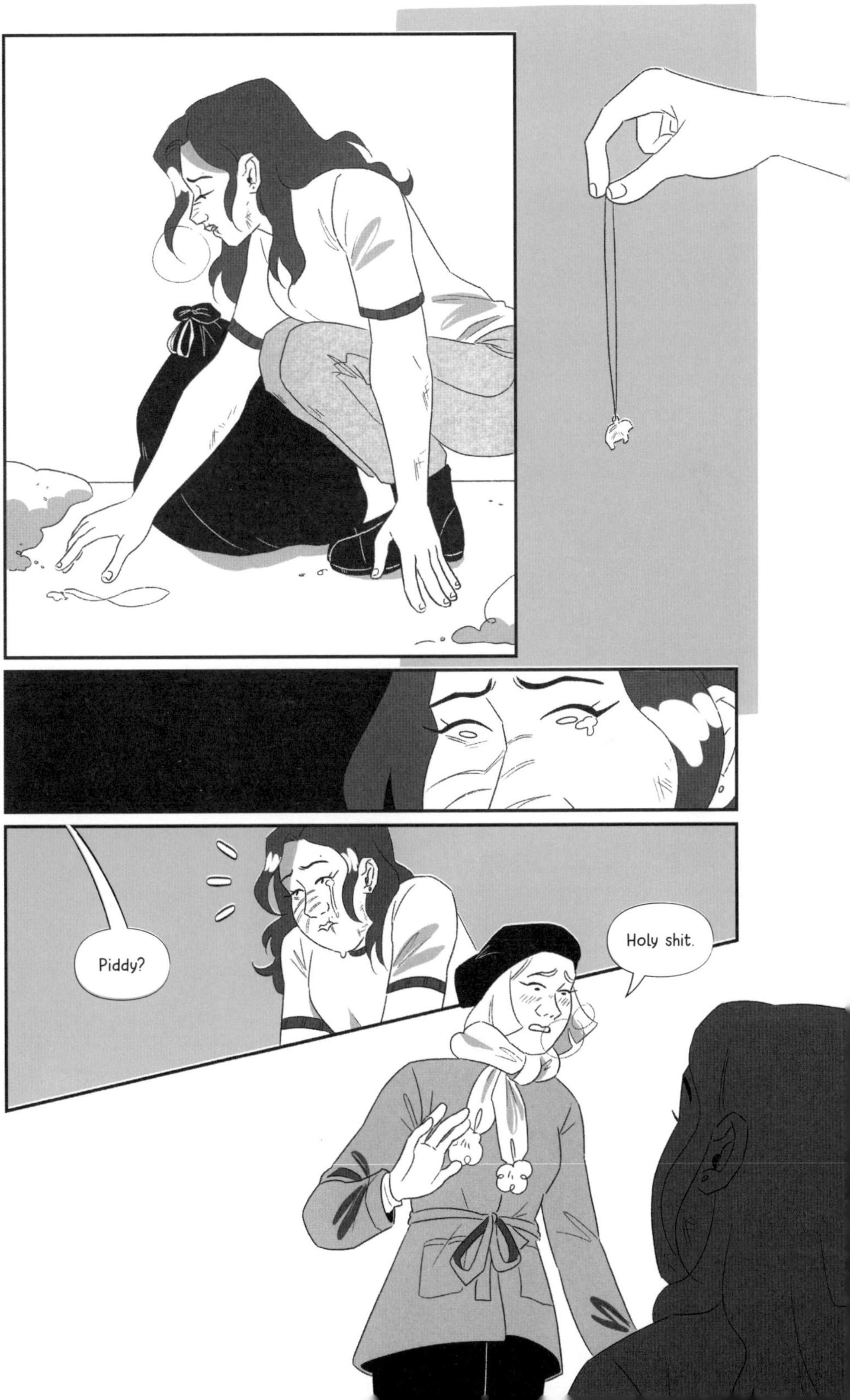
Piddy?
Holy shit.

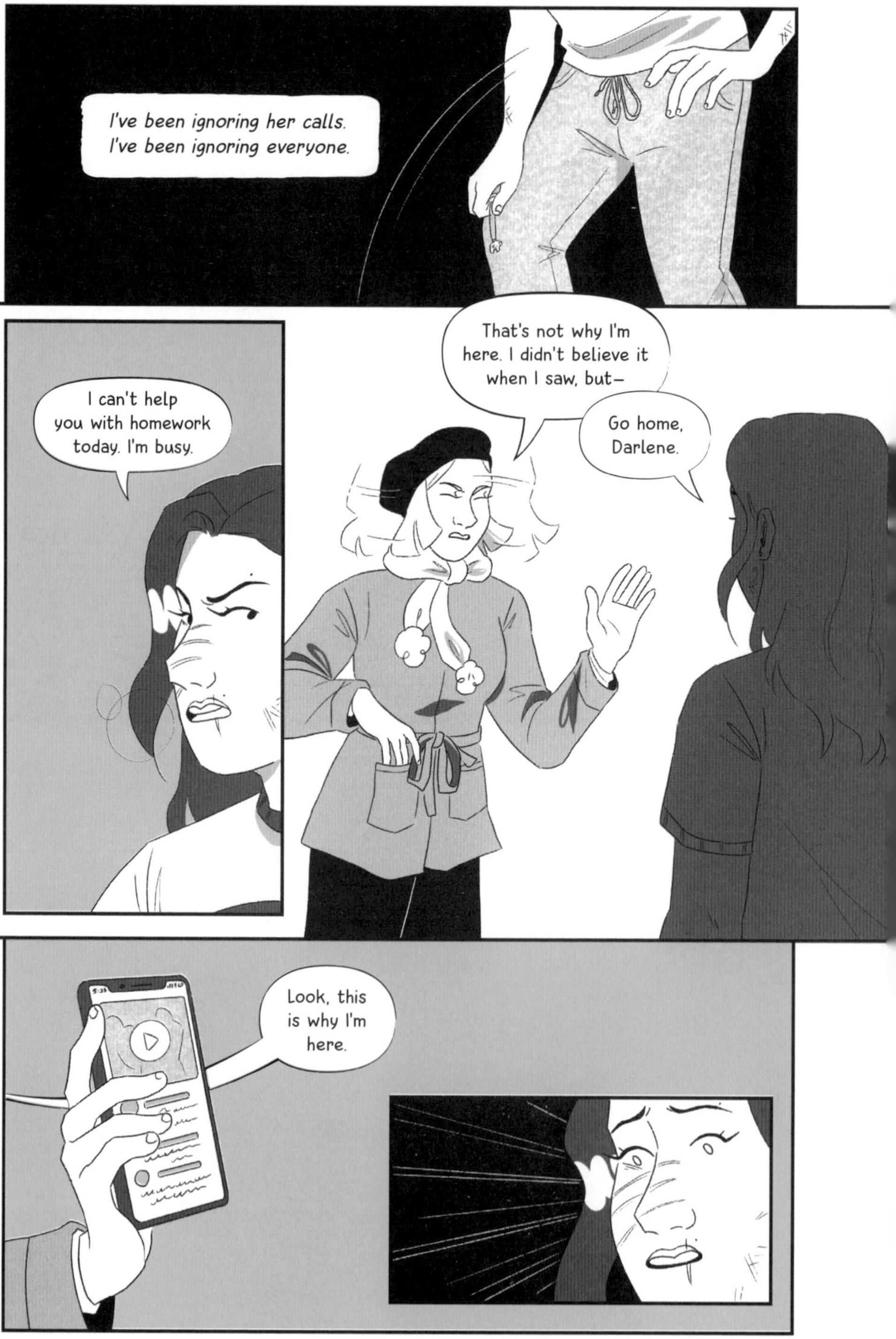

I've been ignoring her calls. I've been ignoring everyone.
I can't help you with homework today. I'm busy.
That's not why I'm here. I didn't believe it when I saw, but—
Go home, Darlene.
Look, this is why I'm here.

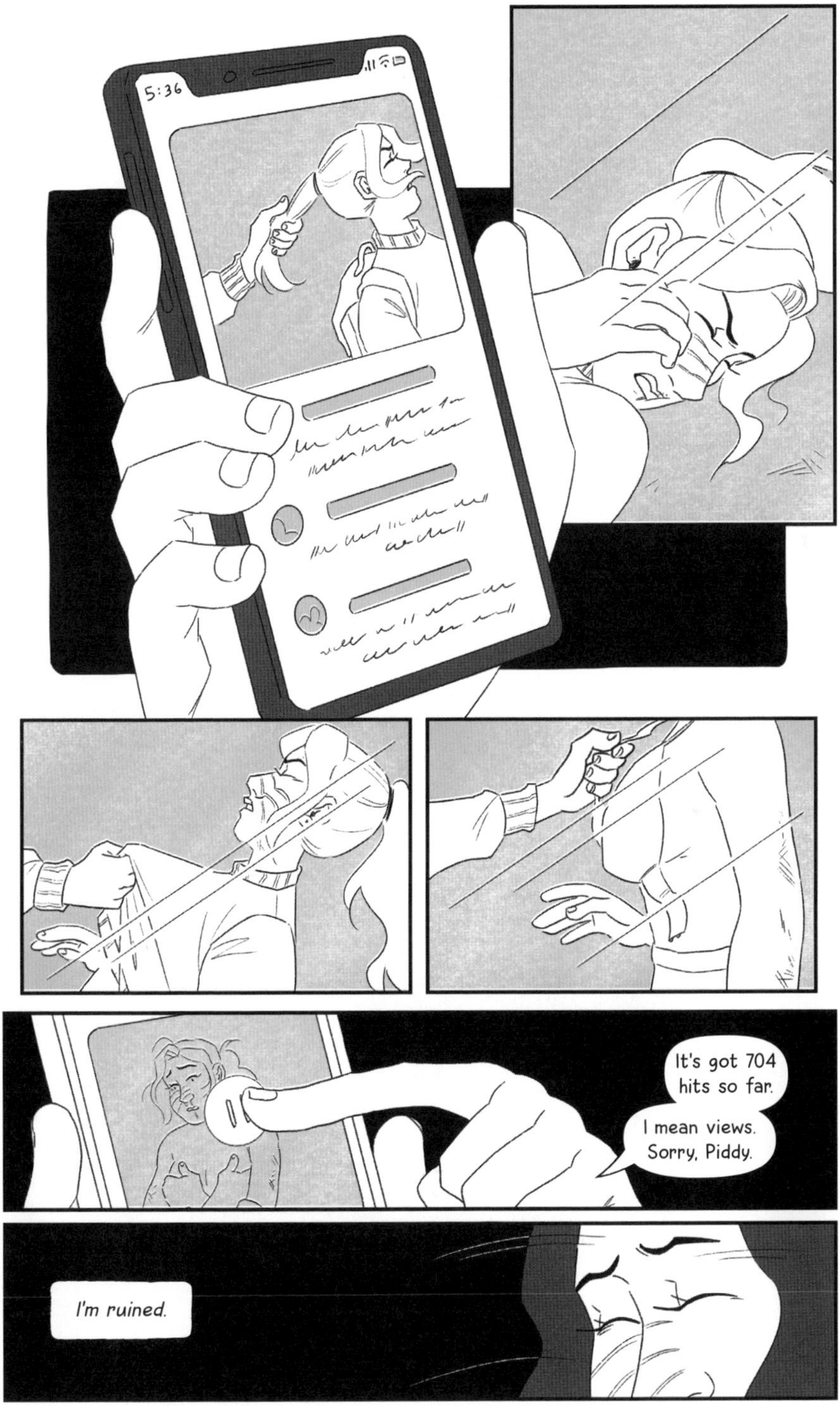
5:36
It's got 704 hits so far.
I mean views. Sorry, Piddy.
I'm ruined.

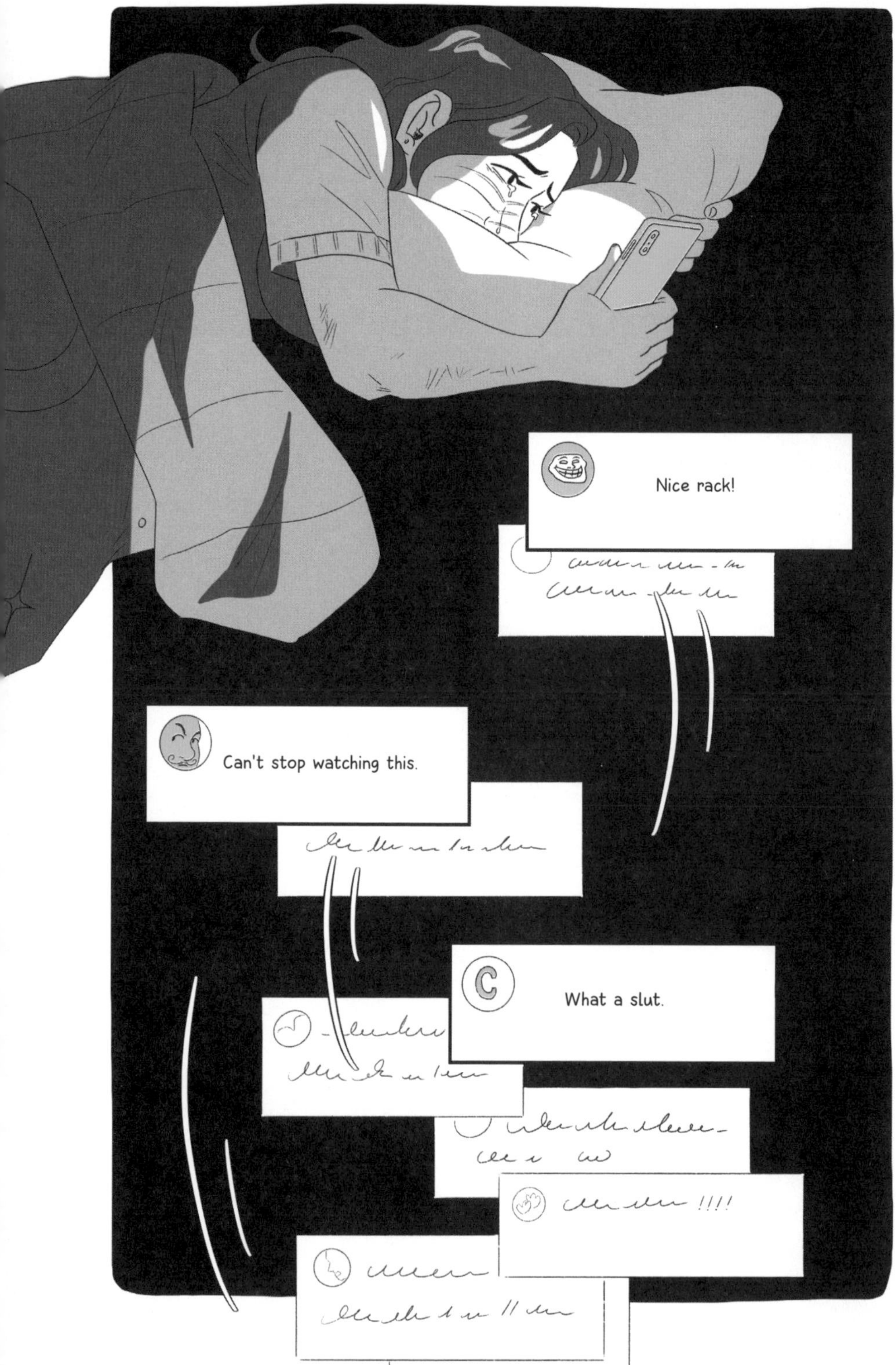
Nice rack!
Can't stop watching this.
What a slut.

I can't hide this tomorrow. No amount of makeup can cover up what the people at school already know.

Yaqui Delgado kicked my ass.

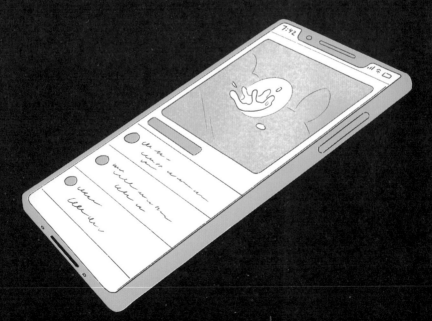

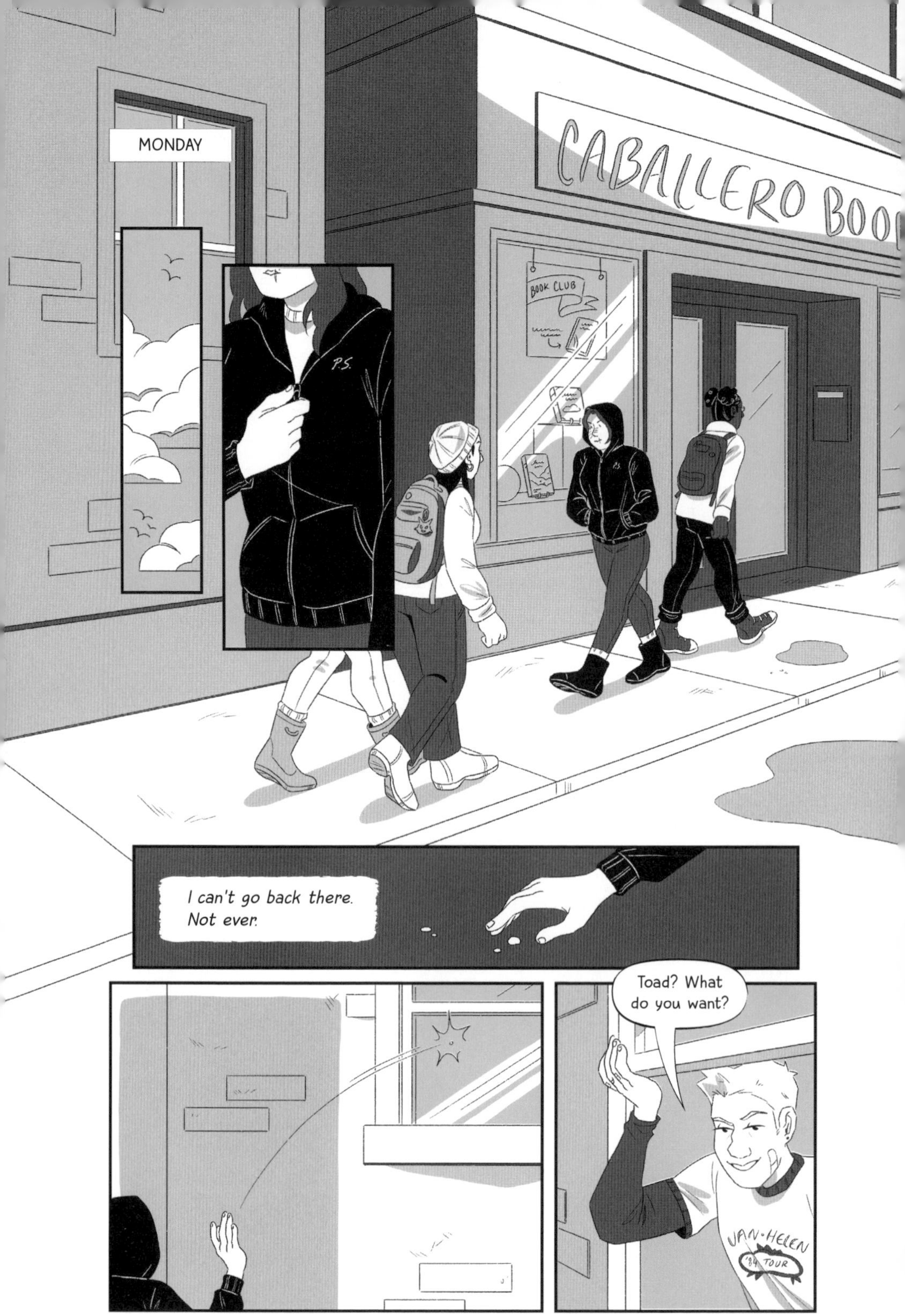
MONDAY
CABALLERO BOO
BOOK CLUB
P.S.
I can't go back there. Not ever.
Toad? What do you want?
VAN-HELEN '84 TOUR

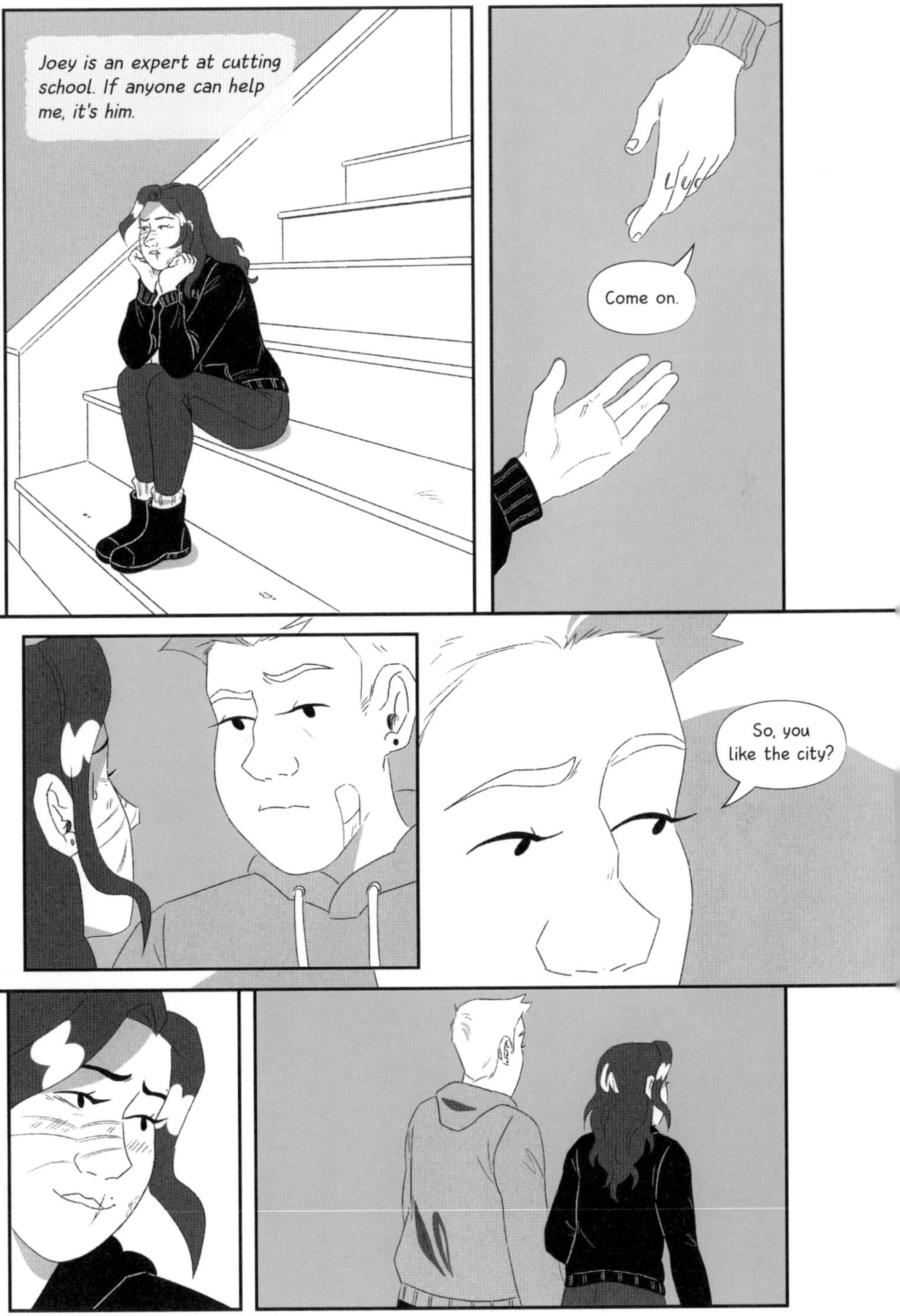
Joey is an expert at cutting school. If anyone can help me, it's him.
Come on.
So, you like the city?

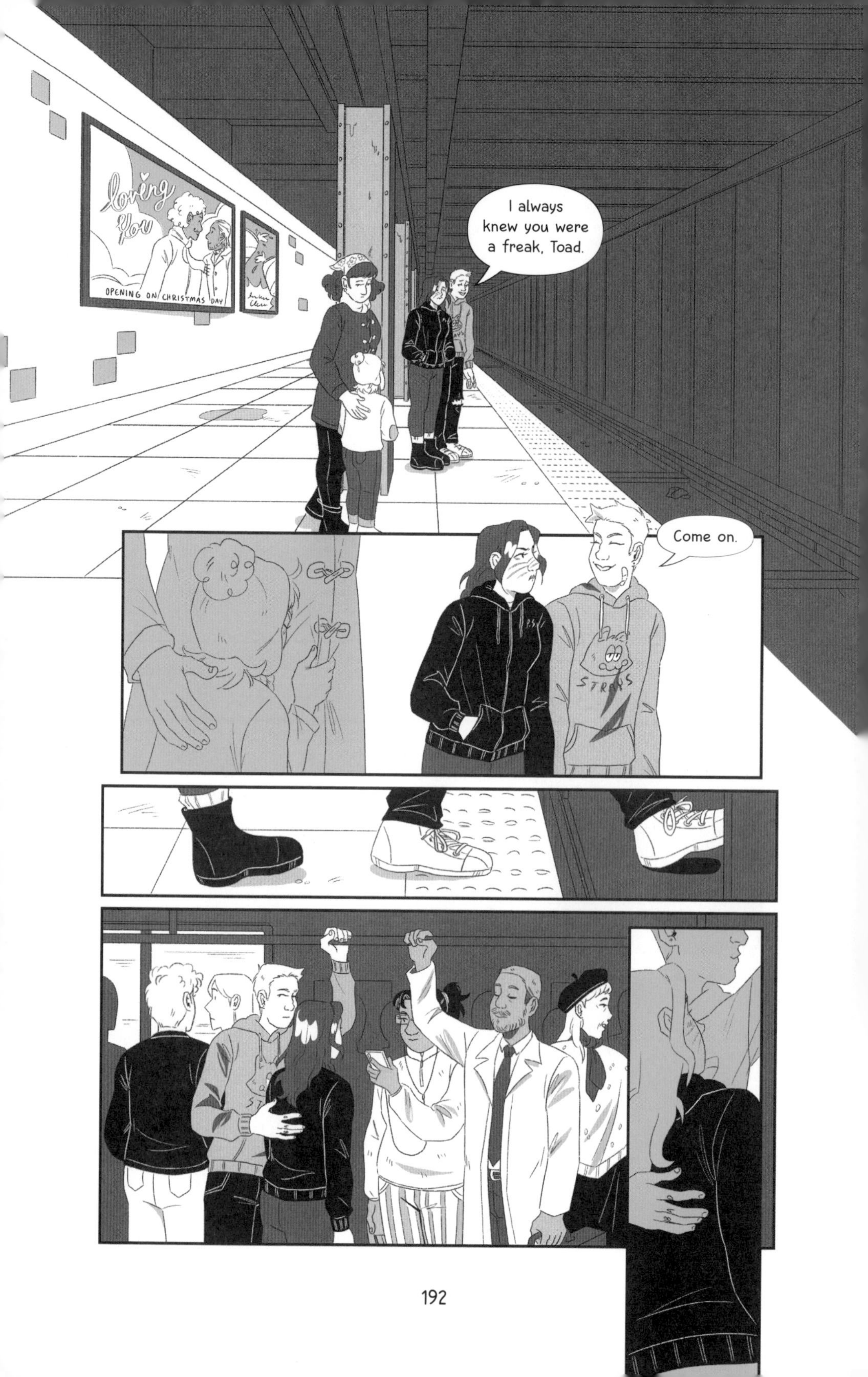
loving you
OPENING ON CHRISTMAS DAY
I always knew you were a freak, Toad.
Come on.
STRAYS

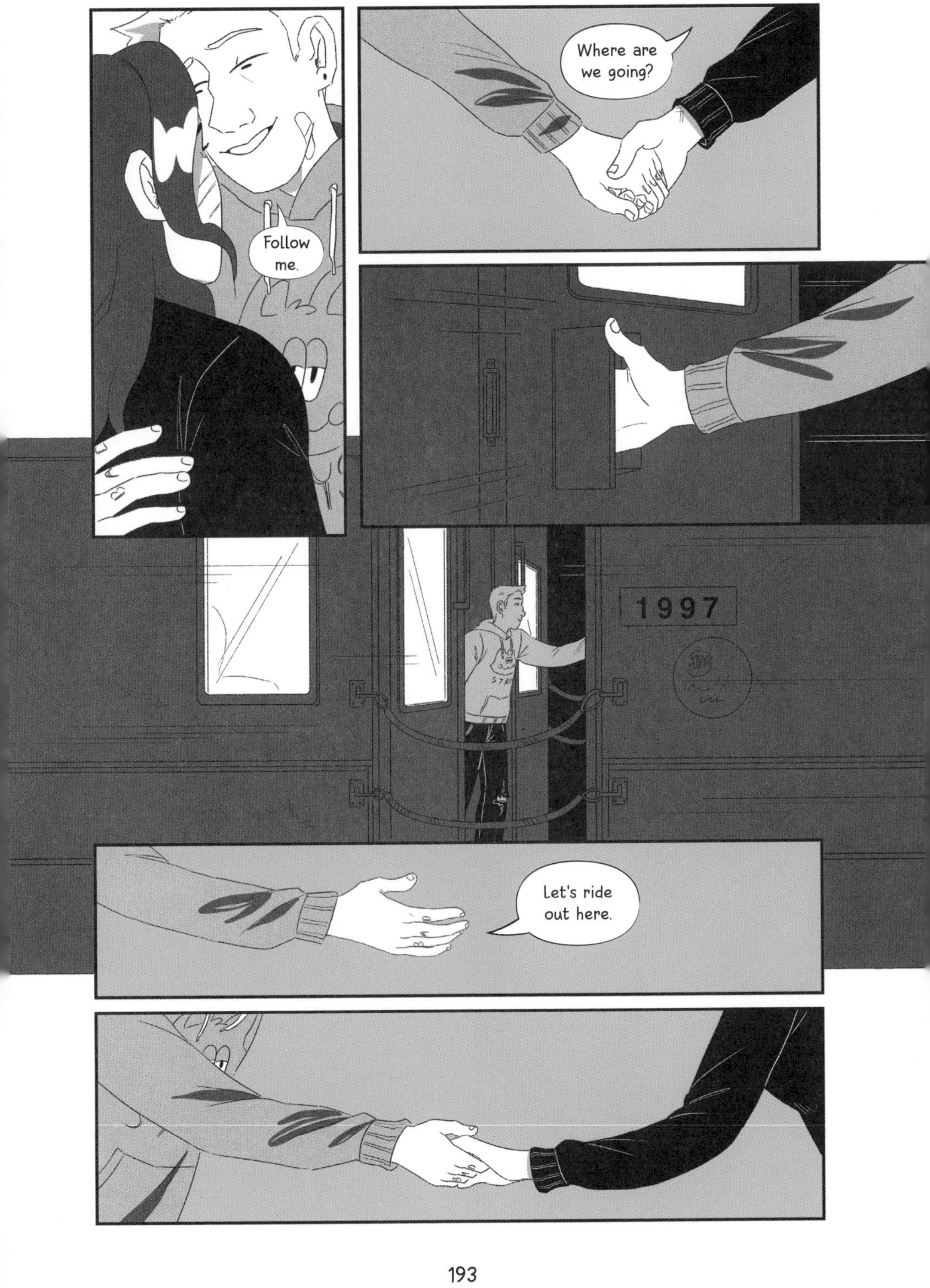
Follow me.
Where are we going?
1997
Let's ride out here.

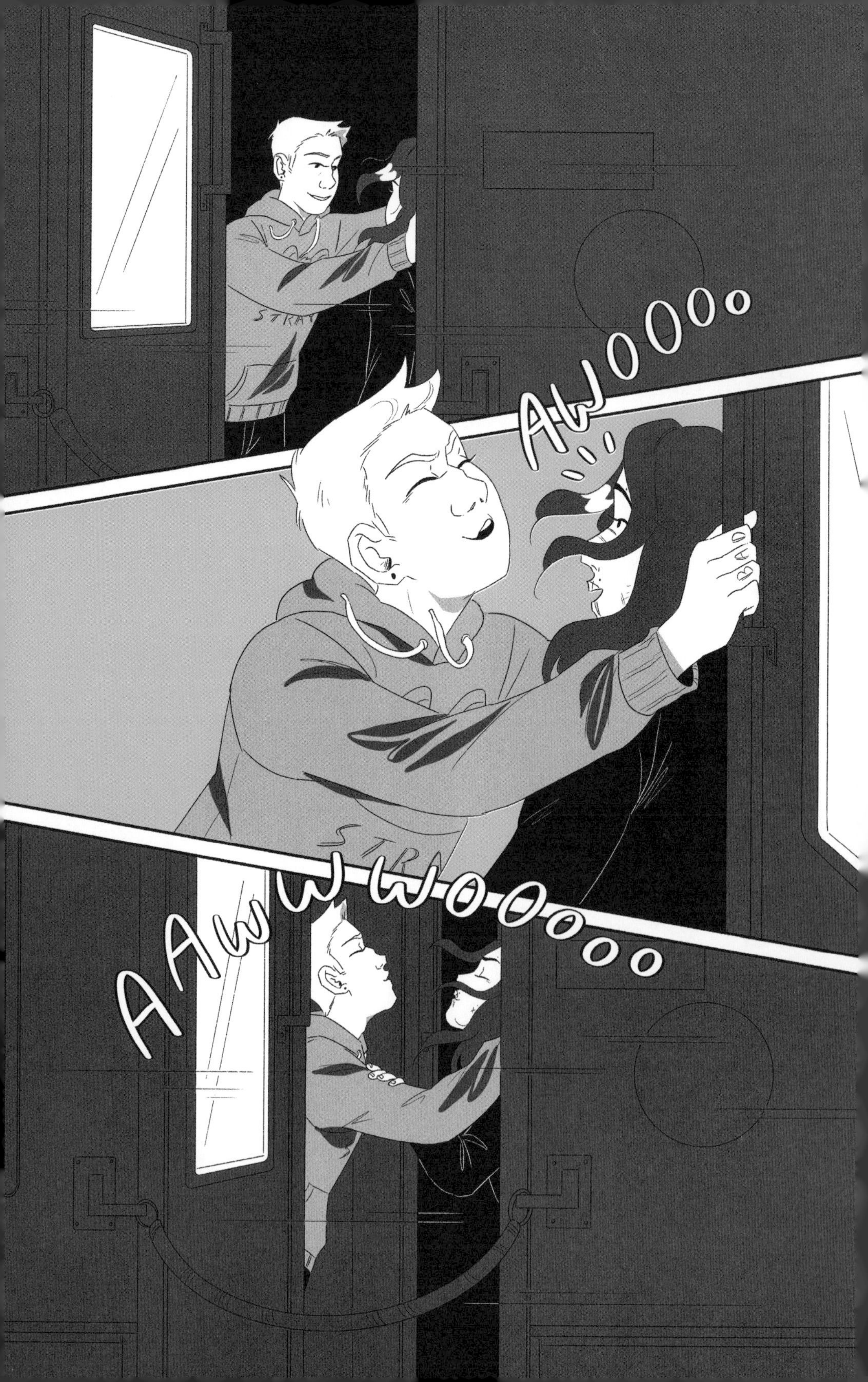
AWOOOo
BAD
AAWWWOOooo

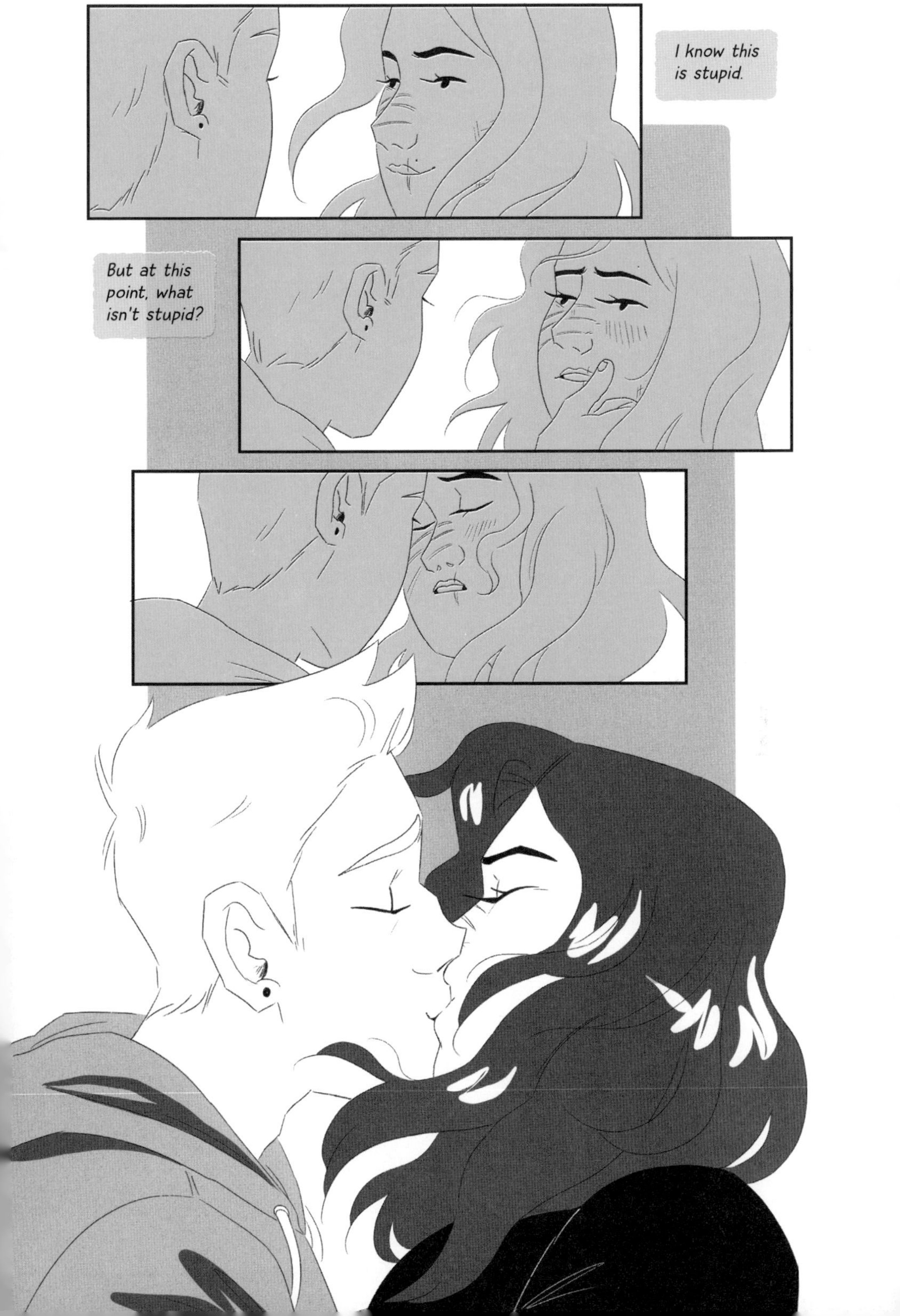
I know this is stupid.
But at this point, what isn't stupid?

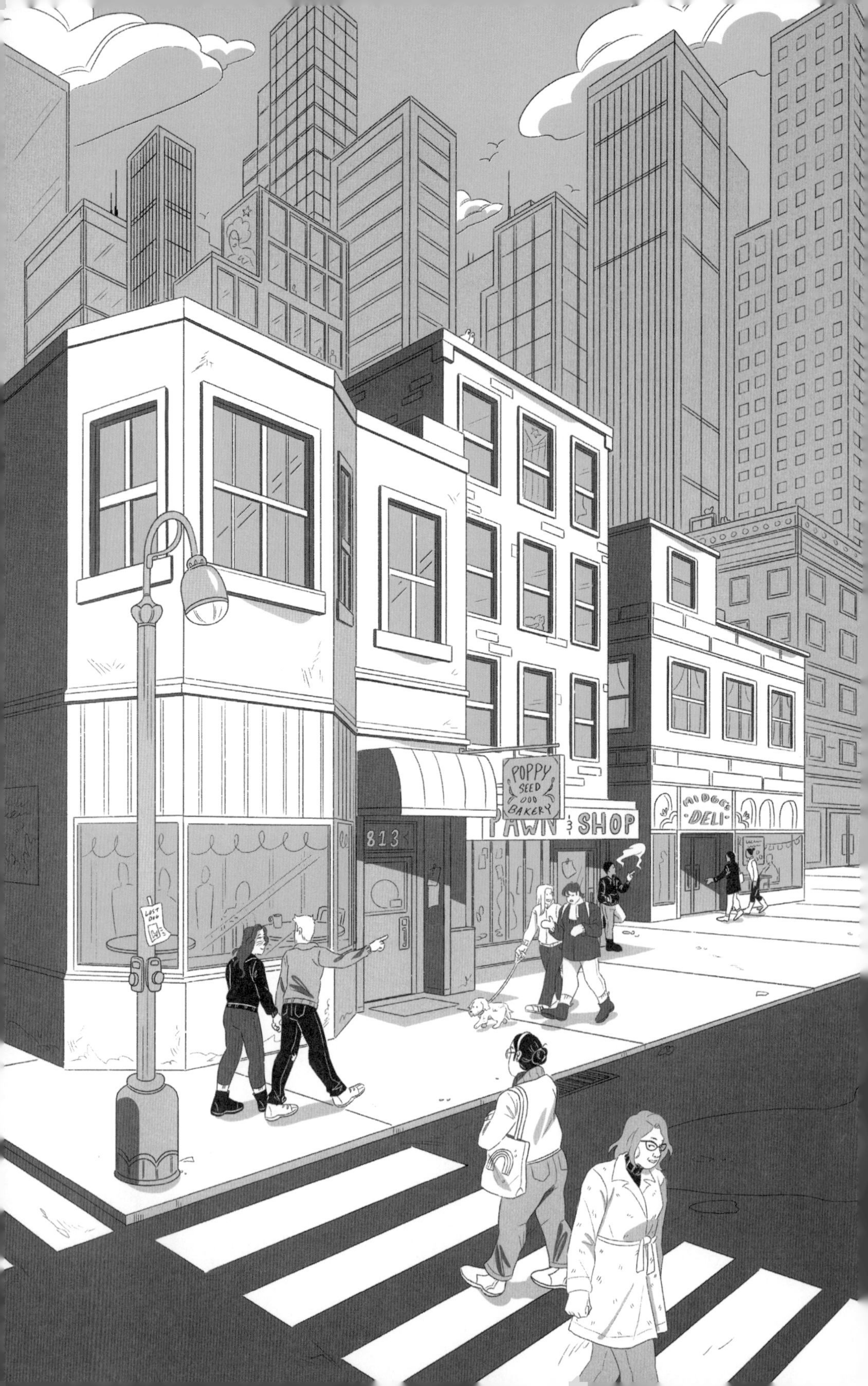
POPPY SEED BAKERY
PAWN SHOP
813
MIDGE'S DELI
LOST DOG

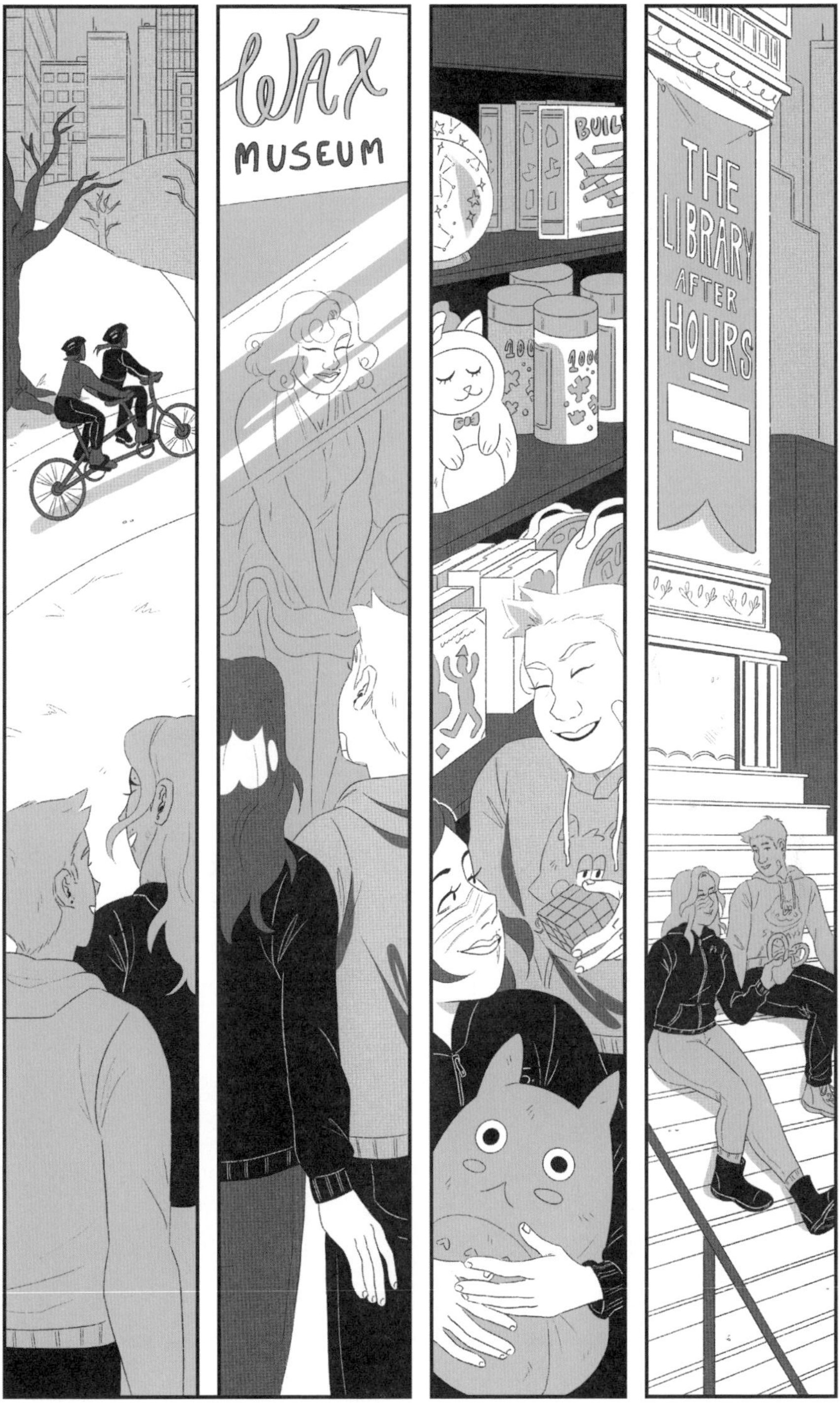
WAX
MUSEUM
BUIL
THE
LIBRARY
AFTER
HOURS

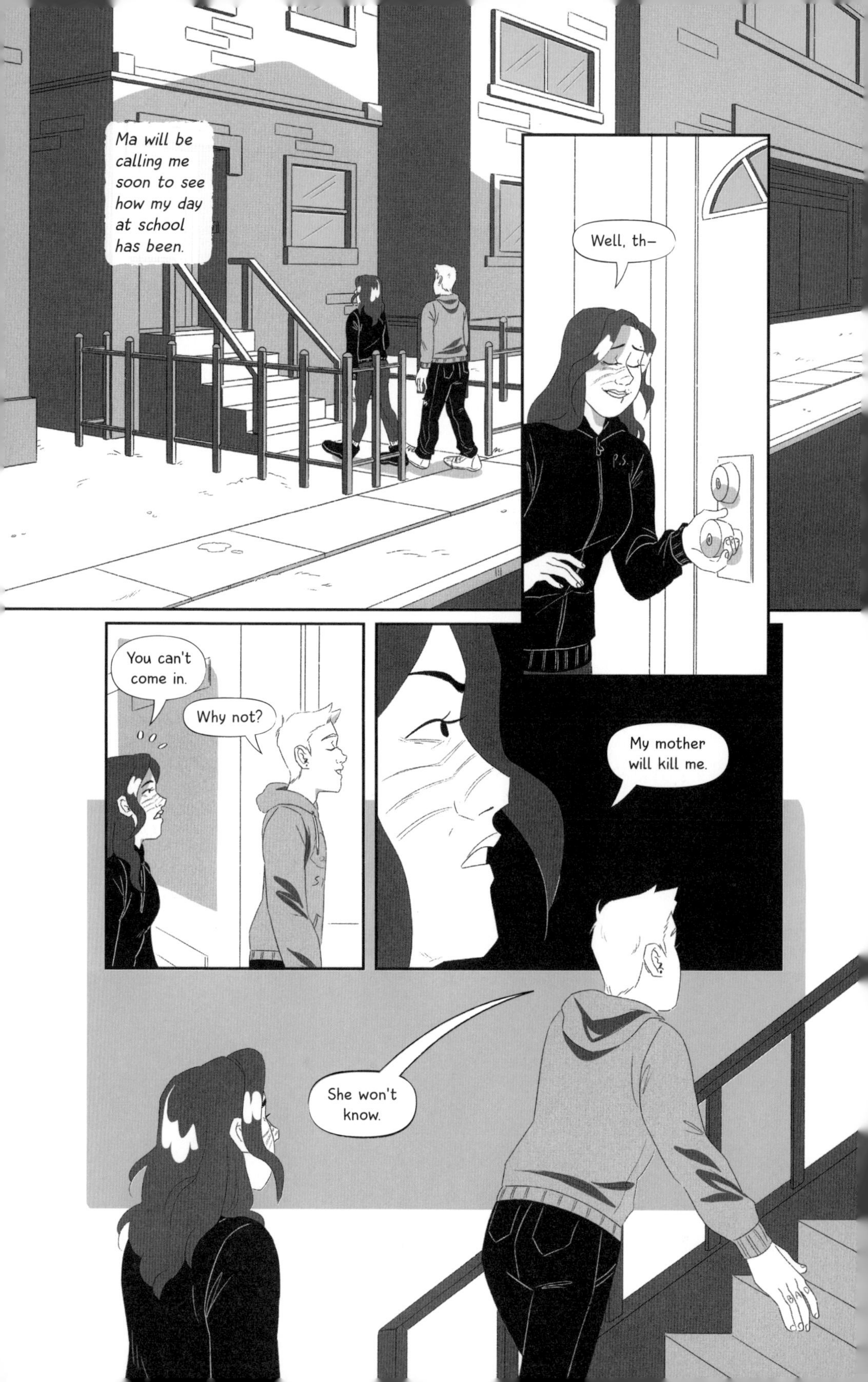
Ma will be calling me soon to see how my day at school has been.
Well, th—
You can't come in.
Why not?
My mother will kill me.
She won't know.

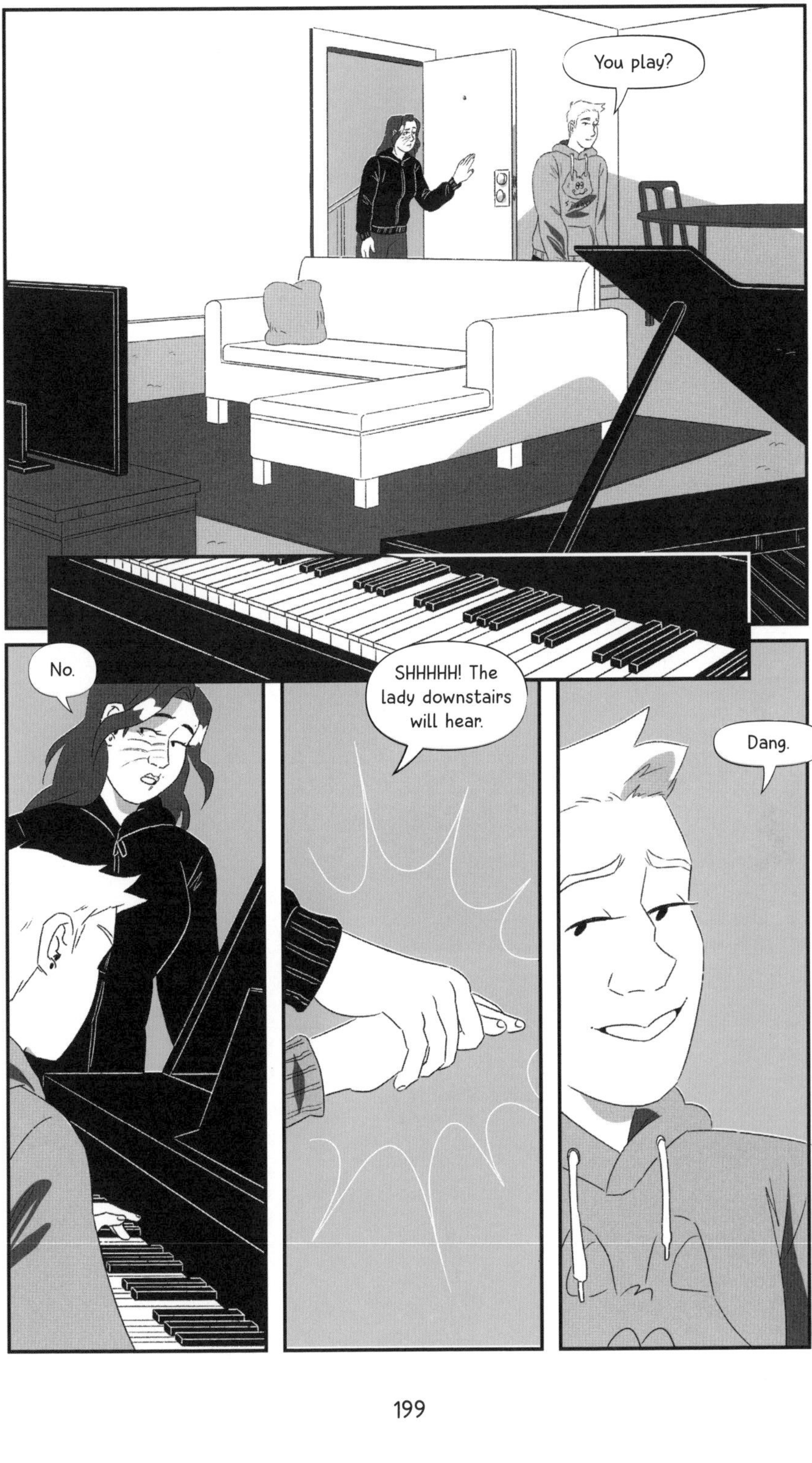
You play?
No.
SHHHHH! The lady downstairs will hear.
Dang.

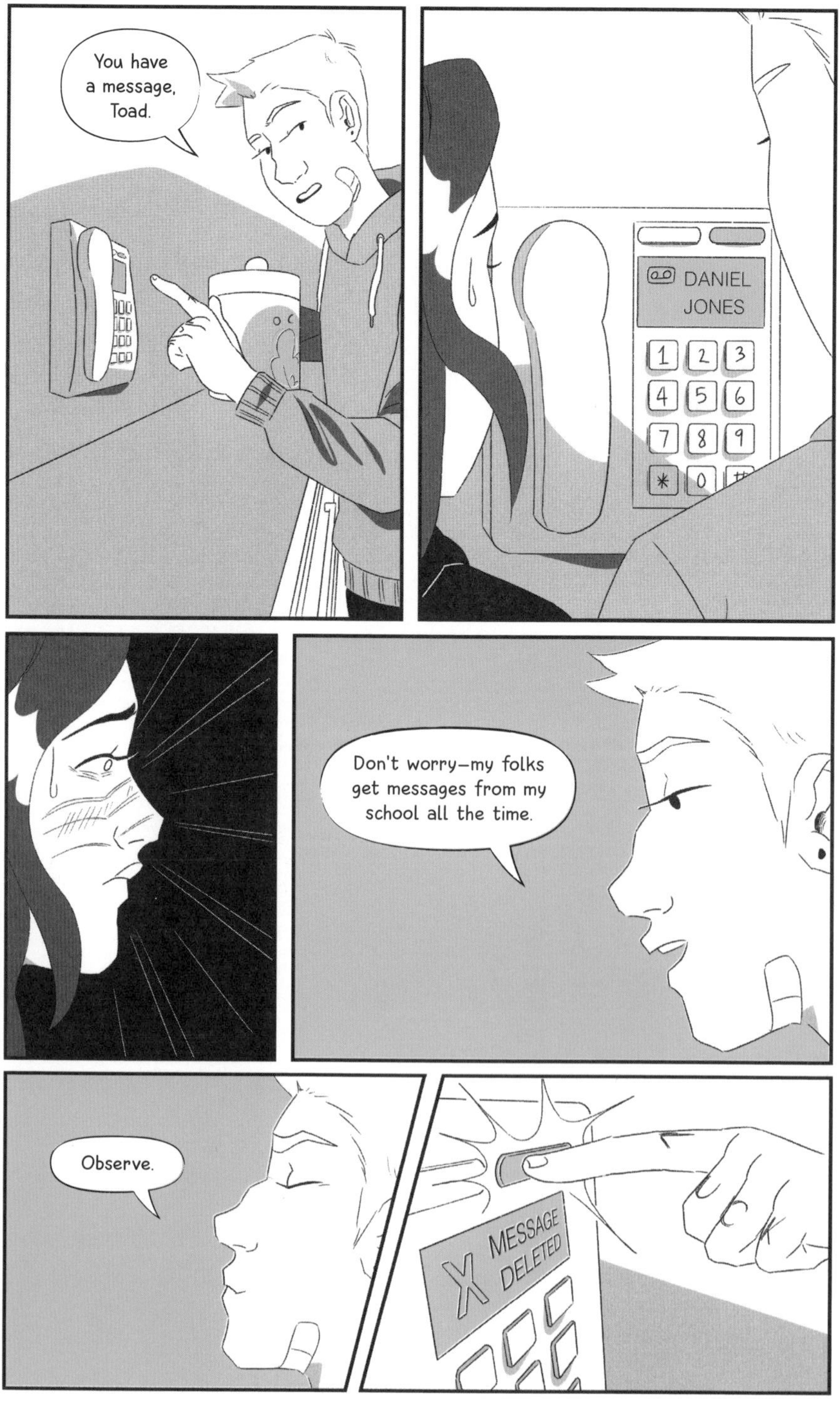

You have a message, Toad.
DANIEL JONES
Don't worry—my folks get messages from my school all the time.
Observe.
MESSAGE DELETED

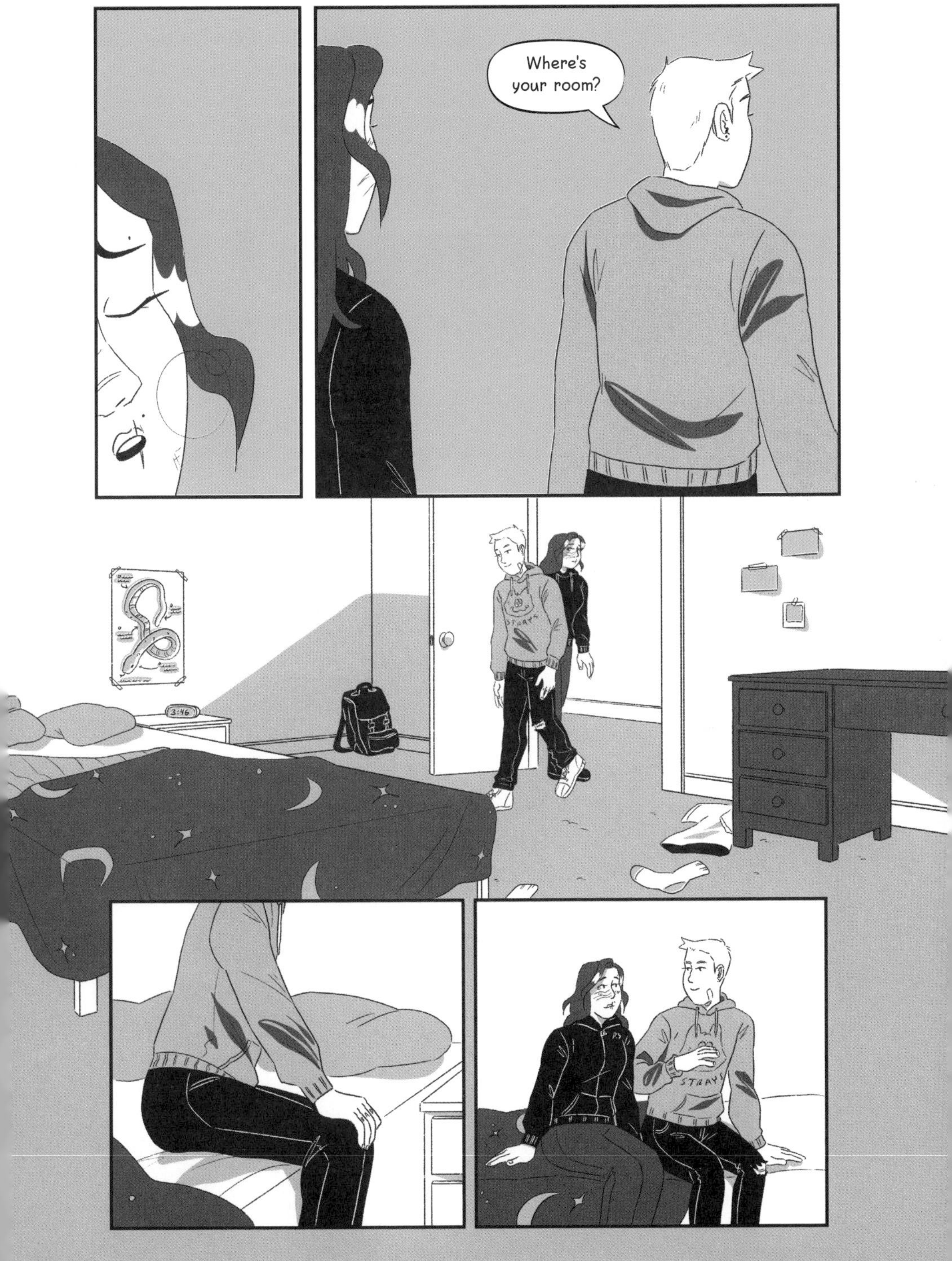
Where's your room?
3:46
STRAYS

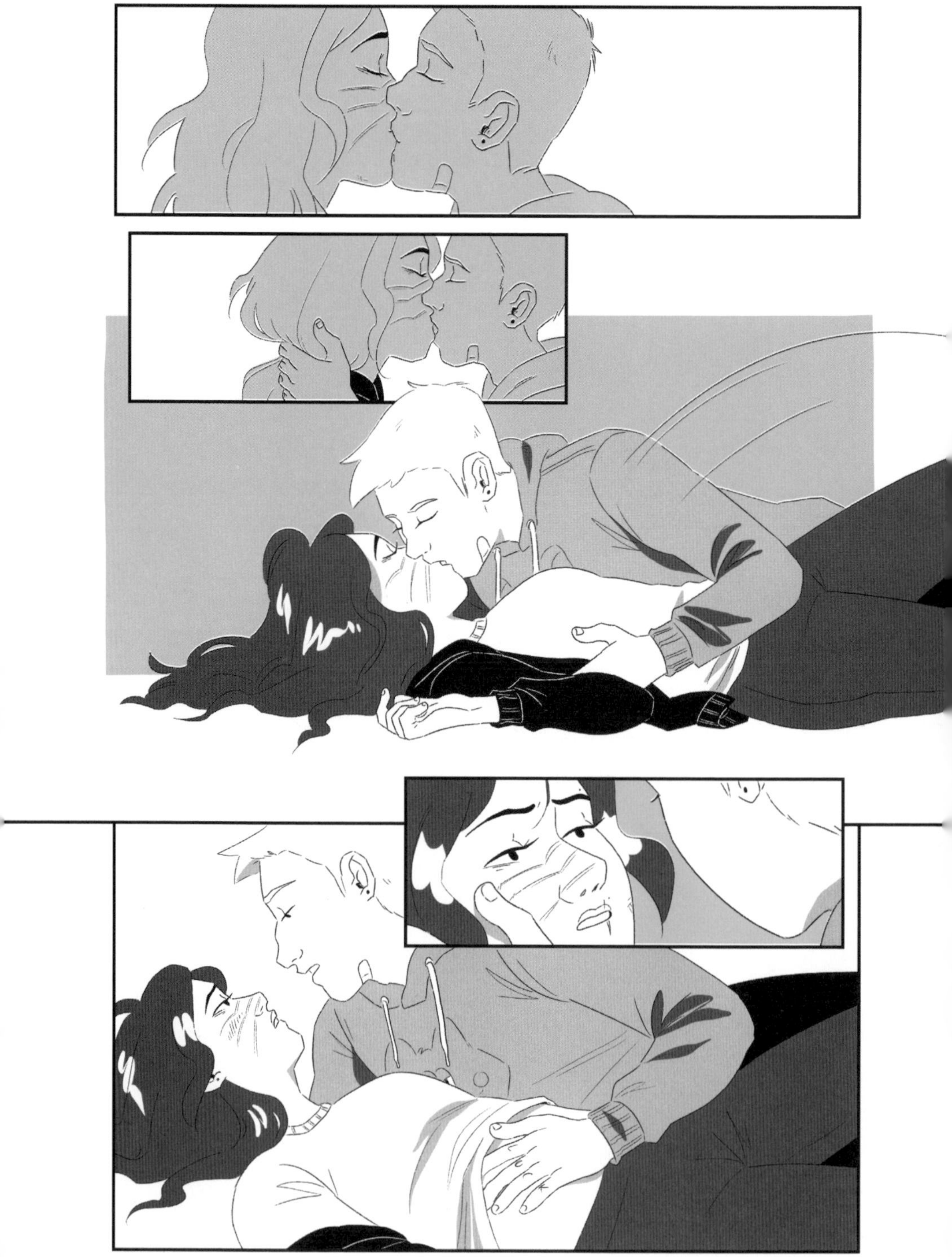

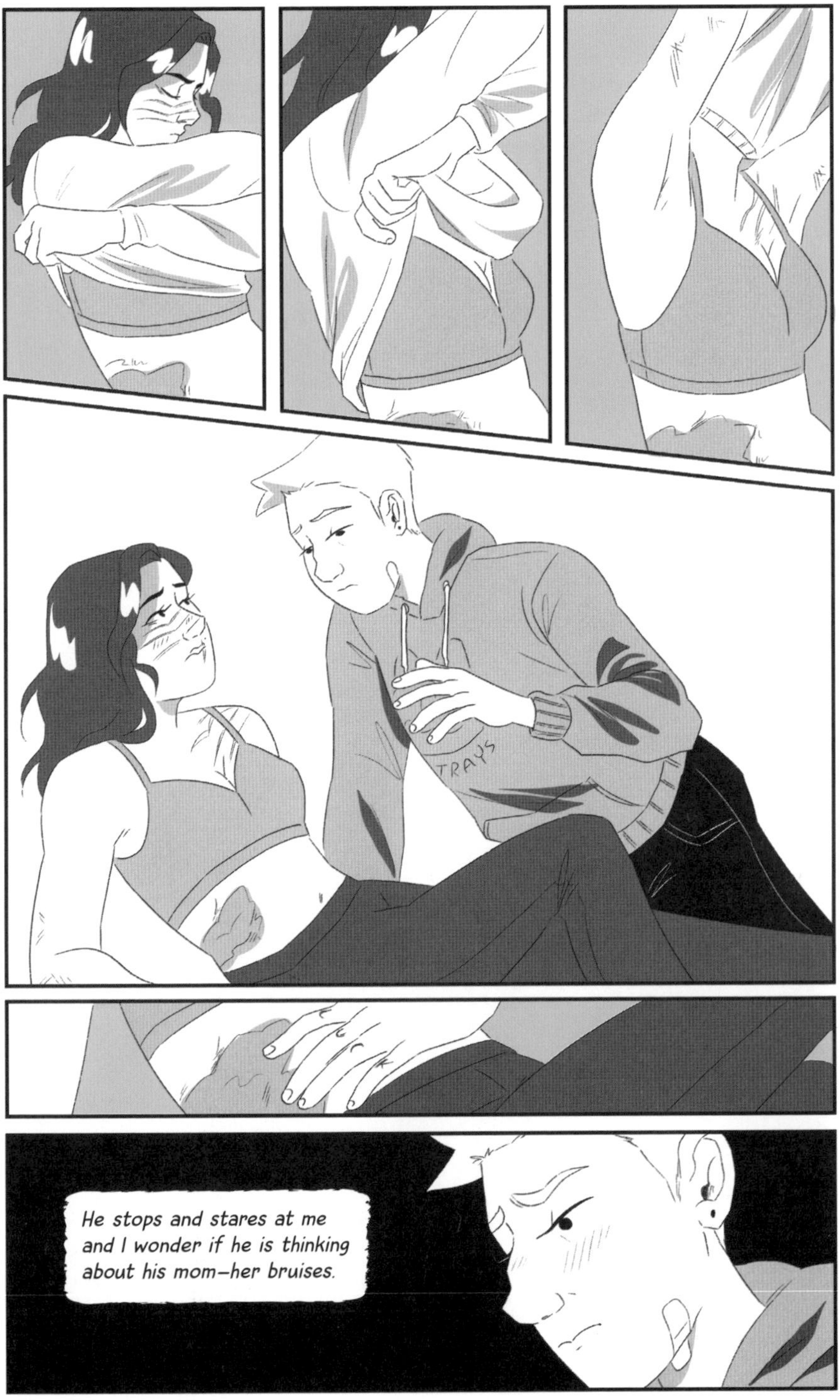
TRAYS
He stops and stares at me and I wonder if he is thinking about his mom—her bruises.

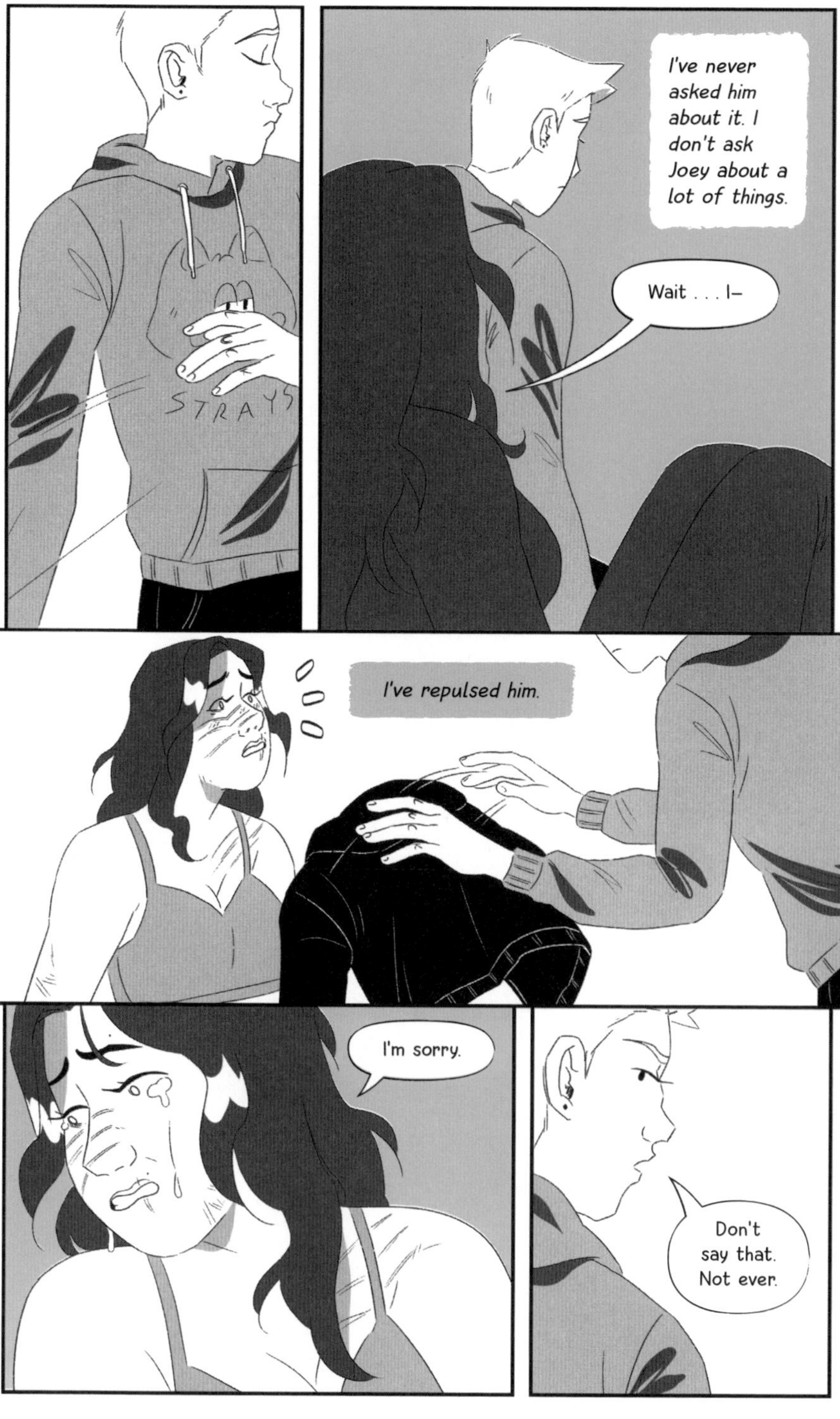

I've never asked him about it. I don't ask Joey about a lot of things.
Wait . . . I–
I've repulsed him.
I'm sorry.
Don't say that. Not ever.

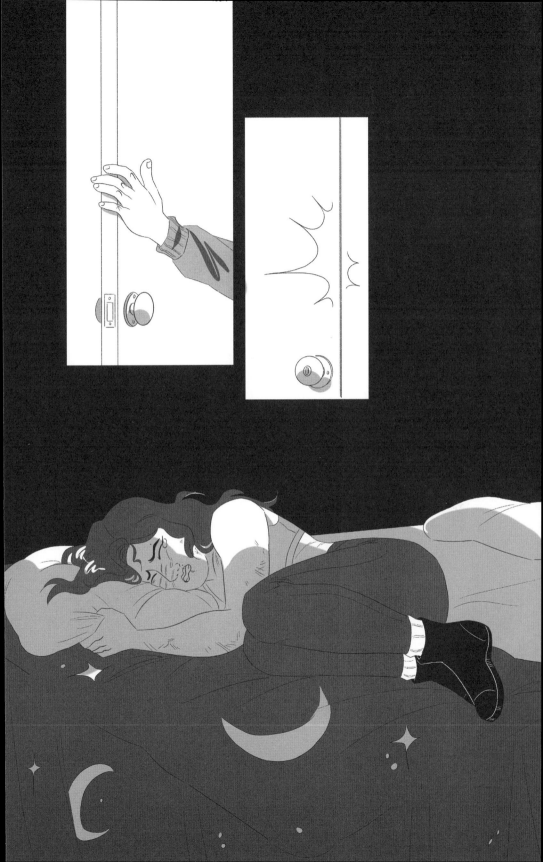

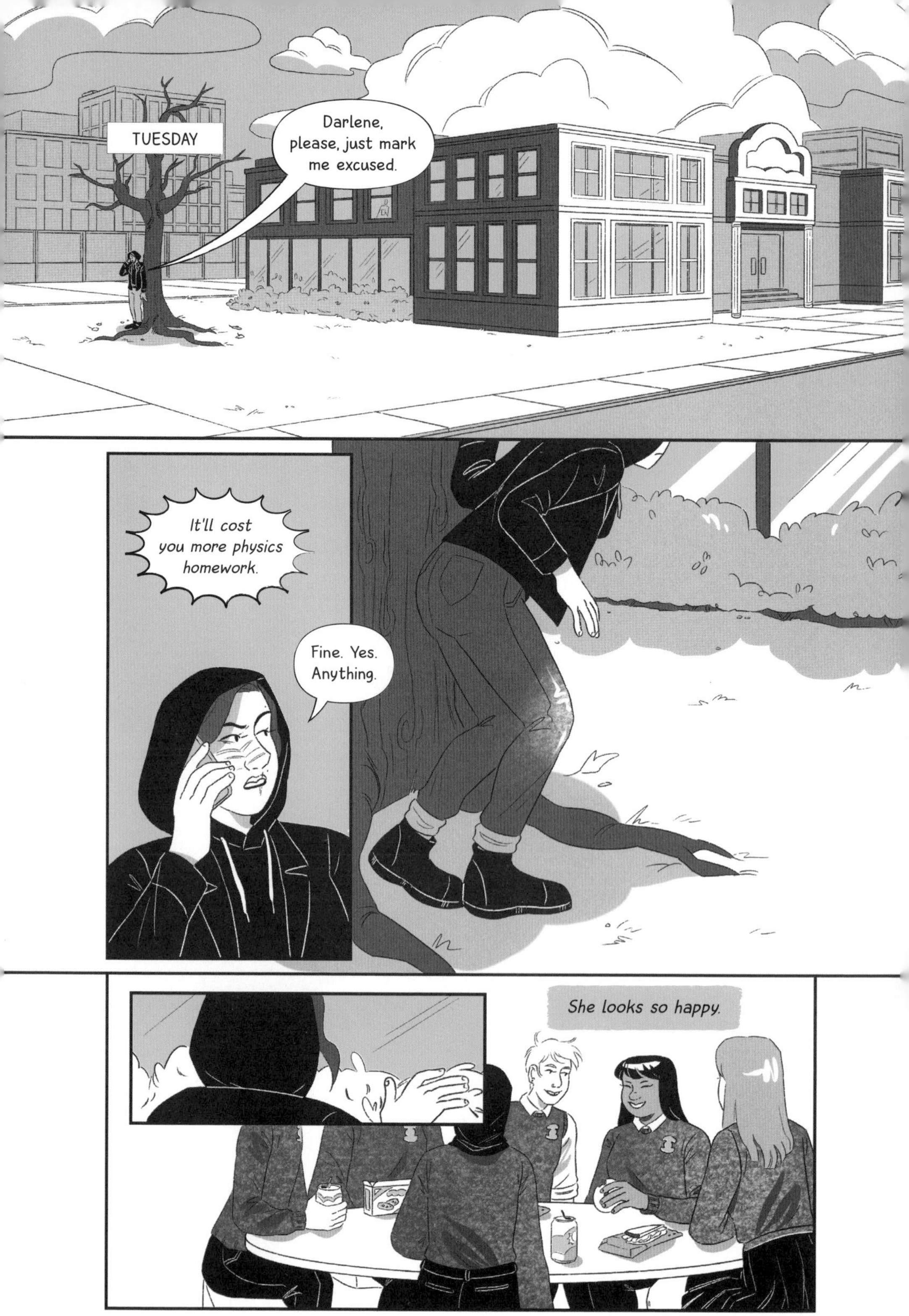
TUESDAY
Darlene, please, just mark me excused.
It'll cost you more physics homework.
Fine. Yes. Anything.
She looks so happy.

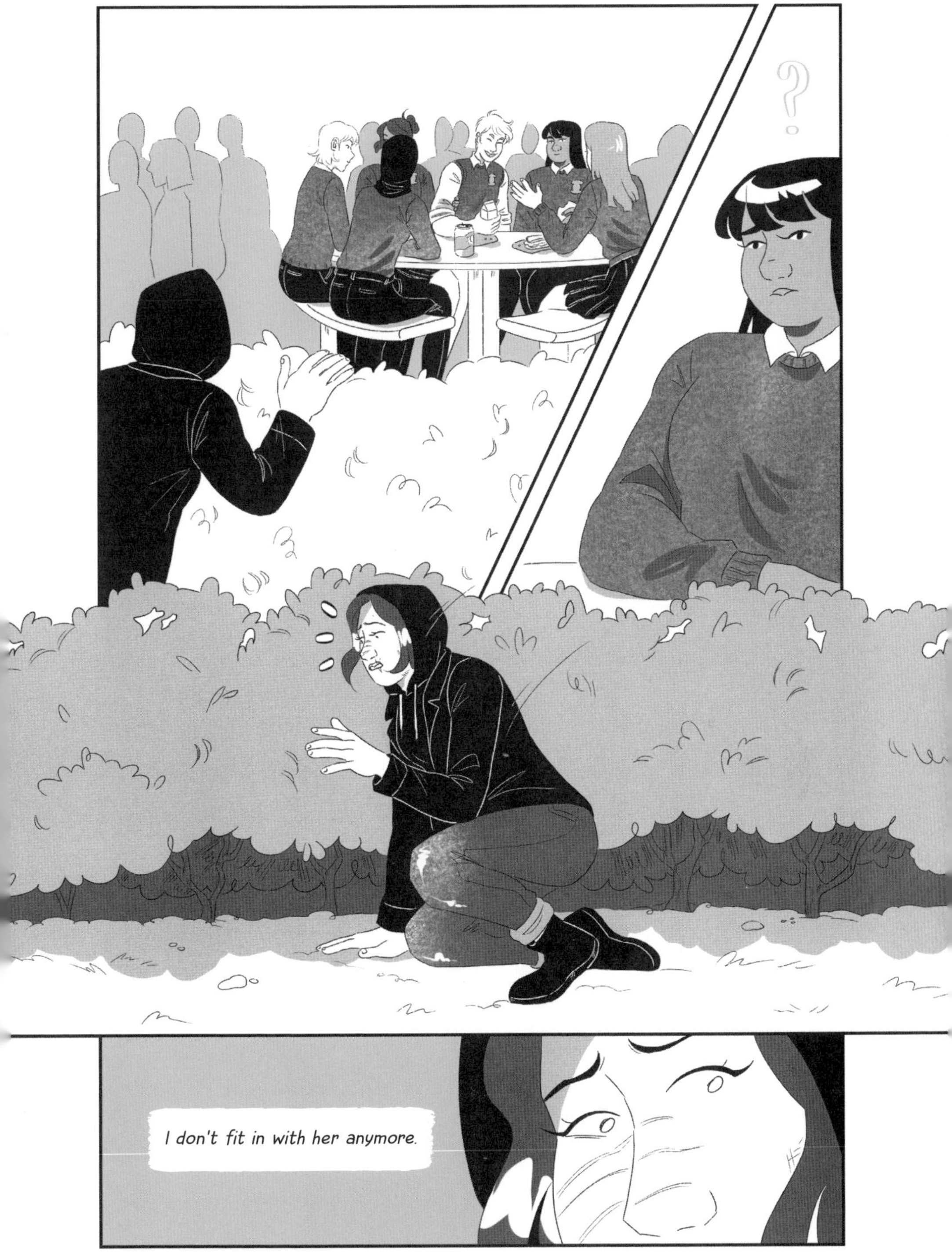
?
I don't fit in with her anymore.

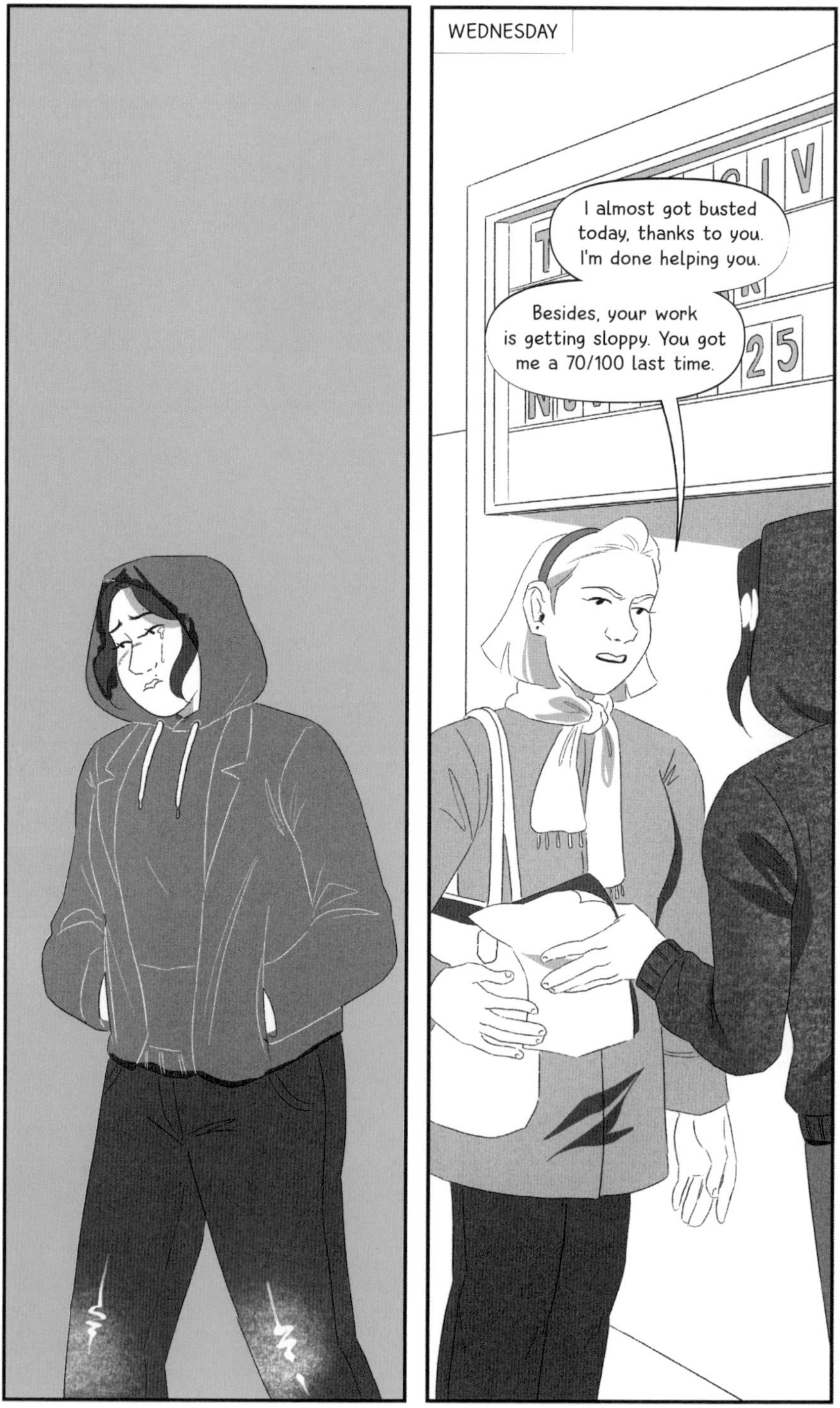
WEDNESDAY
I almost got busted today, thanks to you. I'm done helping you.
Besides, your work is getting sloppy. You got me a 70/100 last time.

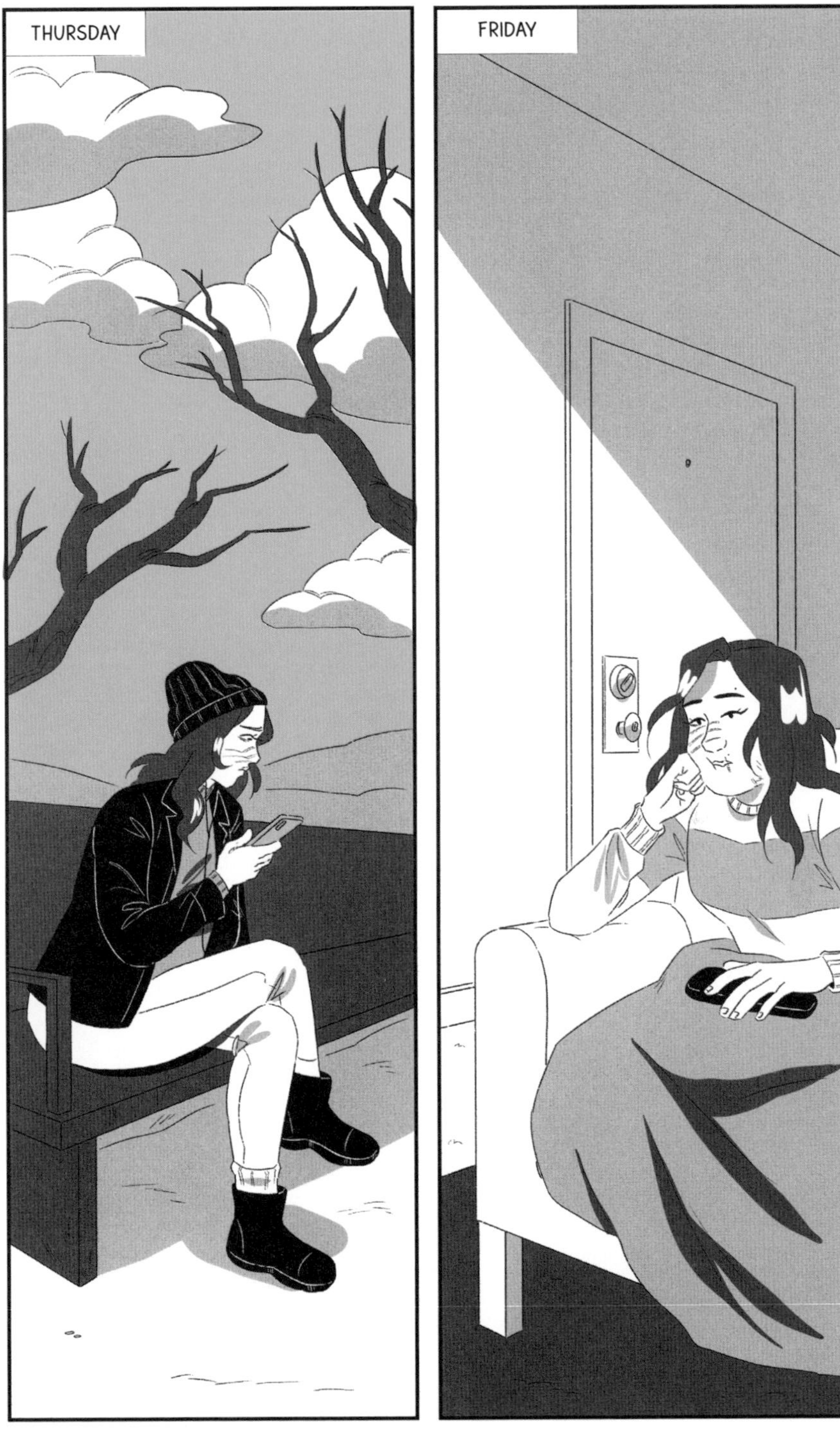
THURSDAY
FRIDAY

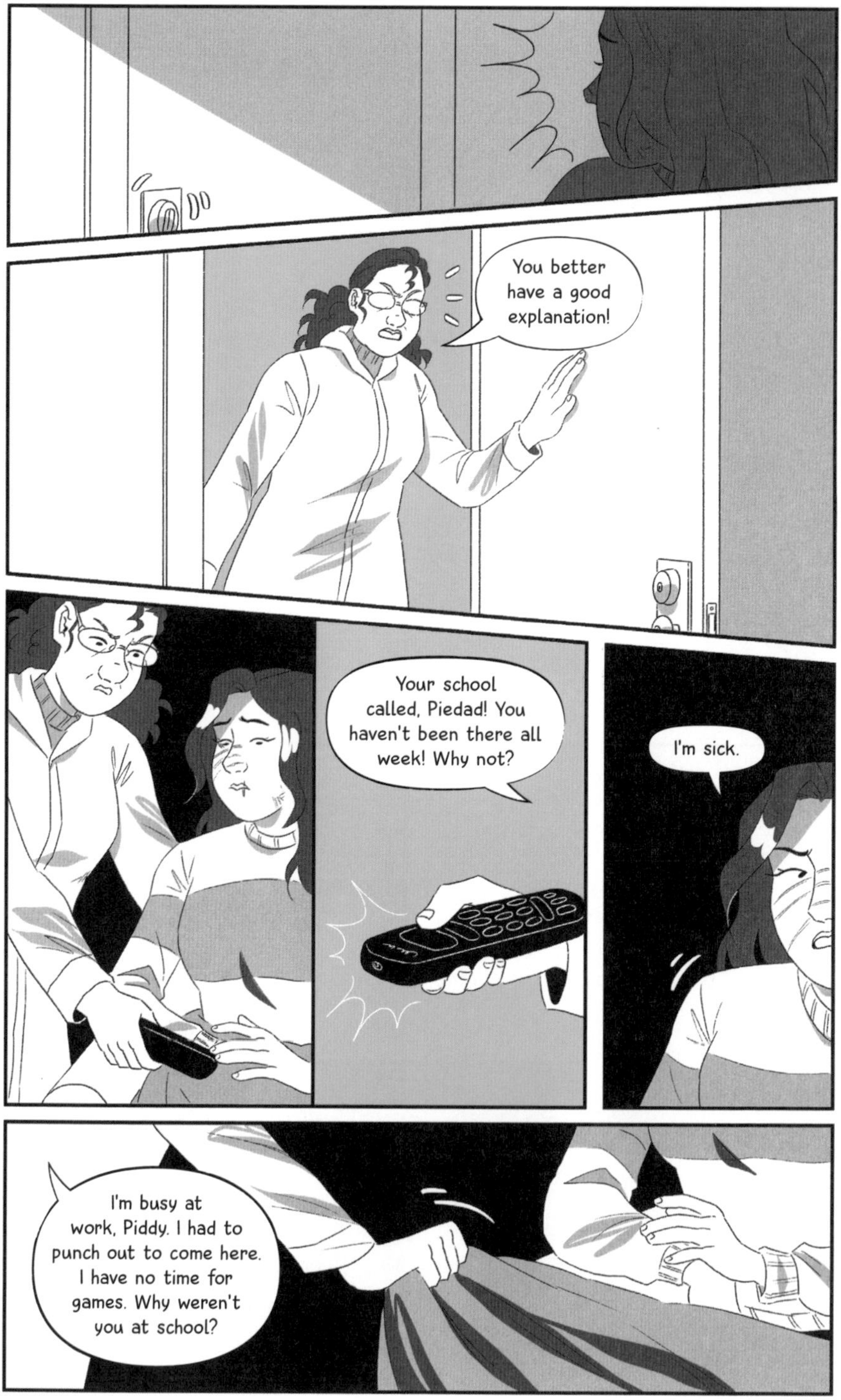
You better have a good explanation!
Your school called, Piedad! You haven't been there all week! Why not?
I'm sick.
I'm busy at work, Piddy. I had to punch out to come here. I have no time for games. Why weren't you at school?

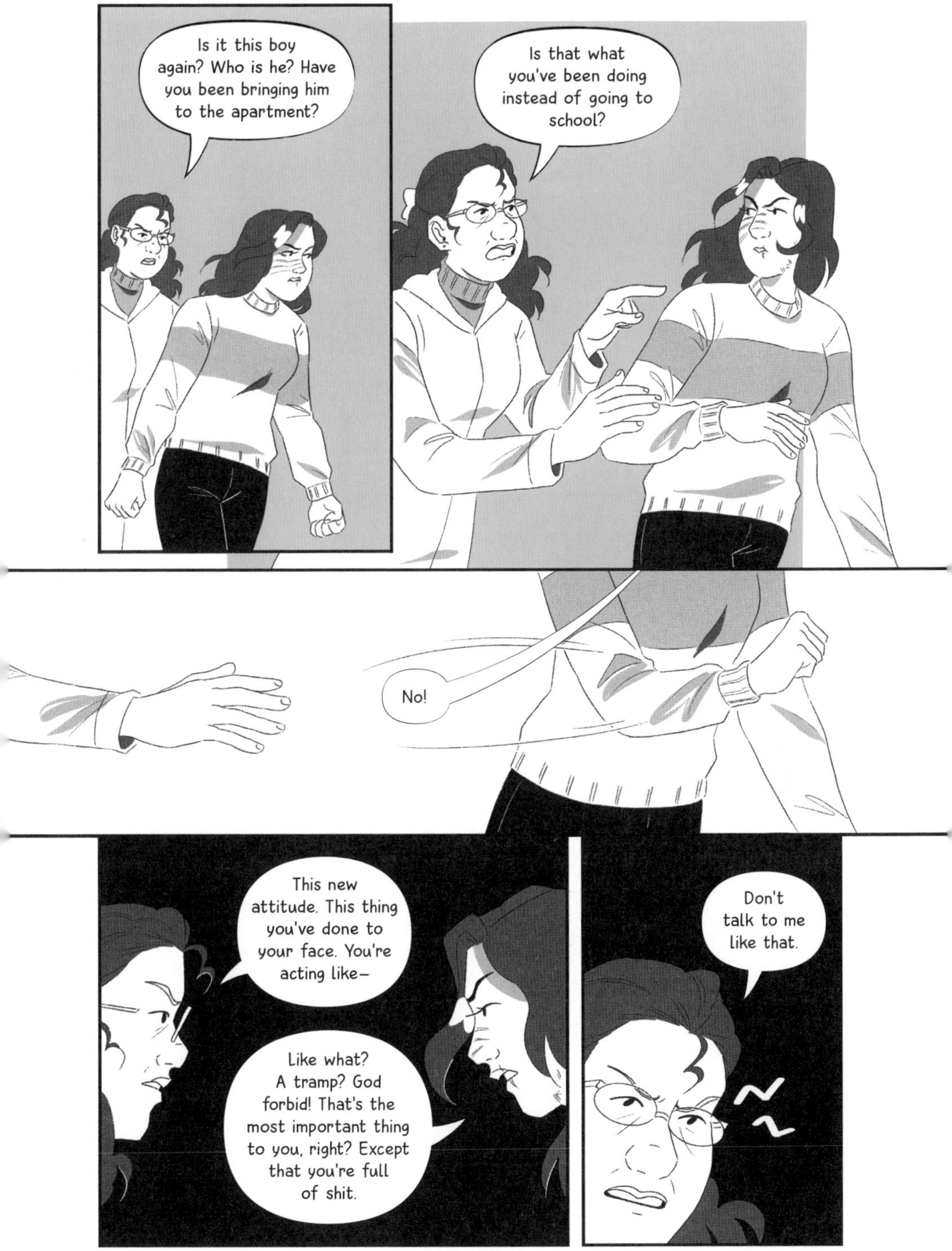
Is it this boy again? Who is he? Have you been bringing him to the apartment?
Is that what you've been doing instead of going to school?
No!
This new attitude. This thing you've done to your face. You're acting like–
Like what? A tramp? God forbid! That's the most important thing to you, right? Except that you're full of shit.
Don't talk to me like that.

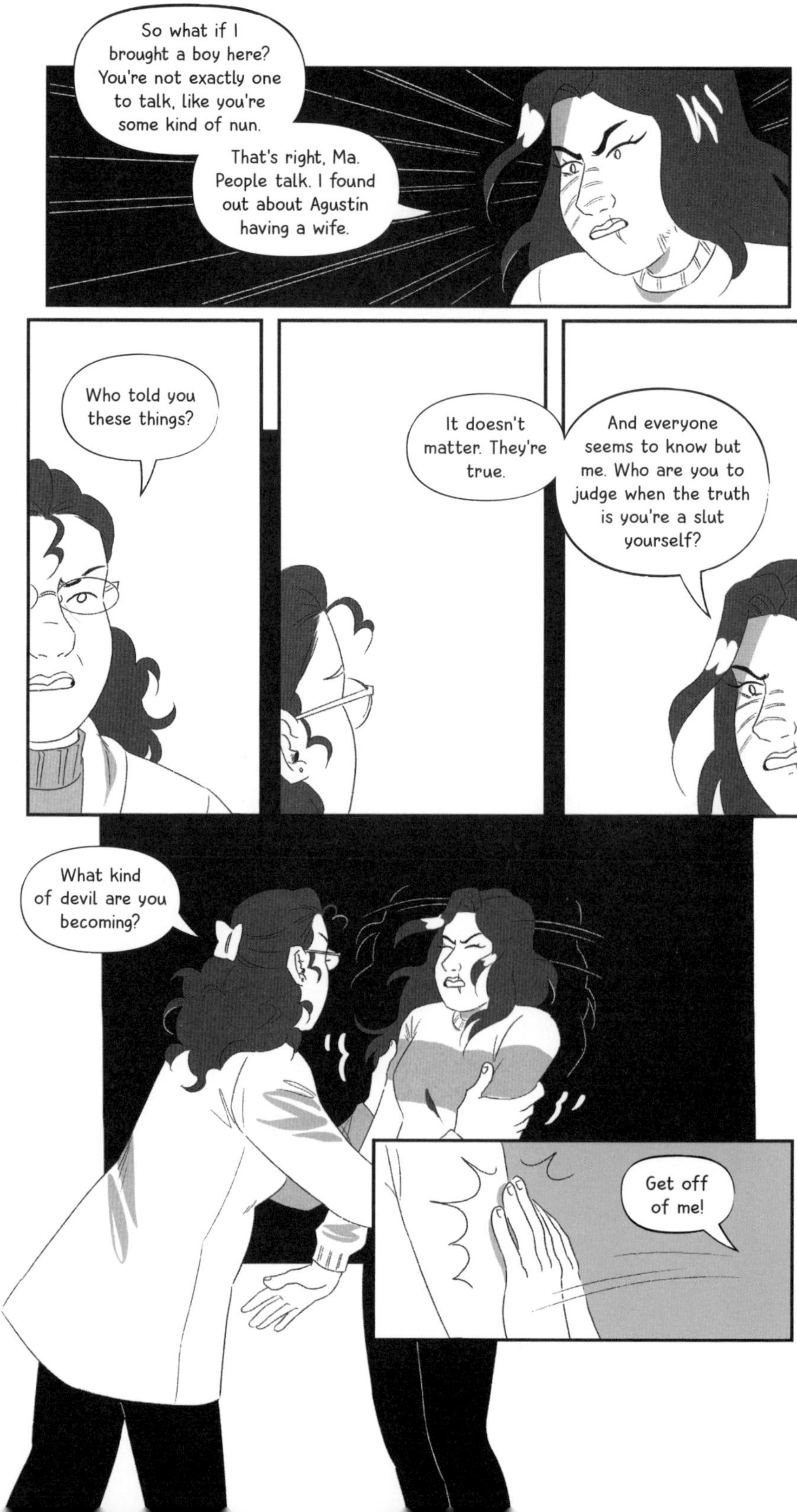
So what if I brought a boy here? You're not exactly one to talk, like you're some kind of nun.
That's right, Ma. People talk. I found out about Agustin having a wife.
Who told you these things?
It doesn't matter. They're true.
And everyone seems to know but me. Who are you to judge when the truth is you're a slut yourself?
What kind of devil are you becoming?
Get off of me!

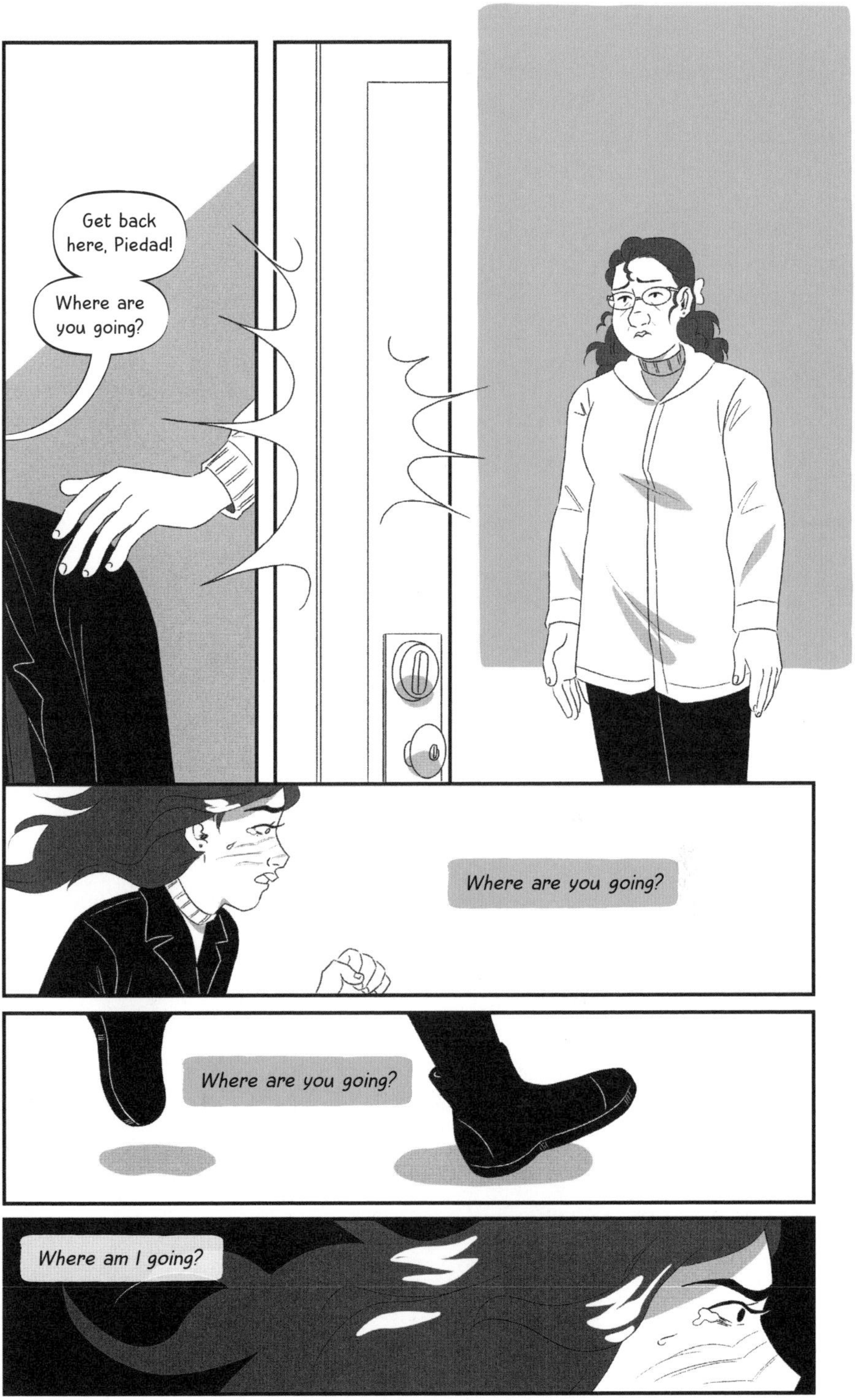
Get back here, Piedad!
Where are you going?
Where are you going?
Where are you going?
Where am I going?

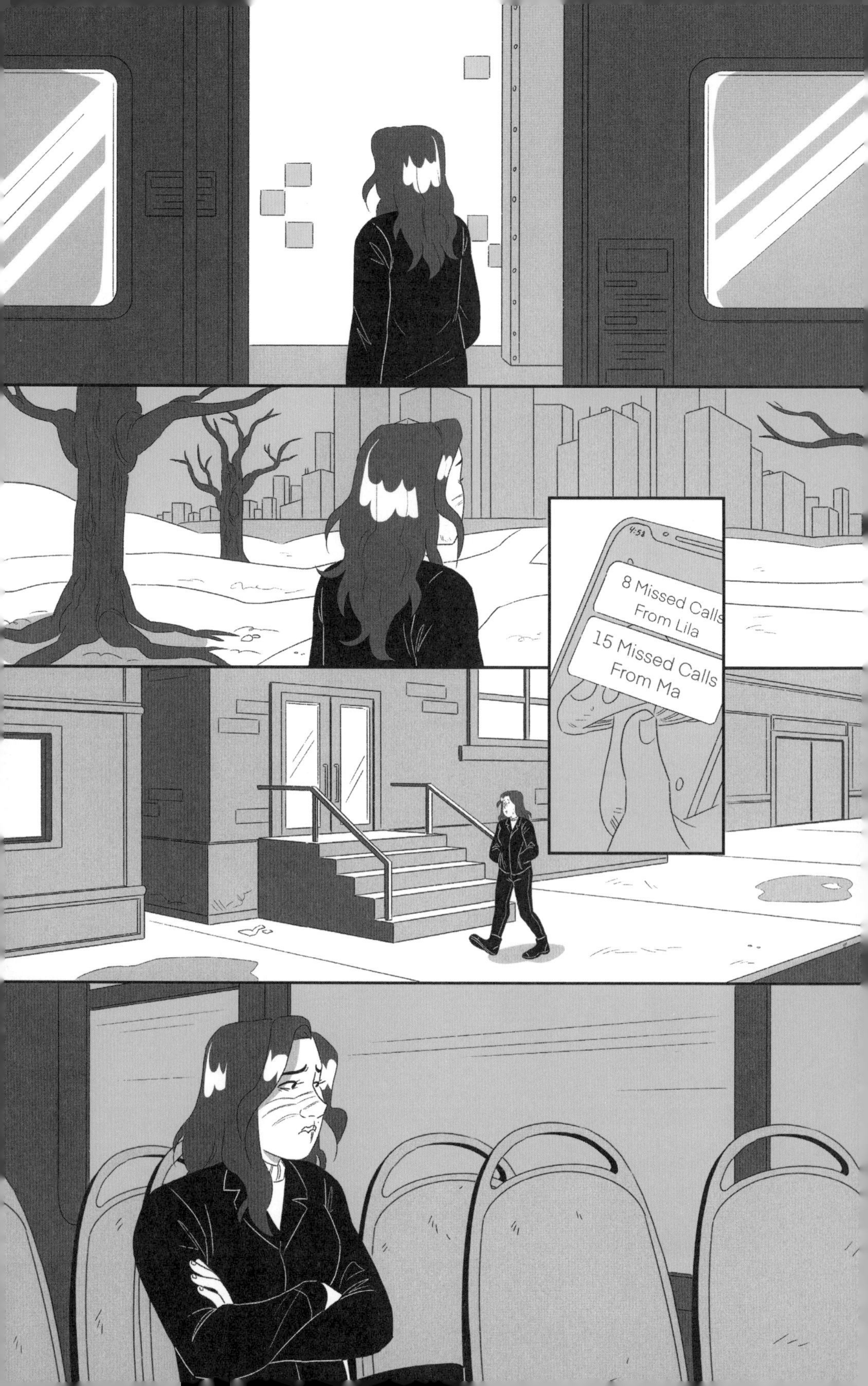
4:58
8 Missed Calls From Lila
15 Missed Calls From Ma

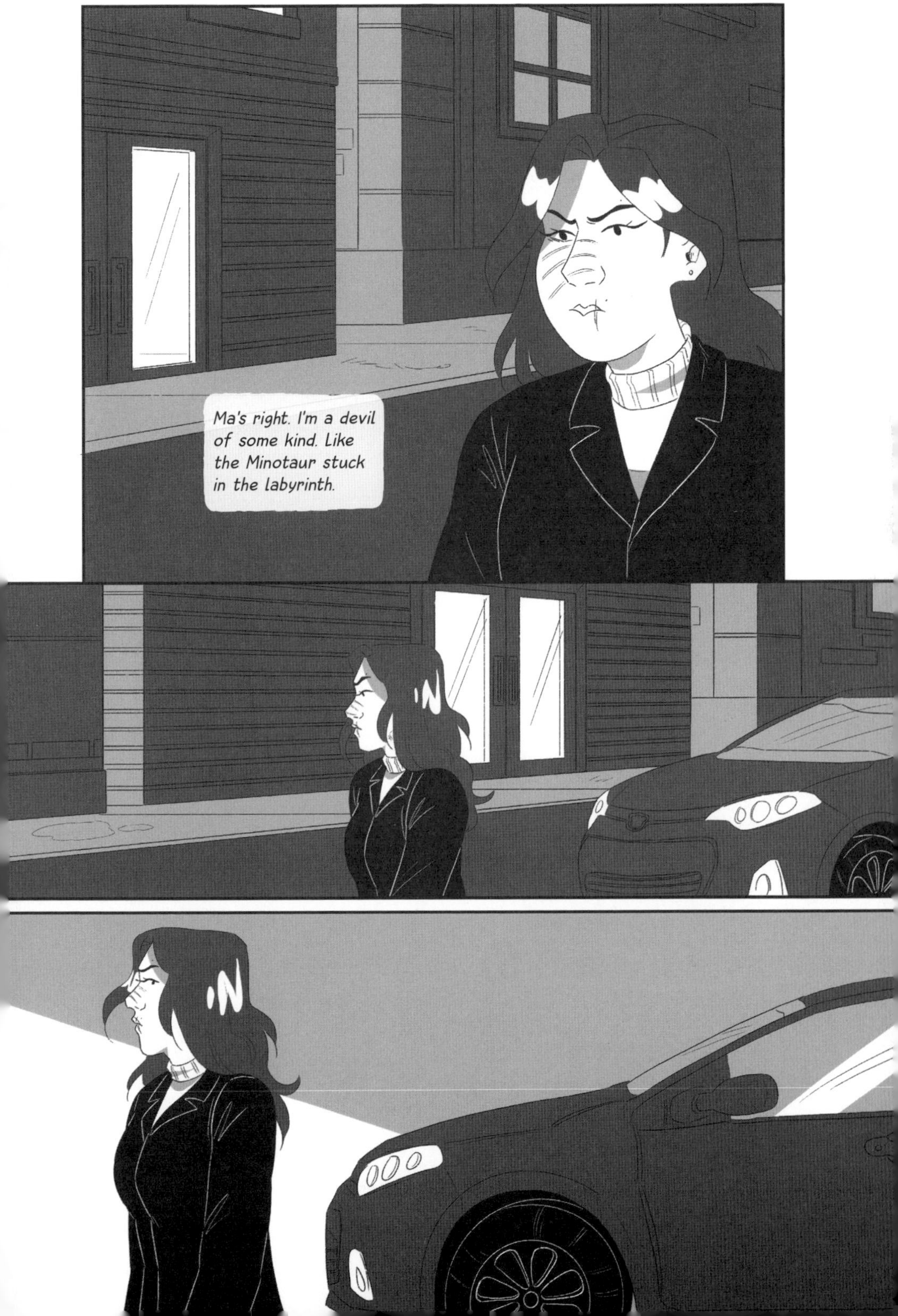
Ma's right. I'm a devil of some kind. Like the Minotaur stuck in the labyrinth.

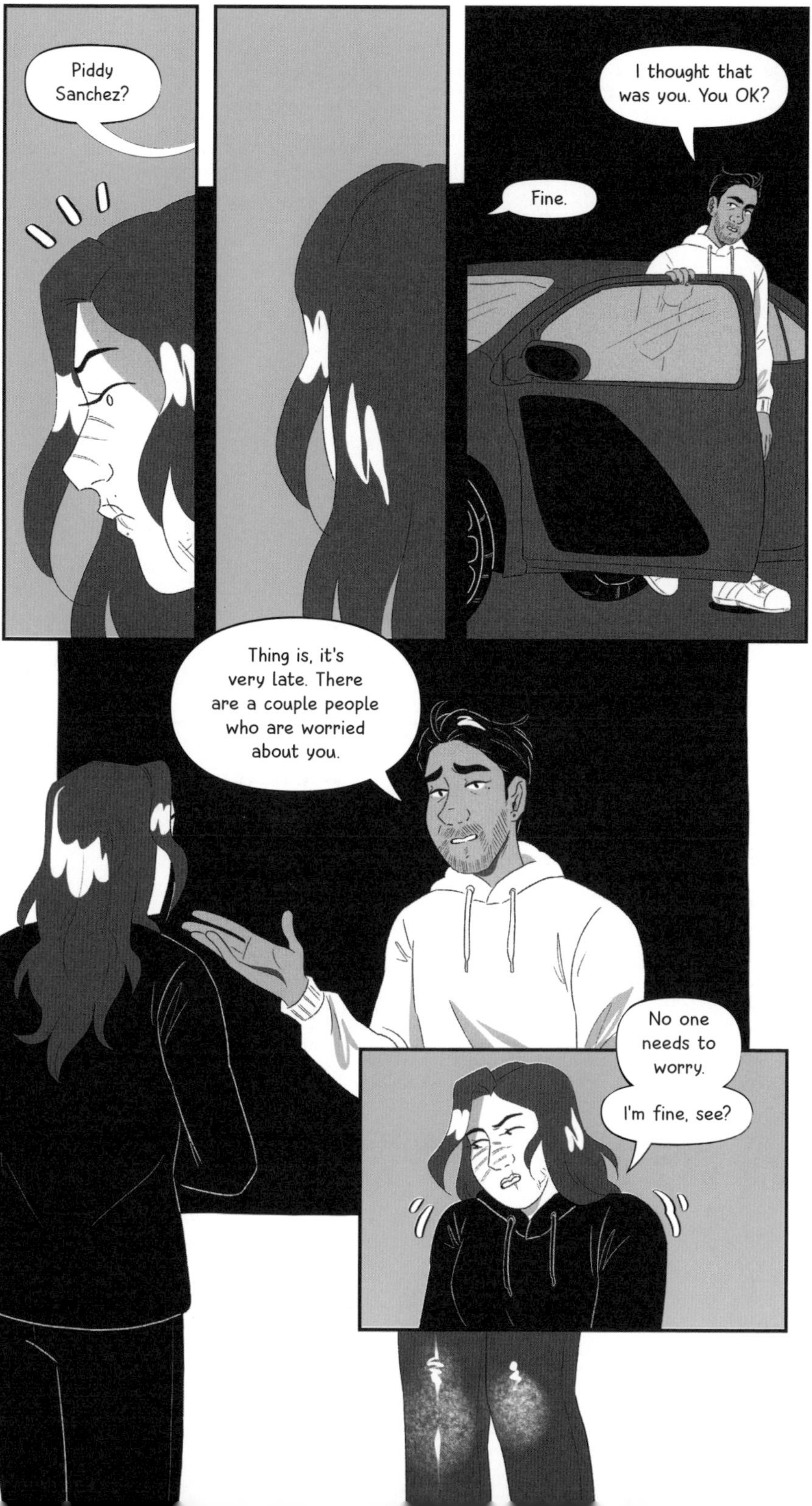
Piddy Sanchez?
I thought that was you. You OK?
Fine.
Thing is, it's very late. There are a couple people who are worried about you.
No one needs to worry.
I'm fine, see?

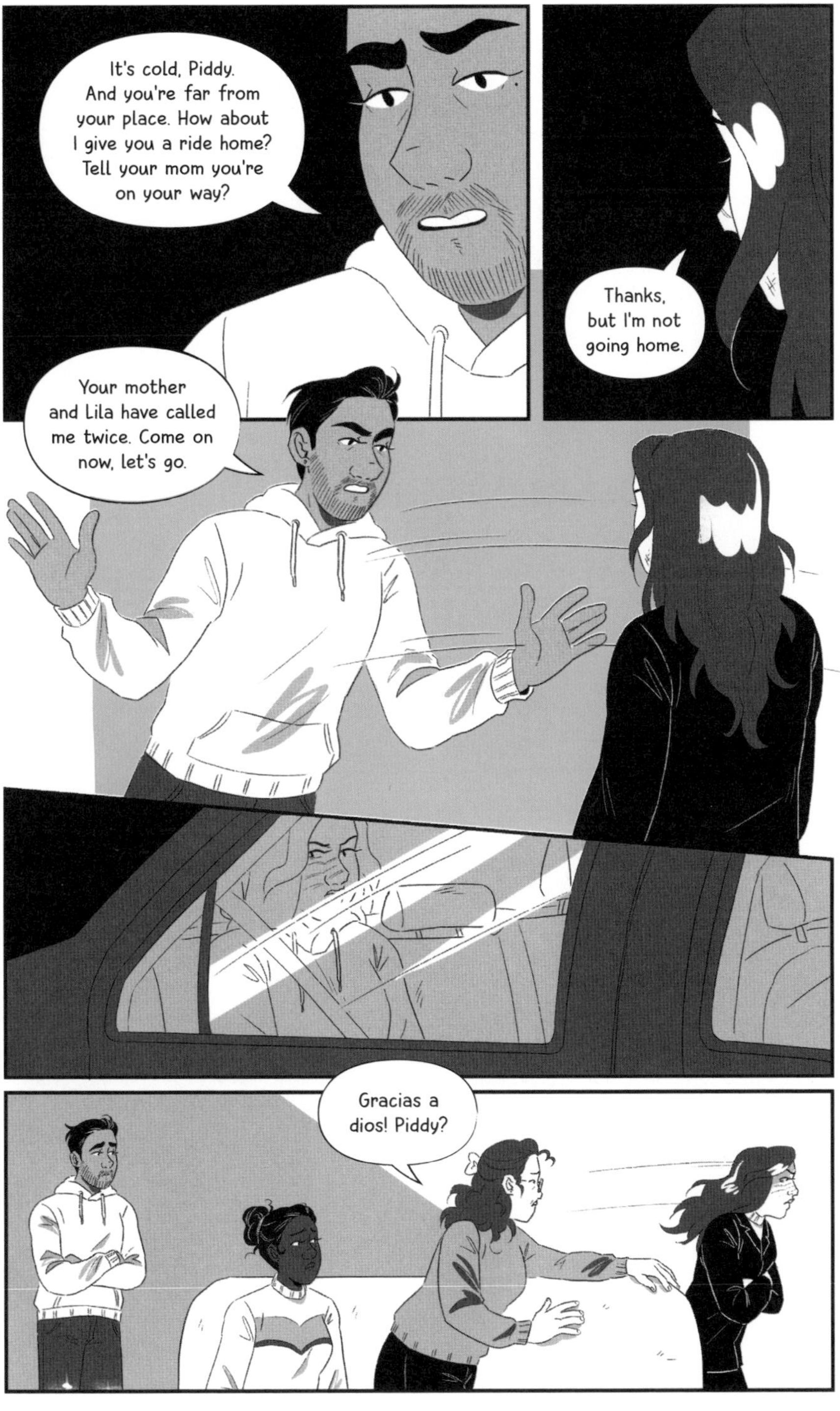
It's cold, Piddy. And you're far from your place. How about I give you a ride home? Tell your mom you're on your way?
Thanks, but I'm not going home.
Your mother and Lila have called me twice. Come on now, let's go.
Gracias a dios! Piddy?

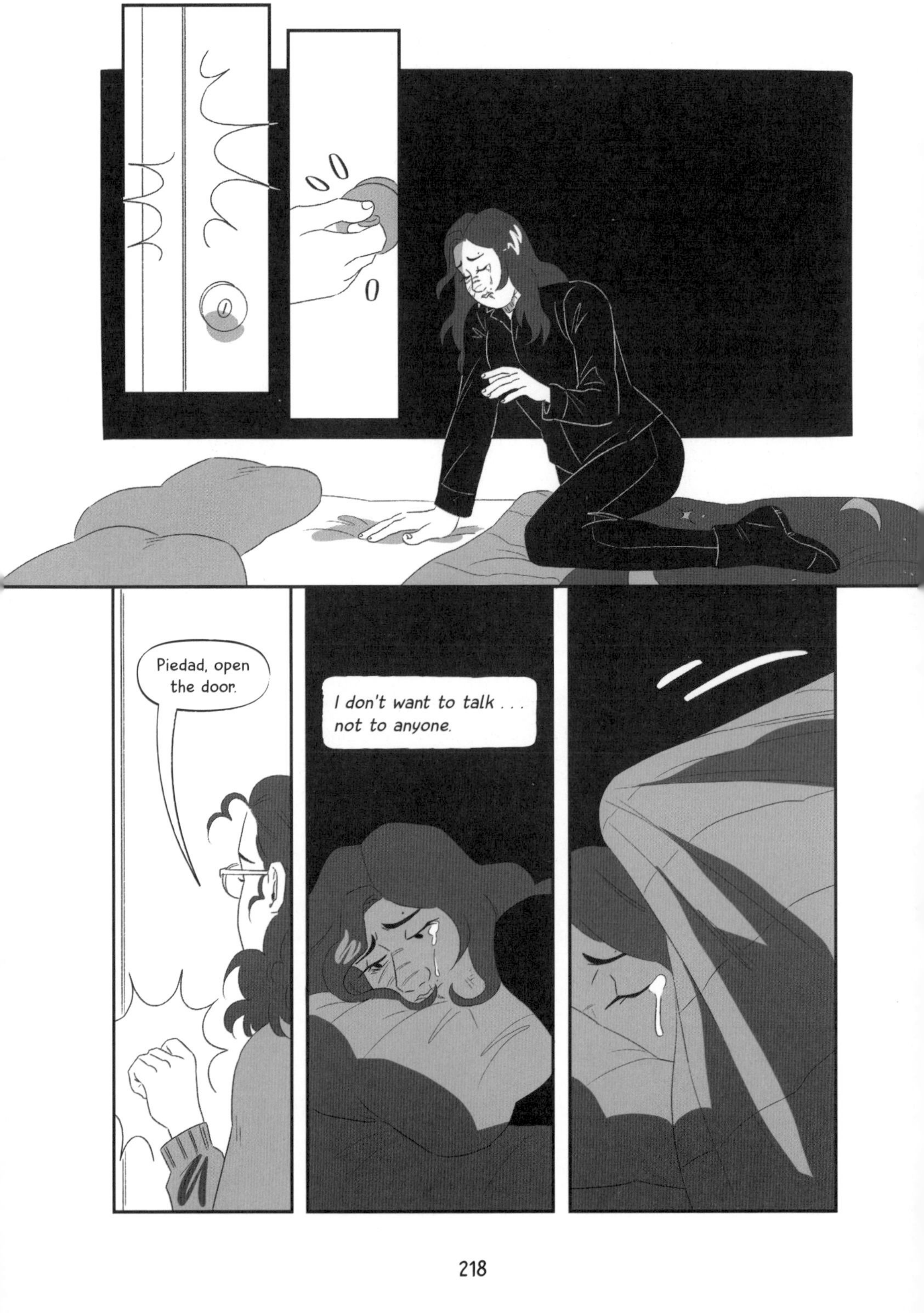
Piedad, open the door.
I don't want to talk . . . not to anyone.

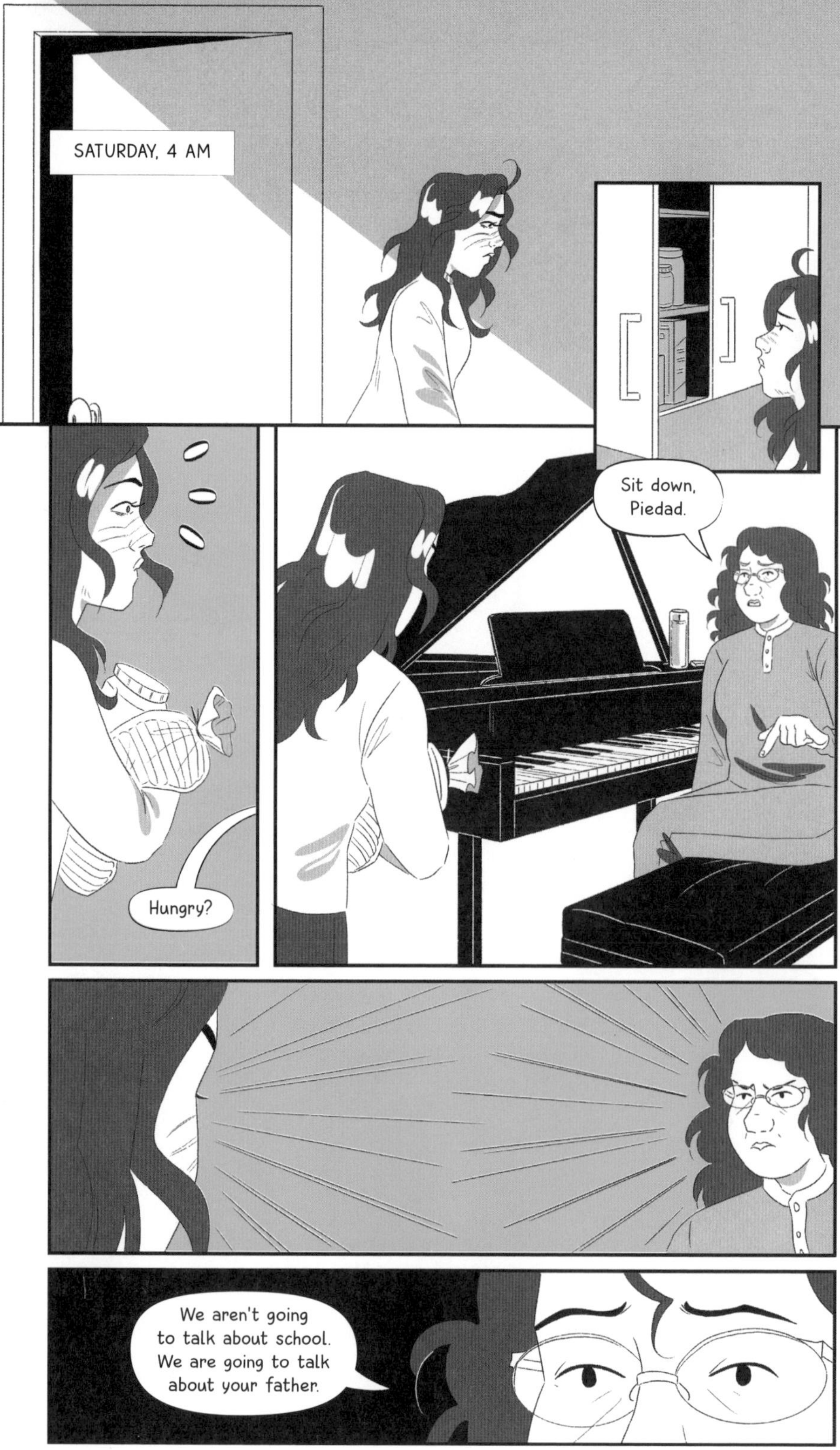
SATURDAY, 4 AM
Hungry?
Sit down, Piedad.
We aren't going to talk about school. We are going to talk about your father.

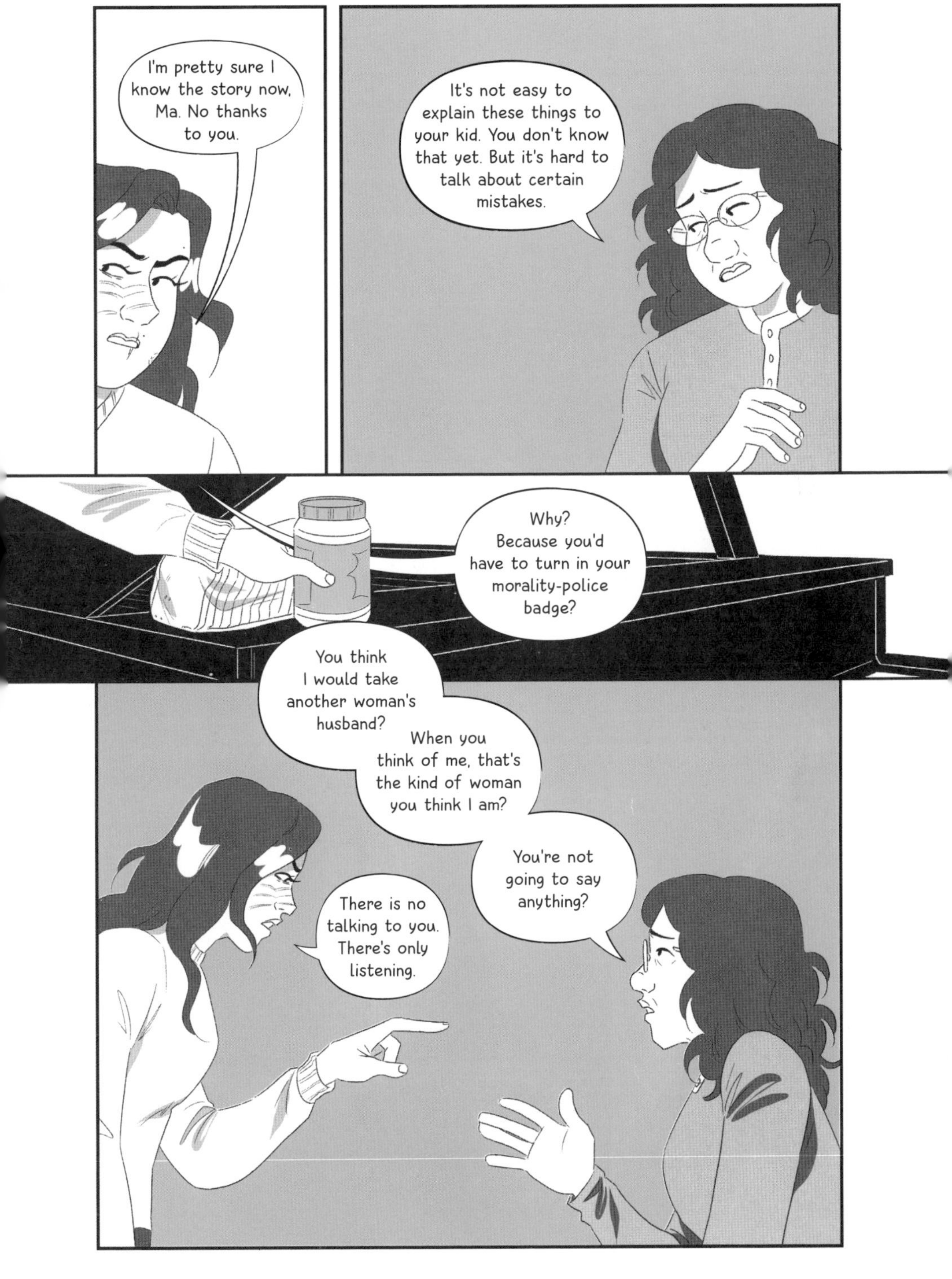
I'm pretty sure I know the story now, Ma. No thanks to you.
It's not easy to explain these things to your kid. You don't know that yet. But it's hard to talk about certain mistakes.
Why? Because you'd have to turn in your morality-police badge?
You think I would take another woman's husband?
When you think of me, that's the kind of woman you think I am?
You're not going to say anything?
There is no talking to you. There's only listening.

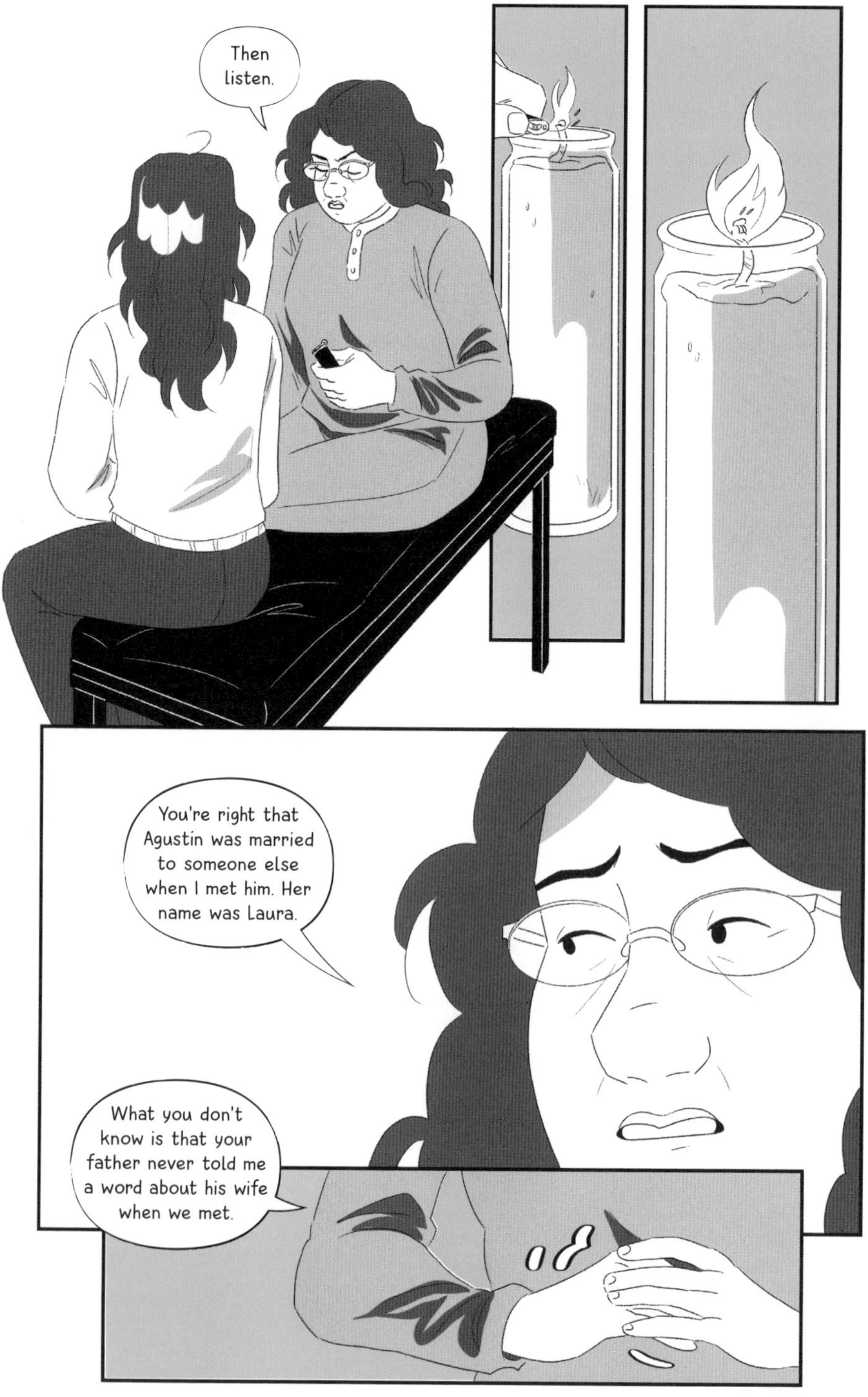
Then listen.
You're right that Agustín was married to someone else when I met him. Her name was Laura.
What you don't know is that your father never told me a word about his wife when we met.

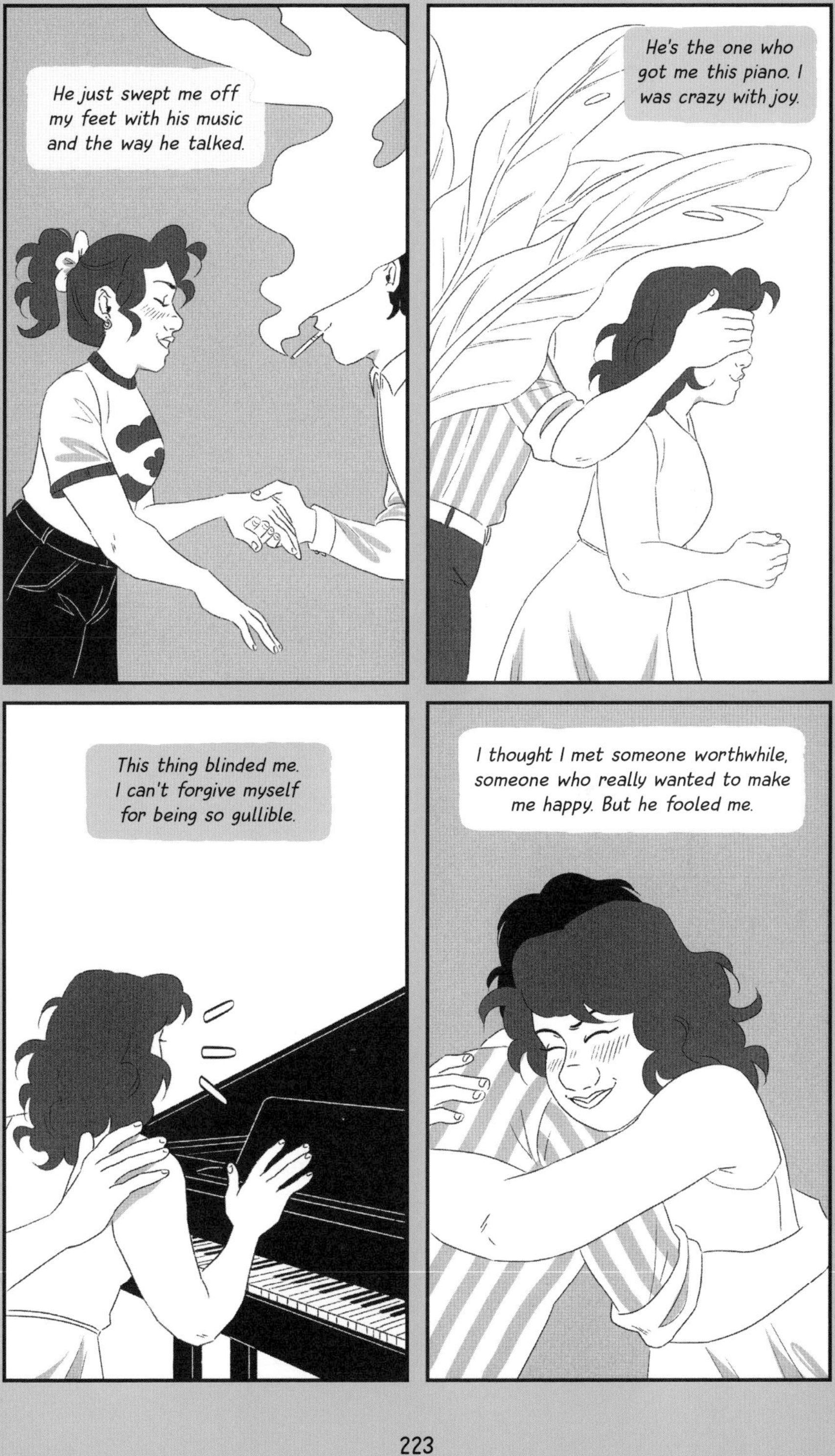
He just swept me off my feet with his music and the way he talked.
He's the one who got me this piano. I was crazy with joy.
This thing blinded me. I can't forgive myself for being so gullible.
I thought I met someone worthwhile, someone who really wanted to make me happy. But he fooled me.

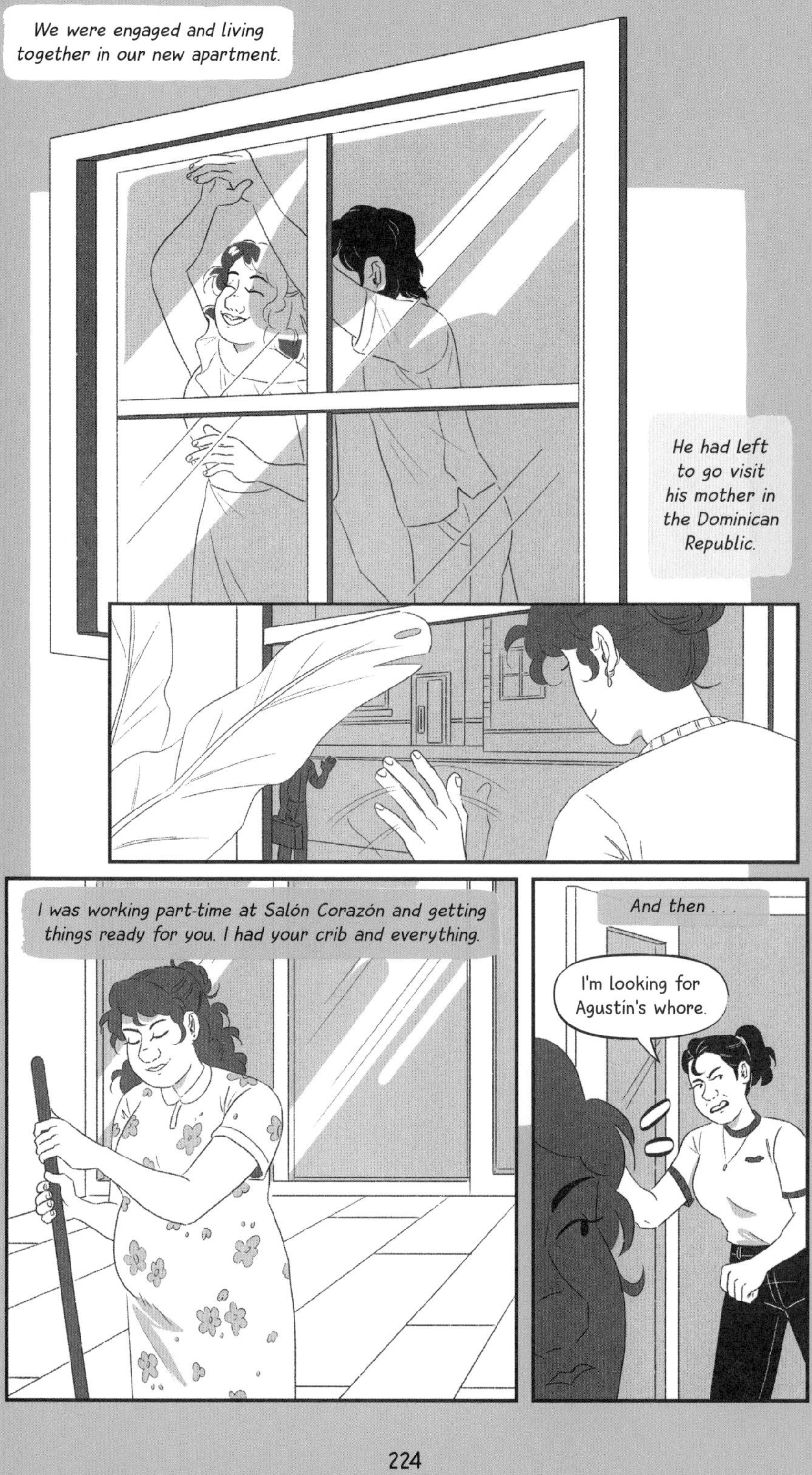
We were engaged and living together in our new apartment.
He had left to go visit his mother in the Dominican Republic.
I was working part-time at Salón Corazón and getting things ready for you. I had your crib and everything.
And then . . .
I'm looking for Agustín's whore.

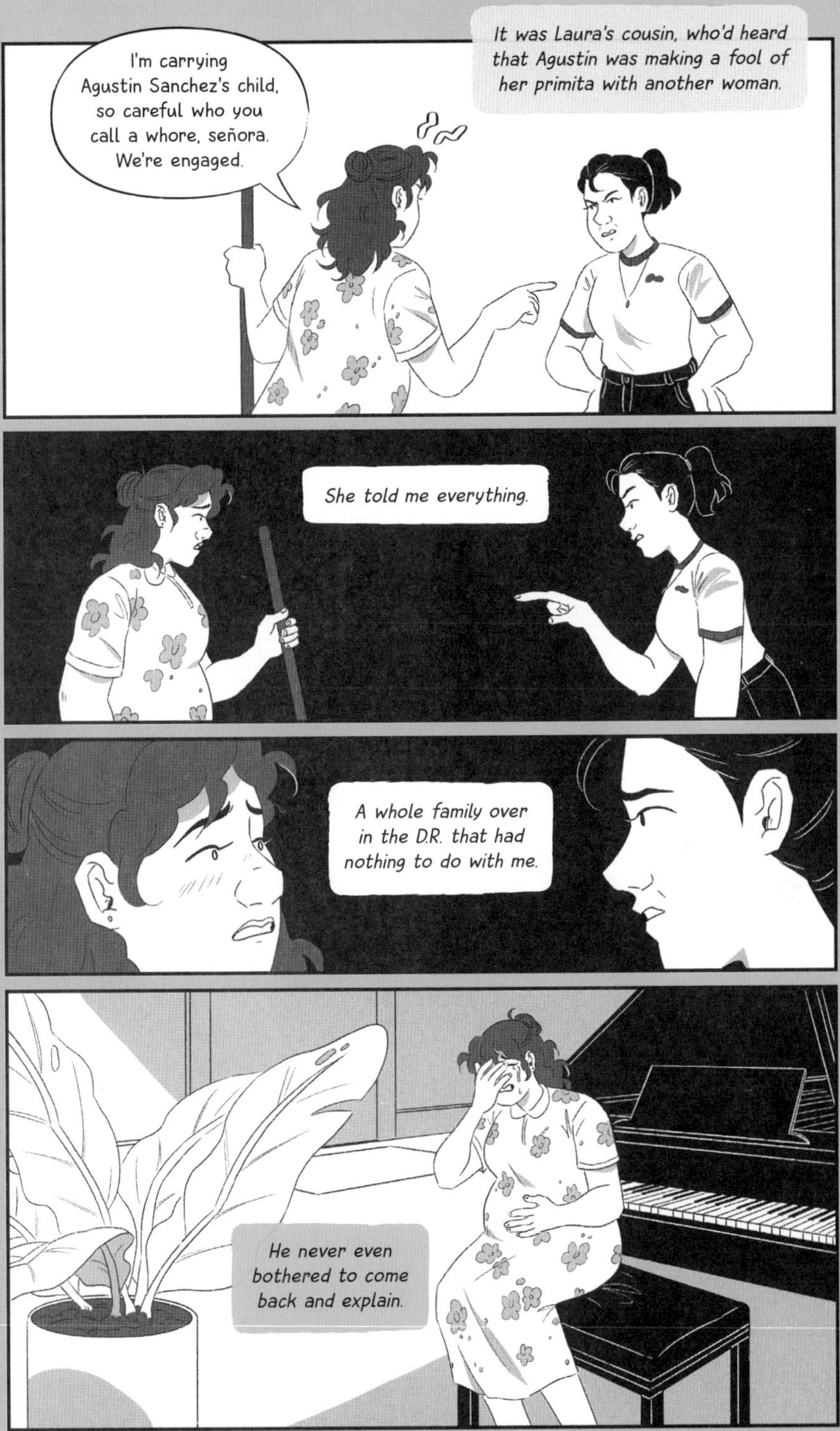
It was Laura's cousin, who'd heard that Agustin was making a fool of her primita with another woman.
I'm carrying Agustin Sanchez's child, so careful who you call a whore, señora. We're engaged.
She told me everything.
A whole family over in the D.R. that had nothing to do with me.
He never even bothered to come back and explain.

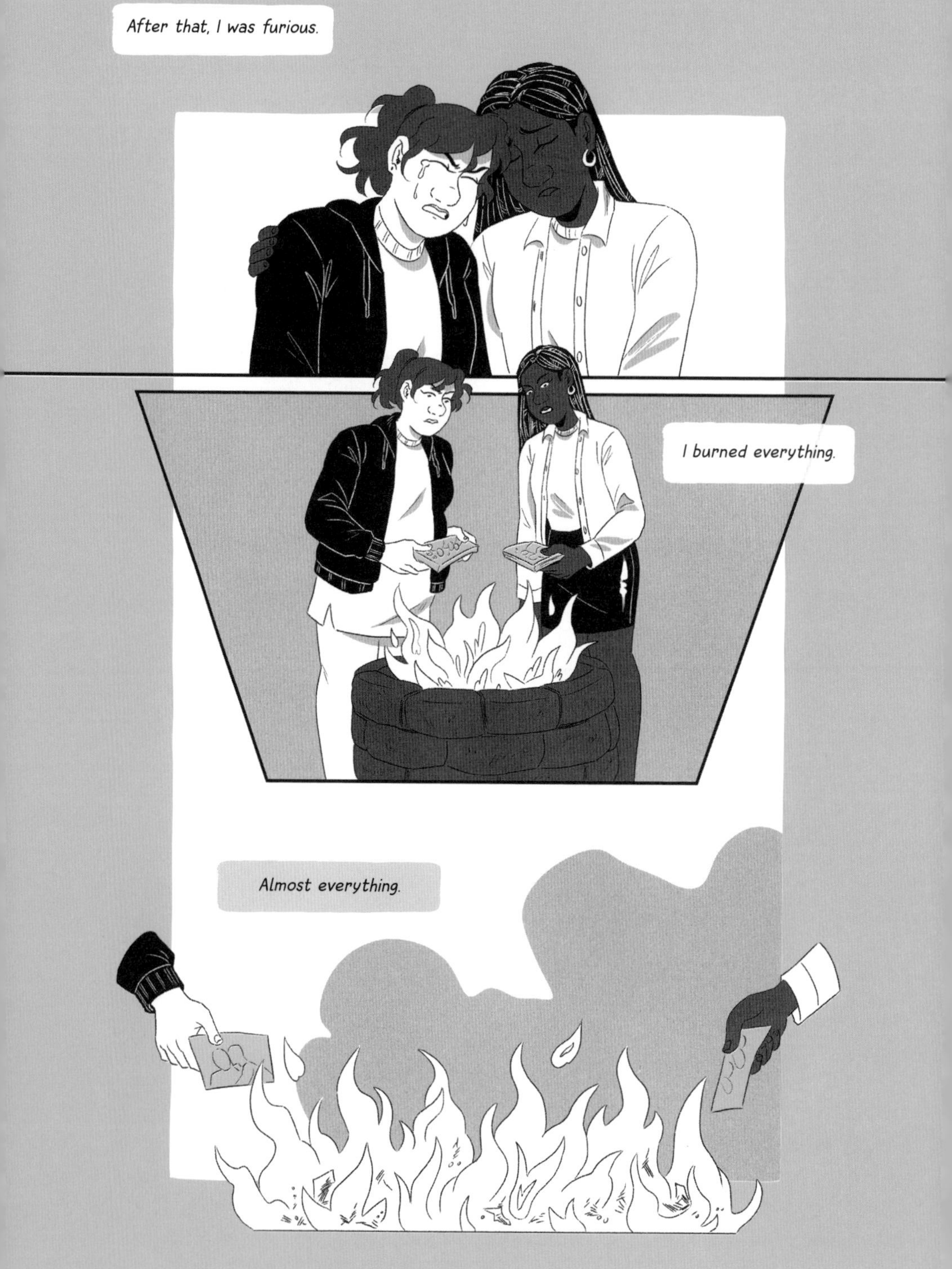
After that, I was furious.
I burned everything.
Almost everything.

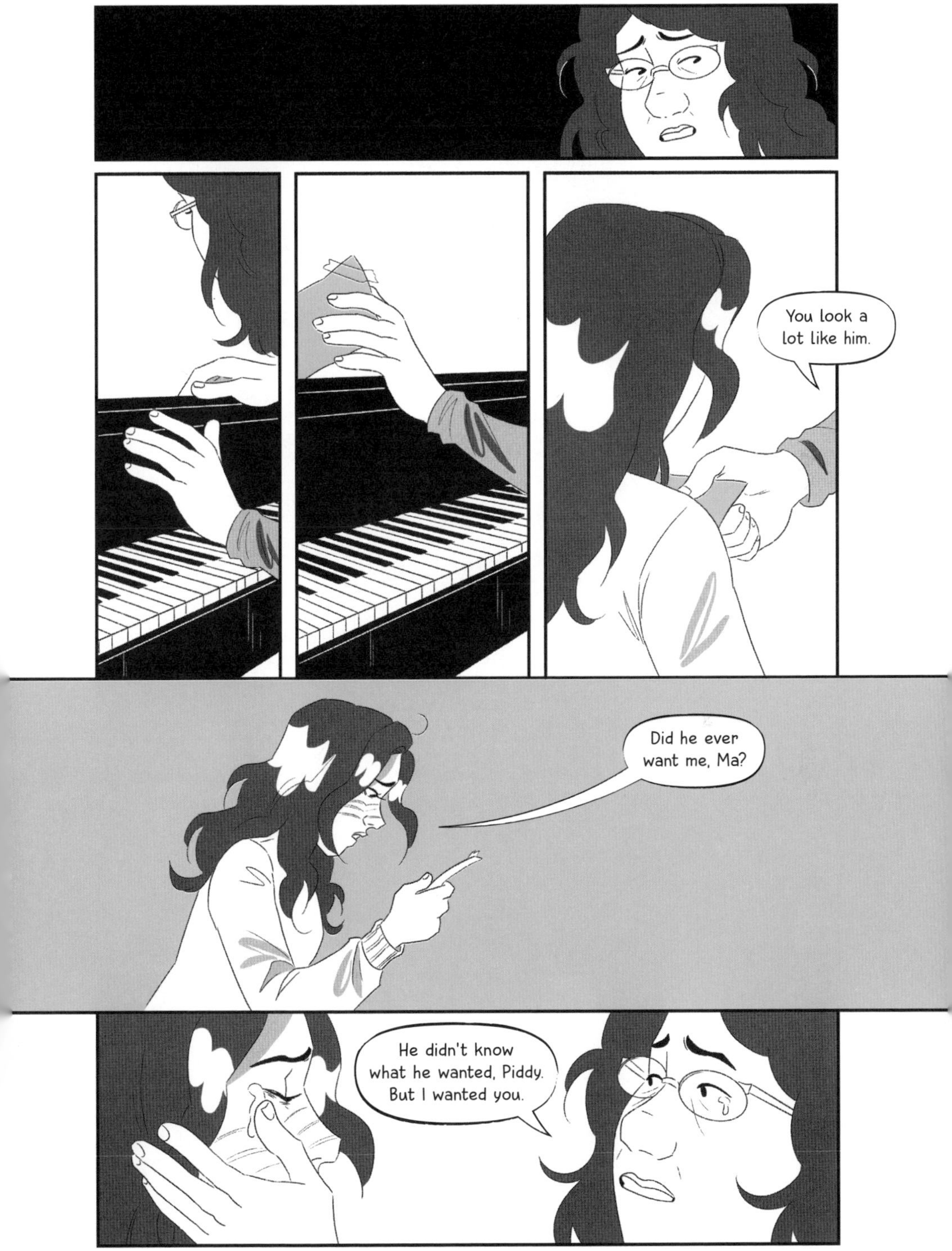
You look a lot like him.
Did he ever want me, Ma?
He didn't know what he wanted, Piddy. But I wanted you.

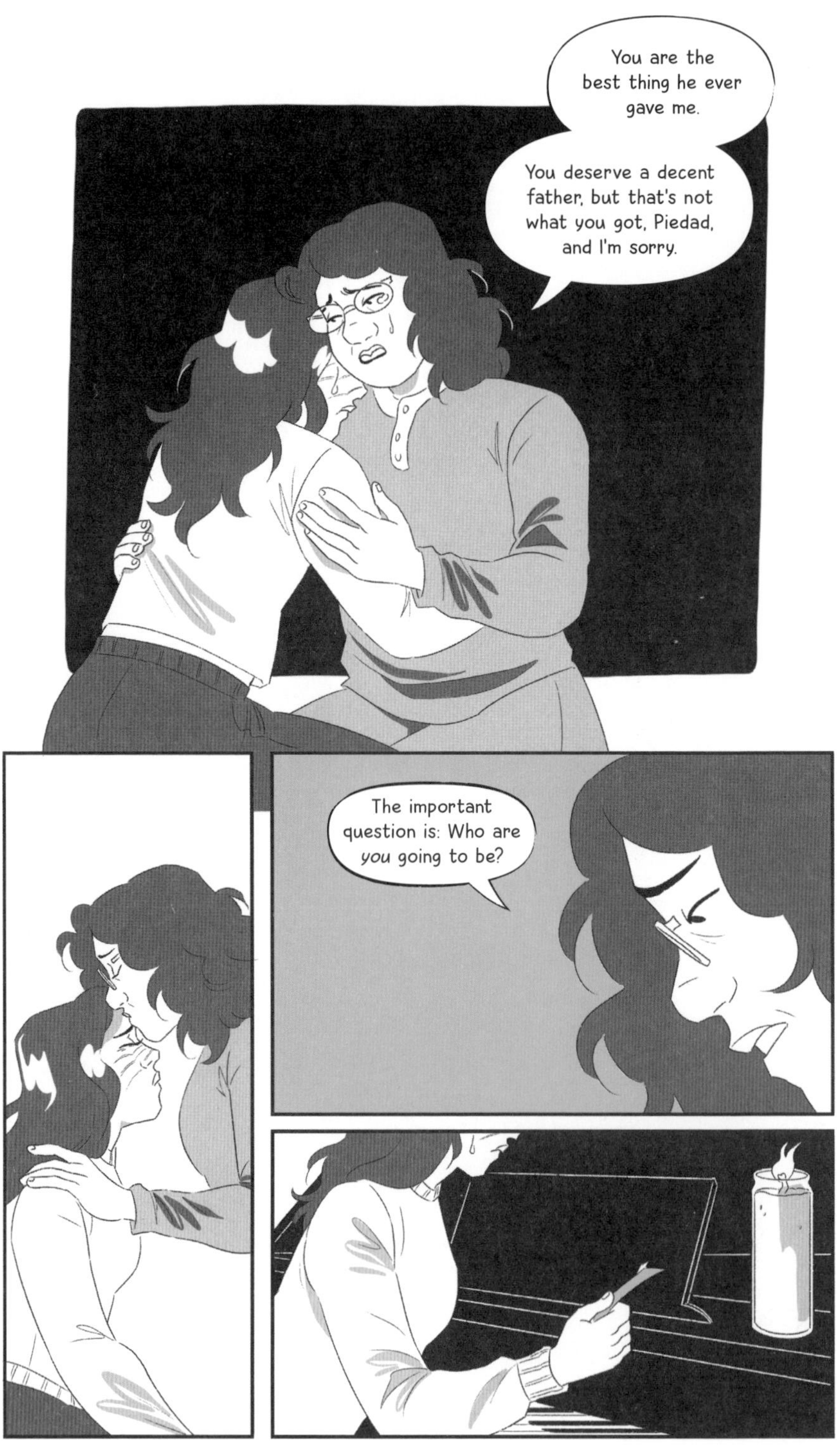
You are the best thing he ever gave me.
You deserve a decent father, but that's not what you got, Piedad, and I'm sorry.
The important question is: Who are *you* going to be?

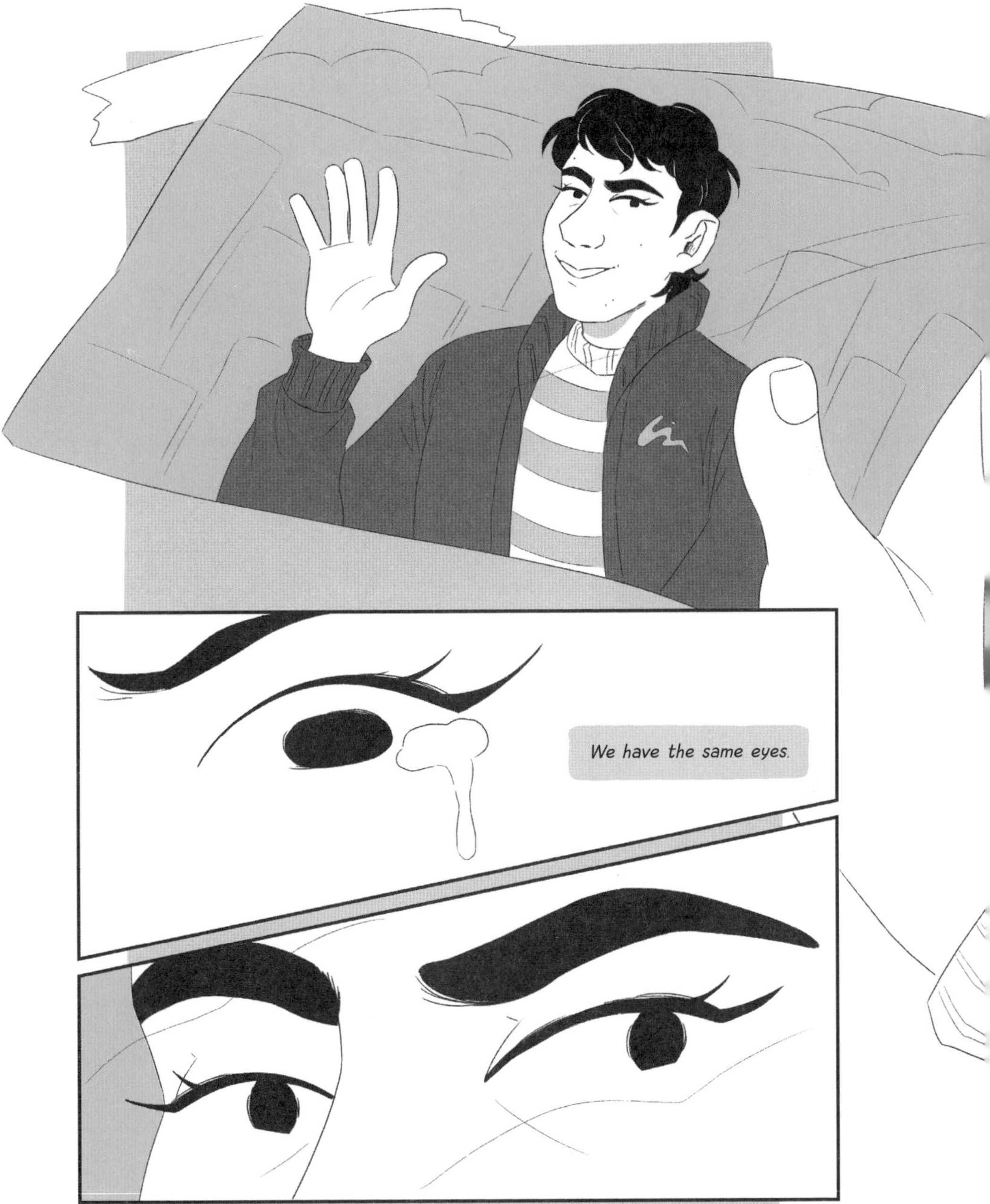
We have the same eyes.

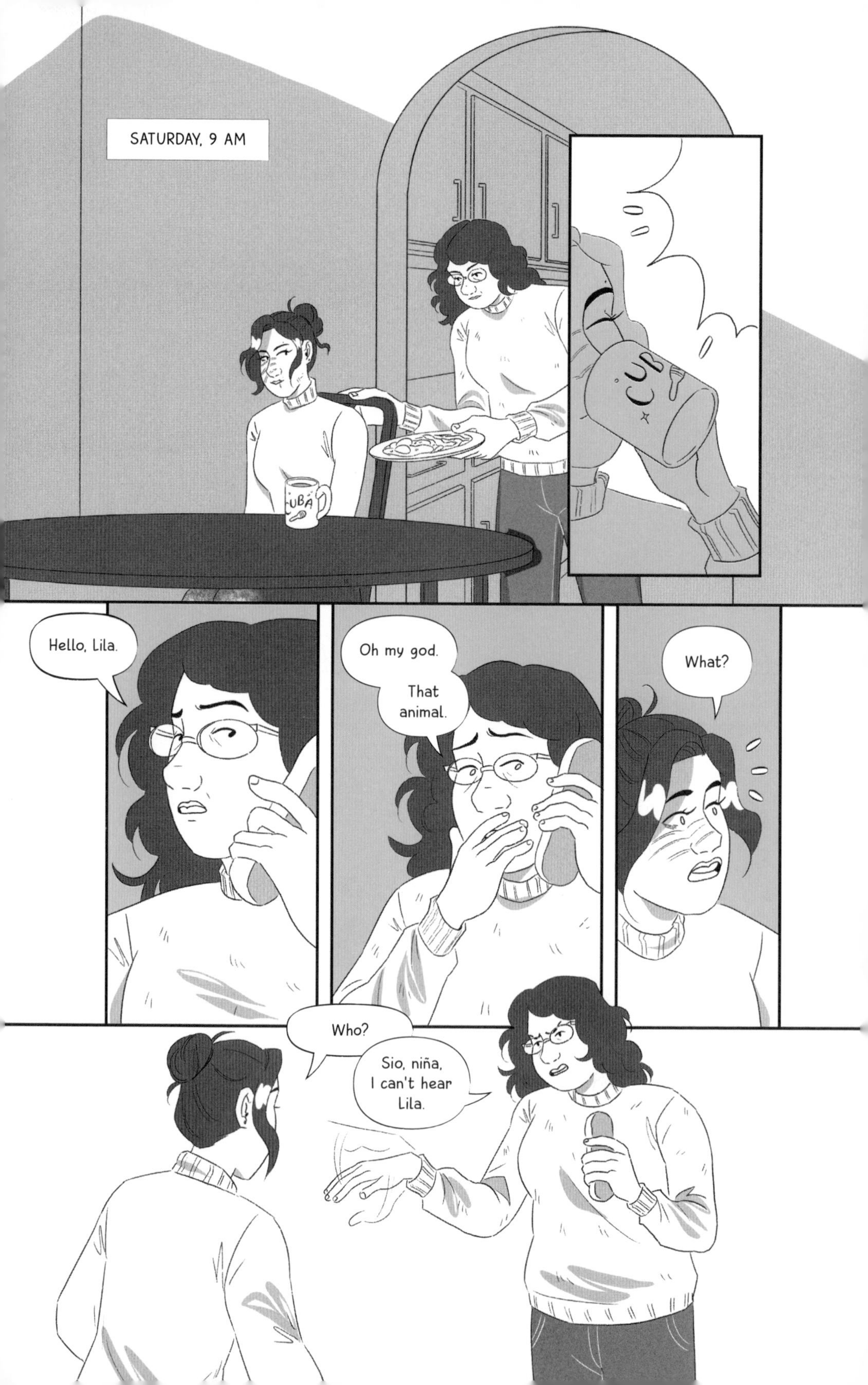
SATURDAY, 9 AM
CUBA
CUB
Hello, Lila.
Oh my god.
That animal.
What?
Who?
Sio, niña, I can't hear Lila.

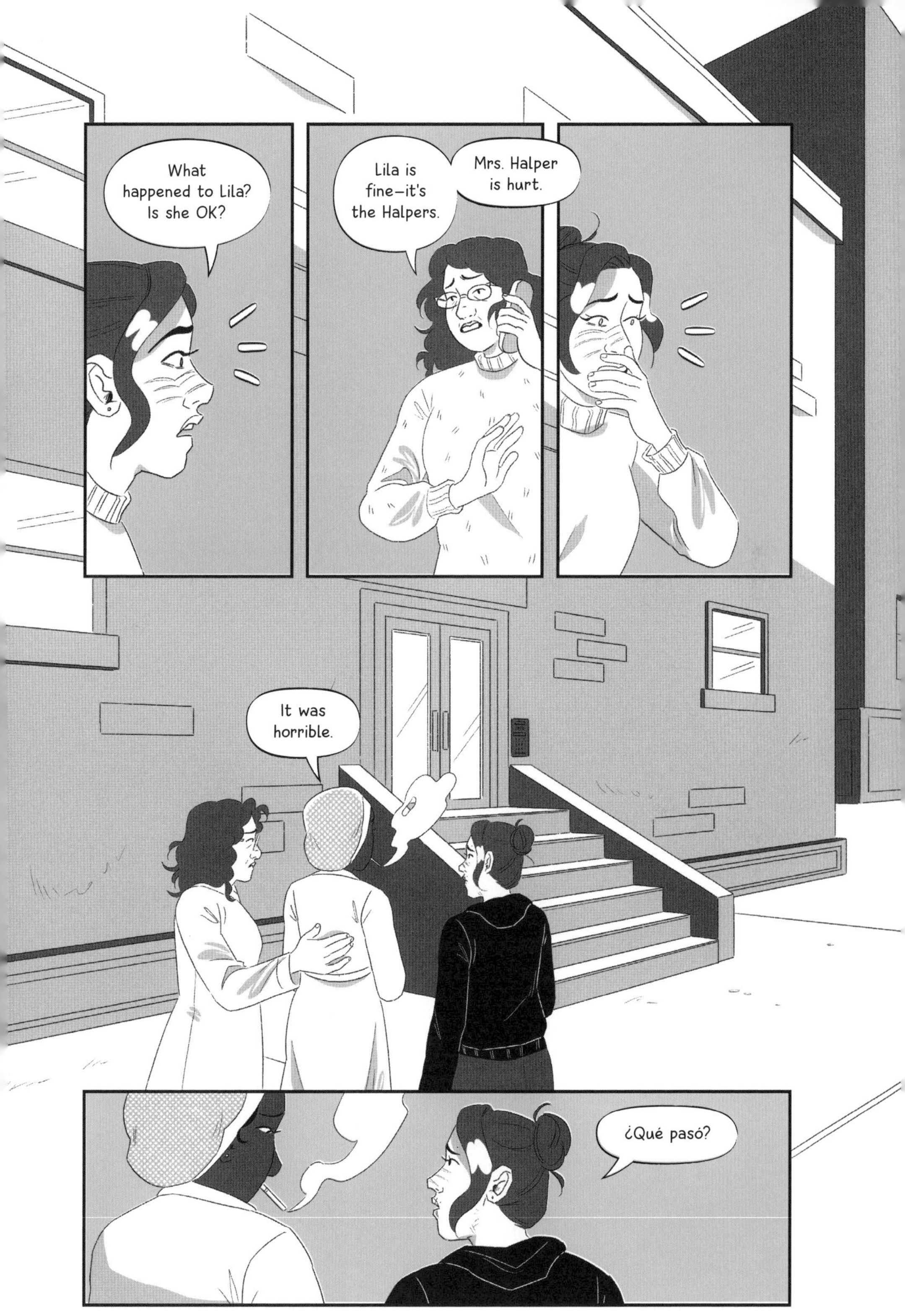
What happened to Lila? Is she OK?
Lila is fine—it's the Halpers.
Mrs. Halper is hurt.
It was horrible.
¿Qué pasó?

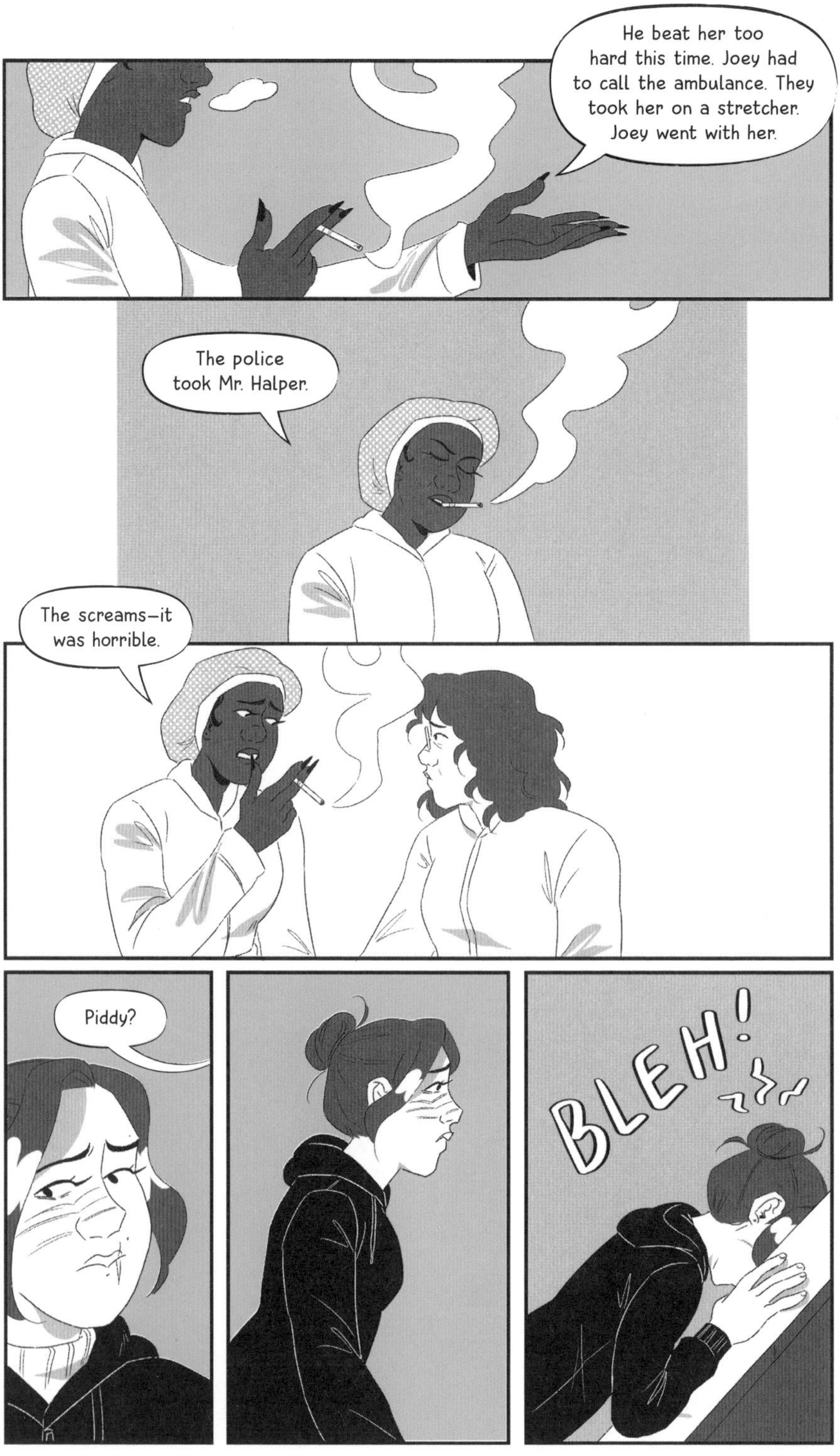
He beat her too hard this time. Joey had to call the ambulance. They took her on a stretcher. Joey went with her.
The police took Mr. Halper.
The screams—it was horrible.
Piddy?
BLEH!

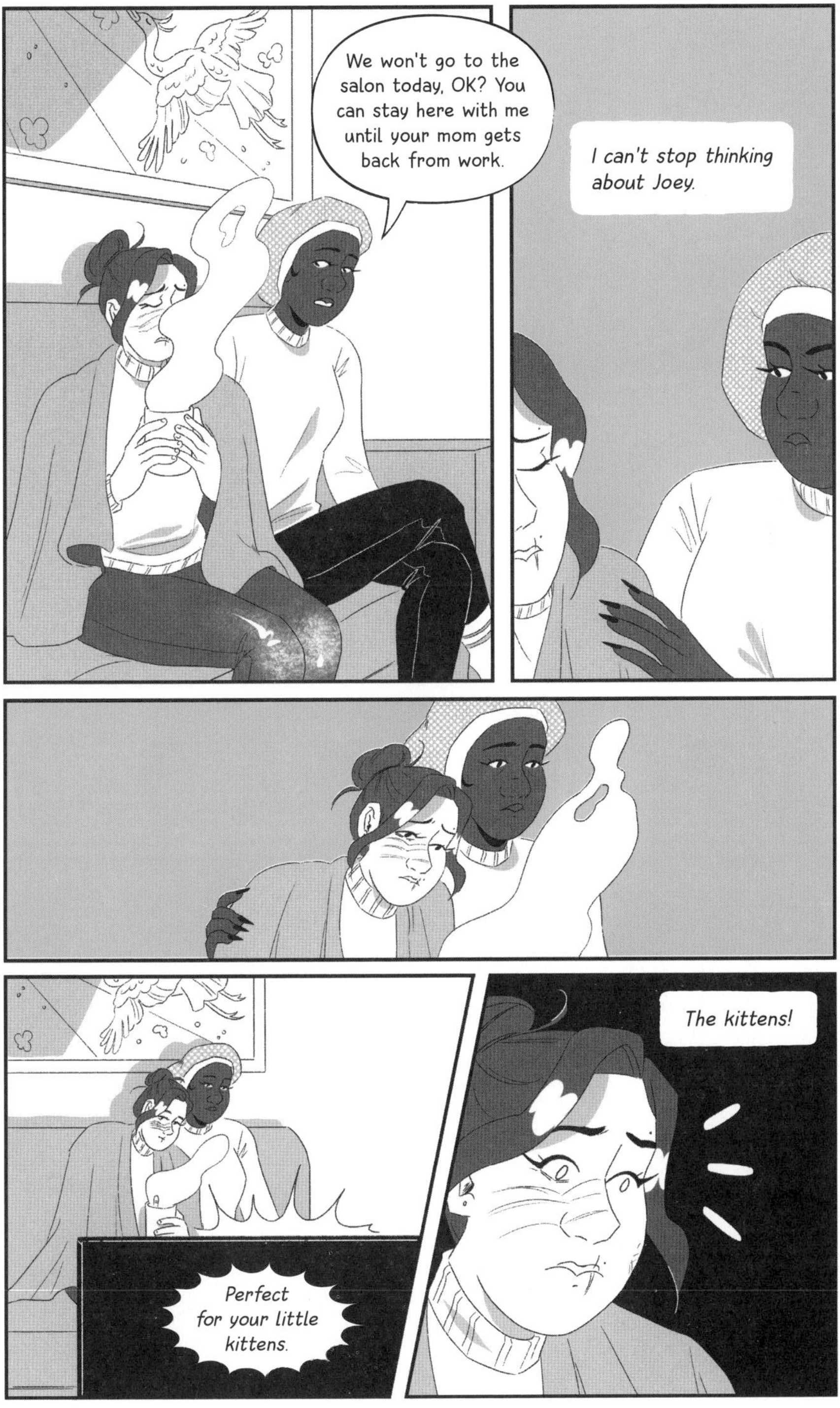
We won't go to the salon today, OK? You can stay here with me until your mom gets back from work.
I can't stop thinking about Joey.
Perfect for your little kittens.
The kittens!

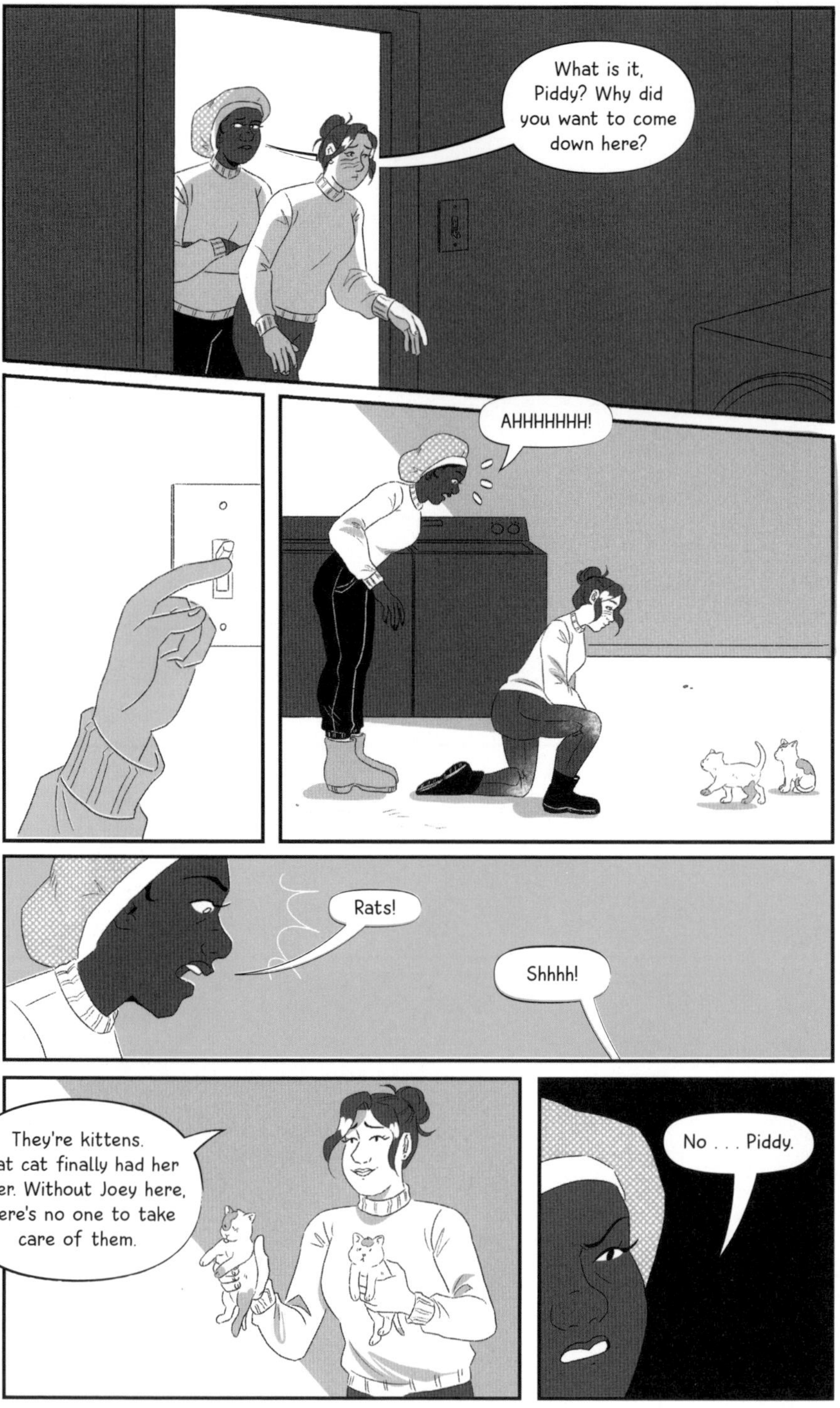
What is it, Piddy? Why did you want to come down here?
AHHHHHHH!
Rats!
Shhhh!
They're kittens. That cat finally had her litter. Without Joey here, there's no one to take care of them.
No . . . Piddy.

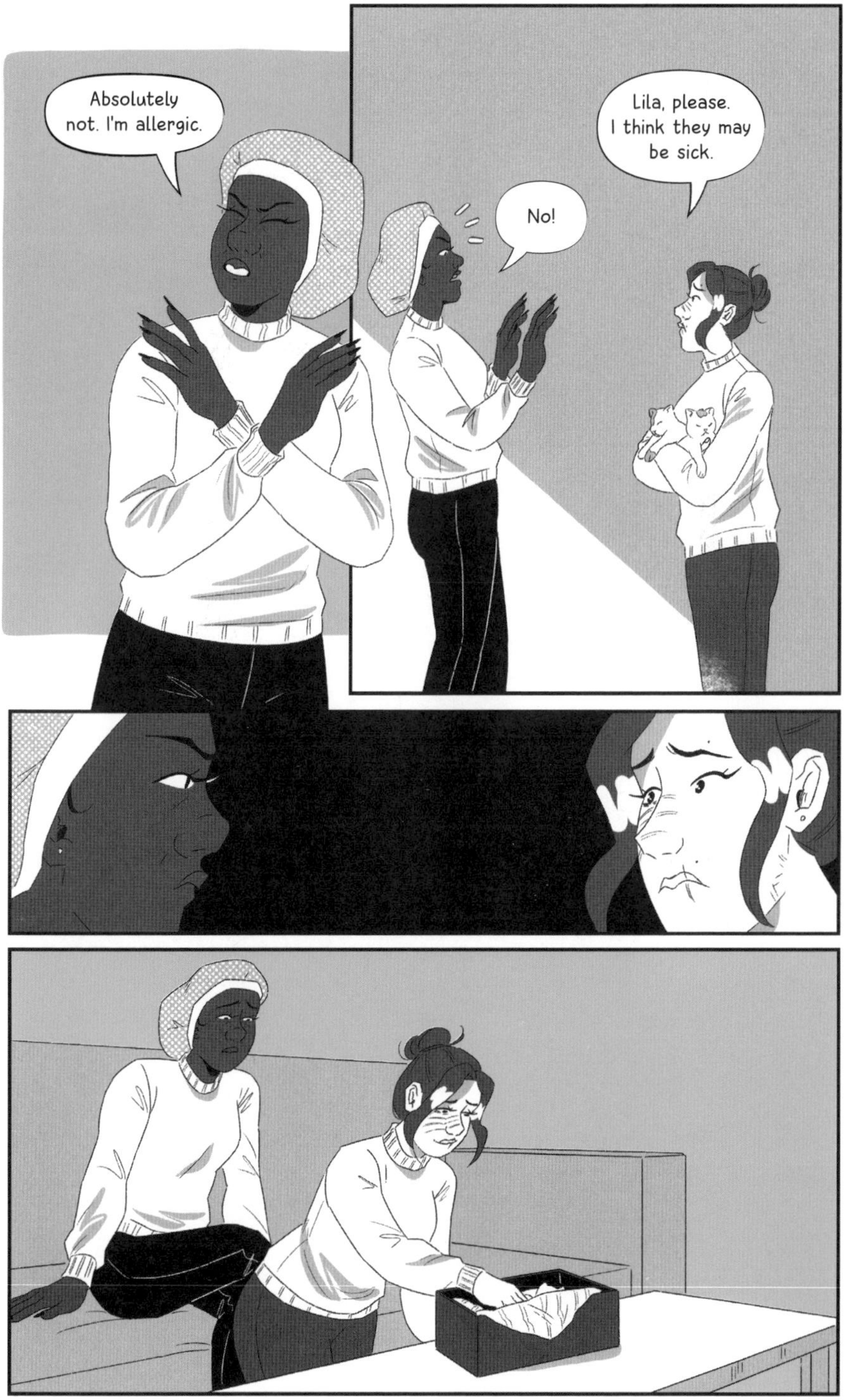
Absolutely not. I'm allergic.
Lila, please. I think they may be sick.
No!

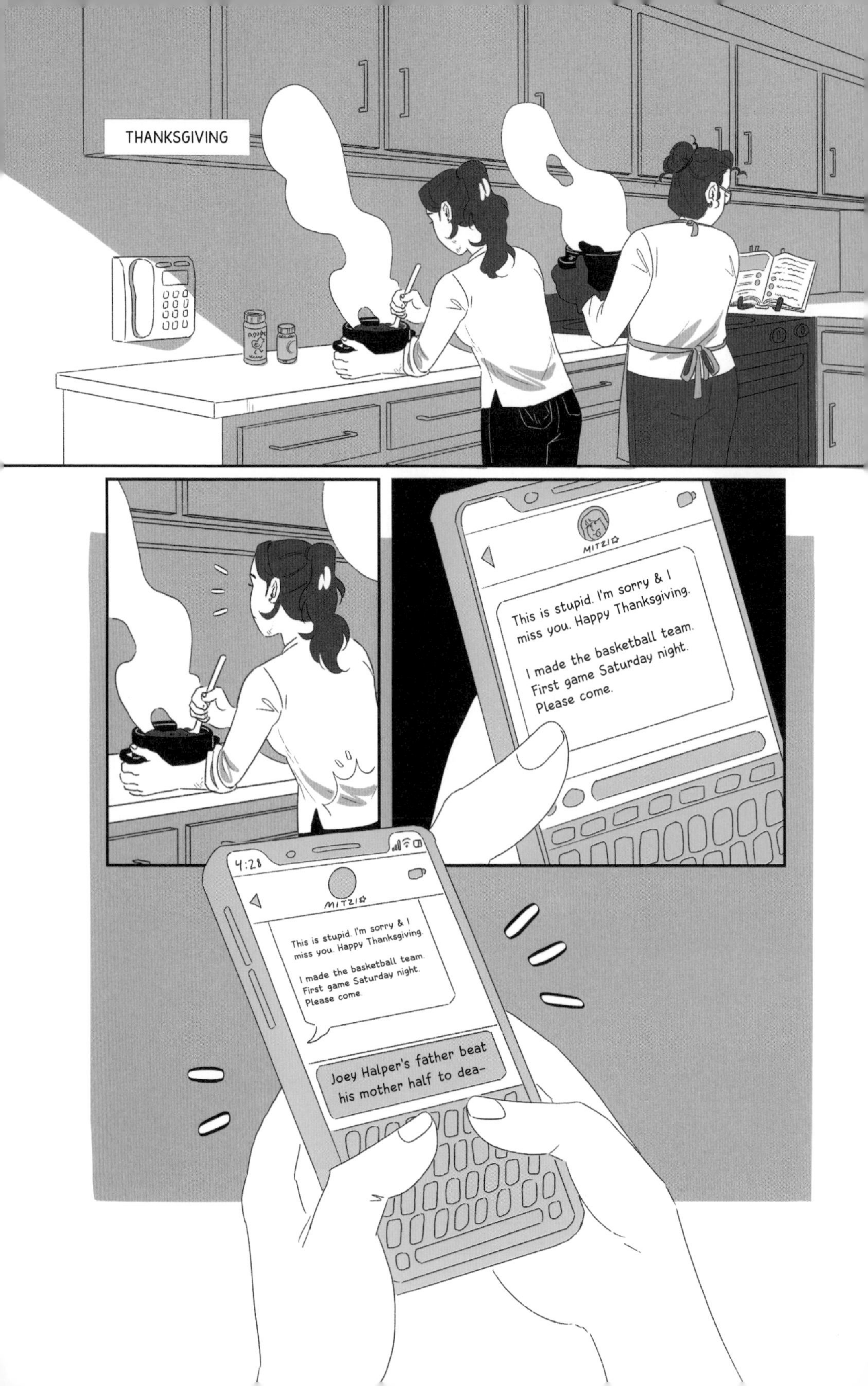
THANKSGIVING
MITZI✩
This is stupid. I'm sorry & I miss you. Happy Thanksgiving.
I made the basketball team. First game Saturday night. Please come.
4:28
MITZI✩
This is stupid. I'm sorry & I miss you. Happy Thanksgiving.
I made the basketball team. First game Saturday night. Please come.
Joey Halper's father beat his mother half to dea-

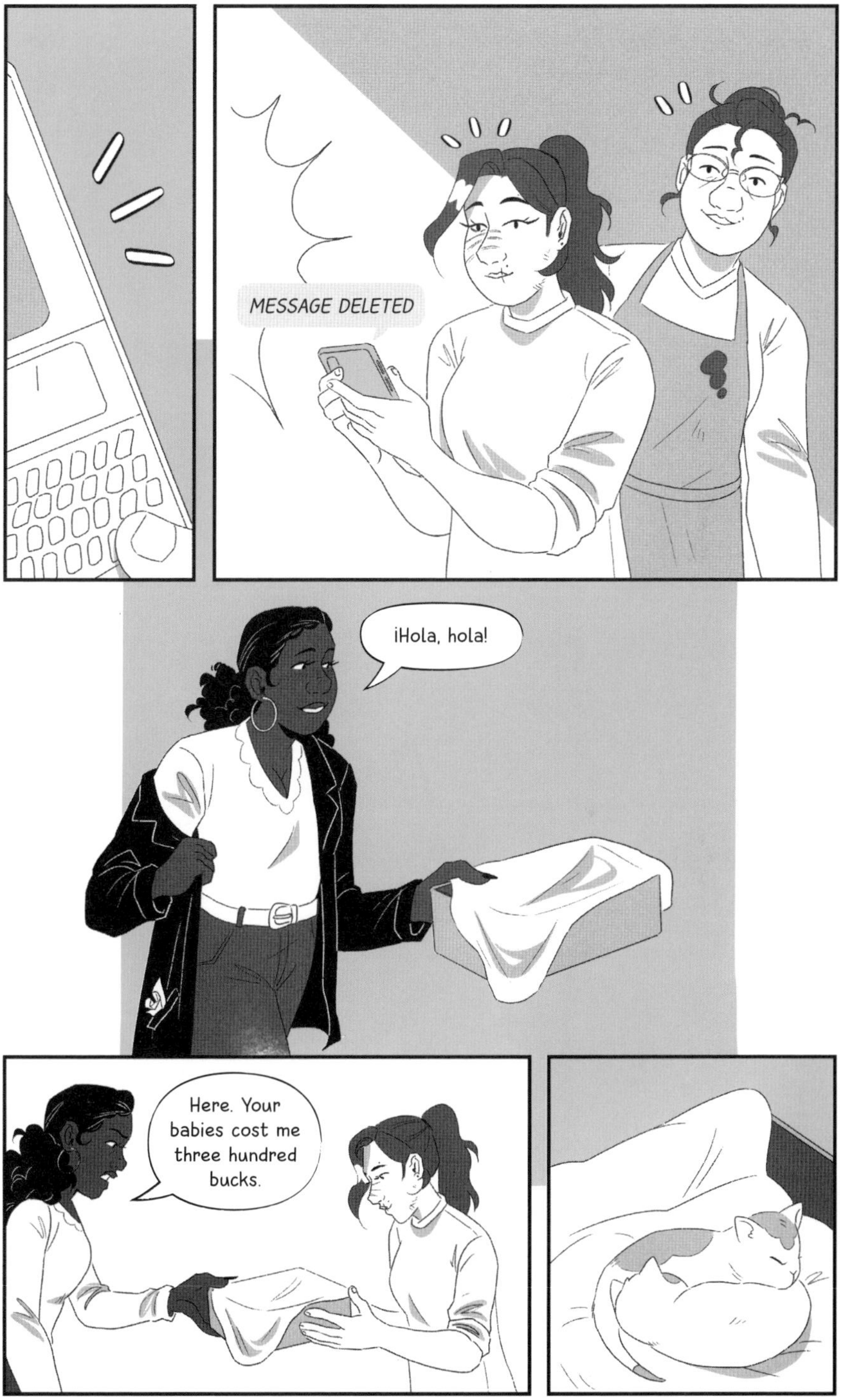
MESSAGE DELETED
¡Hola, hola!
Here. Your babies cost me three hundred bucks.

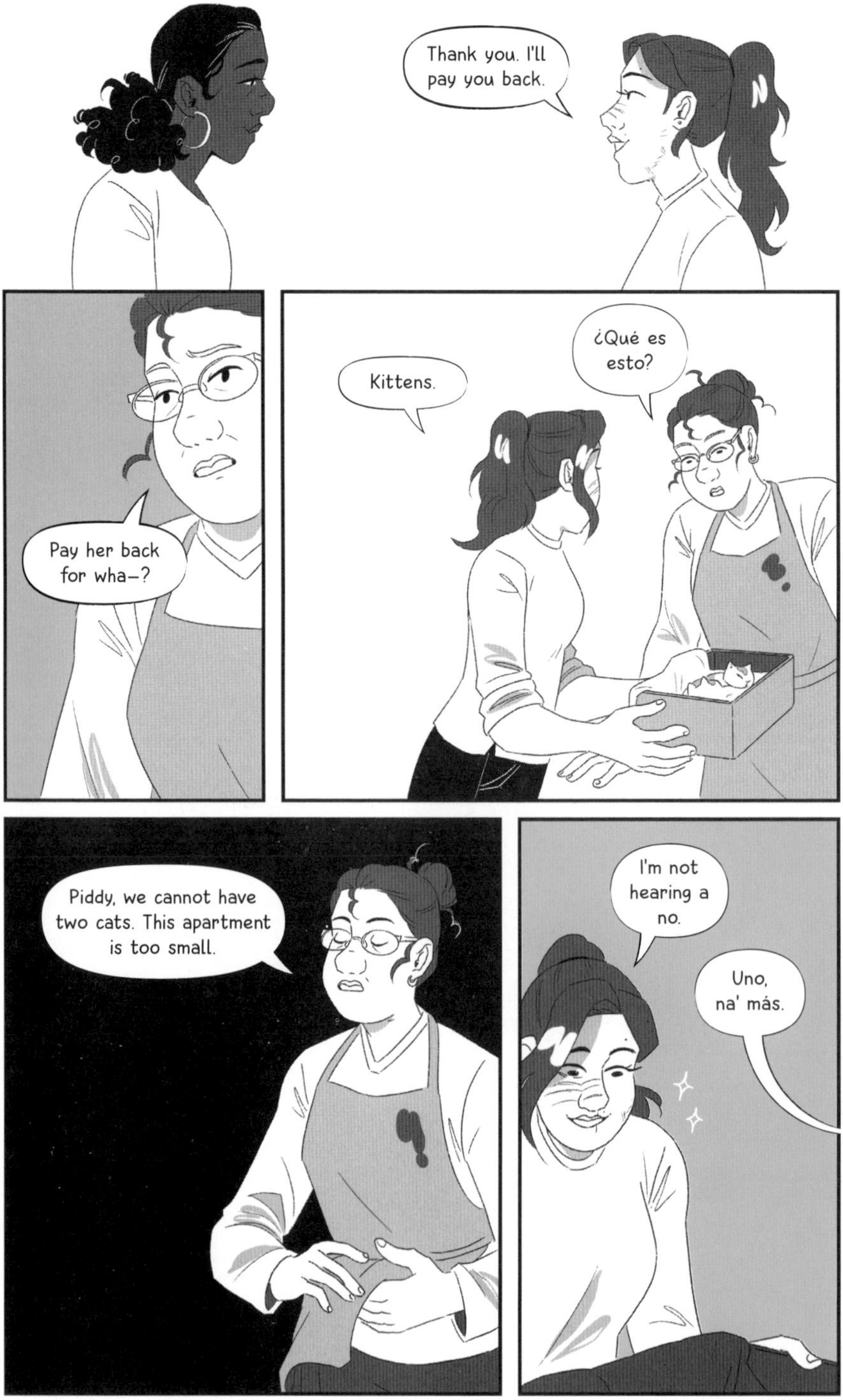
Thank you. I'll pay you back.
Pay her back for wha—?
¿Qué es esto?
Kittens.
Piddy, we cannot have two cats. This apartment is too small.
I'm not hearing a no.
Uno, na' más.

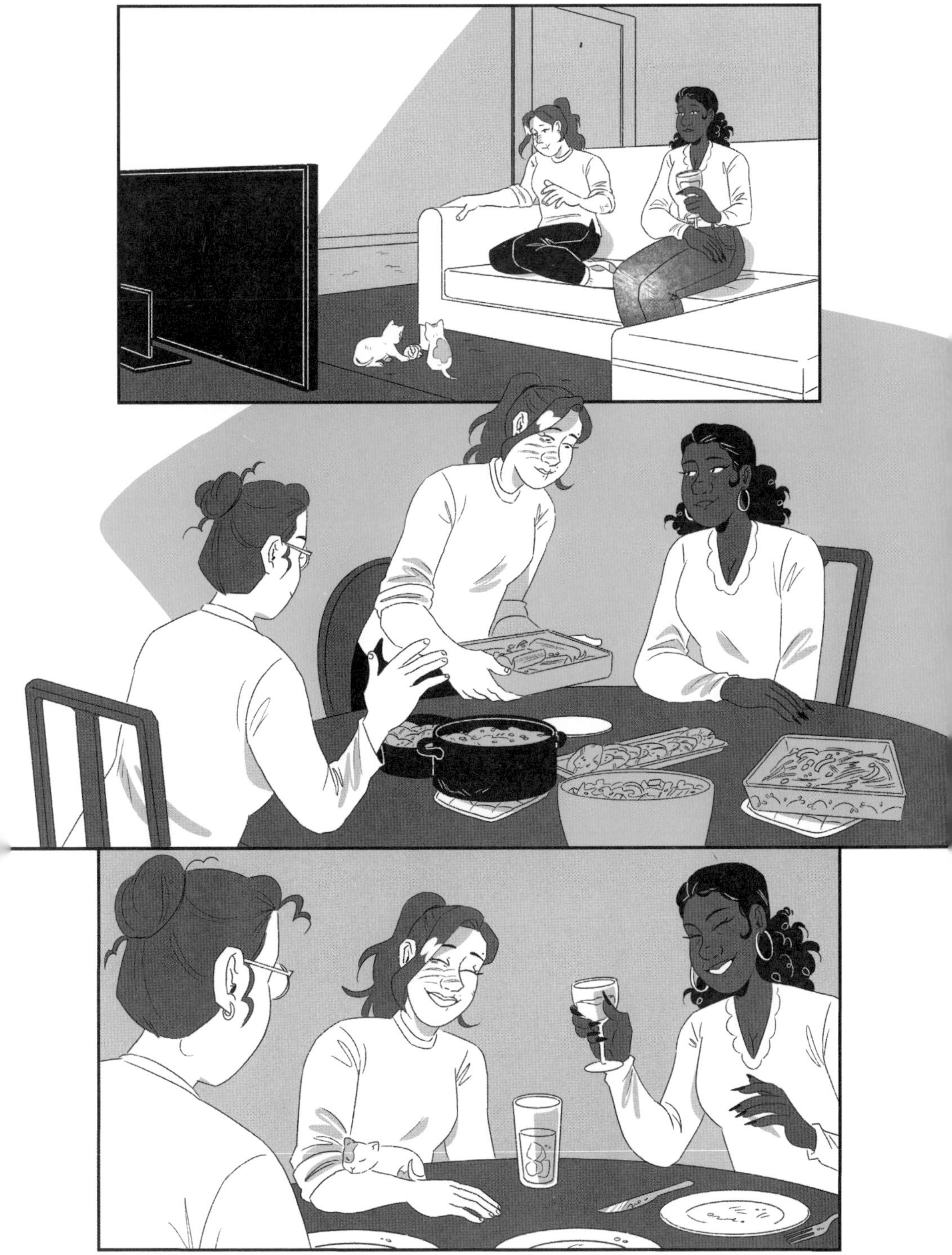

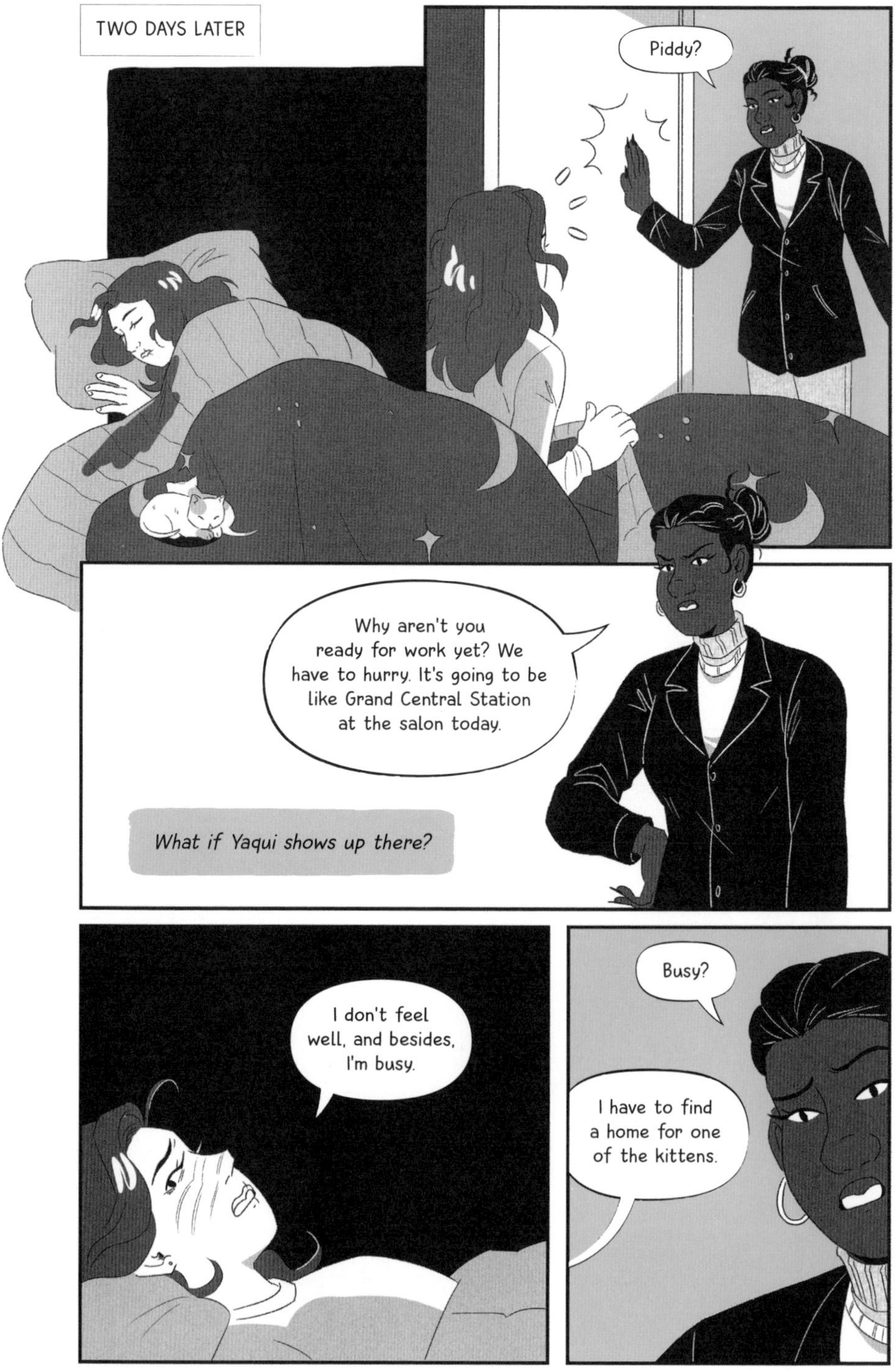
TWO DAYS LATER
Piddy?
Why aren't you ready for work yet? We have to hurry. It's going to be like Grand Central Station at the salon today.
What if Yaqui shows up there?
I don't feel well, and besides, I'm busy.
Busy?
I have to find a home for one of the kittens.

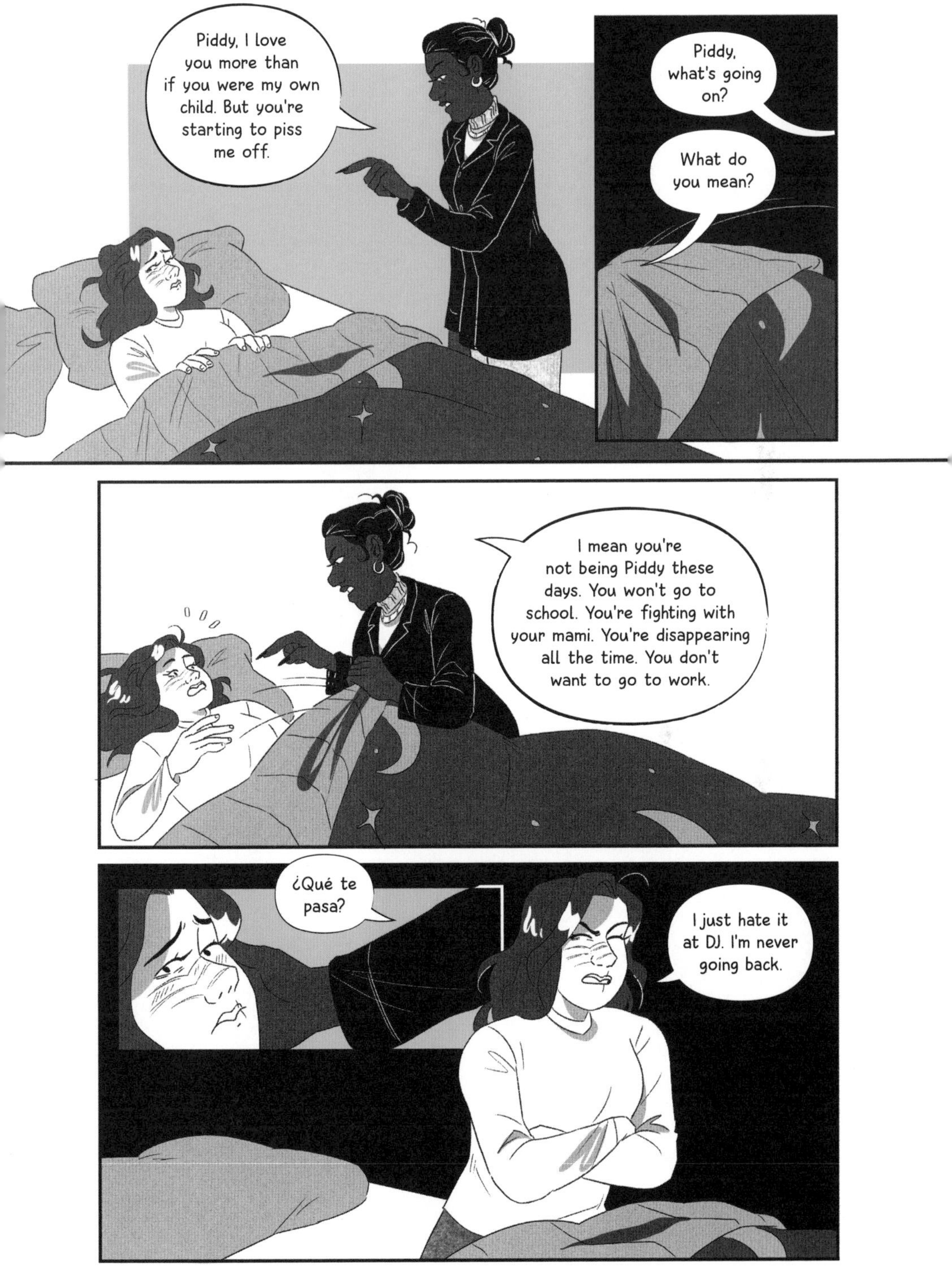
Piddy, I love you more than if you were my own child. But you're starting to piss me off.
Piddy, what's going on?
What do you mean?
I mean you're not being Piddy these days. You won't go to school. You're fighting with your mami. You're disappearing all the time. You don't want to go to work.
¿Qué te pasa?
I just hate it at DJ. I'm never going back.

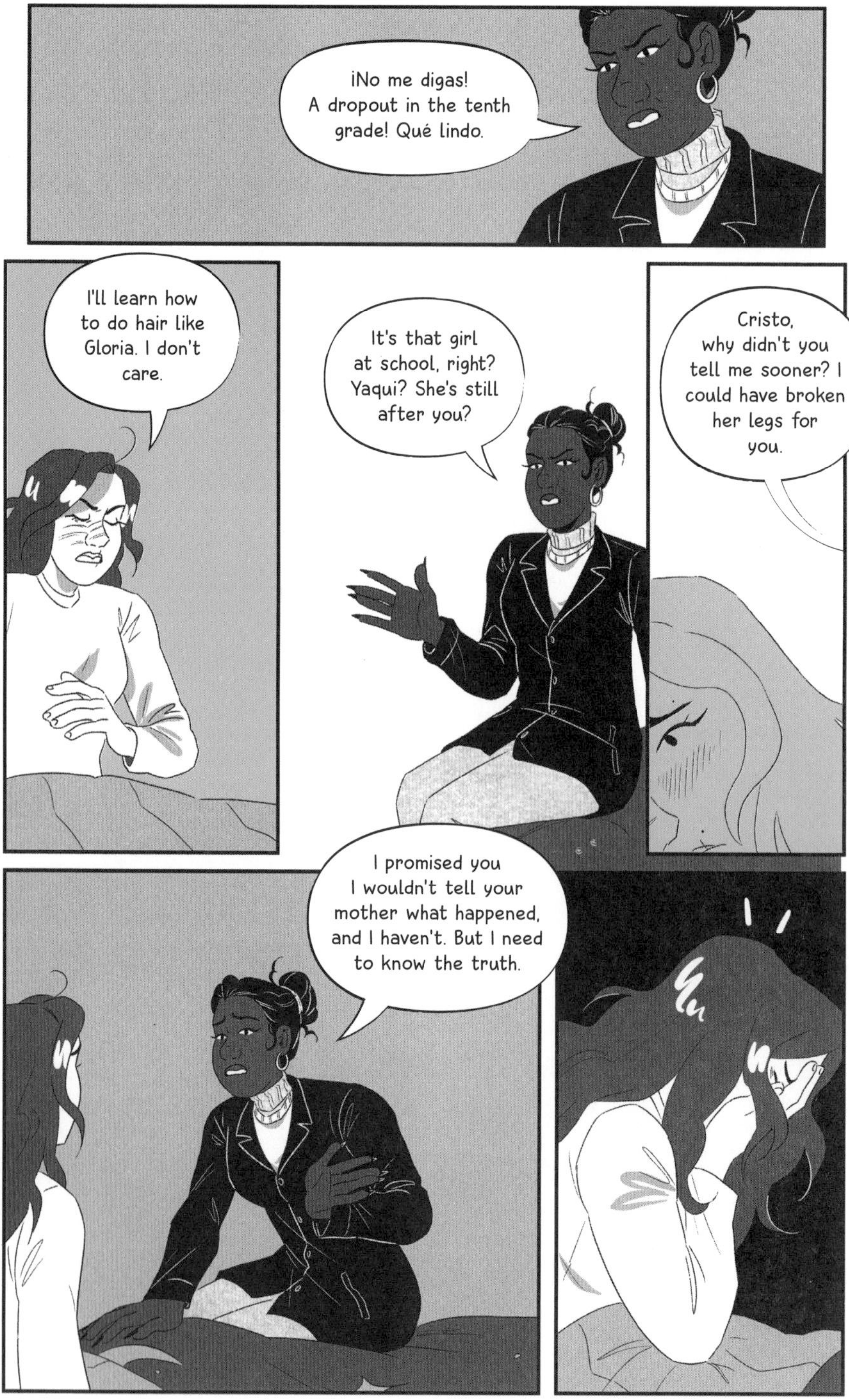
¡No me digas! A dropout in the tenth grade! Qué lindo.
I'll learn how to do hair like Gloria. I don't care.
It's that girl at school, right? Yaqui? She's still after you?
Cristo, why didn't you tell me sooner? I could have broken her legs for you.
I promised you I wouldn't tell your mother what happened, and I haven't. But I need to know the truth.

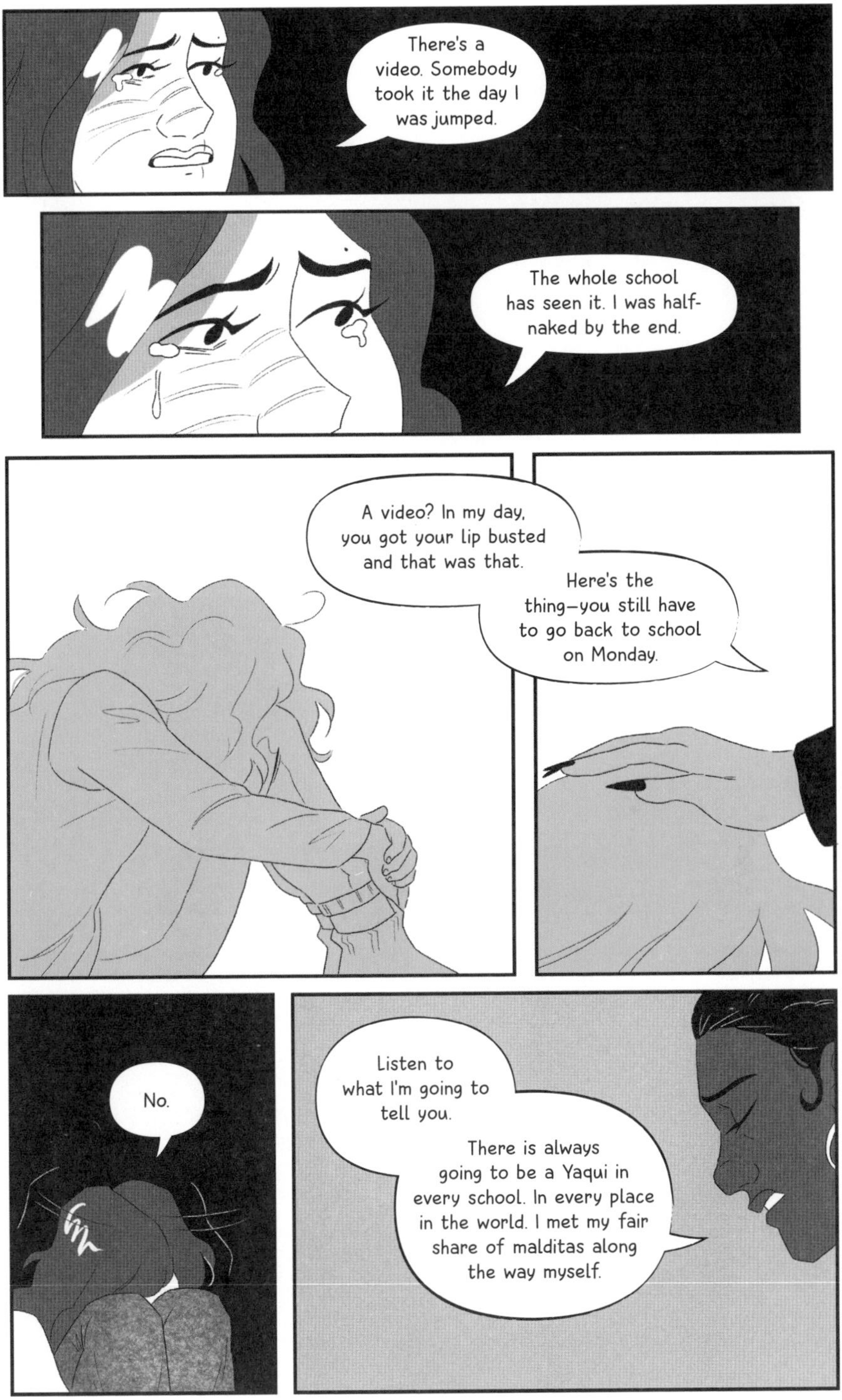
There's a video. Somebody took it the day I was jumped.
The whole school has seen it. I was half-naked by the end.
A video? In my day, you got your lip busted and that was that.
Here's the thing—you still have to go back to school on Monday.
No.
Listen to what I'm going to tell you.
There is always going to be a Yaqui in every school. In every place in the world. I met my fair share of malditas along the way myself.

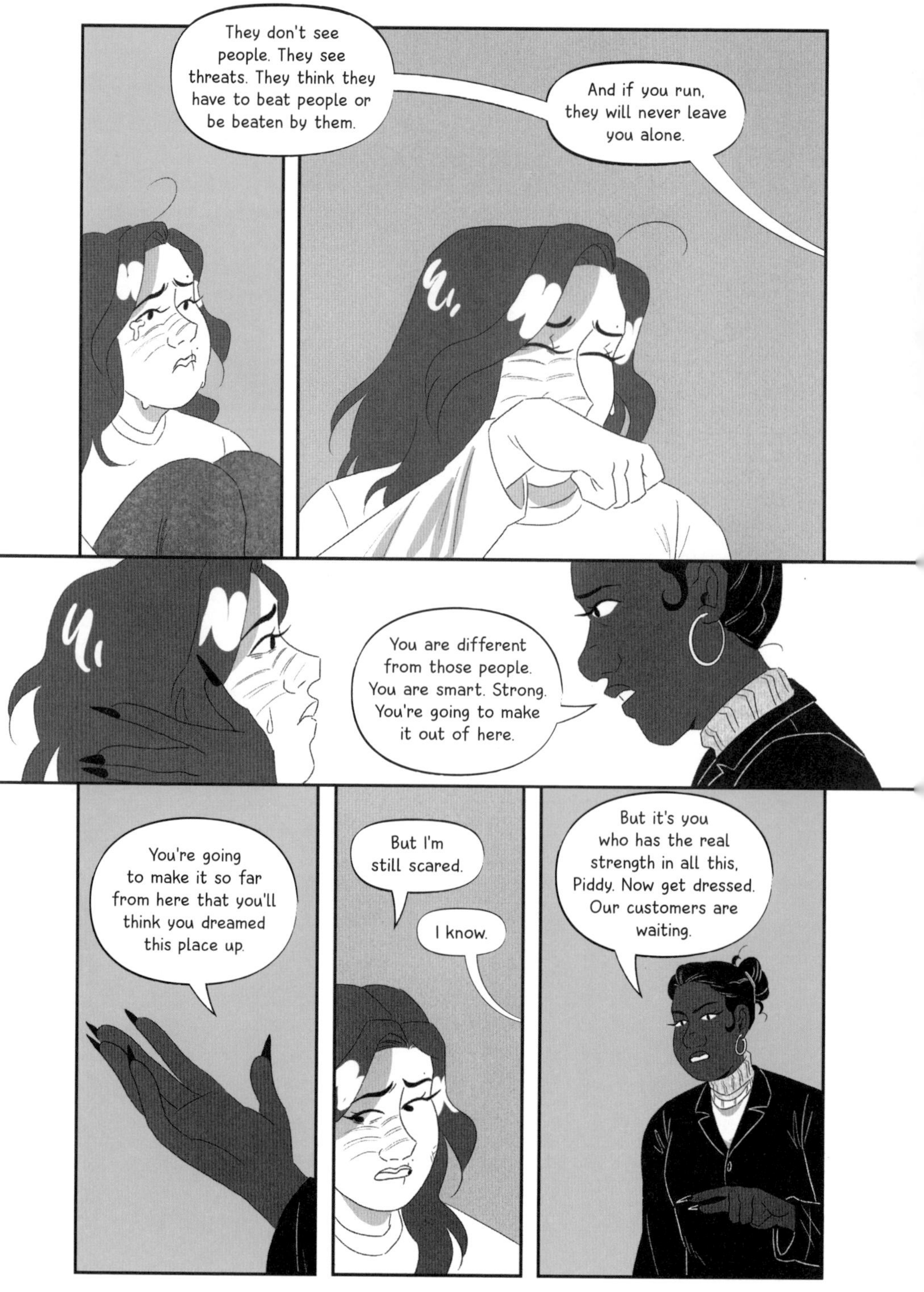
They don't see people. They see threats. They think they have to beat people or be beaten by them.
And if you run, they will never leave you alone.
You are different from those people. You are smart. Strong. You're going to make it out of here.
You're going to make it so far from here that you'll think you dreamed this place up.
But I'm still scared.
I know.
But it's you who has the real strength in all this, Piddy. Now get dressed. Our customers are waiting.

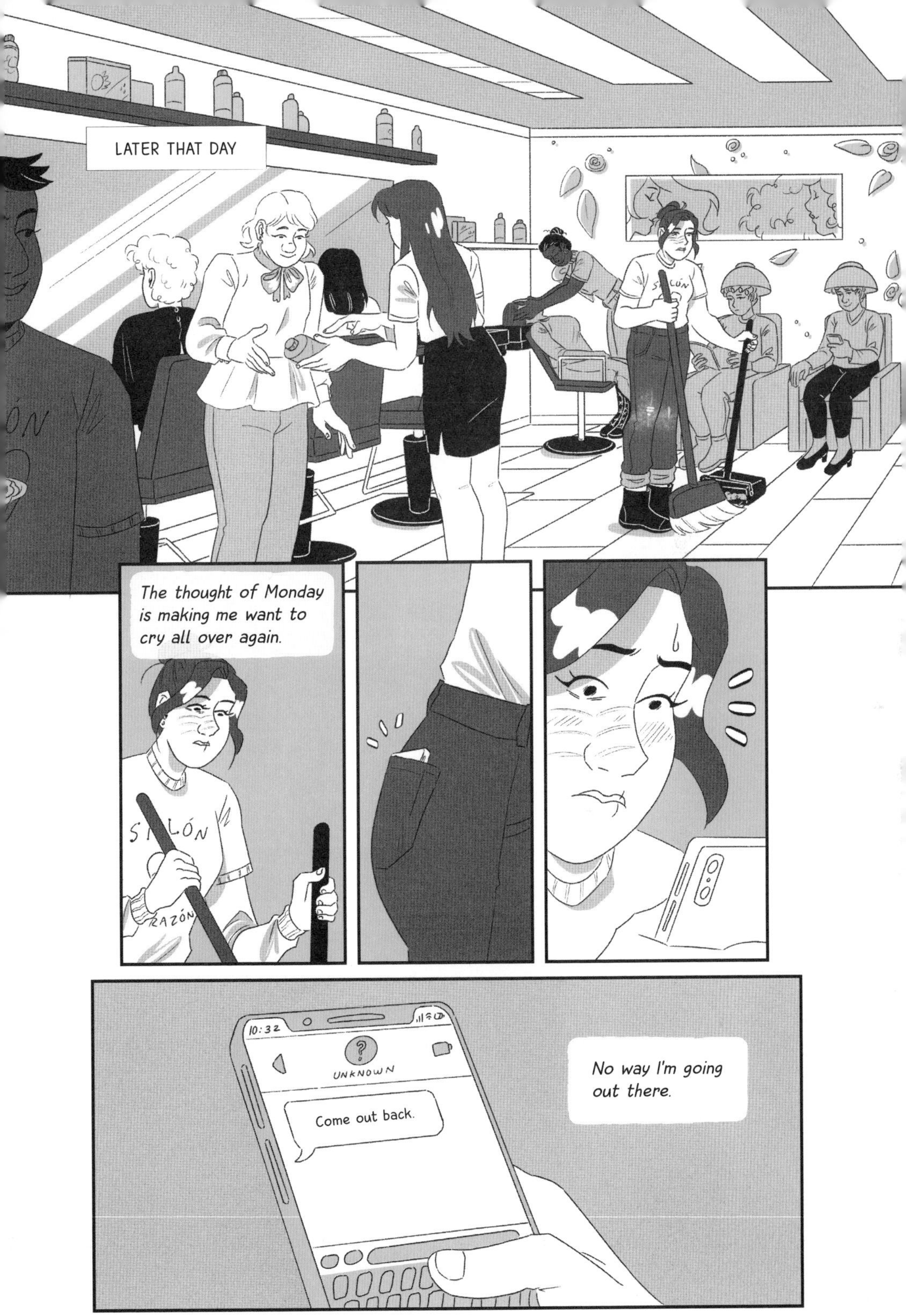
LATER THAT DAY
SALÓN
The thought of Monday is making me want to cry all over again.
SALÓN
RAZÓN
10:32
UNKNOWN
Come out back.
No way I'm going out there.

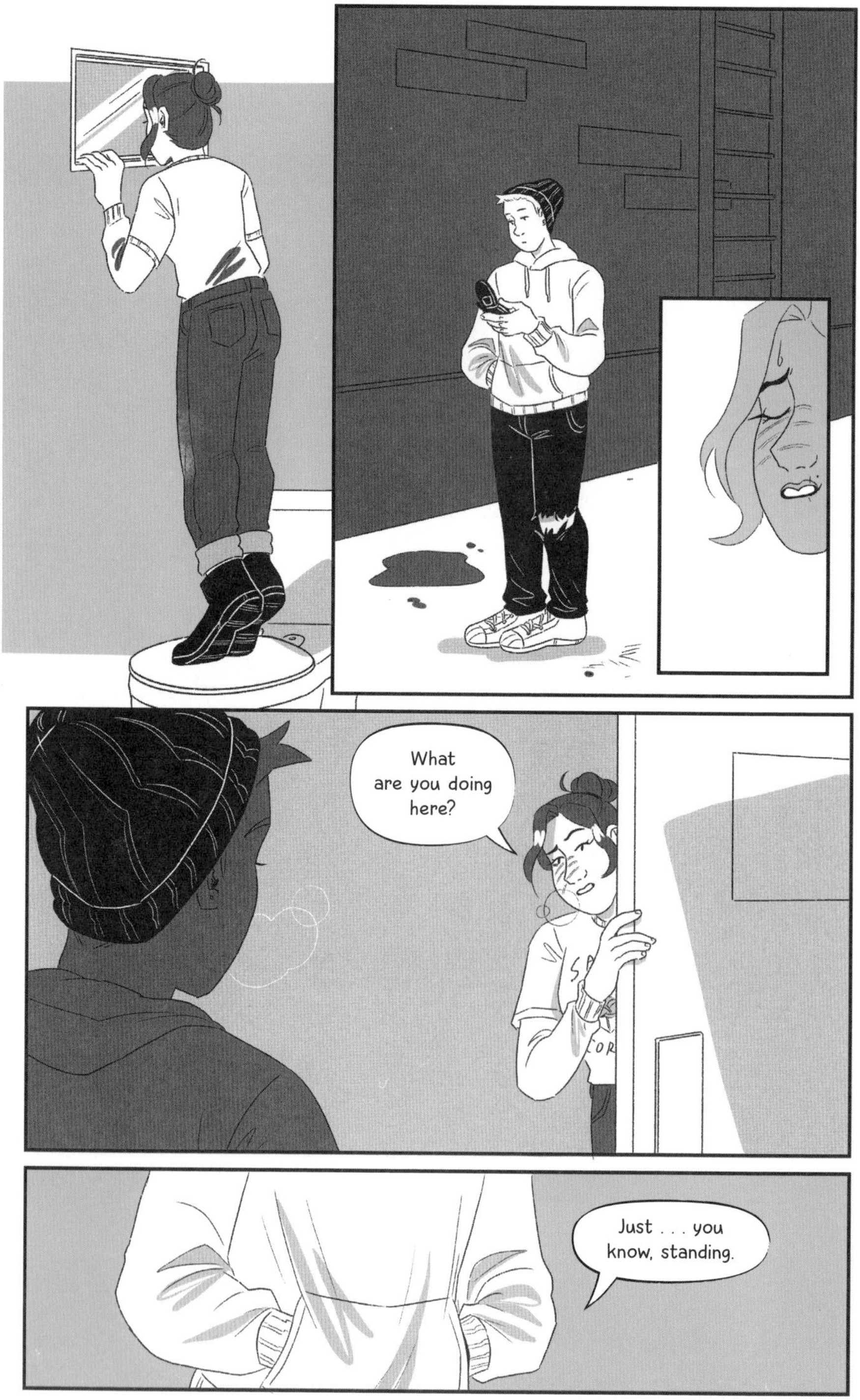
What are you doing here?
Just . . . you know, standing.

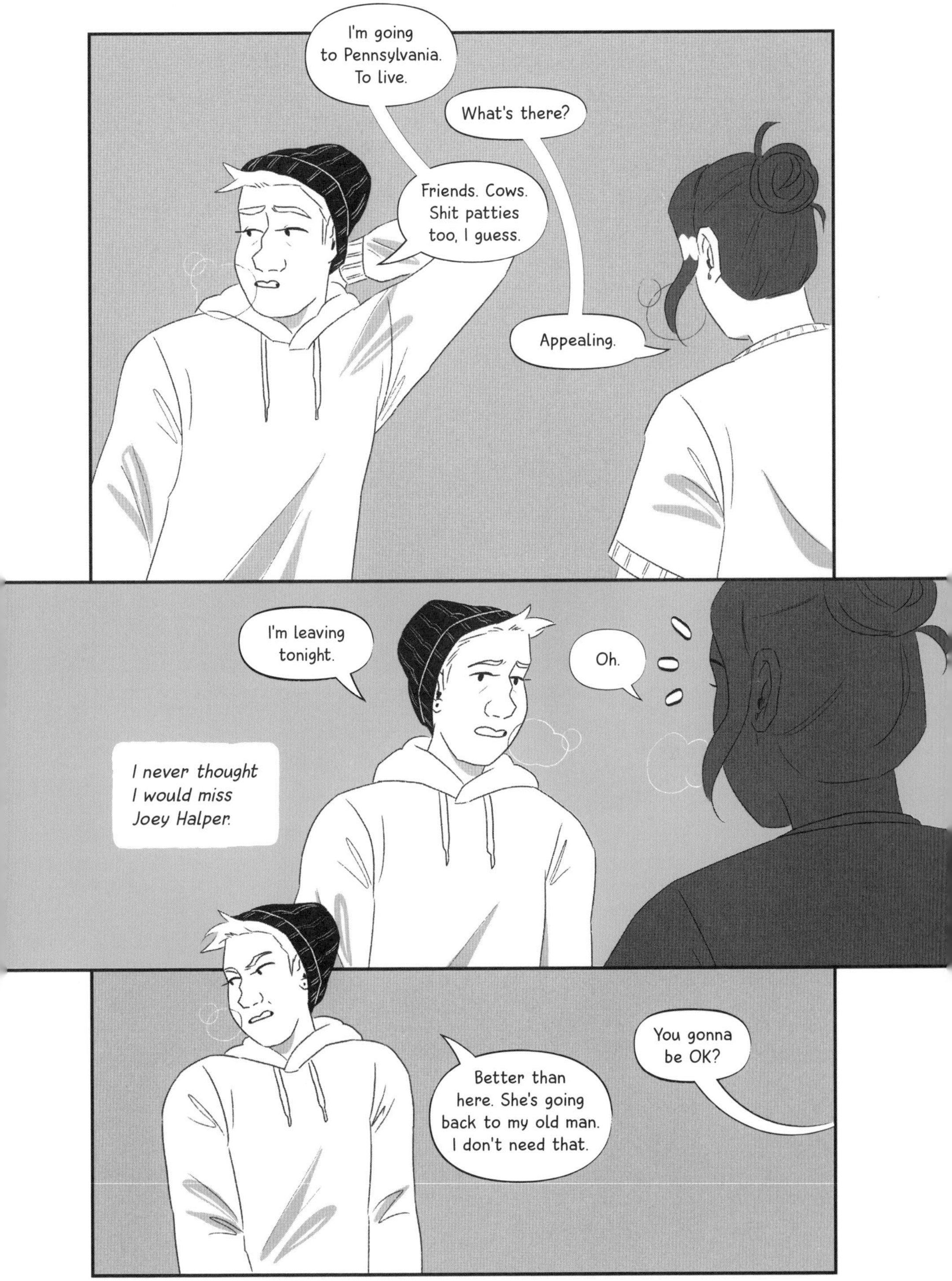
I'm going to Pennsylvania. To live.
What's there?
Friends. Cows. Shit patties too, I guess.
Appealing.
I'm leaving tonight.
Oh.
I never thought I would miss Joey Halper.
Better than here. She's going back to my old man. I don't need that.
You gonna be OK?

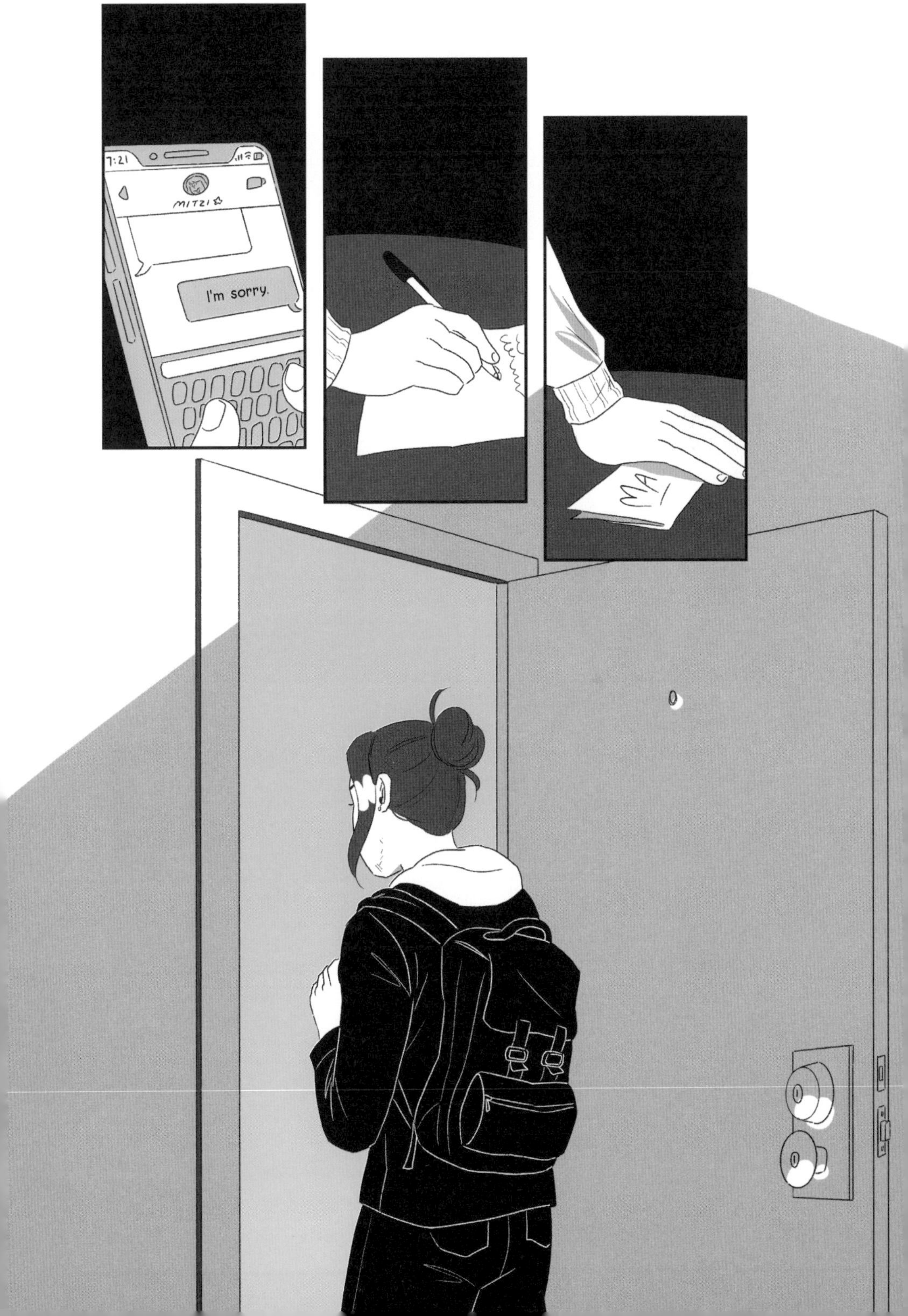

7:21
MITZI
I'm sorry.
MA

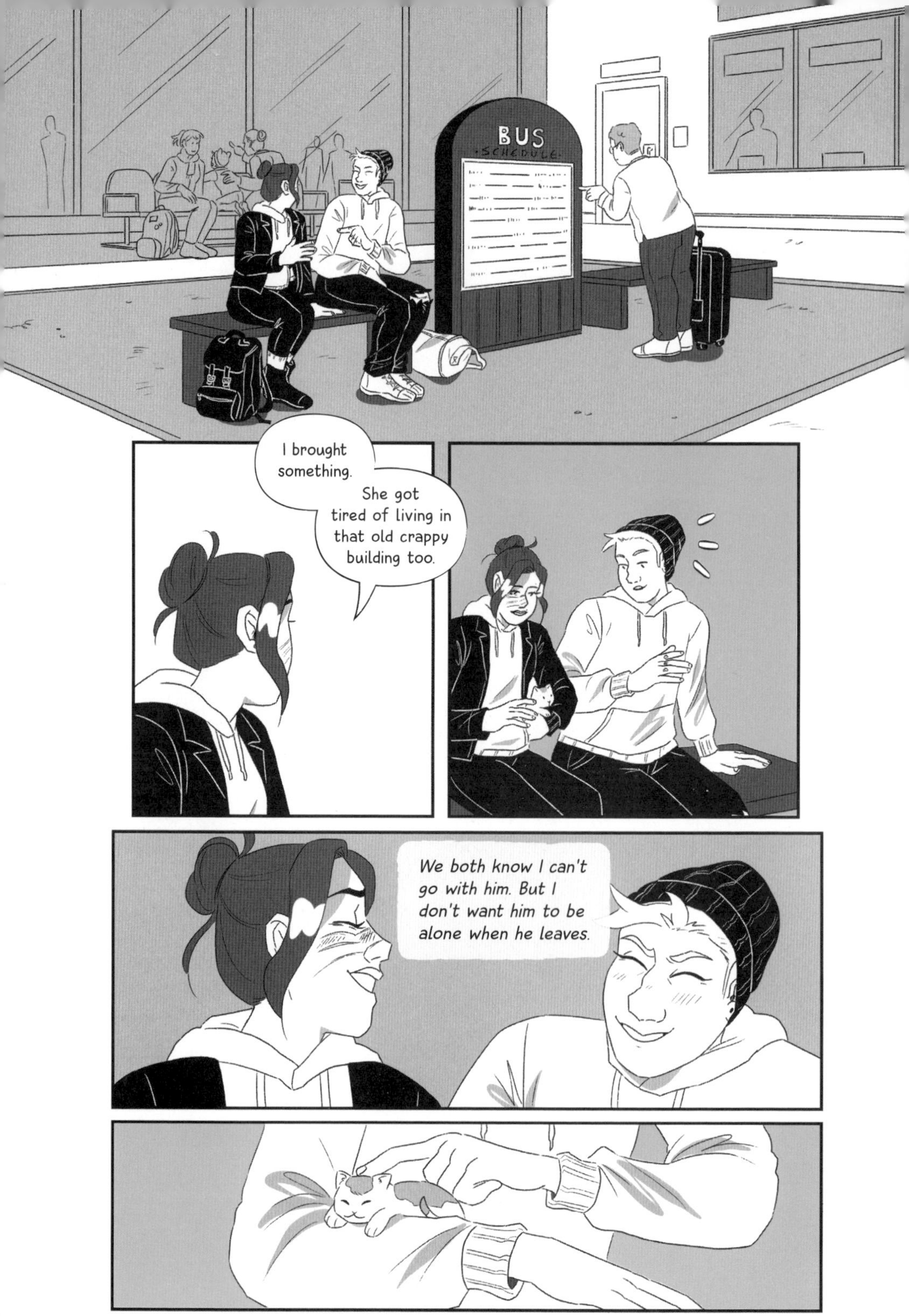
BUS SCHEDULE
I brought something.
She got tired of living in that old crappy building too.
We both know I can't go with him. But I don't want him to be alone when he leaves.

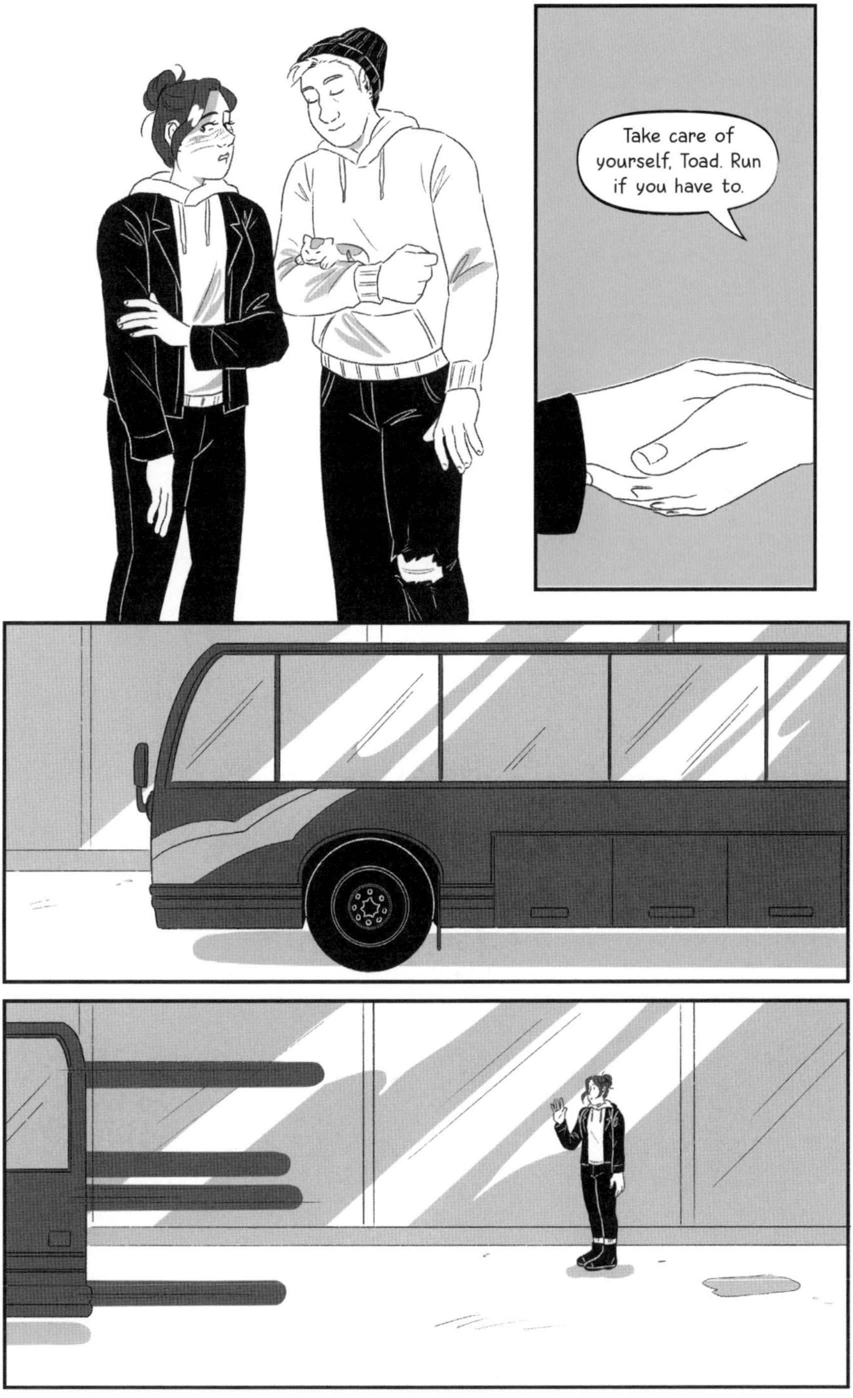
Take care of yourself, Toad. Run if you have to.

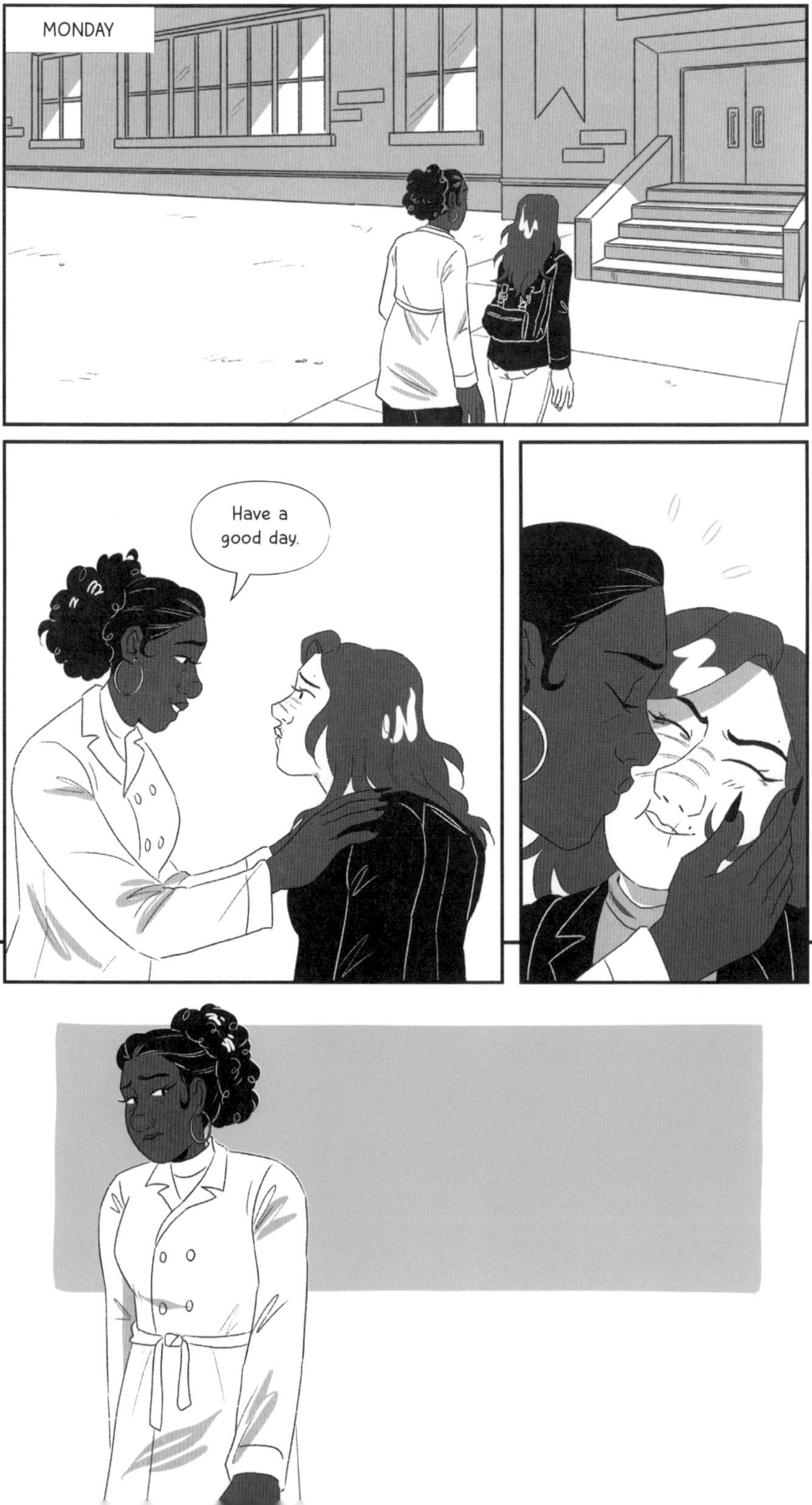
MONDAY
Have a good day.

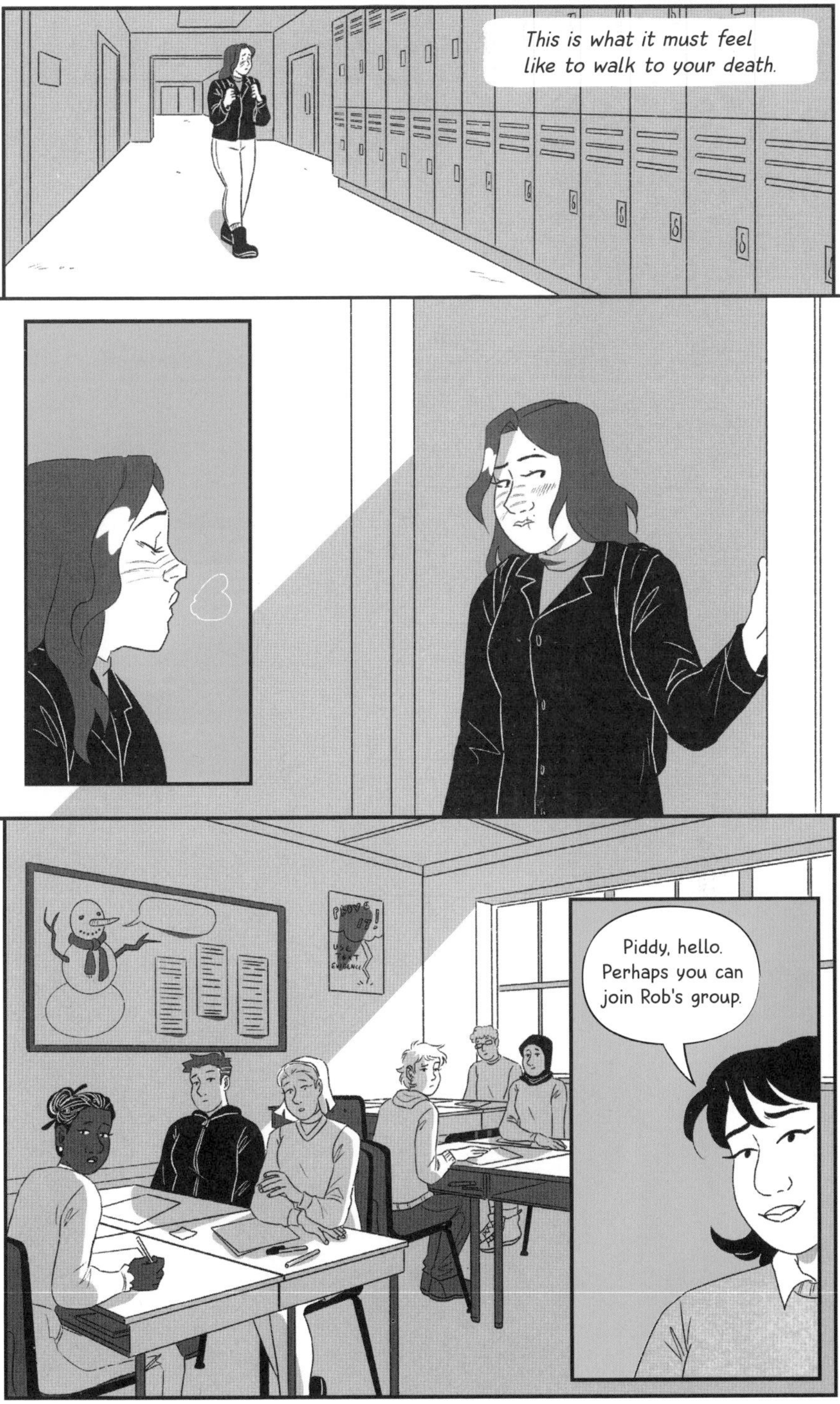
This is what it must feel like to walk to your death.
Piddy, hello. Perhaps you can join Rob's group.

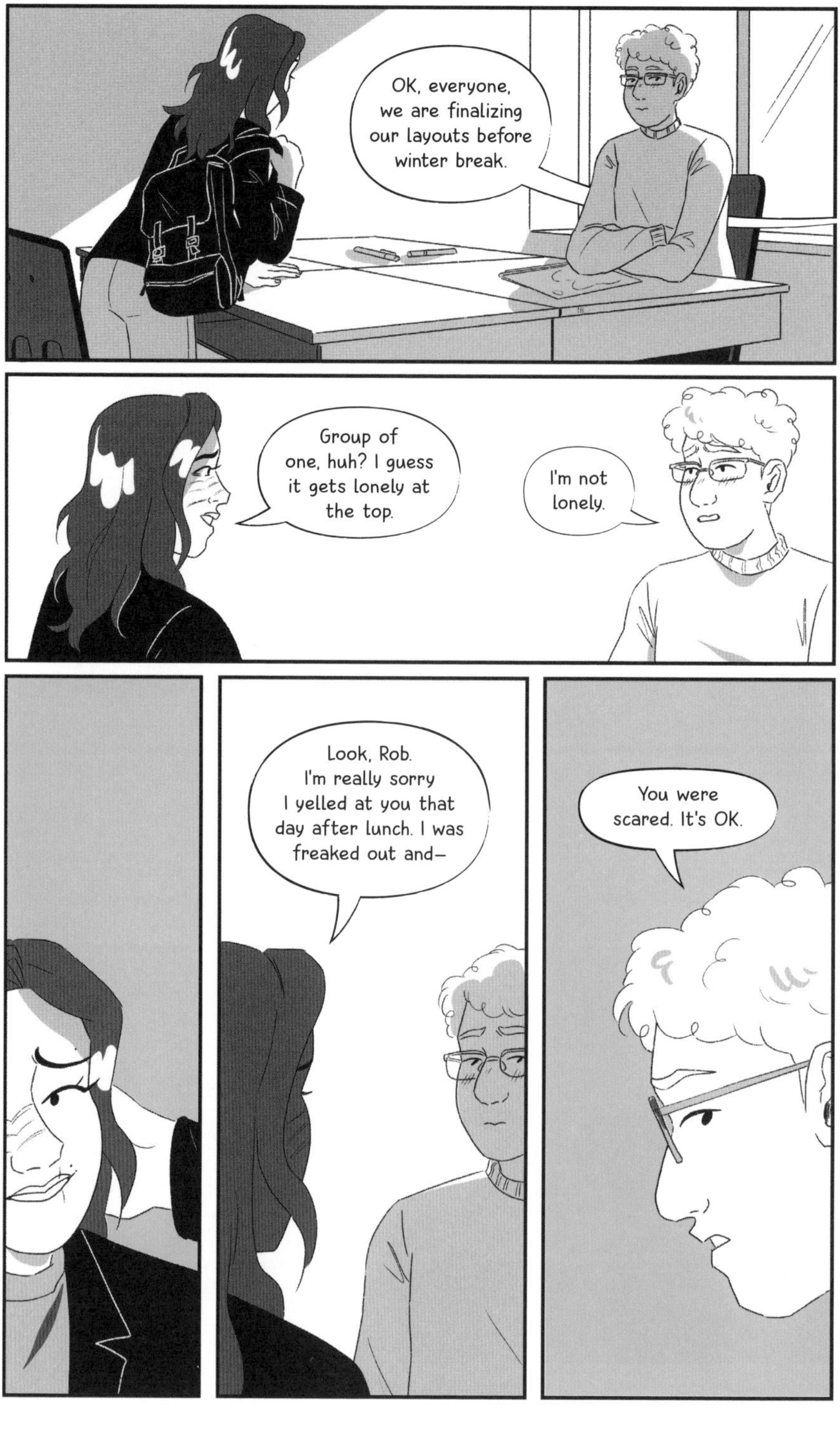
OK, everyone, we are finalizing our layouts before winter break.
Group of one, huh? I guess it gets lonely at the top.
I'm not lonely.
Look, Rob. I'm really sorry I yelled at you that day after lunch. I was freaked out and—
You were scared. It's OK.

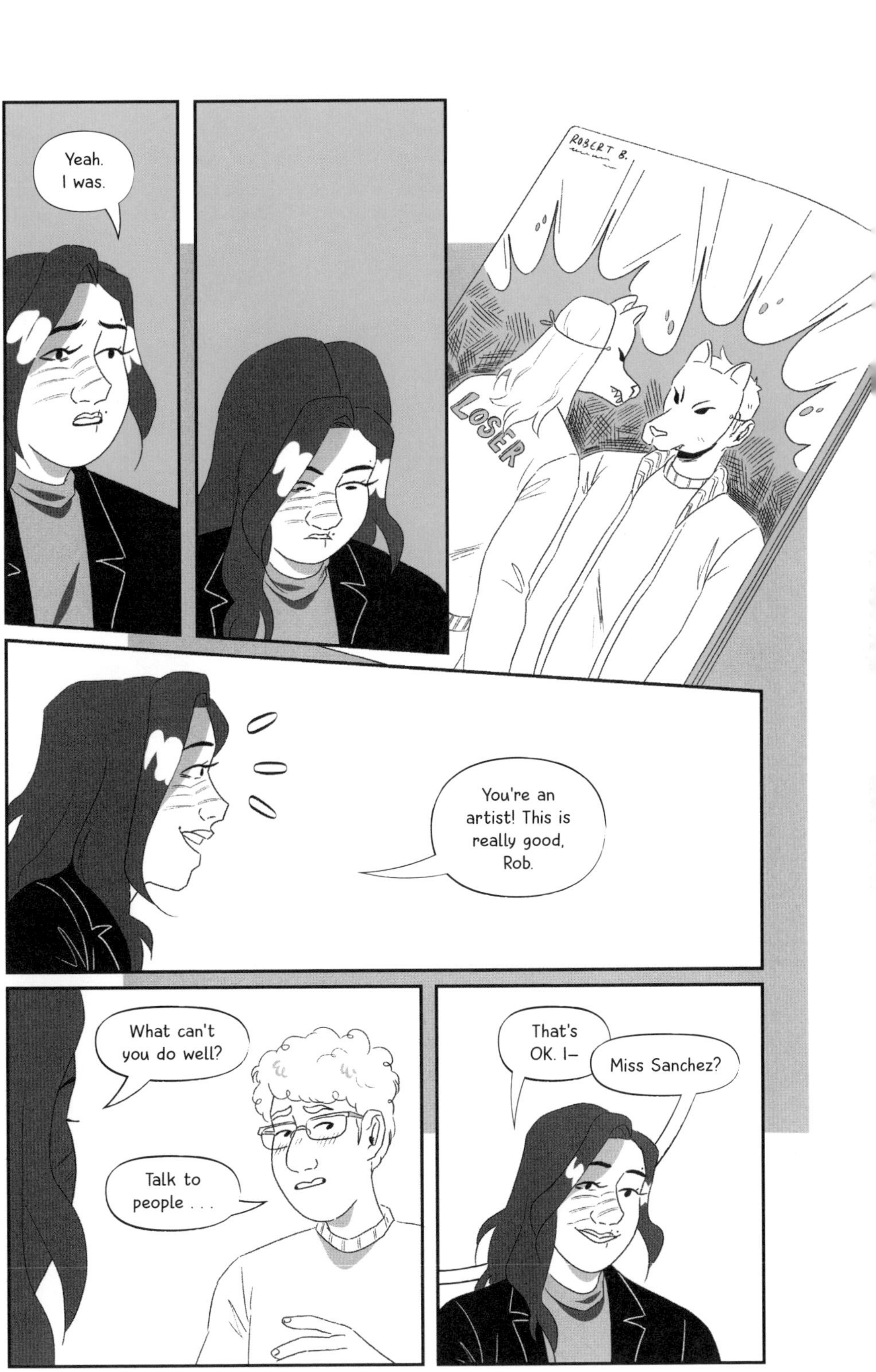
Yeah. I was.
ROBERT B.
LOSER
You're an artist! This is really good, Rob.
What can't you do well?
Talk to people . . .
That's OK. I—
Miss Sanchez?

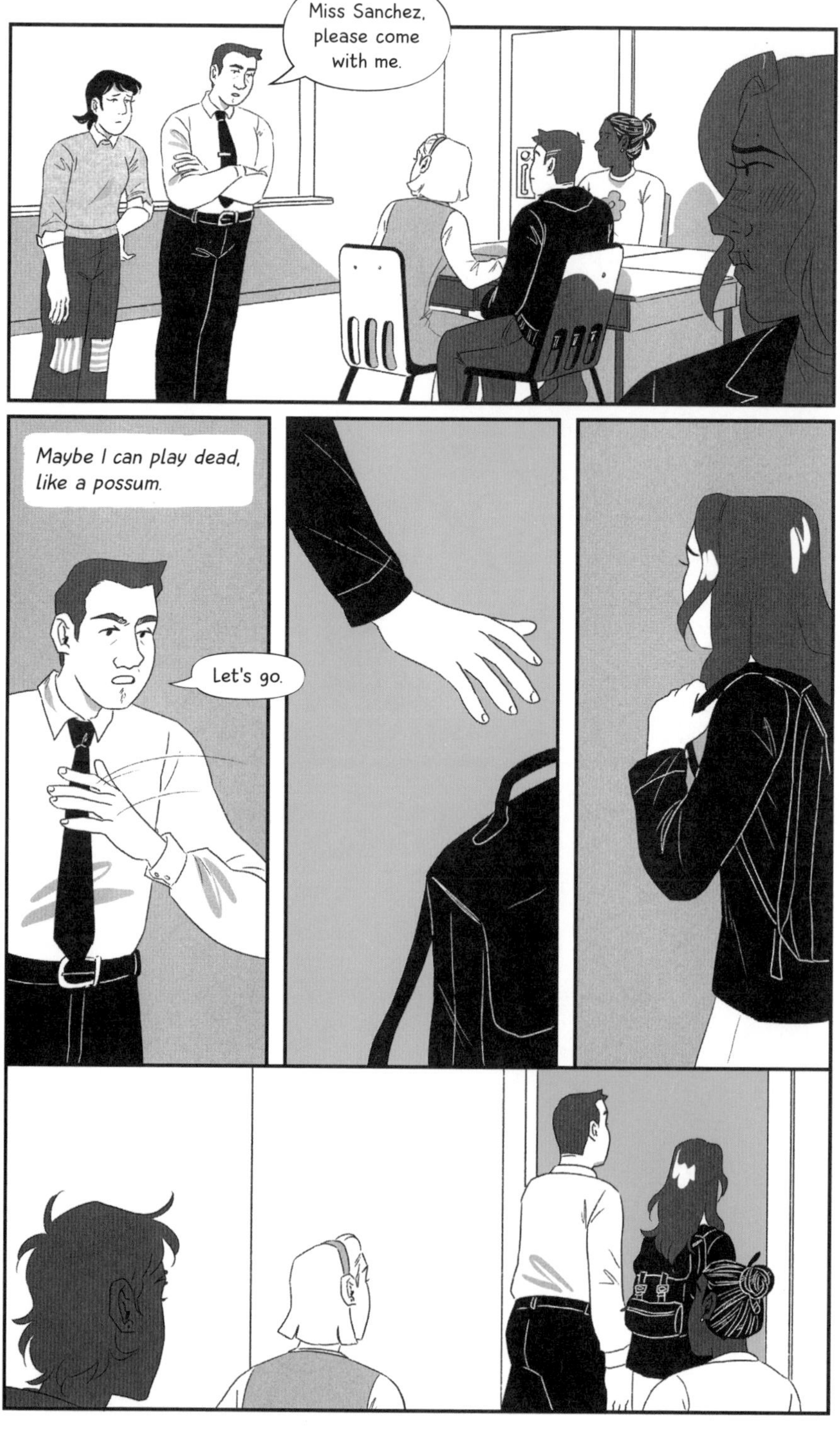
Miss Sanchez, please come with me.
Maybe I can play dead, like a possum.
Let's go.

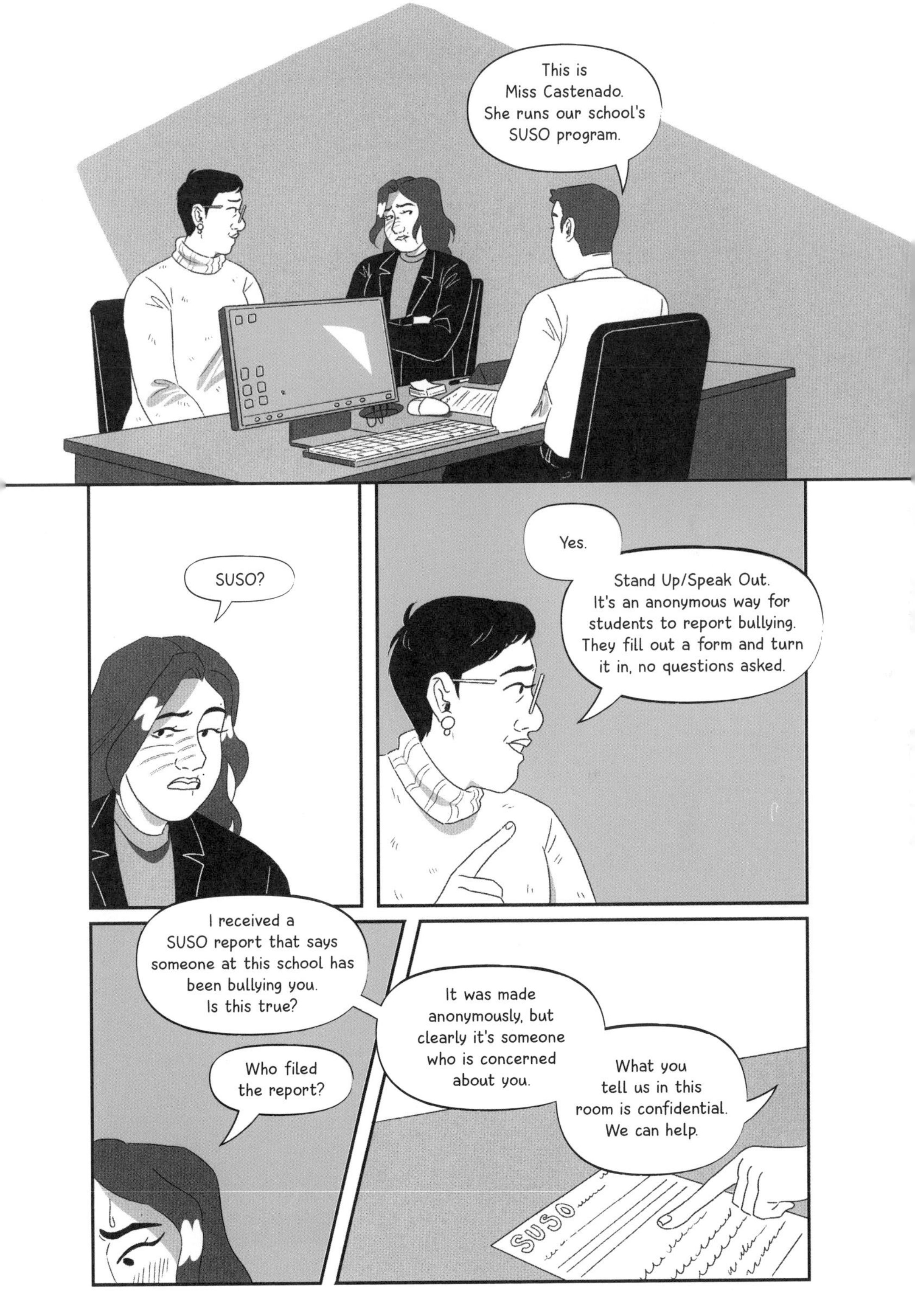
This is Miss Castenado. She runs our school's SUSO program.
SUSO?
Yes.
Stand Up/Speak Out. It's an anonymous way for students to report bullying. They fill out a form and turn it in, no questions asked.
I received a SUSO report that says someone at this school has been bullying you. Is this true?
Who filed the report?
It was made anonymously, but clearly it's someone who is concerned about you.
What you tell us in this room is confidential. We can help.
SUSO

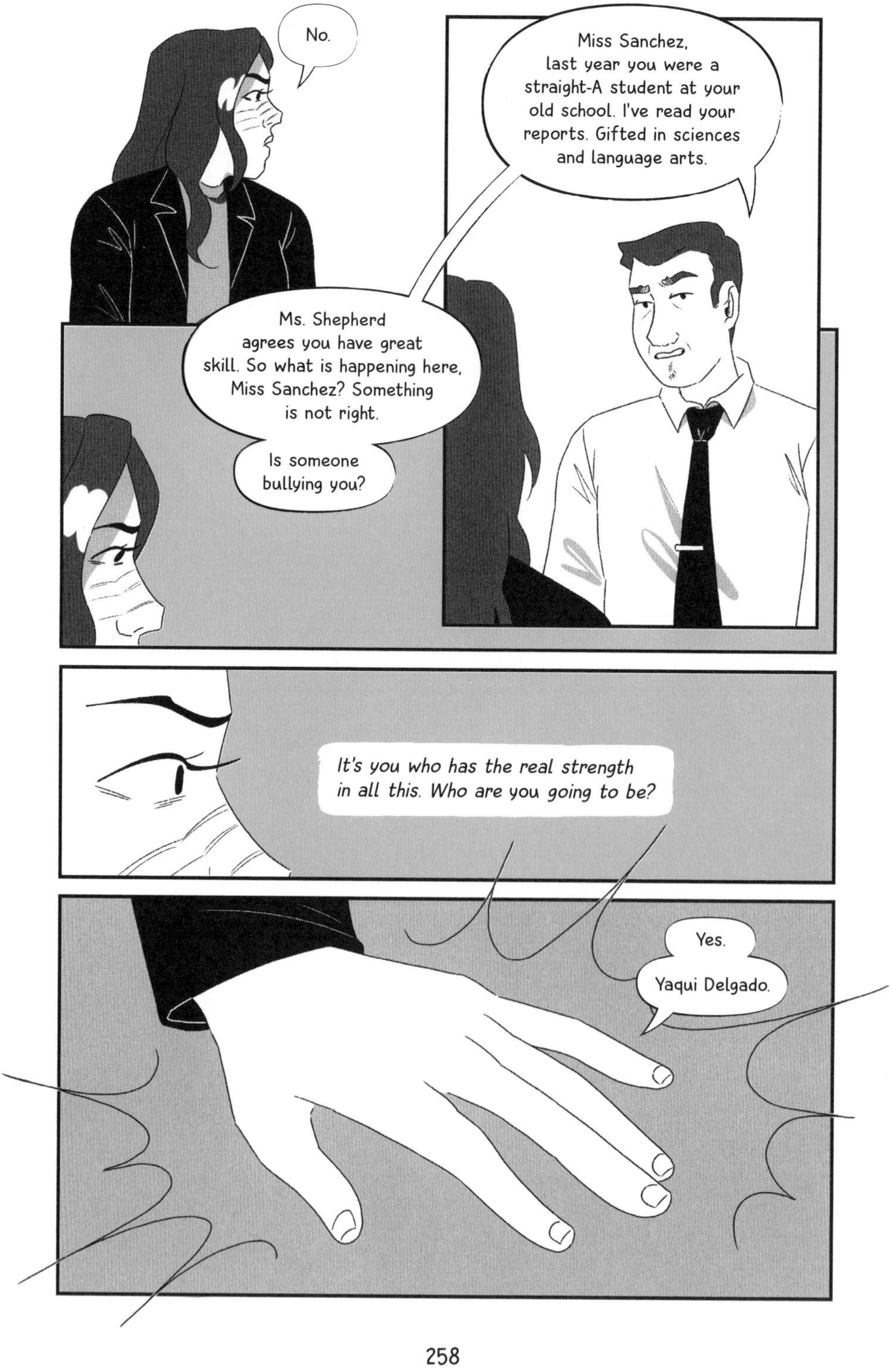
No.
Miss Sanchez, last year you were a straight-A student at your old school. I've read your reports. Gifted in sciences and language arts.
Ms. Shepherd agrees you have great skill. So what is happening here, Miss Sanchez? Something is not right.
Is someone bullying you?
It's you who has the real strength in all this. Who are you going to be?
Yes.
Yaqui Delgado.

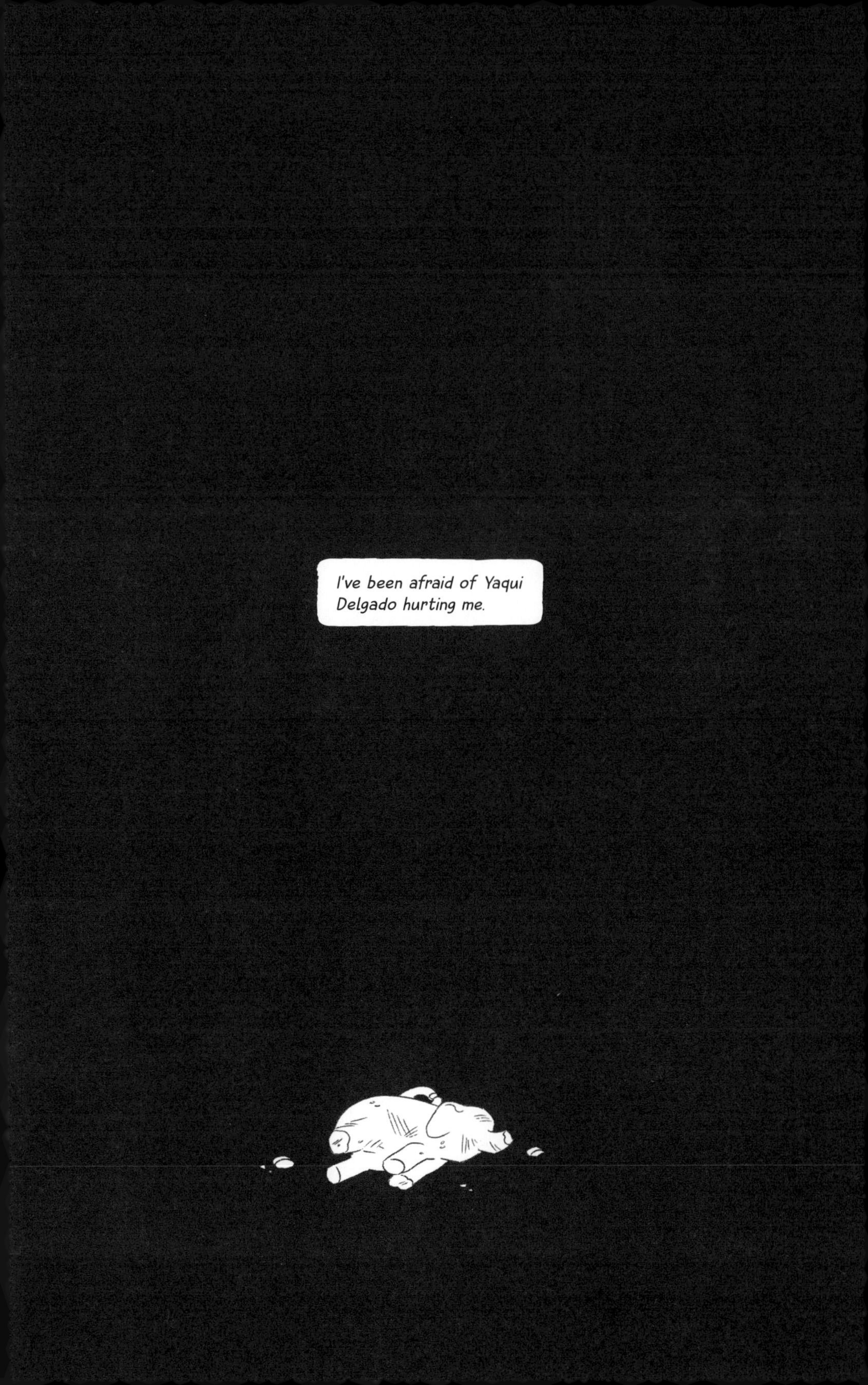
I've been afraid of Yaqui Delgado hurting me.

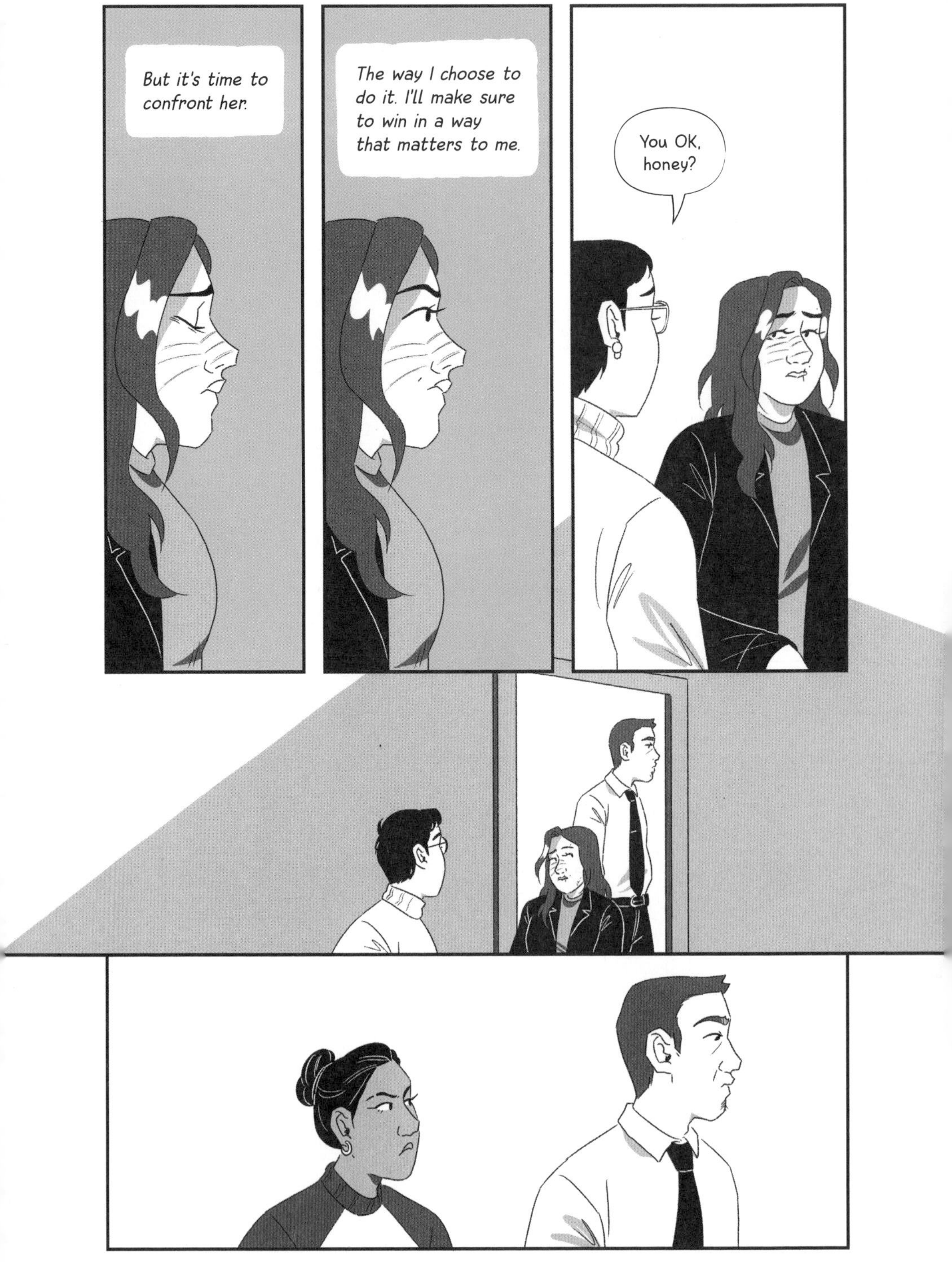
But it's time to confront her.
The way I choose to do it. I'll make sure to win in a way that matters to me.
You OK, honey?

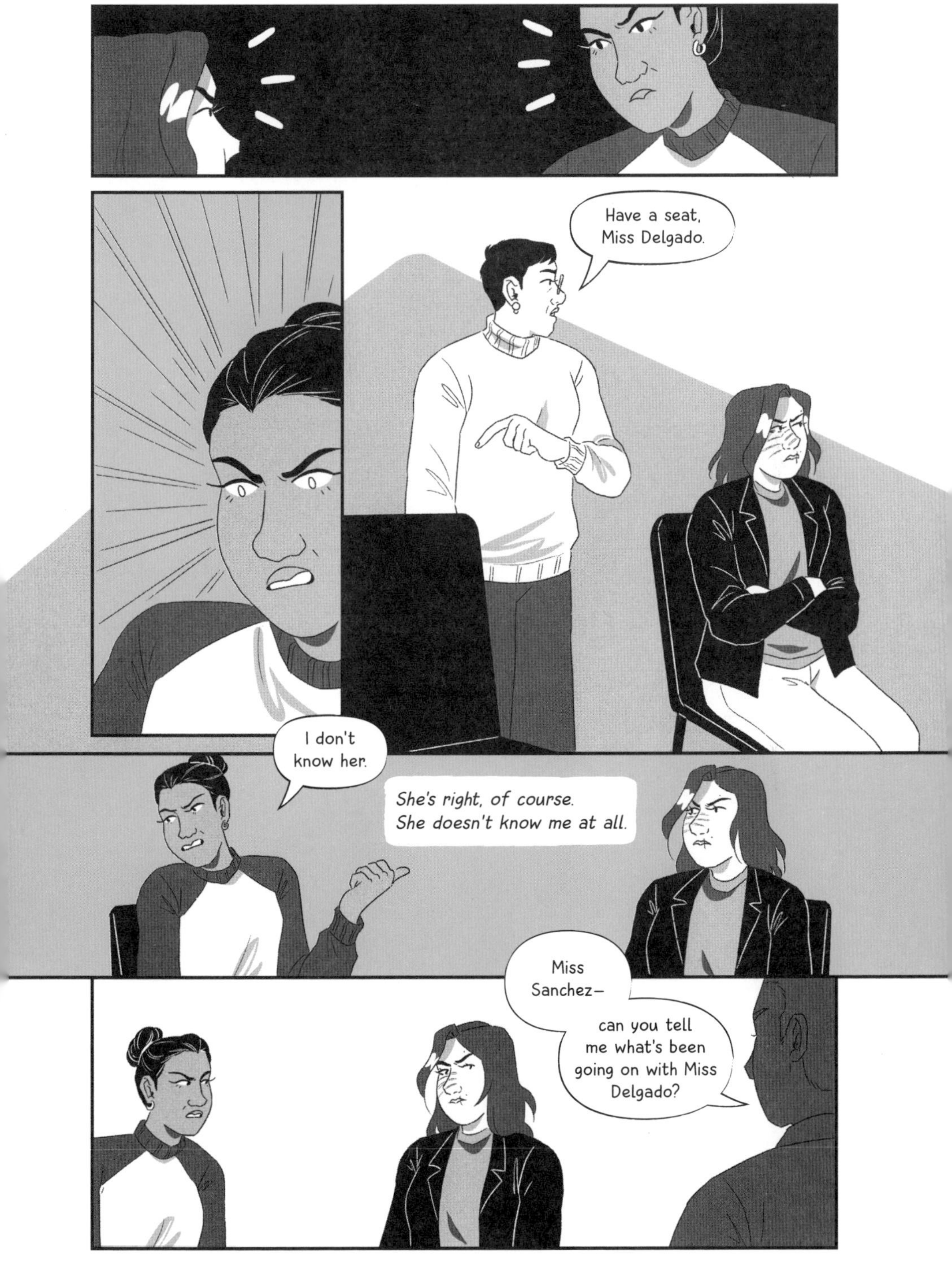
Have a seat, Miss Delgado.
I don't know her.
She's right, of course. She doesn't know me at all.
Miss Sanchez—
can you tell me what's been going on with Miss Delgado?

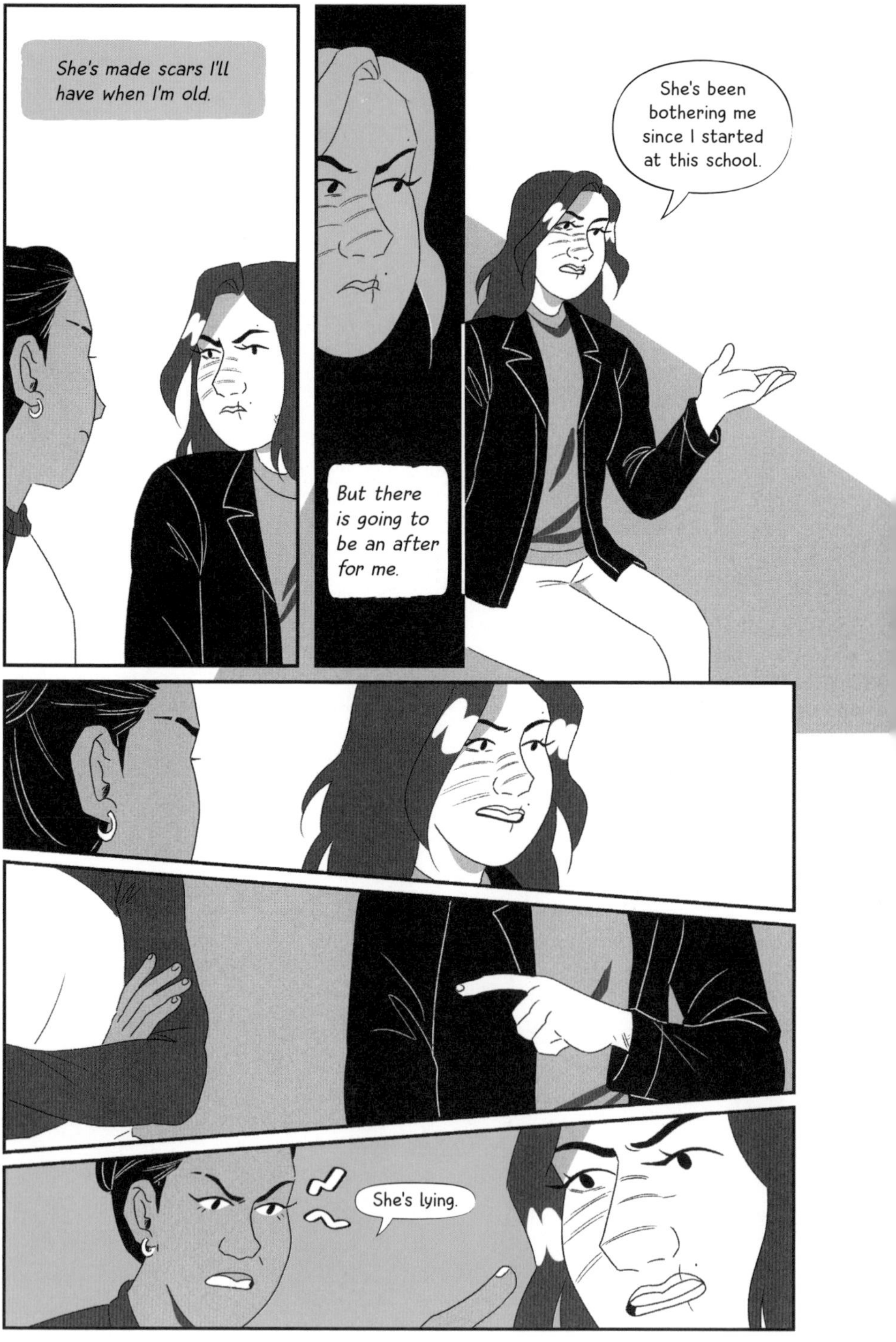
She's made scars I'll have when I'm old.
But there is going to be an after for me.
She's been bothering me since I started at this school.
She's lying.

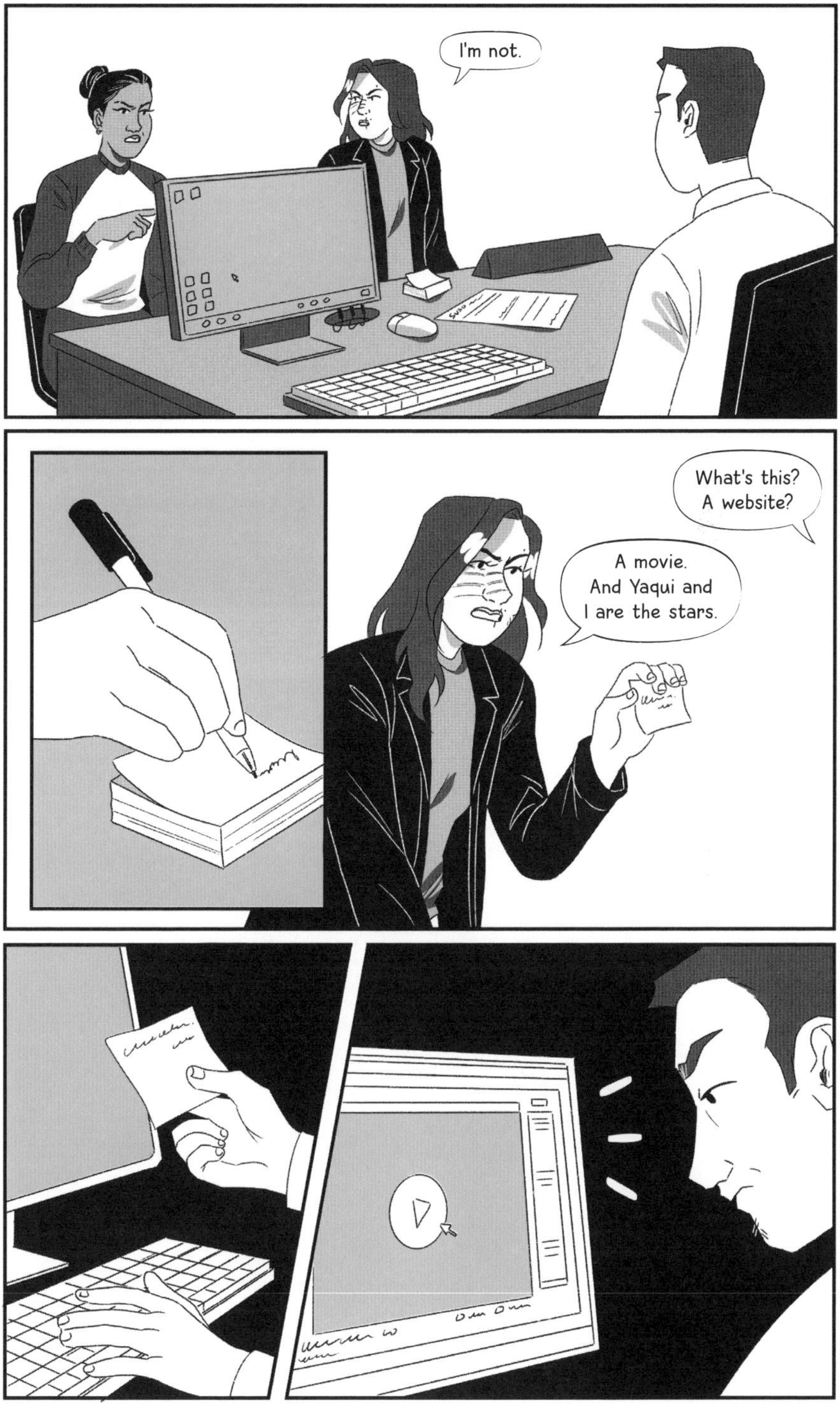
I'm not.
What's this? A website?
A movie. And Yaqui and I are the stars.

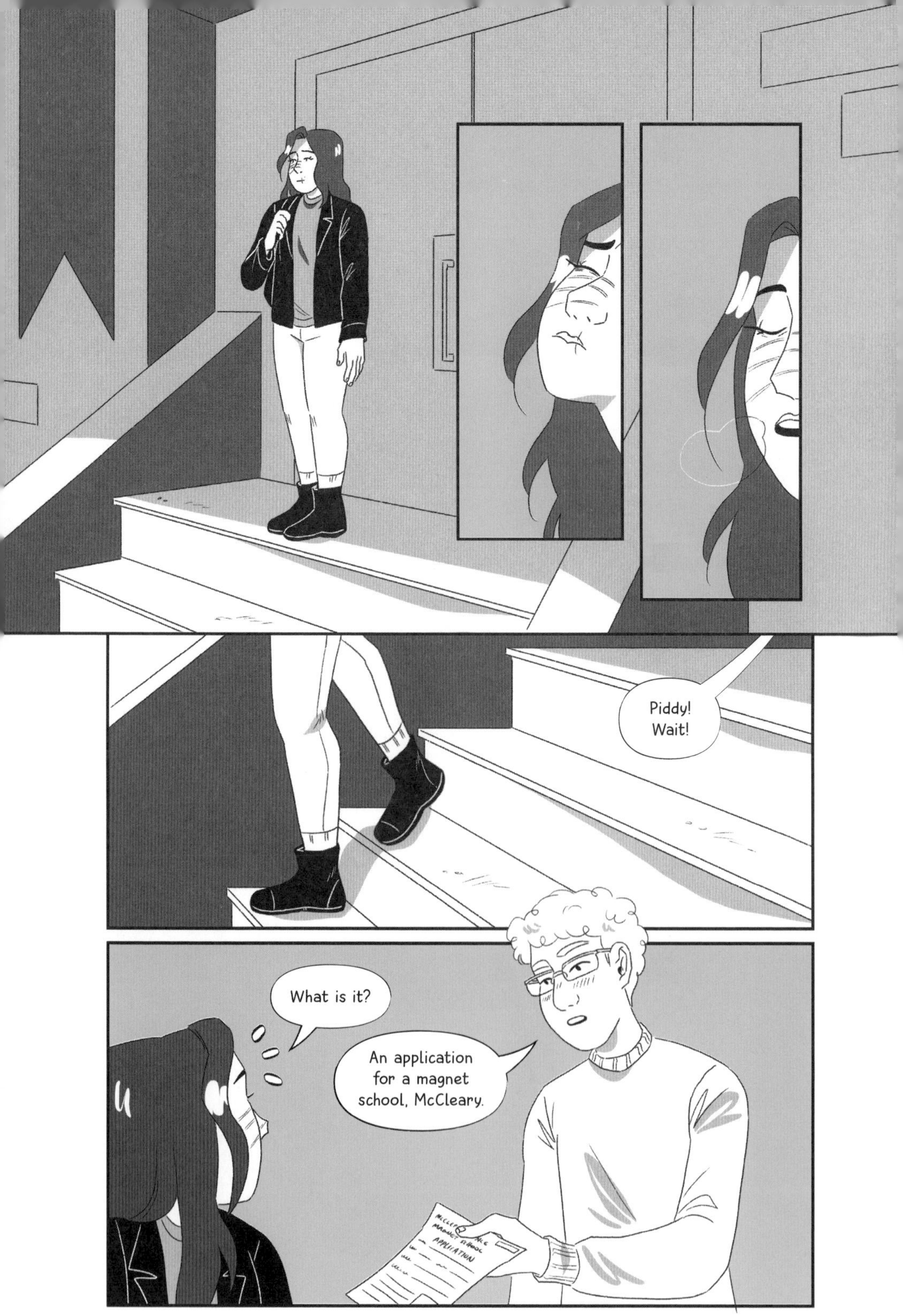
Piddy! Wait!
What is it?
An application for a magnet school, McCleary.
MCCLEARY SCIENCE MAGNET SCHOOL APPLICATION

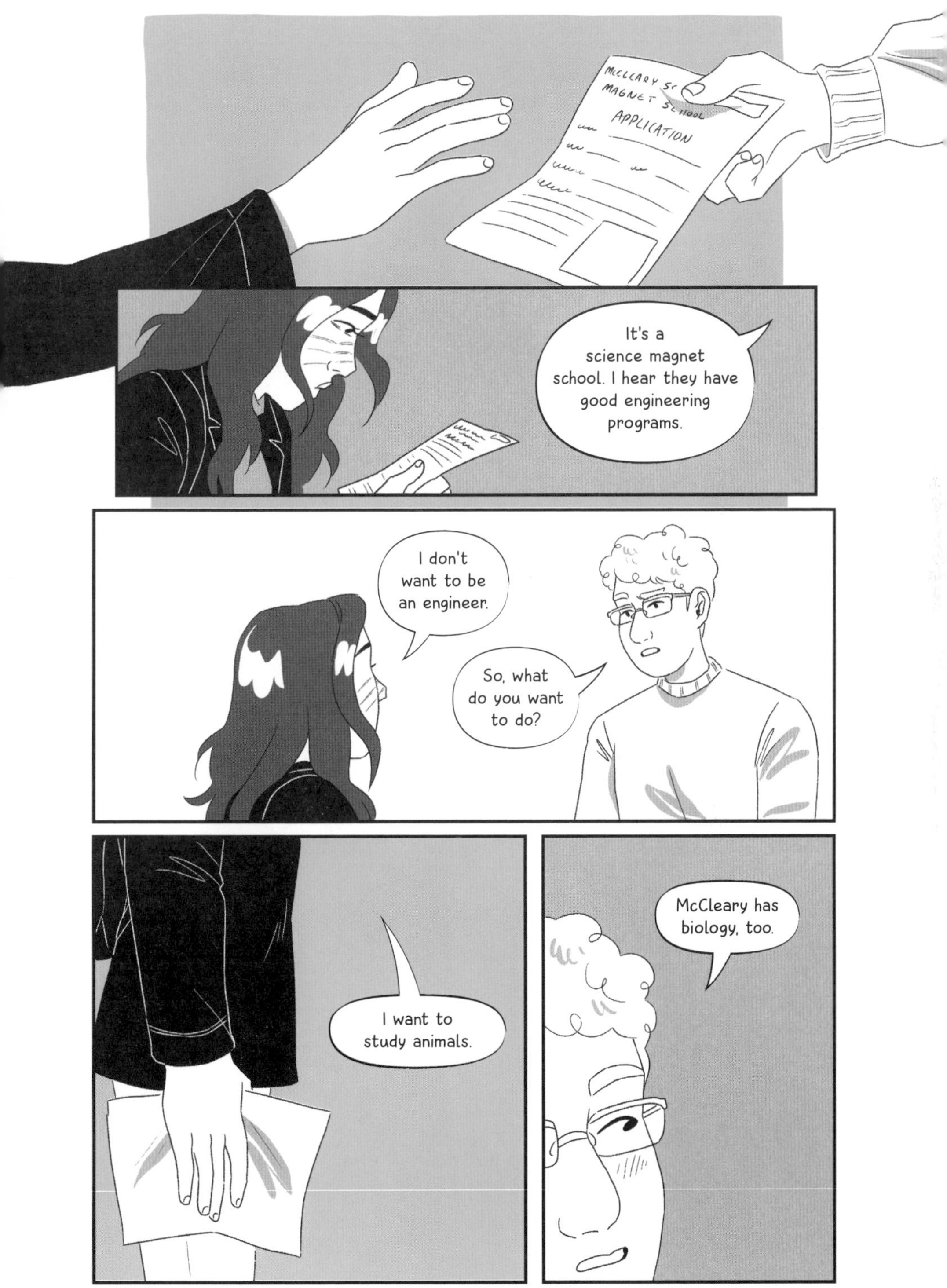

McCLEARY SC
MAGNET SCHOOL
APPLICATION
It's a science magnet school. I hear they have good engineering programs.
I don't want to be an engineer.
So, what do you want to do?
I want to study animals.
McCleary has biology, too.

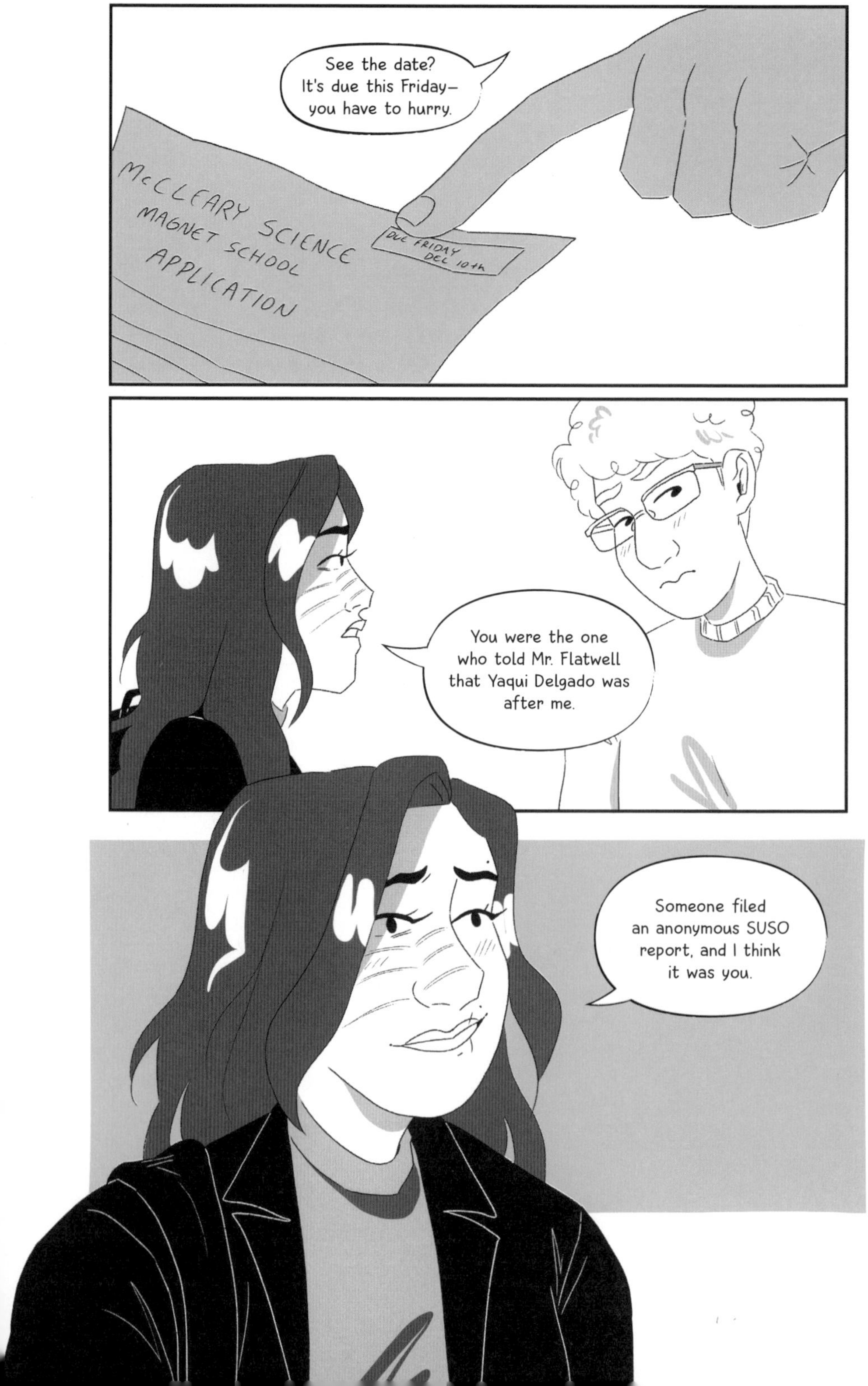
See the date? It's due this Friday— you have to hurry.
McCLEARY SCIENCE MAGNET SCHOOL APPLICATION
DUE FRIDAY DEC 10th
You were the one who told Mr. Flatwell that Yaqui Delgado was after me.
Someone filed an anonymous SUSO report, and I think it was you.

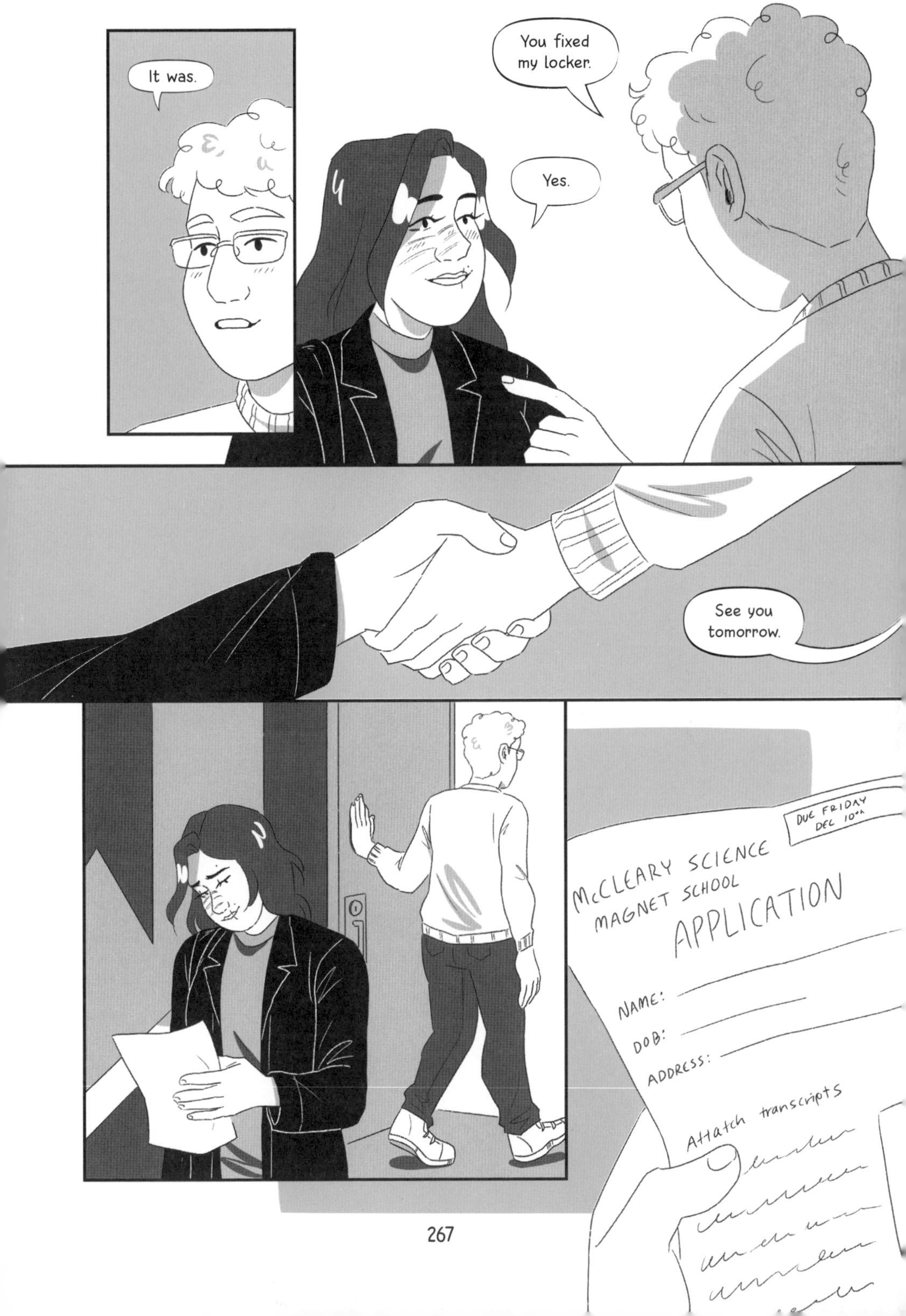
It was.
You fixed my locker.
Yes.
See you tomorrow.
DUE FRIDAY DEC 10th
McCLEARY SCIENCE MAGNET SCHOOL
APPLICATION
NAME:
DOB:
ADDRESS:
Attatch transcripts

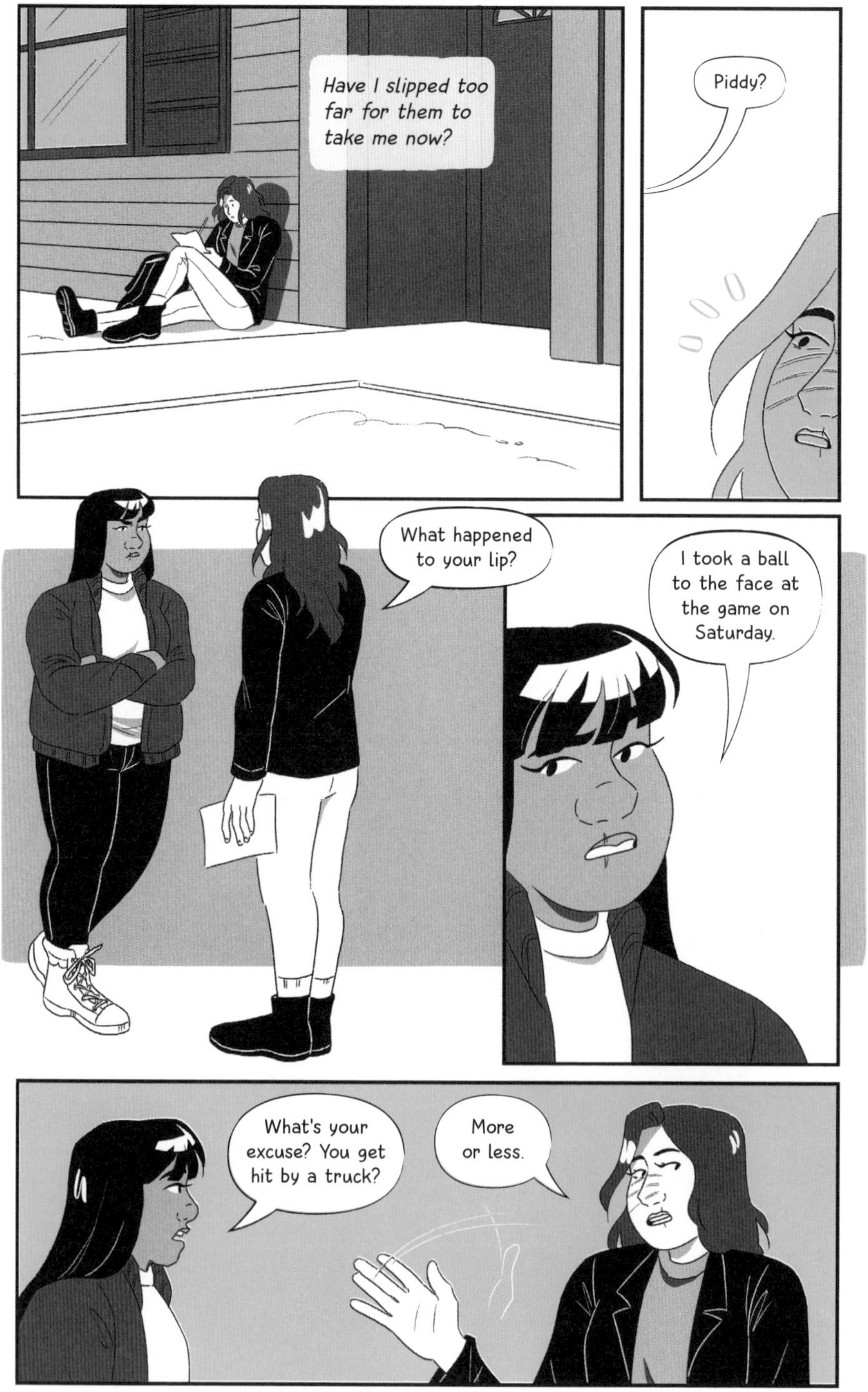

Have I slipped too far for them to take me now?
Piddy?
What happened to your lip?
I took a ball to the face at the game on Saturday.
What's your excuse? You get hit by a truck?
More or less.

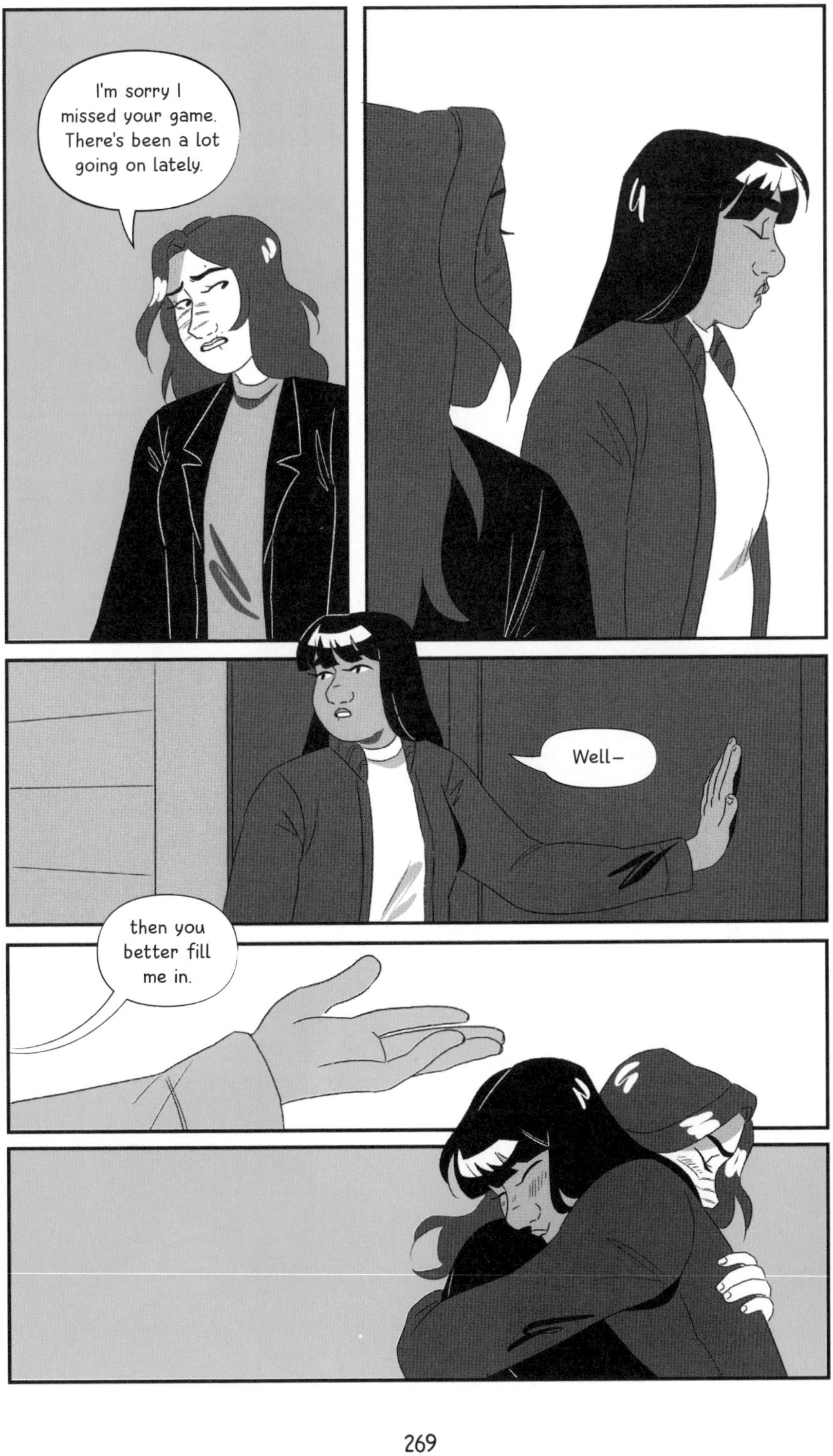
I'm sorry I missed your game. There's been a lot going on lately.
Well—
then you better fill me in.

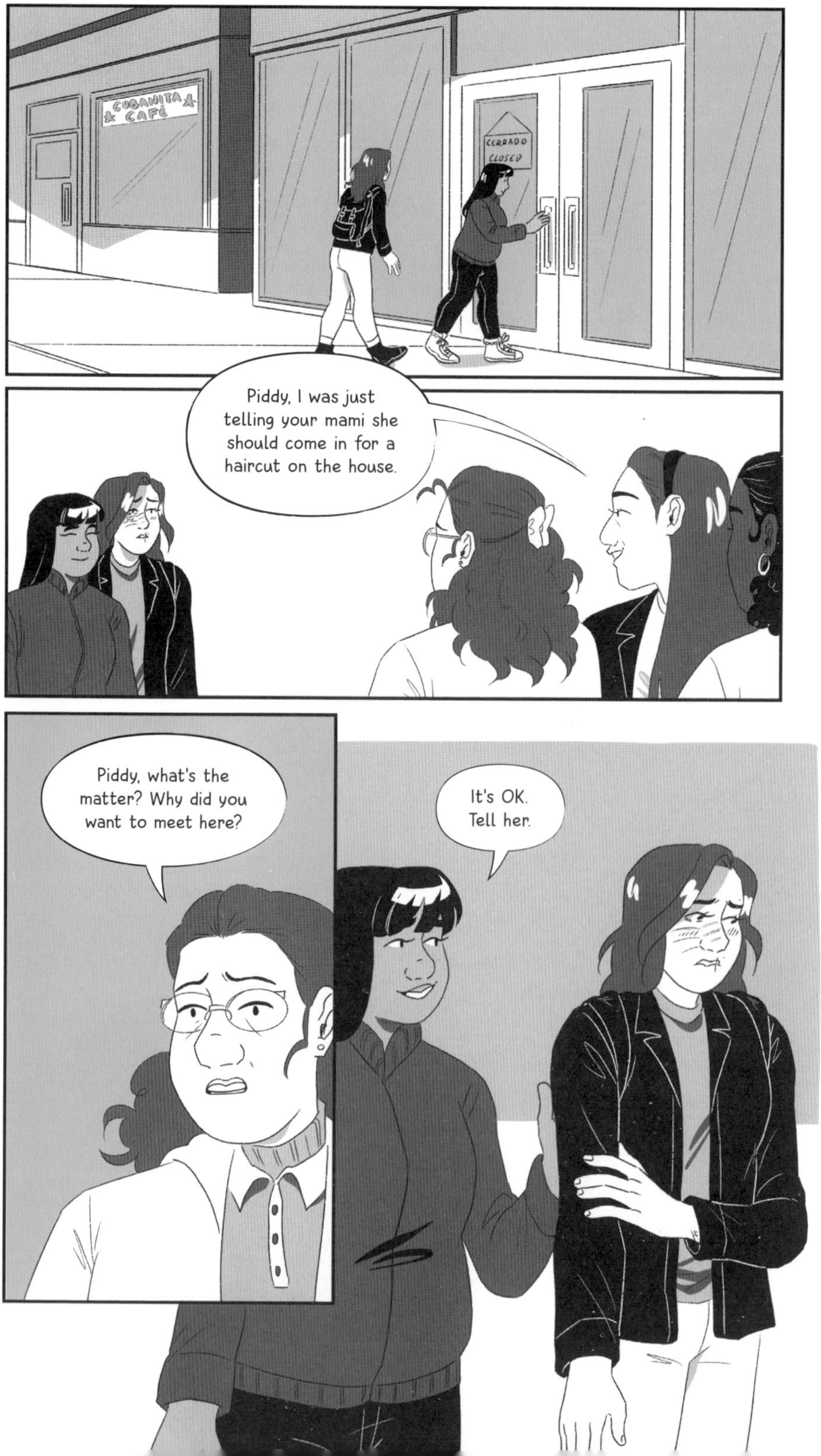
CUBANITA CAFÉ
CERRADO CLOSED
Piddy, I was just telling your mami she should come in for a haircut on the house.
Piddy, what's the matter? Why did you want to meet here?
It's OK. Tell her.

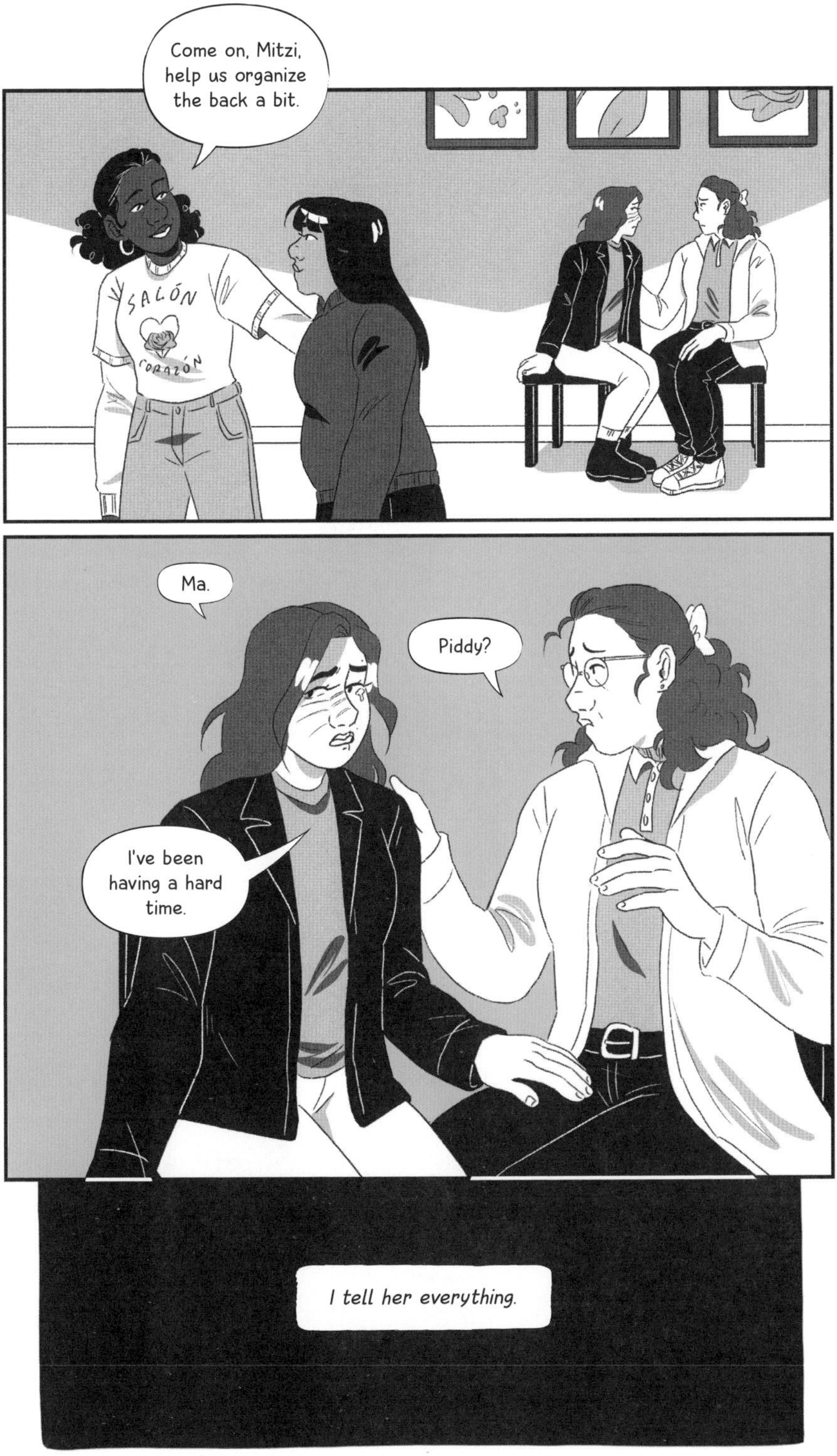
Come on, Mitzi, help us organize the back a bit.
SALÓN CORAZÓN
Ma.
Piddy?
I've been having a hard time.
I tell her everything.

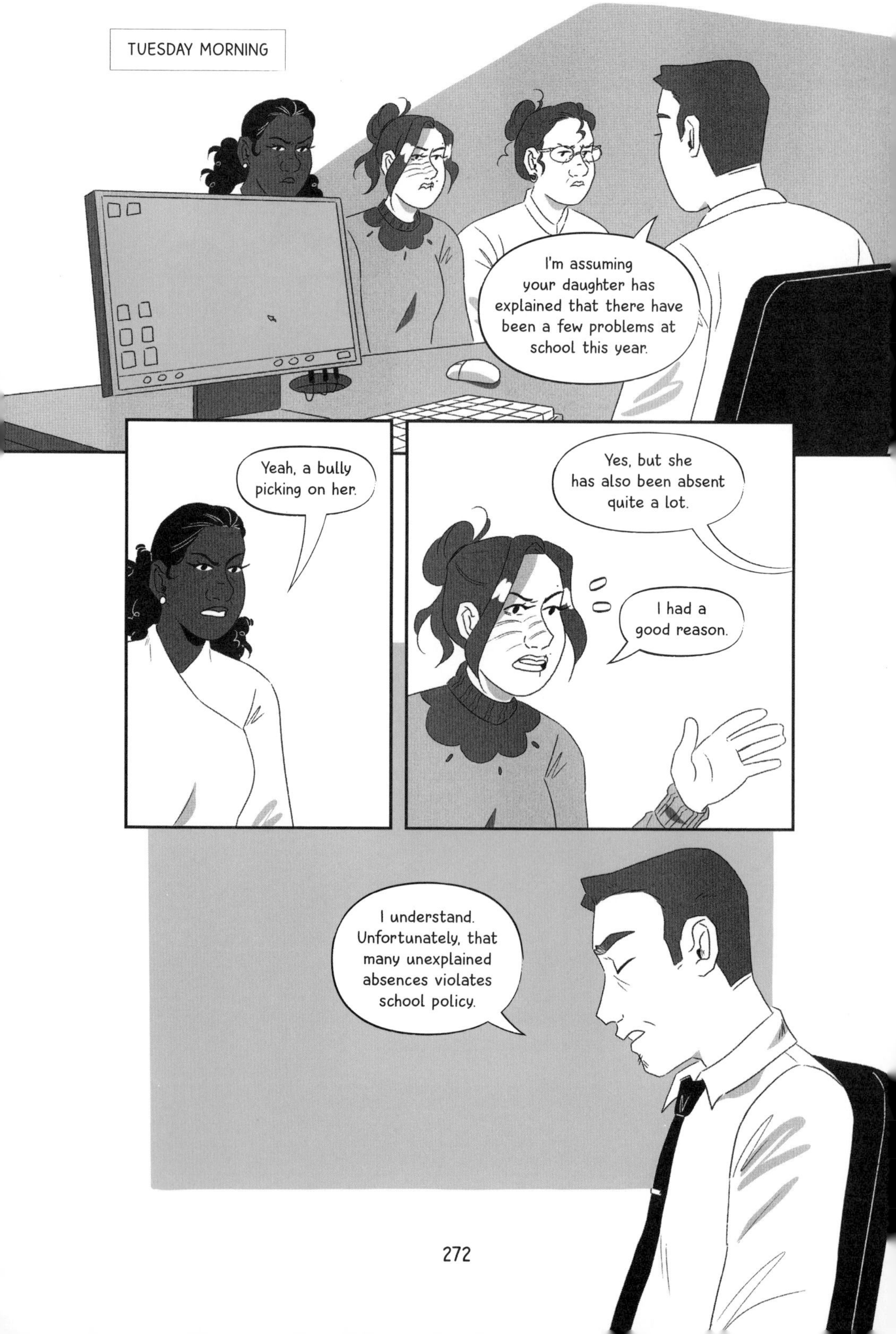
TUESDAY MORNING
I'm assuming your daughter has explained that there have been a few problems at school this year.
Yeah, a bully picking on her.
Yes, but she has also been absent quite a lot.
I had a good reason.
I understand. Unfortunately, that many unexplained absences violates school policy.

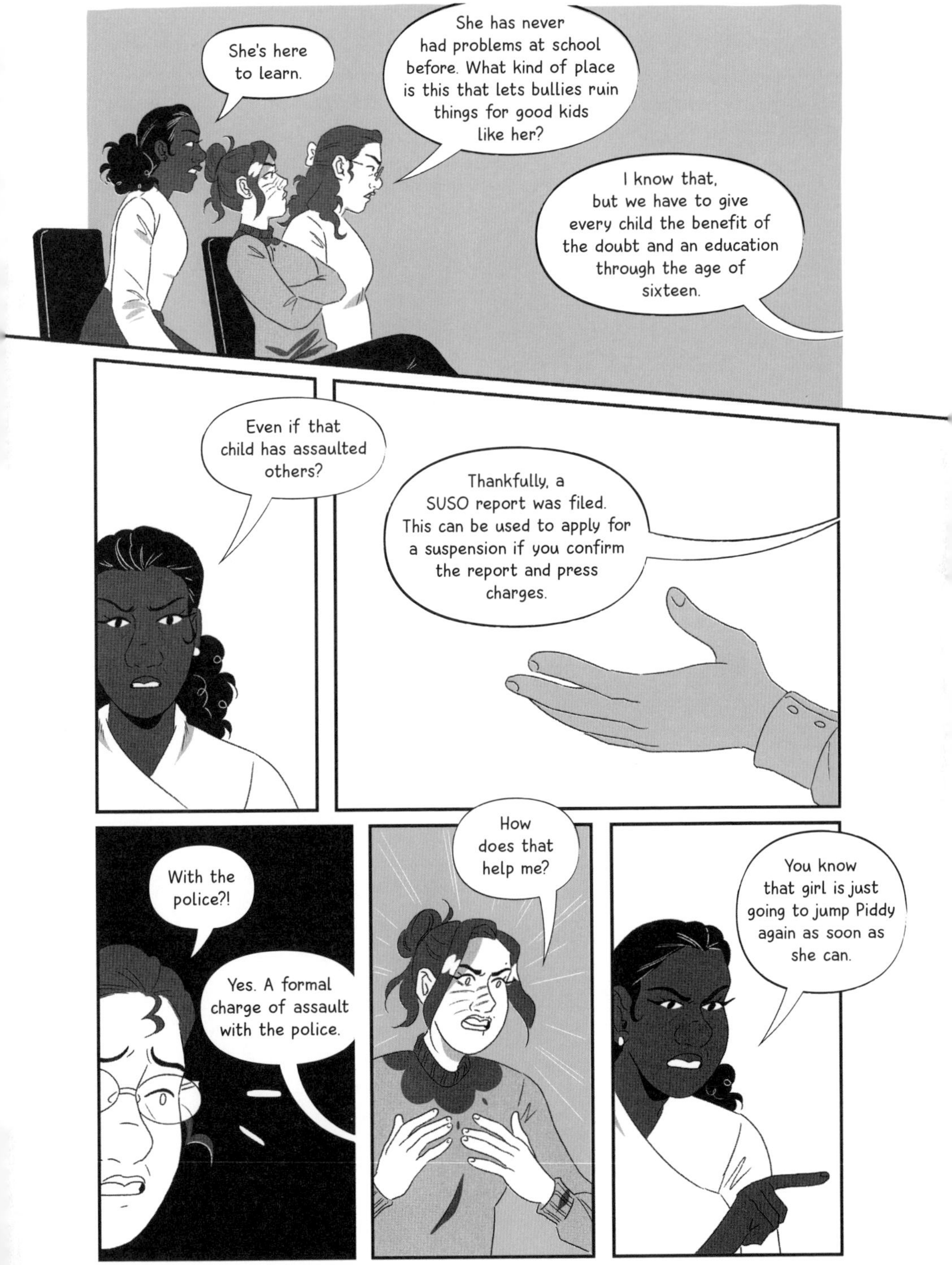
She's here to learn.
She has never had problems at school before. What kind of place is this that lets bullies ruin things for good kids like her?
I know that, but we have to give every child the benefit of the doubt and an education through the age of sixteen.
Even if that child has assaulted others?
Thankfully, a SUSO report was filed. This can be used to apply for a suspension if you confirm the report and press charges.
With the police?!
Yes. A formal charge of assault with the police.
How does that help me?
You know that girl is just going to jump Piddy again as soon as she can.

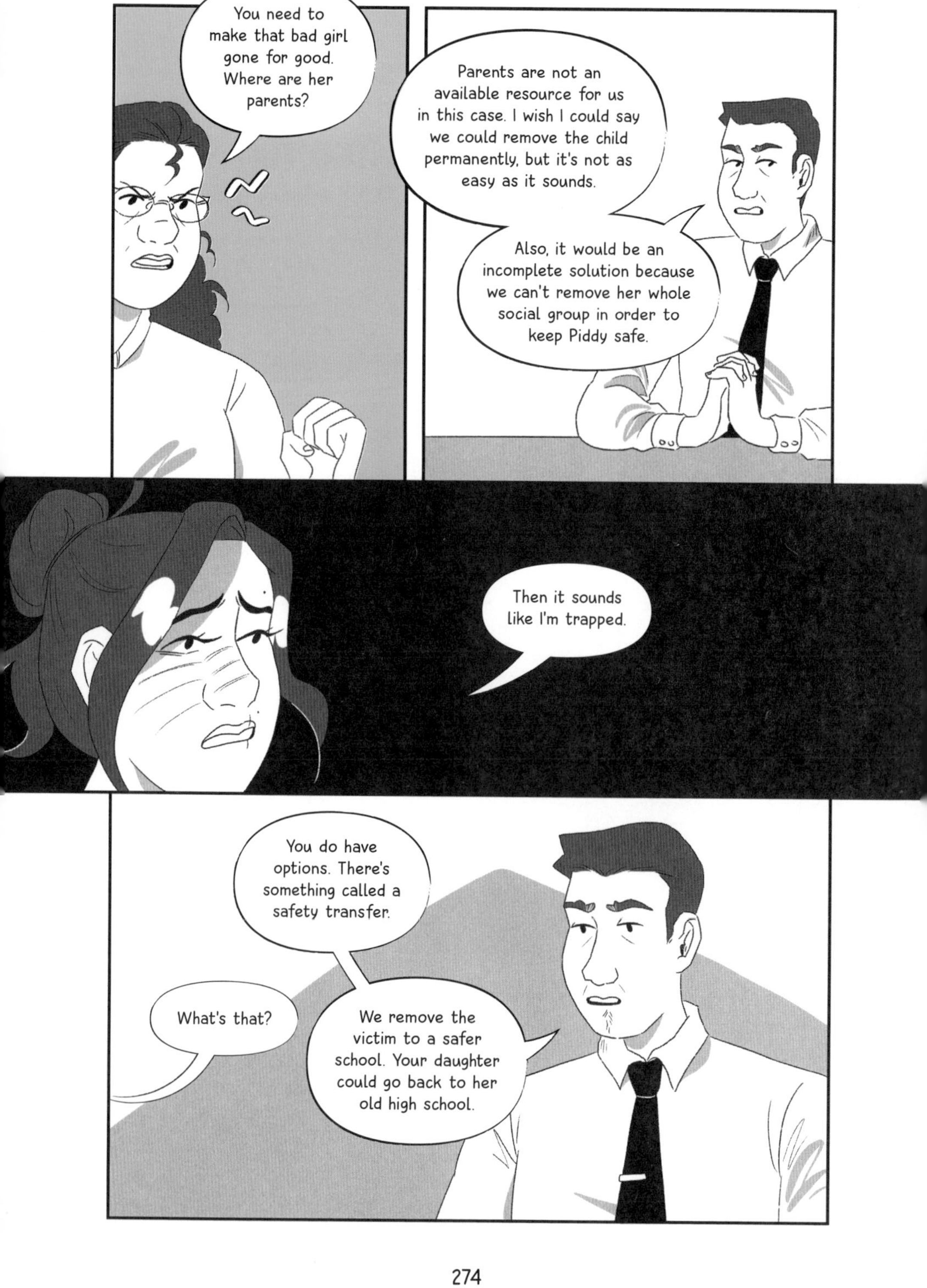
You need to make that bad girl gone for good. Where are her parents?
Parents are not an available resource for us in this case. I wish I could say we could remove the child permanently, but it's not as easy as it sounds.
Also, it would be an incomplete solution because we can't remove her whole social group in order to keep Piddy safe.
Then it sounds like I'm trapped.
You do have options. There's something called a safety transfer.
What's that?
We remove the victim to a safer school. Your daughter could go back to her old high school.

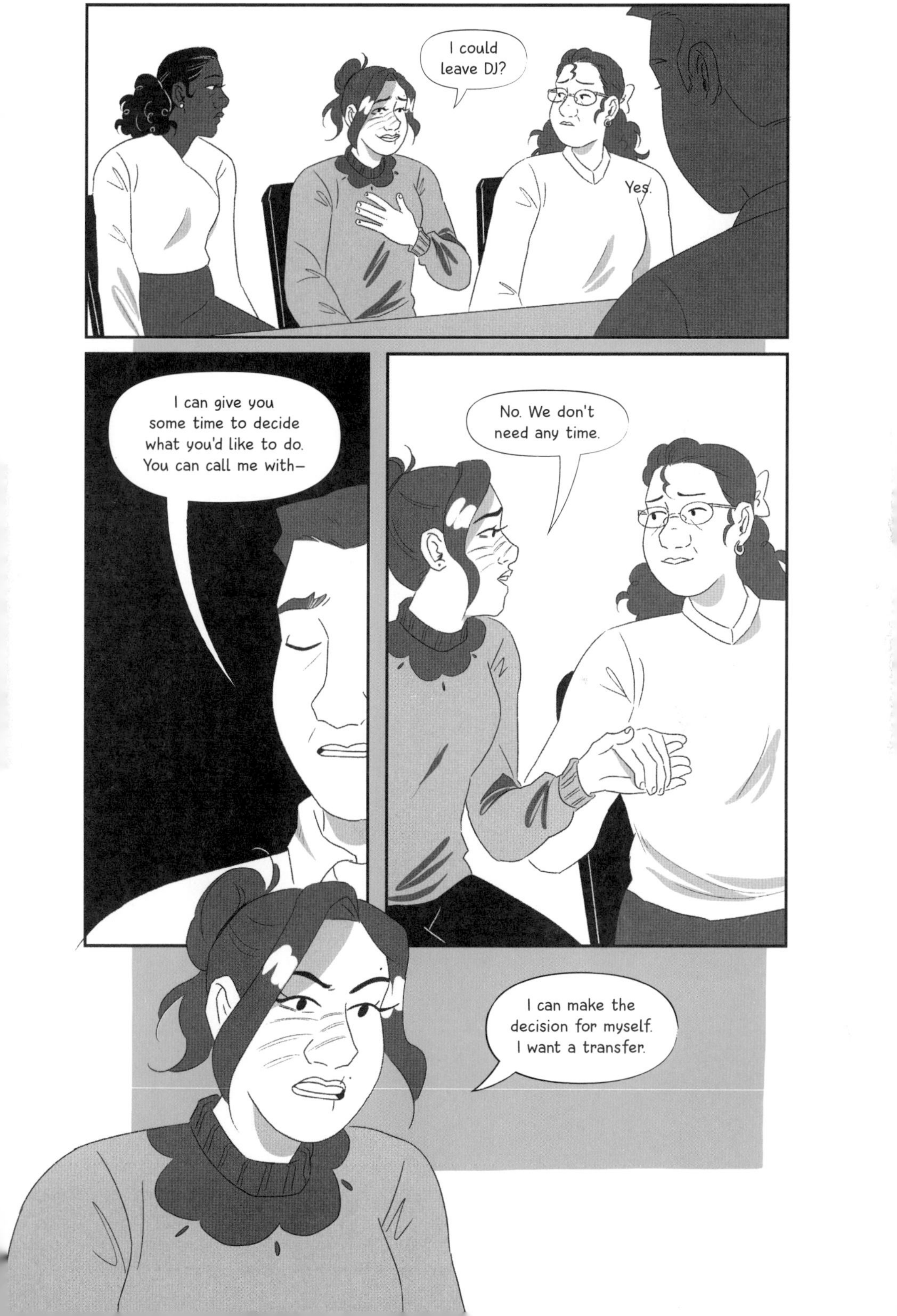
I could leave DJ?
Yes.
I can give you some time to decide what you'd like to do. You can call me with—
No. We don't need any time.
I can make the decision for myself. I want a transfer.

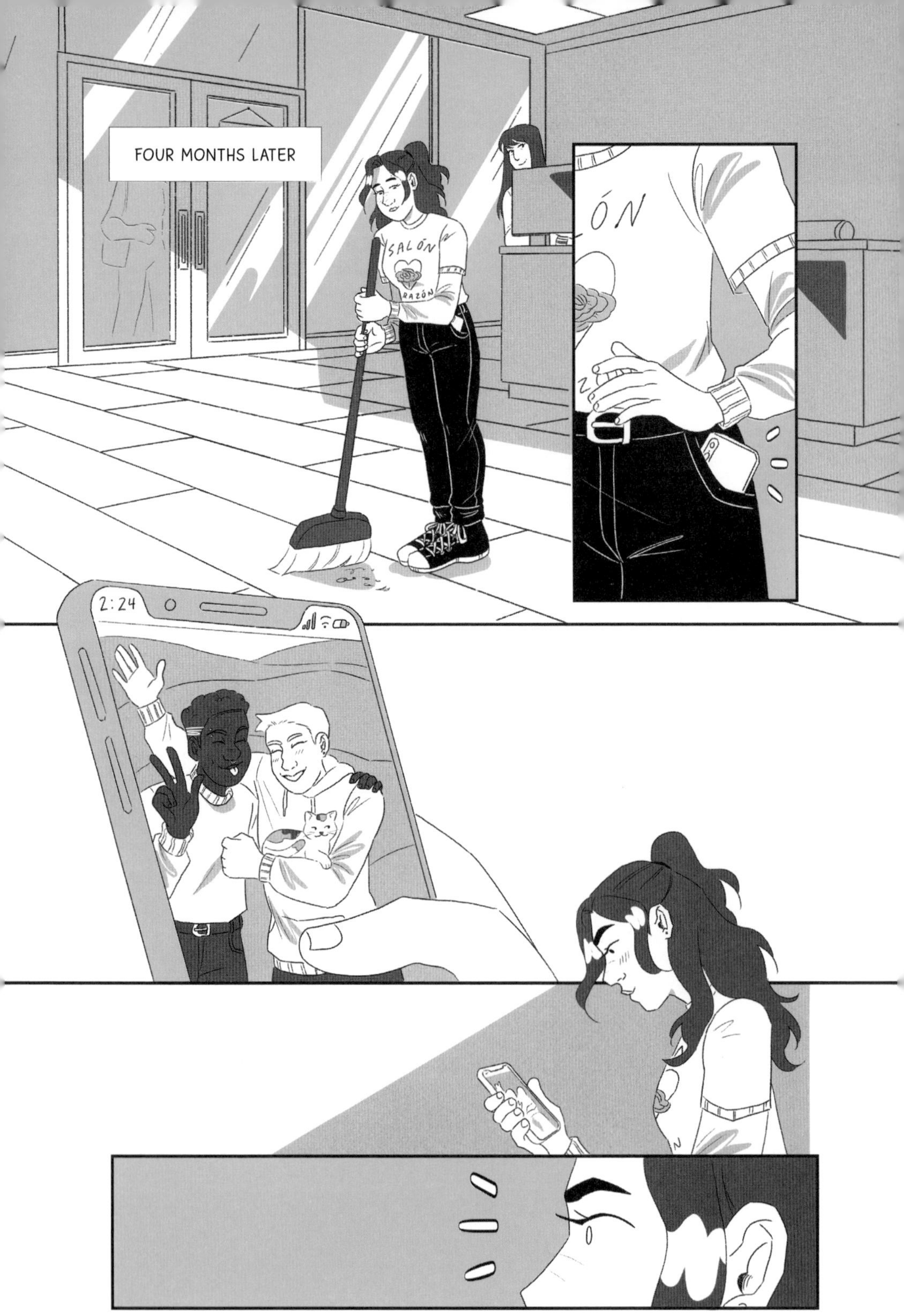
FOUR MONTHS LATER
SALÓN
RAZÓN
2:24

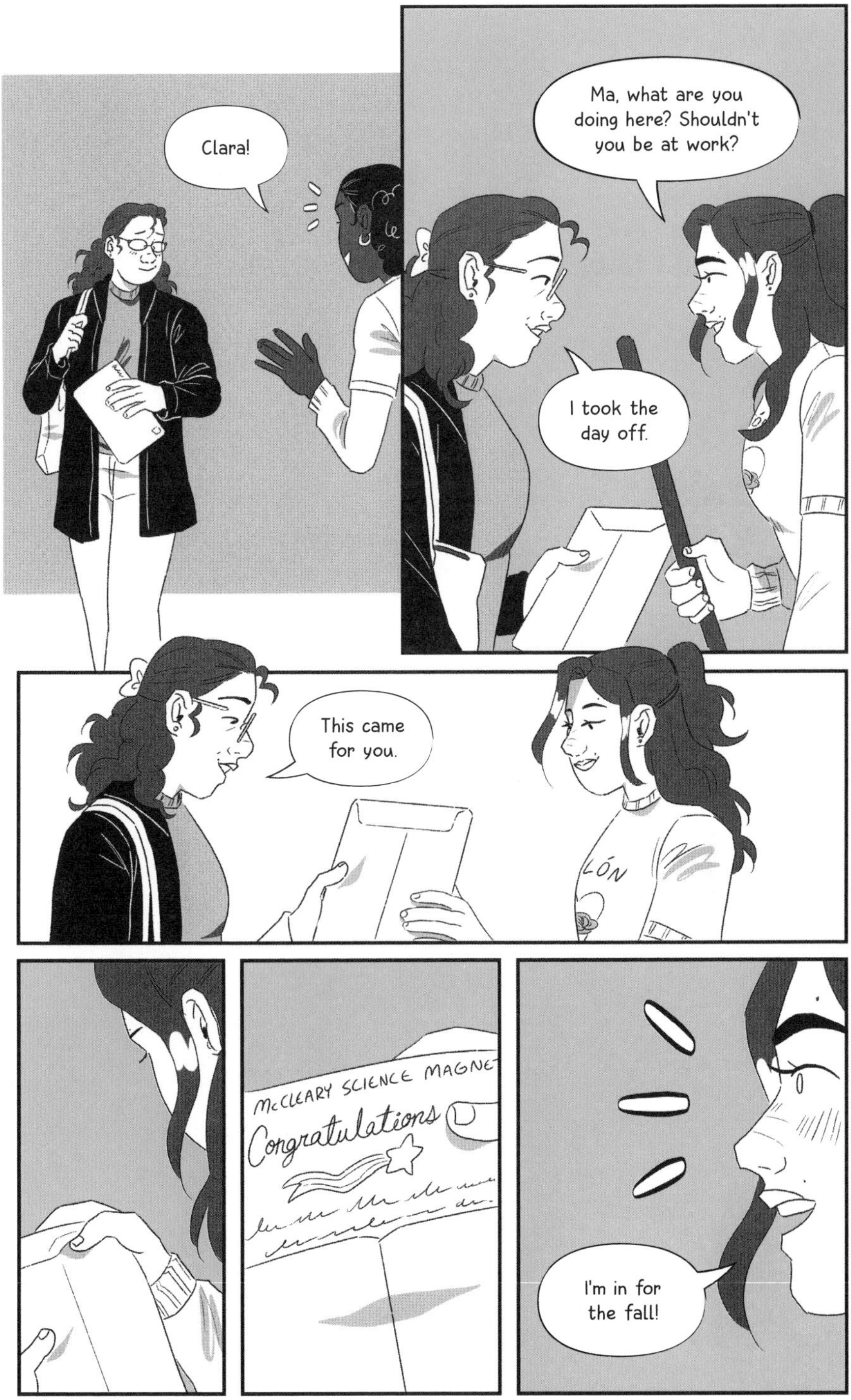

Clara!
Ma, what are you doing here? Shouldn't you be at work?
I took the day off.
This came for you.
LÓN
McCLEARY SCIENCE MAGNET
Congratulations
I'm in for the fall!

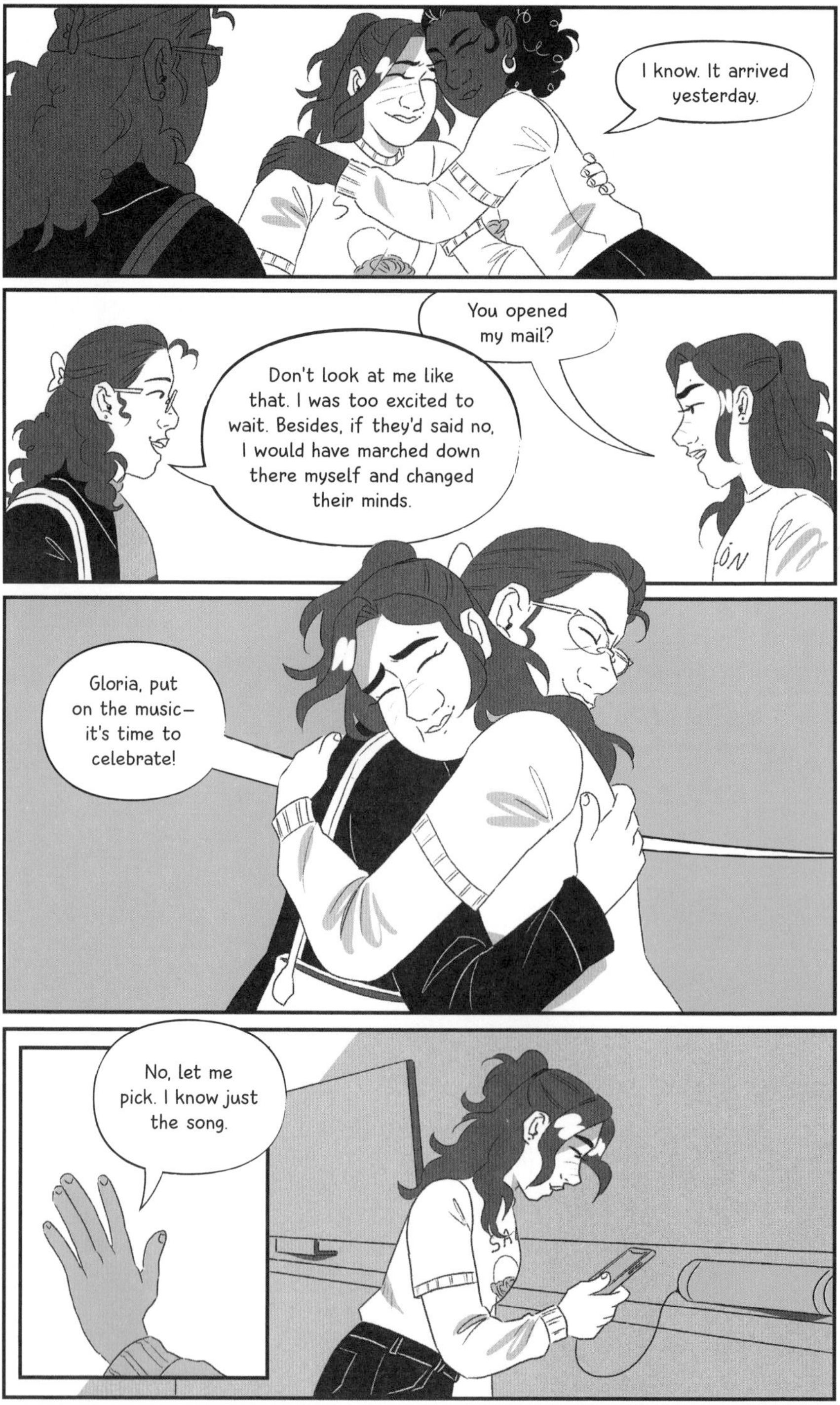
I know. It arrived yesterday.
You opened my mail?
Don't look at me like that. I was too excited to wait. Besides, if they'd said no, I would have marched down there myself and changed their minds.
Gloria, put on the music– it's time to celebrate!
No, let me pick. I know just the song.

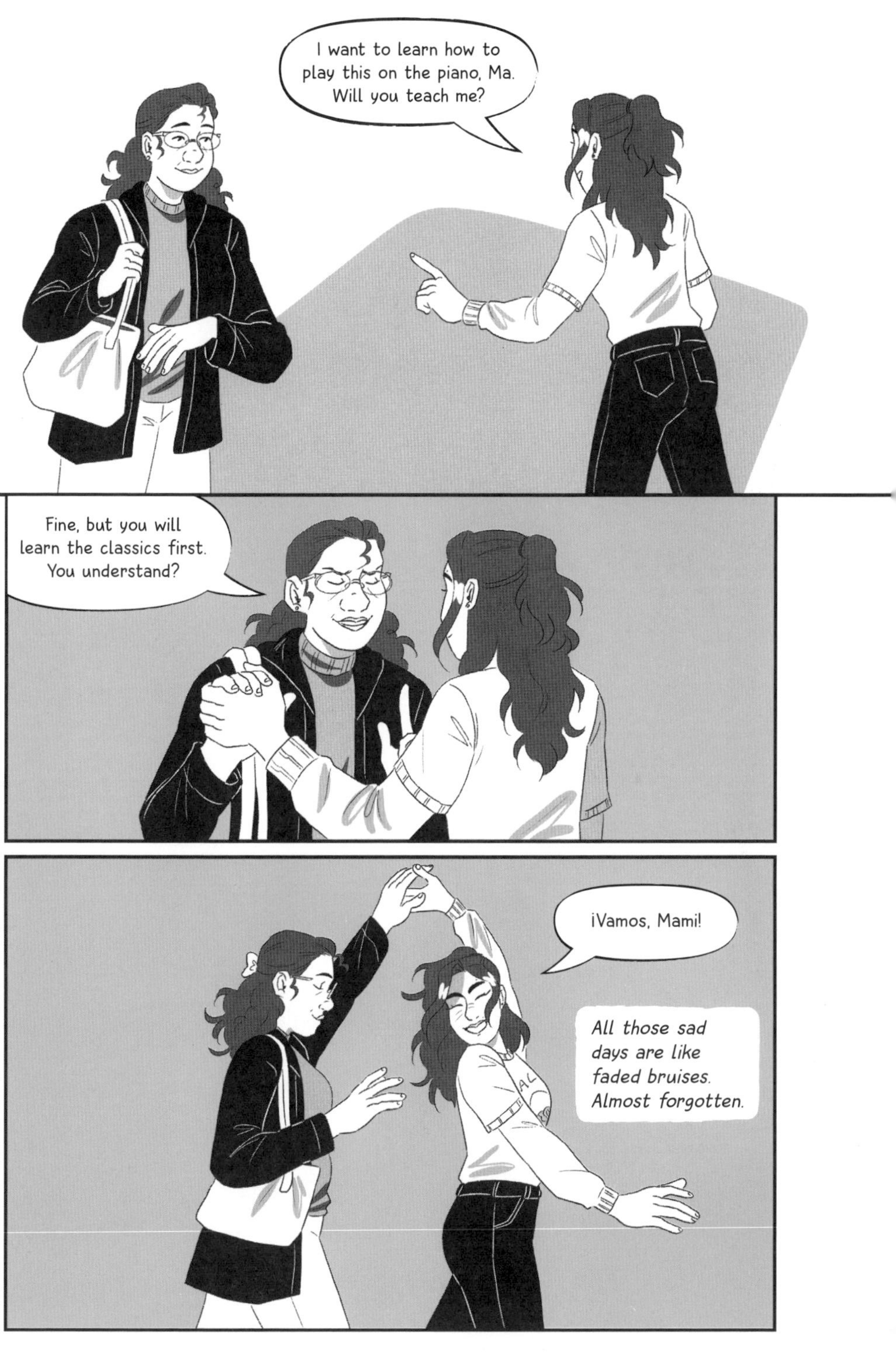

I want to learn how to play this on the piano, Ma. Will you teach me?
Fine, but you will learn the classics first. You understand?
¡Vamos, Mami!
All those sad days are like faded bruises. Almost forgotten.

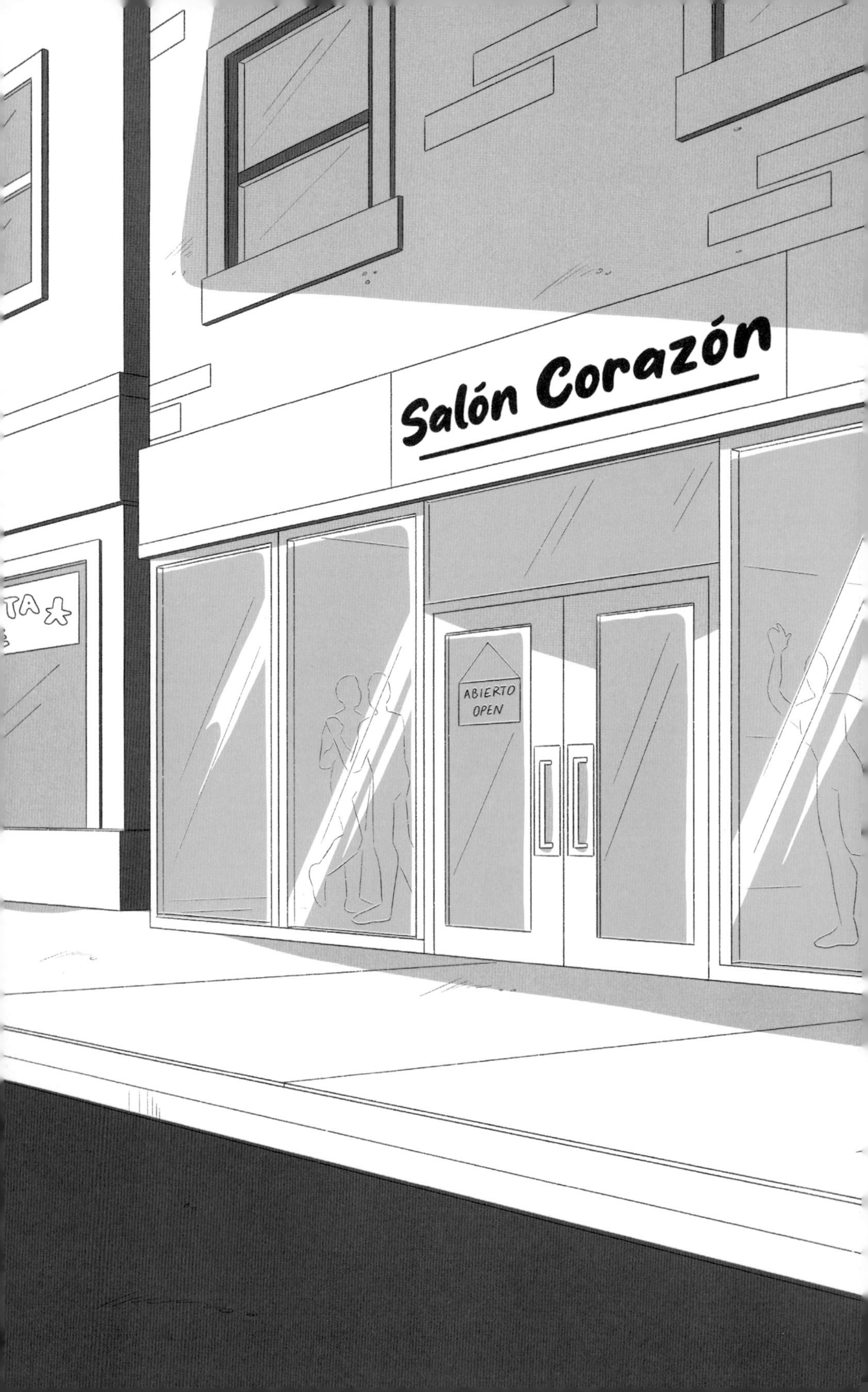
Salón Corazón
ABIERTO
OPEN

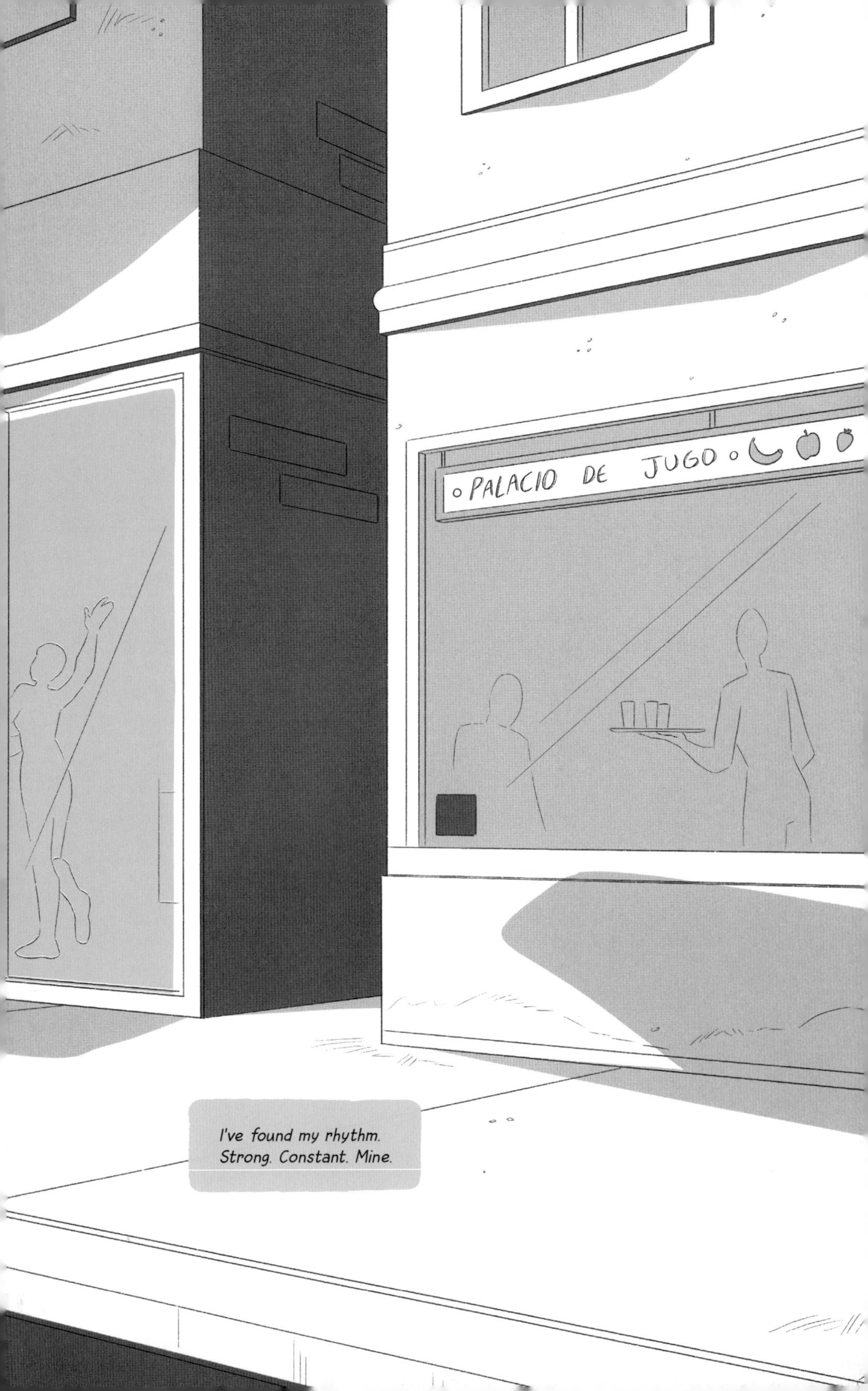
PALACIO DE JUGO
I've found my rhythm.
Strong. Constant. Mine.

To all the muchachas who see themselves in this story
MM

Para mi mamá y papá, quienes me regalaron la
pasión por la vida. Besos. Siempre besos.
MVV

Text copyright © 2013 by Meg Medina
Illustrations copyright © 2023 by Mel Valentine Vargas
Color by Mary Lee Fenner
Lettering by Tif Bucknor

First edition 2023

Library of Congress Catalog Card Number 2023900236
ISBN 978-1-5362-2477-1 (hardcover)
ISBN 978-1-5362-3473-2 (paperback)

23 24 25 26 27 28 APS 10 9 8 7 6 5 4 3 2 1

Printed in Humen, Dongguan, China

This book was typeset in Sunbird.
The illustrations were created digitally.

Candlewick Press
99 Dover Street
Somerville, Massachusetts 02144

www.candlewick.com